SOMMERFELD
TRILOGY

SOMMERFELD
TRILOGY

KIM
VOGEL SAWYER

BARBOUR
PUBLISHING

Bygones © 2007 by Kim Vogel Sawyer
Beginnings © 2007 by Kim Vogel Sawyer
Blessings © 2008 by Kim Vogel Sawyer

Print ISBN 978-1-62029-179-5

eBook Editions:
Adobe Digital Edition (.epub) 978-1-62029-666-0
Kindle and MobiPocket Edition (.prc) 978-1-62029-665-3

All scripture quotations, unless otherwise noted, are taken from the King James Version of the Bible.

Scripture quotations marked NIV are taken from the HOLY BIBLE, NEW INTERNATIONAL VERSION®. NIV®. Copyright © 1973, 1978, 1984 by International Bible Society. Used by permission of Zondervan. All rights reserved.

This book is a work of fiction. Names, characters, places, and incidents are either products of the author's imagination or used fictitiously. Any similarity to actual people, organizations, and/or events is purely coincidental.

For more information about Kim Vogel Sawyer, please access the author's Web site at the following Internet address: www.KimVogelSawyer.com

Published by Barbour Publishing, Inc., P.O. Box 719, Uhrichsville, Ohio 44683, www.barbourbooks.com

Our mission is to publish and distribute inspirational products offering exceptional value and biblical encouragement to the masses.

 Member of the
Evangelical Christian
Publishers Association

Printed in the United States of America.

BYGONES

Dedication

For Connor and Ethan,
my precious grandsons.
You come from a long line of faithful saints.
May you carry that heritage into future generations.

Acknowledgments

Were it not for the support and understanding of my family, words would never appear on the computer screen. So thank you, Don and my daughters, for allowing me the time to write.

My parents, Ralph and Helen Vogel, deserve recognition for letting me sneak off with Daddy's typewriter, peck out my stories, and dream. Little did they realize the childish dreams would one day come true.

A special thank-you goes to Mrs. Erma Raber for taking the time to visit with me about her childhood.

I am deeply grateful to my critique group members—Eileen, Margie, Ramona, Staci, Crystal, and Donna—for their invaluable suggestions and unending encouragement.

So many people in my church support me through prayer—Kathy, Ernie, Ginny, Brother Ray, Don and Ann. . . . May God bless you as richly as you have blessed me.

Three fellow writers are instrumental in bringing me to a belief in myself: Susan Downs, Deborah Raney, and Tracie Peterson—thank you.

To Becky Germany and the staff at Barbour—thank you for the opportunity to work with you. You are a blessing in my life.

Finally, and most importantly, praise be to God for being ever present, ever loving, and ever able to carry me through life's pathway. May any praise or glory be reflected directly back to You.

*But now in Christ Jesus
you who once were far away have been brought
near through the blood of Christ.*
EPHESIANS 2:13 NIV

ONE

Henry Braun paused outside Jimmy's Dinner Stop and pressed his hand to his abdomen. Beneath his neatly tucked shirt his stomach churned. He couldn't decide if it was nervousness or excitement that had his belly jumping like a trout on a line. Either way, it didn't matter.

He hadn't seen Marie in more than twenty years. In his jacket pocket he carried a snapshot of her—one she'd enclosed in a Christmas card to her aunt Lisbeth three or four years back. But he didn't need it to remember her. A man never forgot his first love.

His hand trembled slightly as it connected with the smudged silver door handle of the café. As he tugged open the door, a wave of stale tobacco-scented air washed across him. Stepping inside, he allowed the door to drift shut behind him. He removed his hat, held it against his stomach with both hands, and stood silently, taking in the busy scene.

Nearly every booth and table was filled with noisy patrons, most of them men, probably truckers like Jep Quinn. Two waitresses, wearing pale blue knee-length dresses and white aprons, bustled between tables, pouring coffee from tall plastic containers and bantering with customers. Although both women appeared to be middle-aged, he picked out Marie right away. That nutmeg hair of hers, even cropped short into mussy curls, was unmistakable.

He remained beside a tall counter that held a cash register, waiting for someone to show him to a table. Curious gazes turned in his direction, and one man jabbed another with his elbow, pointing rudely before making a comment that brought a laugh from the other members of his group. Henry was accustomed to this treatment when he stepped out into the world. He averted his gaze and maintained his stoic expression.

After several minutes of waiting, the unfamiliar waitress waved a hand at him and hollered, "Hey, honey! There's a spot over here. C'mon in!"

Henry pointed to his chest, his eyebrows high, making certain she meant him. When she smiled and quirked her fingers at him, he moved forward on legs still stiff from the long drive. He slid into the empty booth.

"You new around here? I don't think I've seen you before."

The woman's bright smile, meant to put him at ease he was sure, made him feel like recoiling instead. But it would be impolite not to reply, so he said in an even tone, "I'm just passing through."

She gave a nod and a wink. "Well, welcome to Cheyenne. Enjoy your stay." Slopping coffee into a thick mug and whacking a menu on the table in front of him, she added, "Just look that over, honey, and I'll be right back to take your order."

He raised a finger to delay her. "I don't wish to order a meal, I only want to—" But she took off, and his request died on his lips. Leaving the coffee and menu untouched, he followed Marie with his gaze. How comfortable she appeared as she moved among the tables, smiling, sometimes teasing, laughing. . . . He had been so certain when she climbed into Jep Quinn's semi she would quickly realize her mistake and return to Sommerfeld. To him. Now he felt foolish.

Marie had obviously found her niche in the outside world.

Disappointment struck him, and he pondered its cause. Had he expected to find her cowering in a corner somewhere, overwhelmed and repentant? No. He had read the letters she'd sent to her aunt Lisbeth over the years. He came here knowing Marie had adopted the worldly lifestyle. The disappointment was personal.

His fingers twitched on the tabletop. Why hadn't she recognized him at once, as he had her?

"Hey, Marie, got a live one in booth thirteen."

Marie balanced three plates on one arm and grabbed a basket of rolls with her free hand. Sally was fond of pointing out the most handsome men who entered the roadside café, figuring Marie needed a man in her life. Marie didn't second the opinion. But she sent her friend a brief grin. "Oh, yeah?"

"Yeah." Sally released a light chuckle and reached past Marie for the plates Jimmy handed through the serving window. "From the way he's dressed, he must be a preacher or somethin'. Check him out."

Marie gave a quick nod. "When I've got a minute to spare." She weaved between tables to deliver Friday's special—fried fish, hush puppies, slaw, and fries—to the truckers at table three. She placed the plastic basket of rolls in the middle of the table, scolding when one of them made as if to pat her bottom. She served him first and quipped, "That should keep your hands busy." All three men roared. Smirking, she moved around the table and plopped plates in front of each customer. Hands on her hips, she asked, "Anything else I can get you fellas?"

The one with the roving hand grinned. "What I want probably isn't on the menu."

"You behave," Marie warned. Although she'd had plenty of opportunity over her years of widowhood, she'd never engaged in flirtation with customers. Sally said she wasn't the flirty type. Marie had always taken that as a compliment.

She backed away from the table. "If you think of something I missed, just wave a hand in the air."

The men hollered their thanks and dug into their food. As Marie turned to head for the serving window, she remembered Sally's comment and glanced toward booth thirteen. Her feet came to an abrupt halt right in the aisle between tables.

That was no preacher. Just a man. A Mennonite man. The plain blue shirt, buttoned to the collar, and black jacket with missing lapels identified him as clearly as advertising on a billboard. Her gaze bounced from his clothes to his face. His brown-eyed gaze met hers squarely, and she gasped. Her knees buckled. She reached for something—anything—to keep herself upright. Her hand connected with the shoulder of the nearest patron, and she heard a gruff voice call, "Hey, darlin', whatcha need?" Her gaze remained pinned to that of the Mennonite man's, who sat unmoving in the booth, his brown eyes unblinking.

"I–I'm sorry," she managed, removing her hand. The customer shrugged and went back to eating. Sally dashed by, and Marie caught the sleeve of her dress.

Sally paused in midstride, her face crinkled in concern. "Hey, what's wrong? You look like you've seen a ghost."

"I think I have."

Sally shifted her gaze toward the booth, then back at Marie. "You know that preacher?"

Marie nodded slowly. "I need a minute. Can you—"

Sally smiled and patted Marie's hand. "Sure, honey. Go ahead. I'll cover you."

Her gaze still on the man in the booth, Marie mumbled a thank-you. Her sluggish feet didn't want to move. *Go. Walk. Have to see what he wants.* Finally her feet obeyed, and she moved as if wading through cold molasses.

He rested his palms on the blue-speckled tabletop and looked up at her. He was older now. His close-cropped dark brown hair was speckled with gray, and lined sunbursts marked the corners of his eyes. But he was still undeniably handsome. Unmistakably Henry.

His Adam's apple bobbed in a swallow. Her throat felt dry, too. One of her hands, as if of its own volition, smoothed her unruly curls. The touch of her hair made her conscious of her uncovered head, and embarrassment struck at the thought of her bare knees and the tight fit of her bodice. Things that had become commonplace over the years now left her feeling exposed and vulnerable. She felt her cheeks flood with heat, and part of her wanted to run away and hide. Yet her feet turned stubborn once more, refusing to move.

What was he doing in Cheyenne, Wyoming—hundreds of miles from Kansas? How had he known where to find her? Had her family sent him? A dozen questions threaded through her mind, but when she opened her mouth, only one word squeaked out. "Hi."

"Hello." His voice had deepened with maturity, but the timidity she remembered still underscored the tone. "You"—he glanced around the bustling café—"are very busy right now."

She licked her lips. "Yes, I am. I—I can't really take a break, but—"

His nod cut her off. "I understand. When are you finished here?"

"Four."

Another nod. "I'll wait."

The simple statement flung her back nearly two dozen years. She heard, in her memory, his pain-filled voice whisper, *"I will wait for your return, Marie."* Now she wondered. . .had he?

13

"Marie?"

Sally's voice jarred her back to the present. She looked over her shoulder. Sally stood in front of the cluttered serving window, her arms held out in a silent gesture of *I need you*. Marie nodded, then spun back to Henry. "Don't wait here." She dug in her apron pocket, retrieved her keys, and twisted her apartment key from the ring. Slipping it into his hand, she said, "You can go to my apartment. The Woodlawn. Take the Broadway Avenue exit off the highway, then go ten blocks north and two east. The apartment building is on the corner of Carson and Twenty-third. I'm in Apartment 4B. Go in, make yourself at home. I'll be there as soon as I can."

She started to turn away, then looked at him again. "How did you get here?"

He pointed out the window. "I drove myself."

She glanced out to the parking area. A solid black four-door sedan waited, dwarfed by semi trucks. Her eyebrows flew high in surprise, and she caught a hint of a grin twitch his cheeks.

"I've worked on cars all my life, and now I drive one."

"Marie!"

Sally's frantic call spurred Marie to action. "I'll be home sometime after four." She dashed to the counter and took the waiting plates. Out of the corner of her eye, she watched Henry exit the café, then followed his tall form as he crossed in front of the window. Moments later, his car backed out of the parking lot and disappeared between semis.

"You gonna deliver those meals or hold 'em till the food is cold?"

Jimmy's sardonic voice captured Marie's attention. Her face flooded with heat once more.

"Sorry." Turning toward the waiting table, she called, "Food's comin' right up, boys."

After serving the men, she sneaked a peek at her wristwatch. Still two and a half hours until quitting time. Her breath whooshed out. *I hope I last that long. . . .*

The brown-brick apartment complex was clean but showed signs of age. Concrete slabs, some cracked, served as porches to each unit. The grass, mostly brown and brittle, was sparse in places, exposing patches of dirt. Henry stepped onto the slab in front of the door marked 4B and shook his head. On the corner of the poor excuse for a porch, a clay pot held a clump of drooping plastic tulips.

So Marie still liked flowers.

Henry couldn't help but think of the large, rambling farmhouse that had been Marie's childhood home, its thick grassy yard scattered with bright marigolds, zinnias, and morning glories. After all that space and beauty, how could she live in a place like this? He sighed, sadness weighing on his chest.

Despite having a key, Henry felt like an intruder as he opened the door and stepped inside. The apartment was quiet except for a ticking clock and a funny noise—a *blurple-blurp*—he didn't recognize. For long minutes he stood on the little rug in front of the door and allowed his gaze to drift around the small area, uncertain what to do.

A long sofa, draped with a bright-colored quilt, stood sentinel along the north wall. In front of the sofa crouched a small chest. Its top held a short stack of magazines, a small black box with white push buttons, and two crumpled napkins. A spindled rocking chair heaped with pillows rested in the corner.

Across from the couch, on the opposite wall, stood a shelving unit with a large center section flanked by open shelves. He crossed to it, his fingers reaching to stroke the surface. He shook his head. At first glance, the unit appeared to be wood, but closer examination proved it to be wood-printed paper glued to a solid base. Artificial wood. . .and artificial flowers. Sadness pressed again.

From the center portion of the shelves, a large television set stared blankly at the sofa. The glass front was coated with fine particles of dust. On a shelf above the television, he located the source of the blurping—a small fish aquarium, with a bright-colored castle and three goldfish. Every now and then a little tube at the back of the square glass box sent up a series of bubbles, which burbled as they rose to the top.

He watched the fish for a little while, his heart aching at the silent message they presented. Marie loved animals, but she probably wasn't allowed a pet in this apartment. Had she purchased the fish as a way to replace the memories of the dogs, cats, and lambs from the farm?

Shifting his gaze from the fish, he turned his attention to the photographs on the shelves. Each frame was unique—some wood, some metal, some pasted with beads or carved with flowers. A few of the pictures he'd seen before, in Lisbeth Koeppler's small sewing room, arranged in a simple album that rested next to the little woven basket that held every letter Marie had sent over the years. All of the photos featured the young girl Henry knew about but had never met.

He leaned closer, examining each photograph in turn, analyzing the girl's features. She had Marie's cleft chin and blue eyes, but not Marie's hair. A shame. That had always been Marie's best feature.

Now that hair was cut short into curls that waved helter-skelter on her head. So many changes. But what had he expected? Shaking his head, he turned from the photographs and crossed to the couch, seating himself on the edge of the soft cushion. Off to the side of the room were two open doorways. One led to the kitchen—he glimpsed a chrome-and-Formica table-and-chairs set—and the other to a hallway that, he surmised, ended with bedrooms. Such a tiny space compared to what she'd left behind. . .

Looking over his shoulder at the clock on the wall, he realized he would have a long wait. He clasped his knees and sighed, wishing he had brought along a book to read. His gaze found the television, and his reflection stared back from the large blank screen. Curiosity struck. What might be showing at two thirty in the afternoon on the television? But he didn't move to turn it on.

Except for the clock's *tick, tick* and the fish bowl's *blurple-blurp*, he sat in silence. Another sigh heaved out. At home he always had things to do, which made the time go quickly. *Blurple-blurp*. He looked at the clock again. *Tick, tick*. Sighed again. "I suppose I could look at one of these magazines."

Suddenly a noise intruded, a scratching outside. He rose as the door swung open and a girl—the one from the photographs—stepped through. She was humming, her head down, fiddling with something in the oversized brown leather bag that hung from her shoulder. She bumped the door closed with her hip and brought up her gaze, swinging her hair over her shoulder at the same time.

The moment she spotted him, she let out a scream that made the fine hairs on the back of his neck rise. Her hand plunged into her bag, and she yanked out a tiny spray can, which she aimed at him. "Don't come any closer. I'll shoot you. I swear I will!"

He brought up both hands in surrender, although he could see no threat in that little aerosol can.

"Who are you?" she barked, her blue eyes wide in her pale face. The hand holding the can quivered, but she didn't back down.

"My name is Henry Braun." He kept his voice low and soothing. The girl's wild eyes made his stomach turn an uneasy somersault. "I drove over from Sommerfeld to see your mother."

"How'd you get in here?"

"Your mother gave me the key. See?" He pointed to the chest in front of the couch, where he'd placed the house key.

Still scowling, the girl inched forward and snatched up the key. Keeping the can aimed at him, she growled, "You stay right there. I'm going to call my mother. Don't you move!"

The girl backed through the doorway that led to the kitchen and disappeared behind the wall. He heard some clicks, then the girl's voice. "Jimmy? This is Beth. I need to talk to Mom."

Henry crept to the front door and let himself out, then perched on the concrete stoop. He would wait out here for Marie. That girl of hers was crazy. For the first time since he headed out on this journey, he wondered if Lisbeth Koeppler had made a mistake.

Two

Although she normally left her sunglasses in the car, today Marie kept them on her face when she walked from the carport toward her apartment. Why she felt the need for the small shield, she couldn't be sure—she just knew she needed it.

Rounding the corner of the apartment complex, she spotted Henry sitting on the stoop in front of her door. Marie's heart caught; her steps slowed. His pose—elbows resting on widespread knees, head down, fingers toying with something on the concrete between his feet—reminded her of when they were teenagers and he would come to visit. Henry's bashfulness always kept his head lowered, his fingers busy spinning a blade of grass or twiddling a small twig.

Long-buried memories rushed to the surface, clamoring for attention. She shoved them aside and focused on the present. Why hadn't he gone in? She had assured Beth he had permission to be there. She stopped several feet short of the porch. Her shadow bumped against his right foot, and he looked up. The slash of shade from his hat brim hid his eyes.

"You didn't wait inside." A foolish statement, considering where she'd found him.

A slight grin twitched one side of his lips. "No."

She took a step closer, her shadow swallowing his foot and the pebbles he had been lining up on the sidewalk. "Why?"

Pushing to his feet, Henry shrugged. "With your daughter home, I thought it best to wait out here."

Of course. He wouldn't be comfortable in the apartment alone with Beth. Remembering Beth's panicked phone call, Marie nearly chuckled. Her daughter had no idea how harmless Henry was. "Let's go inside and we can talk."

He moved aside and allowed her to step onto the stoop, then waited on the sidewalk while she knocked on the door. Three clicks sounded—all three locks. Hadn't Beth believed her when she'd said Henry wasn't dangerous? The knob turned and Beth yanked the door open.

Normally Marie would have greeted her daughter with a cheery hello and a kiss on the cheek. But today, with the clicks of the locks still ringing in her ears, she moved through the doorway and called over her shoulder, "Please come in, Henry."

He followed, his hands clamped around the brim of his hat. He stepped past the little throw rug and waited silently under Beth's scowling perusal.

Marie closed the door, then gestured toward the couch. "Go ahead and sit down." She crossed to the entertainment center and removed her sunglasses, placing them on top of the television. In the glass, she watched Henry's reflection as he crossed to the couch in three long strides, sat, and laid his hat on the seat beside him.

Shifting her gaze, she caught a glimpse of her tousled curls in the fish tank's glass. She smoothed a hand over her hair, feeling exposed and vulnerable in front of Henry without the head covering of her youth. Her hand itched to grab the sunglasses again, but how silly she would look, wearing them in the house. Clasping her hands together, she turned to face her daughter.

"Beth, bring Henry a glass of water. He's been sitting out in the sun for quite a while." She hoped Beth heard the admonition in her tone.

Her mouth in a grim line, Beth disappeared into the kitchen. Soon the rattle of ice in a glass and running water let Marie know her daughter was following her instructions. She sat in the rocking chair in the corner and offered Henry a weak smile.

"It was a big. . ." Shock? Accurate, but too strong. ". . .surprise to see you in the restaurant today."

Beth entered the room, moved stiffly to Henry, and held out the water without a word.

"Thank you." He took a long draw, giving Marie a dizzying sense of déjà vu that quickly disappeared when he wiped his mouth with the back of his hand. "I probably should have called, but—"

Marie drew back, startled. "You know my number?"

He set the half-empty glass near the stack of magazines. "Lisbeth had it."

At the mention of her aunt, Marie's heart melted. Images of the sweet-faced, gentle woman filled her head. Of all the people in Sommerfeld, Marie missed Aunt Lisbeth the most. Leaning forward, she spoke eagerly. "How is she? It's been weeks since I've heard from her."

Henry dropped his gaze. "Your aunt Lisbeth is why I'm here."

His voice sounded strained. Marie's chest constricted.

"I'm going to my room." Beth turned toward the hallway.

Henry jumped to his feet. "No. Please. I need to speak with both you and your mother." He waved his hand clumsily at the couch. "If you'd care to sit, I'll explain why I've come."

Beth sent Marie a puzzled look, but she sat on the arm of the couch near the rocker. Henry remained standing at the other end, and for a few minutes he worried his lower lip between his teeth.

Marie knew he was gathering his thoughts, but she sensed her daughter's impatience. She touched Beth's knee—a silent plea to sit quietly and wait.

Henry cleared his throat. "There is no good way to share bad news. I'm so sorry, Marie, but your aunt Lisbeth passed away six weeks ago."

Marie covered her mouth with her fingers, holding back the words of anguish that rushed to her lips. Dear Aunt Lisbeth. . . dead?

Beth dropped to her knees beside the rocking chair and placed her hands in Marie's lap. Tears glittered in her blue eyes. "Oh, Mom, I'm sorry."

Marie blinked rapidly, managing to give her daughter a wobbly smile of thanks. Beth knew what Lisbeth meant to her. She'd named her baby Lisbeth Marie for her great-aunt. Even though the two Lisbeths hadn't seen each other since Beth was only two weeks old, Beth had read the letters that had arrived over the years, had listened to her mother's stories of time with her favorite aunt. Beth would mourn, too.

Looking at Henry, Marie choked out a single-word query: "How?"

Henry sat back on the couch. Sympathy shone in his eyes. "Her heart."

Marie nodded. The Koeppler bane.

"She'd been ill for the past two years," Henry continued in a tender voice. "The doctor warned her to slow down, but. . ." He shrugged. The gesture communicated clearly, *You know Lisbeth.*

Yes, Marie knew Lisbeth. Always busy, always giving, always smiling. Closing her eyes, she allowed a picture of her aunt to fill her mind. . .Aunt Lisbeth at the table in her kitchen, wrinkled hands kneading a lump of dough, her eyes sparkling beneath her white prayer cap. Marie swallowed the lump of sorrow that filled her throat and gave Beth's hands a squeeze. Beth slipped onto the couch, still holding one of her mother's hands.

"Thank you for coming all this way to tell me." For a moment, Marie longed to reach out and clasp Henry's hand, too. Instead, she coiled her hand into a fist and pressed it to her lap. "Lisbeth always informed me of family deaths in the past, and it was hard to get news like that in a letter. It was kind of you to break this to me gently. Six weeks. . ." She shook her head. "Of course, no one in my family bothered to let me know." She made no attempt to mask the resentment in her tone.

Henry ducked his head. A few moments of silence ticked by before he met her gaze. "There's more." He glanced at Beth, his brow furrowed. "This word is for you."

Beth shot her mother a startled look.

"Your mother's aunt Lisbeth ran a little café in Sommerfeld."

Beth released a little grunt of irritation. "I know. Mom and I talked a lot about Great-Aunt Lisbeth."

Henry's gaze bounced quickly to Marie, an unreadable expression in his eyes, before returning to Beth. "I guess you also know Lisbeth never married, so she has no children."

"Yes."

Henry swallowed, scratching the hair behind his left ear. "Lisbeth and I were. . .close friends."

Marie wondered briefly if they had bonded after her unexpected departure from Sommerfeld—perhaps sharing their heartache at her decision to leave and marry Jep.

"I spent a great deal of time with her, especially when her health began to fail," Henry went on. Beth sat with pursed lips, her fingers tight on Marie's hand. "She asked me to see that her things were cared for after her death. I promised her I would. My sister, Deborah, and her daughter, Trina, have kept the café running, and I've checked her house each day to make sure nothing has gone wrong."

Beth held up her hand. "What does all this have to do with me?"

Henry continued in a calm voice, as if he had rehearsed the words a certain way and they must be delivered as planned. "Two weeks ago, at the prompting of your grandfather. . ."

Beth's fingers convulsed on Marie's hand, and Marie tightened her grip.

". . .I began to clean out the house in preparation for sale of the contents. In Lisbeth's desk, I found her will, written in her own hand. She bequeathed all of her earthly belongings to you, Beth."

Beth jerked back, her hand yanking free of Marie's. "W–what?"

Marie's heart pattered so loudly it nearly covered Henry's quiet statement.

"The café, the house, and everything inside has been left to you."

Beth's wide-eyed gaze met her mother's. "But—but what do *I* want with all that?"

Marie ignored her daughter and looked at Henry. "Do my parents know this?"

Henry's gaze dropped briefly, his forehead creasing, before he offered a nod. "I showed them the will. They couldn't deny it was what she wanted."

"They aren't protesting it?" Marie held her breath. Surely her father would fight to his own death the bestowment of anything to this unclaimed grandchild.

"No, they're not."

Marie released her breath in a *whoosh*.

Beth broke into a huge smile, jumped from the couch, and clapped her hands. "Mom, this is a real windfall. Now maybe Mitch and I won't have to take out a loan to start our business after all. It's like Karma or something!"

Spinning to face Henry, she fired off a rapid explanation. "My boyfriend and I want to open an interior-design shop with one-of-a-kind antiques and specialty items. We were going to get a small-business loan, but now. . ." She paused, licking her lips. "How much do you think you'll get for the house and café? I mean, I know it's in a small town and all, but surely it'll raise at least—what?—thirty thousand? Maybe more?"

Henry rose, holding his hand toward Beth. "You need to sit down."

"I'm too excited to sit!"

Her smile lit the room, but it also cut Marie's heart. This "windfall," as Beth had called it, was at the loss of someone Marie held dear. Beth seemed to have lost sight of that.

The girl paced across the small room. "After everything is sold, go ahead and keep a little for your trouble—maybe 3 or 5 percent—then send me a check for the rest. I trust you."

Henry shook his head. "That won't do."

"Okay," Beth huffed. "Eight to 10 percent."

Henry drew in a breath. "It's not about the money."

Beth tipped her head, scowling. "Then what?"

Once more Henry gestured toward the couch. "Please, will you sit down?"

Beth sent Marie a wary look, then seated herself on the edge of the couch. Looking up at Henry, she flipped her palms outward. "Well?"

"Lisbeth included a condition in the will. Before any of the property can be sold, you must reside in it for a period of no less than three months."

"What?" Beth's voice squeaked out shrilly. She leaped up again and placed her hands on her hips, glowering at Henry. "You must be joking!"

Henry remained calm. "It's not a joke."

"Oh, this is rich." Beth laughed, but the sound held little humor. "These people I've never met kicked my mom and me out of their lives, and now I'm supposed to drop everything, move to Sommerfeld, and live with them for three months? That's the biggest farce I've ever heard of."

"Beth. . ." Marie rose and touched her daughter's arm.

The girl pulled away. "I'm sorry, Mom. I know you loved that old lady, and maybe a part of me loved her, too, just because you did. But what she's asking me to do. . . I won't do it." She pointed at Henry. "You figure some way around that ridiculous *condition*. I don't care how you do it, but get me the money without forcing me to live in that awful town."

Before Marie or Henry could respond, she dashed down the hallway. The slam of her door echoed through the apartment. For long moments, neither of them spoke. They just stood at opposite ends of the couch, looking past each other.

Finally, Henry sighed. Without looking at Marie, he said, "If Beth doesn't fulfill the condition, the property transfers to Lisbeth's brother and sister."

A bitter taste filled Marie's mouth at the thought of her father and her aunt Cornelia sharing the proceeds. Marie wished Lisbeth had just left everything to Aunt Cornelia rather than involving Beth. It was a kind gesture, but that condition. . . It guaranteed heartache. Aunt Lisbeth must have known it would be met with resistance. Why would she place such a requirement on the acquisition?

"I'm reasonably certain you can proceed with splitting the property between Aunt Cornelia and. . ." She couldn't say the word *Dad*. She hadn't had a dad in more than twenty years. Swallowing, she finished, "Beth is very headstrong."

A brief smile flitted across Henry's face. "I can see that."

Marie laughed ruefully. "She won't give in." Even though Beth had never known her father, she had inherited many of Jep Quinn's characteristics. The tendency to act first and think second was very much like him. But even after a lot of thought, Beth was unlikely to concede to Aunt Lisbeth's requirement.

Marie didn't know what to say. There had been a time when she and Henry had spoken freely with each other. But those days were long gone, buried under years of separation. Standing in his presence now was uncomfortable. And sad.

"I'll mail you a copy of the will." Henry's low-toned voice carried a hint of regret.

"Thank you." Marie finally met his gaze. His velvety eyes locked on hers, causing an unusual patter in her heart. "It was kind of you to make the long drive," she blurted out. "I hope your family didn't mind you taking the time off."

Henry blinked twice, his sooty lashes momentarily shielding his eyes. Then he swallowed and picked up his hat, putting it on his head. "Lisbeth was my only family." Without another word, he slipped out the door.

THREE

"Mitch, it was the most aggravating thing!" Beth slammed her fist against her pillow. Clicking the hands-free button on her cell phone, she held the phone like a microphone and continued to vent her frustration. "Can you imagine the nerve of that guy? Standing in my living room, telling me I have to live in some tiny little backwoods town for three whole months just to claim an inheritance. It is so totally stupid!"

She jumped up from her bed and stomped back and forth across the small bedroom. "And Mom just stood there, saying nothing." A pang of guilt struck. "I mean, I kind of understand. She got a shock, finding out her favorite relative died." The ire rose again. "But still, she knows as well as I do that we aren't welcome there. Why didn't she just tell him to get out?"

From the other end of the line, Mitch's husky chuckle sounded. "Maybe because your mama is a lady, and a lady doesn't holler 'Get out' at a visitor?"

Flopping across the bed, Beth threw one arm over her head. She pictured Henry Braun standing uncertainly beside the couch while she aimed her mace can at him, and she laughed. "You should have seen the way he was dressed—straight out of *Little House on the Prairie*."

"Oh, yeah?" Mitch's voice held humor. "One of those bowl haircuts and a beard that hangs down to his chest?"

"No." Beth twirled a strand of hair around her finger. "Real short, neat haircut. And no beard. Actually a pretty decent-looking man for an older guy, except for those clothes. They made him look so. . .backward." She snorted. "Did he really think I'd go live with a whole town full of people like him? No, thanks!"

Mitch's husky laughter sounded again.

She sighed. "I told him to figure out some way to sell the property and send me the money. But I doubt he'll do it. Mom said if I don't meet the condition, my *grandfather*"—she managed to make the title sound like a dirty word—"will get it all instead."

"Is that what you want?"

Beth's throat felt tight. "No! He shouldn't get anything after what he did to Mom—sending her away in disgrace, like she'd done something terrible by marrying my dad and having me." *What kind of a father disowns his child?* Beth wondered for the hundredth time.

"Listen. . ."

Beth's fingers tightened on the phone as Mitch's tone turned wheedling.

"Maybe you ought to back up and look at the big picture."

"What do you mean. . .'big picture'?"

"Now don't get riled."

"I'm not riled!"

Mitch's laugh did nothing to soothe Beth's jangled nerves. Sitting up, she growled into the phone, "I'm going to hang up."

"No, Lissie, come on—listen to me."

Beth crossed her leg and bounced her foot.

"That guy said you'd have to live in. . .what's the name of the town?"

"Sommerfeld." The word was forced between gritted teeth.

"Sommerfeld. But just for three months. You'd be out of there by Christmas. You'd have the money in hand to start our business right after the first of the year."

"But, Mitch—"

"Besides, that town full of. . .what's the religious group?"

Beth huffed. "Mennonites."

"That town full of Mennonites has to be loaded with antiques. I mean, those people don't buy new stuff very often. There's bound to be tons of things you could pick up—probably for a song—to put in our boutique."

Beth stood, her stomach fluttering. "You want me to *go?*"

"Like I said, it's only three months. Drop in a bucket." His chuckle sounded again. "I could live in an igloo in Antarctica for three months if it meant gaining a pocket full of cash and a storehouse of goods for our business."

"Fine." Beth grated out the word. "I'll book you an igloo in Antarctica, and you can leave in the morning."

Mitch's full-throated laughter rang. "Oh, Lissie, you are too cute."

Dropping back to the bed, Beth sighed. "I'm not trying to be. I really don't want to go to that town."

"Not even for the money?"

"No."

"Not even for the antiques?"

"No."

A slight pause. "Not even for us?"

His persuasive undercurrent melted a bit of Beth's resolve. "Mitch. . ."

"Three months, Lissie. That's not such a huge price to pay for our future, is it?"

Beth fell backward, bouncing the mattress. "You are so annoying."

Another chuckle. "But lovable, right?"

Despite herself, Beth released a short giggle. "So. . .if I go, will you come, too?"

A snort blasted. "Yeah, I can imagine how well I'd fit in there. As inconspicuous as a snake in a jar of jelly beans."

Beth giggled, thinking of Mitch's hair that curled over his collar in the back and stuck up in gelled spikes on top of his head. Not even one of those flat-brimmed black hats would make him blend in with the Mennonites if they all dressed like Henry Braun.

"But," Mitch continued, "I think you should take your mom."

Beth released a low whistle. "No way. Mom will never set foot in Sommerfeld again." Flat on her back, she stared at the ceiling, remembering the pain in her mother's eyes when she explained to eight-year-old Beth why she had no grandparents to visit at Christmastime like her friends had.

"But it would give you some company." The persuasive tone returned. "And surely she knows how to run a café after all the years she's spent working in restaurants. A working café would bring in more money than one that's sat empty for a while. She'd help you out, wouldn't she?"

"I couldn't ask her to!" Beth rolled onto her stomach and propped herself up with her elbows. "She hasn't seen her family since I was two weeks old. That's more than twenty years. Imagine how hard it would be for her to go back."

"Aw, let bygones be bygones." Mitch's flippant tone raised Beth's ire. "For the chance at maybe thirty thousand smackers, she can set aside her differences."

Beth set her jaw, allowing her lack of response to communicate her displeasure at his uncaring attitude. After a long pause, Mitch's voice came again, more subdued.

"Lissie?"

"Yeah?"

"At least ask her. There's not much mothers won't do for their kids."

Beth knew that. Mom had given up her entire life for her—sometimes working two jobs to be sure they had a decent place to live and the extras like braces and gymnastics lessons and a vacation every summer. Beth hadn't had to pay a penny for college—Mom had squirreled away enough money over the years to cover the cost of her associate degree in interior design. If Beth asked, Mom would go. But was it fair to ask?

"You gonna think about it?"

Mitch's voice jarred Beth back to the present. "Yeah." She drew in a long breath and let it out slowly. "I'll think about it."

"Good girl."

The approving tone sent a shiver down Beth's spine. He seemed to be counting the money already. "No guarantees, Mitch," she reminded him.

His chuckle, which was becoming annoying, rumbled one more time. "You know, Lissie, I think I know your mama better than you do. 'Bye, babe."

Beth stared at the blank screen on the cell phone for a long time before flipping it closed. She sat up, placed the phone on the whitewashed nightstand, and replayed Mitch's arguments. Maybe he was right. Three months wasn't that much, considering the payoff.

Beth looked around her simple bedroom with its secondhand furniture. Mom had always given her the best she could afford, even if it meant doing without something herself. How many of the clothes in her mother's closet came from Goodwill? Even though she was on her feet all day, she never bought the expensive, cushy shoes but chose discount stores so she could do more for her daughter. Mom gave and gave and gave. Maybe it was time for Beth to give back.

If Beth went to Sommerfeld and met the condition of the will, she'd be in a position to pay her mom back. Take her shopping and let her pick out an outfit that didn't come from the clearance rack. Or maybe take her on a vacation. Mom had told her how Dad promised to show her the United States from shore to shore, but she'd gotten pregnant and couldn't travel. And then, of course, he'd died.

Even though Beth had never met her father, she still missed him. Mom had tried so hard all her life to be both mother and father. . .to keep Beth from feeling as though her life was incomplete. She'd done a great job, but there was that constant spot in her heart where a father's love should have been.

Beth rose and moved to her dresser, picking up the framed snapshot of her parents, taken when Mom was about halfway through her pregnancy. Dad stood behind her, his chin on her shoulder, his hands cupping the gentle mound of her belly. A lump filled Beth's throat. Her daddy would have loved her. She just knew it. And he would never have cast her aside, the way Mom's dad had done.

She set the picture down, her lips pursed, forehead creased. That old man should not get the money meant for her.

"Well," she mumbled, turning toward the bedroom door and sucking in a big breath, "the only way to find out what Mom thinks about all this is to ask her." She headed for her mother's bedroom.

Henry pulled into the first gas station he encountered when he entered Kimball, Nebraska. Dusk had fallen, and the air had a nip in it as it whipped around the pumps and pushed at his hat. The odor of gasoline filled his nostrils, reminding him of the smell that surrounded the truck stop where Marie spent her days.

She was still pretty, he acknowledged, as he forced the nozzle into the opening of the fuel tank and clicked the handle. The modern

KIM VOGEL SAWYER

clothing and short hairstyle hadn't been to his taste, but her blue eyes still had their sparkle, and the cleft in her chin was as appealing as it had always been.

As a young man, courting Marie, he'd wanted to kiss that little cleft, but bashfulness had held him back. Looking at her today, he'd had the same impulse. His stomach clenched. Who would have thought a man of his age would harbor such a boyish whim? It was best to put those thoughts aside. Marie had made her choice. She made it twenty-three years ago when she climbed into Jep Quinn's semi and rolled down the highway without waving good-bye.

Lisbeth had meant well, but her good intentions would accomplish nothing. Henry remembered the brief message enclosed in the envelope with Lisbeth's will, a message meant only for Henry's eyes. *If we can bring her home, home will find its way back to her heart, and she will be ours again.* Yes, Lisbeth had known how Henry still felt about Marie. But Henry knew how Marie still felt about Sommerfeld. He'd seen it in her eyes when he'd given her daughter the condition for receiving Lisbeth's inheritance. Marie would not come home again.

The pump clicked off, signaling a full tank. Henry removed the nozzle, hooked it back on the pump, and closed the gas cap. Leaving the car at the pump, he went inside the convenience store. He selected his supper—a plastic-wrapped sandwich and a pint bottle of milk—and paid for it and the gasoline at the register. Ignoring the curious stares from two teenagers at the magazine rack, he returned to his vehicle, climbed in, and aimed his car east on Interstate 80. He estimated that tomorrow morning's sun would be creeping over the horizon when he arrived in Sommerfeld.

Sunrises. . . New beginnings. . . *My dear heavenly Father, being near Marie again has given my heart funny ideas. It would not bother me a bit if You were to remove all memories of her from my mind.*

Despite his prayer, the image of Marie's tousled hair, blue eyes, and delicate cleft chin refused to depart.

Marie's bedroom door cracked open and Beth leaned in, only her head and one shoulder appearing.

"Mom?"

Marie set aside her book and removed the discount-store reading glasses from their perch on the end of her nose. Patting the patch of mattress next to her knees, she invited, "Come on in, honey."

Beth crossed the floor on bare feet, her head down, long hair hanging in tousled curls over her shoulders. Maternal love swelled up, creating a lump in Marie's throat. In spite of all the regrets she carried, having and raising Beth made them all worthwhile.

Beth sat on the edge of the mattress and picked up Marie's discarded glasses, twirling the plastic frame between her fingers. "I was just talking to Mitch."

As always, mention of Beth's boyfriend made Marie's scalp prickle. She couldn't pinpoint a reason for it—the young man was intelligent, polite, and treated Beth well. But there was. . .something. "What about?"

"Aunt Lisbeth's will."

Marie nodded. "Quite a surprise, wasn't it?"

"I'll say." Beth sighed. Her head still low, she peeked at her mother through a fringe of thick lashes. "Mitch thinks I'm foolish for not meeting the condition."

Marie listened as Beth outlined all of Mitch's arguments. When Beth had finished, she asked, "And how do you feel about it?"

Throwing her head back, Beth huffed at the ceiling. "It makes me mad. I mean, it's not really fair to say, 'I'll give you this if you do that.' It's like what your dad did to you."

Marie tipped her head. "What do you mean?"

"You know—saying you weren't his daughter anymore because you chose to marry my dad and leave the community. It's putting conditions on love."

Marie nodded slowly, lowering her gaze to her lap.

"I guess what makes me madder than the condition on the will," Beth continued, her voice quavering with fervency, "is the idea of your father getting the money that should be mine."

Marie jerked her chin upward, looking at Beth's profile.

Beth turned her face, meeting her mother's gaze. She blinked several times, licking her lips. "Mom, if I decided to do what your aunt Lisbeth said—if I decided to go to Sommerfeld—would you come with me?"

Marie pressed backward against the pile of bed pillows, her hand on her chest. Beneath her palm, her heart pounded like a tom-tom. "Go. . .to Sommerfeld?"

Beth nodded. "I don't know how to run a café, but you do. We could keep it going, which would give us a little income during the months we have to stay there, and Mitch says a functioning business will raise a better price." She set the glasses aside and took her mother's hand. "Mom, I know it's hard for you to think of going there. I know there are bad memories. But the money from that café and the house can give me my dream business and let me do things I wouldn't be able to otherwise."

Marie felt as though something blocked her voice box. She couldn't find words.

"I don't expect you to answer now." Beth squeezed Marie's hand. "Just think about it. If you say no, I'll understand, but. . ." She paused, sucking in her lips for a moment. Giving Marie's hand a final squeeze, she let go and stood.

She zipped across the room and left, closing the door behind her.

Marie stared at the closed door, all the points Beth had made ringing in her ears. Money to start the business, possibility of accumulating items for the boutique, putting Lisbeth's money into the hands she chose. . .

How Marie wanted to help her daughter. But return to Sommer-feld? A rush of memories cluttered her mind—memories she hadn't allowed to surface for years. She closed her eyes, smiling at recalled funny moments, feeling the prick of a tear at touching times. Then one picture loomed over the rest. Her father, his face set in an angry scowl, his finger pointing toward the door, his voice booming, "You made your bed, young woman. Go lie in it!"

Her eyes popped open, sweat breaking out over her body. She trembled from head to toe. Return to Sommerfeld? How could she do it? Then she thought of Beth's pleading eyes.

Marie's head drooped, as if the muscles in her neck had given way. She could not deny her daughter the means to achieve her dream. As difficult as it would be, she would return to Sommerfeld. For Beth.

Oh, Lord, help me. When the words formed in her heart, she wasn't sure if they were a prayer or a command.

FOUR

Henry parked his vehicle behind Lisbeth's Café, in the alley beside the empty storage shed. There had been no room out front, all the parking spaces taken by highway visitors. He wondered briefly if Marie had been gone so long she would fail to recognize the differences between Sommerfeld residents' means of transportation and the vehicles driven by those who lived in the nearby cities.

Her little red car with the white pinstripes would certainly stick out among the Mennonites' plain, black cars. He shook his head, clearing his thoughts. What difference would it make? Marie wouldn't be seeing any of these vehicles. She and Beth had made their choice. His heart felt heavy at his failure to bring them here. Lisbeth would be so disappointed.

With a sigh, he swung open his car door and stepped out. He stood in the V made by the open door and stretched, straightening his arms over his head. His shoulders ached, and he emitted a low groan.

The slam of the café's back screen door caught his attention, and he glanced toward the simple beige block building. His niece, Trina, bustled across the ground toward the trash bins, a black plastic garbage bag in her hands. The white ribbons on her prayer cap lifted in the gentle breeze, twirling beneath her chin. She reached the bins and paused, poising her body for a mighty throw.

"Trina!" He trotted toward her in an awkward gait. His stiff legs didn't feel like moving so quickly. "Let me get that."

Trina grinned at him, her freckled nose crinkling. "Thank you, Uncle Henry. I hate hefting that thing over the edge. Sometimes I dump it on my head!"

With a chuckle, he swung the bag into the high bin, then rubbed his shoulder. "I'm too old to be sitting behind a steering wheel all night."

Trina grinned as she fell in step with him and they headed toward the café. "You aren't old, Uncle Henry."

His lips twitched as he quirked a brow. "Oh?" He touched his temple. "And all this gray hair is just pretend, huh?"

The girl laughed, slipping her hand through the bend in his elbow. "It makes you look distinguished."

Henry shook his head. "I think you're a flatterer, but thank you just the same."

They stepped into the café's kitchen, and Trina scampered to the sink, where she soaped her hands. Based on the sounds carrying in from the dining area, Henry guessed Trina and Deborah were having a typically busy Saturday morning. Deborah stood at the long stove, where she deftly scrambled eggs on the built-in grill.

Trina snatched up two waiting plates from the serving counter behind Deborah and disappeared through a swinging door that led to the dining area.

Henry crossed to Deborah. "Do you need my help?"

She barely glanced at him as she lifted two slices of ham from a tray and placed them next to the eggs. A sizzle sounded, followed by the delicious scent of smoked ham. Henry's mouth watered.

"You look like you need a long rest."

His sister's blunt comment made him grin. "Yes, I suppose I could use one. I've been up for"—he consulted the round clock hanging on the wall—"almost thirty hours now."

"Then go to bed." Deborah poked the ham slices with a fork and flipped them to the other side, then scooped the eggs from the grill with a metal spatula, sliding them onto plates.

Henry shook his head. "Not if you need me."

Trina burst through the door, her cheeks flushed. "Three orders of hotcakes, Mama. One with sausage, one with fried eggs—sunny-side up—and one with sausage and scrambled eggs."

Deborah gave a brusque nod and spun toward the tray of sausage links. Her elbow collided with Henry's midsection. She pursed her lips, shaking her head. "You're no help standing in my way. Go home and go to bed."

Trina's dark eyes sparkled as she took the plates of ham and eggs. "She's right. You look like you're about to fall over. Get some sleep."

Henry opened his mouth to protest, but the telephone by the back door jangled.

Deborah jerked her chin toward the sound. "If you want to help me, answer that. I have hotcakes to pour."

Henry reached the phone as it began its third ring. Pressing the black plastic receiver to his ear, he said, "Lisbeth's Café. May I help you?"

After a pause, a woman's voice—soft, hesitant—carried through the line. "Is—is this Henry?"

He frowned, the café clatter making it hard to hear. He plugged his open ear with his finger. "Yes, this is Henry Braun. May I help you?"

"Henry, this is Marie."

He nearly dropped the receiver.

"Do I need to take that?"

Deborah's strident tone made Henry spin around, tangling

himself in the spiraling cord. He shook his head. "No, it's for me." At Deborah's nod, he turned his back on her and hunched forward, an attempt for privacy.

"Are you there?" Marie's voice sounded again, still timid.

"Yes, I'm here." Henry cleared his throat. "What—what can I do for you?"

A self-conscious laugh sounded. "Well, they say it's a woman's prerogative to change her mind, and Beth has exercised that prerogative."

Henry's heart began to pound.

"Have you notified my. . .parents yet?"

"No." Henry swallowed. "I only just now got into town. I haven't had a chance to talk to them yet."

"So it isn't too late for Beth to meet Aunt Lisbeth's condition?"

The lump returned to his throat. "No, it isn't."

"She'll be relieved to hear that."

"I–I'm sure she will," Henry's voice squeaked. He cleared his throat. "When does she plan to arrive?"

"I expect it will take at least a week to get things squared away here, probably more like two. Do you need to know a specific arrival day right now?"

Henry shook his head, his thoughts racing. "No, of course not. But the house will need airing and a few groceries brought in. If—if you let me know a couple of days ahead of time, I'll make sure things are ready for her."

"Thank you." Her warm tone coiled through Henry's chest. "But don't go to any extra trouble. We'll bring food from our cupboards here, and I'm capable of airing a house."

Henry jerked upright. "Y–you're coming, too?"

"Yes." The word was nearly whispered. "I plan to keep the café running."

Henry looked over his shoulder at Deborah, who stood with her hands on her hips, scowling at the shelf above the grill. A satisfied smile creased her face as she yanked something down and sprinkled it over the sizzling eggs. He pictured Deborah and Marie side by side at that grill. An involuntary snort blasted.

"Henry?"

Marie's questioning tone brought him back to reality. "Yes?"

"Should I use this number to reach you?"

He rubbed his chin. He could give her the number for his shop, he supposed, but for some reason he felt the need to distance himself a bit. "Yes," he said, a niggle of guilt he didn't fully understand twisting his heart. "Deborah will get the message to me."

"All right. Thank you. I—I suppose I'll see you soon."

He wished he could guess what she was thinking. "Yes."

"Good-bye."

The line went dead. Henry held the receiver for another few seconds before slipping it onto its cradle. He looked across the room to Deborah.

She shifted her gaze to meet his, then frowned. "Henry, you're about to fall asleep leaning against the wall. Go get some rest."

He nodded, covering a yawn with his hand. "If you're sure you don't need me."

She flapped a hand at him. "Go. We'll be fine. Trina and I have found our stride."

"All right then. I'll see you later." He didn't wait for her reply, simply exited through the screen door and headed to his car. Not until he was backing out of the little parking area did he realize that Deborah hadn't even asked how his visit had gone.

"So you're really going to do it." Sally sat across from Marie, a coffee cup hooked to her finger. "You're going home again."

The restaurant was blessedly empty after its normally frenzied Saturday. The women sat in a secluded corner booth, away from the two teenage busboys who mopped the floor on the opposite side of the large dining room.

Marie slipped off her shoes and tucked her feet beneath her. She ducked her head at Sally's comment, chuckling ruefully. "I'd hardly call it going home. That denotes some sort of waiting welcome. I doubt I'll have that."

Sally shook her head, her bleached-blond curls bouncing. "Then why do it? That girl of yours is twenty years old—plenty old enough to make the trip alone. Why put yourself through it?"

Over the years of working together, Marie had confided in Sally many times. They had both raised daughters alone, although Sally was alone due to divorce rather than widowhood. Still, the pair had shared woes and worries and laughter. Marie saw genuine concern in Sally's eyes now, and her heart expanded in gratitude.

"If she's going to keep Aunt Lisbeth's café going, she'll need me."

"Didn't you say that man's sister was running it?" Sally placed her mug on the table and played with the handle, running her finger in a circle inside the loop. "She could keep running it. You don't really *need* to go."

The feeling that had plagued Marie for the past two weeks as she packed items and made the dozen arrangements that precede a move now returned. She didn't understand the odd longing; she only knew she had to answer it.

"Yes, I do."

Sally huffed. "Because Beth can't do without you?"

"No." Marie's voice lowered to a husky whisper. "Because I need to. . ." But she couldn't finish. Need to what? Put things to rest? Exorcise a ghost? Burn a bridge. . .or build one? She wasn't sure.

Sally reached across the table and gave Marie's hand a pat. "Listen, honey, you think I don't understand? My daddy did to me exactly what my Cindy's daddy did to her—walked out the door and never looked back. Even though yours didn't leave you physically, he left you emotionally when he sent you away."

Pain stabbed Marie's heart. Even after all the time that had passed, the heartache of that moment—when she stood in her parents' doorway with her fatherless baby wailing in her arms and saw only condemnation in her father's eyes—was as sharp in remembrance as it had been in the living.

Sally tugged her hand. "You're going back there to see if he's changed his mind, aren't you?"

Marie sighed. "Maybe."

Sally took another sip of her coffee, her lowered gaze pinned to Marie. "Well, three months isn't so long, I suppose. A person can bear just about anything for three months."

Marie smirked. "Even handling this place without my help?"

"Humph." Sally plunked her empty mug on the table. "Did you see the replacement Jimmy hired? Can't be more than nineteen and barely a hundred pounds dripping wet. I'll be doing all the lifting and serving while she stands at the counter and flutters her eyelashes at Jimmy all day."

"Oh, Sally." Marie shook her head, smiling at her friend. "At least I know you'll miss me."

"You know I will."

"Thanks for letting Cindy sublet my apartment."

Sally flapped a hand in dismissal. "Oh, that was nothing. It was time for her to spread her wings a bit, find out what it's like not to have Mom around to pick up her dirty socks and pay her phone bill. It'll be a growing experience for her."

"I wouldn't trust anyone else to feed my fish and take care of my furniture." Marie quirked one brow. "She *will* feed my fish and take care of my furniture, won't she?"

Sally laughed. "She's not perfect, but she is kind to animals and isn't a vandal. I'm sure your fish and furniture will be fine."

"Good."

Sally's brow creased. "Marie, can I give you a word of advice?" All teasing had left her tone.

Marie shrugged, offering a silent invitation.

"Be careful. I know it's been a long time, but those hurts haven't completely healed. If you go there with the expectation of being brought back into the fold, and your daddy tosses you aside again, you're going to have open, bleeding wounds."

Marie shook her head, forcing a smile. "Now didn't I just say I don't expect a big welcome?"

"Yes, that's what you said," Sally countered, her eyes flashing. "But saying and believing are two different things." She leaned back, pinning Marie with her steady gaze. "And I know you pretty well, my friend. You and me—we're a lot alike. Underneath, we're still little girls looking for our daddies' approval."

Even though she tried not to think about it, Marie knew Sally was right. The absence of her father's love was a hole that had never been filled.

"Does he know you're coming?"

A weight settled on Marie's chest. "I'm sure he does. Henry told both my father and my other aunt that Beth would be claiming her inheritance. As to knowing *when* I'm coming. . ." She shrugged. "That depends on whether Henry shared my arrival time with my parents. I only called him at noon today. I didn't want him going to a lot of extra work to get things ready for us." A smile tugged at her cheeks. "You see, in Sommerfeld, people don't do physical labor on Sunday. And I didn't leave him anything but Sunday to prepare for us."

"Sneaky." Sally winked, grinning impishly; then her expression sobered. "So. . .what time will you pull out tomorrow?"

"By six, if I can get Beth out of bed." She sent Sally a knowing grin. "It's a ten-hour drive without stops, and I want to be there before it's dark if possible."

"Well, I can see why!" Sally whistled. "Living in a house with no electricity. . ." She patted her hair. "I'd never survive without my blow-dryer and hot rollers."

"Oh, but a person can bear *anything* for three months." Marie threw out the teasing comment, her lips twitching in a grin.

Sally laughed, reaching across the table to clasp Marie's hand. "And I forgot—you don't need to worry about your hair because the ladies all wear those little bonnets." She tipped her head, examining Marie's hair. "I just can't picture you in one of those things."

Marie touched her head, trying to recall the feel of the starched organdy cap. Too much time had passed—the memory eluded her.

"Can I take those?" One of the boys approached their table, pointing at the coffee mugs. "Gonna do the last load of dishes now."

"Sure." Sally handed them over, then sighed. "We should get out of here anyway. It's been a long day, and tomorrow promises to be longer. At least for you."

Marie nodded, locating her shoes beneath the table. She slipped her feet into the comfortable leather loafers and rose, extending her arms toward Sally. The women embraced, the hug lasting several seconds, with Sally rocking Marie back and forth.

When they finally pulled apart, Sally tweaked Marie's chin. "Now, do like I said—take care of yourself. Don't expect too much. Bide your time, get that inheritance for your girl, and come on back here and rescue me from that bodacious young'un Jimmy brought on board."

Marie laughed as Sally slipped her arm around her waist. They walked to the parking lot together. At Marie's car, they hugged again. "I'll see you shortly after the new year," Marie said, a lump in her throat.

Sally nodded. " 'Bye, Marie."

The words were delivered on a light note, but something in Sally's expression as she backed away from Marie's car left Marie feeling as though her friend believed the good-bye was not a temporary one.

FIVE

Henry closed the window over the kitchen sink. Turning around, he leaned against the counter, raised his face, and sniffed deeply. He gave a brief, satisfied nod. Allowing in the crisp fall breeze had done wonders. The house no longer held the scent of neglect.

Heading into the small dining room, he walked through the path made by the late-afternoon sun slanting through Lisbeth's hand-sewn lace curtains. The glow highlighted the layer of dust that coated every surface. The open windows had freshened the air, but now he had a new problem to fix.

With a sigh, Henry returned to the kitchen and scavenged under the sink for a dust rag. He shook his head as he dusted Lisbeth's furniture, wishing he'd used better sense. Uncovering all the furniture had felt like such an accomplishment, but if he had left the sheets in place until after airing the house, he could have simply carried the dust away when he removed the coverings. That was something a woman would have considered, he was sure.

Despite having been the caretaker of his own home for the past twenty-some years, he still found little joy in housekeeping. But complaining didn't make the work go any faster. With another sigh, he turned from the sideboard, which housed Lisbeth's plain, white dishes, to the oak table and chairs. Pulling out one chair, he swept the dust rag over every inch of its surface, humming to fill the quiet. Trina, bless her heart, had asked permission to help him ready the house, but her father had firmly denied the request.

"Sunday is a day of rest," Troy Yoder had scolded his daughter. Then he'd given Henry a stern look, as if he should know better.

Henry squirmed, remembering the embarrassment of the moment. Yes, Sunday was a day of rest—and he rarely abused the fourth commandment—but what else could he do? Marie hadn't let him know until yesterday noon that she and Beth would be leaving the next morning. That had only given him Saturday evening to prepare for her arrival. It wasn't enough time.

Besides, he assured himself as he headed down the short hallway to Lisbeth's sewing room, he had waited until after church service to come finish the tasks. Certainly the Lord understood he was performing a mission of mercy. Two women, tired from a long drive, wouldn't have the energy to do the cleaning necessary to make the house livable.

Running the rag across the top of the waterfall bureau, he scowled. Turning a slow circle, he looked for the photograph album and basket that used to rest on the bureau. They were nowhere to be seen. He opened drawers and peeked into the closet, but the items weren't there. His brow puckered as he contemplated where they might be.

A knock at the back door interrupted his thoughts. His heart skipped a beat as he trotted to the kitchen. Was Marie here now? He began forming words of greeting, but when he peeked through the curtain, he recognized Deborah.

Surprised, he swung the door wide. "What are you doing here?"

She held up a casserole dish covered by an embroidered tea towel. "I brought you our leftover supper." Charging past him, she plunked the dish on the counter. Hands on hips, she glared at him. "I'm sure you haven't taken the time to eat."

He pushed the door closed. "Not yet. I planned to eat when I finished here."

"Men." Deborah shook her head. "What were you doing?"

Henry waved the dust rag, creating a cloud. He sneezed. "Dusting."

Deborah's eyebrows raised. "With that?"

Henry looked at the rag, then back at his sister. He shrugged.

Heaving a sigh, Deborah held out her hand. "Give me that. All you do with a dry rag is push dust around." When he handed the rag over, she pointed at the casserole and said, "You eat while I dust."

After slamming a few cupboard doors, she located a can of furniture polish. Turning, she spotted him still standing beside the counter. "I said eat!"

Henry laughed. "Does Troy know you're here?"

"Of course. As if I would take off without telling him where I was going."

"Does he know you're working?"

With a sour look, Deborah marched through the door that led to the dining room. He heard her muttering, and he couldn't help smiling. Deborah had always been like a toasted marshmallow—crusty on the outside but soft underneath. Although he felt a twinge of guilt, he appreciated her taking over the dusting task. He retrieved one of Lisbeth's forks from a drawer, pulled a stool to the edge of the counter, and helped himself to the creamy chicken-and-rice casserole.

While he ate, he let his gaze rove around the homey kitchen. Lisbeth's penchant for bright colors was showcased in the embroidered muslin curtains bearing red strawberries and green vines. A matching stamped pattern of berries and vines decorated the white-painted cupboards and walls. He frowned when his gaze encountered the little table crunched in the corner of the kitchen. It had always worn a red-and-white-checked cloth. Where might that have been tucked away?

And where were those photographs? Raising his voice, he called, "Deborah, do you remember the picture album and the little basket Lisbeth kept on the bureau in her sewing room?"

A grunt came in response. Henry interpreted it as a yes.

"They aren't there now. Do you know where they went?"

Deborah stuck her head through the doorway. "How should I know? Ask her family—they're the ones who arranged the service."

Henry nodded, thinking back to the day of Lisbeth's funeral. Had the album and letters been there that day? He couldn't remember.

"Where's Lisbeth's broom and dustpan?"

Deborah's brusque question brought him back to the present. He swallowed and stood. "On the inside of the door leading to the basement. I'll get it."

"No. Stay there and finish. I just want to sweep the front room."

"I did that last night," Henry said.

She raised her brows but didn't speak. Obviously he hadn't done it well enough. She disappeared again.

Henry ate as quickly as he could, rinsed the casserole dish and fork, then headed to the front room in time to catch Deborah shoving the couch against the wall. He moved her out of the way and repositioned the couch himself. "You even swept under this thing?"

"Well, certainly. Those dust bunnies always manage to come out of hiding when you least want them to."

Henry brushed his palms together and glanced around the room. In the minimal sunlight remaining, the room looked as neat as it had when Lisbeth Koeppler lived. How many evenings had he spent in this room, visiting with her? She'd been like a second mother to

51

him. His heart twisted as a pang of loneliness struck.

Deborah headed toward the back of the house, broom in hand. She called over her shoulder, "Do the sheets on the bed need to be changed?"

Remaining in the front room, Henry replied, "No. I took care of that yesterday."

"Where did you find clean ones?" The sounds of running water and a cupboard door opening and closing accompanied her words.

"In a chest in Lisbeth's bedroom."

There was an odd clatter, and then Deborah's voice came again. "If they were shut up in a chest, they probably smell musty."

"I took them outside and threw them over the line to air them first."

Deborah didn't respond. He plodded through the house to the kitchen, where he found her washing the casserole dish. She glanced up when he stopped beside the counter. "Light a lamp. I can't see in here anymore."

"Will you need it? There's only that one dish and fork."

Wordlessly, she reached into the soapy water and held up a handful of silverware. "I dumped the drawer full in here. Hated to waste the water."

Henry lit the lamp he had set on the small kitchen table and carried it to the counter.

Deborah released a little snort. "How do you think our city dwellers will survive without electricity?"

Henry opened a drawer, seeking a tea towel. On top of the neat stack of towels, he found the checked tablecloth. He draped it over the table while answering his sister. "Marie's family didn't have electricity when she was growing up, so it won't be new to her." Returning to the drawer, he grabbed a towel and began drying the silverware Deborah placed in the dish drainer.

"Maybe, but it's been awhile. And that girl of hers. . .she won't know how to act."

Henry remembered Beth's reaction when she found him standing in her living room. He smiled. "Oh, I suspect she'll find a way to adapt."

"Where will she sleep? Lisbeth only had one bed."

"I put a cot in the sewing room." The cot had come from his own basement—he kept it on hand for when he hosted summer sleepovers with his nephews. "It doesn't look too bad with one of Lisbeth's quilts over it." He had chosen the red-and-white patchwork quilt with calico hearts embroidered in the centers of selected white squares. It had always been Marie's favorite of the stack in Lisbeth's linen closet.

Deborah shot him a pointed look. "You look forward to their arrival, don't you?" Her voice held a note of accusation.

Henry shrugged, dropping dry forks and spoons into the plastic tray in the silverware drawer. "I don't know what I feel. I just know it's what Lisbeth wanted."

Deborah slammed another handful of silverware into the drainer. "What Lisbeth wanted. . . It would have been better if she'd just given everything to J.D. and Cornelia rather than stirring up this trouble."

Henry paused, leaning against the counter to stare at his sister. "What trouble?"

Deborah didn't look at him. "You know what I mean." She swished her hand through the water and grabbed another spoon. "That girl of Marie's coming here to sell the house and café. I think it's shameful."

"J.D. and Cornelia would have sold it, too," Henry pointed out. "How is that different?"

"It just is!" Deborah snapped out the words. "J.D. and Cornelia

53

had a right to it. This girl. . .Beth. . .she's never even been here!"

Henry could have reminded his sister that it wasn't Beth's fault she hadn't been here, but he knew it would only cause an argument. Instead, he repeated softly, "It's what Lisbeth wanted."

Deborah jerked up the sink plug and watched the water swirl down the drain.

Henry dropped the last fork into the drawer, hung the damp towel on a rack above the sink, and gave Deborah a one-armed hug. "Thank you. Marie and Beth will appreciate this."

She stepped away from him, her expression grim. "I didn't do it for Marie and Beth. I did it for you." She pointed at him. "And you remember something, Henry. Marie has been in the world for a long time. She's not the girl we once knew. I know what Lisbeth was trying to do here, but I have every confidence that three months in Sommerfeld will do little more than make her all the more determined to get away again. Don't—" Her voice cracked, her expression softening. She dropped her hand and sighed. "Don't let yourself get hurt a second time, Henry. Please?"

"Deborah—"

She snatched up her casserole dish and headed for the door. Over her shoulder, she ordered, "Things look fine in here now. Go home."

"Mom, stop at the next gas station, huh? I need a break."

Marie stifled a sigh. "Honey, it's less than an hour to Sommerfeld. Can't you last that long?"

Beth huffed. "I need to go to the bathroom, okay?"

"Well, if you'd lay off the sodas, maybe you wouldn't need a bathroom every half hour." Marie tried to inject humor into her tone, but she was aware of a biting undercurrent.

Apparently Beth heard it, too, because she snapped, "I also need to stretch my legs. I'm tired of sitting."

Marie was tired of sitting, too. She and Beth had traded off driving during the day, but most of the time she'd been behind the wheel. The tug of the small trailer of belongings attached to the back of their car made Beth nervous. Marie's nerves had been frayed, as well—mostly from the early-hour last-minute packing and from having to listen to Beth's lengthy cell-phone conversations with her boyfriend. Marie was just about ready to snap.

She held her tongue, however, recognizing that a large part of her unease was due to what waited at the end of their journey. The closer they got to her childhood home, the more the knot in her belly twisted. Despite Sally's warning, she recognized a small glimmer of hope that someone—Mom or Dad, or one of her brothers or sisters—would be waiting at Lisbeth's to welcome her back. She knew it was unlikely, maybe even ridiculous, and she did her best to squelch the niggling thought. But it hovered on the fringes of her mind, increasing her stomachache with every click of the odometer.

"There's a station." Beth pointed ahead.

Marie allowed the sigh to escape, but she slapped the turn signal and pulled off the highway into the station. Beth hopped out the moment the car stopped and dashed inside. Marie got out more slowly and walked to the hood of the car. She stretched, glancing across the landscape.

An unwilling smile formed on her lips. In the west, the sun had slipped over the horizon, but the broad Kansas sky gave her the final evidence of its bright presence. Deep purple clouds, undergirded with fuchsia, hung high on the backdrop of cerulean blue, and airy wisps with brilliant orange rims hung close to the horizon.

Beth stopped beside her mom's shoulder. "What are you looking at?"

Marie pointed. "The sunset. I'd forgotten how beautiful they could be. Aunt Lisbeth always said there was nothing like a Kansas sunset. She was right."

Beth smirked. "You're not going to get all sentimental on me now, are you?"

Marie shot her daughter a sharp look. "There are worse things than being sentimental. Being insensitive is one of them."

Beth rolled her eyes, and Marie's gaze dropped to her daughter's hand, where she held a super-sized fountain drink. "You said it's just another hour. This won't kick in until well after we get there." Beth's teasing grin eased a bit of Marie's tension.

She gave her daughter a playful tweak in the ribs. "Let's go. We're almost there."

Six

"Well, there it is."

Beth sat up straight in the passenger seat, blinking rapidly to clear the sleep from her eyes. Peering out the window through the dusky light, she caught a glimpse of a sign advertising harness making—*harness* making? Then the vehicle made a sharp left off the highway. Sure enough, there was the town. Sommerfeld. Hardly a town at all, really.

"This is Main Street." Mom sounded as though her tonsils were tied in a knot. The car slowed to a crawl. The headlights illuminated the double-wide, unpaved street.

Main Street. . .unpaved. Beth swallowed a disparaging comment.

Mom pointed to the first building on the left-hand side of the street. "There's Lisbeth's Café. . .now Beth's Café." She grinned, then shook her head, sighing. "My, the hours I spent there when I was a teenager. . ."

My unexpected inheritance. Beth leaned down to squint through the driver's-side window. The evening gloaming and absence of streetlights made it difficult to make out details, but the café appeared to be a rock building, two stories high, fronted by a brick sidewalk. Startled, she glanced right and left. All the sidewalks were brick.

And not a soul was in sight. Anywhere.

She whistled through her teeth and fought off a shiver.

"What's wrong?" Mom's voice dropped to a whisper, adding to the eerie feeling of being in a ghost town.

"Where is everybody?"

Mom shrugged. "It's Sunday. They're all at home. I told you Sunday is a day of rest."

"Yeah, but..." Beth shook her head. The highway traffic less than a half mile to the south, contrasted against the absolute inactivity of the town, was too bizarre.

"Over there is my brother Art's business." Mom pointed to the right.

Out loud, Beth read the sign above the door of the large wooden building. "Koeppler Feed and Seed—Quality Implements and Agricultural Products." Turning to her mother, she whistled through her teeth. "This is wild, Mom. It's like being on a movie set for a Western."

Mom laughed softly. "Well, it is unpretentious. But it's hardly the thing movies are made of."

Beth nearly wore out her neck looking back and forth as Mom made a left turn followed by a second turn one block farther. They drove in silence past two blocks of residential houses, most of which appeared to have been constructed in the earlier part of the twentieth century, increasing Beth's sense of stepping back in time.

The car finally pulled into the dirt side yard of a quaint bungalow with a high-peaked roof and a railed porch that extended halfway across the front and around the north side.

At first glance the house appeared dark, but as their car pulled around to the back, a pale yellow light glowed, gently illuminating the window at the northwest corner. Mom stopped the car behind the house and shut off the ignition. Then, with a huge, heaving sigh, she stared at the building.

"Well, this is it. Your new home sweet home." She sat, unmoving, her hands gripping the steering wheel.

Beth frowned. "Are you okay?"

Mom's laugh sounded forced. "As okay as an old lady can be after driving thirteen hours straight." She rubbed the back of her neck and yawned. The action seemed feigned. "I sure hope that light in there means somebody has made up the bed. I'm not sure I have the energy to do it myself."

Both women climbed out of the car and walked toward the back porch. A black iron gaslight stood along the grassless footpath from the dirt driveway to the house, but it wasn't burning, leaving the path dark. Mom stepped onto the wood-planked porch and twisted the doorknob. "Locked."

Beth tipped sideways, trying to peek through the door's window. "What'll we do?"

For a moment Mom stood there, staring at the knob. Then she bent over to lift the corner of a plastic mat in front of the back door. She held up a key and offered a weak smile. "Just like always."

Beth gaped. "Outside? Where anyone could find it?"

Mom laughed again, the sound more authentic this time. "You're not in the city anymore, Beth. Things are. . .different here." She turned the key in the lock, pushed the door open, then gestured for Beth to enter.

Beth stepped into a dimly lit, narrow room with doorways springing in all directions. She slid her hand along the wall beside the door. "I can't find the light switch."

Mom stepped in and closed the door. "Honey, I told you. No electricity. Follow the glow."

The glow, as Mom called it, came from the open doorway along the north wall. Beth walked through the doorway and found herself in a simple kitchen with white painted cabinets and a small, round table covered with a cheerful red-and-white-checked cloth. A cordless lamp sat on the countertop, sending out a meager amount of light. The only light in the entire house.

Beth shook her head. "Primitive."

Mom moved past her but stopped at the table. She fingered the cloth, her face pinched. After a moment, she released the tablecloth and picked up the lamp by its handle. Smiling in Beth's direction, she said, "Shall we explore?"

With a shrug, Beth followed her mom around a corner and into the dining room. A square wooden table flanked by four chairs filled the center of the uncarpeted floor. A glass-front cabinet holding simple white dishes stood along the west wall—the only other piece of furniture in the room.

Beth resisted another shiver, her feet echoing on the hardwood floor as she trailed behind her mother through a wide doorway to what was obviously the living room. A couch sat beneath one window, with a small wood table on spindly legs at one end. Beside the little table sat a curved-back rocking chair. Mom crossed to it and sat down, placing the lamp on the table. The lamp clearly lit Mom's face. Although she seemed pale and her eyes looked tired—or sad?—a smile curved her lips.

"This was Aunt Lisbeth's favorite seat." Mom's hands caressed the worn arms of the rocker. "When I was little, I used to run in here and climb into it before she could, just to see her put her hands on her hips and scowl at me. She could make the fiercest face while her eyes just twinkled, letting me know she was only teasing. And I would scowl back." She laughed softly. "I wouldn't have dared to scowl at any other adult, but Aunt Lisbeth was different." She stared across the room, seemingly lost in thought.

Beth sank onto the couch. It was stiff and the fabric scratchy, unlike the cushiony velvet sofa at home. "Mom?"

A few seconds passed before her mother turned to look at her.

"If there's no electricity, how will we get heat in here?"

Her mother looked disappointed by the question. Another lengthy pause followed before she pushed off the rocking chair. Picking up the lamp, she said, "Follow me."

She led Beth back through the dining room, through a different doorway, ending in the utility porch. Swinging open a door, she pointed. "There's a coal-burning furnace in the basement. That's what heats the house." She sniffed, and Beth did the same, inhaling a thick, musty odor. "Someone already has it going, but if you're cold, I'll go put in some more coal."

Beth peered down the dark, wooden stairs and shook her head. "No, that's okay. I'll just put on a hoodie." She hugged herself, knowing the chill came from something more than the temperature of the house. "It looks creepy down there."

Mom smiled. "We'll have to go down eventually anyway. Want to see how the furnace works?"

Beth gave an adamant shake of her head. "No, thanks!"

"All right, then." Mom closed the door and faced Beth. "Let me show you Lisbeth's bedroom—there's only one bedroom, so we'll have to share the bed."

Beth made a face. "Great."

Mom sighed. "Beth, I tried to prepare you for all this before we came, but you didn't want to talk about it, remember? You said you preferred to find out everything when you got here rather than get scared enough to change your mind. Now that we're here, I'd rather you didn't complain constantly."

Beth threw her hands outward. "Who's complaining?"

Mom looked at her with one eyebrow raised and her mouth quirked to the side.

"Okay, okay, I'm sorry. I know you said it would be simple, but I had no idea. . . . How did you live like this? Coal-burning furnaces, no lights, everything so. . .bare."

"I suppose when you don't know any different, it doesn't seem like a hardship." Heading for the back door, she said, "Why don't we get our suitcases and then I'll show you the bedroom? And the bathroom. I imagine by now your pop has kicked in."

Beth recognized the teasing note. She matched it, clasping her hands beneath her chin in a mock gesture of supplication. "*Pleeease* don't tell me the bathroom is actually an outhouse."

Mom laughed, and her curls bounced as she shook her head. "Oh, no, we have indoor plumbing."

"Well, let's be grateful for small favors." Beth followed her mom outside. The cool air nipped at her, carrying a fresh scent very different from that of home. A rustle overhead followed by a flapping indicated some kind of night bird took flight from the trees, and Beth involuntarily ducked. Yet when she looked upward, seeking the location of the bird, she found herself mesmerized by the endless expanse of sky.

She'd never seen so many stars, and the plump three-quarter moon appeared as bright as a halogen against the velvety black. "Wow."

Mom swung a suitcase from the back of the trailer and paused, peering upward. She smiled. "Oh, yes. With all the city lights, a person forgets how brilliant the stars truly are." She took in a deep breath, released it slowly, and said, " 'The heavens declare the glory of God; and the firmament sheweth his handywork.' "

At her mother's wistful tone, Beth jerked her gaze to look at her. Mom's eyes glittered as brightly as the stars. Suddenly uncomfortable but not sure why, Beth forced a hint of mockery into her voice. " 'Sheweth'?"

Mom gave a start, looking at Beth sheepishly. "Oh." She laughed lightly. "Something I memorized as a child. Funny. . ." She nibbled her lower lip, her gaze returning to the sky. "I haven't thought about that in years."

Beth waited, her arms folded around her middle. Her mother stared upward, a smile barely tipping the corners of her lips. What was Mom thinking—remembering? For some reason, Beth felt afraid to ask.

After a long while, Mom released an airy sigh, then aimed a bright smile in Beth's direction. "Well, let's get these suitcases inside and unpacked, huh? The rest can wait until tomorrow and sunlight."

Marie pulled the stiff sheet and chenille spread to her chin and stared at the ceiling. From down the hall, a series of squeaks indicated Beth wiggled on the cot. An odd warmth filled her face as she thought about that cot. The second, smaller bedroom had always been Lisbeth's sewing room. Someone had taken down the folding table she'd used to cut fabric or lay out quilt squares and put up the cot, obviously for their use. And she knew who had done it.

When she'd called yesterday, Henry had been eating lunch in the café, so Deborah had called him to the telephone. He had sounded dismayed when she'd said she and Beth would be coming the next day. She could still hear his startled, "But there's no time for preparation." That had been her intention—she hadn't wanted him to feel obligated to get things ready for her. Then he'd asked, "Do you remember Lisbeth only has one bed in her house? Will it work for you and your daughter to share?"

Marie's hesitation before replying that it would be fine no doubt communicated her true feelings about having to bunk with Beth. He must have brought in the cot. And covered it with the bright heart-appliquéd quilt Marie had always loved. Did he remember her preference for bright colors when he'd fixed up the cot?

Her chest felt tight, and she pushed that thought away. How silly to take a trip down Memory Lane. Yet she couldn't deny being in Lisbeth's house, being in Sommerfeld, was tugging her backward in time.

She closed her eyes, her body tired, yet her mind refused to shut down. Outside, under the stars, the Bible verse from Psalms had slipped from her mouth so easily. She couldn't remember the last time she'd quoted a scripture. Yet it had happened effortlessly, as if it had been lying dormant, waiting for an opportunity to present itself.

When she'd first pulled into the yard and seen the light glowing from the kitchen window, her heart had leaped with hope that maybe—*maybe*—someone would be in the house waiting to greet her, to hug her, to welcome her back. But the locked door had let her know no one was around.

The disappointment of that moment stabbed like a knife. Hadn't Sally told her not to expect too much? Yet underneath, an ever-so-hesitant glimmer of hope resided, only to be snatched away by a locked back door. No, no one had been waiting.

Except God.

Marie's eyes popped open. What made her think that? " 'The heavens declare the glory of God.' " She whispered the words into the quiet room. A feeling of comfort followed. A feeling she little understood and was too tired to explore.

"Well, if You're around, God," she muttered with a touch of belligerence, "You might let me get some sleep. It's been a long day, and I've got my work cut out for me tomorrow with cleaning this house and carting in the stuff Beth and I brought."

How strange it felt to speak to God that way, the easy way Lisbeth had always spoken—out loud, without pretension. The way one would talk with a neighbor over the fence. Another constriction grabbed her chest, making her breath come in little spurts. Squeezing her eyes shut, she pushed aside the emotions straining for release and willed herself to sleep.

"Mom?"

The soft voice brought Marie to full attention once more. A shadowy figure stood beside the bed, reminding Marie of the days when Beth was little and would wander in, awakened by a nightmare. "What's wrong, honey?"

"I can't sleep. I'm tired, but it's so quiet here. It's creeping me out."

Marie understood. She scooted over. "Climb in. We'll share tonight, huh?"

Beth slipped in and curled onto her side, facing her mother. "I heard you talking."

Marie's heart caught. "Oh?" She chuckled softly. "I guess I was planning out loud. Lots to do tomorrow."

In the muted shadows cast by moonlight, Marie saw Beth nod. "Do you think I should go to the café tomorrow, or can it wait?"

"It can wait if you want to. It's never open on Mondays."

A long sigh came from Beth's side of the bed. "I guess I should have asked questions before we came. But I was right—I wouldn't have come if I'd had any idea. . . ."

"You know, it really isn't that bad," Marie's voice snapped out more tartly than she'd intended. Why was she so defensive? Sommerfeld was no longer her home. Based on the fact that no one was here to greet them, her family was no longer hers, either. So why tell Beth it wasn't bad?

More kindly, she added, "It's only three months, honey. Think of it as. . .an adventure." She smoothed Beth's hair away from her face. "Who knows, maybe someday you'll write a book about all this."

Beth laughed, pressing her fists beneath her chin. "Who would believe it?"

"Truth is stranger than fiction."

Another laugh. "Oh, yeah."

Marie sighed. "Close your eyes, honey. Get some sleep."

Beth's eyes slipped closed. They lay in silence for several minutes before Beth's voice came again. "Mom?"

"Yes?"

"Thanks for coming with me."

Marie smiled and gave Beth's hair another stroke. "You're welcome."

"I wouldn't want to be doing this alone."

"Well, no worries. You're not alone."

Although Beth finally drifted to sleep, Marie lay awake, gazing out the window at the starry sky, her words to her daughter echoing through her heart. *No worries. You're not alone.*

SEVEN

Marie carried in a box of groceries and set it on the cluttered counter. Looking at the boxes already there, she realized she had been responsible for bringing in each one. Aggravation rose. Was Beth on her cell phone. . .*again?*

Hands on hips, she bellowed, "Beth!"

"In here."

Marie followed the voice and found her daughter in the dining room, lying under the table, flat on her back. Bending forward and propping her hands on her knees, she peered at her. "What in the world are you doing?"

Beth's ponytail lay across the floor in tangled disarray. "Checking out this table. It's solid wood, Mom. I can't even find any nails—just pegs. It's amazing!"

Marie squatted down between two chairs to peek at the underside of the table. "Do you see a brand anywhere—symbols burned into the wood?"

Beth twisted her head, her gaze seeking. Her face lit up. "Yeah! Right there!" She pointed. "It looks like a *K* with an *O* at the bottom right-hand edge." Looking at her mom, she wrinkled her brow. "What does that mean?"

"It means your great-grandfather and great-great-uncle constructed it." Marie straightened and got out of the way as Beth scrambled from her hideaway. "My mother was an Ortmann. Her father joined forces with my father's uncle to open a furniture-making shop." Marie headed through the kitchen, Beth on her heels. "I would imagine if you went door to door around here, you'd find quite a few pieces with that brand."

"When did they start their business?" Beth followed Marie outside to the trailer.

Marie handed a box to her daughter and scowled thoughtfully. "Hmm. Grandpa Ortmann was born in 1907, I believe, and he started the business in his early twenties. . .so maybe the late 1920s?" It felt good to share a bit of family history with Beth. She picked up a box and turned toward the house.

Beth plodded up the back porch stairs and through the utility porch door, which Marie had propped open. "Then that table would be more than seventy years old." Beth's tone turned calculating. "Definitely antique, and certainly unique. I need to do some exploring on the Internet to figure out its value."

Marie put her box on the kitchen table, staring at her daughter. "You're planning to sell it?"

Beth gawked over the top of the box she held. "Well, yeah. I mean, that's why I'm here, remember? To claim all this stuff, sell it, and open my antique shop." With a light laugh, she added, "Duh!"

"Don't get sassy." Marie spun on her heel and headed outside again.

Beth trotted up beside her. "What are you getting so huffy about?"

Marie stopped and whirled on Beth. She opened her mouth, but nothing came out. Beth was right—what was she getting huffy about? The only reason they were here was to meet the condition of Aunt Lisbeth's will, lay claim to everything, sell it for whatever Beth could gain, and get out. Why was she feeling territorial? She sighed and touched Beth's cheek.

"I'm sorry, honey. I didn't sleep very well last night, and I'm tired and cranky. I didn't mean to take it out on you."

Beth's smile returned. "That's okay. I understand." She moved to the end of the trailer, her ponytail swinging. "This afternoon, while I get my computer set up and figure out how to connect to the Internet, you can nap." Then she spun around, her face set in a frown. "I just realized. . .no electricity and no phone line, so no way to connect." She released a disgruntled *uh*. "This really stinks!"

Marie put her arm around her daughter's shoulders and gave a squeeze. "There's a phone line at the café and all the electricity you could need. We'll rig it up over there, okay?"

"Whew!" Beth brightened again. "Thank goodness the café is halfway modernized." Grabbing a box, she moved toward the house. "Speaking of the café, I'm hungry. Can we find something to eat?"

Marie followed Beth into the kitchen. "Let's get some of this stuff put away so we have moving-around room, and we'll have some cold cereal. We'll have to do simple meals until I can remember how to operate Aunt Lisbeth's stove."

The sound of a knock made both women spin toward the utility porch. Marie's heart leaped into her throat. They'd come! Her family was here! She raced through the utility porch to the back door to find Henry Braun in the open doorway. Her hopes plummeted once more.

"Henry."

He took off his hat and offered a smile, apparently unaffected by her flat greeting. "Good morning, Marie. I see you're hard at work."

She took in his neat appearance—crisp twill trousers and dark blue shirt tucked in at the waist, clean-shaven chin, and hair combed smoothly into place. She ran a quivering hand over her tousled waves, aware of how disheveled she must look in faded jeans and an old sweatshirt. As heat filled her face, she decided it was good it wasn't her father at the door—he'd surely disown her a second time if he saw her like this.

A worried frown creased Henry's forehead. "Are you all right?"

Ducking her head, she released a rueful chuckle. "I'm fine. I just. . ." Shaking her head, she pushed aside the jumble of emotions her disappointment had inspired, met his gaze, and forced a smile. "Come on in. I can't offer you coffee or anything. . . ."

Henry remained in the doorway between the kitchen and utility porch. "That's fine. I've had my breakfast."

"Well, we haven't," Beth said, transferring cans of vegetables from a box to an upper cabinet. "And we won't be able to eat decently until Mom figures out the stove."

"It's powered by propane." Henry took a step into the room. "I'm sure there's still some in the tank. Do you want me to get the stove started for you?"

"That would be great. . .if we have something here to cook." Marie looked at Beth. "Have we brought in the ice chest?"

"I haven't."

Henry turned and headed for the back door. "I'll bring it in."

Marie hurried after him. "You don't have to do that."

He didn't look back as he tromped down the porch stairs. His broad shoulders lifted in a brief shrug. "It's not a problem. I came by to see if you needed anything. Carrying in an ice chest is a simple thing to do."

Marie stood at the tail of the trailer while Henry ducked and stepped inside. He took hold of the ice chest and dragged it to the opening. Back outside, he stood upright and grinned at her. "That's heavy. Did you put your refrigerator in there, too?"

Marie slapped a hand to her face. "Refrigerator! Is Aunt Lisbeth's still—"

"In the basement," Henry said. "And it operates on a generator, same as always."

"Beth will love that. She's so fond of the basement." Marie grabbed one end of the ice chest and Henry took the other. She grunted as they lifted it.

They struggled up the stairs and into the house. Henry turned backward to get through the doorways. In the kitchen, his gaze bounced from the tabletop to the counter; both were scattered with boxes.

"Let's just set it on the floor," Marie suggested.

"Are you sure you don't want it downstairs, by the refrigerator?"

Marie lowered her end. "I'm not carrying that heavy thing down the basement stairs. And neither are you. I'd rather make several trips."

Henry released his end with a nod. "I can help you."

They both straightened, their gazes connecting. Marie felt a blush building again and wished she felt less self-conscious. She wouldn't feel comfortable until he left. "That's all right. I'm sure you have things to do."

She was right—Henry did have things to do. Albrecht's tractor still didn't sound quite right when he fired up the engine, and Henry's fingers itched to fiddle with the carburetor until the engine purred. But, he reasoned, Mr. Albrecht could wait another day or so. Who else would help Marie?

He had been so certain when he pulled into the yard he would find other vehicles here—family members come to assist in unloading the women's things and getting them settled. Her parents and siblings knew she was back. He'd made sure he told all of them after she called on Saturday. So where were they? Indignation built in his chest at their standoffish behavior. Had J.D. Koeppler forgotten the parable of the prodigal son? Where was Marie's hug of welcome, the fatted calf?

"I have nothing more important than helping you right now," he insisted, offering a smile to let her know he meant it.

"Have him show you how to start the stove," Beth inserted, "or I'm heading down the highway until I find a McDonald's."

Henry kept his smile aimed at Marie. "I'm afraid it would be a lengthy drive. Salina and Newton are the closest towns with fast food, and they'd both seem pretty far away when you're hungry." He stepped around Marie, heading for the stove. "Did you try to light a burner?"

"Yes." She leaned against the doorframe. "I do remember how to start a propane stove. When it wouldn't light I just assumed it was out of propane."

He nodded. "I turned it off at the valve. I didn't want propane leaking into the house." With a heave, he tugged the stove forward a few inches. The feet screeched against the linoleum floor, and Beth covered her ears. He sent her an apologetic smile. "Sorry." Reaching behind, he found the valve and gave a few twists. Then he pushed the stove back into place. "Hand me a match, please."

Beth removed a match from the tin matchbox holder hanging above the sink and gave it to him. He twisted the knob to start the front left burner. A hiss let him know gas crept through the lines. He struck the match, held it to the burner, and was rewarded by a circle of blue flame.

"Hurray!" Beth clapped her hands. "Okay, Mom, I'll have eggs over easy and toast."

Marie and Henry exchanged grins. Marie said, "Then Henry had better start the oven."

"Oven?" Beth pulled her brows low. "For eggs and toast?"

Henry's lips twitched with amusement as Marie explained.

"For the toast. I'll have to put the bread under the broiler—we can't plug in a toaster, you know."

The girl's eyes rolled upward in a manner Henry had witnessed from his nieces. He turned his back and opened the ice chest, pretending to hunt for an egg carton, before he let loose the chuckle that pressed at his chest.

"Isn't there some way to get electricity here?" Beth pulled out a kitchen chair and sat. "I saw power lines in town, so *somebody* has power."

"Many of our residents have electricity," Henry said. "None of our Amish neighbors do, but nearly all of the Mennonites have chosen to use it."

Marie lifted Lisbeth's iron skillet from the drawer in the bottom of the stove and set it on the burner. Moving to dig through one of the boxes, she glanced at him. "Well, then, how hard would it be to have an electrical line run to the house for this former Mennonite's use?"

The words "former Mennonite" pinched Henry's heart. He was glad Lisbeth didn't hear it—it offered proof that Marie had fully released her childhood faith. He watched Marie pour a scant amount of oil into the pan and spread it around with a metal spatula. "The line to the house would be simple. Wiring the whole house to receive the current would be the hard part."

Marie grimaced, her lips pooching into an adorable pout. "Of course. How foolish of me." She broke eggs into the skillet and a cheerful *sizzle* sounded. "I'm sorry, honey, but we're going to have to put up with things the way they are. It hardly seems worth the expense and effort to wire the whole house for three months."

Henry ducked his head at Marie's blithe words.

"But won't we get a better price for the house if it's wired for electricity?" the girl argued.

Marie sent her daughter a frown. "That's an expense we don't need right now, Beth. Let the next owners worry about it."

Beth sighed. "Oh, all right. But don't plan on me hanging around here much. I'll spend my days at the café, where at least I can access the Internet and listen to a radio." Another sigh released. "No television for three months. Torture!"

Marie laughed, but Henry thought it sounded strained. He looked at Beth. "I'm sure you'll stay busy enough with the café that you won't miss television too much. But if you need entertainment—"

"Oh, please!" Beth held up both palms as if warding off a blow. "Don't tell me there's cow-milking and corn-shucking contests!"

Marie spun around, her face flaming. "Beth!"

The girl's wide, blue eyes blinked in innocence. "What? It was just a joke."

Turning back to the stove, Marie flipped the eggs, but her lips remained set in a grim line.

Henry glanced between the two before completing his statement. "Once or twice a month, the young unmarried people of our community rent the skating rink in Newton and spend the evening there. Maybe you'd like to join them. You could get to know your cousins that way."

Beth opened her mouth. Marie shot a warning look in her direction. The girl closed her mouth for a moment, her eyes sparking, then gave Henry a sweet smile. "I'll give that some thought."

"Butter the bread, Beth. The eggs are done." Marie scooped eggs onto plates and put them on the table. "Henry, would you like me to fix you an egg, too?"

"No, thanks." Henry backed up to get out of Beth's way as she bustled across the kitchen with a loaf of bread and a butter knife in her hand. He reached into the ice chest and pulled out the butter tub.

"Thanks." Beth took the butter and sat at the table.

Henry remained near the doorway, waiting until Marie sat next to Beth. They didn't pray before they picked up their forks. He cleared his throat. "Tell you what, while you eat, I'll empty the rest of your trailer."

Marie half stood, holding her hand toward him. "You don't need to do that."

He waved at her. "It's not a problem. There doesn't seem to be much left. Sit for a while. You've earned it." He hurried out the door before she could offer another argument.

Most of the boxes left in the trailer were labeled either MOM or BETH. Those with MOM, he stacked outside Lisbeth's bedroom; those with BETH outside the sewing room. The few with no label he left on the utility porch. With each journey between trailer and house, his frustration with Marie's family grew. Why hadn't any of them shown up to help?

Based on J.D.'s scowling response when he'd been informed his long-lost daughter was on her way, Henry wasn't surprised that Marie's father wasn't here. But neither her brother, Art, nor her sister, Joanna, had responded negatively. In fact, he was sure Joanna's eyes had lit with happy expectation. So where were they?

He put the last box on the utility porch, then returned to the trailer to close it. After snapping the latch into place, he turned and found Marie standing a few feet away. The morning sun slanted across her face, highlighting her creamy complexion and bringing out the strands of gold in her tousled nutmeg curls. She looked tired.

"Do you have to take the trailer back today?" he asked, to keep from asking something more personal.

"Yes. By noon to avoid another day's rent. But I only have to take it Newton, so I have time yet."

He nodded, then lowered his gaze. They stood silently for a few minutes. He shifted his foot, digging his toe into the dirt. Head still down, he said, "I can unpack some boxes for you if you'd like."

"No. No, you've done plenty."

He glanced at her. She met his gaze directly. A shy smile played on the edges of her lips. "Did you fix up that bed for Beth?"

"Yes."

"That was very thoughtful. Thank you."

He shrugged. "It wasn't so much. Just a cot and some bedding I found in Lisbeth's linen closet."

"The quilt—"

"—was on top of the stack," he said, watching the toe of his boot make an indention in the dirt. "I hope it was all right."

A slight sigh sounded. He sensed disappointment, and he thought he understood the reason for it. She needed remembrances from someone. But it was better if they didn't come from him. She needed her family.

Backing up a step, he waved at his car. "I'd better get out of your way so you can get this trailer out of here."

"Thank you again, Henry. For everything."

He read gratitude in her fervent gaze. Swallowing, he nodded. "You're welcome. Oh!" Digging in his pocket, he retrieved a key ring and held it out to her. "This is for the café. The key with a number one on it unlocks the front door, two unlocks the back door, and three is for the storage closet inside."

She took the ring and fingered each key in turn, seeming to examine the numbers etched into the metal. Eyes downcast, she said, "Thank you."

"You're welcome. Have a good day, Marie. And welcome home."

Her cheeks flooded with pink, and she ran her hand through her curls. He was sure he saw a glint of tears before she blinked and the shimmer disappeared. "Thanks. You have a good day, too."

She turned and headed back toward the porch, her shoulders slumped. Henry slid behind the steering wheel and shook his head. Before he went to his shop, he had another errand to run.

EIGHT

Beth looked up when her mom returned to the kitchen. Wordlessly, Mom dropped a silver key ring next to Beth's plate, the keys sending out a subtle *ting* as they hit the table. Beth picked them up and turned in her chair to follow her mother's progress to the sink, where she washed her hands.

"What are these for?"

"The café. Front door, back door, and storage closet."

Beth smirked, dangling the ring from one finger. "Oh. So they don't keep the café's keys under the doormat?"

Mom offered a weak smile in response. Drying her hands on her pant legs, she faced Beth. "I've got to take the trailer to the rental place in Newton. I can drop you off at the café with your computer so you can get started trying to connect to the Internet. No guarantees you'll find anyone who will provide service here, but I'd think at least one of the dial-up companies would be able to help you."

Beth rose slowly, holding out her hand to indicate the unpacked boxes. "Don't you want me to stay here and get this mess cleaned up?"

Mom shrugged. "We can do that this evening. I know you feel cut off from the outside world. Wouldn't having Internet connection help?"

Beth bounced across the floor and gave her mother a hug. "You're the best, Mom! Thanks."

Mom returned the hug, then set Beth aside. "Yeah, well, you'll be rethinking that this evening when I'm cracking the whip to get all this stuff put away."

Beth laughed and followed her down the hallway to the bathroom. Mom picked up her hairbrush from the edge of the old-fashioned porcelain sink and ran it through her locks, creating some semblance of order.

"Seems kind of silly to get it all put away when we won't be here that long," said Beth.

Mom sent a brief scowl in Beth's direction. "I will not live out of boxes—not even for three months. While we're here, we might as well make things as homey as possible."

Beth shrugged. "Whatever. Should I change before going to the café? Do you think anyone will be offended by my stunning attire?" She struck a pose in her long-sleeved T-shirt and trim-fitting blue jeans.

Mom quirked her brow, her lips twitching. "I doubt anyone will stop in. It's never been open on Mondays. Besides, you should do whatever feels comfortable."

Beth tugged at the hem of her shirt. "This is comfortable."

"Okay, then." Mom moved past her to her bedroom and came out again, purse in hand. "Grab your laptop."

"And my boom box!"

Mom shook her head, chuckling. "Let's go."

An hour later Beth had put the café's telephone to good use by arranging service with an Internet provider that was delighted to finally have someone from Sommerfeld as a customer. They guaranteed she'd be up and running by the middle of the week. Her cell phone was recharging, and her boom box provided background noise. Her telephone calls done, she puttered around the café, becoming acquainted with her new property.

Everything was so *plain*. Walls painted white, with not even a wallpaper border or paneling to break the monotony. White square tiles bearing gray speckles covered the floor. The wide glass windows that stretched across the front of the café at least wore curtains—blue gingham café-style, with little gold plastic loops attaching them to the gold metal rods that divided the windows in half. She stepped onto the front walk to check out the front of the café in the sunlight, but the curious looks from passersby sent her scuttling back inside.

Perched on the edge of the black vinyl seat of one of the high-backed wood booths that lined both sides of the eating area, Beth kept her back to the window. Fifties-style tables and chairs filled the center of the room. Leaning forward, she skimmed her fingertips over the sheeny surface of one table, thinking of a diner back in Cheyenne that had similar tables. In that restaurant, with LPs and music-industry memorabilia decorating the walls, the tables had seemed retro. Here they just seemed out-of-date.

"I suppose," she mused aloud, "someone might consider these trendy. Maybe I should cull a few for my boutique."

The back screen door slammed.

Beth jumped up. "Mom, I'm glad you're back," she said, charging toward the doorway that led to the kitchen. "Guess what? I got—"

She came to a halt when she spotted a teenage girl in the kitchen. Her pulled-back hair covered with a little white cap and the yellow gingham dress that hung just below her knees marked her as Mennonite. Beth nearly giggled when she spotted the girl's white athletic socks and leather sneakers. The footwear seemed out of place with the rest of the outfit. Of course, despite her shoes, she fit the whole town better than Beth ever would.

Beth caught the hem of her shirt and pulled it over the waistband of her low-slung jeans. Meeting the girl's gaze, she offered a self-conscious smile. "Hi. The café isn't open."

The girl giggled, her brown eyes sparkling. "Oh, I know. I waited tables for Miss Koeppler before she died. And my mom and I have kept it going the last couple months. But I saw the lights on and figured someone must be in here, so I thought I'd come introduce myself. I'm Trina Muller." She crinkled her nose. "Well, actually Katrina. But I've always preferred Trina. My grandpa calls me Katrinka." The girl looked toward the radio as an inappropriate lyric blasted.

Beth scuttled over and flicked the OFF button. "Sorry about that." She grimaced.

The girl shrugged. "You didn't select the programming, did you? So don't apologize." She stepped closer to Beth, a warm smile lighting her face. "You must be Marie Koeppler's daughter, but I don't remember your name."

Beth slipped her fingertips into her jeans pockets and leaned against the counter, hunching her shoulders. "Mom named me Lisbeth after her aunt, but I've always gone by Beth."

"Ah." The girl giggled again. She sure was a happy thing. "So you have a nickname, too."

"My boyfriend calls me Lissie," Beth blurted out.

Trina's brown eyes nearly danced. "Did you know my uncle was your mom's boyfriend before she left town?"

This was intriguing. "Who's your uncle?"

"Henry Braun."

Beth's jaw dropped. She straightened, her hands slipping from her pockets. "You mean the Henry who came to tell me about. . . ?"

Trina nodded. The little ribbons that dangled from her cap bounced with the movement. "He and Miss Koeppler—your great-aunt Lisbeth—were very good friends. They both loved your mom a lot. Neither one ever seemed to get over her leaving with that truck driver and not coming back after he died."

That truck driver has a name, Beth's thoughts defended. *Jep Quinn.* She folded her arms across her chest, her heart pounding. "She would have come back if it weren't for my grandfather."

Trina lost a bit of her sparkle. "Oh, I know. My uncle Henry always hoped—"

The screen door slammed again. A tall woman in Mennonite attire stepped across the threshold. Trina looked over her shoulder, and her face flamed pink. She linked her fingers together and pressed them to her ribcage, a smile quivering on her lips. "Hi, Mama."

"It's like Grand Central Station around here," Beth muttered. *Hadn't Mom said this place would be empty on Monday?*

The woman stormed in, her chin held high, her gaze pinned on Trina. Without so much as a glance in Beth's direction, she let loose a tirade that made Beth's ears burn. "Katrina Deborah Muller, you were to go directly to the grocer and home again. I can see from your empty hands that you never even made it to the grocer. What are you doing in here talking to. . ." She waved a hand in Beth's direction, still without looking at her.

Some deviltry made Beth reach out and shake that waving hand. "Hi. It's nice to meet you. I'm Lisbeth Quinn, but you can call me Beth."

The woman jerked her hand free. A brief upthrust of her lips masqueraded as a smile. "I am Deborah Muller." She spun back to her daughter. "To the grocer's, Trina, and then home. We'll discuss this more thoroughly later."

Trina scurried toward the door.

"Good-bye, Katrinka," Beth called. "It was very nice meeting *you.*" She emphasized the last word enough to give Trina's grumpy mother a not-so-subtle message.

Trina sent a quick, impish grin over her shoulder before slipping through the door.

Her mother started to follow but then turned back. "Will you and your mother be handling the café starting tomorrow, or do you prefer to have some help?"

Beth wanted to snap back that she and her mother would be just fine, thank you very much, but she managed to think before she spoke. "If you and Trina are willing to continue for a few more days—to give Mom and me time to settle in and learn the ropes—it would be very helpful." She didn't add a thank-you.

Deborah Muller nodded brusquely. "Very well. The café opens at 6:00 a.m. I am always here by five. I'll see you then." She zipped out the door before Beth could reply.

Five a.m.? Beth groaned. She stomped to the door and peeked out. The alley was empty. Good! Maybe that would be the last of the visitors. She smiled, remembering Trina's grin. How old might the girl be—fifteen? Sixteen at most, probably. A little too young to become a friend, Beth decided, but good to talk to. . .if she would keep her comments about "that truck driver" to herself. And not mention Mom's old boyfriend. Henry Braun and Mom. . . Beth closed her eyes for a moment, remembering Henry's attentiveness and offers to help this morning. Mom had greeted him warmly and invited him in. . . which was more than Beth could remember her mother doing with any man in all of her growing-up years.

A frightening thought straightened Beth's spine. Surely Mom didn't still harbor feelings for that Mennonite man. The idea left her vaguely unsettled, but she snorted and pushed the notion aside. Mom was here to help her, plain and simple. Beth puffed out a breath and shook her head. No sense getting worked up over nothing.

The café seemed too quiet after the Mullers' brief visit. She clicked the radio back on, turning up the volume loud enough so the dining room vibrated with the beat of the music. She grinned. That should keep anyone else from venturing in! Leaning on the counter that held the cash register, she plucked up a menu and examined the café's offerings, humming with the music. When someone tapped her on the shoulder, she released a squawk and nearly threw the menu over her head.

Mom's laughter rang. "I wouldn't have been able to sneak up on you if you didn't have that noise cranked so loud." She covered her ears with her hands. "Can you turn it down?"

Beth zipped around the counter and slid the volume bar to the lowest level. "I'm so glad you're back." She gave her mother an impulsive hug. "It's been lonely here, except for my intruders." Briefly, she described her visits by Trina and Deborah. "That woman!" Beth huffed. "She acted like I had leprosy or something. I know we'll need her help for a while—at least until we get the hang of things here— but I wanted to just drop-kick her out the back door."

Mom stretched her lips into a grimace. She sat on a stool next to a long, metal counter and sighed. "We'll need to continue using Deborah, if she'll stay. We won't be able to run the café ourselves."

"Why not?" Beth slumped against the counter. It felt cold against her hip, and she shivered.

"Honey, I can wait tables and order supplies. But I can't do the cooking. I've never cooked in a restaurant before. And unless you want to learn how to do it. . ."

"Oh, boy." Beth heaved a huge sigh. "You mean I'm going to be with her every day?"

Mom chuckled softly. "Deborah isn't that bad. She's just always been a little. . .bossy."

Beth raised one eyebrow and tipped her chin.

Mom laughed. "Okay, a lot bossy, but we'll need her expertise if you're serious about keeping the café going. Or"—she lifted her shoulders—"we can close it and bide our time."

Beth sighed. "It's tempting, but Mitch said a working café will bring in more cash. One that has sat closed will have to rebuild its customer base."

"Are you sure about this?"

Beth grinned. "Since when do you let me make such important decisions?"

"Since you became the recipient of an extensive estate."

"Oh, yeah." Beth grimaced, flipping her hands outward to indicate her surroundings. "Quite the estate."

Mom rose from the stool and turned a slow circle, her gaze wandering around the quiet kitchen. "Actually, honey, this is a precious gift. This was Aunt Lisbeth's life. Essentially, she's given you everything she valued." Her tone turned wistful, her eyes misting. "It might not seem like much by the world's standards, but to her. . ."

Beth put her arm around her mother's shoulders. "It's hard for you to be here, isn't it?"

Mom blinked rapidly and shook her head. "No. I have a lot of good memories from here. I spent nearly every day with Aunt Lisbeth from the time I left eighth grade until I married your dad. In fact"—she quirked a finger—"come with me."

Beth followed her mom to the dining room, to the table closest to the front door. Mom pressed both palms against the tabletop. "Right here is where your dad was sitting the first time I saw him." She closed her eyes and arched her neck, smiling as she relived some important moment. "He caught my eye. . . ." Opening her eyes, she grinned at Beth. "Even though I knew better than to flirt, I was human enough to enjoy boy-watching. And your dad made boy-watching a pleasure."

Beth sat at the table and rested her chin in her hands. "Tell me about it."

"Oh, honey, I've told you a hundred times how I met your dad."

"So make it a hundred and one." When Mom still hesitated, Beth affected a pout. "Pleeease?"

With a deep-throated chortle, Mom sat across from Beth and imitated her pose—elbows on the table, fingers cupping her face. "Well, when he came in, he was all sweaty. Hair drenched, clothes soppy. . . I could tell he'd been in the sun far too long."

"And you brought him a glass of ice water, which he guzzled in three seconds."

"Yes. So I immediately brought him a second glass, and he looked at me—"

"—and winked and said, 'A girl who knows a man's mind—what a rare find.' "

Mom pulled back, lowering her brows. "Hey, who's telling this story?"

Beth giggled. "Okay, I'll be quiet."

Mom rested her chin in her hands again and grinned. "Even though fraternizing with outsiders was frowned upon, he was impossible to resist. He was so handsome and friendly. . .and so *stuck*." She laughed, her eyes twinkling. "His semi had broken down, he had no way to leave, and the café was the only place in town to hang out."

Beth, remembering the next part of the story, frowned. "Mom, why didn't you ever tell me Henry Braun was your boyfriend?"

To her amazement, Mom's cheeks blotched red. "Who—who told you that?"

"Based on your reaction, it must be true." Beth folded her arms on the tabletop. "You told me Henry fixed Dad's engine, but you never mentioned you were dating him."

Mom dropped her gaze, running her fingertips along the chrome edge of the table. "It wasn't important. And we weren't dating." She shook her head, wrinkling her nose. "At least, not the way you and Mitch are dating. We were just. . . He and I. . ." Releasing a huff, she said, "There was never any formal agreement between us."

Beth thought about Trina's statement that Henry never got over Mom's leaving. Maybe there hadn't been a formal agreement, but Henry must have been serious. "Still, it had to have been weird for him. You know, fixing Dad's semi so he could get back on the road, then seeing you leave, too."

"I suppose." Mom shifted her gaze, seeming to peer out the window.

Suddenly curious, Beth leaned forward. "Do you ever wonder what your life would have been like if you'd stayed? You know, if you'd married Henry instead of Dad?"

Mom jerked her gaze around, her eyes wide. "No."

Beth snorted. "Oh, come on. Be honest."

Mom became very interested in a scratch on the tabletop, her brows furrowed as she ran her fingernail back and forth in the furrow. "In all honesty, Beth, no. When I left Sommerfeld. . .the second time. . ." Briefly, her gaze bounced up to meet Beth's before returning to the scratch. "I never looked back. I didn't *let* myself look back. It was too painful, I guess. I wouldn't be here now if—"

The sound of a clearing voice intruded. Beth looked toward the kitchen. Henry Braun had pushed back the swinging door that separated the kitchen from the dining room. He stood framed in the doorway, and a second man—older, with bushy gray eyebrows and a stern face—stood behind him, peering over Henry's shoulder with a frown. The older man stepped around Henry and took a step into the dining room.

Mom gasped, and Beth shifted her attention to her mother. Her face had gone white. One hand rose to smooth her hair, and her throat convulsed.

Beth looked again to the gray-browed man and understanding dawned. She stood. "Hello, Grandfather."

NINE

Henry waited for J.D. Koeppler to move fully into the room, to return Beth's greeting. But the man stood as if rooted to the tile floor, glaring at his daughter.

Marie stood slowly, her palms on the tabletop as though she needed its support. She licked her lips and blinked several times. "H–hello. . .Dad." Her glance flitted toward her daughter, then returned to J.D. "I'd like you to meet your granddaughter, Beth."

J.D. gave a single nod, his face impassive. Henry considered grabbing the man's shirtfront and propelling him across the floor with a command to say something. But J.D. was known for his stubbornness—any pushing would only make him resist more. The tension in the room increased with every second that ticked by, and a silent prayer filled his heart. *Please, Lord, let someone speak. Let someone reach out.*

But the prayer went unheeded. Instead, it appeared that everyone had turned to stone, resembling a tableau—*Family at Impasse*. Beth stood with her head at an arrogant angle, her narrowed gaze aimed somewhere to the left. Marie seemed to hold her breath, her wide-eyed gaze on her father's face. And J.D. stared back, his carriage stiff.

Beth shifted, an odd grin creasing her face. She approached the doorway, swaying her blue-jean-covered hips in a way that emanated defiance, and held out her hand. "How nice to finally meet you. It's been. . .what? Twenty-one years? Yes, that seems to be about right, give or take a month or two. I believe I was all of two weeks old when you saw me last." She released a brittle laugh. "Of course, I have no memory of that, and since you've made no effort to be a part of my life, well. . ." She raised her shoulders in a shrug that lifted the hem of her shirt, showing her belly button and a tiny silver ring.

Marie jerked to life as J.D.'s frown deepened. She rushed forward a few feet, her hands clasped at her waist. "Beth, please. . ." Her whisper carried over the sounds coming from the radio in the kitchen.

Beth swung her gaze in her mother's direction and held her hands out. "Did I say something untrue? This *is* the man who refused to help you raise me after my dad died, isn't he?"

J.D. finally took a step forward, his eyes blazing beneath his bushy, gray brows. "If I had helped raise you, you would have more respect for your elders." Wheeling on Marie, he gestured to Beth with one hand. "Haven't you given your daughter any training?"

Marie opened her mouth, but Beth jumped in. "My mother has given me plenty of training. She's taught me to always do my best at whatever I do, to be truthful at all times, and to treat others the way I want to be treated." The girl crossed her arms and tipped her chin up, sending a saucy look in J.D.'s direction. "Seems to me you forgot that third one when Mom came to you needing help twenty years ago."

Marie put her hand on Beth's arm. "Honey, this isn't the time—"

Beth pulled away. "Then when is the time, Mom? Look at him!" Beth pointed to J.D., her finger mere inches beneath the man's firmly clamped jaw. "Look at his face. He doesn't want us any more now than he did then."

Henry glanced at grandfather, daughter, and granddaughter. Three different emotions displayed on three faces. Stoicism on the eldest's, resentful anger on the youngest's, and what could only be defined as deep hurt on that of the one caught in the middle.

Marie's throat convulsed as if she fought tears, and Beth snorted. Crossing her arms again, she glared at her grandfather. "Well, don't worry, *Grandfather*. We're not here to stay, so you won't have to put up with our unwanted presence for long. As soon as our time is up and I've got the money from the sale of the house and this café in my pocket, we'll be out of your life. And I guarantee we'll never bother to darken your doorstep again."

The girl charged for the doorway, forcing J.D. to move aside or be run down. She paused at the back counter just long enough to snatch a little silver telephone from its cord, then stormed to the back door. There, she spun briefly to send one more glare in J.D.'s direction. "I'm going back to my house to put a big X on the calendar." Her lips twisted into a snide leer. "One day down. Eighty-nine to go." Then she slammed out the door.

Marie started after her. "I'd better show her the way back."

Henry caught her arm. "It's a small town. She'll find it. And it will do her good to walk off some of that anger."

Tears welled in Marie's eyes, but she blinked them away. "You don't understand. That isn't anger. I know it seems like it, but underneath it's. . ." She looked at J.D. Recrimination flashed in her eyes. "It's a lifelong hurt. From being rejected."

J.D. raised his chin. His eyes narrowed into slits. "*You* rejected *us*."

Marie's jaw dropped. "What? Dad, I didn't reject you."

"You chose that truck driver over your family!"

"I fell in love!"

J.D. reared back at the volume of her statement. Henry's heart launched into his throat.

Marie took a deep breath, and when she spoke again, her voice was under control. "I fell in love with Jep. I wanted to spend my life with him."

Henry shifted backward, a feeble attempt to separate himself from Marie's earnest words.

"I didn't leave with him to get away from you. I just. . .left."

In an instant, a scene from the day of Marie's departure flashed through Henry's mind. A rumbling semi, a man waiting behind the wheel, and Marie beside the open door, confusion on her face.

"Yes, you left. You left your family, your home, and your faith." J.D.'s growling accusation dispelled the memory.

Marie shook her head. A tear slid down her cheek, and she dashed it away with a swipe of her hand. "I didn't. Not at first. I went to a meetinghouse; I honored my beliefs. Yes, I lived somewhere other than Sommerfeld—I was with my husband. But you know all that because I wrote to you. I tried to include you in my life. I didn't *leave* anything until you made me." Sadness underscored her weary tone. "Not until after Jep died and Beth was born and I asked for your help. And you refused to give it. You gave me no choice but to leave, Dad."

"And this is what you choose?" J.D. flicked the short curls over Marie's right ear with work-worn fingers, a contemptuous sneer on his face. "Shorn hair and an uncovered head? Clothing that—"

Henry held up both hands, unable to stay silent a moment longer. "Stop this! What are you accomplishing here?"

J.D. pointed at Henry. "You brought me here. You said I should go see my daughter. Well. . ." His gaze swept from Marie's head to her feet and back again. "I've seen. I come here, out of the goodness of my heart, and all I receive is disrespectful backtalk and blame for her foolish choices." He shook his head, releasing a snort that sounded very much like the one Beth had made. "This is not the girl I raised. This is a woman of the world—a woman who intends to return to the world. And I have no reason to stay here."

He spun on his heel and thumped to the back door. He slammed through without a backward glance.

Henry looked at Marie. He expected tears, but none came. Her face was white, her blue eyes wide, her chin quivering. But she held her emotions inside. His heart ached for her. "Marie, I'm sorry."

She moved stiffly to the noisy box on the counter. She clicked something, and the raucous tune halted midscreech, abandoning them to an uncomfortable silence. Her shoulders slumped. For long seconds she remained beside the counter, head down. He stayed in his spot beside the dining room door, uncertain what to do.

With her back still to him, she finally spoke. "You have no need to apologize, Henry. You meant well, bringing him here. And I admit, when I saw him, I hoped. . ." She sighed, lifting her head as if examining the ceiling. Her nutmeg curls graced her tense shoulders. Turning slowly, she met his gaze. All sadness was erased from her expression. She simply looked resigned.

"I'd better go check on Beth. Thank you for. . ." She swallowed, giving a shake of her head. "Thank you." Moving toward the door, she said, "Would you lock up when you leave?" She didn't wait for his answer but slipped out the door. In a moment he heard her car's engine fire up and then the rumble of tires on gravel as she pulled away.

Henry remained in the middle of the silent café, hands in pockets, heart aching. "Lisbeth, it isn't working."

Marie found Beth at Lisbeth's house. As Henry had predicted, she'd found her way just fine. But judging from the way she was slamming clothes onto hangers and smacking them into the closet, the walk had done nothing to drive out her hurt and anger.

Marie understood Beth's pain. Her chest felt laid open, her heart lacerated and bleeding. She leaned against the doorframe of Lisbeth's sewing room and crossed her arms. "Hey."

Beth barely glanced at her mother. Her lips were pressed in a tight line. She whammed another hanger onto the wooden rod. "Don't tell me I shouldn't have spoken to him like I did, because I won't apologize."

"You're an adult, not a child. You can decide when you believe you owe someone an apology."

"If anyone owes anyone an apology, *he* owes *us* one. Standing there looking at us as if we were scum." She rolled a T-shirt into a wad and slam-dunked it in a dresser drawer. "Couldn't even say hello after two decades of ignoring us. Who does he think he is anyway, some sort of god?"

Beth paused, hand raised to place another hanger in the closet, and released a huge sigh. Plunking the hanger into place, she turned to face her mother. Tears glistened in the corners of her eyes. "Why does he hate me so much? What did I do to him?"

"Oh, honey." Marie rushed forward, her arms outstretched. But Beth eluded her, sidestepping to reach into a box and pull out a sweater. Marie folded her arms across her middle, giving herself the hug she longed to give her daughter. "He doesn't hate you, Beth. How could he? He doesn't even know you."

"And he doesn't want to." The harsh undertone returned. She held the sweater at arm's length, frowning at it. "At least I have a few memories of Grandpa Quinn. Of course, after Grandma died and he moved to Florida, we didn't see much of him. But he was around for a while anyway. It's not like he *disowned* me."

Beth's flippant tone spoke clearly of the hurt she tried so valiantly to conceal with a facade of anger. Marie battled tears as she listened to her daughter share her thoughts.

"But your father. . .and the people in this town. . . That's a different story." Beth popped the sweater onto a hanger but then just stood, holding it two-handed against her ribs. She sucked in her lips, her brow creased. Suddenly she whirled to face Marie. "It's because Dad wasn't Mennonite, isn't it? I'm like a. . .a half-breed to them."

Marie sank onto the cot, causing it to squeak with her weight. She ran her finger around the edge of the neatly appliquéd heart nearest her hip. In her mind's eye, she saw Aunt Lisbeth's veined hand guiding the needle through layers of cloth. A smile tugged at her lips. And then another hand flashed in her memory: her father's hand reaching for her head to flick her curls. She flinched, pushing aside the thought.

"There's so much. . .history. . .behind my father's feelings, Beth. I'm not sure I can explain it in a way that will make any sense."

Beth put the hanger in the closet, then sat on the floor cross-legged. Folding her hands in her lap, she turned her hardened gaze on her mother and barked a one-word command. "Try."

Marie pursed her lips, organizing her thoughts. "I suppose the simplest explanation is this. Outsiders bring in new ideas that don't match the teachings of the church. The church's doctrine is very important. We are to be separate from the world—peculiar, even. When others look at us, we want them to see an outward difference that leads them to the heart, where Jesus resides."

"I don't like it when you say 'us,' like you're a part of them, too."

Marie's heart turned over at her daughter's belligerent tone. "I say 'us' because it's my heritage. Yours, too, even though you weren't raised with it." Beth's frown didn't encourage Marie to continue that line, but she added, "It isn't the doctrine that's wrong here, honey, but the extreme to which it's carried by a few."

Beth scowled. "What I remember about Jesus from Sunday

school is that He was loving to everybody. If Jesus resides in a heart, shouldn't a person's behavior show that? I sure didn't see much lovingkindness in the way your dad treated us today."

Marie turned away, pain stabbing with the reminder of her father's stern, condemning posture. She sighed. "Yes, *Christian* means *Christlike*. And sometimes people don't do a very good job of emulating Him." Turning back to Beth, she leaned her elbows on her knees and clasped her hands together. "But you can't let the way my father treated us today make you think ill of all Christians or all Mennonites. That wouldn't be fair."

Beth pushed to her feet. She flipped her ponytail over her shoulder and reached for another sweater. "Of course not. That would be like your father thinking all non-Mennonites are horrible people. I sure wouldn't want to be like that."

Marie sat in silence, watching as Beth emptied the box of clothing, then reached for a second box. When Beth continued to work without looking in her direction, she finally sighed, rose from the cot, and moved to the doorway. "Well, I guess I'll go make us some sandwiches."

"I'm not hungry."

"Well, then—"

"My phone's recharged. I'm going to try to reach Mitch again." Beth closed the door in her mother's face.

Marie stood for a moment, staring at the wooden door, battling with herself. She understood Beth was upset. Angry. Hurt. When Beth was little and had a problem, Marie had always insisted she talk it out until they reached a workable solution. But now? She wasn't sure they would find a solution to this situation if they talked from now until New Year's. Her father was set in his ideas and unlikely to change.

She'd never thought about it before, but J.D. Koeppler and Beth were a lot alike—both headstrong, unwilling to bend. A humorless chuckle found its way from Marie's chest. She supposed neither would appreciate the comparison. Through the door, she heard Beth's voice and assumed the cell call had gone through. With a sigh, she headed to her own room to put away her clothes. She really wasn't hungry, either.

TEN

Marie wiped her hands on the calico apron that reached from her bodice to below her knees. As had been the case more than twenty years ago, commuters from the surrounding smaller communities on their way to their jobs in the larger cities pulled off the highway to enjoy breakfast at Lisbeth's Café. The place had bustled with activity from six on. Now, at nine thirty, the breakfast rush was over, and she welcomed a moment to lean against the counter and catch her breath.

Her denim midcalf-length skirt felt scratchy against her bare legs, and she shifted a bit so the fabric wasn't brushing her skin. When Beth had spotted her this morning, dressed in the straight denim skirt and button-up blouse, she had raised her eyebrows. Marie had raised hers, too, at Beth's rattiest pair of jeans and skintight baby T that left a half inch of midriff showing. "Wouldn't you like to at least put on a sweater?" The suggestion had been made gently, but Beth immediately flared.

"You told me I could be comfortable, and this is comfortable."

Marie had held up her hands in defeat, but she'd wondered over the course of the morning just how comfortable Beth really was. She'd spent the entire morning hiding in the supply closet, "doing inventory," with her cell phone pressed to her ear, talking in hushed tones with anyone she could rouse.

She could hardly blame Beth for wanting to stay out of sight. Of course, the customers from out of town hadn't reacted oddly to her presence, but the handful of Sommerfeld citizens who came in for morning coffee and conversation had stared unabashedly, their gazes darting away when she met them directly. Their only comments to her had been those necessary for ordering—no friendly greetings or idle chitchat.

Deborah hadn't greeted her or Beth cheerfully, either. Even now, with no customers in the café and the opportunity to visit, Deborah sat on a stool on the opposite side of the kitchen, her back to Marie, her nose buried in the *Mennonite Review*. The only communication with her this morning had been brisk instructions on how things were done. If Marie had her druthers, she'd be hiding in the closet, too, but someone had to wait tables and run the cash register.

A stack of dishes awaited washing. Marie sighed as she stared at the towers of white and blue ceramic plates, bowls, and cups. They'd need to be finished before the noon traffic came in, which Deborah had indicated was so light they might consider closing the café for the midday hours. She and Beth would discuss that later, but whether they decided to close or not, the dishes had to be washed.

Marie decided she wasn't going to be the one to do them. Waiting tables and making sure the café stayed stocked with the needed items for serving was enough of a task without adding dishwashing to the list. Beth would have to carry a share of the load.

She marched to the supply closet and stepped inside, closing the door so their conversation wouldn't carry to Deborah's ears. Beth, engrossed in a cell-phone exchange, held up her hand in a silent bid for patience. Marie waited, leaning against the closed door.

"Okay, I'll start checking. Yes, I'll give it my best shot—you know how persuasive I can be." Beth's soft, intimate chuckle raised the hairs on the back of Marie's neck. "Well, listen, Mom's in here, so I'll talk to you later. Love you, too. 'Bye." Beth flipped the phone closed and smiled. "Mitch has some great ideas for adding to our boutique's inventory. I'm going to start visiting the farms this afternoon, asking if the farmers have any items to sell. He said he'd get a small business loan to pay for the stuff, then we'll pay that back when we sell the café."

"Sounds reasonable." Marie crossed her arms and gestured with her head toward the kitchen. "Honey, Deborah cooks, I serve customers and take the tabs. We need someone to run the dishwasher."

Beth tipped her head, her brows low. "Trina told me she'd been working here with your aunt. I'll bet she knows how to work the dishwasher. I wonder where she is."

"I wasn't speaking of Trina," Marie chided. "I was speaking of you. I need *you* out there."

Beth crunched her face into a scowl. "I don't think I can stand working with that woman. She's such a sourpuss."

"You won't have to work with her. As I said, she's cooking. The stove and the dishwasher are on opposite sides of the kitchen."

Beth huffed. "But I'd really like to start making those visits."

Marie quirked one brow. "Beth, you asked me to come with you and help, which I'm very willing to do, but you've got to help, too." At Beth's grim expression, she suggested, "Maybe you can ask Deborah if Trina can come in tomorrow and operate the dishwasher for you, but for today, I need you."

"I'm not asking Deborah anything."

Marie released a laugh.

"What's so funny?" Beth scowled.

"You. You look exactly like your grandfather with that stubborn set to your jaw."

As Marie had suspected, the reference to J.D. Koeppler provided the impetus for action. Beth tucked the cell phone into her jeans pocket and pushed past her mother. Marie remained in the closet doorway and watched Beth stalk to Deborah's side.

"Mrs. Muller." The use of the respectful title made Marie's chest swell with pride.

Deborah turned her head, meeting Beth's gaze. She didn't smile. "Yes?"

Although Beth folded her arms over her chest in a battle stance, she maintained an even tone. "I wondered if it might be possible for Trina to come in tomorrow and run the dishwasher."

Deborah set the newspaper aside. "Will you be here?"

Beth shrugged. "I'll be in and out."

"Trina is at an impressionable age. Her father and I wish to keep her focused on those things we feel are important to her spiritual and emotional well-being."

Beth glanced at Marie. Irritation flared in her eyes, and Marie held her breath, hoping her daughter would think before speaking. Beth dropped her arms, slipping her fingertips into her back jeans pockets, then faced Deborah again. A slight smile curved her lips. "I assure you I have no intention of corrupting Trina. She's a cute kid, and I wouldn't want to do anything to hurt her. She'll be safe here."

Deborah seemed to examine Beth's face. Beth stood still under the scrutiny, waiting. Finally Deborah gave a brusque nod. "I'll ask her father. If he says it's all right, she can come tomorrow."

Beth shot Marie a triumphant grin before turning back to Deborah. "Thanks."

Deborah returned to reading her paper, and Beth skipped across the tile floor to Marie's side.

"Piece of cake." Slinging her arm around her mother's shoulders, she said, "Okay, show me how to work this big ol' monstrosity."

Beth held her cheerful mood the remainder of the day, much to Marie's relief. Although Deborah never openly spoke to either of them, she lost a bit of the tight look around her mouth as the day progressed, giving Marie hope that she might soften in time. She had no desire to walk on eggshells the entire duration of their three months together. She doubted she and Deborah would return to their old friendship, but she would be satisfied with the loss of tension between them.

Henry was among the supper patrons. When Marie delivered his plate of pot roast, potatoes, and seasoned green beans, he smiled. "When the place is closed, I'll come by."

Marie's eyes flew wide.

His cheeks, wearing a slight shadow of whisker growth, blazed red. "To show you the books from the past several weeks while Deborah has been in charge. She asked me to keep the records since math is not her strong suit."

Business. Nothing personal. Marie nearly wilted with relief. Or regret? She rubbed her eyes. She must be tired if she was having thoughts like that. "Thank you, Henry. I'll stick around." She hurried away before peering into his brown eyes raised any other odd feelings.

Beth left the moment the last plate came out of the dishwasher, but Deborah stayed close when Henry flopped the ledgers open and showed Marie the expenses and income from the past two months. Her heart twisted when she witnessed the change in penmanship in the columns, and she couldn't resist running her finger along the lines penned by Aunt Lisbeth's hand.

"All of the monies made have gone directly into the café account at the bank in McPherson," Deborah said, her brown eyes sharp. "It's all there."

Marie glanced again at the ledger and frowned. "Haven't you or Trina kept anything for your labor?"

Deborah pursed her lips. "Of course not. I wouldn't presume to do that for myself."

"But that's hardly fair." Marie flipped a few pages, searching for prior entries concerning the payment of employees. "If you're working, you ought to be paid. Here." She found what she wanted. Pointing at the numbers, she looked at Henry. "This shows an hourly wage plus tips being paid to Trina when she worked with Aunt Lisbeth. We need to figure out what she would have earned over the weeks after Aunt Lisbeth died and get her caught up. We also need to pay Deborah for—"

"I do not require payment for doing a service for a dear friend." Deborah's firm voice brought Marie to a startled halt.

Marie stared at the woman for a moment. Deborah's brown eyes were as determined as they'd been in her youth. Rarely had anyone won an argument with Henry's sister. Recalling some of their girlhood spats, Marie had to swallow an amused grin.

She processed possible means of convincing Deborah to accept payment for her time in the café, but she came up empty until Deborah's words, *"service for a dear friend,"* repeated in her mind. The smile she'd been holding back found its way to her face.

"Deborah, I very much appreciate you giving to Aunt Lisbeth in such a wonderful way. You were a good friend to her, and I thank you. But as you know, I'm going to need you while Beth and I are here. I can't, in good conscience, allow you to continue working without pay. Not for Beth and me."

Deborah flicked a quick glance at Henry, who seemed to be biting down on the insides of his lips.

Marie continued. "Will you please sit down with Henry and

discuss a reasonable wage? And we'll put you officially on the payroll, starting today."

For long seconds Deborah stood silently, her gaze boring a hole through Marie, but finally she released a sigh. Running her fingers down the black ribbons of her cap, she gave a nod. "Very well. Starting today."

Marie drew in a deep breath of relief. One battle won.

"I'm going home now. Henry, are you coming?" The pointed question left no alternative for him but to rise to his feet.

"Of course. I'll see you again tomorrow evening, Marie." He headed for the back door.

Marie shot a startled glance at his back.

Deborah made another of her pursed-lip faces. She leaned toward Marie and lowered her voice to a conspiratorial level. "Henry has eaten nearly all of his supper meals at the café for the past twenty years." Her stern gaze flicked in his direction for a moment before returning to Marie. "When the café closed for the evening, he took Lisbeth home." Her stern countenance softened a bit. "I'm sure he misses her. They were very good friends." Then she straightened her spine, her grim expression returning. "But he has accepted her loss, and he isn't seeking a replacement."

Marie felt certain Deborah was attempting to deliver a message of some sort, but tired from her long day, she couldn't decipher it. She merely nodded, acknowledging the words. Deborah removed her apron, slipped on her sweater, and followed Henry out the back door.

When Marie returned to Lisbeth's house, she found Beth at the kitchen table with the lamp burning. A crude map, drawn on notebook paper, lay on the checked tablecloth.

Beth looked up and flashed a smile. "Look here, Mom. I drew this from the one on the post office wall. I can use this when I start my antique hunting tomorrow. I plan to hit every house in town, as well as all the farms around Sommerfeld. Maybe all of them in Harvey County. Who knows?" She suddenly frowned. "You look beat. Why don't you go soak in the tub and then hit the hay?"

Marie smoothed her hand over Beth's head and delivered a kiss on her forehead. "Thanks, honey. I think I'll do that." She took a lamp from the edge of the kitchen counter, lit it, and started for the hallway. Before turning the corner, she peeked back at Beth. "Oh, just a reminder, before you take off on your hunt tomorrow, remember to come by the café just in case Trina's father doesn't allow her to come work."

"Oh, he'll let her."

Marie propped a hand on her hip. "You're certainly the confident one."

Beth smirked. "I just have the feeling that mom of hers wants to keep her under her thumb, and what better way to do that than have her stuck at the café all day?"

Marie chuckled and headed to the bathroom. How well Beth knew Deborah already! When she was stretched out in Lisbeth's old-fashioned porcelain tub, staring through the lace-covered window to the starry sky, Deborah's parting comment about Henry accepting Lisbeth's loss returned. She frowned. What was Deborah intimating? When understanding dawned, she almost laughed out loud.

Marie had been given a subtle warning not to try to replace Lisbeth in Henry's life. Sinking a little deeper into the scented bubbles, she closed her eyes, smiling. Deborah had no reason to worry. Those Xs Beth made on the calendar each evening would add up fast, she'd be on her way, and no one need even remember she'd passed through. Including Henry.

For some reason, her heart seemed to pinch with the thought.

Twisting her toe on the hot water spigot, she whispered aloud.

"It's only because being here is bringing back childhood memories. Henry was a big part of my growing up. It's only natural to think of him maybe more than some others."

She reminded herself of that thought as the week progressed. On Wednesday she managed to serve Henry his meal without giving him any extra attention. But on Thursday his hand brushed against hers when she placed a newly filled saltshaker on his table, and she felt her face fill with heat. She escaped before he could see her blush and be embarrassed, too. On Friday she pretended she needed to use the bathroom and asked Trina to take his plate. The gregarious teenager acquiesced so innocently, Marie felt a pang of guilt for the deception.

But Saturday evening, even though Deborah carried Henry's steak and potatoes to the dining room, she didn't avoid him. He called her name as she scurried by on her way to the kitchen. Pausing several feet away, she peered at him with raised brows, hoping she gave the illusion of great busyness even though the café was only marginally crowded.

"I wanted to ask you a question." His gaze flicked to the tables on his right and left, communicating his unwillingness to speak loudly enough for any other patrons to overhear.

With a sigh, she approached his table, stopping on the opposite side. "Yes?"

Now that he had her attention, he hesitated, his thick eyebrows knitted. "It's about. . .attending meetinghouse."

Marie took a backward step. "That's a subject best left alone, Henry." She softened the words with a smile, but before he could say anything, she dashed to the kitchen. She made sure she stayed there until he dropped a few bills on the table, rose, and left.

ELEVEN

Marie poured a cup of coffee from Lisbeth's tall aluminum percolator, then doctored it liberally with sweet cream purchased from a local farmer. She sank down at the kitchen table and cradled the warm mug between her palms. Across the house, Beth still slept. She'd probably sleep until noon. Marie shrugged a little deeper into her chenille bathrobe and sipped her coffee, wondering what time it might have been when her daughter had put the cell phone away and finally went to bed. The wee hours of the morning, that's for sure.

She sighed. Beth's venture wasn't turning out as she'd hoped. She had visited two families a day, and despite her most polite demeanor and generous top-dollar offers, no one had agreed to sell her anything for her planned boutique. Marie's heart ached as she remembered her long conversation with Beth last night.

"Mom, I don't understand it. A lot of the stuff I've tried to buy is just out in barns or on back porches—not even being used except to stack more stuff on or take up space. Why won't they sell it to me and make a little money?"

Marie had tried to explain that the Mennonites, traditionally, weren't interested in gaining earthly wealth, so money wasn't a motivator to them. Beth had demanded to know what was a motivator. At Marie's response that helping a neighbor was of more importance than accumulating wealth, Beth had turned derisive.

"These people are so backward."

Her daughter's statement had brought a rush of defensiveness. "They aren't backward, just different. Frankly, I find it refreshing that there are still people in the world who look out for each other rather than constantly scrambling for the ever-loving dollar."

At that point, Beth's face twisted into a scowl, and she pushed away from the table with a curt, "Well, they sure aren't looking out for *me* by keeping that stuff to themselves. I'm going to call Mitch." Her conversation with her boyfriend had lasted long into the night. Which meant Marie would have a quiet morning to herself.

She raised the cup to her lips and breathed in the rich aroma of the brew. Having grown accustomed, over the past week, to the fuller flavor of coffee brewed in a percolator, she wondered if the drip-machine coffee from home would seem bland. She chuckled softly. Bland. . . Would she have ever thought she would apply that term to anything in Cheyenne?

She rose from the table and crossed to the window, peering across the stubbly pasture that stretched west of the house. As a little girl, she had stood at this same window with Lisbeth, "watching the wheat grow," as her aunt had put it. A smile of fond remembrance tugged her lips. She could almost feel the tickle of the ribbons from Lisbeth's cap trailing along her cheek as her aunt had leaned forward to whisper in her ear, "Can you see the stalks stretching toward the sun, sweet girl? A wise wheat stalk reaches toward the sun, and a wise person reaches toward the Son."

Marie had dashed into the backyard to dance in circles, her hands reaching upward to catch a sunbeam, laughing out loud while Lisbeth watched from the window, laughing, too. When she'd grown a little older, she'd realized Aunt Lisbeth referred to the Son of God rather than the sun in the sky. The day she'd found the courage to tell Aunt Lisbeth she had finally grasped her meaning, her aunt had tickled her nose with the end of her long braid, making her giggle. "And that proves to me, my darling girl, that you are growing wiser." Tears had winked in the woman's eyes as she'd advised, "Always reach for the Son, Marie. Draw Him closer and closer, and your wisdom will grow more and more."

That afternoon, with Aunt Lisbeth's gentle guidance, Marie had invited Jesus, the Son of God, to enter her heart and forgive her sins. Lisbeth's expression radiated joy as she folded Marie in her arms and whispered, "Welcome to the family of God, my Marie." The look on her aunt's face was permanently etched in Marie's mind.

Something trickled down her cheek, and she brushed her fingers over her face. They came away wet, and Marie gave a start. Why was she crying? The answer came at once. How disappointed Aunt Lisbeth would be to know how far her beloved niece had strayed from the Son.

"I'm sorry, Aunt Lisbeth," she whispered, the pain of her loss striking more harshly than at any time since Henry had delivered the news of her aunt's passing.

A strong desire to see her dear aunt just one more time washed over Marie. Visiting with her in person was impossible, but she could at least visit her final resting place. She set her now-cold cup of coffee on the red-checked tablecloth and hurried to Lisbeth's bedroom, shedding her bathrobe as she went.

Fifteen minutes later she was behind the wheel of her car, dressed in blue jeans and a hooded sweatshirt. But as she turned the key in the ignition, she remembered it was Sunday. The cemetery was next to the meetinghouse. And the meetinghouse would be filled with worshipers. She pressed her forehead to the steering wheel, emitting a low groan. She couldn't go there now. . .or could she? She closed her eyes and forced her mind to picture the layout of the meetinghouse and its surrounding grounds, including the iron-fenced cemetery.

If she didn't use the large driving gate in the corner closest to the back doors of the meetinghouse—if she parked outside the fence and walked through the small gate at the back corner of the cemetery—surely she would be unobtrusive enough to escape notice. No doubt Aunt Lisbeth had been buried in the Koeppler plot, which was in the northwest corner, completely opposite the meetinghouse building.

Maybe she should wait until tomorrow. She wouldn't be working. Maybe tomorrow would be better, she tried to convince herself. But the need to spend time with Aunt Lisbeth became a gnawing ache Marie could not ignore. She twisted the key, bringing the engine to life, and backed down the driveway.

Henry opened his Bible to the book of Ephesians, as directed by Brother Strauss, then lifted his gaze to the minister. Something—a slight movement outside the window—caught his attention. *Probably geese taking flight.* He shifted his eyes without turning his head and peered through the simple glass pane to prove his guess. Instead of birds, a slender human form slipped between headstones at the far side of the cemetery.

Henry's heart lurched. Even though the person wore a hood, which hid the face and hair from view, he knew it had to be Marie. Seeking Lisbeth. He wondered how he could be so sure, and he realized he just knew. Because—even after all this time—he knew Marie.

Although his face remained attentively turned toward the front of the simple sanctuary as if listening to the minister, his mind wandered backward. To another meetinghouse service in another time, when he was a lad of twelve. That was when Marie had first captured his heart.

The Saturday before, she had gone to the creek with the visiting bishop and been baptized in recognition of her acceptance of Jesus. The sight of her on the opposite side of the meetinghouse, with her nutmeg hair smoothed back and her sweet face framed by the white prayer cap and dangling ribbons, had distracted him throughout the entire service. Afterward, he had sidled up to her in the meeting-house yard. Bashfulness had kept his chin low, but somehow he'd managed to tell her how pretty she looked.

Marie's smile had lit the countryside, and although she hadn't thanked him with words for his compliment, her glowing expression had given him all the thanks he needed. After that, no other girl had ever mattered. It was always Marie. Right up until the day he watched her climb into a semi truck and ride away, the white ribbons dancing in the breeze that coursed through the open window.

He swallowed, his eyes once more jerking to the side to peek out. Yes, she was still there, hunkered beside the mound of dirt where Lisbeth had been put to rest. His heart twisted for the pain of loss she must be feeling. He understood it—he felt it, too. Lisbeth had been so special to him. More, even, than any of his own relatives. They had a bond—an affinity—that grew from their sorrow at Marie's departure.

Lisbeth was gone, but now Marie was back. His heart pattered.

His gaze sought and found J.D. Koeppler several pews ahead, in his usual spot. The man sat ramrod straight, his face aimed toward the front of the meetinghouse. A window was at his left. Had his eyes found his daughter, crouching in the cool wind, grieving beside a grave? Henry stifled a snort. Sympathy wouldn't swell in J.D.'s chest. The man's heart had turned to stone over the years.

He hadn't always been so cold. Henry remembered a warm twinkle in the man's eyes when he'd approached Marie's father, at the age of fifteen, and stammered out his desire to court her. J.D. had put his big hand on Henry's shoulder and said, a grin twitching his cheek, "Son, she'd be hard-pressed to find someone finer. But she's just turned thirteen. Can you give her a few years to grow up first?"

Henry had slunk away in embarrassment, but as J.D. had suggested, he'd given Marie a few years. And when she was finally old enough to make a commitment, Jep Quinn's semi had broken down on the highway at the turn that led to Sommerfeld, and within a week she was gone.

Henry sighed. On the bench beside him, his brother Claude poked him with his elbow. Claude's low brows let Henry know he'd been caught daydreaming. He sat up straight and forced his ears to absorb today's sermon. But he couldn't resist giving one more glance out the window.

Marie was gone.

"Where have you been?" Beth met her mother at the back door. She hugged herself and shivered as a gust of wind whisked through the open door. "I woke up and couldn't find you."

"I went to the cemetery." Marie passed through the utility porch to the kitchen and peeled off her sweatshirt while Beth followed, continuing to scold.

"Couldn't you leave me a note or something? I mean, it's unnerving to wake up and be all alone. What were you doing at the cemetery?"

Marie picked up her coffee cup from the table and poured the cold contents down the drain. "Visiting Aunt Lisbeth." A band constricted around her heart. Sitting beside the grave hadn't provided the comfort she had gone seeking. Cup in hand, she headed for the percolator.

"I was hoping we could do some laundry today. I need jeans

washed, and we're out of our towels in the bathroom. I don't want to use the ones your aunt left. They smell funny."

Marie clamped her jaw and held back a sharp retort. She poured coffee into her cup, focusing on the swirl of dark liquid.

"I tried some of your coffee, but it tasted bitter to me." Beth leaned against the counter, her shoulders hunched. "So I haven't had any breakfast. And it's cold in here. Can't that furnace put out more heat?"

Marie took a deep breath, seeking patience. "Beth, all you have to do is add coal to it and adjust the damper, and the heat will increase. I've told you that."

Beth tossed her head. "And I've told *you* I'm not going into that basement. It creeps me out."

"Well, I haven't done your laundry since you turned fourteen, and I'm not going to start now," Marie retorted sharply. "The washer is in the basement, so if you need clean clothes, you'll have to go downstairs."

Beth pushed off from the counter, her lips puckering into a startled pout. "Why are you being so grumpy?"

"Why am I—" Marie shook her head, swallowed, and took another calming breath. "I'm not trying to be grumpy, but you have done nothing but grumble since I stepped through the door." What bothered Marie more than Beth's complaints was the fact that her daughter didn't seem to recognize how difficult visiting the cemetery might have been. She needed sympathy, and it wasn't forthcoming.

"I'm not grumbling," Beth protested, a slender hand pressed to her chest.

Marie fixed her daughter with a pointed stare.

The girl blew out a breath that ruffled her bangs. "Okay, maybe I was." She yawned, not bothering to cover her mouth. Running her hands through her tangled hair, she said, "I didn't get much sleep last night."

Neither had Marie, but she didn't share that with Beth. She raised her coffee cup and took a cautious sip of the hot liquid. "And that's my fault because. . . ?"

"I didn't say it was your fault, I just. . ." Beth stared off to the side for a moment. Finally she brought her gaze around and released a sigh. "I'm frustrated, Mom, and so is Mitch. We put all our hopes into getting our start-up inventory from this town, and no one is cooperating. I know we'll have some stuff if we use all the furniture and quilts and dishes from this house. . ."

Marie's heart skipped a beat.

". . .but we'll need more. And I don't know how to talk people into selling."

Sipping at the steaming coffee, Marie gathered her thoughts. The idea of Lisbeth's things being purchased by strangers made her feel sick to her stomach. But that had been the intention all along—to sell everything and make money. She just hadn't realized how much being in her aunt's home would resurrect childhood memories. Selling Lisbeth's belongings would be like selling a part of herself.

"Mitch is coming up sometime in the next couple weeks, when he can get away."

Marie jerked, pulling her focus back to Beth's words.

"He said maybe if I have cash in hand and I flash it around, people will be more willing to let their stuff go."

Although Marie doubted a fistful of dollars would make much difference, she decided not to discourage Beth right now. Instead, she said lightly, "Well, let's hope it helps. Now. . .about your laundry."

Beth grimaced. "Can't we go to a Laundromat or something?"

Marie put down her coffee cup and folded her arms. "If you want to go to a Laundromat, go ahead. But I think it's a waste of gas and quarters when we have a machine in the basement."

Beth nibbled her lower lip, peering at her mother through a narrowed gaze. Suddenly her eyes widened. "Say. . .what kind of washing machine doesn't use electricity?"

Marie grinned. "Come see." She snatched up a lamp, lit it, and led the way.

Beth tiptoed, holding her arms tightly across her middle as if trying to make herself smaller as she followed Marie down the narrow, open-back stairs. When they reached the dirt floor, Beth glanced at the overhead support beams and shuddered. "I bet there are spiders down here just waiting to drop on my head."

"You're bigger than they are," Marie retorted. She walked past the refrigerator and ducked through an opening in the cinder-block wall that divided the basement in two halves. In the center of the second room, on a sheet of plywood, waited Aunt Lisbeth's 1936 Maytag washing machine.

Beth's eyes bulged. "That's nothing more than a tub on legs!"

"It works," Marie insisted. She tugged Beth by the arm until they stood beside the white porcelain washer. "Look. You turn on the water over there." She pointed, and Beth tiptoed across the floor to the copper line that poked through a hole in the basement's ceiling. She fingered the small iron valve dissecting the pipe.

A rubber hose, clamped to the end of the line, ran across the floor and draped over the edge of the tub. Beth followed the hose back to the washer, leaned over, and peered beneath the tub. "Where does it drain?"

"There's a plug down here." Marie reached inside the tub and pointed out a rubber stopper. "When you pull it, the water goes through this tube and into a drainage hole over there." She pointed to a dark corner of the basement, where the rubber tube disappeared.

Upright again, she reached inside the tub and gave the metal agitator a spin. "After the clothes have agitated, you drain the soapy water, refill the tub for a rinse, and put the clothes through this wringer to remove the excess water. Then you hang them on the clothesline outside." While she explained, she mimed the actions.

Beth's expression grew more disbelieving by the minute. "You've got to be joking."

Marie raised one brow. "I assure you, I am not. I've washed many a load in this old Maytag." She gave the machine a pat. "Aunt Lisbeth hid it down here because she didn't want the neighbors to know how spoiled she was."

Beth choked. "Spoiled?"

Marie nodded, grinning. "See the motor underneath? It's gas powered. You didn't have to crank the agitator yourself."

Beth burst out laughing. Marie couldn't stop her own smile as she witnessed her daughter's mirth. When Beth was under control, she circled the washer, stepping over the water lines to examine every inch of the ancient machine. Her survey complete, she grinned at her mother.

"Well, I have no intention of using this thing to do my laundry, but I think it will make a great addition to my boutique. I can picture it on someone's sun porch with impatiens spilling out of it." Her eyes sparkled. "Or filled with ice and cans of pop for entertaining." She clapped her hands once. "I'm going to go call Mitch. He won't believe this thing!"

Beth hurried upstairs, but Marie stayed in place, her fingers curled over the cold rim of the cast aluminum tub. Her father's question rang through her mind: "Haven't you given your daughter any training?" Beth's coldheartedness concerning the things Marie valued made her wonder if she had failed somehow.

Standing beside the washing machine brought back a rush of pleasant childhood memories. But to Beth, the machine only meant one thing: the almighty dollar.

TWELVE

Marie closed the basement door and headed toward the kitchen, but a shadowy figure outside the back door brought her to a halt. Someone stood on the porch, hands cupped beside eyes, peering through the lace curtain. Squinting, Marie stared. Then her jaw dropped.

Dashing to the door, she swung it open. "Joanna?"

A shy smile played at the corners of the woman's lips. "Hello, Marie. May I come in?"

Marie jerked backward a step, gesturing. "Yes, please. It's so good to see you." How Marie longed to throw her arms around her sister. Only a year apart in age, the pair had been inseparable growing up. With their similar hair color—although Joanna's leaned toward brown while Marie's leaned toward red—and identical clefts in the chin of their heart-shaped faces, the two had often been mistaken for twins. Both had loved this, and they'd sewn matching dresses clear into their teens to perpetrate the myth.

Now, looking into Joanna's face, framed by her white mesh cap and black ribbons, Marie felt as though she were looking into a mirror of what might have been had she remained in Sommerfeld. Instead of reaching for her sister, she took a step back.

115

Joanna's face clouded. "Would you rather I not be here?"

Marie's hand shot forward, her fingers barely brushing the sleeve of her sister's coat. "Oh, no! I just—I'm so surprised." She waved toward the kitchen, releasing a nervous giggle. "Please. Come in. Sit down. Or would you rather go to the front room? There's still coffee in the pot, but I haven't started lunch yet, so—"

Joanna's blue eyes twinkled. "Stop blabbering, Marie. You always were one to blabber when you didn't know what to say."

Marie gawked at Joanna for a second or two, then burst into laughter. Joanna joined her. For a few glorious moments they were teenagers again, elbows linked, sharing a private joke. The laughter faded, and they stood, smiling into each other's matching eyes.

"Well. . ." Marie cleared her throat and pulled out a kitchen chair to sit down. "What brings you here?"

Joanna tugged out a chair, too, and started to sit. At that moment, Beth bounced into the kitchen with an overflowing laundry basket held against her stomach. Joanna jerked upright and stared at her.

Beth came to a halt and stared back. Her gaze bounced between the two women several times; then she released a low whistle. "Wow. This one's got to be related. For a minute, I thought you were Mom in dress-up clothes."

Marie sucked in a sharp breath, but Joanna's tinkling giggle rang. She shook her head, smiling at Marie. "And this one has to be yours. Despite that blond hair, she's got your eyes and chin, as well as your frankness."

Beth raised one eyebrow and fixed her gaze on Marie. "You always told me that whole being-too-frank thing came from Dad's side of the family."

Joanna laughed again. "Did she? Really, Marie. . ." She shook her head, still chuckling. Looking at Beth, she said, "I'm your aunt Joanna. And I could tell you stories about your mom that would make your head spin."

Beth's lips quirked. "Oh, yeah?"

"But she won't," Marie inserted.

Beth and Joanna laughed and shared conspiratorial winks.

"Later?" Beth asked.

"Later," Joanna promised.

Marie glowered, but her heart sang at the instant camaraderie of these two women who meant so much to her.

Beth's expression turned sheepish. She set the basket down and dug underneath, removing the quilt that had been on her cot. "Can you tell me how to get nail polish out of fabric?"

Marie jumped up and rushed forward, snatching the quilt from Beth's arms. A bright pink splatter filled the center of the quilt. "Beth! How did this happen?"

She shrugged. "I was doing my toenails, and the bottle spilled. I tried to blot it, but. . ."

Joanna stepped between them, fingering the stain. She shook her head. "I think you'd ruin the fabric if you used something strong enough to remove that stain. This quilt has to be at least forty years old."

Beth groaned. "Oh, that means I won't get a penny for it."

Marie bit back the words that longed for release. This quilt was much more than a dollar sign to her. Why couldn't Beth see the sentimental significance?

"Oh, well." Beth rolled the quilt and tossed it aside. "I can always sell it as a 'cutter.' Someone may want to chop it up and make a teddy bear out of it or something." She hefted the basket. "So, where are the car keys? I'm going to hunt up a Laundromat."

Joanna spun, staring at Marie with an open mouth. "Laundry. . . on Sunday?" Then she clapped her hands to her cheeks and moaned. "Oh, I told myself I wouldn't do that." Clamping her hands together and tucking them against her ribcage, she drew a deep breath and smiled at Beth. "There's one on West First in Newton. Just follow Highway 135 North. There's a First Street exit off the highway, so you can't miss it."

"Is there a McDonald's near there?"

Joanna laughed. "Aren't there McDonald's everywhere? Just follow the signs."

Beth grinned. "Thanks!" Turning to Marie, she raised her eyebrows. "Keys?"

Marie pulled them from her pocket and handed them over. She forced herself to set aside her sorrow over the ruined quilt and focus on the issue at hand. "Do you have money?"

"Yep." Beth headed for the door, her ponytail swinging. "See you later!"

At the slam of the door, Joanna removed her coat, hung it on the back of the chair, and sat down. "She's a pretty girl, Marie."

Did a hint of accusation linger in her tone? Marie picked up the quilt, folded it lovingly, and carried it to the table. After setting the quilt aside, she seated herself. "Yes, she is. She's a challenge at times, but I can't imagine my life without her." She glanced at the quilt, reminding herself that Beth was infinitely more important than squares of fabric pieced together.

Joanna nodded. "I feel the same about my three. My oldest one, Kyra, has the fiery personality I see in your Beth. It's too bad—" She jerked her face away, the black ribbon of her cap crumpling against her shoulder.

"Too bad they didn't know each other growing up?" Marie finished her sister's thought.

Joanna bit down on her lower lip and gazed outward for several seconds before facing Marie again. The hurt in her eyes was unmistakable. "I've missed you so much. Not a day has gone by that

I haven't thought of you, wondered how you were, wished I could talk to you. It's been very hard."

Marie tried to swallow the resentment Joanna's gentle reprimand stirred, but a question found its way out. "Then where were you last week when I pulled into town? Do you know how hard it's been to sit in this house every evening, knowing my family is out there but doesn't care enough to come by?"

Joanna dipped her head. Marie stared at the spot where Joanna's part disappeared beneath the nearly translucent mesh of the cap. Joanna sighed, her head still low. "I wanted to come. But how could I know if I'd be welcome?" Her chin shot up, and tears winked in her eyes. "Twenty years, Marie, and you never wrote or called. How is a person supposed to know what to do?"

Marie's thoughts sniped, *You never called or wrote to me, either.* But she held the words back, aware they would do more harm than good. The silence lengthened.

Finally Joanna sighed. "I didn't come here to start an argument. I just wanted to know how you are. To see you again. I—" Joanna lurched from the table and held out her arms.

Marie pushed to her feet and fell into her sister's embrace. They hugged, laughing and crying at once, and Marie felt as though her heart might burst with happiness. Hurts melted away in the warmth of the hug, and when Joanna pulled loose to slip her elbow through Marie's, Marie knew things would be all right between the two of them.

They walked to the front room and perched side by side on the couch. For the next three hours they caught up, sometimes giggling like young girls over remembered silly times, other times vying for who could tell the most outrageous story of parenting. When Marie's stomach growled, it reminded her that lunchtime had come and gone. She pulled back, guilt striking.

"I'm keeping you from your family. They're probably wondering where you are and when they'll be fed."

Joanna shook her head. "They know where I am, and Kyra and Kelly are plenty capable of putting a meal on the table."

Marie grimaced. "Won't Hugo fuss about you spending the afternoon away from home?"

"What are Sundays for except to visit?" Joanna's gently lined eyes sparkled. "But if you offered me a sandwich, I wouldn't decline it."

They returned to the kitchen, where they made sandwiches and then sat at the table to eat. Marie felt a twinge of discomfort when Joanna prayed aloud, asking a blessing for the simple meal. It had been a long time since she'd offered grace before eating. But the easy conversation that followed erased the discomfort.

At nearly five o'clock Beth returned, the clothes folded neatly in the basket. Her face reflected surprise when she spotted Joanna. "You're still here? I figured you'd be long gone by now."

Joanna glanced at the red plastic wall clock and jerked. "Oh, my. It is growing late. I should go home." She stood and reached for her jacket. Slipping her arms into the sleeves, she looked at Beth. "I'll have to come back sometime and bring my daughters so we can all get acquainted. Your mother assures me she won't be such a stranger from now on."

Beth shot her mother a quick questioning look, but she recovered quickly and smiled at Joanna. "That would be great. How old are your daughters?"

"Kyra is nineteen and Kelly is thirteen." She smirked. "I also have an eleven-year-old son, Hugo Jr. We call him Gomer. But he isn't one for visiting. Too active." Turning to Marie, she added, "I didn't tell you—Kyra's engagement to Claude Braun's son Jacob was published today at the end of service. They plan a January wedding."

Marie's chest tightened. She and Beth would need to be gone

before the wedding. As nonchurch members, they wouldn't be welcome. Being in town, knowing the celebration was going on without them, would be too hard. She nodded. "I wish them well."

Joanna paused, her gaze narrowing, as she examined Marie for a few thoughtful seconds. Then her face relaxed. "Well, I need to go." She gave Marie a quick hug. "But I'll be back, Kyra and Kelly in tow." Pulling away, she cupped Marie's cheek with her hand. "Soon?"

Marie swallowed the lump that formed in her throat. "Very soon."

With another quick smile, Joanna slipped out the back door.

Beth put her hand on her hip. "Careful, Mom."

Marie jerked her gaze to Beth. "What?"

Pointing at the doorway where Joanna had disappeared, she said, "They're pulling you back. I can see it your eyes. This is *temporary*." She drew out the word, exaggerating each syllable. "Remember?"

Marie nodded, forcing a light chuckle. "Of course I remember." She scooped out the towels from the top of Beth's basket. "I'll go put these away," she said, changing the subject, "and you take care of the rest."

Beth gave her mother a wary look before turning toward the bedrooms. Marie headed for the hallway leading to the bathroom, but as she passed the kitchen window she paused, looking across the landscape behind the house. Aunt Lisbeth's words echoed through her mind. *"A wise person reaches toward the Son."* For a moment she wondered—was the pull Beth mentioned coming from her family, or from the One she once called Savior?

The telephone jangled on the corner of Henry's desk. He wiped his mouth with a napkin, dropped it beside his plate, and crossed the floor. He lifted the receiver in the middle of the second ring. "Hello?"

"Henry, this is Joanna."

"Don't tell me you're having trouble with the starter in your car again."

Joanna's light laugh sounded, bringing a pang of remembrance. The airy tremble at the end of her laugh sounded so much like Marie's. After Marie had left, he'd considered pursuing Joanna. Fortunately, good sense had reigned. Who could ever replace Marie? His good friend Hugo Dick had asked for Joanna's hand, and the two enjoyed a happy marriage. While he remained a bachelor.

"No, no, I'm not calling about my car. This is. . .personal."

Henry straightened his shoulders.

"I finally went to see Marie."

His heart began to thud.

"And I'm so glad I did. We spent the whole afternoon together and had a wonderful chat."

Henry smiled. "That's good. And she. . .welcomed you?"

A slight pause. "Yes. I think she was apprehensive at first, but so was I! We had a good time, though, and we plan to get together again soon so our girls can get acquainted."

Henry imagined outspoken, wild-haired Beth in her denim pants and shirts three sizes too small next to Joanna's sweet girls with their white caps and modest caped dresses. He shook his head. "I hope that goes well."

His tone must have communicated his doubt, because Joanna laughed. "I suppose it will be interesting, but they're cousins. They need to know each other."

"I agree," Henry said. "I'm glad you're trying to work things out." He paused, wondering if he should keep his next thought to himself, but finally decided to share. "I know Lisbeth would be pleased."

A long sigh came from Joanna's end of the line. "Every time the family was together, Lisbeth mentioned Marie and Beth. Her way, I think, of keeping them alive for us. Dad rarely let her give many details, but I found it comforting to know at least someone was keeping in touch with Marie." Her voice caught. "Being with her today made me realize how much we've missed through this separation. I wish. . ."

Although Joanna let the sentence go unfinished, Henry read the final thought. "Me, too," he said softly.

After a lengthy pause, Joanna's light chuckle sounded. "Well, aren't we a pair, throwing imaginary pennies in a wishing well."

Henry forced a laugh in response.

"I'd better go. I just wanted you to know I followed your advice and went to see my sister. Thanks for pushing me."

He smiled. "That's what friends are for."

"Good-bye, Henry." The line went dead.

Henry hung up the phone and smiled at the receiver. His gaze rose to a framed needlepoint sampler, a gift from Lisbeth. He read the words aloud. "But now in Christ Jesus ye who sometimes were far off are made nigh by the blood of Christ." He ran his finger along the top edge of the simple wood frame.

"Don't worry, Lisbeth," he said. "I'll keep trying until we bring her home again."

THIRTEEN

Marie examined the tumble of black lumps on the hard-packed ground next to the monstrous furnace. Over the two weeks of their stay in Lisbeth's house, Marie had grown accustomed to shoveling fuel into the belly of the iron beast twice a day, but she hadn't paid close attention to the dent its ravenous appetite had made in the supply.

The Kansas plains could be unpredictable during the winter months. If she didn't replenish the coal supply soon, she and Beth might end up facing some cold days ahead. She hooked the coal hod on its nail and brushed her palms together. She wondered where she could get coal around here. She was certain things had changed tremendously since she'd left with Jep.

Ask Henry, her thoughts immediately prompted. That would be simple since he continued to come to the café for supper every evening. For a moment she allowed a smile to twitch at her lips. Although the conversations with Henry were always brief, both of them aware of Deborah's watchful gaze and listening ear, she had come to enjoy sharing a few moments of chatter with him at the close of each day.

Despite her initial determination to keep a chasm between them, Henry was slowing building a bridge toward friendship. He wouldn't mind if she asked how to get a supply of coal delivered. But she pushed the idea aside. No sense in relying on him any more than necessary. He was already keeping the books at the café and would oversee the distribution of property when the time came. She shouldn't take advantage of his friendship. Besides, she acknowledged with a sigh, leaning on him too much might give him the wrong idea.

Might give her the wrong idea, too.

She trudged up the stairs and went to the kitchen sink to wash the remnants of coal dust from her hands. Outside the kitchen window, the sky looked bleak, the color of an old iron washtub. Rain might spoil Beth's plans for the day. Last night, after she and Beth were in their pajamas and ready for bed, Mitch had arrived to assist Beth in her quest for boutique items. Marie's scalp prickled as her mind replayed the image of her daughter throwing herself into her boyfriend's arms, lifting her face for his kiss.

He slept on the sofa, having collapsed there about a half hour after his arrival. Marie blew out a breath of relief, recalling how Beth had asked for bedding to put together a sleeping spot in the living room for Mitch. Even though Marie hadn't been faithful in church attendance since Beth was a little girl, she had raised her daughter to have morals. Sharing a bed with her boyfriend wasn't something she was willing to do. "Thanks for Beth's appropriate choice," Marie murmured.

She froze. That thought seemed awfully close to a. . .prayer. Had she really *prayed*? She shook her head. No, probably not a true prayer, more an inward statement of relieved gratitude. But it had felt like a prayer. A shiver shook her frame, spurring her to action.

"Breakfast." She tried not to bang things too loudly as she got out a cookie sheet and a knife to slice bread. Humming, she buttered the front and back of each slice. Just as she'd grown to prefer the flavor of percolated coffee, toast made from home-baked bread purchased from the grocer and browned under the broiler before being slathered with Joanna's peach preserves had become her favorite breakfast. Even though Beth continued to grouse about the lack of conveniences, Marie didn't mind the additional steps.

In fact, when she was home again, she planned to put the toaster away and continue to use the broiler. She also intended to keep Aunt Lisbeth's red-speckled percolator separate from the sale items. It was going back to sit on her electric stove and be put to use there.

She opened the oven door to check the bread, smiling as the aroma met her nostrils. The slices were browned to perfection. Just as she pulled the cookie sheet from the oven, Mitch appeared in the kitchen doorway.

"Morning, Marie." Bare-chested, his hair on end, Mitch stretched his mouth in a wide yawn and scratched his toned stomach with both hands. It had been two decades since a male had stood in her kitchen in the morning, sleep-rumpled and relaxed, and Marie found herself blushing profusely at the rush of memories his arrival conjured.

Aware of her gaping robe, which exposed her pink polka-dot flannel pajamas, she turned her back to him, dropped the cookie sheet on the counter, and quickly tied the belt on her robe. Once she was covered more modestly, she faced him. "Good morning, Mitch. Did you sleep well?"

"Pretty well, but that sofa's as hard as a concrete slab." He placed his hands against his lower spine and leaned backward, flexing his shoulders.

Marie turned toward the counter and unscrewed the lid on the jar of preserves. She scooped out a spoonful and plopped it on a piece of toast. "That sofa's been around for a while. I'm sure it's stuffed with sawdust. I'm sorry it wasn't more comfortable."

A low chuckle rumbled, and he cleared his throat. "It's okay. When a person's tired enough, he can sleep just about anywhere."

The shuffle of his feet let her know he'd moved farther into the kitchen. His face appeared over her shoulder. "Wow, that toast smells good."

Without looking at him, Marie offered a suggestion. "Go wash the sleep out of your eyes, put on a shirt, then sit down and have some. I made plenty."

His chuckle came again, and the amused undercurrent made Marie's face grow hot. "Thanks." He ambled around the corner toward the bathroom.

Abandoning the toast, Marie dashed to her bedroom and slipped into a pair of jeans and a button-up oxford blouse. Glancing at her glowing face in the small mirror above the dresser, she wondered if he realized the effect he'd had on her. She snorted. Of course he did! What else was that chuckle about?

Well, it wasn't *him* specifically that had her so rattled. She was wise enough to recognize that. It was just having a male, in such a state of dishevelment, so near. Not since Jep's death had a man spent the night under her roof. It could have been anyone standing out there, and she would have experienced the same embarrassed discomfort.

Worry struck. If his presence was this rattling for her, how might Beth respond?

She set her jaw as she lifted her hairbrush and ran it forcefully through her errant curls. If he planned to stick around, he would need to find a hotel in one of the larger towns nearby. Having him in the house day and night might prove to be too tempting for both of the young people. She would mention that to Beth as soon as she woke up.

As she placed the hairbrush back on the dresser, she heard a knock at the back door, followed by Mitch's call: "I'll get it."

She trotted around the corner in time to see Mitch, still shirtless, swing the back door open. Henry stood on the porch.

Henry took a step back when a half-dressed young man opened the door to Lisbeth's utility porch. A flurry of movement behind the man captured his attention, and he peered over the muscular shoulder to see Marie hurrying down the hallway.

She pushed in front of the man. "I've got it, Mitch. Go finish dressing."

The man grinned, scratching his whiskered chin. "Okay, Marie." He lifted his hand in an indolent wave and ambled down the hall, disappearing into the bathroom.

Henry gawked after him, curious about his presence but unwilling to ask.

Marie faced him, her cheeks stained pink. She crossed her arms over her chest and held the door open with her hip. "Good morning. W—would you like some toast?"

Henry shook his head. "No, thank you. I've had breakfast."

"Well, at least come in out of the cold." She pushed the door wider.

Aware of the other man inside, he remained on the stoop, holding his jacket closed against the morning breeze. "That's all right. I came to see if you—"

"Marie?" the man's voice intruded. "Can I borrow your toothpaste?"

Marie turned her face toward the bathroom. "Yes. Whatever you need." Her voice sounded tight. She faced Henry again. "I'm sorry. You came to see. . . ?"

"If you need some coal. I'm ordering a ton for my folks' place. I thought maybe you could use some, too."

Her eyes widened. "How could you possibly—"

"—know you need coal?" Henry smiled. "I always got Lisbeth's coal when I got it for my folks. They seem to run out about the same time."

She stared at him for several silent seconds, her brows low, puzzlement in her eyes. Then she shook her head, making her curls bounce. She took in a deep breath. "I was just noticing this morning that I need coal, but I didn't want to bother you. I can get it myself if you'd be kind enough to tell me where."

Henry released a light chuckle. "You'd have a time getting it in that car of yours. I borrow a truck from one of the local farmers and deliver it to my folks. The railroad brings it to town, but the train won't come to your house."

She ducked her head, laughing softly. When she raised her gaze, she looked a little less embarrassed and standoffish. "Thank you, Henry. Once again, your kindness is beyond the expected. Do—do you think you might advise me on how much I'll need to get me through December?"

December. The reminder of her short time here struck again, making Henry's heart race. "You could start with a quarter ton. If you need more, we can always get it later."

She bit down on her bottom lip, her forehead creased in thought. Finally she nodded. "Thank you, Henry. I appreciate your help."

The young man wandered back into the porch. He had slipped on a shirt that was covered in big flowers, but he hadn't bothered with the buttons, leaving it flap open. He stepped beside Marie and draped one arm over her shoulders, holding his free hand toward Henry.

"Hey. I'm Mitch Rogers, Beth's significant other. You must be the Henry Beth told me about."

Henry shook the younger man's hand, disconcerted by his familiarity with Marie. Her cheeks blazed again. He wanted to knock the boy's arm from her shoulder.

"I'm Henry Braun. I'm pleased to meet you." He hoped the Lord would forgive him for his fib.

Marie shifted her shoulders, and Mitch's arm slid away. "Henry is bringing us a load of coal today so I can keep the furnace running."

"Oh, yeah?" Mitch leaned against the doorjamb, as if providing chaperonage. "Good. We can use the heat. Pretty chilly in here in the mornings."

Henry thought the man would stay warmer if he'd button up his shirt. He backed up, reaching for the stair railing. "I'll have that coal here late this afternoon, Marie. I'll just dump it through the basement window, like always."

"That sounds fine."

He felt reluctant to leave, yet had no excuse to stay. "I'll see you later." He turned and jogged to his waiting car, hoping his face wasn't as red as the heat behind his cheeks indicated.

Driving toward his shop, he wondered about his strange reaction. Why should he care if some young man put his arm around Marie? It wasn't any of his concern. Marie had been taking care of herself ever since Beth was a tiny baby. She could continue to do so. Yet he couldn't deny the protectiveness he felt toward her.

Pulling behind his shop, he killed the motor and sat in the car for a few minutes, gathering his thoughts. "I promised Lisbeth to do all I could to bring her home. But home meant Sommerfeld, not my heart," he reminded himself sternly. "I can help her as a Christian brother concerned for her well-being, but I have to stop being jealous."

Jealous. The word made him set his jaw. He had no right to feel jealous toward anyone who showed attention to Marie. And he knew just how to get over that feeling.

Slamming out of his car, he headed to the back door of his shop and punched the key into the lock. "I'll just get busy," he said as he swung the door open and flipped on the lights. Unfortunately, no matter how busy he kept himself, the image of Mitch's arm draped over Marie's shoulders would not leave him alone.

"So you've been to each of these farms and everyone said no?"

Beth nodded at Mitch, irritation rising again at the memory of all those polite yet firm refusals. "And there's some neat stuff there, too." She sighed, brushing aside the remaining crumbs on the tabletop. "But there are plenty more places to go. We'll just have to hope for the best."

Mitch shook his head, his dark eyes gleaming. "First we'll go back to each of these farms. Give them a second chance." Slipping his hand into his back pocket, he removed his wallet. He flopped it open and grinned, rifling his thumb over the stack of twenty-dollar bills. "Ammunition, dear Lissie. We'll capture 'em yet."

Mom interrupted. "Don't make pests of yourselves. If the people don't want to sell, they don't have to. It's their right to keep their own belongings."

Beth turned in her chair and scowled at her mother, who stood at the sink, drying the last of the lunch dishes. Mom had been uptight all morning, fussing about Mitch being here and how it wasn't appropriate to have him in the house. Now it seemed she didn't want them to buy things for the boutique, either. Didn't she understand how a successful store would benefit all of them? "What's your problem today?"

Mom blinked in surprise. "I don't have a problem. I'm just saying, don't get pushy. If they don't want to sell, they don't have to."

Mitch hooked his elbow on the back of the chair and grinned. "Aw, c'mon, Marie, I'm not going to threaten anybody. But the opportunities are too good here. Beth told me about some long bench with a lid that had a feather tick inside it. You'd never find anything like that in the city."

Mom nodded. "A sleeping bench. They were fairly common when I was growing up." She leaned against the counter, and a slight smile graced her lips. "My mom kept one in the basement, and she'd sleep down there during the summer when it got too hot in the house."

Mitch nudged Beth's shoulder. "See there? Another one available. Where do your grandparents live? We can ask about theirs, too."

Mom's smile turned into a grimace. "Don't bother. They won't sell." She reached for another plate.

Beth huffed. She flipped her hand toward her mother. "That's the attitude around here, Mitch. 'They won't sell.' " Irritation mingled with hopelessness. Sighing, she raised her shoulders in a defeated shrug. "We might as well just catalog everything in this house and plan on it being our starting inventory. Maybe we can use some of the money you got to hit some auctions and buy stuff that way."

Mitch's gaze narrowed, his eyes snapping. "Absolutely not. I took my vacation to come out here and build our inventory. That's exactly what we're going to do." He took Beth's hand and raised it to his lips. His chin whiskers pricked her skin. Rubbing his fingers over her knuckles, he leaned forward and whispered, "I'm a salesman, remember? Together we'll convince 'em, Lissie. Trust me."

Beth giggled, her earlier despondence melting away under his fervent gaze. She bounced to her feet. "Let's go to the café and get on the Internet. We can scope out some of the stuff I've already seen and get an idea of secondary market value."

Mitch rose more slowly. His lazy amble was only one of the things that drew Beth to him. His laid-back attitude was in direct contrast to her whirlwind emotions, and she loved how they balanced each other. They'd no doubt be very successful together in business. . .and in love. Her heart pounded with the thought.

She leaned into him, snuggling against his chest and releasing a sigh of contentment when his arms closed around her. Still nestled, she peeked at her mother. "We're going to the café, Mom. Be back by suppertime, okay?"

Mom gave a nod, but she didn't push any words past her tightly clamped lips.

FOURTEEN

"Hi, Aunt Marie." Joanna's daughter, Kyra, slid into the corner booth and took the menu Marie offered.

Marie's heart fluttered, just as it had the first time one of Joanna's children used the title. The feeling of acceptance the simple word *aunt* delivered made her want to close her eyes and savor it. "Hi, honey. What brings you out this afternoon? Didn't you like what your mom was fixing for supper?"

Kyra laughed, the trickling tone very much like Joanna's. "No, it isn't that at all." She laid the menu on the table and folded her hands on top of it. "I really came to see Beth, but she isn't here. Again. I haven't been able to track her down all week."

Marie frowned. Beth had spent the entire week with Mitch, rarely appearing in the café except to grab something to eat and leave again. Mitch had indicated his vacation was nearing its end, and Marie admitted she'd be relieved to see him go. Beth's dissatisfaction with Sommerfeld had increased tenfold during her boyfriend's stay. The last few Xs on the calendar had been penned with force.

"She's been pretty occupied with Mitch." Marie managed to smile.

Kyra tipped her head, her cap ribbons shifting with the movement. "Has she had much success in buying items?"

Marie shook her head. "Not much, I'm afraid. A few things, but not nearly what she'd hoped. But in true Quinn fashion, she isn't willing to concede defeat. She intends to visit every house in Harvey County before she's finished."

Kyra laughed again. "She is determined!"

"More like stubborn," Marie said on a sigh.

"You know, I really admire her," Kyra said thoughtfully. "She sees what she wants, and she's willing to go after it. A lot of people, when faced with the kind of negative responses she's gotten, would just give up. But Beth continues to move forward because it means so much to her."

Marie wasn't sure Kyra fully understood Beth's motivation—achieving financial security at any cost—but she appreciated her niece's kind response. "Maybe you're right."

"I know I am." Kyra giggled, peeking around at the nearly empty café before leaning forward and whispering, "I had to be determined when it came to my relationship with Jacob. He's as bashful as his uncle Henry, and he would never have made a move if I hadn't let him know I was interested." She shook her head, her blue eyes sparkling. "But determination pays off." Pausing, she licked her lips. "You and Beth will be here for the wedding, won't you?"

Marie's heart sank. Despite having spent time with Joanna and her family over the past couple of weeks, no other relatives had approached to welcome Marie back. She was fairly certain she would not be welcome at a family event, but she hated to hurt Kyra's feelings. She spoke cautiously. "I'm not sure right now, honey. We'll probably go back to Cheyenne right after Christmas."

Kyra nodded, a sweet smile tipping up her lips. "I understand. Well. . .if it works for you to be there, I'd sure like that."

Marie's heart melted. "Oh, I would, too." She took in a deep breath, changing the subject. "You said you were looking for Beth. What did you need?"

Kyra sat up straight, eagerness showing in her bearing. "A bunch of us are driving to Newton tomorrow night for a skating party. I wondered if she and Mitch would like to join us. Several of her cousins are going, along with our friends, and we thought it would be a good way for her to get to know us better."

Marie slid into the opposite side of the booth. "Oh, Kyra, it's so nice of you to want to include her, but. . ." Beth spending an evening with the Mennonite young people? While Mitch was in town? Marie couldn't envision it.

"We won't be out late," Kyra added. "With service on Sunday, we need to be home by ten at the latest. We all plan to meet at Uncle Art's business and carpool, and we always eat at McDonald's before we go to the skating rink, so we'll leave at five o'clock."

Marie sat silently, uncertain how to avoid hurting Kyra's feelings.

Kyra leaned back, linking her fingers together. "Just tell her, okay? If she and Mitch are there, they can ride over with Jacob and me. If they're not, I'll know they didn't want to go."

"I can't believe I'm doing this." Beth stood in the hallway, hands on hips, a scowl marring her pretty face. "Skating. . .in a skirt, yet!"

Marie glanced over Beth's outfit—meshy-looking pink sweater, flaring peasant-style skirt, and brown T-strap flats. Six inches of bare leg showed between skirt and shoes. "You'll need socks."

"They're in my purse. There's no way I'm wearing them in public until I have the skates on my feet." She shook her head, her ponytail swaying. "I'm going to feel like such a misfit."

Marie recognized the insecurity beneath Beth's adamant statement. She stepped forward, cupped her daughter's cheeks, and gave
her a kiss on the forehead. "You'll be fine."

Beth grasped her mother's wrists and gave them a squeeze. "I
wish Mitch were coming."

"Why isn't he?"

The girl scowled. "He said he needed to get all his stuff packed
to head back to Cheyenne tomorrow morning. But I think he just
doesn't want to hang out with Kyra and Jacob and the rest. He feels
funny around them."

Marie nodded. "I suppose that makes sense."

Resting her weight on one leg, Beth tipped her head and sighed.
"Tell me again why I'm doing this?"

Marie imitated Beth's stance. "Number one, because it will do
you good to get out with people your own age. And number two,
because you'll get to know some of your cousins. . .at least a little bit.
They are family, you know."

A lengthy, melodramatic sigh followed Marie's comments, but
Beth made no disparaging remark. "Okay. Maybe if the young people
get to know me, they'll tell their folks to sell stuff to me after all. I
guess that would make this all worthwhile."

The reference to money-making made Marie clench her jaw.

"I just hope I stay on my feet, or everyone will see what I have
on underneath." With a smirk, Beth lifted the hem of her skirt to
reveal knee-length Spandex biking shorts.

Marie burst out laughing.

"I know, I know," Beth groused, "but I didn't have anything else.
I'd stick out even worse if I wore my jeans."

"You could borrow my denim skirt. At least it won't flare out."

Beth shook her head. "Huh-uh. It's not my style. Besides"—she
grinned impishly—"when I whirl around the floor, this one will be

bee-yoo-ti-ful to watch." Rising on one toe, she spun in a circle, the batik-patterned fabric becoming a blur of color.

Tears stung behind Marie's eyes as another picture formed in her memory—Beth on the first day of kindergarten in a pink polka-dot dress, twirling to make her skirt flare, a huge smile on her sweet face.

"All right then." Marie gave her daughter a hug, holding on tight. For some reason, letting Beth go was as bittersweet as it had been on that first school day so long ago. "Have a good time."

"I'll do my best." Beth headed for the door, her arm around Marie's waist. "What are you going to do while I'm out?"

"Empty Aunt Lisbeth's closet and bureau so I can put my own clothes away. I've been putting it off, but I can't handle living out of boxes any longer."

"Okay. Well—" They reached the back door and Beth grabbed the doorknob. "See you around ten."

Marie held the door open and watched Beth skip down the porch steps. When she reached the bottom, she lifted her hand in a brief wave, then rounded the corner to the car. Marie waited until the car had pulled out of the driveway before closing the door and heading to Lisbeth's bedroom.

She sat on the bed for a long moment, an odd loneliness filling her. The need to talk to someone, to share her concerns about Beth, struck hard. It wasn't a new feeling—she'd experienced it often during her years of raising a daughter alone. But it was one to which she'd never grown accustomed.

Over the years, the need to share her life with someone had often welled up. Sally had pushed her to date, to explore relationships, but something always held her back. Fear. Fear of choosing someone who wouldn't be able to love Beth, or who might even mistreat her. She read reports weekly in the newspaper about men abusing their stepchildren. Marie couldn't bear the thought of bringing someone home who would prove detrimental to Beth's well-being. So she'd always forced the loneliness aside, focusing instead on the relationship with her daughter.

But now Beth was grown, fumbling out into the world on shaky wings. It wouldn't be long before those wings would grow strong enough for her to fly, and Marie would be alone. What would she do then for companionship? But sitting here thinking wasn't getting her clothes put away.

Sighing, she pushed to her feet and crossed to the closet. She opened the single door and peered into the shadowy depths. Only about a dozen dresses hung there, all made from the same pattern. Although the dresses worn by Joanna and Deborah and many other women in the community were made from patterned fabric, all of Aunt Lisbeth's were solid colors—mostly deeper shades of blue, brown, or green.

Marie pulled one out and held it at arm's length, taking in the rounded neckline and attached modesty cape. Running her finger along the edge of the cape, she mentally compared the dress to the things in her clothes box. How her wardrobe had changed since she left Sommerfeld.

She laid the dress on the bed, then stacked the others on top of it, slipping the hangers free. When she had her own clothing hung up, she turned back to the stack of dresses and began folding them to put in the now-empty box. Before placing the last one in, she paused. Almost without thought, she slipped off her shirt and pulled the dress over her head.

A smile formed on her lips. She remembered Aunt Lisbeth as being very petite and slender, but she must have gained weight as she aged—the dress hung loosely on Marie's frame. She smoothed her fingers along the cape, her eyes closed, recalling how Mom had often scolded her for running her fingers up and down the cape edge of her dresses and leaving difficult-to-clean smudges in the fabric.

Turning to the small mirror above Aunt Lisbeth's dresser, she examined her reflection. A laugh blasted. She was glad there was no full-length mirror available to see the complete effect. The Mennonite dress's simple neckline combined with her untamed curls looked ridiculous.

But if her hair were smoothed down and a cap in place. . .

She hurriedly removed the dress and put her shirt back on. But as she picked up the dress to fold it and put it away, she found she couldn't do it. For some reason, sealing that dress in the box would be like sealing away her past. For good.

She shook her head. What was wrong with her? She dropped the dress on the bed and padded out to the living room, where she curled up in Aunt Lisbeth's rocker, one foot tucked up on the seat. Rocking gently, she looked out the window at the deep evening shadows and let her mind drift across the community. Several blocks over, Joanna probably had the ironing board out, pressing crisp creases into the pants her husband and son would wear to the meetinghouse tomorrow. She smiled, remembering the hubbub of getting things ready for Sunday when she was a little girl.

Caught in the middle of seven siblings, she had to listen to oldest sister Abigail's bossing and ignore her younger brothers' teasing. Her job had always been to make sure everyone's shoes were shined. She wondered if Mom still used a cold biscuit on Dad's shoes on Saturday nights or if they'd finally resorted to shoe polish and a buff cloth.

The sense of unity and belonging that came from the family piling into the buggy together on Sunday morning and rolling over the country roads, meeting other buggies and other families, was something she hadn't experienced since she was a teenager. Loneliness had been alien to her as a child. There was always someone—whether a brother or sister or friend—close at hand. The close-knit community had met every need for companionship. She would have never imagined feeling this alone.

Pain stabbed at her as she thought about all she'd lost when Jep died. She clutched her stomach as she remembered the horror of learning that his semi had gone off an embankment just weeks before Beth's birth. With his death, her dreams of family also died. From that point forward, it had only been her and the baby—no husband, no brothers or sisters for Beth. And with her father's refusal to allow her to return home, not even cousins and aunts and uncles and grandparents. Just a young mother and her little girl.

Marie shot out of the rocking chair. She didn't want to revisit those pain-filled days. She paced through the dining room to the kitchen, seeking some task to fill her hands so her mind would stop reminiscing. Everything was put neatly away, so no work waited. There was no television with which to numb her senses. A glance at the clock told her it was too early to go to bed. Besides, she wanted to be awake when Beth came home.

Restlessness drove her to the bedroom, where Aunt Lisbeth's dress waited, mocking her with the differences between her childhood and her adulthood. She yanked up the dress, folded it into a bulky square, and shoved it into the box with the others. After sealing the box, she pulled on a jacket and stormed to the back door. A long walk should clear her mind. She'd walk until the memories faded away.

Even if it means I walk all the way back to Cheyenne.

Henry held a napkin around his peanut butter sandwich and ambled to the front-room window. While he ate, he watched two squirrels play a game of tag, their bushy tails fluffed out behind them. If he still had his old dog, Skippy, those squirrels would have a third playmate. Skippy had always enjoyed chasing the furry pests up into a tree. His barks would drown out the squirrels' scolding chirps.

He missed that old dog. He'd been a good companion. Between Skippy and Lisbeth, there'd always been someone to talk to in the evenings. Now? He sighed. Only squirrels.

He started to turn from the window, but a movement caught his eye.

Leaning forward, he focused on the street. A woman charged down the road, hands deep in the pockets of a jacket, hood shielding her profile from view. But the blue jeans identified her. Marie. No other woman in Sommerfeld would wear jeans.

He ducked away from the window, concerned she might turn her head and spot him watching.

Back in his kitchen, he leaned against the counter and finished his sandwich, the image of Marie's low-chinned pose making his heart thud. He wondered if she were heading out to the cemetery again. She was moving in that direction. She'd looked forlorn. Lonely. Henry understood that feeling.

He wadded up the napkin and threw it away before returning to the front room. Leaning into the corner of the couch, he closed his eyes and replayed evenings in Lisbeth's front room, seated beside her, peeking at an open letter in her lap. Lisbeth had shared every one of Marie's letters with him.

Marie hadn't been a prolific writer—sometimes entire months passed without word. But each time a letter arrived, Lisbeth would save it until Henry drove her home from the café, then she would read it out loud.

Snippets of letters came back to him—Beth's learning to walk, the loss of her first baby tooth and her delight at the quarter the tooth fairy left behind, starting new jobs, mourning the loss of Jep's mother to cancer, Beth's graduations from junior high, high school, and college.

A lifetime of memories were contained within Marie's letters, and Henry had lived each one of them vicariously through the words on the page.

He'd always held his breath when Lisbeth started reading, afraid she would announce that Marie had found another man to share her life. But no mention had ever been made of dating—her focus was always on providing for her daughter. The little girl who meant everything to her had grown into a young woman, who meant so much to her that Marie was willing to come back to a place she didn't want to be.

From the slump of her shoulders as she'd paced by his house, he knew being here was a heavy burden. In the nearly three weeks she'd been here, he hadn't witnessed many people reaching out to her, other than her sister Joanna. How hard it must be for her to go to the café every day and not be accepted.

He longed to relieve some of the sorrow she carried. As much as his heart twisted with the admission, he still loved her. It seemed odd, this long-held feeling for someone he hadn't seen on a daily basis for more than two decades. Yet his love for her had stayed alive, thanks to Lisbeth's willingness to share the letters. A part of him wanted to tell her that someone besides Joanna loved her. But he wouldn't do it.

On the shelf in his closet, a small box bore mute testimony to his love for her. For a moment he considered going in and opening the box, peeking at the white Bible he'd purchased as a way of proposing to her without having to rely on speech to communicate. How he hated his penchant for growing tongue-tied! But he'd known the little white Bible, traditionally carried in place of a wedding bouquet, would let her know what his heart felt.

He had tried to speak of his love that day long ago when he realized she intended to leave with Jep Quinn. He'd touched her arm and whispered, "I'll wait for you, Marie." How he had hoped she would look into his eyes and realize how much he loved her—and that he would take her back the moment she chose to return. And even though he still felt the same, he was older now. Wiser. He remembered too well the searing pain of watching that semi roll away, carrying the woman he loved.

A heart could only bear that kind of pain once in a lifetime. So he'd keep his feelings to himself this time. Apparently his love hadn't been enough to hold her in Sommerfeld twenty-two years ago. He wouldn't risk it again. This time, when she drove away, he wouldn't be watching.

FIFTEEN

Beth waved good-bye to Kyra and the others before sliding into the car and starting the engine. She released a huge breath of relief. The evening was over, and she'd survived. Actually, she mused, once she got over the initial embarrassment, it hadn't been so bad. Awkward, yes—especially in McDonald's, where people kept staring at the oddly dressed Mennonites—but not awful.

Beth angled the vehicle onto First Street, shaking her head. How did Kyra stand all that gawking every time she ventured out? It wasn't as if Beth wasn't accustomed to people looking at her. She realized she was attractive, and she dressed in a way that showcased her attributes, essentially inviting second glances. But tonight, the way people gaped and whispered behind their hands. . . Those stares weren't out of admiration, but morbid curiosity. She hadn't liked it at all.

She made the turn onto Cottonwood, and the headlights illuminated a dark-clothed pedestrian. Beth recognized the gray hoodie—Mom. She came to a stop and rolled down the window. "What are you doing wandering the streets this late?"

Mom popped the door open and slid into the seat, even though the house was only a few yards ahead. "I went for a walk and ended up at the cemetery."

"At night?" Beth stared at her mother.

Mom leaned her head against the headrest. "Whew! I'm worn out. That was more of a hike than I expected at the end of a day."

Beth shook her head and pulled forward, turning into the driveway of the house. "Honestly, Mom! Walking to a cemetery at night? You would never have done that at home."

Her mother laughed softly. "Of course not. The cemetery is miles away. Everything here is within walking distance." She angled her head to smile at Beth. "How was the skating?"

Beth popped the car into PARK, jerked off the ignition, and scowled. "The skating part was fine, believe it or not. I had fun once I figured out how to turn corners without waving my arms all over the place and looking like an idiot. But how did you stand all those people staring at you? I felt like part of a circus freak show!"

Mom sighed, shifting sideways in the seat to face Beth. "You get used to it. Or you learn to ignore it."

"Well, I hated it. If I were a Mennonite, I'd change the dress code."

Mom burst out laughing.

"It's not funny!"

Mom's chortles continued. "Oh, honey, I'm not laughing at you. But if you could have seen your face. . ."

Despite herself, a smile twitched at Beth's cheek. It was good to hear Mom laugh, to see her happy. Being here had been tough on her—Beth had seen evidence of that in how she often stared off into space or stood alone in the corner of the café's kitchen, her head low. But as soon as their three months' stay here was done and she had the money in hand, she'd make it all worthwhile for her mom.

Reaching across the console, she gave her mother's hand a

loving squeeze. "Come on. Let's go put another X on the calendar—celebrate another day closer to being able to go home."

Marie rolled over, teased awake by the song of a cardinal from the spirea bushes outside the window. She lay, eyes closed, listening to the cheerful tune, and suddenly a hymn replaced the bird's song. *"Faith of our fathers, living still. . ."*

Her eyes popped open as the hymn filled her heart, seeming to echo through her soul. A strange tug brought her out of bed, to the window, to peer across the landscape of stubbly fields to the barely visible gray line of highway. Last night Beth had been eager to follow that highway back to Cheyenne. But, oddly, the X on the calendar had filled Marie with an unexplainable sadness.

"Faith of our fathers, holy faith. . ."

Last night's sadness returned, wrapping around her heart like a band. Her gaze fell to the box tucked in the corner—the one holding Aunt Lisbeth's clothes, the outer trappings that told of her inward beliefs. Beliefs Marie had held so long ago.

"I want your faith, Aunt Lisbeth," she whispered aloud, finally acknowledging the root of the tug on her heart. But how to regain it? With a pang, Marie realized she didn't know the answer to that question. Sinking onto the edge of the bed, she covered her face with her hands as loneliness smacked again—a loneliness that had haunted her for too many years.

In the past, she'd managed to push past the loneliness with busyness. Being a single mother, she'd poured herself into her daughter. As the only breadwinner, she'd poured herself into her work. But here, with Beth pursuing her own dreams, and hours of freedom away from the café, she had no escape. It engulfed her, increasing her longing for something—someone—to fill the void.

"Aunt Lisbeth, I wish you were here to advise me." She uttered the words on a note of anguish. And immediately an answer came: *Look to the Son.*

Of course. Aunt Lisbeth had always said the answer to any problem lay in God's handbook, the Bible. Marie knew where her Bible was—on the bookshelf back in her apartment in Cheyenne, no doubt covered with a layer of dust from lack of use. But surely Aunt Lisbeth's was here somewhere. Marie sat up, her gaze bouncing from the bureau to the chest in the corner to her aunt's desk to the closet and finally to the stand beside the bed.

Her hands reached toward the drawer in the little bedside stand. Holding her breath, she eased the drawer open, and her heart leaped with relief. There it waited, its faded black cover with the gold letters—HOLY BIBLE—inviting Marie's entrance.

She slipped it from the drawer, cradling it between both palms, and carried it to the front room. She tugged Aunt Lisbeth's rocker until it faced the east window, then sat. For a moment she hesitated— where should she begin? *"Faith of our fathers, holy faith. . ."*

With a deep breath, she rested the book's spine against her lap and let it fall open. Psalm Twenty-three, all underlined in blue ink, came into view. Marie leaned over the Bible and read.

Dimly aware of her surroundings—the shifting shadow across the hardwood floor, the creaking of Beth's cot, the occasional sounds of vehicles outside the house—she moved from Psalms to Isaiah to John, thumbing in search of places where her aunt had underlined passages or written notes in the margins. Then she sought favorite verses from her childhood, reading entire chapters, absorbing, renewing, accepting.

When someone called her name, she jerked, half surprised that the voice was feminine and not a deep, masculine, heavenly timbre. Looking up, she spotted Beth in the wide doorway between the front room and the dining room. Her daughter's brow furrowed as her gaze landed on the book.

"What are you doing?"

"Reading." Marie's fingers twitched, eager to seek more passages. "If you're hungry, there's cereal and milk." She hoped Beth understood the message: *Please take care of your own needs right now so I can take care of mine.*

"Yeah, okay. Want a bowl?"

"No, thanks. I'm fine."

Beth scratched her scalp with both hands, tousling her hair. "You okay?"

Marie smiled. "I'm fine, honey. And getting better by the minute. Enjoy your morning."

"I'm going to run a bath, then." Beth sent an odd look over her shoulder as she headed for the bathroom.

Marie returned to her reading. She continued until the banging of pots and pans in the kitchen disturbed her focus enough that she had to set the Bible aside and investigate. Beth, a towel wrapped turban-style around her head, gave her mother a scowl. "Are you finally done?"

Marie ignored the sarcastic bite in Beth's tone. "For now." She glanced at pans on the stove. "What are you doing?"

Beth shrugged and pulled a fork from a drawer. "Fixing lunch. You obviously weren't going to do it. I asked you twice."

Marie stared at her daughter. "You did?"

"Yes."

Marie lifted lids and discovered canned corn, potatoes, and pork chops. She turned to Beth in surprise. "Why so much food?"

Beth's jaw dropped. "You invited Joanna and her family for lunch today." She flapped her hand toward the living room. "Then you sat out there and didn't bother to fix anything. They'll be here in less

149

than half an hour. I haven't even gotten dressed because I've been in here peeling potatoes." Looking pointedly at Marie's pajamas, she added, "What's the matter with you this morning?"

Marie reached out to give Beth a hug. The girl remained stiff and unresponsive. "There's nothing wrong with me, honey. In fact, I think I'm more right than I've been in quite a while. But we can talk about that later. I've got to take a bath."

"A bath?" Beth put her hands on her hips. "What about all this?" She gestured toward the stove.

"You're doing great." Marie blew Beth a kiss as she scampered around the corner. "Just watch the pork chops—don't want them to get too brown."

The water spattering against the porcelain tub covered Beth's grumbles.

Over the next two weeks, Marie started and ended each day with time in Aunt Lisbeth's Bible. Prayer grew from the Bible reading, and by the end of the second week Marie found herself whispering little prayers over the course of the day, conversation with her heavenly Father springing naturally from an overflowing heart.

She wanted to share with Beth the changes taking place inside her, but her daughter resisted speaking of spiritual issues. Beth's attitude seemed to grow more surly by the day, complaining about Mitch's departure and the slow progress she'd made in securing items for her planned boutique. The highlight of her day was drawing a big, black X in the box on the calendar.

Joanna, however, had squealed with delight when Marie told her she was finding her way back to her childhood faith. "Oh, Marie! How? When?" Joanna wrapped her in a hug that stole her breath. "Oh, never mind—I don't need the details. It's enough just to see the sparkle in your eyes." Pulling back, she had cupped Marie's face and beamed with tears glittering in her eyes. "Oh, Marie. . .welcome home."

"*Welcome home.*" As much as Marie had celebrated hearing those words from Joanna, she still held a deep longing to hear them from the lips of her father. When she'd mentioned that to Joanna, her sister's face had clouded.

"Marie, don't put your faith on Dad's shoulders. He'll only let you down."

Marie's mind replayed Joanna's warning as she loaded the last of the dirty dishes into the dishwasher at the café. Tiredness from the busy Saturday made her shoulders ache, but it couldn't compare with the ache that stabbed her heart every time she recalled her father's condemning tone and harsh expression. She knew she would never feel as though she had truly come home until she made peace with her father. But how?

The back screen door squeaked. Her focus on emptying the bin of dirty dishes, she didn't look up. "Hey, Beth."

"It's me, Henry."

Marie jerked upright and spun toward the door. Automatically, she smoothed her hand over her hair. The curls had grown, becoming less manageable over her weeks in Sommerfeld. She'd pulled her hair into a ponytail at the crown of her head, but errant strands sprang free in every direction. She wasn't sure why it bothered her to have Henry see her in a state of unkemptness. She only knew discomfort struck with his presence.

She went back to transferring plates from the bin to the dishwasher, jabbering to cover the erratic beat of her heart. "Deborah and Trina aren't here. I told them I could finish up and they should go home. W—what brings you back? Deborah said you'd finished the bookwork for the week."

"A storm is brewing. There's sheet lightning in the east."

Marie glanced at him. His dark-eyed gaze followed her every move. She swallowed and turned back to the plates. "A lightning storm in November?"

He shrugged. "It's unusual but not unheard of. Kansas is unpredictable."

So are you. "I—I haven't heard any thunder."

He took a forward step, bringing himself into her line of vision. "It's not close enough yet. But the wind is picking up. It won't be long before we'll hear it."

That still didn't explain why he was here. "Thank you for telling me. Guess I'll hurry home then."

"I could drive you."

The quiet statement sent Marie's heart into her throat. She didn't look at him. "I can walk."

"I know you can. I've seen you walking all over the place."

The gently teasing undercurrent forced Marie's gaze around. His smile invited her to respond with one of her own.

"These storms can come up fast, and I don't want you caught in it. I'll be happy to drive you."

Marie stood, hands curled around a plate, peering into Henry's eyes. The realization that he'd observed her restless strolls, that he'd returned out of concern for her safety, brought a rush of gratefulness. . .and something else she couldn't define. "I appreciate that, Henry. Thank you." She focused on the dishes, stacking the last few as quickly as possible into the tray. "Beth went into Newton earlier. I have no idea if she's back yet."

Henry leaned against the far end of the rinsing trough. "She isn't."

Marie chuckled as she pushed the tray into the dishwasher, slid the door closed, and flipped the switch. The pound of water against the metal walls of the washer drowned out the sound of her laughter.

"What's so funny?" Henry raised his voice above the noisy machine.

Marie removed her apron, shaking her head. "I'd forgotten there were no secrets in Sommerfeld. I should have just asked you if Beth had returned."

Henry grinned. "Speaking of no secrets. . ." He hesitated, his grin fading and his neck blotching with red.

Marie's hands froze in the process of rolling the apron into a ball. She waited, the pulsing beat of the dishwasher matching the pound of her heart. She had to strain to catch his next words.

"Joanna tells me you're praying and reading the Bible every day." He swallowed, the bob of his Adam's apple capturing her attention. "I'm happy for you, Marie. Lisbeth would be, too."

Her gaze bounced up to meet his, and the twinkle of tears in the corners of his eyes made her heart lurch. Unable to reply, she merely nodded.

He blinked quickly, and the shimmer disappeared. He held his hand toward the door. "Are you ready?"

She nodded, scooped up the basket of dirty linens, and scurried toward the door while Henry turned out the lights. The cool air, heavy with the essence of rain, filled her nostrils. The first gentle rumble of thunder in the distance echoed in her ears. Henry's trembling fingers on her back ignited her senses.

"Come on, Marie. Let's get you safely home."

Sixteen

Marie stood in front of Lisbeth's closet, remembering her reaction to the whisper touch of Henry's fingers on her back as he'd guided her to his waiting car so he could transport her safely home last night. *Just loneliness,* she told herself. Like her flustered reaction when Mitch stepped into the kitchen. She would have had the same response with anyone. It had been a long time since she'd been shown that kind of consideration.

It wasn't Henry. It was loneliness.

She told herself this again as she dressed for service. Her heart pounded as she considered the possible ramifications of her showing up this morning. She knew Joanna would be thrilled. So would Henry. But everyone else? She hoped no one—her father, in particular— would make a scene that would embarrass her sister or Henry. But it was time for her to worship formally again.

Beth didn't understand. When she had returned from Newton in the midst of a pouring rainstorm, Marie had told her she planned to start attending church. Beth had argued, pointing out all the things Marie herself feared. "You're just going to get yourself hurt," she shouted, her voice booming more loudly than the thunder that shook the house. When Marie remained determined to go, Beth had stomped off to bed.

Well, Marie decided as she buttoned her blouse beneath her chin and tucked the tails into her skirt, *Beth might be right.* She could get hurt. But she knew she would hurt more, in her heart, if she ignored the tug of the Holy Spirit to return to the fold. Even if people rejected her, she had to at least try.

In the bathroom, she pulled her hair into a ponytail and formed a makeshift bun. Using bobby pins, she anchored the strands that were too short to reach the tail. She had found Lisbeth's caps in a box on the shelf of the closet and had even considered putting one on, but in the end she decided against it. She wasn't a meetinghouse member, and she wasn't sure she would seek membership again. Right now, she only wanted to attend, to listen, to learn, to rediscover a portion of what she'd left behind when she drove away with Jep.

One step at a time.

She peeked in at Beth. Her daughter slept soundly, her hair spread across her pillow. The familiar swell of mother-love rose in her breast, and she tiptoed across the room to smooth the tangled blond locks and place a kiss on Beth's forehead.

Beth stirred, her face crunching. Her eyes slid opened, and she blinked several times, her bleary gaze on Marie's face. "Mom?" her voice croaked.

"I'm sorry. I didn't mean to wake you."

Beth scowled at her mother. "You're going, aren't you?"

Marie nodded.

"But it's still raining, isn't it?"

The patter on the roof gave the answer. Marie smiled. "I won't melt. I'm not made of sugar." How often had she told Beth she needn't fear the rain because only sugar melted in the rain. Her own mother had told her the same thing.

Beth rolled over. "Well, have fun."

Her daughter's tone stung a bit, but Marie smoothed her hair again and focused instead on the calling of her heart. "I'll be back by noon; then I'll fix us some lunch."

Beth didn't reply. Marie tiptoed out, pulling the door closed. She took a jacket from the hooks by the back door and held it over her head as she hop-skipped around puddles on the way to the car.

When she reached the meetinghouse parking lot, she felt a lurch of discomfort. How obvious her bright red car looked among the plain black ones lining the side of the meetinghouse.

"No more obvious than my uncovered head," she reminded herself. Reaching under the seat, she located an umbrella. She heaved a sigh of relief when she discovered it was her own solid blue one rather than Beth's bright orange, daisy-covered one. Much less conspicuous.

Headlights cut through the curtain of rain as another car pulled up next to hers. Marie squinted through the foggy glass and saw a familiar face—Joanna's. Heart leaping with gratitude for the perfect timing, she popped her door open and thrust out the umbrella. Joanna stepped from her car and joined Marie under the plastic cover.

"You ready?"

Marie took in a fortifying breath. "As ready as I'll ever be."

Joanna's husband and children jumped from their vehicle and dashed toward the white clapboard meetinghouse. Hugo and Gomer entered the door at the right corner in the front of the building, and Kyra and Kelly ran side by side to the door at the back. Joanna and Marie followed the girls, their elbows linked, sidestepping around puddles.

A musty smell from the coats dripping on hooks assaulted Marie's nose as she entered the cloakroom. Several women stood in the room, quietly chatting. When Marie entered, the talk immediately stopped, leaving an uncomfortable silence. Marie put her coat on a hook and then turned to face Joanna.

Joanna offered an encouraging smile. "Let's go find our seats."

A shiver shook Marie's frame. She no longer had a seat. After she'd left with Jep, the leaders had voted on her excommunication. What would happen when she entered the worship room? Would people point fingers and send her away, as her father had done?

Joanna took Marie's arm. "Come on." Her voice was gentle, understanding.

Swallowing, Marie stayed close to Joanna as they stepped past the quiet women who watched their progress. A flurry of voices sounded behind them the moment they left the cloakroom. "That was Marie! Yes, Marie Koeppler—remember?" Marie ignored the hushed remarks.

When she and her sister entered the simple square worship room, Marie let her gaze sweep the area. Memories rushed back as she found the preachers' bench along the side wall behind the unstained wood pulpit. Two rows of benches faced the pulpit. Several men and boys, dressed in black suits and white shirts, sat on the right-hand side. A hat rack, suspended from the ceiling, hung over the last row of men's benches. The hats, wet from the rain, dripped onto the heads of the men seated beneath them.

Joanna tugged on Marie's arm, leading her to a center bench on the left-hand side. Joanna slid in first, followed by Marie; then Kyra and Kelly sat on Marie's other side, surrounding her with their comforting presence. A quick glance confirmed her parents had not yet arrived. She aimed her gaze at her lap, her heart pounding, fearful of what might happen when her father came through the front door and spotted her uncovered head.

She knew, even without looking, the instant he arrived. A hush fell over the room, followed by an air of expectancy. Her scalp prickled, and she wondered if her father's large hand would grab the back of her neck and pull her from the seat. Her heart pounded with the *thud* of footsteps on the wooden floorboards. Then the *creak* of a bench and a sigh as collective breaths were released.

Marie peeked sideways to see the swish of a dark blue dress moving down the side aisle. Allowing her gaze to drift upward, she focused on the profile of the woman who moved into an open spot two benches closer to the front. Her heart skipped a beat and tears stung her eyes. *Momma.* Her throat convulsed with the desire to rush forward, to cry out the name she hadn't uttered in more than twenty years, to embrace the woman who once held her to her breast.

Joanna's hand clamped over Marie's fist in her lap, and Marie jerked her head to peer into her sister's eyes. Joanna's eyes also glittered. Marie's gaze moved past Joanna to the other side of the church, to the man who had raised her. His face was aimed forward, his jaw firm, his eyes steely.

Marie swallowed. He didn't want her here. She read that clearly in his stiff bearing and clamped jaw. But he stayed silent on his bench. Throughout the entire service—the entry of the ministers, the hymn singing, the prayer and scripture reading, the sermon, the closing hymn and announcements—her father remained silent on his bench, never so much as flicking a glance in her direction.

When the benediction was complete, he stormed to the hat rack, snatched his hat from its hook, and charged out the door. His wife followed.

Marie's heart leaped with hope when, just before slipping through the cloakroom door, her mother paused and looked over her shoulder, meeting Marie's gaze. A tender longing lingered in the brief, silent exchange. Then she disappeared from view.

Joanna squeezed Marie's hand as three men stepped to the end of their bench. Marie swallowed the tears that choked her throat and turned to face the men. She held her breath, waiting for them to tell her she should not return. But to her surprise, the tallest one offered a hesitant smile.

"Marie?" He clutched his hands against his stomach, his blue eyes searching hers. "Do you remember me?"

She frowned, looking into lined eyes. Suddenly recognition dawned. "Art?"

He nodded, his smile growing. He gestured to the two younger men standing behind him. "And Conrad and Leo, too."

Marie met each of her brothers' gazes in turn. Still holding Joanna's hand, she stammered, "Oh, my. You–you're all grown up, you little pests."

Her face filled with heat as she realized what she'd just said, but all three men laughed, earning a stern look from the residing preacher.

Art touched her arm. He kept his voice low. "Where can we go and visit?" His gaze swept across the other family members standing in an awkward circle.

"My house," Marie blurted. *My house? Since when is it* my *house?* She remembered too late that Beth was there, maybe still in her pajamas, not expecting company.

Joanna shook her head as Hugo and Gomer joined the little circle. "My house is bigger, and I have a turkey in the oven. Let's all go there today, hmm?"

Marie's eyes filled with tears. Obviously Joanna had planned—in advance—a welcome-back-to-the-family celebration for her. Knowing her parents wouldn't be there made the situation bittersweet, yet how wonderful to experience the warmth of her sister and brothers' acceptance.

"Thank you. I'll need to go home first and—" She intended to say, "Tell Beth where I'll be." But Art offered a suggestion.

"You could pick up your daughter. We'd like to get to know her, too."

Tears of gratitude spilled down Marie's cheeks. Swallowing, she offered an eager nod. "I'll be there soon."

She turned to retrieve her jacket from the cloakroom but froze when she heard her sister's words: "Henry, if you don't have lunch plans, please come to our house. We have plenty."

Her heart pounding, she waited for his response.

"I usually have lunch with Deborah's family on Sundays. They're expecting me. But thank you for the invitation. Maybe another time?"

Joanna's laughter rang. "Sure. There'll be plenty of other times."

Marie experienced a brief roller-coaster ride of emotion—relief, followed by disappointment, followed by elation. Before she could examine the odd feelings, she dashed to the cloakroom, grabbed her jacket, and ran through the drizzling mist to her car.

Henry slapped his hat on his pant leg, shaking off the raindrops, before knocking on Deborah's front door. Normally he entered through the back, but on Sundays his sister insisted on formality. Trina opened the door to him and took his hat with a twinkling grin. He chucked her under the chin to thank her, smiling when she giggled.

Trina scampered to the hall tree, hung up his hat, then headed toward the back of the house. "C'mon, Uncle Henry. Mama's just about got everything on the table."

Henry smiled and followed. Of all his nieces and nephews, Trina was his favorite. Her infectious giggle and freckled nose had always been impossible to resist. There were times when sympathy swelled for her—he believed her parents were too strict, their expectations unreasonable. But he was cautious enough to keep that opinion to himself. No need to incite rebellion in the teenager's heart. He also carefully refrained from giving her preferential treatment to avoid conflict with her cousins. But he couldn't deny she possessed a special piece of his heart. If he had a daughter, he'd want her to be like Trina. Suddenly an image of Beth Quinn in her faded blue jeans and tight shirt flashed in his memory. He scowled. There was no comparison between Beth and Trina. And hadn't he decided to come to his sister's house today so he wouldn't be faced with Marie Koeppler Quinn and her daughter? There was no sense in thinking about either of them.

Still, as he sat at Troy and Deborah's table, eating his sister's good cooking and participating in the conversation, his mind kept flitting down a few blocks, to where half of the Koeppler family had gathered. He chewed Deborah's baked ham and wondered if Marie and Beth were enjoying Joanna's turkey. He listened to Troy's opinion on the proper irrigation of winter wheat and wondered what kind of reminiscing was taking place around Joanna's dining room table. He watched Trina and her brother Tony engage in a quick exchange of elbow pokes and wondered if Beth was feeling at ease with Kyra and her other cousins.

By the time Deborah served dessert, Henry knew he wouldn't be able to relax that evening unless he could find out how the reunion between Marie and her brothers had gone. He excused himself as soon as he could, experiencing a prick of guilt at Trina's hurt look when he refused a game of Wahoo, their usual Sunday afternoon activity. He gave his niece a one-handed hug and promised, "Next Sunday we'll play two rounds, okay?"

Trina nodded, releasing a sigh. "I'll just play with Tony." She shot her brother a pointed look. "Unless he cheats. Then I'm putting it away."

Henry shook his finger at the thirteen-year-old. "No cheating, Tony. Playing fair in games leads to playing fair in life."

The boy sent him an innocent look. "I don't cheat. . .much."

Henry stifled the chuckle that rose in his throat. Affecting a stern look, he said, "Any is too much. Understand?"

Tony shrugged, offering a sheepish grin. "Okay." He punched Trina in the arm. "I get the blue marbles."

Both scurried off. Henry called good-bye to his sister and brother-in-law, then headed for his car. The rain had stopped, but the sky still looked overcast and dark, much like a late winter evening. A glance at his wristwatch told him it was still early afternoon. He snorted. He'd been foolish to leave his sister's place so soon. Surely the Koepplers were all still visiting, getting reacquainted. He should have stayed and played Wahoo with his niece and nephew. Should he go back in?

No, he wouldn't be able to focus on the game anyway. He put the car in gear and drove slowly through the rain-drenched streets, his tires slipping in the softened earth. His windows fogged, and he cracked one open, allowing in the fresh scent of after-rain. Passing Hugo and Joanna's house, he cranked his head around, searching for Marie's car. It wasn't there.

With a frown, his heart pattering in concern, he faced forward again. Why would she have left so early? Maybe the reunion hadn't gone well after all. Worry struck hard, and he curled his fingers around the steering wheel and increased his speed slightly, eager to reach his home and telephone Hugo.

He cleaned his feet on the doormat and headed to his telephone without removing his hat. He dialed with a shaking finger and waited through four rings before a female voice answered. "Hello?"

"Is this Kyra?"

"No, it's Kelly."

She would do. "This is Henry Braun. I just wondered. . ." Suddenly he felt foolish asking the teenager about Marie. He blurted, "Is your father or mother there?"

"Just a moment, please."

After a scuffle, accompanied by the mumble of voices, he heard Joanna's voice. "Hello, Henry. What can I do for you?"

The telephone tight against his chin, he whispered, "Did Marie leave already?"

"No, she's still here." Joanna kept her voice low, too—as if they shared a secret. "She and the boys are having a wonderful time visiting."

Henry frowned. "I drove by, and when I didn't see her car, I became concerned."

"Ah." Joanna didn't question why he was driving past her house when it was out of the way between his home and Deborah's. "Beth left with the car about an hour ago. Said she had some things to do this afternoon. But she's coming back around seven to pick up her mother."

"Oh." A relieved breath whooshed from his lungs. "I hope all went well."

"Very well." Joanna's tone held an undercurrent of joy.

"Good." Henry swallowed, suddenly wishing he could be at Joanna's, be a part of the circle accepting Marie home. "Well, I'll let you go then."

"All right. Good-bye, Henry."

He placed the receiver in its cradle, then stood, his hand still cupping the black plastic, his gaze on Lisbeth's sampler. He smiled. Marie had been welcomed home, first by her sister and now by three of her brothers. Surely it was only a matter of time before her parents and remaining siblings accepted her as a member of the family again. Just as Lisbeth had hoped and prayed.

Unless. . . His smile faded. Unless Beth created problems. Why hadn't the girl stayed, become acquainted with her uncles and aunts and cousins? Beth meant so much to Marie. The rebellious young woman could pull her away again.

SEVENTEEN

Marie refilled a customer's coffee mug, offering a smile and a cheery, "Can I do anything else for you?"

The man glanced at his wife, then shook his head. "No, thanks. Just the check, please."

"Coming right up." Marie nearly skipped to the back to tally the tab. Her heart continued to sing despite the gloomy weather outside the café. The wonderful afternoon two days ago with Art, Joanna, Leo, Conrad, and their families—talking, laughing, hugging, bonding—still lingered, offering a peace and acceptance that resulted in an explosion of joy. *Thank You, Lord, for this step toward reconciling with my family.* She couldn't stifle the smile on her face, even when patrons didn't respond to it.

They would respond someday, she assured herself. If her family could welcome her back, the community would, too, given time. And if they didn't? She shrugged as she wrote the final dollar amount at the bottom of the ticket. She would be fine. She had her God, her daughter, and her sister and brothers again. That was more than she'd ever hoped to have. More than enough.

She returned to the table and slipped the square of paper next to the man's elbow. "Have a good day, and come see us again."

"We will," the man responded. "And maybe when we come back, you will have solved your mystery."

Marie tipped her head. "Mystery?"

The couple exchanged a quick look. "The whole town is buzzing," the man said. "We even got wind of it in Lehigh."

Marie moved closer to the table, her curiosity piqued. "What's the buzz?"

The woman leaned forward, her eyes snapping with eagerness. "This past Sunday, two families returned from afternoon visits to discover their homes had been burglarized."

Marie jerked back. "In Sommerfeld?"

The man shrugged, his thick eyebrows pulling down. "To be honest, I'm surprised it hasn't happened before. You don't have any police force on duty here, and you're right off the highway. That's an open invitation to criminals."

Marie looked back and forth from the man to the woman. "Were the homes vandalized, as well?"

"Oh, no," the woman said. "No damage was done."

Marie blew out a short breath. "That's a relief."

The man's expression turned thoughtful. "From what I heard, there was no disruption of property at all, and only one or two items were taken from each residence. It's almost like the thief knew exactly what he wanted and where to find it."

At the man's words, a warning bell clanged in Marie's head. She forced a quavery smile. "Let's hope it was just a fluke. I'd hate to think of the town being targeted by thieves."

"I'm sure it was just a one-time thing," the man said, pushing himself from the table. "It's too bad, though. After all these years of peaceful living, your little community has to be impacted by the world's evil."

Marie stood beside the table while the man and his wife shrugged into their jackets, picked up the tab, and headed to the cash register. Burglaries. In Sommerfeld. That explained the subdued behavior of many customers this morning.

The sounds of the café drifted into the distance as she replayed the man's comment about the thief knowing what he wanted and where to find it. An unpleasant idea formed in her head, washing away the happiness of the morning.

As soon as the couple left, Marie charged across the floor to Trina, who was closing the cash drawer. The girl released a gasp when Marie touched her arm.

"Trina, do you know anything about the burglaries that took place Sunday?"

The girl's gaze flitted to the side, and she nibbled her lower lip.

Marie gave Trina's arm a gentle squeeze. "Please, honey. I really want to know."

Trina's wide-eyed gaze met Marie's. "All I know is what I've heard in passing. Maybe you should ask Mama."

Marie looked toward the kitchen doorway. Even though the other woman had loosened up a bit over their time of working together, Deborah had been exceptionally tight-lipped today, reminding Marie of her first days in the café. Her heart pounded, fear taking hold. Did Deborah suspect what Marie was now thinking?

After giving Trina's arm a light pat, Marie entered the kitchen.

Deborah sat on a stool near the dishwasher, her head back and eyes closed. Marie cleared her throat, and the woman opened her eyes and shifted her gaze. When she spotted Marie, she pursed her lips. "Did you need something?"

Marie moved in front of Deborah. "Yes. I need you to tell me what happened in town Sunday afternoon."

Deborah's eyes narrowed. "I don't like to gossip."

Marie sucked in a deep breath. "I'm not asking you to. But

I need to know what happened."

Deborah sighed. "Marie." She shook her head. For a moment she appeared to falter, her forehead creasing with a pained expression. But then she thrust out her lower jaw in an expression of stubbornness. "I can't say. I don't have facts, only hearsay, and I won't repeat it." She charged across the floor to the stove and banged pots around.

Marie stood for a moment, staring at Deborah's back. Her heart pounded so hard she feared it would leave her chest.

Pulling her apron over her head, she called, "The breakfast rush is over. I'm taking a break. I'll be back in half an hour or so."

Deborah nodded without turning around.

Marie left the café and followed the sidewalk to Henry's shop. A cool breeze nipped at her bare legs, and her feet slipped on the rain-slick bricks, but she kept a steady pace.

The overhead garage door hung half open, and she heard muffled clanging from the depths of the metal building that housed Henry's mechanic shop. She ducked through the opening and blinked as her eyes adjusted to the bright fluorescent lights that hung on chains from the ceiling. A truck stood in the middle of the concrete floor, and two legs stuck out from beneath it.

Marie walked to the legs, her wet shoes squeaking. "Henry?"

His legs jerked. Then his feet rose slightly, and his body glided out from beneath the truck on a flat, rolling platform. Once he was clear of the vehicle, he sat up, gaping at her. A smudge of grease adorned his left cheek, and he held a wrench. "What brings you here?"

Marie crouched down, bringing her eyes level with his. "Henry, will you tell me about the burglaries that happened Sunday?"

He grimaced, rubbing his hand over his face. The action smeared the grease almost to his jaw. Had the situation been less serious, she might have teased him about it.

"I don't know a lot," he said slowly, placing the wrench on the floor beside him with a light *clank.*

"Please." Marie detested the tremble in her voice. "Tell me. I need to know."

He met her gaze, and she saw sympathy in his dark eyes. "Apparently, while the Albrechts and Goerings were visiting neighbors Sunday afternoon, someone broke into their houses and took some things."

Marie frowned. Her mouth went dry. "Antiques?"

He fiddled with the wrench, his head low. "Yes."

She swallowed hard. "Do you know what?"

His sigh sounded pained. "A Russian trunk from the Goerings and a mantel clock from the Albrechts."

Marie's heart caught.

His gaze still aimed downward, he added, "They might not be the only ones missing things."

"What do you mean?"

"After the news came out, people started checking their barns and sheds. Some found things missing they didn't notice right away because they weren't items they used every day."

Marie lurched to her feet.

Henry pressed one hand to the concrete and stood. He held his dirty hand toward her. "Now don't jump to conclusions."

Whirling on him, Marie's temper flared. "I don't have to. The whole town will jump to conclusions for me. You know they'll blame Beth."

His silence confirmed her statement.

She laughed. "All morning, people were giving me funny looks, whispering behind their hands. I thought it was because I'd dared to show up at the meetinghouse, but now it makes sense. They're all thinking my daughter is a thief!"

"Marie—"

She spun away from his reaching hand and tender look. "Just because I raised her in the world doesn't mean I raised her poorly. I taught her right from wrong."

"Of course you did."

His calm reply deflated her anger. Did he truly believe her? Did she truly believe it herself? Tears stung her eyes. "But no one else will believe it, will they?"

Once again, Henry fell quiet.

Marie shook her head. "I'd better let you work. Thanks for telling me." She heard him call her name as she dashed toward the door, but she didn't turn around. As she hurried down the sidewalk, her heart thumped out a fear-filled message: *Not Beth, not Beth, not Beth.*

Marie bypassed the turn to the café and went directly to Lisbeth's. She walked around to the back. The car wasn't there, which meant Beth was still hunting. Or stealing. *Stop that!* Maybe they hadn't attended church regularly after Jep's mother died, and they hadn't prayed together the way her parents had with her, but she had taught Beth morals. Beth would not steal. She wouldn't!

Marie repeated those words in her mind as she moved from room to room in the small house, peeking in closets and under the cot in Beth's room. She found nothing that didn't belong there, unless she counted the two mismatched socks hiding beneath the cot. Given Beth's irrational revulsion for the basement, she didn't bother to check there. As she stood in the middle of the dining room, realization struck.

There wasn't any place in the house to hide things, but there was a shed behind the café. At one time it had sheltered Lisbeth's buggy, but the buggy had been sold years ago. Deborah had said it stood empty, too run-down to be of any real use. It would be a perfect place to hide things.

Marie took the shortcut between the houses that led to the alley behind Lisbeth's café. Despite the cool temperature, she broke out in a sweat. By the time she reached the double doors that opened out onto the alley, she found herself taking great heaving breaths. She examined the ground in front of the shed, looking for evidence of recent activity, but the rains had swept the area clean.

Her heart pounding, she clasped the board that lay across metal hooks, sealing the doors closed. She hefted the weathered board aside and slipped her fingers through the hole that served as a handle in the right-hand door. Her chest boomed with each heartbeat as she tugged the door. The metal hinges resisted her efforts, and she grunted, giving a mighty yank that swung the door wide. An unpleasant odor greeted her nostrils—mildew and mouse. She covered her nose with her hand and forced herself to step inside.

Only thin slivers of murky light sneaked between cracks in the planked walls. She squinted, forcing her eyes to adjust to the shadows. When she could finally focus, her legs nearly gave way.

Except for a pile of mouse-chewed burlap sacks and two rusty tin cans, the shed was empty.

She stepped back into the alley and slammed the door shut, sagging against it, her chest heaving with breaths of relief. Eventually her quivering limbs returned to normal, allowing her to stand upright. She dropped the board in place, berating herself. Of course Beth was innocent. How could she have thought otherwise, even for one moment? Guilt struck hard. She wouldn't let Beth know of her momentary fears.

Tonight, when they were alone, she would find out where Beth had gone Sunday afternoon. Armed with that information, she would be ready to defend her daughter to anyone who dared suggest she had something to do with the burglaries.

She headed for the café, sucking in big gulps of the clean air, ridding herself of the worry that had driven her across town in search of the truth. As the customer from Lehigh had said, with no police force in town, it was inevitable that something like this would happen. Beth had nothing to do with it.

Marie entered the café, her head held high.

That evening, when she and Beth sat at the kitchen table enjoying glasses of milk and leftover apple pie from the café, Marie leaned back in the chair and let out a sigh. "I suppose you've heard the scuttlebutt around town."

Beth raised one eyebrow, a bite of pie halfway to her mouth. "I haven't been in town the past few days. But the people have sure been acting whacky. I actually had a door slammed in my face this morning." She put the bite into her mouth.

"I hear there have been some burglaries." Marie watched Beth's face.

Beth went on eating. "Oh, yeah?"

"Antiques from houses, and items from barns and sheds."

The fork paused in its path, then lowered to her plate. "Oh, great."

Marie nodded. "That's what I thought this morning when I found out."

Beth pushed her plate away. "I suppose as the newcomers we're being held accountable."

Marie shrugged. "It does probably look suspicious—first you going door-to-door, soliciting antiques and unusual items. Then those same items being taken."

Beth pressed her palms to the table, ready to jump up.

Marie put her hand on her daughter's arm. "But we can eliminate the suspicions very easily."

Beth sank back into the chair, a scowl marring her face. "How? Let them invade our privacy and search the house? They won't find anything."

"I know." Marie slid the half-eaten slice of pie back in front of Beth and picked up her own fork. "All we have to do is account for our whereabouts. If we can prove where we were on Sunday when the thefts took place, no one should be able to point fingers."

Beth sat back in her chair and crossed her arms. "Why should I do that? Isn't my word good enough?"

"Honey—"

"No!" Beth held up both hands, as if deflecting a blow. "I'm not *accounting* for anything. I didn't do it, and I'll tell that to anyone who asks. That's going to have to be good enough."

Shaking her head, Marie fixed her daughter with an imploring look. "Beth, I understand how you feel, but unless you set the community's mind at ease, things could get very uncomfortable here. . .for both of us."

"I don't care." Beth pointed to the calendar and gave an arrogant toss of her head. "See all those Xs? That means my days here are limited. These people can think what they want to. It doesn't matter to me."

Marie's hand trembled as she put down her fork. "Will you at least tell *me* where you were?"

"Where I was is my business. No one else's." Beth rose, her eyebrows high, her head held at a haughty angle. "You're just going to have to trust me, Mom. I know what I'm doing." She stormed from the room. The slam of her door signaled the end of the conversation.

EIGHTEEN

Henry sat at his usual table in Lisbeth's Café, an untouched plate of scrambled eggs and bacon in front of him. He was the only Sommerfeld resident in the café. Every other customer was an out-of-towner. Each morning over the past two weeks, he'd noticed fewer and fewer townspeople coming into the café, but this was the first time absolutely no Sommerfeld residents started their day with one of Deborah's fresh-baked cinnamon rolls.

As the month marched toward the Thanksgiving holiday, the tension in town increased. Talk had started about foregoing Sunday afternoon visits so everyone could go home and watch their properties. Henry wasn't in favor of this—the tradition of Sunday visits was something that went back through generations, and he feared if it stopped for a short time, it might permanently drop away. These kinds of changes had led to congregation splits in the past.

Although he'd been very young, he still remembered the upheaval of the last split, when the decision was made to allow church members to have electricity and drive automobiles. Some of those who were in fierce opposition to making use of the worldly conveniences joined a community in southeast Kansas. His own parents and Lisbeth, like a few other families in the community, hadn't adopted the changes, but had left it to individual conscience rather than condemning those who elected to make use of the technologies.

But now, with burglaries continuing to take place every week, the murmurs were rising, the cry for protection heard from several corners of the community. Henry feared what might happen if the thief was not caught soon.

Marie bustled past, plates in hand. She flicked a glance in his direction but didn't smile. His heart ached. She looked haggard, the lines around her eyes pronounced, the bounce gone from her step. Although she had continued to attend service at the meetinghouse, which thrilled him, he wondered when she would finally grow weary of the members holding themselves aloof and stop coming.

She headed back into the kitchen, and he stared at the doorway for long minutes, wishing Lisbeth were there. Lisbeth, in her wisdom, might have ideas on how to bring everyone together, to eliminate the fears and find the truth.

Truth. Henry lowered his gaze to the tabletop. What was the truth? Marie had been adamant when she'd come to his shop two weeks ago seeking answers. He wanted to think as she did, that her daughter had nothing to do with the disappearance of those belongings. Yet part of him couldn't help but wonder about the coincidence. Beth had asked about purchasing certain items, the owners declined, and the items disappeared.

The town had already tried and convicted Beth. He knew that's why people were staying away from the café—they didn't want to support a person they viewed as immoral. *Lisbeth, this isn't what you had in mind when you established the conditions of your will, was it?* How could Marie even think about staying in Sommerfeld permanently with everyone thinking ill of her and her daughter? He pushed his plate away, his appetite ruined by his thoughts.

Dear Lord, why did this have to happen now, when Marie was turning back to You and her faith?

Marie came around the corner with a bin on her hip. Normally Trina bussed tables, but Deborah had been making her stay home the past few days. She gave the excuse that, with the dwindling clientele, she wasn't needed, but Henry suspected it had more to do with trying to keep her from having any contact with Beth and Marie.

Another heartache.

Marie paused beside his table, frowning at the untouched plate. "Was something wrong with the food?"

Henry shook his head. "No. Just not hungry."

She sighed, glancing at the nearly empty room. "That seems to be going around."

Henry peeked over his shoulder. The few customers appeared to be eating, not needing attention. He pointed to the chair across from him. "Want to sit down for a minute?"

She tipped her head, and the hint of a smile curved her lips. "On one condition—you don't mention the word *thief*."

The sadness in her eyes stabbed his heart. He smiled and nodded toward the chair. "Agreed."

She sat, plunking the bin on the corner of the table. She looked at him, quiet and waiting, and he found himself tongue-tied. With her hair pulled back, the errant curls held in place by a kerchief tied around her head, and her blue-eyed gaze pinned expectantly on his face, she had the same effect on him that she'd had at fifteen. The silence grew lengthy, uncomfortable. She squirmed.

"What are your plans for Thanksgiving?" he blurted before she could get up and move away.

Marie blinked, her long lashes sweeping up and down. She took in a breath and gave a graceful shrug. "Joanna has asked me to join her family, but I'm not sure I will."

Henry scowled. She shouldn't be alone. "Why not?"

"Well. . ." She linked her fingers together and rested them on the edge of the table, then seemed to examine her thumbs. "If Joanna has her own dinner, that means she won't be with my parents. The only reason she's doing this is because she knows Beth and I aren't welcome at the farm. I don't want her to separate herself from the family because of me."

The sadness in her tone tugged at Henry's heart. Here she was, in the community, so close to her family, and yet so far from them. He wished he could build a bridge that would bring them together. He reached across the table and placed his hand over hers. Her gaze bounced up, meeting his.

He felt heat building in his cheeks, but he didn't avert his gaze. "Joanna wouldn't do it if she didn't want to."

"I know, but. . ." She paused, shifting her gaze to the side for a moment, as if gathering her thoughts. "I don't want people to have to choose sides." She looked at him again, one eyebrow quirked. "There's no sense in stirring up trouble when our time here is so short."

Henry jerked his hand back, then regretted his hasty action when he saw her expression cloud. He cleared his throat. "Regardless of the length of your stay, any reconciliations will be beneficial to your family, don't you think?"

Another hesitant shrug communicated her apprehensions. "One can hope, I suppose. I'd like to think that, after Beth and I return to Cheyenne, I'll stay in touch with my family. But it will be up to them."

Henry nodded, and silence fell between them. Once more, he wished for Lisbeth's presence. She would have been an excellent mediator between Marie and her family, he was sure. His skills in that department were lacking—he didn't have an inkling how to bring things to right.

"Well," Marie said, but she was cut short by the call of one of the customers requesting a refill on coffee. Henry watched her bounce to her feet and dash to the table that held the coffeepots and carry one to the table. From there, she made the rounds, avoiding his table.

He knew what his breakfast cost without needing a check. Shifting his weight to one hip, he tugged his billfold from his back pocket, removed a five-dollar bill, and slid it under the edge of his plate.

Out on the sidewalk, he drew in great breaths of the cool air, attempting to clear his cluttered mind. Turning toward his shop, he processed his thoughts.

Henry knew Marie's family was more important to her than the community, but less important than Beth. If the girl decided to make Sommerfeld her home, Marie would no doubt settle in, as well. If that happened, surely her entire family would eventually come to accept her.

Turning the key in the lock of his door, Henry released a snort. Beth wouldn't stay. Not after the way everyone had pointed fingers. If she were guilty, she would have to take her stolen goods and go. He flipped on the light switch, then sank onto a metal stool beside his work counter. The situation seemed hopeless.

No, nothing was ever hopeless. He knew that. Ducking his head, he closed his eyes, a prayer rising in his chest. *She's back, Lord, and she's seeking You. Please let this mess be fixed to the betterment of all.* He recognized the underlying selfishness of his request, knowing much of his motivation was his long-held love for her. He wanted her here, with him. But he also wanted her happy. He knew she couldn't be happy until all of the relationships were restored.

Slapping his knees, he rose and reached for his toolbox. Sitting here worrying about Marie wouldn't get Lucas Schrag's oil leak repaired. He'd have to leave Marie in God's hands.

Beth put another piece of gravy-drenched turkey in her mouth, chewed, and swallowed. She might as well have been eating sawdust. Despite the lace tablecloth and candles, the array of foods and polished silverware, despite Joanna's tremendous effort to make this first Thanksgiving together in more than twenty years a festive event, it was a flop.

Tension hung so heavy it was palpable, making it hard to swallow. A glimmer of tears shone in Mom's eyes, and at times in Joanna's, too. Beth felt a stab of sympathy, but there wasn't much room for sympathy with the amount of anger she held.

Her uncle Leo and his wife and kids had come to Joanna's for this meal, but neither Art nor Conrad were there. They'd chosen to go the farm, to have Thanksgiving with Beth's grandparents. From the whispers she'd overheard in the kitchen, an aunt and uncle she had yet to meet, who lived in neighboring communities, were also at the farmhouse. They'd been invited to come by Joanna's to see Mom but had refused.

Little wonder Mom battled tears. Beth understood her mother's heartache, but she also resented it. Hadn't Mom figured out by now these people weren't worth tears? The two of them had always made it just fine on their own. When Grandma Quinn passed away and Grandpa moved to Florida, Mom had wondered how they'd get by alone, but they'd managed. To Beth, that proved they didn't need anybody except each other.

They especially didn't need this town full of righteous blame finders.

She'd observed the way customers reacted to Mom in the café. From her spot in the corner, hunched over her computer, she'd seethed with frustration when Mom's friendly overtures were ignored. And now that Mom was going to that church, it was even worse! Beth's solution was to spend less time at the café and more time away from the town. But Mom was stuck. Beth stifled a frustrated snort. She wished she'd never come to Sommerfeld. It was all a huge mistake.

On her left, her cousin Kyra asked quietly, "Would you pass the pickled beets, please?"

Beth handed them over, her gaze meeting Kyra's briefly. Beth couldn't help but feel a prick of guilt for lumping Kyra and her family in with the rest of the community. Joanna and her husband and children hadn't pushed Mom or her aside. Beth appreciated that, but it wasn't enough. Mom needed all or nothing. There was no way she'd ever have it all, so. . .

Beth shoved her chair back and stood. Every person seated around the table stopped in midbite and stared at her. "I'm sorry, but I'm not feeling well. Will you excuse me, please?" Without waiting for a response, she charged through the kitchen to the back door. As she expected, Mom came around the corner a moment later, her brow creased in worry.

"Honey, are you okay?"

Beth shook her head. "No. And neither are you." Taking her mother's hand, she implored, "Let's go back to the house."

Mom's face puckered in concern. "Are you feeling that bad?"

Beth huffed. "I'm not sick, Mom, unless you count sick of this town and these people. We should never have come. I'm sorry I dragged you here. I—" She shook her head and gave her mother's hand a tug. "Let's just go."

"In the middle of dinner?" Mom slipped her hand free. "Sweetheart, Joanna went to a lot of trouble for us. She and Leo and their families chose to be here for us. I can't leave."

"Yes, you can."

"No, honey, I can't." Mom lowered her voice to a whisper, but

179

her tone was firm. "I will not walk away from a dinner that was set up just so we could spend some time with family this holiday."

Beth stared at her mother, ire rising higher by the minute. Couldn't Mom see that staying only created more problems? More heartache? She had to get her mom out of here. She grabbed her jacket off the hook and jammed her arms into the sleeves. "Well, I've had enough family for one day. I'm leaving."

Mom wrung her hands. For a moment Beth hesitated. She hated to see her mother so torn. But this family had cut her off a long time ago. And they would abandon her again when it came time to leave. Having the money from the café and house would enable Beth to repay her mom in some way for all the sacrifices she'd made over the years. But surely the gift wouldn't be worth the heartache she was experiencing now. It was better to make the break now, before her mother got in too deep.

Mom touched her arm. "Will you be okay at home by yourself?"

Home? Since when was Lisbeth's house *home*? Beth's heart twisted. She forced a sarcastic tone. "I'll be fine. All by myself on Thanksgiving."

Mom shook her head, her eyes sad. "Honey, it's your choice to leave. You can stay here with us."

Beth turned away, her chin quivering. "Us" used to mean her and Mom. She closed her eyes for a moment, gaining control of her emotions. When she felt she could speak without her voice breaking, she looked at her mother. "Enjoy yourself. I'll call Mitch. I know he'll have time for me today."

She slammed through the door, thrusting her hands deep into her pockets. She and her mother had walked to Joanna's—she followed the same route back to Lisbeth's.

As she passed houses, she couldn't help but peek through plate-glass windows to the groups gathered inside. The scenes she witnessed—smiling, laughing groups—provided a stark contrast to the isolation she felt as she walked under leafless trees across brown yards. Back in Cheyenne, even with only Mom for family, she'd never felt as alone as she did right now, in this community where grandparents and aunts and uncles and countless cousins resided.

Hunching into her jacket, she forced her gaze straight ahead and moved as quickly as she could over the uneven ground. How she wished Lisbeth hadn't sent Henry Braun with that message. How she wished Mitch hadn't talked her into heeding the request. How she wished. . . She sighed. Wishing was a waste of time. Nothing would ever be the same.

When she reached Lisbeth's, she went into the house and grabbed the car keys from the corner of the kitchen counter. No way was she staying here by herself. Not when there were things she could be doing. Things that would benefit her—and Mom—once her time in Sommerfeld was over.

"I'm doing this for you, Mom," she muttered, "and you'll understand it all when I finally get you out of here." Beth started the engine, backed out of the drive, and headed for the gravel road that led out of town.

NINETEEN

Marie handed a dripping plate to Joanna, then plunged her hands back into the warm, sudsy water. With a chuckle, she said, "I never thought I would actually enjoy washing dishes after having an automatic dishwasher for so many years."

Joanna laughed. "If someone's sharing the chore, it can be almost pleasant. We used to have some good conversations over the dishpan, didn't we?"

Marie sent her sister a smirk. "Yes, when Abigail wasn't listening in so she could run and tattle if we said something we shouldn't."

"As if we ever said anything we shouldn't have." Joanna winked and bumped Marie's arm with her elbow.

Marie giggled, relishing the kinship she'd renewed with her sister. She gave Joanna a sideways glance and dared to share a piece of her heart. "One of my biggest regrets with Beth is she never had the pleasure of brothers or sisters. You and I had such fun growing up, and she never experienced that."

"She never had any fun?"

Joanna's feigned expression of shock made Marie laugh, but she shook her head. "You know what I mean. She missed out on a lot."

Joanna put down her dish towel and gave Marie a quick hug. "I'm sure she never realized she was missing anything. It's obvious she adores you."

Marie quirked her brow.

Joanna shook her finger under Marie's nose. "Now stop that. What you're going through with Beth right now is growing pains, pure and simple. It happens. But she loves you as much as you love her. Nothing will ever change that." She took another plate and swished it dry with the embroidered tea towel.

Pain stabbed anew as Marie considered the shattered relationship between herself and her parents. Her hands stilled in the water as she remembered how many precious things had been destroyed by her decision to leave with Jep.

Joanna's mind must have drifted in the same directions as Marie's, because she dropped her gaze, her forehead creasing. "Sometimes, I suppose, relationships do change. But—" She met Marie's gaze, her tone turning fervent. "Things can always be put to right again with a little effort."

Considering her father's behavior thus far, Marie wasn't sure she agreed with Joanna, but she decided not to argue. No sense in upsetting her sister any more than Beth's untimely departure three hours ago had. Lifting out a bowl, she forced a smile. "Effort. . .and time. . .and prayer."

Joanna hugged the bowl to her chest, creating a wet circle on her apron bib. Her eyes filled with tears. "Oh, Marie, it thrills me to hear you say that. Do you know how much Lisbeth and Henry and I have prayed over the years for you to allow God back into your life? And now I see it happening. I'm so thankful!" Her voice broke.

Marie felt the sting of tears herself. She imagined her sister, her aunt, and Henry kneeling in prayer. . .for her. . .and felt humbled by their steadfast concern. She would have expected Aunt Lisbeth and Joanna to maintain their desire to bring her back to faith—they were family. But Henry? Wonder filled her heart. The man she'd jilted had spent twenty years praying for her faith. How did one say thank you for that kind of dedication?

"And I believe," Joanna went on, sniffling, "that our prayers will bring Dad around, too. If he bends, everyone else in the family will follow suit, from Abigail down to Conrad. So don't lose heart, okay?"

Marie didn't have to force this smile. She tipped her head to touch Joanna's forehead, the little sign of affection she had used often as they were growing up. "I won't." Straightening, she added, "But I hope—"

A rap at the front door interrupted her words. Joanna's eyes flew wide. "See! I bet that's Abigail, Ben, and Conrad with their families, here to spend a little time with you."

Marie's heart pounded, and she licked her lips as her breathing increased. She mentally prepared a greeting for her older brother and sister as she followed Joanna to the front room, wiping her hands on the apron. Kyra, Kelly, and Gomer came from their bedrooms at the same time, and they were all gathered together when Hugo pulled the front door open.

To Marie's disappointment, two men from town stood on the porch, hats in their hands, their expressions somber. Hugo invited them in, and Joanna bustled forward.

"Kurt, Robert, how good to see you this evening. I have some pumpkin pie and whipped cream left over if you'd like a piece."

The men exchanged glances, and the taller of the pair shook his head. "That's kind of you, Joanna, but we didn't come for socializing."

Hugo crossed his arms, his brows pinching together. "Oh?"

Marie's scalp prickled when both men fixed their gazes on her.

The second man said, "There's been some trouble in town today, and we thought you needed to know about it."

An arm slipped around Marie's waist. Marie jerked her gaze and found Kyra close. She gave the young woman a quick smile of thanks before looking back at the men.

"What trouble?" Hugo asked.

"Leonard Dick returned to his home after spending the afternoon at his daughter's place. His front door stood open. The sleeping bench from his second bedroom was gone."

Marie's knees buckled, and she would have gone down if Kyra hadn't supported her. Joanna guided her to the sofa, where she sank onto the cushion, her ears ringing, her heart pounding furiously. Beth had mentioned a sleeping bench when speaking of the items she hoped to buy. But she wouldn't. . .would she?

"We're telling everyone in town to be careful," the taller man said. "Be sure your doors are locked, and maybe put the things you value under cover so they can't be seen by peeking in windows."

"Thank you, Kurt. We'll do that." Hugo's voice sounded strained.

The man shifted his feet in a nervous dance. Marie focused on his hands, which twisted the brim of his hat. "Some of the men in town are going to set up a community watch day and night. If you want to be involved—"

"I sure do," Hugo inserted.

"We're getting together at eight this evening at the meetinghouse. We'll see you there."

The men left. Hugo closed the door, then turned his grim expression on Marie. "It sure would have been better if Beth had stayed here with us today."

Joanna gasped. "Hugo! You don't think—"

"I don't want to." Hugo pushed his hands into his pockets and hunched his shoulders. "But everyone else in town was with family, celebrating the holiday."

Marie rose on shaky legs. "She went home. I know she did. She'll be there, waiting for me. You'll see."

Hugo looked at Joanna, who beseeched him with her eyes. Turning back to Marie, he said, "It's getting dark. I'll drive you."

Marie knew it was a desire to satisfy himself to Beth's whereabouts that brought about the offer, but she nodded mutely. She hugged her sister, nieces, and nephew, then followed Hugo to his car.

Lights shone in every house—more lights than Marie had seen before. People stood in yards in small clusters, talking. They stared as Hugo drove slowly down the shadowy streets. *Please be there, Beth. Please, let's be able to prove them wrong.*

When Hugo pulled into Lisbeth's yard, Marie noticed windows glowing in the front bedroom—Beth's room. Her tense posture sagged with the rush of relief that swept through her. Hugo drove to the back of the house, where Marie's car waited a few feet from the back porch, in the same spot she had left it yesterday when she returned from the café.

Her chest flooded with elation. "See? The car's here, and Beth is here."

Hugo walked her to the porch, but instead of stepping onto the wooden platform, he moved to Marie's car and placed both palms on the red hood. He jerked his gaze toward Marie. The look on his face made her break out in a cold sweat.

"It's warm."

"I'm telling you, we need to go to that house, knock on the door, and demand to look around." Jay Albrecht stood with crossed arms at the end of his bench, his dark eyebrows pulled down in a ferocious scowl.

Albrecht had assigned himself as leader of the meeting. Having had his grandfather's mantel clock taken, he was the angriest of all the thief's victims.

Henry noticed several men nod in agreement of Albrecht's bold suggestion. Every male over the age of twenty-one appeared to be in attendance at this community meeting, including all four of Marie's brothers, two adult nephews, and her father, who sat in a silent row on the preachers' bench behind the empty podium.

"And if we found things, what then?" The question came from the back of the room, offered by Allen Wedel. The Wedel place had lost several enamel buckets and a hand plow.

"That would be proof," Albrecht declared in a booming voice. "We could then take the Quinns to the police."

The thought of Marie and Beth being hauled to the police station in one of the larger nearby towns made Henry feel as though someone had kicked him the stomach. He wanted to speak out in their defense, but his tongue seemed glued to the roof of his mouth.

Henry's nephew Jacob rose and faced Albrecht. "Even if we did find the missing items, we wouldn't be able to prove the Quinns stole them. Not unless they were seen taking them."

Albrecht snorted. "Why would they have them if they weren't responsible for the stealing?"

Jacob shrugged. "Maybe someone else took the things and hid them there."

A snicker went across the room. Doug Ortmann asked, "For what purpose?"

"To make it look as though the Quinns were responsible."

Albrecht waved his hand. "Bah! No one else has a reason to take those things. We all know why those women are here—to get whatever they can lay their hands on. And that's exactly what they've been doing!"

The murmur of concurrence made Henry's stomach churn.

Hugo Dick stood and joined Jacob. "I don't agree, Jay. Maybe the daughter came to get what she could, but I don't think we can say that about the mother."

"Then why do you think she's here?" Albrecht's tone turned derisive.

Hugo glanced at Henry. "As an answer to prayer."

Henry looked at his feet, certain his face was glowing red.

"My wife, Joanna, her aunt Lisbeth Koeppler, and Henry Braun here have all prayed for years that Marie would return to this community. That she would be able to restore lost relationships. I think Marie came for that reason."

Mumbled voices rose and fell. Henry couldn't resist the urge to look at Marie's family. All faces were stoic, their gazes downcast except for J.D., who stared straight ahead with his arms folded tightly across his chest.

"Don't be ridiculous." Albrecht's scowl deepened, his angry glare fierce. "You know as well as I do that nothing like this has ever happened in our community. But these two women arrive, and immediately there's trouble."

Ortmann turned in his seat to face Jacob and Hugo. "I agree with Jay. I believe that girl wants our things badly enough to take them."

"No one saw Beth take anything," Jacob said, raising his voice to be heard over the rumbles that rolled across the room. "No one has even seen the goods." His gaze swept the room, silencing the murmurs. "I thought we came here to organize a community watch to prevent future burglaries, not form a trial and jury."

"You're being sassy, boy," Albrecht growled.

Henry's ire raised with Albrecht's condemnation. With a silent prayer for strength, he pushed to his feet and put his arm around his nephew. "Jacob has a right to speak his opinion, just as you do, Jay." He spoke calmly. "And in this case, he's right. We're not accomplishing anything here with all this faultfinding. Let's organize our watch and wait to see what happens."

"And if the thief never shows again? What then?" Ortmann demanded.

"Then we've been successful," Jacob said.

Albrecht threw his arms outward. "But we don't get our things back!"

"Maybe not." Henry looked around the room. "But I think we need to look at our motivations here." His gaze flitted toward Albrecht. "Some folks here seem bent on revenge. But the Bible says vengeance belongs to the Lord."

An uneasy silence fell over the gathered men. Albrecht's face turned scarlet. He sat down abruptly, his mouth set in a grim line.

"Who brought paper?" Jacob asked.

Henry patted his shirt pocket. "I have a small pad and a pen."

Jacob smiled at him. "Good. Uncle Henry, would you please write down the names of all the men in attendance?"

Henry flipped open the pad and jotted down the names. He looked up, pen poised. "Jay?" He waited until Albrecht lifted his head. "Would you like to schedule everyone's time for watching?"

The man's gaze narrowed, and for a moment Henry feared he would storm out of the room. But he gave a brusque nod. "Four-hour shifts?"

Several nods and mumbles came from the group.

Albrecht fired out time slots and called for volunteers. Henry carefully recorded the information. In the midst of the planning, he heard a shuffle along the side bench.

J.D. Koeppler stood, his sons and grandsons following suit. The entire Koeppler family filed out of the meetinghouse without volunteering for a shift. Henry watched them go, his heart heavy. None of them had said a word in support of Marie throughout the entire meeting.

But then something else occurred to him. Neither had any of them condemned her.

TWENTY

"This is nice." Beth cupped her hands around her coffee mug and smiled across the table at her mother. "With all the hours you've been spending at the café, we don't get much time together anymore. I'm glad we decided to leave the place closed all weekend."

Marie's throat tightened at her daughter's words. She, too, had missed time with Beth. Lately, even when they were together, the tension made it difficult to enjoy Beth's company. Last night, when Hugo discovered the car's engine was warm—evidence that it had been driven recently—Marie approached Beth, intending to ask where she'd gone. But her daughter's defiant attitude made her change her mind. Maybe a part of her feared knowing the answers to the questions that pressed her mind.

But this morning she saw no sign of yesterday's defiance. Beth seemed relaxed, open, more like the girl she'd been back in Cheyenne. Marie's heart rose with hope that what Joanna had said was true—Beth was merely experiencing growing pains and their relationship wouldn't be irreparably damaged by their time in Sommerfeld.

"What should we do today?" Marie gave a cautious sip at her mug.

"How about packing our bags and taking a quick trip?" Beth's eyes danced. "If we left here in the next hour, we could be in Kansas City by midafternoon."

Beth's enthusiasm gave Marie's heart a lift. "What would we do there?"

Beth shrugged. "Rent a room in a nice hotel, sit in a hot tub, watch television. . .something *normal*. Since the café won't open again until Tuesday, we could stay clear through Monday. It'd be like a minivacation."

"But I have service Sunday." Marie was struck by two simultaneous emotions—surprise that attending service had become so important to her, and regret that her daughter's enthusiasm immediately deflated.

Beth shook her head, her hair spilling across her shoulders. "Mom, I don't get you. You'd blow an entire weekend away from here just to go to that little church?"

Marie lowered her head. She wished Beth understood the changes taking place in her heart. But she couldn't quite comprehend it herself, let alone explain it to someone else. All she knew for sure was she didn't want to miss service at the meetinghouse. Reaching her hand across the table, she touched Beth's rigid arm.

"Honey, I don't mean to disappoint you."

Beth jumped up and moved stiffly to the stove, where she poured another cup of coffee. Leaning against the counter, she fixed her mother with a unwavering glare. "The last thing I expected when we came here was for our family to fall apart."

A pang pierced Marie's heart. For many years "family" had meant the two of them. But now it was so much more. Even if the rest of Marie's family never came around, surely Beth would benefit from having Joanna and some of her cousins in her life. How could she help her see that?

"You aren't the same mother I've had for twenty years. You

dress different—I can't remember the last time you wore a pair of jeans. You talk different—bringing God and prayers into nearly every conversation. And you act different—all quiet and accepting instead of standing up for yourself. I don't feel like I even know you anymore!"

Marie tipped her head, narrowing her gaze as she reflected on Beth's statement. "I suppose I have made some changes since we arrived. Being here has helped me remember the teachings of my childhood and how important they were to me. They've become important to me again. I hope the changes aren't bad ones." She spoke slowly, thinking carefully as she formed words. "But I've seen you change, too. You've become resentful, snappy, and. . .sneaky."

Beth jerked upright, her brow creasing sharply.

Marie knew she'd struck a nerve. She proceeded with caution. "What do you do while I'm at the café all day?" Although she kept her tone soft and noncombatant, Beth's face blazed pink.

"Here we go again. Crazy Beth is robbing everybody blind."

"If it isn't true, why not prove them wrong? What are you trying to hide?"

Beth shifted her gaze to the side, the muscles in her jaw twitching. Although Marie waited for several moments, Beth didn't answer.

Marie released a sigh. "It's okay. You don't have to tell me."

Beth swung back, flinging one arm wide. "See? That's exactly what I mean! Back home, if I tried to keep something from you, you'd bug me until I caved in."

"You want me to bug you?"

"No."

"Then what do you want?"

Beth stared, her body angled forward as if poised for a fight. "I want us to go back to how we were before. You and me against the world. Maybe it wasn't perfect, but it was secure."

Marie shook her head. "Sweetheart, I love you, and I always will. You're my daughter—my precious gift." Her throat went tight as love filled her so completely she ached. "But I don't think we'll ever be the way we were before. I've found something here that I lacked for too many years. And I know I'll never be able to let it go again."

Beth poked out her lips, her expression sour. "You're talking about God, aren't you?"

Marie wasn't sure which feeling took precedence at that moment—elation that Beth had recognized the light of God in her mother's bearing, or sorrow that she spoke of it with such disdain. "Yes, I am."

Beth marched to the sink and dumped the coffee. Dark spatters rose with the force of her swing. "And I suppose you'll choose Him over me, just like you've chosen your family over me."

Marie bolted from her chair and rushed across the floor to envelop Beth in her arms. Even though her daughter stood stiffly, keeping her arms at her sides, Marie held her close, stroking her hair with a trembling hand. "Sweetheart, I'm not choosing anything over you. Nothing will change how much I love you. But I can't give God up for you. I hope you understand that."

Beth allowed the embrace for a few more seconds before she pulled back. The hurt in her eyes stabbed Marie. "No, Mom, I don't understand. And frankly, I don't want to." She moved to the doorway leading to the hall and then paused, her shoulders tense. "Since you don't want to go away this weekend, I guess I'll go on my own. I could benefit from some normalcy. Maybe I'll call Mitch, see if he wants to fly in and meet me."

Marie clamped her jaw, refusing to respond. There was no point—Beth already knew how Marie felt about her spending time with Mitch. Instead, she posed a practical question. "How will you pay for your minivacation?"

"Maybe I'll take some of the money out of the account in McPherson. . .unless you have a problem with that."

Marie sighed. "That account will be yours soon anyway. I won't oppose it."

Peeking over her shoulder, Beth sent Marie a brief questioning look. When Marie met her gaze, remaining silent, Beth released a huff and disappeared around the corner.

Marie sat back at the table and buried her face in her hands. *God,* her heart cried, *I won't choose Beth over You. But please don't let me lose her. She means so much to me. . . .*

Henry glanced at the overcast sky as he slid into his vehicle. He released a shiver. The temperature had dropped overnight. The gray sky and the snap of the air gave the promise of snow. He smiled. From the time he was a boy, he had anticipated the first snow of the season. Often it came right after Thanksgiving, which always brought a rush of eagerness for Christmas.

Pulling his car onto the fog-shrouded road, he let his thoughts drift ahead to Christmas. It would be different this year, without Lisbeth. Fondness brought a smile as he remembered past years and the traditions he'd shared with his dear friend. He would miss her homemade noodles and spicy mince pies. He would miss shopping for fabric for her quilts. How she teased him about choosing such unattractive patterns! He could still see her crinkly smile, hear her teasing comment, "What do men know?" The comment always brought a laugh, never indignation.

Mostly he would miss *her*—their time together.

He supposed it seemed odd to others, how close he had been to Lisbeth. But there was no denying how much he had come to love the old woman. And he was sure she loved him like the son she never had.

His tires crunched on the hard ground as he rolled slowly toward the church, the empty seat beside him serving as another reminder of Lisbeth's absence. Even when she'd still had her buggy, he had driven her to the meetinghouse on days of inclement weather. If she were alive, he'd have her company today.

Through the murky morning light, he glimpsed a figure hunching forward into the wind and moving in the same direction as he. He squinted, and his heart lurched. Marie? Bringing his car to a stop beside her, he reached across the seat to pop open the passenger door.

"Marie!" He heard the concern in his tone but did nothing to squelch it. "What are you doing walking in this cold? Get in!"

She made no argument, but slipped into the seat and yanked the door closed behind her. "Brr!" She hugged herself as she smiled at him. Her nose was cherry red, her eyes watery. She still looked wonderful. "Thank you. I didn't realize how cold it was. The wind bites this morning."

"Yes, it does. You should have more sense than to walk." He shifted the car into gear, his heart thudding at his own audacity. Had he scolded her?

But she laughed. "It had nothing to do with sense. My feet were my only transportation today. I don't have a car."

He shot her a sharp look before turning his attention back to the road. "Is something wrong with the engine?"

"No. Beth went away for the weekend, and she needed the car." He detected a hint of sadness beneath her statement. "So if I wanted to attend service, I had to walk."

"Well," he blustered, "the next time you need a ride, let me know. You shouldn't be out when it's this chilly. You could get sick."

He sensed her pleasure by the upturning of her lips although she kept her gaze aimed ahead. "I appreciate that, Henry, but I wouldn't want to put you out."

"I always took Lisbeth to service." He glanced at her. "I was just thinking how the seat seemed empty without her. It's nice. . .to have someone there." He was rewarded by her smile. He drew a breath and made a brave offer. "I can pick you up every Sunday if you like. That way if Beth wants the car. . ."

Marie looked at him, her face pursed into a thoughtful expression. When she spoke, her voice was soft, hesitant, yet he also detected gratitude. "I appreciate that, Henry. Thank you."

"You're welcome." He pulled into the churchyard and parked close to the women's entrance rather than his normal place at the front of the church. She got out before he could rush around and open the car door for her. Disappointment struck, but he pushed it aside. "I'll give you a ride back to your house afterward, so come out here after service."

She flashed him another quick smile before ducking into the hood of her furry coat and dashing for the door. Henry had a difficult time focusing on the singing and sermon, knowing he would have time with Marie that afternoon. Brief time, certainly, since the drive to Lisbeth's was less than a mile, but any time was a treat.

His heart pattered hopefully as he recalled her decision to attend service despite having to brave the cold morning. Her desire to return to her faith must be strong. He offered a silent prayer for the work that had started in her soul to continue, as Lisbeth had hoped, and bring her completely back to the fold.

His gaze flitted to the back of J.D. Koeppler's head. The man's thick, steel gray hair stuck up in the back, exposing a tiny bit of his freckled pink scalp. He stared at that spot of skin, wishing he could peel back the layers of J.D.'s heart and get to the soft center. How the man had hardened himself over the years.

Lisbeth once said the pain of Marie's departure had given J.D. a heart callus. At the time, Henry had been dealing with his own pain and hadn't wasted any sympathy on J.D. Now, however, he had to wonder how much the man was hurting by being so near to his daughter yet holding himself at a distance. Or had his heart grown so hard that he didn't experience any discomfort? Henry couldn't tell by looking.

He turned his head slightly and located Marie's mother. He was certain Erma would embrace Marie if given the opportunity. He'd witnessed her sidelong glances, the longing in her eyes each time she looked at her daughter. But if J.D. didn't bend, Erma wouldn't make any overtures. She honored her husband in every way, even at the expense of her own heartache.

Henry admired Joanna for making a stand against her family and welcoming Marie back into her life. She knew the woman paid a price, being ostracized by her parents and siblings, but Joanna followed her own heart. She and Marie were a lot alike. Marie had followed her heart twenty years ago. . .right out of Sommerfeld.

But would she do it again? Henry's chest grew tight as the question formed in his mind. He didn't dare speculate on the answer to that question.

The congregation shifted, slipping to kneel at the benches for the final prayer. Henry knelt, too, and when he folded his hands and closed his eyes, he repeated the prayer that had been a part of him since he was a young man of twenty-two. *Bring her back to us, Father.* He knew he meant not only spiritually but also physically.

When the service ended, Henry reached for his hat from the overhead rack. Someone caught his arm, and he turned to find Doug Ortmann beside him. The man crooked his finger, indicating for Henry to follow him to the corner. Once separate from the crowd,

Doug spoke in a hushed tone.

"Have you heard, Henry? There haven't been any thefts since Thanksgiving Day."

Henry nodded. Apparently the watch system was working. Of course, no one watched during service—the men had agreed service was too important for any of the members to miss. "I'm thinking the thief knows people are actively seeking him. He's probably moved on."

Doug nodded. "I hope so. I didn't like thinking Marie. . ." He shook his head, sadness in his eyes. "She's a cousin, you know."

Henry clamped his hand over the man's shoulder. "I know. It's been hard on many people, the speculation and worries."

Doug nodded. "But if no more thefts take place, things will settle down, won't they?"

Henry took in a big breath. "I pray so, Doug."

"Me, too." The man smiled. "My family's waiting. I'd better go."

The man's blithe words cut Henry. What must it be like to have family waiting? Then his heart lifted—today he had someone waiting. Marie. He hurried his steps to his car.

TWENTY-ONE

Marie slipped her hood over her head and crossed her arms, tucking her hands in her armpits, while she waited beside Henry's car for his return. She watched the men's door, standing on one foot then the other in an attempt to keep warm. When she spotted him she bounced forward two steps and met him in front of the hood.

"Henry, Joanna invited me over for lunch, so I'm going to ride with Hugo. I just wanted to let you know."

His smile immediately faded. "Oh. All right." He shrugged, his lips forming the semblance of a grin that didn't reach his eyes. "Of course, that makes sense for you to ride with them."

The depth of his disappointment seemed disproportionate to the situation. Guilt wiggled through Marie's heart when she recalled his comment about the empty seat in his vehicle serving as a reminder of Lisbeth's absence. Maybe she should let him transport her. But no, she wasn't Lisbeth, and serving as a replacement wouldn't be healthy for Henry. Or her.

She risked grazing his sleeve with her fingertips in lieu of the squeeze she wanted to deliver. "I do appreciate your willingness to give me a ride." She licked her lips, her heart suddenly racing. "I would appreciate a lift next Sunday morning if the offer still stands."

"Sure it does. The wintry weather seems to have arrived. No need for you to get frostbite."

The hint of teasing in his tone made Marie smile. "Thank you." She sidled toward Hugo's waiting car. "I'll see you Tuesday, right?"

For a moment he looked baffled, then his expression cleared. "Oh! At the café. Yes, sure. You know you will."

She gave a quick wave, then jogged the final few feet to Hugo's car. Sliding into the backseat with Kyra, Kelly, and Gomer, she released a giggle. "Whew! Maybe I should have let Henry take me. This is a tight fit!"

Gomer scooted forward and draped his arms over the back of the front seat, giving the girls more space. "How's that?"

Marie tousled his short hair with her fingers. Although the Kansas seat-belt laws prohibited Gomer's position, Marie knew no police officer was likely to swing through Sommerfeld and ticket Hugo for not having his son belted in. "Thanks, kiddo."

He grinned.

Kelly tapped Marie on the arm as the car backed out of the churchyard. "Aunt Marie, are you and Mr. Braun courting?"

"Kelly!" Joanna gasped and abruptly shifted to stare into the backseat.

Kelly pressed herself farther into the seat, her gaze bouncing between Marie and her mother. "What did I say?"

Kyra bumped her sister's arm. "It's a nosy question, Kel."

Kelly folded her arms, her lower lip puckered. "I wasn't trying to be nosy. I just wondered."

Marie swallowed. "W–what would give you that idea, honey?"

The girl shrugged. "I don't know. You used to court. Mom said so."

Joanna spun to face the front. The back of her neck, visible between her coat collar and her hairline, turned bright pink.

"And sometimes," Kelly continued, "people who courted when they were young get back together when they're old."

Marie nearly giggled at being referred to as "old," but she suspected Kelly would take offense.

Hugo, his hands clamped over the steering wheel, glanced into the backseat. His forehead creased into a scowl. "Have you been reading romance books again?"

Kelly blushed crimson and ducked her head.

Kyra burst out laughing. "Kel!"

"I don't see anything funny." Kelly's tone turned defensive.

Huge sent his daughter a glowering look. "I don't see anything funny, either. Those books give you wrong ideas. No more of them, Kelly."

The girl kept her head low. "Yes, Dad."

Kyra continued to chuckle.

Kelly socked her in the arm. "Stop laughing!"

Kyra brought herself under control as Hugo pulled into the driveway. Gomer clambered over Marie's legs and shot out of the car. Marie followed more slowly, slipping her hand through Kelly's elbow so they could walk together behind the rest of the family.

On the porch, after everyone else had gone inside, Marie gave Kelly a one-armed hug. "Honey, I'm not upset with you."

Kelly's blue eyes shimmered as she peered into Marie's face. "Are you sure? I didn't mean anything bad when I asked. I just. . ." She lowered her gaze.

Marie cupped her chin and lifted her face. "Tell me what you're thinking."

Kelly shrugged. "I just think it would be neat if you and Mr. Braun got together. Then you could stay here and not go back to Cheyenne."

A teasing grin twitched at Marie's cheek. "What, I can't stay here alone?"

Kelly released a self-conscious giggle, hunching her shoulders. "Well. . .I suppose you could." Tipping her head to peer at Marie out of the corners of her eyes, she said, "But wouldn't it be more exciting if you had a beau?"

Marie pinched the end of her niece's nose. "You *have* been reading romance novels."

The girl giggled, her eyes sparkling. "Don't tell Daddy, but my friend Abbie Muller gave me one about this couple who dated all through high school. They were going to get married, but they split up when the girl got swept off her feet by a traveling salesman. But the salesman died, and the girl came back to town, and she and her high-school boyfriend got together again." Kelly released a deep sigh. "It was a really good story."

Marie shook her head.

"It reminded me of you and Mr. Braun," Kelly went on eagerly. "The couple in the story was really happy they got back together. Don't you think you'd be happy with Mr. Braun?"

Marie smoothed a wisp of hair behind Kelly's ear. "Honey, life never works out like storybooks. It's a good idea in theory, but. . ."

Kelly tipped her head to the side. "But what?"

"In storybooks, people often don't think about what God wants for them." Marie smiled, her heart lifting at the realization of how important God's will had become in the past few weeks. She hadn't even considered whether leaving with Jep was what God wanted for her back then—she'd just gone. Now she didn't want to proceed on anything without His blessing. "I need to do what God would have me do, not what sounds romantic. Do you understand?"

Kelly nodded, but Marie could see by the loss of sparkle in the girl's eyes that she was disappointed. Flinging her arm around Kelly's shoulders, Marie aimed her toward the door. "I tell you what. If God lets me know He has romance in mind for me, you'll be the first one to hear about it, okay?"

The thirteen-year-old's face lit with pleasure. "Okay!"

That evening, in Lisbeth's bedroom, snuggled beneath one of her aunt's quilts, with a lantern illuminating the pages of Lisbeth's Bible in her lap, Marie reflected on her conversation with Kelly. As much as she hated to admit it, she felt haunted by the girl's innocent question: *"Don't you think you'd be happy with Mr. Braun?"*

She had many memories of Henry, and none of them were unpleasant except the one from the day she left Sommerfeld with Jep. The image of his stricken face, tears glittering in the corners of his dark eyes, brought a stab of guilt as sharp as the one she'd felt that day. Even though she hadn't looked back, she knew Henry stood beside the road until the semi was out of sight. She knew he had mourned her leaving. Even if Lisbeth hadn't shared Henry's heartbreak in her letters, Marie would have known.

But she had loved Jep. They'd been happy. He'd teased her about being his little Mennonite girl, but he'd never been put off by her cap and simple dresses. He hadn't even insisted she adjust her attire after they recited vows in front of a justice of the peace. Jep had been raised in the Baptist church but slipped away due to his job as a truck driver. All the traveling pulled him away from regular church attendance, but Marie had insisted on finding a church to visit every Sunday when she began traveling with him.

She smiled, her heart swelling with gratitude as she remembered Jep holding her close, whispering, "Marie, honey, you've been so good for me. I feel like Jesus is my friend again. Thanks for getting me back on track." She had been so happy with him, so certain God meant for them to be together.

But their time together had been short-lived—not quite two

years. She hugged the Bible to her chest, pain stabbing with the memory of the day the police officer knocked on the apartment door and told her Jep was gone. He'd fallen asleep at the wheel, the man had said, and rolled the semi over an embankment. He'd been killed instantly, so he hadn't suffered. Marie hadn't found much comfort in that fact at the time.

In the numb days following Jep's funeral, his parents had been wonderful, supportive, assuring her they would help her with the baby, who would never have the opportunity to know the father who had celebrated her conception. But Marie had wanted her own mama. So as soon as she could travel—when Beth was a mere two weeks old—she had climbed on a bus and returned to Sommerfeld.

Only to be sent away by her father.

So she had left, disgraced and aching, and moved in with Jep's parents, relying on their help. The day she moved under their roof she discarded the outer coverings that told of her Mennonite faith.

Marie touched her tangled hair, recalling how odd it had felt those first days without her cap in place.

A sudden desire struck. Almost against her will, she set the Bible aside and slipped from the bed. Padding on bare feet to the closet, her heart pounding, Marie sought the old, familiar covering. Lisbeth's caps rested in a box on the closet shelf. She removed the box, set it on the bed, and lifted out one cap. Her hands trembled as she fingered the white ribbon—white, because Lisbeth had never married. Her cap would require black ribbons.

Her breath caught. Did she truly want a cap again?

She licked her lips, her mouth dry, and crossed to the bureau and the round mirror that hung above it. Placing the cap on the bureau top, she smoothed her unruly hair from her face and examined her image. When she lowered her hands, the strands flew in disordered curls around her cheeks. The lantern light brought out the gold and red highlights. Henry had always admired the red in her hair.

Shaking her head, she pushed thoughts of Henry away. This had nothing to do with him. Picking up the cap, she held her breath and slipped it over her curls. With quivering fingers, she tucked the errant curls beneath the sides of the cap. Her reflection blinked back at her, her face pale, her eyes wide. The white ribbons trailed down her neck. Time melted away, and Marie looked into the face of her youth. A tear slid down her cheek.

Closing her eyes, she dropped to her knees beside the bed. "Oh, my Father God, I've missed You. I'm so glad to have You back in my life. I know when I leave here, You will go with me. I can worship You away from Sommerfeld. But I don't know what to do." For long moments she remained beside the bed, hands folded beneath her chin, her knuckles digging into her flesh, her heart crying out for guidance.

When she got to her feet again, she had no sure answers, but she knew one thing. If she were to stay in Sommerfeld, she wanted to be part of her childhood congregation once more. Her decision to leave with Jep had resulted in excommunication. But her fellowship could be restored if given approval by the bishop.

She experienced a sense of loss as she tugged the cap free and returned it to the box. One ribbon hung along the cardboard side, and she lifted it, twisting it around her finger. A smile formed as she envisioned God twisting Himself around her heart. "All right," she whispered. "I'll try to regain my membership. If they refuse me, then I'll leave. . .again. But this time—" Her heart caught, tears filling her eyes. "This time I won't leave You behind."

"Are you sure?" Henry leaned his elbows on the table, bringing himself closer to his brother-in-law. He and Troy shared a corner booth in the café. Henry was pleased to see business returning since the town had enjoyed a full week without thefts. The café didn't bustle with Sommerfeld residents, but members of the community filled three tables. It was a step in the right direction. And if what Troy said was true, there was an even bigger reason for celebration.

"She told Deborah about it herself." Troy lifted his mug and sipped the steaming brew, his eyebrows high. "And Deacon Reiss told me this morning that the bishop is coming on Sunday to visit with her."

Henry slumped in his seat, his spine suddenly unable to hold him erect. After all the years and countless prayers, it seemed Marie was returning to the church. And if she did, she would no doubt remain in Sommerfeld. "Well, I'll be."

Troy set his mug down and frowned across the table. "Now, Henry, Deborah asked me to tell you about it, but she also wanted me to tell you something else."

Henry angled his head.

"Don't get your hopes up. Just because she wants to come back to the church doesn't mean. . ." Troy turned his gaze away.

Henry nodded. Troy didn't need to finish the sentence. Marie's return to the church didn't necessarily mean she would return to him. She'd made her choice long ago, and based on what he'd overheard the day he'd brought her father to the café, her love for Jep Quinn had gone deep. There might not be room for another love.

Releasing a little huff of laughter, he shifted forward again. "Tell Deborah not to worry." He waited until Troy met his gaze. "God has brought Marie back to faith, and that's a real answer to prayer. It's what Lisbeth wanted. I can be happy with that."

Troy nodded and went back to sipping his coffee, pulling in noisy slurps. It was clear he was pleased to be finished with the conversation.

Henry leaned into the padded seat, his thoughts racing. What he'd told Troy was truthful—he could be happy for Marie if she managed to regain fellowship with the congregation. But he also knew it would be difficult to be happy for himself if Marie were to remain in Sommerfeld and not be a part of his life.

TWENTY-TWO

Beth closed the cover on her laptop, sighed, and massaged her neck with both hands. When would this tension ease up so she could relax? Her weekend away, although enjoyable—especially after Mitch arrived, even though he looked ridiculous sporting a new, short haircut—hadn't accomplished what she'd hoped.

Her gaze flitted to Mom, who lifted two plates from the serving counter and headed toward the dining room. Tears stung behind Beth's eyes. Instead of her time away making Mom see how important it was for them to stick together, it had pushed her in the direction of the church. This past Sunday she had even talked to the head honcho about becoming a member again!

In four more weeks, she would be able to officially claim the inheritance, sell the house and café, gather up Lisbeth's antiques, and return to Cheyenne to open her boutique with Mitch. He'd located a shop area they could rent in one of the older buildings on Capitol Avenue. It would be pricey, but he was certain they'd be able to make it work. The thought of having a successful decorator boutique thrilled her on many levels. But—her throat tightened—Mom might not be going with her. And if Mom didn't come, how could Beth possibly do all the things she'd planned in order to repay her?

How could her mother betray her this way? All her growing-up years, Mom had been there—the one stable, unwavering, un-shakeable relationship in a world where others came and went. But now her mother was slipping away, choosing others over the child she had claimed meant everything to her.

Beth felt as though her dreams were crumbling at her feet.

Trina turned from the dishwasher and flashed Beth a bright smile. "All done researching?"

Beth lowered her hands. She didn't feel like talking to anyone, but Trina was hard to resist. The girl was incurably cheerful. Despite her controlling mother, bleak surroundings, and dismal wardrobe, she always wore a smile. Kind of like Mom these days.

"I wasn't researching." She swiveled on the stool and watched Trina load plates. "I was making sure the café and house were listed on the Realtor's Web site."

Trina's expression clouded. "So you're really doing it, huh?"

Beth flipped her hands outward. "That's what I came to do. I follow through on my plans." *Unlike someone else I know.*

Trina went on stacking, her hands moving rhythmically between the bin and the washer tray. The little ribbons from her cap swayed with the steady movement. What would Mom look like if she started wearing one of those caps?

"Well, I'm glad you're getting to do what you want to, but. . ." Trina paused for a moment, pulling in her lower lip and furrowing her brow. "Are you sure you want to sell everything?"

"Why wouldn't I?" Beth propped her elbows on her knees. Out of the corner of her eye, she saw her mother hand Deborah an order ticket. Mom said something Beth couldn't hear from this distance, and Deborah smiled in return, resulting in Mom's low-throated chuckle.

Her heart caught at how at ease her mother appeared. And how left out that ease made her feel. She fit her thumbnails together and stared at them, her chest tight. Speaking loud enough for everyone in the kitchen to hear, she said, "I'm absolutely sure. In fact, I'm counting the hours until I'm outta here."

Trina gave a quick nod, then focused on the dishes, clearing out the bin and sending the tray through the washer. She flipped a switch, and the roar of running water almost covered her comment. "I'll miss working here. Daddy probably won't let me work anywhere else. He trusted Miss Koeppler to keep an eye on me."

Trina bustled off, pushing the metal cart in front of her, and Beth sat upright, realizing something for the first time. Selling the café didn't only affect her—it affected Trina and Deborah, too. Did they rely on the income? Trina certainly relied on the opportunity to mingle with people. She'd never met a more gregarious kid than Henry's niece. She had no idea why it suddenly bothered her to think of Trina and Deborah being ousted, but she couldn't deny a pang of guilt.

Maybe she could tell the new owners the Muller mom-and-daughter team was part of the bargain. She snorted at the thought. Why should she care about grumpy Deborah and her happy offspring? They were nothing to her. Just as this town was nothing to her.

Pushing from the stool, she headed for the back door. Cool air slapped her face when she stepped into the alley, and she sucked in a sharp breath. It wasn't as if she had never experienced a cold winter—she was raised in Cheyenne, after all—but for some reason the Kansas cold seemed to penetrate deeper.

Or maybe she just had less tolerance for anything related to Kansas.

Deciding not to dig too deeply along those lines, she climbed into the car. She jammed the key into the ignition and started the engine. This bad mood wasn't her fault. It was Mom's. *Mom and all her changing*. Beth's hand stilled on the gearshift as a realization struck. Despite the lack of creature comforts, the continued rejection by the majority of her family, and the undeniably long days of working in the café, Mom seemed more content than Beth could ever remember.

Slapping the gearshift into position, Beth shook her head and pushed on the gas. Maybe Mom *thought* she was content, reliving all her childhood stuff, but just wait until Beth had money in hand and finally told her everything she'd been doing to ensure their brighter future. That would win her back. That's when real contentment would begin.

The first smile of the day found its way to Beth's face as she aimed the car toward the highway. Her future awaited.

Henry licked the tip of the pencil before recording the total at the bottom of the column in the ledger. He ran his gaze down the line of numbers, mentally adding. Convinced the calculator had figured correctly, he underlined the total and closed the ledger. He lifted his head to find Marie watching him.

Heat flooded his chest. He forced a wobbly smile. "You're still here."

"I'm waiting for Beth." She perched on a stool at the end of the counter, near the back door. Over her blouse she wore a hip-length, thickly knit sweater that had belonged to Lisbeth. The collar was folded under on one side, and his fingers twitched with the desire to straighten it for her. But if he touched the collar, her nutmeg curls would certainly brush his knuckles, and he might end up doing more than fixing her collar.

He looked back at the ledger. "She knows you're finished here?"

Marie sighed. "I'm sure she does. The café closes every day at eight o'clock, and I'm always ready to leave by eight forty-five." She glanced at the clock hanging above the stove. "I suppose she's not terribly late. It's not quite nine yet."

"But you've had a long day."

Marie laughed lightly, her blue eyes tired. "I've had a long *week*."

Henry wondered what meaning hid beneath her blithe statement. He rose. "I'll take you home. If the lights are off here, Beth will know you've gone on."

Slipping from the stool, Marie covered a yawn with slender fingers. "Thank you. I'll take you up on that offer."

After he shrugged into his jacket and joined her at the door, she turned off the lights. They were immediately plunged into darkness, giving an intimacy to the setting. Henry fumbled for the doorknob, heaving a breath of relief when he located it.

Swinging the door open, he said, "Go ahead. But be careful— the ground is uneven."

Marie preceded him, and he followed slightly behind and to her left, his hand poised to steady her in case she tripped. But she moved with her typical grace through the shadows to his vehicle. She reached for the door handle, but he caught it first, opening it for her. The interior lights lit the underside of her jaw, bringing out the little cleft in her chin and highlighting a few wisps of hair that had slipped free of their bobby pins.

He swallowed and gestured silently for her to slide into the car. She did so, first sitting and then drawing in her legs in a fluid movement. He slammed the door a little harder than necessary, his heart in his throat. Maybe it hadn't been such a good idea to give her a ride home. On Sundays, with the sun lighting the landscape and worship on his mind, it was easier to distance himself. But under the stars, with shadows showcasing the delicate curve of her jaw and deepening the color of her eyes, old feelings ignited.

Walking around the car, he sucked in big gulps of cold air, trying to cool his racing thoughts. Behind the wheel, he flashed her a quick smile. "Okay, let's get you home."

They rode in silence through the still streets. He wanted to ask her how her meeting with the bishop had gone, if she'd heard anything from the deacons who would determine her future position within the congregation. He wanted to tell her he'd been praying that she would be granted membership. But fearful of her answers— would he be able to hide his disappointment if the response was their refusal?—he kept his mouth closed.

His gaze bounced along the houses, noting how many places hadn't bothered with porch lights this evening. The town finally seemed to be settling down from its scare with the thief. The watchers would continue through December, just to be safe, but Henry believed the worst was over. They could all relax.

He pulled behind Lisbeth's house, as he had so many times over the years of transporting Lisbeth. Marie craned her neck as they rounded the back corner, and he heard her breath release in a sigh as he stopped beside the porch. Something in her pose made his heart turn over. The engine still idling, he faced her. "Is something the matter?"

She glanced at him. Her eyes appeared black with the absence of light. "I just hoped Beth might be here. She–she's been gone so much lately."

The sadness in her tone pierced Henry's heart. He forced a chuckle. "Well, she's young. Stretching her wings."

"I suppose." Marie remained in the seat, her hands in her lap, her head tipped thoughtfully. "But her wing-stretching was different before we came here. It didn't concern me the way it does now."

Henry put the car into PARK but left the engine running. The gentle hum provided a soothing lullaby. The dash lights illuminated the interior enough to highlight her features but little more. The cover of night gave him the courage to speak openly. "Tell me why."

Her head jerked backward as if she were surprised. She blinked several times, her lips sucked in, and for a moment he expected her to grab the door handle and let herself out. But instead, she shifted slightly in the seat, angling her body to face him, and licked her lips.

"I think I messed up when I raised Beth. I was so hurt by Dad sending me away, I turned my back on the way he raised me. I didn't make knowing God a priority for Beth." She shook her head, grimacing. "I took her to Sunday school when she was little—we went with Jep's parents. But when Beth was six, her grandmother died, and the next year, her grandfather moved to Florida. After that, I had to work more hours since I didn't have their financial support, and. . .well, church just went by the wayside."

Henry nodded. He already knew all this—Marie had shared with Lisbeth in letters, and Lisbeth had shared with him. But he stayed silent and let her talk.

"Beth's always been a good girl, though. Respectful to me. Respectful to others. I did teach her that." She turned her head, her gaze out the window. "Since we've been here, though, I've seen so much resentment in her. I'm not sure where it's coming from, and I don't like it. But I can't seem to talk to her anymore."

Looking directly at Henry, she offered a sad smile. "We were always lucky that way—we could always talk. More than other moms and daughters. I really miss that."

"You'll get it back," Henry said, unable to keep himself from giving some small encouragement. She seemed so forlorn. "Beth is balking at the restrictions here, that's all. She isn't accustomed to this simpler lifestyle."

"But that's just it." Marie's frustration came through clearly in her tone. "It's more than the lifestyle that's bothering her. I think she's gone so much because she's trying to avoid what I've found here—a relationship with God. It frightens her, and that's the last thing I'd want her to feel."

"The unknown is always frightening." Henry wove his fingers together to keep from reaching for her hand. The longing to give her comfort became difficult to resist. "The more Beth sees evidence of God's touch on your heart, sees how it brings you joy, the more open she'll be to it."

"Are you sure?"

The uncertainty in her quavering voice pained Henry. He gave in to the impulse and placed his hand over hers. "Yes, I'm sure. How did you come to accept it? By witnessing it in the lives around you— in the lives of those you loved who loved Him."

Marie made no effort to extract her hand from his clasp. Instead, she turned her hand palm up and slipped her fingers around his hand. Henry felt certain she was unaware of the action, but the simple touch filled him with heat.

"Of course." Her whispered voice barely carried over the engine's gentle rumble. "How could I have been so foolish as to forget?" Her fingers trembled within his grasp. "Lisbeth always lived her faith quietly, yet it was evident. If I try to emulate her, surely the reality will eventually reach Beth's heart, opening her to receiving God's love." A smile broke across her face. "Thank you, Henry. I feel much less worried now."

He forced even breathing, bringing his racing heart under control. "You're welcome."

They sat, their hands joined, for several seconds before Marie spoke again. "Do you realize you're the first man I've ever talked to about Beth?"

He didn't know how to respond. One word squeaked out. "Oh?"

Her nod rearranged the wisps of coiling hair. "Since Jep's father moved away, there hasn't been a man in our lives."

Henry thought his heart might pound out of his chest.

"I've thought. . .so many times. . .how Beth and I could both benefit from a man's point of view. Admittedly, I—I always hoped my father. . ."

Her stammered words, and her convulsing fingers, nearly melted Henry. But his throat was too tight to speak. So he increased the pressure on her hand, letting her know he cared. She returned the contact, curling her fingers more securely around his, giving a silent *Thank-you*.

Henry remembered a conversation he'd had with Lisbeth about J.D.'s stubborn refusal to read any of Marie's letters. Lisbeth's theory had been that J.D. knew he was wrong for sending his daughter away, and by ignoring her, he could ignore his guilt. His self-righteous grumping, she had concluded, was just a cover-up for the unhappiness underneath. Could Marie benefit if he shared Lisbeth's wisdom now?

"Your father. . ." Henry's voice cracked. He cleared his throat and started again. "Your father lost a great deal by his hasty actions. He lost you, and he lost Beth. He isn't a foolish man—he recognizes his mistake. But his pride. . . Lisbeth prayed, and I keep praying, that he will swallow his pride and choose to reach out to you."

A tear rolled silently down Marie's cheek, dripped from her chin, and landed on Henry's hand. Without thinking, he lifted his fingers and brushed the moisture away. She caught his wrist, pressing his fingers against her cheek for a moment. Then, with a jerk, she released him. Even in the faint light, he saw the color in her face deepen.

Turning from him, she grabbed the door handle. "I'd better go in."

"Let me walk you."

"No." She swung her feet out and looked over her shoulder. "I'm fine." Stepping from the car, she stood for a moment in the triangle of soft light. She leaned forward slightly to meet his gaze. "Thank you again, Henry." She slammed the door and moved quickly around the front of the vehicle.

He watched her shadow gain substance as she ran through the paths of white created by the headlights, Lisbeth's sweater flapping. He watched her clamber up the porch steps, snatch open the door, and disappear inside. Then he watched the window until a pale glow indicated she'd managed to light a lantern.

He could go now. She was safe.

When he reached for the gearshift, he realized his hand was shaking. He released a snort of self-deprecation. Marie might be safe, but he most certainly was not.

TWENTY-THREE

"Henry, it's only right that you come for lunch today." Joanna's blue eyes sparkled as she looked at Henry. "After all your years of faithful prayer, you need to join us in celebrating Marie's return to our fellowship."

Henry's heart certainly celebrated. Deacon Meiss had announced at the close of service that morning the decision to accept Marie Quinn as a member of the Sommerfeld congregation. Art, Conrad, Leo, and their families all intended to meet at Joanna's in honor of Marie's official return. He wanted to be there, yet he hesitated. He would be the only nonfamily member. If Lisbeth were there, too, it would be fine, given their unique friendship, but. . .

Snowflakes danced by, reminding him they were standing out in the cold while Joanna waited for an answer. He looked into her eyes, their hue the same as Marie's, and he gave a nod. "I'll be there. Thank you."

Her smile lit her face. Touching his sleeve, she said, "Good. Don't dally—we want as much of the afternoon as possible to make merry!" She turned and scurried to her car, where Hugo waited with the engine running. In moments, Hugo's vehicle left the churchyard. Marie waved from the backseat, her smiling face pressed to the glass.

He answered with a smile and wave of his own, then turned toward his car.

Across the churchyard, he spotted J.D. Koeppler assisting his wife into their buggy. Like a handful of other older members, the Koepplers hadn't adopted the use of more modern transportation. Their ride home would be chilly today.

As Henry reached for his door handle, something in his soul compelled him to cross the hard ground to Koeppler's buggy. He reached it just as J.D. picked up the reins.

The man gave a start when Henry touched his arm, and he turned a stern scowl down on Henry. "What do you want?"

The growl was certainly intended to put Henry off, but he didn't back away. Giving the man's arm a gentle squeeze, he said, "Are you coming to Hugo and Joanna's?"

Erma leaned forward slightly, her gaze flittering between J.D. and Henry. There was no denying the longing in her eyes. But J.D. didn't look at his wife—he looked firmly ahead, his jaw thrust forward. His mouth barely moved as he grated out his response. "I have nothing to celebrate."

Henry jerked his hand back. Although he had witnessed J.D.'s stubbornness frequently over the years, his adamant denial of what had taken place inside the meetinghouse today still took Henry by surprise. "Mr. Koeppler, the lost has been found. The prodigal has returned. There is much to celebrate."

But J.D.'s gray brows pulled down, giving him a fierce look. "I don't buy into her games. She and her daughter only came when the opportunity to carry away the spoils was presented to them. They have no interest in relationships, only riches."

Erma dropped her gaze to her lap, and Henry was certain he saw tears glint in her eyes.

J.D. went on. "Kyra told us how they count down on a calendar, marking off the days until they can be away from us again. The lost is not found, Henry, but merely biding her time until she can discard us once more. I will not celebrate that." Clicking his tongue, he encouraged the horse to pull away from the hitching rail.

Henry stood silently as the buggy rolled backward several yards. With a tug of the reins and a call to "Giddap," J.D. directed the dappled gray beast to pull the buggy toward the road.

Henry watched it go, his heart heavy. J.D. was wrong in his assumptions about Marie. Yes, Beth had come for riches, but Marie was here for relationships. Henry was certain of that. His conversation with her last night in the car spoke clearly of her inner battle of balancing the important relationships in her life. She wanted her family—*all* of her family.

His sigh hung in the crisp air. Shaking his head, he moved toward his car once more. Perhaps J.D. wouldn't celebrate, but Henry would. He, with Marie's brothers and sister, would make merry and praise God for Marie's decision to return to Sommerfeld.

As he pulled away from the churchyard, his gaze found Lisbeth's simple headstone. What would Lisbeth say to J.D. if she were still alive? Even though Henry had spent time nearly every day for the past twenty years with the dear woman, he was unable to determine the answer to that question.

Although Marie relished the long afternoon with Henry, her siblings, and their families, she would have been lying if she said she didn't regret the absence of some important people. Beth's and her parents' lack of attendance cast a pall over the celebratory mood, and she suspected she wasn't the only one to feel it.

Many times she'd seen a glimpse of something in Henry's or Joanna's eyes that expressed a hint of sadness. In those moments, their gazes had locked, and she felt a silent kinship of understanding. She knew, even without saying the words, they wished as deeply as she did for the circle to be complete, for the entire family to meet and rejoice together.

By midafternoon, the young people, who ranged in age from four to twenty-one, gathered in various bedrooms for quiet activities or naps, leaving the adults alone to chat. Hugo carried in chairs from the dining room, creating a misshapen circle of seats in the front room. Marie found herself in the center of the sofa between Joanna and Art's wife, Doris. Henry sat on a ladder-back chair across from her. Having him directly in her line of vision proved distracting, and she played with the buttons on her blouse to avoid gazing into his warm brown eyes.

Doris gave Marie's knee a pat. "So, what are your plans now, Marie? Will you stay permanently?"

Marie looked at Doris, aware of Henry's attentive gaze from across the circle. "Now that I'm part of the congregation again, I would like to stay. But there are many things to work out. I'll need a place to live and a way to take care of myself."

Art leaned forward, placing his elbows on his widespread knees. "Seems to me you've already got that covered with the café and Lisbeth's house."

Marie smiled at her brother. "No. Those are Beth's, not mine."

"She wouldn't let you have them?"

Art's frown brought a rush of defensiveness. "It's not a matter of her letting me. I wouldn't ask. She's depending on the proceeds from the sale of that property to start her own business. I won't take that away from her."

"Well," Doris suggested, her brow puckered thoughtfully, "maybe you could buy the properties?"

Marie allowed a light laugh to escape. "If I had money to buy a café and a house, I would have offered to help Beth fund her business without coming here." Her words created a stir around the room, and she realized how ungrateful she sounded. She held up her hand. "Please don't misunderstand. I don't regret coming. But if it hadn't been for Lisbeth's unusual will"—her gaze met Henry's, and she felt her lips twitch in a smile—"there would have been no motivation for me to return to Sommerfeld. I would never have found the courage to do it had it not been a means of helping Beth."

Henry looked away, a hint of something—pain? regret?—flashing in his eyes. Before she could explore his reaction, Art spoke again.

"I understand." He sighed, shaking his head. "You know, the new owners of the café, whoever they might be, will still need workers. So even if it sells, you'd probably have the opportunity for a job. But a place to live. . .that's a little harder."

Conrad crossed his leg and looked at his wife. "When Sonja and I got married, we wanted to find a place to rent. But there was nothing available. If old Mr. Brandt hadn't passed away, we wouldn't have had a house. There's just not much turnover in Sommerfeld."

"Maybe. . ." Joanna's pensive tone captured Marie's attention. But before she completed her thought, she shook her head and emitted a rueful chuckle. "No, that wouldn't work."

Hugo prodded, "What?"

Joanna's gaze bounced around the room, as if gathering courage, before returning to Marie. "I was just thinking. . .there's so much room at the farm now that all of us are on our own. With just Mom and Dad rattling around out there, I know they have space for Marie."

A negative murmur made its way around the circle.

"See?" Joanna threw her hands outward, her expression regretful. "I told you it wouldn't work."

"It would work," Art inserted, "if Dad weren't so obstinate. I think Mom would be okay with the idea."

Leo nodded. "I know she would. She told Phyllis at Thanksgiving how hard it was to know Marie was in town yet not at the house for the holiday."

Marie stared at Leo's wife. "She really said that?" Her heart lifted with hope, then plummeted. "But she'd never cross Dad. He's the head of the home."

"And she's right to honor him." Henry spoke, surprising Marie. He'd been largely silent through most of their time together. Everyone looked at him, and he squirmed in his seat. His Adam's apple bobbed before he spoke again. "God can't honor her if she doesn't honor her husband—you all know that. I'm not saying J.D. is right in what he's doing, but Erma is right in what she's doing. Asking her to cross J.D. wouldn't be. . ." He shrugged, red mottling his cheeks. "It wouldn't be right."

Another mumble sounded, each husband and wife conferring quietly. Marie stared across the room at Henry, who stared back, a silent apology in his eyes. Marie felt her heart double its tempo. She understood the meaning behind his words. He wanted J.D. to accept her as much as she did, yet he didn't want any more conflict while they waited for her father to bend. The same feeling of kinship that had swept over her at other times in Henry's presence returned, rising higher and causing her pulse to pound.

"Marie—"

Reluctantly, she turned her attention back her older brother.

"Doris and I have a room you could use."

Marie's breath came out in a sigh, tears stinging her eyes. "Oh, Art, I appreciate that so much." She glanced at Henry. "But you know, what Henry just said about Mom needing to honor Dad. . ." She let her gaze sweep the room, briefly touching each of her siblings. "I think all of us need to honor him, too. I am thrilled to be here today, but I know your choosing to be with me instead of with the folks creates conflict between you and them. My moving in with any of you would only expand that conflict. I don't want to be responsible for creating any more trouble than I already have."

"So what will you do?" Joanna asked, tears in her eyes.

Marie took her sister's hand, looking at their intertwined fingers. "I don't know. But I know who does know, and we can petition Him in prayer. If I'm meant to stay in Sommerfeld permanently, He will provide whatever is needed. And if those needs aren't met. . ." The next words had to be forced past a knot in her throat. "Then I know it's His will for me to go back to Cheyenne."

Marie lifted her gaze to look around the room at each person. "But this time, I'll make sure God is a permanent part of my life. I won't cast Him aside again." Smiling through the tears that blurred her vision, she added, "I can be Mennonite in Cheyenne. And I will visit. Often. I won't separate myself from any of you again."

A lengthy silence followed, in which each person appeared introspective, their gazes aimed unseeingly at various spots in the room. Except for Henry, whose gaze remained pinned to Marie's face. She returned his unwavering gaze, hoping he read in her steady contact that she meant the promise for him, too.

Eventually, the silence was broken by a *thump* and a startled wail from one of the bedrooms.

"That's got to be Sharolyn," Phyllis said, bouncing to her feet and heading for the hallway.

Conversations broke out again, the topics less serious. Phyllis returned, carrying her daughter, who tumbled into Leo's arms and snuggled her tear-streaked face against his shoulder. Marie settled back on the sofa and absorbed the typical, boisterous, clamoring scene, a lump of gratitude in her throat for having the opportunity to be part of this large family once more. At the same time, she offered yet another prayer for the circle to extend to include Beth, Abigail, Ben. . .and her parents. She missed them with an intensity that created an ache deep inside. Looking at Sharolyn in Leo's arms provided a reminder of the long-lost relationship between herself and her father, as well as Beth's lifelong absence of a father.

The clock on the mantel chimed five times, signaling the approach of suppertime. Joanna slapped her hands to her knees, pushing herself to her feet. "Well, I guess I'd better pull out some lunch meat and—"

A knock at the door interrupted her words. Hugo started to rise, but she waved her hand at him. "Stay put. I'm up."

She opened the door, and a slightly younger, more slender version of Art stepped over the threshold. Marie leaped to her feet, her arms automatically reaching for the brother who, two years her senior, had alternately teased and protected her while growing up. "Ben!"

But Ben remained rooted on the little braided rug inside the door, his unsmiling gaze sweeping around the room.

Art rose haltingly. "Is something wrong?"

Ben's jaw thrust out, reminding Marie of her father's stern posture. When he spoke, his voice thundered with accusation, bringing another reminder of J.D. into the room. "My house was broken into this morning."

Gasps filled the air. Marie's legs trembled, and she sat back down, her eyes dry but unblinking. A hand descended on her shoulder— Joanna's. She clutched it, grateful for her sister's comforting presence.

"The thief is still in Sommerfeld?" Leo's disbelieving query hung in the room.

Ben nodded stiffly. "Apparently so. And he strikes at the only time the watch isn't active. That tells me this thief is knowledgeable of the town's activities." His glare turned on Marie. He took one step toward her. "Only one person in this town knows all the goings-on but avoids the meetinghouse. You know, too, don't you?"

Marie gaped at her brother, her jaw flapping uselessly. She knew. Lord help her, she knew.

TWENTY-FOUR

Marie drew in a deep breath as Henry turned into the driveway of Lisbeth's home. Her car waited at the back of the house, indicating Beth was there. She released the breath slowly through her nose, praying for strength.

Her gaze on the car, she gave a start when a hand closed over hers. Turning her head sharply, she found Henry fixing her with a concerned look.

"Would you like me to go in with you. . .to support you?"

Marie's heart turned over. Henry had been such a good friend in her younger days. It amazed her that, after the number of years that had slipped by and all the changes, he could still offer his friendship so easily. A part of her wanted him to come in with her, to stand beside her, to face Beth with her. But the greater part knew she couldn't depend on him that way.

With a sigh, she said, "I appreciate your offer, Henry, but it's better I go alone." She gave the hand holding hers a quick squeeze, then pulled away. A chill struck with the removal of his warm touch. Before she changed her mind, she opened the car door and stepped out, then hurried to the back porch. She stepped into the house without looking back at Henry.

Beth sat at the kitchen table, a newspaper spread in front of her. At Marie's entrance, she looked up, and her face broke into a huge smile. "I've been waiting for you! I can't wait to show you something."

Marie's heart pounded. "Honey, I need to talk to you."

Beth jumped up, her blue eyes dancing. "Can't it wait? I think you're going to be surprised."

Removing her coat with trembling hands, Marie debated the best thing to do. She draped the coat over the back of a chair and looked once more into Beth's eyes. Suddenly she couldn't ask the question that pressed at her mind. She forced her lips into a smile. "What surprise?"

Beth grabbed her mother's hand and led her down the hallway to her bedroom, chattering as they went. "I originally planned to save this for Christmas, but I can't wait. I hope it's okay if you get a present two weeks early."

It had been weeks since Marie had seen Beth so cheerful. She offered a silent prayer for guidance, then managed to answer in a teasing tone, "I'll take a present anytime. What is it?"

With a giggle, Beth pulled her through the door and pointed at the cot where a teddy bear sat, its arm outstretched as if reaching for a hug. Tears filled Marie's eyes, blurring her vision, but she recognized the fabric used to create the bear. Lisbeth's appliquéd heart quilt.

On shaky legs, she moved to the cot and lifted the bear. She turned to face Beth, who beamed from the doorway.

"Are you surprised?" Before Marie could answer, she bubbled, "I'm sorry to have been so secretive, but I really wanted to surprise you. I've been spending a lot of time in Newton with an older lady who is teaching me different crafts. I saw her advertisement in the paper, and I thought having some unique craft items in addition to the one-of-a-kind antiques for the boutique would draw in more customers. So I've learned how to turn cutter quilts into stuffed animals or wall hangings, and I've even learned to make stained-glass windows. It's been fun!"

Beth crossed to Marie's side and touched the wide ribbon tied around the bear's neck. "Mrs. Davidson actually did most of the sewing on this one, because I wanted it to be absolutely perfect." Her expression turned uncertain. "You're not upset, are you, that I cut it up? After I dumped that nail polish on it, there wasn't any other way to salvage it."

Marie set the bear on the cot and enfolded Beth in her arms. The quilt became secondary as the full magnitude of Beth's admission sent a wave of relief through her. Beth wasn't the thief. She had been working on the furtherance of her business, but not the way the town had surmised. Marie berated herself for believing the worst of her daughter. How grateful she was that she hadn't accused Beth when she'd arrived home!

Still in her mother's embrace, Beth released a light laugh. "Does this hug mean it's okay I chopped up the quilt?"

Marie pulled back and cupped Beth's cheeks. "It's beautiful, Beth. Thank you." Picking up the bear again, she gave it a hug, smiling over its head. "I think Lisbeth would be pleased, too."

"Oh, good!" Beth hurried toward the closet and pulled the door open. Pushing her clothes aside, she said, "There was enough of the quilt left to make two smaller ones, too." Turning to face her mother, she held twin versions half the size of the one Marie had been given. "I'd like to keep one, and if it's okay with you, I'd like to give the other one to Trina since she worked so closely with Lisbeth at the café."

Once again, tears gathered. Marie nodded and forced words past the knot in her throat. "I think that's a wonderful idea."

With the two bears in her arms, Beth sat on the cot and tipped her head. Blond hair spilled across her shoulders, the strands shimmering in the light of the lantern that glowed on the dresser top.

"Now, what did you want to talk to me about?"

Marie swallowed, shaking her head. "Nothing. It's not important now." Leaning forward, she gave Beth a kiss on the forehead. "Thank you for my gift, honey. I'll treasure it."

Marie left Beth's room, carrying her bear. In her own bedroom, she set the animal on the bed, resting it against the pillows. She sat and fingered one ear. A question remained unanswered. If Beth wasn't the thief, who was?

Beth crept into her mother's room Monday morning and touched her shoulder. "Mom?"

Her mother stirred, scrunching her face and blinking rapidly. She turned blearily in Beth's direction, rubbed her eyes with both fists, and finally sat up. "What is it, honey?"

Beth smiled at the croaky tone. Maybe she should have brought in a cup of tea to clear the sleep from Mom's throat. "I'm going in to Newton to finish a stained-glass project. I wondered if you'd like to come along and meet Mrs. Davidson."

Mom pushed the covers down and swung her feet from the bed. Seated on the edge of the mattress, she peered groggily at Beth. "I'd like that." She yawned and ran her hands through her hair, making it even more mussed. "And maybe I can do a little fabric shopping while we're in town."

Beth crossed her arms and smirked. "You gonna make teddy bears, too, and compete with me?"

Mom's soft laughter sounded. "No. But I need to pull out Lisbeth's machine and make some dresses. I think I can remember how to sew."

Taking a step back, Beth frowned. "Dresses? What for?"

Her mother pulled in her lower lip, a sure sign of nervousness.

Beth's heart rate increased.

Mom patted the mattress beside her. "Sit down for a minute, honey. I need to talk to you."

With some trepidation, Beth approached the bed and perched on the edge of the mattress. "About what?"

"You know I talked to the bishop about rejoining the church."

"Yeah."

Mom sucked a breath through her nose, as if she needed strength. "Well, yesterday the announcement was made that I've been accepted back into fellowship."

Beth's jaw dropped. "So you're staying here? For good?" The apology in Mom's eyes pulled at Beth. She jumped up and moved several feet away before whirling on her mother. "You aren't coming back to Cheyenne with me?"

Mom stood, reaching her hand toward Beth. "It's not for sure yet. I'd need a place to live and a way to support myself here. Both of those are big needs, and I'm not sure how they'll be met. But if I'm meant to stay, I know God will provide."

A band of pressure seemed to wrap around Beth's heart at her mother's words. How could she choose the town over her own daughter? She took a backward step, shaking her head slowly. "I wish we'd never come here."

Mom leaned her head back, her eyes closed. Beth knew she battled tears. She ping-ponged between wanting to rush forward and hug her mother or rush out of the house and not return. Finally Mom lowered her head and looked at her.

"Honey, I'm glad we came here. It hasn't been an easy time for either of us. But being here has restored something I've missed for many years. Now that I'm back in fellowship with God, I feel. . .whole again. I can't regret that."

Her mother's quiet, sincere tone made Beth ache with a longing to understand what Mom meant by being "whole." Yet she rebelled at the insinuation that her mother had lacked something all her years away from Sommerfeld.

"Are you telling me you haven't been happy since you left here? That my dad and me—" Beth couldn't continue. She clenched her fists, pressing them to the sides of her head. "I can't listen to this anymore. I've got to—" She raced toward the back door.

Mom's pounding steps came behind her. "Beth, wait!"

Beth grabbed the door handle, wrenched it violently, and threw the door open. It banged against the wall and bounced back. Beth charged through the storm door, allowing it to slam on her mother, who followed closely on her heels. Mom stood on the porch, stretching out her hand in a silent bid for her return, but Beth ignored her. She revved the engine and squealed out of the drive.

Escape. . . Escape Sommerfeld. Escape Mom. Escape the odd longing that rose up from her breast and tried to choke her breath away. *Just. . .escape.*

The remainder of the week passed in a dizzying blur of tumultuous emotion. Marie's elation at being welcomed back into the fellowship of believers battled with despair at Beth's reaction; her delight at being a part of the lives of Joanna and three of her brothers warred with the pain of continued distance from Abigail, Ben, and her parents; relief at the knowledge of Beth's innocence concerning the thefts couldn't quite eradicate the concern that somewhere in Sommerfeld the thief still existed, casting a spirit of unease over the entire community.

She leaned against the counter and caught one black ribbon that dangled from her cap, twisting the satin strip around her finger. After only a few days, the cap felt as natural as it had in her youth.

Even the dresses—a far cry from the clothing to which she'd become accustomed since Jep's death—offered a sense of coming home. Aware that the articles of clothing were merely exterior trappings, she still experienced a sense of security in the donning of the simple symbols of her restored faith and fellowship.

Deborah turned from the stove, wiping her hands on her apron, and gave a slight start when she spotted Marie. She shook her head, her ribbons waving, before heading into the storeroom.

Marie stifled a giggle. She'd grown accustomed to the double takes. It seemed the community was having a harder time adjusting to her cap and dress than she was.

With the exception of Henry.

Her heart skipped a beat as she remembered his reaction the first time she came around the corner from the kitchen, attired in the caped dress and mesh cap of their sect, to take his order. His eyes had grown wide, filled with tears, and then his face had broken into a smile that sent her heart winging somewhere in the clouds. His joy—so evident—had brought a sting of tears to her eyes.

He had swallowed, brushed his hands over his eyes, and said in a voice thick with emotion, "Lisbeth would be so pleased."

Tears stung again now, remembering. Regret smacked hard. She should have returned sooner. Should have spent time with her aunt. Resolutely, she pushed the regret aside. She couldn't change the past—she could only change the future. And from this day forward, her heart and her will would be in alignment with God. It would be her aunt's legacy, one she would do her utmost to pass on to Beth.

Beth. . . Marie closed her eyes and prayed again for her daughter. The open rebellion pained her heart. *Father, I give her to You,* she said, repeating words that had become almost a mantra in the past few days.

The jingle of the bell that hung over the dining room entry door captured Marie's attention. Customers. She headed to the dining room, snatching up a handful of menus on the way.

The remainder of the day stayed busy. Saturdays always brought in the highway traffic, and Marie had little time to herself throughout the afternoon and evening. As was his custom, Henry ate his supper at the café, then stayed to tally the receipts and balance the books.

Deborah and Trina took care of the kitchen cleanup while Marie placed the orders for next week's supplies and Henry finished the bookwork. They all completed their tasks about the same time, and as he always did, Henry offered to take Marie home. She accepted, but on this evening they spoke little. Marie pondered the odd silence and decided her reticence had to do with the change in her standing in the community.

No longer could she be considered an "outsider." She was now an accepted part of the fellowship. Tomorrow she would attend the meetinghouse for the first time in more than twenty years as an official member. Why that seemed to impact her relationship with Henry, she couldn't be sure. She only knew it felt different—as if a barrier had been removed. But a barrier from what?

Her heart thumped. She knew from what.

She risked a glance in his direction. The muscles along his jaw looked tense, as if he gritted his teeth. It increased the tremble in her tummy. Could Henry be thinking the same thing as she—that her acceptance in the fellowship would mean a community acceptance of their relationship moving beyond friendship?

Jerking her gaze out the window, she tried to eliminate those thoughts. Yet they niggled, increasing her discomfort as they rode silently through the star-laden evening.

When he pulled into the drive behind Marie's car, Henry put his vehicle into PARK and faced her. Her heart pounded at the uncertainty reflected in his eyes.

"Do you—do you need me to drive you tomorrow?"

"No, thank you." Marie swallowed, regret and relief bouncing back and forth and wreaking havoc in her soul. "I'll have my car. Beth was running a slight fever this morning, so I doubt she'll be going anywhere tomorrow."

Concern etched his brow. "Is she all right? Do you need to take her to the hospital?"

Marie's heart welled at his kindness. "No, I'm sure it isn't serious. Just a cold that got out of hand. It's that time of year."

He nodded, his expression thoughtful. "Well, then, you take care of yourself." The dash lights gave his face a rosy glow. At least, she blamed the color on the dash lights. "I'll see you tomorrow, at our meetinghouse."

She couldn't deny the rush of pleasure that came with his words. *Our meetinghouse.* Hers now, too. She gave a quick nod. "Yes. Tomorrow. Thank you for the ride, Henry." Hand on the door handle, she turned back and added, "And for your friendship. It's meant a lot to me."

His lips tipped upward, the left side climbing a fraction of an inch higher than the right. It gave him a boyish appearance that sent Marie's heart fluttering. "You're welcome."

With another nod, she bounced out of the car and hurried inside. After checking on Beth and insisting she drink some more juice, she readied herself for bed. Sleep tarried, her thoughts cluttered with the odd emotions Henry had stirred.

When morning came, his face—the sweet, lopsided smile of last evening—lingered in her memory and teased her as she prepared for service.

Her hands trembled as she slipped her cap into place, and she gave herself a stern command to gain control. She would miss the point of the sermon if she spent her morning daydreaming about

Henry Braun! A quick check on Beth showed her fever had broken during the night, but she had no desire to get up, so Marie gave her a kiss and headed for the car with the promise she would come straight back after service rather than going to Joanna's.

Her thoughts on the service, she almost didn't stop for the brown van that crossed her path on Main Street, heading north. The driver, his black, flat-brimmed hat pulled low, glared in her direction as he rolled past. Marie lifted a hand in silent apology, and his nod acknowledged it.

Heaving a sigh of relief that she hadn't pulled in front of him, she started to cross Main. But then something struck her, and she stared after the van. The driver had appeared to be Mennonite in his dark suit and familiar hat, yet vans were not on the list of approved vehicles. She had reviewed the list only last week, knowing she would need to trade her red car for something more conservative if she remained in Sommerfeld.

A feeling of dread wiggled down Marie's spine. Without another thought, she made a sharp left and followed the van toward the edge of town.

TWENTY-FIVE

Knowing her red car would be conspicuous on the brown landscape, Marie fell back, her heart thudding with fear of being spotted. When the van turned right on the second county road outside of town, her instincts told her to go to the next intersection and double back. She craned her head as she continued north past the intersection, watching. The van increased its speed, kicking up puffs of dust that nearly swallowed the entire vehicle.

Her hands felt damp and her stomach churned with nervousness as she increased her acceleration to reach the next corner. She made a sharp right, holding her breath as her tires slid on the gravel, but she clutched the steering wheel with both hands and kept the car on the road. Looking off to her right, she spotted the swirl of dust that indicated the van's progress.

She smiled. "Thanks, Lord, for the cloud." Speaking aloud offered some comfort, so she continued talking to God as she drove, the van's telltale cloud of dust pointing the route. The cloud disappeared behind the dilapidated barn of a farmstead long since abandoned and surrounded by scrub trees. If it weren't for the bare branches of winter, the farmstead would have been hidden by the barrier of wind-shaped trees.

Marie slowed to a crawl, aware that the same dust that had notified her of the van's progress would alert the driver to her presence. The crunch of the tires on the hard gravel road made her cringe as she let off the gas and coasted to a stop on the east side of the barn.

She found the van parked on the north side, its back doors standing open. The van's radio blared out a rock tune, which told her in no uncertain terms the vehicle was not being driven by a Mennonite, no matter how he was attired.

She sat in her car, leaning forward to peer around the corner, her heart booming so hard she feared it might burst. As she watched, the man came into view, carrying something that appeared to be heavy by the slope of his back and his staggered steps. He pushed the item into the back of the van, brushed his hands together, then turned toward the barn again.

He came to a halt, his head jerking sharply in her direction.

Marie sank against the seat, her mouth dry. She grabbed the gearshift with a trembling hand, prepared to ram the car into DRIVE and speed away if needed. The man rounded the corner of the barn and came directly to her window. Her jaw dropped as he leaned forward and tapped on the glass.

Rolling down the window, Marie gasped. "Mitch!"

He had the audacity to laugh as he snatched off his hat and ran his hand over his close-cropped hair. "Surprised you recognized me in these duds. I'm as stylin' as you, Miz Mennonite Lady." He struck an arrogant pose, his grin wide.

Marie opened the door and stepped out. "What are you doing?"

Mitch's grin faded, replaced by a sneer of displeasure. "Trying to load up and get out of here. I guess I should've waited another half hour. If you were already in that chapel, you wouldn't have seen me." A disparaging snort of laughter burst from his chest. "Guess I got impatient."

He slung an arm around her shoulders and herded her around the corner. "Well, c'mon. Might as well confirm what you're suspecting, huh?"

Marie's feet felt leaden as she moved unwillingly alongside Mitch. When they entered the barn, she nearly collapsed. The hodgepodge of items, stashed haphazardly, provided evidence of Mitch's illicit industry.

She swung to face Mitch, flinging her hand outward to indicate the collection of items. "You took all this?"

He crossed his arms and shrugged. "With a little help."

Marie stumbled forward, grasping the back of the sleeping bench that had been removed from the Dicks' home. Her disappointment was so deep she didn't know if she could form words, but somehow the quavering question came out in a strangled whisper. "Beth was in on this?"

Mitch's laughter rang. "You really think Lissie had anything to do with this? Oh, no, Marie, you raised a real little goody-goody. Your darlin' daughter won't even keep an extra dime from a cashier who's too stupid to make correct change." He moved forward and stood at the other end of the bench, his grin mocking beneath the brim of the hat he'd slapped on at an angle. "No, I just took careful note of all her complaining about the stuff that got away. Then I went to the locations and made sure I got it for her."

Marie shook her head. Even with the evidence in front of her, the unreality made her feel as though she were caught in a bad dream. "So all this time. . .you haven't been in Cheyenne, you've been in Sommerfeld?"

"Well. . ." Mitch scratched his head. "Not Sommerfeld. I've spent most of my time in Salina. I knew Lissie was hanging out in Newton with some old lady, and I didn't want to accidentally run into her and ruin the surprise."

Marie's head spun, trying to absorb the truth. "But you met her in Kansas City Thanksgiving weekend. How did you explain being able to get there so quickly?"

Mitch released a snort. "Do you think I was dumb enough to *drive* there? Lissie's not stupid—she would've figured out I had to be close by to reach her in a few hours by car. No, I drove to Wichita, left my car there, and caught a plane."

He advanced along the back side of the bench until he stood only a few inches from Marie. "I've kept her completely in the dark on this. I knew she'd kick up a fuss, and I didn't want her knowing anything about it until it was all set up in our boutique back home. But boy, it's been tough being this close and not being able to spend time with her." He winked. "Thanks for getting in that fight with her so we could have our weekend alone."

Marie's knees went weak at his secretive grin. "You—you didn't. . . ?" She couldn't bring herself to ask the question.

Mitch laughed. He leaned forward and whispered into her ear, "You mean did we sleep together?"

She jerked back, heat filling her face.

His laughter rang again. "No. Little Lissie won't do that, either." He scowled, surveying the items in the room. "She'd never approve of this, but I had to do it. It was too good to pass up. Plus there was no other way to recover the money I'd borrowed."

"You'd have the money from the sale of the house and café," Marie argued.

Mitch pulled his face into an impatient scowl. "Honestly, Marie, how far would that go in purchasing at auctions? Antiques are becoming harder and harder to come by. There's no way we'd pull a profit." He turned introspective, pinching his chin between his thumb and forefinger. "No, this was necessary."

Turning back to Marie, his scowl deepened. "And now I'm stuck.

Because here I am, caught with the goods, and here you are, ready to talk."

Her breath coming in little gasps, Marie took an uncertain backward step. "W–what do you intend to do?"

He stared at her for a moment, his brows low in a scowl. Then he jerked back, eyes wide, and burst out laughing. "Oh, you think I'm gonna—"

Slapping his knee, he continued to laugh while Marie contemplated making a run for it. But her quivering legs convinced her she wouldn't be able to go ten feet without collapsing.

Mitch shook his head, bringing his laughter under control, and fixed her with a smirking grin. "Gimme a break, Marie. I might've helped myself to some things without paying for them, but I wouldn't resort to murder. Not when I know you're going to keep my secret."

Marie raised her chin and peered at him through narrowed eyes. "What makes you so sure I won't tell?"

Mitch's posture turned calculating, giving Marie a chill. "You wouldn't want to hurt Lissie, would you? She loves me. How would she feel, knowing the man she loves and wants to spend her life with is capable of"—he waggled one brow—"larceny?" Settling his weight on one hip, he crossed his arms and twisted his face into a knowing leer. "And based on our conversations of late, she isn't so sure you really give a rip about her. Just last night, in a weepy little voice, she told me how you chose the church over her. She's all broken up about it. You try to tell her I'm the Sommerfeld thief, and she'll just see it as a ploy to pull her away from me."

Another arrogant shrug made Marie want to slap his smooth-shaven face.

"It's a no-win situation for you, the way I see it."

Marie considered Mitch's comments, and with a sinking heart she realized he was right. Telling Beth that Mitch had been stealing from the citizens of Sommerfeld could drive another wedge between her and her daughter. Even if Beth believed it, it would hurt her deeply. Marie hung her head.

Mitch laughed again and brushed past her, heading toward the open doors. "That's what I thought."

Marie scurried after him, taking in great gulps of the cold air. "But you can't take these things!"

He whirled on her. "Why not?"

"They aren't yours."

"They are now."

"How do you plan to explain to Beth how you got them? She knows they've been stolen. You can't just put them in your shop and expect her not to recognize them. It'll kill her to know you took these things!"

Mitch paused, quirking his lips to the side as his gaze narrowed. "She'll understand. She'll know I did it all for her. Because I love her."

"Do you really believe that?"

He stared at Marie for a long time, the silence heavy between them.

Marie forced out a quavering question. "How could you hurt her that way? Don't you care for my daughter at all?"

Anger flashed in Mitch's eyes. "That's hitting below the belt, Marie."

"You know as well as I do, Beth is the one who stands to lose the most through all this." As Marie pled her case, she prayed for him to realize the extent of distress he would cause if he carried through on his plan to take the items to Cheyenne.

The look on his face changed from arrogance to regret, confirming to Marie that the Lord was answering her prayer.

"The only way to save Beth's feelings is for you to drive away. Leave all this stuff here."

"I don't know," he said weakly. "I've spent a lot of money on motels and food while I've been hanging around here, storing this stuff."

"I'll help you pay it back."

He raised one brow, his expression doubtful. "You'd help a thief?"

"For Beth. . .yes." Marie quivered from head to toe. Wrong or right, she would protect her daughter. She had no idea how she would come up with the money; she only knew she had to do it, for Beth's sake.

"What about all this stuff? How do you plan on returning it?"

"I don't." At his startled look, she said, "The acreage around this barn will be farmed, come spring. Someone will stumble upon these things and make sure they're returned to the rightful owners. I won't have to do anything except wait." Her chest felt tight. Keeping this secret would be deceitful, but she had no other ideas.

His eyes turned into malevolent slits. "You'll do that? Just wait, and not say anything?"

She looked him square in the eyes. "Yes."

"Okay then." He yanked off the hat and sailed it through the open doorway into the barn. Marie heard a light *clup* when it hit the back wall. "Help me put the stuff from the van back in the barn, and I'll head out."

Marie caught his sleeve. "And what about Beth?"

"What about her?" he snarled, jerking his arm free of her grasp.

"You. . .you plan to continue seeing her?"

"Why wouldn't I? We have our plans set, Marie. For the past year, it's all we've talked about—going into business together, combining our lives. That won't change." He glanced at the stolen items and smirked. "After all, what Lissie doesn't know won't hurt her, right?"

Having a boyfriend who would sink to the level of common thievery *would* hurt Beth! But Marie knew nothing she said right now would make a difference. So with a silent prayer that Beth would recognize Mitch's true character before it was too late, she moved woodenly to the end of the van.

Mitch had only had time to load a couple of antiquated washtubs and a beautifully carved mantel clock. When he set the clock on the sleeping bench's seat, Marie felt a pang of remorse. Surely being left in the weather—this barn was far from airtight—would ruin the clock's workings.

"Well, I'm outta here." Mitch clapped his hands together and headed out of the barn.

Marie watched him swing up behind the steering wheel. He slammed the door, offered a mocking salute, and roared away in a squeal of tires and a wild churning of dust.

Coughing, Marie backed into the barn, waving her hands to clear the air. When she could breathe easily again, she moved slowly through the dimly lit barn, examining the items for damage. Although Mitch had stored them without much thought for orderliness—things stood helter-skelter—he must have exercised care when moving them. And everything, from old buckets to the Dicks' sleeping bench, seemed to be there.

Sinking down onto the sleeping bench, she traced the delicate rose petals carved on the face of the mantel clock, her heart heavy. Letting Mitch go hadn't been right, yet she couldn't bear the thought of Beth's broken heart if she learned the truth. Somehow she would have to keep this secret, let someone discover these things on their own. At least, she comforted herself, everything would eventually be returned.

"No real harm will be done." She spoke the words aloud, trying to convince herself.

A gust of wind burst through the open doors, and she shivered. She should shut the doors to at least provide some protection for the items inside. She stood and turned toward the doorway. And froze.

A man lingered in the open doorway. The sun behind him put his face in full shadow, but when he stepped out of the bright shaft of sunlight, recognition dawned. Marie gasped and covered her lips with trembling fingers.

TWENTY-SIX

W hat are you doing here?" Her shielding fingers muffled the words.

Henry took one more step forward, his gaze sweeping the barn. His chest constricted when he recognized the jumbled scattering of stolen contents. Facing Marie again, he said through gritted teeth, "I was about to ask you that question."

Her face seemed pale in the barn's muted light, her blue eyes wide. Slowly, she lowered her hands and wove her fingers together, pressing the heels of her hands to her coat front. "I—I—" She clamped her lips together and fell silent.

Henry felt as though something hot and stifling rose up inside him, and his tone turned hard. "When you didn't show up at the meetinghouse, I got worried. Gil Krehbiel told me he'd seen your car heading north out of town. I was concerned, so I left to look for you. But I never imagined. . ." He broke off, unable to finish the thought.

All this time he'd felt sorry for her, defended her, befriended her. . . and she had been stashing her neighbors' things away, one by one. The evidence shattered his heart. The years of loving her, praying for her, now seemed wasted. How could he have been such a fool?

"Now I know why you refused my ride this morning. So you

could come out here, check on your *stash*." The harshness of his tone surprised him. Had he ever spoken to anyone the way he was now speaking to Marie? He didn't think so. But he'd never felt as betrayed as he did now. He had a right to be harsh.

Raising his chin, he fired off another question. "Did you burglarize another home on the way out, or have you and your daughter decided you've collected enough?" He glared at her, taking in her nutmeg hair combed back under the pristine white cap. What did that cap mean to her? Was it only a ruse to keep the community from pointing fingers of blame in her direction? Hadn't his and Lisbeth's prayers accomplished anything?

Pain rose from his chest, closing off his voice box. Spinning on his heel, he stomped toward the opening.

Marie flew up beside him, her slender fingers wrapping around his forearm. "Henry! Please. . .it isn't what you think."

He stopped, his body stiff, and glowered down at her. Her fingers, tight on his sleeve, burned him, yet he didn't try to shake loose. "Then tell me. Tell me how you came to be sitting here on Sunday morning while the rest of the fellowship—the fellowship you joined—sits in the meetinghouse in worship."

She blinked rapidly, her breath coming in spurts of white fog, but she remained silent.

Lifting his hand, Henry peeled her unresisting, cold fingers from his sleeve and took a step away from her. The depth of her deception created an ache in his heart so crushing he knew it would never completely heal. "It looks like your father was right. You didn't come here for the relationships—you came for whatever you could gain."

The knowledge weighed him down, the truth striking like the slash of a knife, searing his soul with anguish. "You said you'd do anything for your daughter. I guess. . ." His gaze swept across the items once more before returning to her. He forced his words past a knot of agony that refused to be swallowed. "I guess the world is too deeply ingrained in you after all."

He waited for her to speak, to explain, to defend herself. But she stood silent before him, tears trailing down her pale cheeks, her fingers twisting together. When several minutes passed and still no words of explanation spilled forth, he shook his head and stared at the spot of ground between his black boots.

"I'll go to the meetinghouse and let people know where they can find their belongings. You. . ." He tried once more, unsuccessfully, to dislodge the painful lump blocking his throat. "Go back to the house. I won't say anything except that I found the stolen goods."

"Oh, Henry, you can't—"

He held up his hand, his head still low. "I'm not protecting you. I'm protecting Lisbeth's memory. I won't have this shame attached to her in any way." Lifting his head, he met her gaze. "You leave with Beth when the time period of the will's stipulation is over." The words came out in a hoarse whisper, burning in his belly like an ulcer. "I'll stay silent about your actions only if you promise to take your worldliness away from Sommerfeld and never bring it back again."

She gasped, clasping her hands to her throat.

He waited, but she didn't answer. He thundered, "Will you promise?"

Still no words came, but she shrank away from him and gave a quick nod, her eyes glittering with tears.

"Now go to Lisbeth's." He made a deliberately insulting sweep from her toes to her head. "And remove that cap. You make a travesty of it."

A sob broke from Marie, stabbing all the way through Henry's chest. But he remained rooted in place as she dashed past him. He heard her engine start, heard the crunch of gravel, heard the car drive away. He waited until he heard nothing except the beating of his own heart.

Yes, it still beat despite his certainty that Marie's deception had split it in two. With a sigh, he straightened his shoulders, ran his hands down his face, and returned to his vehicle. He had a happy message to deliver to the congregation, and somehow on the drive he must find the ability to smile through his heartbreak.

Marie burst through the back door, stumbled down the hallway to her room, and fell across Lisbeth's bed. How could a heart that ached this badly still manage to pump blood?

The look on Henry's face. The tone of his voice. The emotional withdrawal. Marie hadn't experienced such a depth of pain since the day she learned of Jep's death. On that day she'd lost something precious, too. Something irreplaceable. Something that could never be restored.

Until that moment—that horrible moment when Henry's face reflected both the anger of accusation and the hurt of betrayal—she hadn't realized how important his friendship had become in her brief time back in Sommerfeld. But now she'd lost him as surely as she had lost Jep.

"Oh, God, what should I do?" She wanted to pray, but no words would come. She merely groaned, the sounds of her distress stifled by Lisbeth's pillow. She thought her chest might explode with the force of her sobs, but holding them back was worse.

Her face buried and eyes closed, she gasped in surprise when hands closed on her shoulders. Someone pulled, rolling her to her side, and she opened her eyes to find Beth kneeling on the bed.

"Mom? What happened?"

Her daughter's concerned voice and worried face brought a new rush of tears. Beth reached for her, and Marie found herself being cradled the way she had held Beth when she was little and was afraid or hurt. She clung, sobbing against Beth's shoulder, all of the pain and frustration of the past several weeks seeking release.

Beth rubbed her back, murmuring in her ear. In her daughter's sympathetic embrace Marie finally brought her crying under control. Pulling back, she reached for a box of tissues on the corner of the bedside table and noisily blew her nose. Beth, still on her knees, watched with her brow furrowed.

Marie took in several shuddering breaths and sank against the pillows, closing her eyes. Her head pounded painfully, and her eyes felt raw. She brought up her hand and pulled the cap from her head, dropping it in her lap. When she opened her eyes and glimpsed the rumpled ribbons lying across the skirt of her simple dress, she remembered Henry's command that she remove the cap.

He'd said she made a travesty of it. A mockery. A pretense. He thought she put it on just to fool people into thinking she wanted to restore her fellowship. To trick people while she stole from them. Henry, her dear childhood friend, believed she was capable of such horrendous acts. And if Henry, who should know her, thought this, surely the town. . .

She would have to follow his demand and leave. She had no choice. Tears welled again, and she covered her face with both hands.

Beth tugged her hands down. "Mom, what in the world happened?" Beth's cold distorted her words and made her voice raspy, yet the concern carried through. "Did they kick you out of church or something?"

Marie shook her head violently.

"Then what is it?"

Different explanations paraded through Marie's mind, but none could be shared without divulging secrets. She turned her face away, pressing her trembling chin to her shoulder.

Beth took Marie's hand between hers and squeezed. "Please tell me why you're crying. You're scaring me, Mom."

When Beth's voice broke, Marie's eyes flew wide. The purpose was to avoid hurting Beth, not worry her. When she saw the tears shimmering in her daughter's eyes, she reached out and stroked Beth's cheek.

Finally she forced a few words past the sorrow that tightened her throat. "I'll be okay. It's just. . ." Squeezing her eyes closed, she once more envisioned Henry's accusing glare, heard his command that she remove her cap, that she leave.

She shook her head, determined to dislodge the memories, and the movement loosened her hair from the pins. Locks tumbled against her cheeks, and she smoothed them away from her face, her gaze dropping to her lap. The cap still lay there, and suddenly another picture filled her head—Henry, wearing a smile of approval while tears winked in his eyes when he'd seen her in the cap. Pain stabbed anew, and she groaned out one word: "Henry. . ."

Beth leaped off the bed, her brows forming a sharp V. "Henry hurt you? How? What did he do?"

Marie couldn't speak, regret closing off her voice box.

Beth slowly moved toward the bedroom door, her gaze on Marie. Her expression remained hard, angry. But when she spoke, her voice held nothing but kindness. "Do you want some tea? Some of that spearmint kind from the café that you like so much?"

Tea wouldn't fix anything, but she sensed Beth's need to do something to help. So she nodded wordlessly.

Beth paused in the doorway. "You stay here, Mom. I'll be back with that tea. Just rest, okay?"

Marie nodded, and Beth slipped away. When she heard the *click* of the back door latch, she rolled over, hugged the bear that Beth had crafted from Lisbeth's quilt, and once more allowed the tears to flow. Henry's words continued to echo through her mind.

"Take your worldliness away from Sommerfeld and never bring it back again."

Beth turned the car onto First Street. Her stuffy head throbbed from her cold, but it couldn't compete with the pain in her chest. Seeing Mom that upset. . .it hurt. A lot. And Mom had said Henry was the one who had hurt her.

She clamped her gloved fingers around the cold steering wheel and clenched her jaw until her teeth ached. Who did he think he was, making Mom cry? She drove straight across Main Street rather than turning toward the café. The tea could wait. Her talk with Henry couldn't.

Henry put the plate holding a cold ham sandwich on the table, pulled out a chair, and sat. He sighed deeply, staring at the food. Although breakfast had passed hours ago, he wasn't really hungry. Food wouldn't fill the void he felt.

Loneliness overwhelmed him, as heavy and enveloping as one of the lap robes from his boyhood days. Grandmother had always made their lap robes several layers thick to block the cold wind that rushed through their buggy during winter rides. He'd never liked sitting beneath one—he preferred frigid air to the feeling of suffocation from having to crouch under that heavy square of layered cloth. But right now there was no escape from the smothering layers of loneliness.

At least the citizens of Sommerfeld were rejoicing. He had

managed to deliver the message to the congregation: "The lost has been found." In their excitement, no one had asked more than where to find their belongings. While people bubbled with relief, he had quietly slipped away and come home. Yes, for the citizens of Sommerfeld the lost had been found.

He had used those same words when speaking of Marie to J.D. Koeppler. Now he realized nothing had been found. For him, everything had been lost. He fingered the top slice of bread on the sandwich. Maybe he should just wrap the sandwich in aluminum foil and put it in the refrigerator. The lump in his throat would surely prevent him from swallowing.

Before he could decide what to do, a pounding on his front door intruded. Frowning, Henry rose and crossed to the door. He peeked out the window and drew back sharply in surprise when he recognized Beth Quinn on his porch. When he opened the door, a gust of chilly air rushed in, followed quickly by Beth. She charged past him into the middle of the room, faced him with her hands on her hips, and attacked.

"Mister, you've got a lot of explaining to do."

Her words were colder than the December wind. Henry closed both the storm and interior doors, then stood in the misshapen rectangle of sunlight filtering through the door's window. "Good afternoon, Miss Quinn."

At his droll greeting, her gaze narrowed. "This isn't a social call and you know it. What did you do to my mom?"

Raising his chin, he spoke in a flat tone. "I did nothing to your mother."

Beth shook her head, her uncombed hair wild. "You must have done something. She's more upset than I've ever seen her, and all she said was your name."

Based on the girl's red-rimmed eyes and chapped nose, it appeared

Marie had spoken the truth when she said Beth was ill. Henry gestured to the sofa. "Sit down, please."

"No!" the girl's voice croaked hoarsely. She angled her body toward Henry, her stance reminding him of a rooster preparing to battle for kingship of the chicken yard. "Tell me what you did to make my mother cry!"

The girl's defiance stirred Henry's anger. Marching across the floor, he captured her arm and propelled her to the sofa. With a slight push, he managed to seat Beth on the edge of the cushion. Jamming his thumb against his chest, he said, "I did nothing. If your mother is crying, it's over her own guilty conscience, nothing more."

"Guilty con—" Beth shook her head, her fingertips pressed to her temples. "Mom has nothing to feel guilty about."

Henry snorted. "Is your sense of right and wrong so distorted you can't see the truth? She steals, yet she shouldn't feel guilty?"

"Steals?" Beth's head shot up, her eyes wide. "What in the world are you talking about?"

Henry stared at Beth, unable to believe she didn't know. Was it possible Marie had acted alone? She loved her daughter desperately. Would she have done all this without Beth's knowledge as a way of protecting the girl should she be caught? It was the only logical explanation. For one moment, Henry experienced a twinge of sympathy for Beth. How would she feel when she discovered her mother's love for her had driven her to such extremes?

Sitting on the opposite end of the sofa, he linked his shaking fingers and rested his elbows on his knees. "I'm sorry to be the one to tell you, but your mother is responsible for the thefts that have been taking place in town."

Beth sat bolt upright, her eyebrows crunching downward to create a scowl of disbelief. "No way."

Henry admired the girl's loyalty, but she had to face the truth.

"It's true. This morning, when she should have been in service at the meetinghouse, I found her in the barn of an abandoned farm about three miles outside of town. All the stolen goods were there with her."

Beth shook her head slowly, her breathing erratic. Holding up both hands, she said, "There's got to be some mistake. My mom wouldn't—"

"There's no mistake." Unintentionally, a hard note crept back into Henry's tone. "I saw her with the stolen goods. And she offered no explanation."

"But why would she steal?"

Henry drew a breath through his nose, gentling his voice. "For you."

Beth jerked to her feet, swaying. Henry rose, too, poised in case the girl fainted. But she held her footing. "You're wrong."

"How can you be sure? Isn't that why you came—to gather items for the business you plan to open? When people told you no, your mother found a way for you to have the things after all." Henry's chest constricted as he spoke the words. How it hurt to condemn Marie this way.

"You're wrong." Beth's voice quivered with conviction, tears glimmering in her eyes. "My mother is the most moral person I know." Her chin jutted forward. "Once, when I was in first grade, I took a candy bar from the store without paying for it. One of my friends from school was having a birthday, and I planned to give it to her as a gift. When mom found me wrapping it, she took me back to the store and made me apologize to the manager. I had to give the candy back *and* pay for it. When I told her I had taken it for a present, she said, 'You don't steal for *any* reason; stealing is wrong.' " Crossing her arms, Beth glared at him. "Mom wouldn't steal. I know she wouldn't."

"Maybe not for herself, but—"

"Weren't you listening to me? She wouldn't do it for anyone!" A tear slipped free and rolled down Beth's cheek, and she brushed it away with a vicious swipe of her hand. "I don't know why she was out there. I don't know why she wouldn't explain herself to you. But I do know my mom would not steal. Not even for me. She—"

Beth's voice broke, and she jerked her gaze away, her chin crumpling. She took a few ragged breaths, her shoulders rising and falling with each heaving inhale and exhale. When she was somewhat controlled, she looked at him again. "She taught me that the only thing a person can truly call her own is her character. Mom's character is as pure as anyone's. And since we've been back here, all her talk about God. . ."

Shaking her head, Beth fixed Henry with a look of pained betrayal. "You hurt my mom a lot. I've never heard her cry that hard—never. She wasn't feeling guilty. She was just. . .hurt."

Beth drew herself up, her chin high. "All this time, I thought you were her friend—someone she could depend on. But you're just like all the rest of them." She charged past him and slammed out the door before he could say another word.

Henry stood in the middle of the front room, staring at the storm door, his thoughts racing. His throat convulsed as he envisioned Marie crying harder than she'd ever cried before. Because of him.

Beth's description of Marie's moral character is what he wanted to believe. But the evidence was against her. He had caught her red-handed! And she hadn't offered any explanation.

A need to discover the truth drove Henry out the door to his car. Behind the wheel, he turned the vehicle toward the county road he had traveled that morning. He would search the barn for answers. *Please guide me, Lord.* He would not rest until he found the truth.

TWENTY-SEVEN

Beth slipped back into the house with her pocket full of packets of spearmint tea. She found her mother in the kitchen in front of the wall calendar, her fingers pressed to the square representing December 25. Beth crossed to her quickly and put her arm around her shoulders.

"You okay?"

Mom shrugged, releasing a dismal sigh. "I'll be all right."

After all that crying, Mom's nose was as stuffed up as if she had caught Beth's cold. Beth snatched three tissues from a box on the corner of the counter and pressed them into her mother's hand. "I'll get your tea started."

"Thanks."

Mom remained at the calendar while Beth filled the teakettle and set it on the stove. She lit a burner with a flick of a match, then returned to her mother's side while the water heated. For a few moments she stood silently, her gaze on her mother's profile. Mom simply stood there, her focus on the calendar, almost as if she were frozen in place. Beth touched her shoulder with her fingertips.

"What are you doing?"

Mom glanced at her, her tousled hair seeming incompatible

with the Mennonite dress of hunter green. "Thinking. About Christmas." She heaved a sigh. "We haven't gotten a tree or any-thing, and it's only a week away. Do you want to drive into Newton tomorrow morning and find one? I'm sure they'll be pretty picked over, and we don't have any decorations, but. . ." Mom's eyes swam with tears.

Her chest tight, Beth put her arms around her mother's unresponsive form. "Don't worry about what Henry told you. He's just a jerk. Forget about him."

Mom pulled free and stared at Beth, her eyes wide. "How do you know what Henry said?"

Beth offered a quirky grin and scratched her head. "I went to see him. I gave him what for, too."

Sinking into a chair at the kitchen table, Mom continued to stare, wide-eyed. "Oh, honey."

Beth sat, too, and took her mother's hand. "I know there's no way in the world you took that stuff."

Mom lowered her gaze to their joined hands. Her shoulders lifted and fell in a sigh.

Beth tipped her head. "But what were you doing out at some abandoned farmstead? I thought you went to church, but Henry said you didn't."

Mom turned her gaze to the window that looked over the pasture behind the house.

Her curiosity increasing with each silent second that passed, Beth said, "It is odd that you knew where to find the stolen things. Did somebody tell you where they were hidden?" Her mother re-mained silent. "How did you know to go there?"

Mom's clamped jaw let Beth know she didn't intend to answer. She gave her mother's hand a tug. "Mom?"

A soft whistle from the teakettle intruded. Mom removed her

hand from Beth's grasp and rose. "The water's ready. Do you want a cup, too?"

Beth watched her mother cross the floor on stiff legs and prepare two cups of tea. But when she set one cup in front of her, Beth shook her head and rose, backing away from the table. "Why won't you answer me?"

Mom fitted her hands around the mug and lifted it, the steam swirling up around her face. Fixing Beth with a serious look, she said softly, "Honey, remember when I asked you where you were spending your time, and you told me I should just trust you?"

Beth gave a small nod.

"Well, now I'm telling you the same thing. You have to trust me." She sipped the tea, her gaze returning to the calendar.

Beth, her heart pounding, turned and quietly headed to her bedroom.

Henry stood in the middle of the abandoned barn, his brows pulled low and hands shoved deep into his pockets. The floor was stirred up, showing signs of recent activity. All of the items were gone, claimed by their rightful owners, but if he closed his eyes he could remember the scene he'd discovered earlier that day. Marie, on the Dicks' sleeping bench with her arm around Albrecht's mantel clock. Off to the side, the Flemings' Russian trunk had waited, and behind it, a stack of enameled pans.

Suddenly something struck him, and his eyes flew wide. He gaped, his gaze jerking here and there as other pictures cluttered his mind. The barn had been in disorder—no specific space designated for furniture, another for implements, all just thrown in with no thought given to organization. Even as a child, Marie's school desk had always been neatly arranged, the pencils here, the paper there.

The restaurant was now attended with the same care. Would she have been careless in the storing of valuable antiques? That didn't make sense.

Henry ambled around the interior of the barn. So many people had come and gone this afternoon, the soft dirt floor wore scuffs and gouges. He came to a halt and crouched down, his heart skipping a beat, when he discovered, in one corner, a shoe print that didn't fit with the others. Wafflelike markings left by some sort of athletic shoe.

He swallowed. Like Deborah and Trina, Marie wore athletic sneakers in the café. He put his hand beside the print, measuring it against the length of his fingers, then jerked to his feet and placed his foot alongside it. He nodded, a smile of satisfaction tugging at his lips. A man made that print—a man who wore sneakers rather than the boots of a Mennonite.

Turning a slow circle, Henry's gaze meticulously scanned the floor for more prints matching the one he'd just found. He located two more complete ones and a partial one. His heart pounding harder with each discovery, he continued searching for clues. Along the far wall, in the shadows, he spotted something.

He crossed quickly to the item in question. A black hat, lying upside down in the dirt. At first glance, it appeared Mennonite, but when he picked it up and carried it to the yard, where the sun sent down its light, he discovered it was constructed of tightly woven straw painted black rather than felt. No man from town owned a hat like that.

Which could only mean one thing. At some point, a man wearing athletic shoes and a hat meant to look Mennonite had been in this barn.

An idea took shape in Henry's mind. He tapped his leg with the straw hat, his thoughts racing. From Lisbeth's letter-sharing, he knew

Marie had no man in her life who would assist her in any endeavors, whether wholesome or unwholesome. However, Beth did—and that man had an equal stake in the business she wanted to open.

Maybe. . .just maybe he had forced Marie into helping him. Perhaps he had threatened her into silence.

Hope tried to blossom, but he squelched it. No more speculations. He needed truth. Tossing the hat into the backseat of his car, he headed to town.

With a heavy heart, Marie slipped the dress she'd sewn only last week onto a hanger. She placed the hanger on the closet rod, then lifted the sleeve, admiring the color. She'd chosen deep green because once Henry Braun, with his face glowing pink, had said green brought out the red in her hair. How foolish. She released the sleeve and closed the door with a snap.

Smoothing her hands along the hips of her blue jeans, a rueful chuckle found its way from her chest. Who would have thought that, after such a short time, blue jeans could feel foreign? Yet they did. She reached for the closet door handle, fully intending to put on the dress again, but she snatched her fingers back before they closed around the tarnished brass knob. No longer would she wear the Mennonite trappings.

But I'll still wear God in my heart.

The thought brought a rush of comfort. Moving to the window, she peered outside. Dusk had fallen, painting the surroundings with a rosy hue. Across the street, lights glowed in windows. Families were sitting down to their evening meal of lunch meat, cheese, crackers, and pickles. Always a simple evening meal on Sundays.

Marie's mind replayed other Sundays and their evening meals, some from her childhood, others more recently with Joanna's family.

She shook her head, forcing the memories aside. It was best she start separating herself now. Less than three weeks remained before Beth could sell everything, and then they would return to Cheyenne. To their old life.

No Sommerfeld, no café, no Joanna and Deborah and Trina, no simple meetinghouse, no Henry.

A lump filled her throat. If she didn't think of something else, she would cry again, and that would only upset her daughter more. Worn out from her cold and her excursion to Henry's, Beth now slept. Determined not to wake her with another noisy crying jag, Marie searched her mind for something to do. Her gaze fell on Aunt Lisbeth's small desk, and an idea struck. A shopping list for Christmas items would surely occupy her mind and cheer her at the same time. If it were going to be the last one in Sommerfeld, she wanted it to be special.

Crossing to the desk, she pulled open a drawer and searched for paper. A tablet of white lined paper came into view, along with a half-empty box of envelopes. She lifted both out and sat at the desk, placing the items in front of her. Then she pulled out the center drawer and withdrew a pen. She gave the pen's push button a *click* and flipped back the cover on the tablet.

Her heart leaped into her throat. Writing went halfway down the page, obviously penned by Aunt Lisbeth. The first line read, *"My dearest Marie. . ."*

Beth rolled over, and the cot let out a now-familiar squeak of complaint, bringing her awake. Yawning, she slipped her hands outside the covers, stretched, then balled her hands into fists and rubbed her eyes. Opening her eyes, she found the room blanketed in darkness. Apparently the sun had slipped behind the horizon while she napped. What time was it?

By squinting at her wind-up alarm clock—the one she'd purchased for her stint in this house with no electricity—she managed to make out the position of the black hands. Seven thirty. Her stomach growled, confirming the hour. But she didn't get up.

Instead, she slipped her hands beneath her head and stared at the white-painted plaster ceiling, which appeared gray in the absence of light. She wiggled, trying to reposition herself on the lumpy mattress provided by Henry Braun.

Henry Braun. . .

A picture appeared in her mind of his face when she'd stormed into his house that afternoon. She sure had surprised him. But that was only fair—he'd surprised her, too, by turning on Mom that way. After everything he'd done to help them out, too. It made her mad all over again to think about it. And confused.

Rolling to her side, she pulled the covers to her chin and stared across the room. At least she had accomplished one thing. Mom wouldn't be staying in Sommerfeld now. They'd go back to Cheyenne together after Christmas. Somehow the thought didn't cheer her the way it once would have.

Tears stung Beth's eyes as she realized her mother had seemed happier here than she ever had in Cheyenne. Mom had never been one to wallow in despair or complain—that wasn't her way—but here, in Sommerfeld, she exuded an element of deep contentment. Despite the conflict with her parents, despite the lack of enthusiastic welcome by the community, her mother had found something here that gave her joy.

How had Mom identified it? She pressed her memory, straining to recall the exact words. They came in a rush—*"a fellowship with God."* With the remembrance came a splash of regret. She and Mom had always shared everything. Big things like an apartment and a car. Little things like toothpaste and shoes and banana splits. But this God fellowship thing belonged to Mom alone.

Beth felt left out.

When they returned to Cheyenne, God would surely go, too. She recalled her Sunday school teacher saying God was everywhere. He didn't just live in Sommerfeld. Beth swallowed, her throat aching. Would she feel left out even in Cheyenne, when Mom took her fellowship with God home to Wyoming?

Then there was this thing about Mom being in a barn with a bunch of stolen goods. Why wouldn't she tell Beth what she was doing there? Sure, Beth had kept a few secrets since they'd come to Sommerfeld—she'd had to if she didn't want to ruin a good surprise. There was still one more she was saving for Christmas. But Mom had always been open with her. Holding back something as important as a reason that could exonerate her didn't make sense.

Tossing aside the covers, Beth sat up. She groped under the edge of the cot for the fuzzy socks she had discarded before climbing under the quilt—the wood floors were cold in spite of the blast of warm air from the iron heater grates. Once her feet were covered, she headed for the hallway. She needed her mother. And some reassurance.

TWENTY-EIGHT

"M om?"

Marie lifted her gaze from the unfinished letter at the sound of her daughter's voice.

"You're crying again."

She touched her face, startled to find tears. Wiping them away, she offered a tremulous smile. "Don't worry. I'm okay. Look." She held the tablet toward Beth. "I found a letter from Aunt Lisbeth."

Beth squatted next to the chair and reached for the pad. She read the brief passage quickly, then looked at her mother again. "It's not finished."

"No." Marie took back the pad, her gaze on Lisbeth's neat, slating script. "I'm not sure what interrupted her, but I'm sure she intended to finish it and get it mailed." Hugging the tablet to her chest, she closed her eyes for a moment. "Aunt Lisbeth never stopped loving me, Beth. Never. We didn't have to be together for our relationship to continue. And that gives me such comfort right now."

"Why?"

Beth's gently worded query brought Marie's eyes open. She looked at her daughter and forced words past a knot in her throat. "Because soon I'll be away again—away from Joanna and Art and

265

the others—but somehow we'll stay in touch. Through letters, just like Aunt Lisbeth and me."

Beth took the pad and tapped one paragraph on the page. "This must have been written shortly after my graduation. She thanks you for a picture from my big day."

Marie laughed softly, looping a strand of hair behind Beth's ear. "I included her in all your big days—your first tooth, first haircut, first day of school, first ballet recital." Suddenly something struck her. With a frown, she began opening and closing desk drawers.

"What are you doing?" Beth stepped back, clearing the way for Marie to open the drawers on the left side of the desk.

"Through the years I sent Aunt Lisbeth enough photographs to fill a small album. It just occurred to me I haven't seen them anywhere." Looking up at Beth, her heart fluttered. "She wouldn't have discarded them. . .would she?"

Beth shook her head adamantly. "They've got to be in a box somewhere. Want me to look?"

Marie closed the last drawer and slumped back in the chair "No. That's okay. When we get things ready for the auction"—pain stabbed with the comment—"we'll probably come across them. Who knows where they might be right now?"

Beth hung her head. "Mom, about the auction. . ."

Her daughter's shamefaced pose brought Marie to her feet. "Yes?"

Meeting her mother's gaze, Beth licked her lips. "I–I've sounded really selfish about all the stuff in this house. I wanted to make as much money as I could so I would be able to do something nice for you. You've always put me first, and just once I wanted to put you first and pay you back."

Relief washed over Marie as the motivation for what she had perceived as money-grubbing became clear. Her heart swelled with love. "Oh, honey."

"Now I think maybe I could pay you back the best by letting you keep the stuff from your aunt's house. It means a lot to you, I know. So maybe we should just forget the auction."

How much her daughter had matured over the past weeks. Marie embraced Beth, giving her a kiss on the cheek. "That is the best gift you've ever given me."

Pulling away, Beth offered a wobbly grin. "Even better than that ceramic frog I made in third grade?"

Laughing, Marie hugged Beth again. "I loved your purple, six-legged frog! I still have it tucked in the sock drawer of my dresser back home."

At the word *home*, both women froze for a moment.

Looking into her mother's eyes, Beth posed a quiet question. "Mom, do you want Sommerfeld to be your home now?"

To Marie's chagrin, tears stung her eyes. A deep part of her longed to remain in the place of her birth, but Mitch's actions—and Henry's accusations—had sealed her fate. What she wanted didn't matter anymore. She couldn't stay. Not now.

Blinking, she cleared the tears from her eyes and forced her lips into a smile. In the brightest tone she could muster, she said, "This was to be a three-month adventure, right? And it's nearing its end, so. . ." She flipped her wrists outward in a glib gesture she didn't feel.

Beth crossed her arms and quirked a brow. "You aren't fooling anybody."

"Well, I—" Before she could complete the thought, a knock interrupted. She glanced at her wristwatch and frowned. "Visitors at this hour? I hope nothing's wrong." She hurried down the hallway to the front room with her daughter on her heels and pulled the curtains aside. Seeing Henry and Joanna standing on the porch, she glanced at Beth, who shrugged and said in a hard tone, "Might as well let 'em in. Knowing both of them, they'll stand out there in the cold until you do."

Henry allowed Joanna to precede him through Marie's front door. In the past, he had always entered this house through the utility porch in the back. Coming in the front door gave the visit a feeling of formality that left him vaguely unsettled. Yet he knew, given the topic that must be covered, formality would be a good shield for the emotions that churned in his belly.

Marie closed the door behind them, then stood, hugging herself, her wide-eyed gaze flitting from her sister to him. His heart plummeted when he scanned her attire. Blue jeans and a sweater. Standing there with Beth, who wore similar clothes, she seemed oceans away from him again.

Joanna stepped forward and embraced her sister, her white prayer cap and neatly pinned hair incongruous to Marie's tousled, uncovered locks. Henry looked away, turning back only when Joanna touched his arm.

"Let's all sit down."

Henry appreciated her taking charge. His tongue felt thick, incapable of functioning. Fortunately he'd had full use of it when he went to Hugo and Joanna's and told them what he'd found at the barn. The need to confide in someone, to seek someone's advice, had overwhelmed him as he'd driven back to town earlier that evening. Not having Lisbeth to turn to, he chose the one who had most fully embraced Marie's return. In Joanna he'd found his advocate, and her presence now gave him confidence that, together, they would get to the bottom of things.

Beth inched toward the double doors, her narrowed gaze boring a hole through Henry. "If you don't need me, I'm going to my room."

She pointed to her red nose. "Not feeling too good, you know?"

Marie crossed to her quickly and gave her a kiss on the cheek, whispering something to which Beth responded with a nod, before the girl disappeared around the corner. The evidence of Marie's deep care for her daughter twisted Henry's heart. It seemed to point, once again, to the extremes she would go to for Beth.

Marie sat in Lisbeth's well-worn rocking chair, and both he and Joanna took seats on the sofa—Joanna at the end closest to Marie, he at the farthest end. Joanna stretched out her hand toward her sister, and Marie reached back.

"Marie, Henry made sure everyone knew where to find their belongings today. So all of the goods are back with their owners."

Henry watched Marie closely. Her shoulders slumped slightly with the news, but she didn't seem dismayed.

Joanna continued. "When he told us at the meetinghouse they'd been found, he didn't tell us how he came to find them." She glanced at Henry, then turned back to Marie. "He only told everything to Hugo and me. The town doesn't know you were with the things when he found them."

Marie's face drained of color, and her gaze shifted in his direction. "Thank you." The words came out in a wavering whisper. "You kept your word."

He managed a nod. Yes, he had told her he wouldn't tell—to protect Lisbeth's memory. Yet he knew, deep down, he'd also done it to protect her.

"But Marie," Joanna went on, capturing Marie's attention, "we need to understand. You rejoined the church. You told us you wanted to stay. You—you weren't being dishonest with us, were you?"

Marie's pale face mottled with red. Henry's heart pounded. Could that rush of high color indicate a guilty conscience? His body angled forward slightly, leaning toward Marie, inwardly praying for her to share an explanation that would set everyone's mind and hearts at ease.

"I wasn't being dishonest." Marie's voice was tight, as if she were being strangled. "I truly wanted to regain fellowship and remain in Sommerfeld. But. . ." She drew in a deep breath and released it slowly, the splashes of pink fading from her cheeks with the dispelling of breath. "But apparently it isn't meant to be."

Joanna turned toward Henry. Her brows were low, her lips pursed. "Henry, I'm thirsty. Would you get me a glass of water, please?"

Henry nodded, understanding the silent message. She wanted time alone with Marie. He welcomed the distraction and the separation. Marie's last statement had been like putting a knife through his heart. He headed for the kitchen with his head low, his heart aching.

The moment Henry disappeared through the dining room, Marie felt Joanna give her hand a sharp jerk. "All right, Marie," her sister whispered, "we're alone now, and I want the truth."

Marie reared back, sending the rocker into motion. She stared at Joanna, surprised by the vehemence in her tone. "I—I—"

"And no avoidance! I don't for one minute believe you had anything to do with the thefts." Tears glittered in Joanna's blue eyes, pain evident. "So you must be protecting somebody. It was Beth, wasn't it? Beth and her boyfriend."

Marie yanked her hand free and clasped it against her ribcage. She felt her own heartbeat against her hand. "No!" She, too, kept her voice low, but she matched Joanna in passion. "My daughter is not a thief!"

Joanna's forehead crinkled. "Then who, Marie? Henry found footprints out there, man-sized, that didn't match the boots our men wear."

Even now, the reference to "our" made Marie's heart pine with longing to be a part of that "our."

"He suspects, as do I, that Beth's boyfriend is involved."

Marie looked away, certain her face would give away the truth.

Joanna leaned forward, capturing her hand again. "Are our suspicions true?"

Marie's chin quivered with the effort of holding back her secret.

With a long sigh, Joanna released Marie's hand and slumped back on the sofa. "Why are you protecting him?" Her voice reflected confusion. Suddenly she sat up straight again, her eyes wide. "Did he threaten you?"

Shaking her head, Marie faced her sister. "No. Not really. He just. . ."

Joanna leaned forward, bringing her face near. "What, Marie? Tell me."

Her body trembled. Marie drew up her knees and wrapped her arms around them. Yet her voice quavered when she replied. "He just made me realize how terribly hurt Beth would be if she knew the truth about him. She loves him. . .and he's a thief."

Joanna sat in silence, her gaze never wavering from Marie's, her brow knitted and her lower lip pulled between her teeth. She nodded, the movement so slight Marie almost sensed it rather than saw it. "I see."

Marie thumped her feet on the floor and tipped the rocker forward, grasping both of Joanna's wrists. "I can't tell, Joanna—not without hurting Beth. And I can't stay here with Henry thinking—" A dry sob burst out, and she lowered her head, regret weighing her down. "If only it could be different."

Joanna raised her hands to cup Marie's head and draw it to her shoulder. Marie sat within the circle of her sister's arms, absorbing the love and understanding offered through the wordless embrace.

After long moments, Joanna spoke softly, her voice hoarse. "So you'll let the one who loves you think you are capable of being involved in something morally and legally wrong in order to protect Beth's feelings?"

Slowly Marie removed herself from Joanna's hold. Settled against the back of Lisbeth's wood rocker, she answered, "Yes."

"I think you're a fool."

Marie nodded. "You're right. I'm a fool for thinking I could come back. I would be miserable, trying to live here and attend the meetinghouse regularly with Dad feeling like he does. Maybe this is God's way of sending me back to Cheyenne. That's where I belong."

Joanna's eyes flooded with tears. "No, Marie. *Here* is where you belong. I've seen you blossom here. We all have—Henry and Hugo and Kyra and Deborah. How can you even think of leaving?"

"How can I even think of staying?" Marie countered. She released a sorrowful sigh. "No, God brought me back for a reason—to rediscover my relationship with Him. I've done that, and I know I'll never let Him go again. So. . .at the end of Beth's and my three-month time period, I'll move on."

Her sister stood, glaring down at her. "You're just as stubborn as our father. Well, I'm not going to argue with you. But I am going to pray very hard, between now and the end of the month, that God brings you to your senses." Moving to the doorway leading to the dining room, she called, "Henry, I'm ready to go."

Henry returned and followed Joanna to the front door. Marie remained in the rocking chair as he opened the door. Poised in the doorway, Joanna looked back.

"We're all meeting at Mom and Dad's after service Christmas Day for dinner and presents. This is your official invitation. You and Beth are my gift to me this year, so I expect you to be there." She stepped outside. Henry followed, pulling the door closed behind him.

TWENTY-NINE

Through the wall, Beth heard the front door latch and knew the guests had left. She flumped back on the creaky cot, her thoughts racing. No doubt Joanna and Henry had come to harass Mom about the stuff in the barn. She hoped her mother hadn't told them anything. Not because she didn't want the truth to come out, but because she wanted Mom to tell her before she told anyone else.

Her relationship with her mom had gone through some rough water lately, but once they were back in Cheyenne, things would settle down again. Maybe her business wouldn't start off with the bang she'd imagined, but it would still start. Things would be okay. Especially with the new skills she'd picked up from Mrs. Davidson over in Newton.

A smile formed as she thought about the surprise she had waiting for Mom, thanks to Mrs. Davidson's tutelage. Slipping from the cot, she tiptoed out the door and down the hallway. She peeked into the front room and spotted her mother in the rocking chair, head back and eyes closed. Satisfied she wouldn't be caught, she returned to her room and opened the closet door.

On the floor, wrapped in old towels, waited the gifts she had made of stained glass. For Mom, a two-foot square of bright tulips, with the sun beaming down from the upper left-hand corner. She had drawn the pattern and chosen the colors herself. Pride welled as she remembered Mrs. Davidson's words of praise for her accomplishment. Beth's heart lifted, imagining her mother's pleasure. Mom loved flowers and bright colors.

Several smaller pieces also waited, all made of the same design— a frosted-center cross with brightly colored beams shooting from behind it. She had fashioned each in a different color scheme and had enough for Joanna, Kyra, Trina, and Deborah, plus one more. She had toyed with the idea of giving the last one to Henry, to thank him for his help. But given his recent actions, she was not about to follow through with that idea.

Folding the towel back around the colorful window, Beth wondered if this type of craft would sell well in the city. Mitch would have an opinion on that. She slid her mother's gift back in the closet, closed the door, and picked up her cell phone, eager to discuss the possibility with him.

The phone rang four times before Mitch's voice answered. The line was staticky, with wind noise in the background. He sounded harried.

"Hey, what're you doing?" Beth greeted.

"Driving—snowsto—"

The connection broke in places, and Beth frowned, struggling to comprehend. "If there's a snowstorm, don't go out."

"—ing home. I—to get there—ly."

Beth sat on the edge of the cot, pressing the phone to her ear while she ran her free hand through her hair. "Can you hear me okay?"

"—es."

"Then listen, okay? I need to talk to you about making stained-glass windows to sell in our boutique. When you're not driving, call me back, okay?"

Between breakups, she heard his laugh. "Our—still on?"

"Our boutique?"

"Yeah."

"Of course it's still on. Why wouldn't it be?"

"—eason. Th—mom for me, huh?"

Dread settled in Beth's stomach. "What about Mom?"

The line disconnected. Beth sat, stunned, thoughts whirling through her mind like the snowflakes she envisioned swirling by Mitch's car. Mitch wanted her to tell Mom something. . .thank you, maybe. . .but why? When had he been in communication with Mom?

A sickening picture began to take shape. She shook her head, an attempt to keep it from forming. Despite her efforts, little bits and pieces of conversations with Mitch from the past several weeks whizzed back, dropping into place like puzzle pieces.

"So tell me, Lissie, where did you see that mantel clock?"

"Don't worry, baby—we'll get your antiques."

"They've formed a community watch, huh? All the time? Well, yeah, of course not during church."

And that weekend in Kansas City. At one point he'd chuckled for no reason she could discern. When she questioned him, he'd said, "Oh, I was just thinking how quiet it is in good ol' Sommerfeld right now." At the time she'd thought he was unfavorably comparing the tiny town to the bustling city. But now the choice of words—it *is* rather than *must be*—haunted her.

She leaped up, her heart pounding. Charging out of the bedroom, she sobbed out one word: "Mom!"

On Christmas morning Beth joined Marie in attending the special service at the meetinghouse. Her daughter looked so nice in a simply styled blue skirt, white blouse, and loose-knit blue sweater, with her long hair pulled into a sleek bun on the back of her head. Not quite as conservative as Marie's hunter green dress and white cap, but it thrilled Marie that Beth had selected the outfit herself, giving careful thought to what would be appropriate for the service.

The past week had been a time of talking, crying, and praying together that had bonded mother and daughter more firmly than ever before. Just last night, seated with Beth at the little table in the corner of Lisbeth's kitchen, with the glow of the lantern illuminating the pages of Lisbeth's Bible, Marie had guided her daughter through the steps necessary to become a child of God. When Beth prayed the sinner's prayer, inviting Jesus Christ to enter her heart, Marie's heart soared with a joy beyond description.

After Beth went to bed, Marie wrote a note to her daughter on the inside cover of Lisbeth's Bible, wrapped it in shiny paper of the brightest red, and placed it under their Christmas tree with "To Beth, from Great-Aunt Lisbeth" on the tag. She knew Lisbeth would approve.

Gratitude filled Marie so completely, she felt she would burst from happiness. With God in her heart and Beth at her side, she could face her parents today with a sense of peace.

During the closing hymn, she stood between Beth and Joanna, holding their hands, linking her past with her future. With God at the center, everything would be fine. Of that, Marie was certain.

When the service concluded, she and Beth exchanged wishes of Merry Christmas with worshipers as they made their way out of the meetinghouse. Her gaze collided with Henry's, and it lingered, her heart straining toward him. Although they had seen each other in the café every day since his visit last Sunday, they hadn't spoken.

She longed to bridge the gap between them, especially now that her leave-taking was just around the corner, but a part of her feared reaching out to him. If what she suspected was confirmed—that she had grown to love Henry in the past weeks—then leaving him would be impossible. The gap must remain, no matter how painful.

She allowed her lips to form the words, "Merry Christmas," waited for his answering nod, then forced her gaze away. Taking Beth's arm, she said, "Let's get to your grandparents' place, shall we?"

Neither she nor Beth spoke on the short drive to Marie's childhood home. Turning into the lane that led to the house, she broke into a cold sweat. How she wished this homecoming was like the story in the Bible about the prodigal son, with the father watching, waiting, arms outstretched, an embrace and celebration at the end. Her gaze swept the house, the yards, the outbuildings. With a chuckle, she observed, "It all looks so much smaller."

Beth sent her a sympathetic look. "You know, Mom, we could just go back to Lisbeth's and have a quiet day together."

Marie considered Beth's suggestion but shook her head. "As tempting as that sounds, this may be my last Christmas in Sommerfeld. I really want to be with my family—my whole family—and I want all of them to at least meet you, see what a beautiful daughter I've raised."

"Aw, Mom." Although her tone sounded embarrassed, Beth grinned. She looked out the window and frowned. "Looks like we're the only ones here so far."

"They'll be here." Marie got a sudden idea. "While we're alone, let's snoop."

"Snoop?" Beth released an amused snort. "Seriously?"

"Seriously. Come on." Marie swung her door open and stepped out of the car. A light covering of snow dusted the ground, but the sky was clear and bright, and no wind whipped from the north. "I'll show you around—let you see my childhood playing spots."

Beth grinned. "Okay."

Knowing time was short, Marie chose her favorite location first—Dad's woodworking shop. Linking arms with Beth, she guided her to the cement-block building behind the barn. "We kids were never supposed to play in here because some of Dad's tools could be dangerous. But I never touched the tools, and he knew it, so he let me go in. It made me feel special."

Releasing Beth, she turned the knob on the heavy wood door and swung it open. The hinges groaned in the cold, and a familiar smell greeted her, sending her back a quarter of a century. Marie closed her eyes and inhaled, allowing the odors of cut wood, leather, paint, and turpentine to fill her senses, igniting memory after memory.

"Mom?" Beth's startled tone brought Marie's eyes open. She turned and spotted Beth at one end of the long, homemade workbench that stretched along the entire north wall of the sturdy building. "You've got to see this."

Marie crossed to Beth, and her jaw dropped when she realized what her daughter had discovered. Pictures—dozens of them—tacked to a board that had obviously been mounted for the sole purpose of displaying them. Marie touched the crisp, white pine board. It had been recently erected.

Stunned, she turned her attention to the array of pictures, recognizing every one. The photos she had sent to Aunt Lisbeth, arranged chronologically, starting with the snapshot of her and Jep on the steps of the courthouse where they had recited their vows and ending with the day of Beth's graduation from junior college. Marie's life laid out in silent snapshots.

She stared, unbelieving, her heart thudding out a message. *Dad, Dad, Dad.*

"Why would he have done this?" Beth asked.

The groan of the door intruded, stopping Marie from answering. She turned to face the entry, and her heart doubled its tempo. Her father stood framed in the doorway, his face unsmiling.

"Dad." Marie took a step away from the workbench, her fingers linked together. "I—I just wanted Beth to see the places where I spent time as a child. I didn't—"

He moved over the threshold into the building, closing the door behind him. "I always trusted you not to touch things in here." His voice rumbled, low and stern, yet Marie sensed no anger in the tone.

She gave a quick nod. "And I haven't touched anything today, either. I didn't abuse your trust."

His gaze shifted from her face to the wall behind her, and his chin quivered.

Marie's heart melted. "Dad. . .you took Aunt Lisbeth's photos?" She made certain she spoke softly, gently, with no hint of recrimination.

"I did."

"Is it because. . . ?" She held her breath, waiting, hoping, praying. *Please, Lord. Please.*

Tears glittered in her father's blue eyes. His face crumpled, and he lowered his head. His gaze aimed downward, he rasped, "I missed so much. I needed to—to somehow know you again."

Marie heard Beth's sudden intake of breath, felt her daughter's hand on her arm. The desire for reconciliation was so strong it became a flavor on her tongue. Giving Beth's hand a quick squeeze, she stepped forward, making the first move.

"Dad, I'm right here. And I want to know you again, too." Her breath came in tiny spurts. "Can we let go of the past and start over?"

He stood so stiff and unresponsive, Marie wasn't sure he'd heard her quiet words. Her heart pounding with hope, she waited.

Slowly her father's gray head lifted, his tear-filled eyes meeting hers. His hands quivered, then inched upward, reaching, the hands open and inviting.

With a little cry of joy, Marie ran across the concrete floor and flung herself against her father's chest. His arms came around her; his head tipped to rest on her white cap. Warm tears soaked the top of her head.

His "Please forgive me" and her "Oh, Daddy, I'm sorry" spilled out at the same time. They broke away for a moment to look into each other's faces. They both released a brief laugh before embracing once again.

A second pair of arms came from behind Marie—Beth, joining the hug. Marie felt one of her father's arms slip away, and she didn't have to look to know it now enveloped her daughter.

Marie closed her eyes, memorizing the moment. The smells of the shop blended with the smell of snow trapped in her father's suit coat. Beneath her cheek, she heard the thud of her father's heartbeat; on her head, she felt the pressure of his jaw. The sting of cold against her bare legs juxtaposed the warmth of the embrace, becoming a symbol of the sting of resentment being replaced by the warmth of acceptance. Silently she praised her Father God for allowing her this precious time of communion, of connection, of bygones becoming bygones, of hurts melting away.

They stood in a tight circle, with Marie at its center, for long moments until finally, reluctantly, her father's hold loosened and he stepped away. Looking down at her, he said, "I can't let you go again without saying. . .I love you, Marie. You–you're still my girl." He grazed her jaw with thick, callused fingers. She clasped his wrist, pressing the broad hand to her cheek.

His fingers quivered. "Your mother has a dinner waiting. . .and presents." His gaze turned to include Beth. "For both of you."

Beth smiled. "Then let's go in, Grandpa."

THIRTY

Marie allowed Beth to drive back to Aunt Lisbeth's from the farm. A light snow fell, the tiny flakes taking on the appearance of tossed glitter in the headlights as they drove along the silent country road toward town. She leaned against the headrest, tired yet blissfully happy. Her prayers had been answered—her family's full acceptance was the best present she could have received this Christmas.

The gift Beth had given her was a close second, however. Although she had already thanked her, she took advantage of their time alone to express her appreciation again. "Honey, I love the stained-glass window you made for me. I'm so impressed with the arrangement of colors—it almost looks as if the tulips are in the foreground and the sun far behind. I've never seen stained glass with the illusion of depth before."

Beth shot her a quick, quavery smile. "Mrs. Davidson said I had a rare talent—that creating three-dimensional stained-glass art is difficult."

Marie's eyebrows shot high. "Honey! Perhaps you've discovered a gift."

"Could be." Beth turned her attention back to the road, but Marie could tell by the way she nibbled her lower lip that her thoughts drifted beyond the dirt pathway.

Marie sighed, settling back in the seat again, reflecting on the teary good-bye at the farmstead just a few minutes ago. Leaving town would be difficult, but miles could be traveled both ways. She would be back, frequently. The next twenty years would be different from the past twenty.

The headlights scanned the front of Aunt Lisbeth's bungalow as they turned into the drive. Beth slowed, leaning forward over the steering wheel to squint out the windshield. "Mom, is there something on the porch?"

Marie looked. It appeared a square package had been wedged between the front door and storm door. "I'll go see what it is." She hopped out and stepped under a shimmer of moonlight that created a bluish shadow of her form as she crossed the snowy yard. When she lifted the box, her fingers slipped, surprised by the heft. She hugged it to her chest and returned to the vehicle.

Inside the car, she shook snowflakes from her hair and read the printing on the brown paper wrapping. "To Marie, from Henry." She stared at it, unmoving, wondering what it could be.

Beth nudged her. "Well, open it!"

Her stomach jumping nervously, Marie did as her daughter bid. Under the brown paper, she discovered an age-yellowed box. She opened the box and released a gasp.

"What is it?" Beth asked.

Marie slapped the lid back in place. "Honey, I—I need to go see Henry."

"Now?"

The girl's incredulous tone made Marie smile. "I'm afraid so. Do you mind being alone for a little while?"

Beth's slack-jawed expression changed to one of understanding. "I'll be fine, Mom." She put the car in PARK and slipped out the door.

Leaning back inside, her lips formed a quavering smile. "Good luck."

Marie's face filled with heat as Beth laughed and closed the door. Sliding behind the wheel, she reversed the vehicle and headed to Henry's. She used one hand to drive; the other caressed the box on the seat beside her.

Henry ran his hands over his face. Fingers pulling at the skin along his jaw, he looked out the window. Again. Then glanced at the clock. Again. Grimacing, he turned away from the snow-laden night and released a groan.

It had been a foolhardy thing to do, leaving that package. It probably embarrassed her. Or scared her. Or both. While it had seemed a good idea at the time, he now realized it could lead to more heartache and regret. What had he been thinking?

Well, he'd just have to go get it. Maybe she hadn't returned from her folks' place yet. He could fix this if he could get there before she did. He hurried across the room to the coatrack in the corner, but as he raised his arm to lift down his coat, he spotted headlights. He froze, watching, as the car turned into his driveway.

Marie.

Too late.

His legs turned to jelly, but he managed to move the few feet needed to reach the door and open it just as she stepped onto the porch. Snowflakes graced her head and shoulders, glistening under the light of the moon. Her blue-eyed gaze met his, and although she didn't smile, neither did she frown. His gaze dropped to her hands. She held the box. He swallowed.

"May I come in?"

Her tremulous voice spurred him to action. Jerking out of the way, he said, "Yes. Please." With an awkward bob of his head, he gestured to the box. "You found the gift."

She stood hesitantly in the doorway, her coat buttoned to her throat, her sweet face lifted to him. "Thank you, Henry. It means so much to me to have it."

He nodded, unable to find his voice.

"You've kept it all this time?"

"I couldn't take it back. I wrote in it."

At her crestfallen expression, he could have kicked himself. Why had he blurted out something like that? Shaking his head, he took hold of her arm. "Come in, please, and sit." He guided her to the sofa and waited until she perched on the center cushion. He sat on an overstuffed chair at the end of the sofa, clasped his hands together, and pressed them to his lap.

"I wouldn't have taken it back anyway." What a relief to see her expression change. Her blue eyes flickered in his direction. He found the courage to finish what he wanted to say. "It was meant for you. You should have it."

She nodded. Her graceful hands lifted the lid on the box and set it aside. With her chin still low, she glanced at him. "May I read what you wrote inside?"

She hadn't done that yet? His neck and ears grew hot, but he nodded.

He sat in silence while she peeled back the cover of the white Bible and read it out loud. It only took a few seconds—he'd never been a man of many words. But he sensed by the way she traced her finger over the writing that she found pleasure in the brief message. She faced him again, and he swallowed.

"Henry, thank you for this Bible. That's why I came here tonight—to say thank you."

He nodded stupidly. Of course that's why she'd come. What other reason would there be?

"But may I also tell you thank you for so many other things?"

"Like what?"

She tipped her head back a moment, as if gathering her thoughts, then met his gaze once more. Tenderness showed in her expression. He tightened the grip of his fingers, the tips biting into his own knuckles.

"Thank you for being such a wonderful friend to Aunt Lisbeth. She loved you like a son. You were very special to her."

As she was to him. He nodded.

"Thank you for your prayers over the years. Most people would have given up, but you didn't. And now I am reaping the benefit of your steadfast devotion."

His second nod was jerky, his neck muscles so stiff he felt he had no control of them.

"And thank you for your efforts to reunite me with my family. They were successful. This was the best Christmas I've ever had. I'm a part of the family again, welcomed by every member."

"*Every* member?" his voice croaked out hoarsely.

Her smile told him she understood the simple question. "Even Dad. We made our peace. It was precious."

Henry blew out a breath of relief. "I'm so glad."

"Me, too."

They sat in an uncertain silence, with their gazes aimed at their own laps. Marie seemed to examine the Bible she continued to hold; Henry begrudged the grease he could never completely remove from beneath his fingernails.

After a long while, Marie set the Bible aside and looked at him again. "Henry, about last week. When you found me—"

He held up his hand, meeting her gaze squarely. "It doesn't matter."

"It *does* matter. It must. You haven't spoken to me all week."

Henry ducked his head. He hadn't known what to say to her. If she were innocent, his accusations were inexcusable. If she were guilty, he couldn't reconcile himself with it.

"I need to tell you the truth, and I hope you'll forgive me for being less than honest with you when you found me."

Raising his head, Henry said, "I'm listening."

Briefly, Marie explained how she had come to be in the barn that morning and why she had kept the details to herself. Henry remembered his promise to keep silent in order to prevent any negative light being cast on Lisbeth. He realized, with a start, that Marie's motivations for silence were no different than his had been.

She finished quietly. "So now that you know it was Mitch, charges could be filed by everyone who had items taken. I'll understand if that's what you choose to do. And I'll accept my responsibility for letting him go. I won't lie about it anymore."

Henry thought carefully before speaking. "Thank you for telling me. I think, since everyone has back what was taken, they would be willing to let the matter lie. We could talk to the deacons if it would make you feel better."

"What would make me feel better," she said, her eyes flooding, "is if you would forgive me. I don't want to leave again with regrets between us." Touching the Bible with her fingertips, she licked her lips. "You meant to give this to me before I left. . .with Jep." She looked at him, her expression uncertain. "I don't want another message to go unstated."

Henry drew in a ragged breath. "Marie, my biggest regret right now is having, for even a brief time, believed you capable of thievery. I should have known. Please, will you forgive me?"

Her eyes sparkled, her lips tipping into a smile. "Yes. And can you forgive me?"

"Yes."

Her smile grew, and she released a light bubble of laughter. "Oh, that feels good."

Henry smiled. Yes, it felt good to have past mistakes erased, to start with a clean slate. Another silence followed, but this one lacked the unease of the last. Instead, it was a time of settling, of finding a comfortable ground together. It made his heart feel light, and although he hated to interrupt it, he had a question he wanted to ask.

"Marie, do you think Beth would be willing to sell the café to Deborah and Troy?"

She tipped her head, her fine brows coming down for a moment. "Deborah is interested in running it?"

"Yes. She and Trina would keep it going. She's come to enjoy being there."

Another light laugh spilled out. "Well, this is a day for surprises. I'll have Beth get in touch with Deborah. I'm sure they can work out the details with the Realtor."

"Good." He cleared his throat. "And when it sells. . .you'll be leaving?"

For several seconds she seemed to hold her breath, looking at him, something in her expression making his heart increase its tempo. Then, in a hesitant voice, she said, "Do I have a reason to stay?"

Slipping to her side on the sofa, Henry took her hand. "I hope you do." Reaching across her, he lifted the Bible from its box and put it on his knee. He opened the cover and read the words he had penned there the week before Jep Quinn arrived in town. "What God brings together, let no man put asunder." Giving her hand a squeeze, he said softly, "Marie, can I hope that. . .perhaps. . .I might be a reason for you to stay?"

Tears blurred his vision as he admitted, "I've never stopped loving you. Lisbeth knew it. She hoped, like I did, that one day you would return. I know you loved Jep—I wouldn't try to replace him in your heart or Beth's. But if you gave me a chance—"

Marie touched her fingers to his lips. "Henry, I would never see you as a replacement for Jep."

His chest constricted as he waited for her to continue.

"Jep was the love of my youth, and I don't regret loving him. He once told me I helped bring him back in step with the Lord. He gave me Beth. I can't imagine my life without her. Our relationship had a purpose."

Her tender tone, her gentle expression—even though she spoke of another man—held Henry captive.

"But you've been faithful to me, expressing care for me, even when I didn't return it. There is no substitute for that kind of dedication and love. Jep was the love of my youth. But you, Henry, are the love of my life."

He opened his mouth, closed it, swallowed, and finally formed words. "Do you mean. . .you love me, too?"

A tear burst from its perch on her thick lashes and spilled down her cheek with her nod.

He scooped her into his arms, pulling her against his shoulder. "What about Beth? Will she return to Cheyenne alone?"

She made no effort to extricate herself from his embrace. Her face against his neck, she murmured, "God has brought us back together. He'll take care of Beth—I trust Him with her."

He crushed her close, burying his face in the scent of her hair, before setting her aside. Tears trailed down her smiling face, and he brushed them away with his thumbs.

Her sweet lips curved into a smile that sent his heart racing. "Merry Christmas, Henry."

For once, Henry's clumsy tongue found the perfect words. "You are my God-bestowed gift. I love you, my Marie."

Discussion Questions

1. Marie has spent over two decades separated from her family. What kind of emotional toll did this separation take?

2. Beth never knew her father and didn't meet her mother's extended family until she was a young woman of twenty. How did this lack of family affect her?

3. Because Henry never married, his friendship with Lisbeth and his extended family play an important role in his life. Do you think this would have been different if he had married and had children of his own? Do circumstances dictate how we live or do we dictate how we live?

4. When Marie and Beth return to Sommerfeld, they each have very different reactions to the simplicity of the community. Compare and contrast these reactions. Are these differences based on personality or experience?

5. Lisbeth's will was the impetus for bringing Marie and Beth to Sommerfeld, but she had prayed consistently for Marie's return. Was the stipulation of the will a manipulative tactic or a means of answering the prayer?

6. Marie's father held himself aloof from Marie even when she was in the community. Why did he refuse to welcome her home? What did his choice cost him?

7. The community viewed Marie and Beth with suspicion, especially after the thefts. What was the reason for the community members' reticence in reaching out? Were they biblical in their response?

8. Marie reached the conclusion that, even if she leaves Sommerfeld again, she will take God and her faith with her. Do we live our faith inwardly, outwardly, or both? Explain.

9. Lisbeth served as a prayer warrior and peacemaker. Do you know someone like Lisbeth? What traits could be adopted into our own lives for the betterment of those around us?

10. Marie realized she hadn't prayed for God's will before leaving with Jep as a young woman, yet she believed God used her in a positive way in Jep's life. Can God use our steps even when we are outside of His will?

11. Ephesians 4:32 encourages us to forgive one another as God has forgiven us. How might the story have been different had Marie's father and extended family put that verse into practice when Marie chose to marry Jep?

12. Returning to Sommerfeld opened up the opportunity for reconciliation for Marie in many relationships. Which reconciled relationship was the most important, and why?

13. Marie, Henry, and Marie's family carried many regrets based on past decisions. Living our lives without regret is an important goal. What steps can be taken to avoid the sting of regret?

BEGINNINGS

DEDICATION

For Rylin,
the precious new addition to our family.
Your life is just beginning, sweet boy. . . .
May you seek the Lord's wisdom early and grow
in the knowledge of Him.

ACKNOWLEDGMENTS

To my family: Don, Mom and Daddy, my girls, and my little boys. Thank you for walking this pathway with me. I love you all muchly.

To my critique partners: Eileen, Margie, Darlene, Ramona, Crystal, and Donna. Thank you for your support, suggestions, prayers, and encouragement.

To the "brainstormers": Deb R., Judy, Pat, and Deb V. You brought Beginnings to life. Thank you!

To my prayer warriors: Rose, Carla, Connie, Cynthia, Kathy, Don, and Ann. God bless you—you are so special to me.

To Joyce Livingston, my "stained-glass expert." Thank you for your advice, but mostly for your friendship.

To Patricia MacDonald, my "neonatal expert." Thank you for reading the scenes and getting the vernacular right. You made it real.

To Becky and the staff at Barbour. Thank you for the opportunity to work with you. I'm grateful to be a part of the Barbour family.

And finally, most importantly, to God. You blessed me with a new beginning, and You've been with me every step of the way. I am nothing without You. May any praise or glory be reflected directly to You.

The fear of the LORD is the beginning of wisdom:
and the knowledge of the holy is understanding.
PROVERBS 9:10

ONE

Sommerfeld, Kansas

Awash of melted colors splashed across the concrete floor of Quinn's Stained-Glass Art Studio, coloring the toes of Beth Quinn's white leather sneakers. She raised her gaze from the reflection on the floor to the windowsill, where a scene of a dogwood branch with a cardinal nestled among white blossoms perched. Backlit by the late-afternoon sun, each carefully cut piece of colored, leaded glass glowed like a jewel.

As always, Beth got a chill of pleasure from seeing one of her finished creations. "Ooh, yes." She hugged herself and gave a satisfied nod. "Perfect."

The back door to the studio burst open, bringing in a gust of chilly wind. Beth spun toward the door, her hand on her throat. She slumped with relief when she recognized Andrew Braun, her lone employee, stepping through.

Andrew held up both hands as if in surrender. "I'm sorry—the wind caught the door. I didn't mean to startle you."

Beth laughed, shaking her head. In mannerisms and appearance,

Andrew reminded her a lot of her stepfather, Henry, who was Andrew's uncle. He was tall, with short-cropped brown hair covered by a billed cap that shaded his dark, walnut-colored eyes. He was so shy it had taken weeks before he would say more than *Hi* to her in conversation. But over the past two months of working together in the studio, they had finally formed a friendship.

At least, it was only friendship from her angle. She sensed a need to tread carefully. Getting romantically involved with Andrew Braun would open a can of worms the likes of which Sommerfeld had never before seen. And she'd already opened plenty.

"No harm done. And look!" She pointed to the stained-glass piece.

He carefully latched the door and glanced at the window. His eyes widened in surprise. "You got that cardinal one done already? I was going to solder the reinforcement bars for you."

Beth smirked. "All done. I didn't need'ja." She laughed at his crestfallen expression. "But you know if this one goes over well, there will be plenty of other opportunities for you to put the soldering iron to work." Oh, she hoped her statement proved true! Skipping across the floor, she grabbed his elbow and tugged him over to the window. "Well, look at it, and tell me what you think."

Andrew stood before the scene, pinching his chin between his thumb and forefinger. Beth waited, hands clasped in front of her, while he took his time seeming to examine every inch of the finished piece. Even though he had witnessed the creation of this window from her first drawings, there was always an element of excitement when pieces were viewed away from the worktable.

Finally, he gave a nod. "Yes. It's a well-done piece. I like the little yellow bits between breaks in the branches, which make it look like the sun is shimmering through. You were right not to put the cardinal in the center. Even though it's the focus of the piece, its placement to the lower right gives a better balance to the scene overall."

Beth smiled, basking in the approval of another artist.

"But"—he leaned forward, tapping one dogwood blossom with a blunt finger—"should this petal have been placed lower to give the illusion of lapping over the cardinal's tail feathers a little more? It would have added more dimension, I think."

She sent him a brief scowl. "I think it's fine the way it is. I've built in dimension with the varying background sky colors and the deeper green on the undersides of the leaves, which creates shadows." Defensiveness increased the pitch of her voice as she pointed to the elements she mentioned. "And look at the cardinal itself—the way it's positioned at an angle on the tree branch. There's plenty of dimension."

He looked at her with one eyebrow raised. "Yes, there is. But you asked me what I thought, and I think if the flower right above the cardinal had been brought down some—maybe a quarter of an inch—it would have enhanced the dimension."

Beth set her jaw, wishing she could return to the days when all he said was *Hi*.

Nudging her with his elbow, he grinned. "I made you mad."

She jerked away. "I'm not mad!" But even she recognized the irritation in her voice. Taking a deep breath, she said through gritted teeth, "Thank you for your opinion. I'll take it under advisement if I choose to duplicate this piece. Now. . ." Tipping her head, she pushed her long ponytail over her shoulder. "What are you doing here again? I thought you went home."

He shrugged. "I came back to do that soldering. But I guess I don't need to."

She grinned, satisfaction filling her as she looked once more at the cardinal. "Nope. You don't." Much work went into the completion of a stained-glass project, but Beth enjoyed each step of the process, from drawing the design to adding the reinforcement bars that prevented buckling of the leaded-glass piece. Yes, whether creative or structural, she relished every facet of stained-glass art.

With the tip of her gloved finger, she traced the line of soldered zinc that bordered the cardinal's wing. She shook her head, chuckling to herself. Never would she have thought when she made the journey from Cheyenne, Wyoming, a little over a year ago that she would stay in Kansas. Her goal had been simple—sell off the unexpected inheritance from her great-aunt, collect as many antiques as possible from the Old Order Mennonite community citizens, and return to Cheyenne to open an antiques boutique.

But those three months in Sommerfeld had turned everything upside down.

Clamping her hands around the edges of the glass, she lifted the scene from its perch on the windowsill. She grunted with the effort. The piece was larger than any others she'd made so far and heavy from the metal that bordered each glass segment. Andrew reached for it, but she shook her head.

"I can do it." She shuffled across the floor to the display bench along the back wall of her small studio. Sweat broke out across her forehead and between her shoulder blades. Once the scene was secured behind the wood strip that kept the finished pieces from sliding, she wiped her forehead and sent Andrew a triumphant grin. "See?"

His frown let her know he wished she would let him handle the heavier tasks, but Beth was determined not to depend on Andrew too much. Beth was determined not to depend on *anyone* too much.

She offered a suggestion. "As long as you're here, you could put away the shipment of glass that came this morning."

Andrew shrugged and turned toward the crate in the corner. Beth removed her gloves and put them in the top drawer of her storage cabinet. *This cabinet is really too pretty to simply house supplies,* she thought as she ran her hand over the smooth pine top. Two of her mother's cousins had built the cabinet for her, varying the sizes of the drawers and inserting dividers to keep everything organized. A quick glance around the steel building that served as her studio brought a second rush of appreciation. Watching the building go up in one day, reminiscent of an old-fashioned barn raising, had been thrilling—and scary.

She still marveled at the support she'd received from the community after their initial mistrust. Yet she realized their willingness to help didn't indicate approval of her. Since she hadn't joined their meetinghouse, she was still an "outsider." But Mom had rejoined, so they offered their newly claimed member's wayward daughter a helping hand. And now that they'd all had a hand in getting her studio up and running, she felt a real obligation to make it a success.

Her gaze returned to the dogwood and cardinal scene, her heart pounding with hope. A gallery in Wichita had commissioned the piece—her first real commissioned work after nine months of selling smaller, copper-foil pieces at craft fairs. If the gallery owners were pleased, it could lead to more work, and eventually she would be able to establish herself as a bona fide stained-glass artist.

So far, the response to her work had been favorable—her unique blending of colors that created a three-dimensional effect was unique to the stained-glass community—and she credited God with giving her the special talent. She longed to glorify Him through this gift.

Heading for the corner to retrieve the broom, she couldn't help smiling at her thoughts. A year and a half ago, she wouldn't have considered including God in her conversation, let alone being concerned about pleasing Him. But so many things had changed for Beth, both inside and out, and God was the most important addition to her life.

Andrew paused in transferring glass squares to felt-lined shelves, his brows puckered. "I swept just before I left at noon. You're sweeping again?"

"Uh-huh."

"Did you run the cutter while I was gone?"

"Nope." She ignored his sour look and drew the broom's bristles across the floor, collecting tiny shavings of glass. No matter how many times they swept, they could never get it all. The carbide cutter sent out miniscule fragments, and they had a way of traveling to every square inch of floor rather than politely staying beneath the cutting table. The small pile of multicolored bits took on the appearance of sugar crystals, but eating them would be a huge mistake. She'd have to exercise caution when the babies her mother was carrying were big enough to come visit.

Beth paused in her sweeping, her heart skipping a beat with the thought of the twins who would arrive in another four months. That was a change to which she still hadn't adjusted. After twenty-one years of having her mother to herself, she now shared her with a stepfather, a host of relatives, and soon, a new brother and sister. Although it had once been Mom and her against the world, now Beth often felt as though it was Mom's world against her.

Pushing the thought aside, she whisked the glass bits into a dustpan and dropped the broom. She crossed the floor and held the dustpan out to Andrew. "See? Glass sugar. I could sweep again right now and find more. I think it comes up through the concrete."

Andrew chuckled—a deep, throaty sound that always made Beth feel like smiling. "Oh, I doubt that."

She shivered as she dumped the glass fragments into the trash bin right outside the back door, lifting her gaze briefly to the crystal blue sky. No clouds, which meant no more snow. At least for now. She had discovered the weather could change quickly here where the wind pushed unhindered across the open plains.

After clamping the bin's lid back in place, she scurried through the doorway and nearly collided with Andrew, who stood right inside the threshold. His nearness made her pulse race, and she took a sideways step as she slammed the door closed with her hip.

He reached into his pocket. "I almost forgot. I got you some horse-shoe nails like you wanted." Holding out a small, crumpled, brown bag, he added, "There's a dozen in there, but if you need more, I can get them."

Beth took the bag and unrolled the top to peek inside. "Thanks. I'll probably need more eventually, but this will get me started." She offered a smile. "This will work so much better for keeping the assembled pieces in place when I work with larger sections. The lead scraps are fine for holding my smaller works, but as I try to enlarge. . ."

Andrew nodded. "Just let me know when you want more." He started for the door, then paused and turned back, giving his forehead a bump with the heel of his hand. "Oh. Uncle Henry and Aunt Marie are coming to our house for supper tonight. My mom said to ask if you'd like to come, too."

Beth rolled the bag closed as she considered his question. While she appreciated the efforts made by her stepfather's family to include her, she always ended up feeling out of place with her worldly clothes and pierced ears. Andrew's father was one of the worst—his scowling disapproval made her want to disappear. Not once had the man smiled at her, even in her mother's presence, and Mom was his sister-in-law!

As she sought an answer, she felt a yawn build. She gave it free rein and then pushed her lips into a regretful pout.

"I'm sorry, Andrew. Tell your mom thanks for the invitation, but I've been putting in some long days finishing up the cardinal piece. I think I'll just head home, eat a sandwich, and turn in early."

Andrew shrugged. "Okay. Have a good evening then." He stepped out the door, leaving her alone.

Andrew pressed his fork through the flaky layer of crust topping the wedge of cherry pie in front of him and carried the bite to his mouth. His mother made the best pie of anyone in Sommerfeld, where every girl learned to bake as soon as she was old enough to wield a wooden spoon. If he could find a girl who cooked as good as his mother, he'd marry her in a heartbeat.

Heat filled his face at his bold thoughts, and he glanced around the table at the visiting adults. They seemed oblivious to his flaming cheeks, and he released a small sigh of relief before digging once more into the pie.

Lately his thoughts turned too frequently to matrimony. Part of it, of course, was his age. At twenty-three as of a month ago, he was old enough to assume responsibility for a wife. . .and children. He chewed rapidly, dislodging that thought. Part of it was being the only son still living at home, his brothers all having established homes of their own. And part of it was Beth.

His hand slowed on its way to his mouth as an image of Beth Quinn filled his mind. Her long, shining ponytail, her bright blue eyes, the delicate cleft in her sweet chin, the way her slender hands held a pencil as she sketched her designs onto butcher paper. . .

"Andrew?"

Mother's voice from across the table brought him out of his reverie.

She pointed at his fork, which he held beneath his chin. "Are you going to finish that pie or just hold it all evening?"

A light roll of laughter went around the table. Andrew quickly shoved the bite into his mouth, certain his cheeks were once again blazing. On his right, Uncle Henry gave him a light nudge with his elbow.

"If a man's not eating, he has something important on his mind. Want to share?"

If the two had been alone, Andrew probably would have asked his uncle's advice on how to cope with these odd feelings he harbored for Beth. After all, Uncle Henry had loved Beth's mother for years—even during the period when she wasn't a part of the fellowship of their meetinghouse. Surely he, of all people, would understand Andrew's dilemma.

But they had an audience—Henry's wife, Marie, and Andrew's parents. So rather than approach the topic that weighed heavily in his thoughts, he blurted out the first thing that came to mind.

"Beth got that commissioned cardinal scene finished, and it's a beauty."

Both Uncle Henry and Aunt Marie smiled, their pleasure apparent. Equally apparent was Mother's worry and Dad's disapproval.

Dad cleared his throat. "One picture doesn't make a career, son. Don't put too much stock in it."

The cherry pie lost its appeal. He pushed the plate aside. For as long as he could remember, his father had discouraged his interest in artistic endeavors. How many times had he been told in a thundering tone that a man couldn't make a living with pictures, that he needed to set aside such foolishness and choose something practical? More times than he could count. The only reason Dad tolerated his time at the studio now was because during the winter months he wasn't needed as much on the farm. Yet Andrew knew that even when spring arrived he'd want to be in the studio. Unlike his brothers, his heart wasn't in farming or hog raising.

Mother put her hand on Dad's arm. "Andrew's doing Beth a big favor by helping in her studio."

"I know that," Dad countered, his gaze fixed on Andrew. "And I'm not telling him he shouldn't help her out. It's a Christian thing to do. We've all offered Marie's girl assistance in that undertaking of hers. I'm glad she's enjoying it and doing well. But neither should he start thinking that one commissioned stained-glass art piece is going to lead to a career that could take care of a family, which is what Andrew needs to consider. I want him to *think*."

Mother's hand gave several pats before she pulled it away. She sent Andrew an apologetic look. Andrew gave her a slight nod to show his appreciation for her attempt at support, but he knew any further talk would only lead to an argument with his father. He'd endured enough of those in the past. Didn't need one now.

Pushing his hands against the edge of the table, he said, "May I be excused?"

Mother nodded, her expression sad. As Andrew headed for his bedroom, he admitted having his mother's sympathy was a small consolation for the constant disapproval he received from his father when it came to using his talent. His God-given talent. . .

Andrew paused in his bedroom doorway, absorbing the phrase *God-given talent*. Didn't the Bible say that God gave gifts? And didn't the Bible say man should not squander what God had given? Why couldn't his father see past the end of his sunburned nose and recognize his way wasn't the only way?

Too restless to turn in, Andrew reversed direction and returned to the dining room, where the four adults still sat sipping coffee and chatting. "I know Beth has plans for that February craft fair at the mall in Salina. Since she's spent so much time on the cardinal piece, she's behind on cutting glass for the cross suncatchers that sell so well. I'm going to head over to the studio and do some cutting—help her out."

Mother's lips pursed, no doubt a silent reprimand for him having interrupted the conversation. Dad's lips pinched, too. Andrew knew him well enough to read his mind. Dad didn't want Andrew involved in the world of art. And he didn't want Andrew entangled in Beth's world. But it was too late. Andrew's interests were fully entrenched in art. . .and in Beth.

Before Dad could form an angry blast, Andrew turned and headed for the door.

Two

Beth stretched out on the sawdust-stuffed sofa and crossed her ankles. Although she appreciated not having to purchase furnishings, she was considering replacing Great-Aunt Lisbeth's ancient sofa with something modern. And soft.

Picking up the television remote from the little wood table at the end of the sofa, she aimed it at the glass box across the room and clicked through the stations. Thanks to the satellite dish on the roof of the house, she had a variety of programs from which to choose, but nothing caught her interest. With a sigh, she turned off the television and leaned her head back, closing her eyes.

Her great-aunt Lisbeth probably wouldn't recognize her house anymore. In the year since Beth had assumed ownership, she'd made good use of the money from the sale of Lisbeth's Café to update the house according to her own preferences. Electricity, which made possible the use of a central heating and air-conditioning unit; carpet over the hardwood floors; two telephone lines—one of which was used for the Internet; the addition of a washer and dryer set up in the utility porch; and a modernized kitchen. Not that she did a lot of cooking. But the microwave worked great for frozen dinners and for reheating leftovers frequently delivered by Mom.

Mom had slipped—with few bumps in the road, it seemed—back into the simple Old Order way of life in which she'd been raised, but Beth couldn't imagine doing without the conveniences of modern life outside of this little community. She wouldn't be here were it not for her mother and her studio.

And needing to distance herself as much as possible from Mitch. Even now, the pain of his betrayal stung. She turned her attention elsewhere.

Her thoughts drifted to the studio, where her newly completed project awaited packaging and transporting to the gallery in Wichita. A rush of nervous excitement filled her as she wondered how the gallery owners would respond to the piece. *Oh, please, let them like it!* her thoughts begged.

Her mother had told her God wouldn't have opened the doors to her discovering her unique talent for stained-glass art if He didn't intend for her to use it. But Beth still harbored a touch of insecurity. Her relationship with God was still new enough that—even though it carried a great deal of importance to her—she hadn't quite found her niche. She wasn't 100 percent sure where God wanted her to be.

Everything had fallen so neatly into place for her establishing the studio and getting started with stained-glass art. Mom believed this meant it was God's will. Beth still worried it might simply be a series of coincidences. Things had seemed to fall neatly into place for her to start an antiques boutique, too, but that hadn't turned out so well, thanks to Mitch. How could she be so sure this new undertaking would be successful?

She longed for the peace and assurance her mother possessed. Perhaps, she reasoned, it would come when her relationship with God had time to mature. She certainly hoped so. One thing was certain:

She would not involve someone else in this business venture. Not as a partner. She wouldn't put that much trust in anyone else ever again.

Swinging her legs from the sofa, she headed to the kitchen and poured herself a cup of water. Sipping, she looked out the window at the soft Kansas evening. The velvet sky scattered with stars still amazed her with its beauty. The sky seemed so much bigger here on the plain than it had in the city. It was quiet, too, with only the occasional hum of distant traffic offering a gentle reminder of life outside this peaceful community. At times, Beth appreciated the solitude and simplicity, and at other times, this life felt stifling.

Like now.

She slammed the plastic tumbler onto the countertop and headed to the utility porch. She plucked her woolly coat from a hook on the wall and slipped it on, pulling the hood over her tangled ponytail. The President's Day Extravaganza at the Salina Mall was just a few weeks away, and she needed to add to her inventory of small pieces if she wanted to fill the booth she'd reserved.

Tomorrow she'd be transporting the cardinal piece to Wichita, which meant a shorter workday. She might as well take advantage of these evening hours and get the pieces cut for at least one suncatcher. It would put her a step ahead. And a walk through the frosty January evening, listening to her feet crunch through the remaining crust of snow and breathing in the crisp air, might help release the restiveness in her heart.

Bundled, she headed out the door.

Andrew removed his goggles and picked up the glass pliers. Pinching the length of blue glass below the score line, he gave a quick downward thrust, and the first side fell away. He turned the square of glass and repeated the process until he held a perfectly shaped wedge of blue flat on the palm of his gloved hand.

Grasping the narrow end of the wedge between his finger and thumb, he held it to the light for a moment. The color changed from the deep hue of a blue jay's wing to the soft shade of a periwinkle blossom, and he allowed a smile of pleasure to grow on his face. Others might scoff at the joy Andrew found in admiring something as simple as the color variation in a piece of leaded glass held to a fluorescent light, but right now, he was alone. He could enjoy himself.

Humming, he pulled open the small top drawer that housed the carborundum stones and removed one. He carried the glass piece and the stone to a little bench in the corner, sat down, and began to smooth the rough edges of the glass.

Tiny bits of glass sugar, as Beth called it, dusted the tops of his boots and the floor around his feet as he filed. Hunkered forward, he carefully filed just enough to smooth the glass but not grind so much that it changed the size of the piece. There was little margin for error when it came to making the pieces fit together properly. His tongue crept out between his lips as he slid his gloved finger along the edge to search for snags. Finding none, he gave a satisfied nod and turned the glass to file another side.

He was busily filing the fourth and final edge when the back door burst open, allowing in a gust of wind that swept the particles of glass off the toes of his boots. Startled, Andrew leaped to his feet, and the slice of glass fell from his hand. It landed on his boot and then bounced onto the floor, one corner breaking off when it plinked against the concrete.

Lifting his gaze from the ruined glass wedge, he found Beth glowering at him.

"What in the world are you doing in here?" Hands on hips, her nose bright red, she faced off with him in a battle stance that might have intimidated a lesser man. But Andrew had confronted a much tougher adversary—his own father—so he found Beth's attack more disheartening than frightening.

"I wanted to help you get started on some new pieces for the show in Salina." He shook his head, looking once more at the piece of blue glass at his feet. "That piece won't be usable, I'm afraid." He bent over and picked it up, and as he rose, Beth took two steps toward him.

"Well, it scared me half to death when I saw all the lights on in here. I thought someone had broken in or something."

That explained the way she had come barreling through the door. Andrew frowned, rubbing his thumb over the length of glass in his hand. "I'm sorry. I didn't mean to scare you. I really just wanted to. . . help."

She plucked the piece of glass from his hand. She examined it, scowling a bit when she encountered the chipped corner. But when she looked at him, he read a hint of remorse in her eyes. "You had this one ready to go, didn't you? And I scared it right out of your hand."

A grin tugged at his lips. "I guess we're even then, huh, for scaring each other."

Without answering, Beth walked over to the storage cabinet, pulled a ruler from one of the drawers, and measured the piece of glass. "Well, this won't work for one of the long rays anymore, but you might be able to trim right below the chipped spot and salvage this for a shorter ray. Want to see if it works?"

Nodding, Andrew took the piece and placed it over the paper pattern for one of the suncatchers. To his relief, three of the four sides matched perfectly. A trim on the chipped fourth side would make it usable. He shot Beth a wide grin. "It'll work."

She heaved a sigh of relief Andrew fully understood. The sheets of leaded glass were not inexpensive. She salvaged every piece she could to make the twelve-by-twelve-inch sheets stretch as far as possible. He knew she harbored dreams of purchasing a kiln, which would enable her to fire her own glass in all the colors of the rainbow. In the meantime, however, she had to purchase the colored glass from a manufacturer in Canada. Wasting it wasn't an option.

Beth pointed to the table holding the carbide cutting wheel. "Good! So get to hacking." Slipping off her coat, she threw it onto the display bench and moved to the box that held sizable glass scraps. She reached into the box.

"Gloves first," Andrew cautioned.

Glancing over her shoulder, she grimaced. "Bossy."

"No more than you."

She grinned.

He grinned.

She headed to the cabinet and retrieved a pair of yellow leather gloves. Waving them at him, she said, "Okay. Now cut, huh? We've got work to do."

For the next two hours, they worked in companionable silence, the *whir* of the carbide wheel and the *snip* of the pliers providing a familiar, soothing lullaby. By the time nine thirty rolled around, they had pieces for four more suncatchers, ready to be filed and fitted together into finished products.

Side by side, they organized the pieces on the worktable in readiness for tomorrow's work. He left the carborundum stone out, knowing it would be needed. But Beth picked it up and returned it to its drawer. He hid his smile. Meticulous in all areas, she would make an excellent housekeeper.

Swallowing, he focused once more on the pieces of glass laid out neatly across the worktable, shifting them around with his finger. "I'm glad these smaller projects can be done using copper foiling rather than lead caming."

Beth paused, her hand in the cabinet drawer, and glanced over her shoulder. "They do go together much more quickly, and I know they're easier to work with. But. . ." She closed the drawer, turned, and faced him. Her face wore an expression of uncertainty. "You are willing to help with larger pieces, which require the lead came, aren't you?"

Andrew felt his heart thud beneath his shirt. Her question told him he was needed. Wanted. Maybe even. . .desired. Only as an employee, he reminded himself. *For now, but maybe, in time. . .* "I'll help you as long as I can, in any way that you need." Then he felt obliged to add, "When spring arrives, though, when we need to cut the winter wheat and plant the new crop. . ."

She nodded, biting down on her lower lip. Her fine brows pinched together. "I know. Your dad will need you."

Her concern was no doubt directly related to the workload she would face alone, but his was much more personal. Being in the fields with his father could never satisfy him the way working in the studio—with Beth—could. But if Beth made a success of the studio, expanded it the way she hoped, and proved to his father a man could make a decent living at this art business, then perhaps. . .

"Well, I'll be taking the cardinal piece to Wichita tomorrow." She picked up their coats and handed his over. "Which means you'll probably be filing all alone here tomorrow. By the time I'm back, maybe we'll be able to start putting the suncatchers together, huh?"

"That's the goal." Andrew forced a lighthearted tone as he pushed his hands into the sleeves of his heavy coat. He wished he had picked up the coats first. Then he would have been able to hold hers for her while she slipped her arms into the sleeves. Maybe he would have been able to lift that ponytail from beneath the collar and find out if the strands felt as soft and silky as they looked. But she was already buttoning up, with her blond ponytail draped across her shoulder, so all he could do was open the door for her, which he did.

The wind greeted them as they stepped outside, cutting off Andrew's breath with unexpected force. He lifted his gaze to the sky, observing that the stars had been extinguished. He blew out a breath, which hung on the cold air, and pointed upward. "Uh-oh. Clouds have gathered. And it smells like snow."

Beth swung her gaze to the sky, too, her eyes wide. "Oh, no. No snow. I have to go to Wichita tomorrow, and I *hate* driving in snow."

He looked at her. "I could take you if you like."

But she shook her head. "No. I need you here, finishing those sun-catchers." She sighed, her breath creating a small cloud that a fresh gust of wind quickly whisked away. "I guess I'll worry about it tomorrow." Shivering, she hunched into her coat. "But no more talking right now. It's cold. Let's get home."

THREE

The alarm clock blared, jarring Beth from a sound sleep. She slipped one hand from beneath the covers and smacked the SNOOZE button on top of the black plastic case. Silence fell. Shivering, she pulled the covers over her head to enjoy a few more lazy minutes. She'd never been an early riser. Being her own boss meant she could set her own hours. Since she usually worked into the evening, it didn't bother her to indulge herself with some extra snooze time in the morning.

She lay in her snug nest, ears tuned for the alarm. Her windows were no longer rattling, and the tree limbs weren't clacking together. Something else occurred to her. It was *cold*. Apparently, the wind she'd heard last night had done more than interrupt her sleep. By the chill in the house, she was certain Andrew's prediction had come true. There had to be fresh snow on the ground.

Flopping the covers back, she bounced out of bed. Hugging herself, she crossed to the windows and pushed the curtains aside. She groaned. At least two inches of glistening white coated the ground, and flakes continued to fall from the sky. The wind, thankfully, had departed, but. . .the snow. . .

For a moment, Beth stood transfixed by the sight. Big, fluffy puffs drifted down from a bleached sky. The sharp contrast of darks and lights—white sky, whiter snow, stark brown tree limbs, deep green leaves, and bright red berries on a bush outside the window—teased her artist's eye.

"Wow, God," she whispered, her fingers pressed to the glass and her breath steaming the pane, "that is absolutely gorgeous. . . ."

Then frustration struck. How she hated driving in snow! Turning from the window, she hurried to the hallway and pushed the little lever on the thermostat up two degrees. The heater kicked on, sending a rush of warm air through the iron grate. She remained beside the scrolled square and enjoyed the warmth for a few minutes before forcing herself to get moving.

Mom and Henry had given her a devotional Bible for Christmas, and she started each day by reading a brief passage of scripture and an object lesson based on it. After reading, she spent time in prayer. There was still an awkwardness to her prayer time. Deep down, she believed God listened and cared. It wasn't a lack of faith that created the discomfort but more a lack of familiarity. She hadn't grown up with it. It was all so new. She appreciated being able to talk to God and found herself addressing Him at odd moments during the day, but times of formal prayer still felt stilted to her. She hoped eventually she would find an ease with the practice.

After dressing, she put on her coat and gloves, grabbed her car keys, and headed to her car. She squinted against the glare of white, listening to the squeak of wet snow beneath her feet. Snowflakes dusted her shoulders, and she swept them away with a quick flip of her hand. When she spotted the accumulated snow on her windshield, she wished for a garage where she could keep her car under cover, but fortunately the blanket of white brushed off fairly quickly. Sliding behind the wheel, she turned the ignition and sat, arms crossed, while the engine warmed up. With the defroster on full blast, it didn't take long for the remaining bits of snow on the windshield to melt into racing droplets.

Watching the droplets zigzag down the glass windshield made Beth dizzy, and she turned on the wipers to whisk the moisture away. "If I get dizzy from the water drops on my own windshield," she muttered as she put the car into DRIVE, "what will the snowflakes rushing at me do?"

She got the answer to that question as she drove the short distance from her house to the studio on the edge of town. By the time she reached the studio and pulled in next to Andrew's older-model pickup, she knew she would not be able to drive to Wichita unless the snow stopped.

Disgusted, she hurried through the back door and announced, "It's all your fault!"

Andrew, bent over the worktable, straightened and sent her a blank look. "Huh?"

"You." She pointed at him, puckering her lips into a forced pout. "You had to go and say the word *snow* last night, didn't you?"

His lips quirked. "You're blaming that on me?"

Beth threw her arms outward. "Who else can I blame it on?"

A chuckle rumbled, and he offered a one-shouldered shrug. "Sorry, but I don't have that much power."

"Well. . ." She removed her coat and threw it on the display bench. Walking over to the cardinal picture, she traced one blossom with her fingertip. "I guess I won't hold you responsible then." She turned and caught Andrew staring at her. For some odd reason, heat filled her cheeks. "What?"

He shook his head, and his ears flamed red. He jerked his head in her direction and said, "You're all dressed up. You won't want to do any grinding in that gear."

Beth glanced down. She had chosen a pantsuit and high-heeled boots in lieu of jeans and tennis shoes to make a professional appearance at the gallery in Wichita. She groaned. "I just figured I'd load up and go, but you're right—if I'm stuck here, I won't want to work in these clothes." She heaved a huge sigh and reached for her coat. "I guess I'll run home and change. If the snow clears off by noon, I can still make it to Wichita with the cardinal picture."

"You want me to grind or cut more pieces?"

Beth paused, one finger pressed to her lips, as she considered the best use of Andrew's time. "Cut." She spoke decisively, adding a firm nod. "And I'll be back in a jiffy." Grabbing up her coat, she drew in a big breath and murmured in an ominous tone, "Back into the blizzard." Andrew's laughter followed her out the door.

Per Beth's request, Andrew set aside the carborundum stone and collected the snipped pattern pieces for the suncatchers. Beth had designed the suncatcher herself, centering a cross with bursts of colored wedges seeming to come from behind it. The design was simple, but her way of choosing colors—especially glass squares that faded to a lighter shade from one side to the next—gave the piece a three-dimensional appearance. Andrew marveled at how such a small thing changed the overall impact of a design.

He placed glass squares across the worktable, then laid a paper pattern on top, holding the paper in place with his fingers while he carefully drew around it with a paint pen. When he had first started working for Beth, she had insisted he glue the pattern piece to the glass before tracing around it. Over time, she'd developed confidence in his ability to keep the paper from slipping and allowed him to skip that additional step. Not only did this shorten the length of time needed to prepare the glass for cutting, but it made Andrew swell with pride. It felt good to be trusted.

By keeping the darker color at the center and the lighter at the outside of the parts of the sunburst, a greater portion of glass was wasted, so Andrew used extra care in the placement of the pattern. "No wasted pieces," he muttered to himself. He was just finishing up the fourth piece when a knock at the door intruded.

Startled, he looked toward the back door. It wasn't locked. Were Beth's hands full so she wasn't able to get in? He darted to the door. Opening it, he found nothing but a flurry of snowflakes. The knock came again, and he realized it was coming from the front. Giving the back door a firm yank, he dashed across the floor and unlocked the seldom-used front door.

A man with melting snowflakes on his uncovered head waited on the small concrete stoop. The moment the door opened, he stepped through with a broad smile and extended his hand. His snow-covered shoes left wet blotches on the floor. Andrew was pretty sure this would aggravate Beth. He'd have to remember to ask Mom if he could bring over one of her rag rugs to put in front of the door.

"Good morning." The man spoke in a cheerful tone. "There are no hours of business posted, but I saw the lights on. I hope it's okay to come in. Are you Quinn?"

Andrew gave the man's hand a solid shake. "I'm Andrew Braun. I work for the owner. She stepped out for a few minutes, but she'll be back. You can wait."

"Thank you." He looked around the studio, his shrewd gaze absorbing every detail. "I've never been in a stained-glass studio before. It's interesting."

Andrew raised his eyebrows and followed the man's gaze, trying to see the surroundings through the eyes of someone unfamiliar with the craft. He remembered his own awe when he first started—the pleasure of combining colors and shapes to create scenes, the patience required to prepare each piece of glass to fit the overall scene, the efficiency of the flowchart of steps that Beth had posted on the wall to make certain he did things in the proper order, and finally the satisfaction of viewing a finished product.

His gaze located the cardinal piece, still resting on the display bench and awaiting packaging. He hadn't created anything that elaborate yet, but he looked forward to the day Beth trusted him with larger projects. Suddenly he wondered if this stranger was an artist, too, seeking employment. Andrew's heart skipped a beat. The man was obviously worldly. His clothing and mustache set him apart from the Mennonite men of Sommerfeld. Would Beth, who had been raised in the world, prefer his assistance?

"Are you a stained-glass artist?" Andrew blurted out the question, his words loud in the peaceful shop.

The man shook his head, the corners of his eyes crinkling with mirth. "Huh-uh."

But he didn't expound on his answer, leaving Andrew floundering. After a few more awkward seconds of silence, Andrew waved his hand toward the worktable and said, "Well, I was busy cutting pieces. If you don't mind, I'll just. . ." He backed toward the table.

"That's fine. Do you mind if I look around?"

Andrew shrugged. He had no authority to tell him yes or no. Knowing how the glass fragments flew with the use of the cutting wheel, he set aside the task of cutting and took up a stone to grind the rough edges of the glass pieces laid out on the worktable. He kept a furtive eye on the stranger, who walked slowly around the periphery of the small building, his hands clasped at the base of his spine, his expression bland.

It seemed hours passed before the sound of a car's engine alerted Andrew to Beth's return. He hurried to the back door and opened it for her.

She bustled through with a smile on her face and quickly removed her coat. In place of the purple suit, she wore faded jeans, a blue T-shirt that brought out the bright hue of her eyes, and a flannel shirt with none of the buttons fastened. How could she be so cute in such sloppy attire?

"The weatherman says this will all clear off by midmorning, so—" Her cheery patter stopped when she spotted the stranger. Handing her coat to Andrew, she walked to the man. "Hello. Welcome to Quinn's Stained-Glass Art Studio. I'm Beth Quinn."

Andrew experienced a prickle of discomfort at the ease with which Beth greeted the man. He didn't care for the way the man gave Beth a quick once-over with his eyes, perusing her as thoroughly as he had the studio. But Beth didn't seem bothered by it. Her smile remained intact.

Andrew's fingers crushed her coat in a stranglehold.

"My name is Sean McCauley. It's nice to meet you."

Beth tipped her head, tumbling her shining ponytail across one shoulder. "What can I do for you?"

Sean McCauley slipped the tips of his fingers into his jacket pockets and smiled at Beth. "I'm a shopper."

Andrew's chest constricted at Beth's light, friendly laughter.

"Well, I don't often have shoppers come by the studio. As you can see"—she held out her arms, indicating the space—"I don't have a gift-shop area at all, although I hope to expand as my business grows."

The man gave a slow nod, his mustache twitching. "Would you

mind sharing your expansion plans with me?"

Andrew bristled. How were Beth's plans this man's concern? But Beth didn't seem to see anything wrong with the question. She didn't hesitate.

"Certainly. Right now it's a fairly small working studio, appropriate for preparing pieces for craft fairs. I've been working craft fairs for the past nine months, marketing myself and my creations." She moved slowly toward the display bench as she spoke, with the man following, his gaze pinned to her face. "The craft fairs brought interest, and I was commissioned by the Fox Gallery in Wichita for this piece."

Pausing in front of the cardinal scene, she looked up at McCauley. "Are you familiar with the Fox Gallery?"

The man offered a slow nod. Andrew waited for him to say something, but he remained silent. By now, Andrew had nearly twisted Beth's coat into a knot. He dropped it on the end of the display bench as Beth continued.

"I'm hopeful this piece will garner enough interest to lead to more commissioned pieces. My heart really is in the larger works. As that opportunity opens, I want to expand the shop, doubling my work space, and build a small gallery onto the front of the building where people can come and purchase finished pieces, eliminating my need to attend craft fairs. Although it can be fun to go out and mingle with the public, the fairs take me away from the studio. I also hope to eventually have an Internet Web site offering pieces for sale and making myself available for special orders."

"High aspirations," McCauley commented.

Andrew couldn't see the man's expression, since McCauley faced the cardinal piece, but he clearly heard the note of praise. Yes, Beth had high aspirations. Her aspirations had become Andrew's in the weeks he had worked with her. He wasn't sure of this man's interest, but he sensed trouble brewing for some reason he couldn't quite understand.

McCauley leaned one way, then the other, seeming to take stock of the cardinal scene. Standing upright again, he said, "What is it, about thirty-two by twenty-four inches?"

Beth shot him a startled glance, and even Andrew found the man's accuracy impressive. Beth replied, "Thirty-two by twenty-five, but that was a great guess. Are you an artist?"

Andrew blurted out the answer. "No."

Both Beth and McCauley cranked their necks to look at him.

He felt heat build in his neck. With a lame shrug, he said, "I asked him that earlier."

McCauley's mustache twitched again. He turned from Andrew to face Beth. Holding out his hand, he said, "Let me finish my introduction. I'm Sean McCauley of McCauley Church Construction out of Kansas City. I'd like to talk to you about the possibility of making you a part of our team."

FOUR

Beth took a step back, her heart leaping into her throat. She had hoped the stranger was a gallery owner or a crafts buyer—someone who might purchase a few of her pieces for retail. But an offer to become a part of his company? Her knees felt weak, and she wasn't sure she could remain standing. Turning, she stumbled to one of the tall stools next to the worktable and propped herself against it.

"I–I'm afraid I don't quite understand what you're saying."

Sean McCauley laughed lightly, showing even white teeth beneath the straight line of his neatly trimmed, reddish gold mustache. His blue-green eyes crinkled with the broad smile. "I'm sorry. I do need to slow down a tad." Crossing to the table, he pointed to an empty stool. "Do you mind?"

With a wave of her hand, Beth gave him permission to sit. As Sean seated himself, Andrew approached and stood beside her, his steadfast presence appreciated.

Slipping his hand inside his jacket, Sean retrieved a small card, which he handed to her. "So you know I'm legitimate. . ." His tone held a hint of teasing.

Beth examined the card, then handed it to Andrew, who scowled at it as if it held an inappropriate message.

"McCauley Church Construction has been in business for nearly forty years. We have three crews, and we've been involved in the building of churches from one coast to the other. We've built everything from simple chapels to three-story complexes. There is a McCauley building of worship in every state of the continental United States."

He leaned his elbow on the edge of the table, using his finger to trace the outside edge of a rose-colored piece of glass. "We've commissioned stained-glass windows from other companies, and we have no complaints. But. . ." His smile broadened. "You've captured our attention."

Beth put her hand against her chest, rearing back in puzzlement. "Me? How?"

Sean released a chuckle. "My aunt purchased one of your suncatchers at a craft fair in Olathe—a purple butterfly."

Beth nodded. "One of my best sellers."

Sean's smile sent a spiral of warmth through her middle. "I can see why. It's a great design. My dad and I were astounded when she showed it to us. The illusion of depth. That's really quite rare in stained glass."

"I don't claim credit for it," Beth said, her heart pattering. "It's a gift from my Creator. I simply want to use it."

The approval in Sean's unique eyes increased the tempo of her heartbeat. "That appeals to me, too. As a Christian company, it's important to us to glorify God through our business dealings. You seem to be a good fit for us between your commitment to working for God's glory and your amazing ability in stained-glass art."

Andrew, always quiet around strangers, surprised Beth by inserting a question. "How would you go about putting Beth on your payroll?"

Sean shot Andrew a quick look before turning back to Beth. "You wouldn't officially be an employee of McCauley Church Construction.

We'd commission you the same way you were commissioned by the gallery in Wichita."

Andrew nodded, and Beth felt a prick of aggravation. Since when did her business dealings require his approval? Shifting on her stool, she angled her shoulders to partially block Andrew from Sean's line of vision. "How many windows are we talking about here?"

Sean shrugged. "There's no way to say. It depends on many factors." He picked up a piece of glass from the table and examined it. "Have you worked with the heavier leaded glass?" Without waiting for an answer, he continued. "What's the largest piece you've constructed? Are you willing to sign a waiver that, if the piece doesn't meet our standards of excellence, you will absorb the loss? Can you set aside other projects and focus on designing for us exclusively when under deadline?"

Beth's head spun. Although she'd tried to exclude Andrew, she now found herself turning her head to seek his advice. He stared dumbly at Sean, his mouth open slightly as though he were as taken aback as she felt. She'd get no help from him. She turned back to Sean.

"Let's try one question at a time." Taking a deep breath, she began a series of careful replies. "First, this is the weight of glass I've used so far, but my equipment can handle the heavier glass. It's just that I've done smaller projects, so I've only had need of the lighter weight. Second"—she gestured toward the display bench—"the largest piece I've constructed so far is the cardinal piece."

Sean glanced at it again. "Impressive, but small compared to what we would need for most churches."

A wave of panic pressed from Beth's chest. "What size do you need?"

Sean removed a slip of paper from his pocket, unfolded it, and handed it over. Beth looked at it, her eyes widening. The dimensions were three times the size of the cardinal piece. She showed the paper to Andrew, sucking in a deep breath of fortification when his eyebrows shot to his hairline.

Andrew whistled through his teeth. "That's a good-sized piece."

"Yes, it is," Sean agreed, "but it's smaller than some. In one of our churches, we commissioned a stained-glass window that was nine feet wide and twelve feet high."

Beth had seen projects of that size and had wondered what it would be like to create something of that magnitude. Now the opportunity lay in front of her, if she could only prove her ability.

Sean continued, speaking directly to Andrew. "The windows we've commissioned in the past have all been beautiful, but they've lacked the three-dimensional effect Beth is capable of creating. That's why I'm here." He faced Beth again. "Is it too much of a challenge?"

Before Beth could respond, Andrew cut in. "Beth can do anything she sets her mind to."

Sean's mustache wiggled as if he fought laughter, but Beth gave Andrew an appreciative smile. His confidence in her gave her a needed boost. "I'd like to try."

"Try?" Sean angled his chin to the side, peering at her through narrowed eyes. "And if it doesn't work?"

Beth squared her shoulders and met his gaze directly. "I wouldn't expect you to pay for something that doesn't please you. However, I would like to be fairly certain before I go to the expense of creating a project of the size and weight you've indicated that you would be satisfied."

"And how can we make that happen?" Sean leaned forward, his eyes sparkling.

At closer range, Beth made out a spattering of pale freckles across his nose and cheeks. It gave him a boyish appearance that contrasted with the mustache. How old was he? A few years older than herself—midtwenties probably. She momentarily lost her train of thought. But when his red-gold eyebrows rose, she realized she'd allowed long seconds to slip by without answering. She swallowed and formed a reply.

"Perhaps I could do several preliminary drawings—in color, of course—so you could see what I envision as the final project. If you approve the drawing, I'll proceed. Then, if for some reason the window is not constructed properly, you would have the option of not purchasing it. I would ask to be compensated for my expenses and time, however. Does that seem fair?"

"All but the compensating for your expenses and time."

Beth's scalp prickled. "Oh?"

Sean raised his shoulders and held out his hands. "If you were on our payroll, then yes—we might offer an hourly wage in addition to reimbursement of expenses. But as a commissioned artist, the payment comes with the delivery of a finished, suitable project. Perhaps, eventually, if this business venture proves to be mutually satisfactory, we could consider making you a permanent employee of McCauley Church Construction, but—"

"Let's stick with commissioned work." Beth heard Andrew's sigh and sensed his relief at her resistance to becoming a part of McCauley's team. She didn't understand his reason, but she knew she was reluctant to combine forces with anyone. On her own, she could call the shots. Get someone else involved, and she wouldn't be in control any longer. She wasn't ready to sign that away, no matter how large the contract.

"That's fine." Sean reached into the pocket inside his jacket once more and withdrew a packet of papers. "This is the contract my father drew up in case you were interested. Please look it over, mark any questions you have in the margin, and I'll be back tomorrow to see what you think." He stood, his smile building once more. "It's been very nice meeting you, Miss Quinn and. . ." He looked at Andrew, snapped his fingers, then added, "Andrew." His gaze on Beth again, he finished in a warm tone. "I look forward to working with you."

Beth nodded, the papers as heavy as a sheet of leaded glass in her hands. "Thank you. I'll. . .I'll give this some thought and prayer."

"Good. Until tomorrow, then." Sean buttoned his jacket and headed out the door.

Beth turned from the closed door to look at Andrew. She had considered asking him what he thought, but the glimpse of thunder in his expression sealed off her words.

In his car, the engine running and the heater blasting him with cold air, Sean flipped open his cell phone and said, "Dad," in a clipped tone. Beeping indicated the phone understood the command. He tapped the steering wheel with his fingers, impatience pinching his chest as he waited for the call to be answered.

"How'd it go?"

Sean grimaced at his father's greeting. *Don't waste time with pleasantries. Just get straight to the purpose.* He had to admit, finding out the artist Quinn was a young, attractive female had nearly set him off course. It took some effort to put his focus back where it belonged.

"She's willing to try, but I don't know. It's a pretty small studio, and she doesn't have experience with the heavier glass."

"Gut reaction, Sean. Could she do it?"

The line crackled, letting Sean know they didn't have much time before the snowy weather disconnected the service. He answered from his gut. "I think she could."

"Then follow through on what we planned."

Sean nodded. "Will do. See you tomorrow evening sometime, hopefully with signed contract in hand."

The line disconnected, and Sean dropped the phone onto the seat beside him. *Well, Lord, we'll see what happens from here.* Sean put his car in gear and angled it toward the waiting highway. He'd find a hotel down the road—maybe that one outside of Hillsboro he'd passed on the way—and spend a leisurely day holed up with a television and remote control. By this time tomorrow, he'd be on his way to securing the artist Sean was sure would be a household name in the stained-glass art industry before the year was out.

His mind hop-skipped along a pathway: Her success would mean his success; his success would mean the company's success; and the company's success would mean Dad's approval. Yes, everything would work out perfectly.

FIVE

Andrew went back to grinding the rough edges of the pieces of glass on the worktable, allowing Beth to study the unexpected opportunity provided by the thick contract in her hands. At least, he hoped she was studying—and finding favor with—the unexpected opportunity. By her introspective expression and silent tongue, he surmised she was deep in thought.

He stayed quiet and allowed her to think while he replayed the offer made by McCauley. His heart pounded at twice the beat of the rhythmic *scritch–scritch* of the carborundum stone. If Beth took on the task of designing windows for that company, she'd be busy. Possibly wealthy. And successful.

Very successful. . .

He licked his dry lips, considering how her success would become his means of convincing his father a person can support himself with art. Beth couldn't possibly keep up with her smaller projects and the larger ones for McCauley. She'd need him full-time. Ah, yes. Andrew closed his eyes for a moment, a smile tugging at his lips. His deliverance was near.

Unless, of course, she decided not to do the smaller things at all and just focus on windows for churches. Would she be able to handle that on her own?

"Andrew?"

Beth's timid query brought him back to reality. The wariness in her blue eyes made his heart thud. "Yes?"

She flapped the contract. "In looking at this, most of the benefits are on the side of McCauley Church Construction. If I follow through on projects, meet their deadlines, and design to their satisfaction, then the benefits flow toward me. There are quite a few 'ifs,' especially since I run such a small studio. But"—she tucked her lower lip between her teeth for a moment, her brow pursed in thought—"if I meet this first challenge, if I manage to prove myself, all the plans I have for the studio could come to pass."

Andrew nodded, setting aside the stone. He spoke slowly. "You know I'll do whatever I can to help you."

"Yes, I know. Thank you."

"So. . ." Andrew's mouth went dry again. He swallowed hard. "Do you think you'll sign it?"

Beth looked at the contract again. "I want to talk to Mom and Henry about it first."

For a reason he couldn't explain, Andrew experienced a wash of disappointment.

"But for now"—she hopped off the stool and carried the contract to her coat, tucking it beneath the thick folds of fuzzy fabric—"I need to focus on these suncatchers for my craft booth."

"I can do this," Andrew blurted. "Go talk to them now."

She sent him a funny look. "Henry's at his shop. It'll have to wait until suppertime." A smile crept up her cheeks. "I've never known you to be so impatient. What gives?"

Andrew shrugged, forcing aside the eagerness that twisted in his chest. "I guess I just want to see your dreams come true. You've earned it."

Her expression became almost tender as she looked at him, and he felt heat building in the tops of his ears.

"That's really sweet. Thank you."

A twinge of guilt struck. His dreams were directly related to her dreams coming true. His wish for her wasn't exactly without strings attached. But he kept that thought to himself. He nodded to acknowledge her words, then suggested, "Instead of working on these, why don't you start some drawings and get ideas for the window so you're ready to knock Sean McCauley off his feet tomorrow?"

Her eyes sparkled as her laughter rang. "Okay. I am itching to draw." She moved to the storage cabinet with an eager bounce in her step and plucked out a pad of graph paper, drafting tools, and pencils. Back on the stool, she pushed the glass pieces aside to create a drawing space on the worktable and bent over the paper.

Andrew tried to focus on the piece of glass in his hand—he needed to be cautious not to file inside the score line—but it was hard not to watch the lines of graphite creating a geometric pattern on the paper just across the table. It was equally hard to keep his eyes off the artist.

Beth was so cute when deep in concentration. She hunched over the pad of paper, her blond ponytail slipping across her shoulder now and then only to be pushed back with an impatient flick of her wrist. Her thick lashes swept up and down, her gaze zipping from one corner of the drawing to the other. The swish of the pencil across the paper came in short, thoughtful strokes. Her lips sometimes tipped up in satisfaction and other times pursed just before she dropped the pencil and used the rubber eraser with force.

An hour slowly ticked by while Beth sketched and Andrew sanded. Snowflakes ceased their flutter outside the window. Finally,

Beth straightened on the stool, put down the pencil, and rubbed the back of her neck with both hands while emitting a low groan.

Andrew set aside the carborundum stone. "All done?"

She grimaced, stretching her arms over her head. "With a very rough draft, yes. I'll set it aside and look at it later. I need a little distance now."

Andrew nodded. He understood what she meant. Taking a break from a design allowed the artist to view it with a fresh perspective. He always needed at least three hours between first and second drafts. He jerked his head toward the window. "Snow's stopped. You could probably make that run to Wichita now."

Beth swiveled to look at the window, and her face lit. "Oh, good!" Hopping off the stool, she put the drawing pad and pencil in the drawer. Then she headed for the stack of cardboard and Styrofoam sheets they used to cushion the finished projects for travel. "I'll probably grab a sandwich at home and eat it on the way. Feel free to take your lunch break whenever you like." The squeak of Styrofoam nearly covered her words. "Do you plan to stick around all afternoon? You don't have to if you don't want to."

Andrew watched as she put a layer of foam over the top of the cardinal scene, hiding it from view. "I'll stick around. Maybe by the time you get back, I'll have one of these suncatchers put together."

She flashed a quick grin over her shoulder. "Only one? I figured a half dozen at least."

He smiled. These teasing moods of hers were fun. He just was never sure how to tease back. "Well. . .we'll see."

She laughed lightly as if he'd said something humorous and wrapped the package with wide, clear tape. Standing, she swished her hands together. "Would you mind putting that in the trunk of my car?"

"Sure." Andrew slipped his coat on, then lifted the scene and followed Beth to her car. Fresh snow clumped on their shoes, and Beth banged her feet on the lower edge of the car door opening before swinging her legs inside the vehicle. He slammed the trunk lid, then gave it a pat. "Have a safe drive."

Beth peeked out the open door and waved. "Thanks. Enjoy your afternoon." She yanked the door closed, and the engine revved to life. Andrew remained on the concrete slab by the back door, watching bits of snow fly from her tires as she pulled away. When she turned the corner from the alley, he stepped into the studio and closed the door against the chill.

He removed his coat and his boots, leaving the wet boots beside the door, and walked on stocking feet to the storage cabinet. He reached for the drawer that contained the copper foil, but he didn't open it. His gaze shifted to the drawer where Beth had put her drawing for McCauley's window.

Curiosity shifted him two drawers to the left. Feeling like an intruder, he slid the drawer open slowly. The sketch tablet came into view, showing Beth's drawing by inches. He kept sliding until the entire design was revealed. At first glance, it reminded him of looking into a kaleidoscope. Almost a starburst pattern. He lifted it out and held it at arm's length, examining it. He scowled. Although the design was pleasing in balance, something was missing.

Propping it on the cabinet, he took a step back, pulling his lips to the side in contemplation as he allowed his focus to shift from the center to the outward edges. He snapped his fingers, recognizing the problem.

Snatching up the pad, he tore Beth's sheet loose and dropped it on the worktable. He placed the pad with its clean top sheet next to her drawing. Looking back and forth from her design to the page in front of him, he began to draw.

"This is beautiful, Beth." Marilyn Fox, owner of the Wichita gallery, sent Beth a huge smile. "I'm sure the interest in this piece will be high."

Beth released the breath she'd been holding. It came out with a light giggle. "Oh, I'm so relieved. This is still so new to me."

"It won't be new for long," Marilyn predicted, giving Beth's shoulder a squeeze.

Beth nodded, thinking of the contract in the passenger seat of her car. If she ended up working with McCauley Church Construction, she would be thrown into the world of stained-glass art. Her pulse accelerated at the thought.

"Well, let's talk about your next piece for us, shall we?"

The words captured Beth's attention, and she jerked her gaze from the cardinal scene to the smiling gallery owner. "But this one hasn't even sold yet."

"Oh, it will." Her arm still around Beth's shoulders, she herded Beth into her small, cluttered office at the rear of the store. "I've been in the business long enough to recognize the keepers. And you, Beth, are a keeper." The woman's arched brows rose with her words of praise.

Beth twisted her fingers together. "I really appreciate your vote of confidence," she said, hoping her tone didn't sound as uncertain as she felt, "but I'm not sure I have the time to do another commissioned piece right now."

Marilyn sank into the chair behind her desk. Resting her elbows on the arms of the chair, she made a steeple of her fingers and stared at Beth. "Oh?"

"No." Beth stood on the opposite side of the desk, seeking an explanation that wouldn't divulge the possibility with McCauley's. She wasn't sure she should speak of it until it was final, but if she signed that contract, her time would be wrapped up in the large window. She latched onto the only certainty. "I am in the middle of making several small pieces for a crafts fair which is coming up quickly, and—"

Marilyn waved a manicured hand. "Beth, that little stuff is fine for someone who dabbles. But you are an artist. You can't afford to dabble."

In doubt about how to respond, Beth remained silent.

"Let someone else do the little stuff if you still want to have things in craft fairs." Marilyn raised one brow. "Didn't you say you had a man helping?"

Beth nodded. "Yes, and he's quite capable, but—"

"Then let him fry the small fish, and you work on reeling in the whale." Marilyn shook her head, her chandelier earrings catching the light. "Really, Beth, you have the talent to go far as an artist. The question is do you have the drive?"

"Of course I do." Beth's reply came automatically.

Marilyn's smile grew. "Good. Then let's talk about the second piece." She pointed to a plastic chair in the corner.

Beth dragged the chair to the desk and sat down. An hour later, Beth had in hand a one-page contract for a second commissioned design that would feature a cardinal on a lilac bush. Ideas for that scene competed with the image of the window for McCauley's as she drove back to Sommerfeld, and worry made her clench the steering wheel so hard her fingers ached.

"God, have I gotten myself in over my head?" She spoke aloud, feeling comfortable sharing her thoughts in the privacy of the vehicle. She sucked in a breath of apprehension. "Should I have prayed before agreeing to a second commissioned piece?" Marilyn had seemed so certain it was the right thing to do, and Beth did want to use the talent God had given her. How often should she seek the Lord's guidance in these decisions? Uncertainty made her heart race. "Oh, I hope I did the right thing."

She continued to stew the remainder of the drive, but by the time she pulled behind the studio, she had calmed herself with the reminder that she wasn't working alone. Andrew was helping. As Marilyn had said, if he assumed responsibility for the little things, it would free her to focus on the larger projects.

Although she had changed back into her suit for the trip to the gallery and it wasn't appropriate for the studio, she couldn't resist pulling in to see how much progress Andrew had made with the suncatchers during her nearly five-hour leave of absence.

She hop-skipped through the slushy snow to the back stoop and stepped inside. When she entered the studio, she saw Andrew at the worktable and smiled. But when she spotted the loose pieces of glass still scattered across the wood surface, her smile faded.

Andrew's head jerked up. "Beth. . ." His cheeks blotched red. He slapped a drawing pad upside down, creating a current that sent a single sheet scooting from the table. Beth walked over and picked up the paper. Her scowl deepened when she recognized the drawing she'd made that morning.

She looked at him, suspicion creating a sour taste in her mouth. "What are you doing?" Looking pointedly at the unconstructed sun-catcher pieces, she added, "Obviously not what I had anticipated."

Andrew raised his shoulders in a sheepish gesture. "I guess I lost track of time."

Beth released a little huff. "So what are you doing?"

When he didn't answer, she held out her hand. After a moment's hesitation, Andrew slid the pad of paper across the table to her. She turned it over, and her jaw dropped.

"You're reworking my design?" Who did he think he was, sitting here doodling on something that didn't concern him rather than completing the work she'd assigned?

"Well, I looked at yours, and it seemed like something was missing—the depth just wasn't there. So I thought—"

"So you thought you'd fix it, huh?" Her voice squeaked out two decibels higher than normal. Slapping the pad onto the table, she glared at him. "I can't believe this! I leave you with a simple task: finish some suncatchers. And instead you spend the day working on a design that I fully intended to complete when I returned. This was a rough draft!" She waved the drawing. "You knew that! So why mess with it?"

Andrew opened his mouth, but nothing came out.

Beth's anger burned hotter with his lack of explanation. "Andrew, I trusted you to work on these." Her hand quivered as she pointed to the glass wedges on the tabletop. "And you let me down. If I can't trust you, then. . ." She didn't complete the thought, but she knew by the way Andrew's face went white that he understood the unspoken threat.

Shaking her head, she crushed her drawing and the pad holding his drawing to her coat front. "I'm going home now. I need to talk to Mom and Henry. I need to. . .think. You"—she backed toward the door, taking the drawings with her—"just lock up and go home."

Six

Beth pulled behind the simple, ranch-style house her mother and stepfather shared, turned off the ignition, and took a deep breath to calm her rattled nerves. Finding Andrew fiddling with her design had brought a dizzying sense of déjà vu followed by a wave of panic. She could not allow another man to sabotage her plans!

Peering through the car's window, she focused on the concrete foundation that would eventually support the two rooms Henry was adding to the west side of the house. She remembered his elation when Mom told them the doctor had detected two heartbeats. Henry's laughter echoed in her memory along with his joyous comment, "Well, Marie, we hoped to be blessed with two children. I just didn't expect to have both blessings at once!" He had immediately begun planning the addition so each of the new family members would have their own space.

Suddenly the concrete slab wavered, and Beth realized tears swam in her eyes. She brushed them away impatiently. What was wrong with her, sitting here getting all teary? Tired. That's all. She was tired from her long days at the studio. And they didn't promise to get shorter.

With a sigh, she snatched up the contract Sean McCauley had left and stepped out of her car. Henry had apparently put a snow shovel to work—the walkway was clear—so her feet stayed dry as she walked to the back porch. Although Henry had encouraged her to forgo knocking and just walk in, she didn't feel comfortable doing it. This wasn't her home. She tapped on the door and waited for an answer.

Mom's smiling face appeared in the window before the door swung wide. "Honey!" Mom tugged her across the threshold and delivered a hug made awkward by her bulky front. "I was hoping you'd stop by. Andrew said you finished the cardinal piece and it was beautiful. Did you bring it with you so I can see it?"

Beth pushed the door shut behind her, twisting her lips into a scowl. "No, I didn't even think about bringing it by. But I took some digital pictures. I'll show you after I get them downloaded."

Mom sighed, feigning a quick pout before flashing a grin. "Well, I guess that will have to do." Then she linked arms with Beth. "Come on in, then, and talk to me while I finish dinner. Do you want to stay?"

Beth sagged into a chair, plopping the contract onto the little table tucked into the corner of the kitchen. "I have something I need to talk to you and Henry about, so that'd be great. Thanks." She pushed her coat from her shoulders, allowing it to droop over the chair back, and watched her mother putter around the modest kitchen.

Her mother had changed so much since they'd left Cheyenne, there were still times when Beth did a double take. Home-sewn dresses instead of jeans and a button-up shirt; hair pulled into a bun beneath a white cap trailing black ribbons instead of tousled, loose curls; and a relaxed countenance rather than the lines of tension she'd often worn around her eyes and mouth. Returning to her childhood home had been good for Mom.

"So what did you do today since the cardinal piece was done?" Mom stirred something in an iron skillet on the stove, and the scent of peppers and onions filled the room.

"Drove to Wichita to deliver it." Beth sniffed, and her stomach turned over in eagerness. "And commissioned a second piece, this time with the cardinal in a lilac bush."

Mom sent a quick glance over her shoulder, her eyebrows high. "A second piece? That's great! A lilac bush. With those tiny flowers, that should be a challenge."

Beth flicked the stack of pages on the table with her thumbnail. "I'll probably find a piece of mottled lavender glass, maybe with some texture, to emulate the petals. I'll have to play around with it." She hoped she'd have time to play around with it.

"Sounds fun." Mom slipped a lid on the skillet and waddled to the sink. The added girth around her middle stole her usual grace, and her ankles seemed thick.

Beth frowned. "Are your feet swollen?"

Mom tipped forward, tucking her skirt against the underside of her extended belly to look at her own feet. She straightened with a soft laugh. "Oh, that's not so bad. Sometimes my ankles seem to disappear, and my toes stick out in all directions."

A stab of worry struck. "Did you do that when you were carrying me?"

Mom paused for a moment, sending Beth a crinkly smile. "Now, honey, you have to remember I've aged a bit since you were born."

Despite herself, Beth smiled. Never would she have imagined becoming a big sister at twenty-one. She teased, "Yes, I guess it's a good thing you have all your brothers and sisters, Henry's brothers and sister, plus their assorted offspring to give you a hand."

Mom tipped her head, one black ribbon trailing down her neck. "And you?"

Beth shrugged, looking at the contract. A band seemed to constrict her heart. "With all of them, you don't really need me."

A hand descended on Beth's shoulder, bringing her attention around. "Beth, you realize these babies can never replace you, don't you?"

The tenderness in Mom's eyes brought the sting of tears. Beth sucked in her lips, gaining control, before she answered. "It's just that everything is so different, Mom. So many changes. . . Sometimes it's hard to stay on top of it all."

Mom went back to the stove, turned the dial, and joined Beth at the table. She took Beth's hand, stroking her knuckles with her thumb. "You realize you don't have to stay on top of it all alone, don't you? You can ask God for help, and He'll answer every time. As for other helpers, you have Henry and me, and Andrew."

At Andrew's name, an image of him hunkered over the worktable, redoing her drawing instead of constructing suncatchers, flashed through Beth's mind. She jerked her hand free.

Mom frowned. "Beth?"

Beth shook her head. "I appreciate having you and Henry, and of course I know God is there for me. I'm still learning how to lean on Him, but I do know He's there. But as for Andrew. . ." She puffed her cheeks and blew out a breath. "I must not be a very good judge of character when it comes to men. They let me down every time."

"What has Andrew done?"

"Oh, nothing much. Just ignored my direction to put together suncatchers for the show in Salina and spent his time reworking a drawing he had no business reworking." Beth attempted a glib tone, but she heard the sharp undercurrent.

Mom's face pinched. "I'm sure his motivations were good."

Beth bounced from the chair, marching to the stove to stir the contents of the skillet. "Just like Mitch's motivations were good when he illegally 'collected' antiques for our boutique?" Vegetables and chunks of chicken caught the fury of the wooden spoon before she clanked the lid back in place. Facing her mother, she crossed her arms. "No, I'm better off working alone. That way, things get done the way *I* want them done without any misunderstandings or deceptiveness."

Her gaze fell on the contract, which lay on the table. Her heart skipped a beat. How would she keep up with everything on her own? A wave of panic struck, a silent prayer forming without effort. *God, how am I going to meet these demands?*

Mom struggled from the chair, arching her back to lift herself. With one hand pressed to her lower back, she crossed the kitchen to cup Beth's cheek with her free hand. "Honey, don't sell everyone short because Mitch made a mistake. Being alone is. . ." She heaved a sigh, her eyes drifting shut for a moment as if reliving something. "Lonely. Don't cut yourself away from everyone out of fear."

Beth felt tears sting behind her nose again. She sniffed. "I don't want to, Mom, but—"

The back door banged open, and Henry Braun entered the kitchen. His nose and ears were red from the cold, his hair stood on end, and he carried in the odors of cold air and gasoline. He bestowed a huge smile on both women. "Well, good evening! My two favorite girls." He crossed the kitchen and kissed Beth's cheek and then his wife's lips.

Beth, watching their kiss of greeting, felt a pang of envy. It must be wonderful to fully belong with someone the way her mother now belonged with Henry. She shoved that thought aside. Belonging to someone meant depending on them. And it meant being let down.

"Are you staying for dinner?" Henry asked Beth as he lifted the lid from the skillet and peeked at the contents.

"If that's okay." Beth watched Henry waggle his eyebrows in her mother's direction, his face creased in a grin. The serious Henry who had shown up unexpectedly at their apartment in Cheyenne fifteen months ago had transformed into a lighthearted, teasing man nearly impossible to resist.

"Perfectly okay." He slipped the lid in place and rubbed his stomach. "I'll try to control myself, even though your lovely mother has prepared stir-fry, one of my favorites."

Mom's tinkling laughter rang as she shook her head at her husband. Beth wondered if she should creep away now and leave the two of them alone. But Mom turned to her and pointed to the cupboard.

"Would you set the table, Beth? I'll make sure the rice is done, and then after Mr. Braun here has washed up"—she looked pointedly at Henry's hands, which he examined with mock dismay—"we can eat."

Half an hour later, the last of the rice had been scraped onto Henry's plate, and Beth's stomach ached from the second portion she hadn't needed but had eaten anyway. Leaning back in her chair, she took a sip of water and sighed.

"That was really good, Mom. Now I know why it's one of Henry's favorites."

Mom sent a fond smile across the table to her husband. "You know, he puts the title 'one of my favorites' on everything I fix, even if it's just a bologna sandwich."

Henry grinned. "That's because no one spreads mayonnaise on a slice of bread like you do—just the right amount to bring out the flavor of the bologna without overpowering it."

"Oh, Henry." Mom released an amused snort, shaking her head.

Even Beth had to laugh. Honeymooners. That's what her parents were. And at their ages! Still, she had to admit it was wonderful to see them so contented. She only wished they didn't seem so. . .complete. Where did that leave her?

Henry swallowed the final bite of rice, wiped his mouth, and fixed Beth with an intent look. "Now, your mother said you have something to discuss with us."

Beth appreciated the way her stepfather removed all teasing from his tone before addressing her. Never had Henry treated her with anything except respect and kindness, the way she had always wanted a father to treat her. Sometimes she wished she could set aside her inhibitions and accept him as readily as he had accepted her. Yet the remembrance of another father—one she'd never had the opportunity to meet—always reared up, tangling her emotions and distancing her from Henry.

But he was right: She did have something to discuss, and she did respect his opinion. She plucked up the contract, which she had placed on the floor beside her chair, and handed it across the table. While Henry leafed through it, Beth shared the details of the visit from Sean McCauley and their conversation. Both Henry and Mom listened intently, interrupting occasionally to ask a question.

Beth finished, "It looks like it would be a wonderful opportunity if I can satisfy them with that first project."

Henry looked over the top of the contract, his eyebrows high. "And all the expense falls on you if they don't like it. Can you absorb that?"

Beth grimaced. "It would be painful. It would take quite a few craft-fair sales to make up for it, that's for sure. But the risk would be worth it considering the potential payoff if they do like it. Lots more work, plus the income to expand the studio and buy the equipment I need to be completely self-sufficient."

Henry nodded and went back to reading.

"What about the gallery in Wichita?" Mom, leaning sideways to peek at the contract, shifted her gaze in Beth's direction. "Can't they keep you busy enough?"

With a shrug, Beth stifled her frustration. Being torn between the gallery opportunities and the construction company's opportunities left her feeling bruised. "I don't know. They did commission a second piece, and Mrs. Fox indicated there would be more, but it's still small scale compared to what McCauley is after."

Henry shot a startled glance at his wife. "The gallery commissioned Beth to do a second piece?"

Mom nodded, pride shining in her face. "Yes, they did. She delivered the first one, and they immediately asked for a second."

Beth wriggled on her chair, feeling as though she'd been forgotten.

But Henry set the contract aside and fixed his gaze on her. "There's no doubt this could be financially lucrative if it works out, Beth. I guess what it comes down to is what you want to accomplish with your studio. Do you want to be strictly an artist, creating your own designs on your own time clock, which gives you freedom but maybe lacks security? Or do you want the security of knowing you'll have steady jobs, putting together windows with someone else's idea at the heart, and you serving as the constructor?"

Steady, secure work opposite sporadic, unreliable contracts. Designing her own projects opposite following someone else's lead. The thoughts ping-ponged in Beth's mind, making her dizzy with the possible pros and cons of each position. Finally, she threw her hands out and huffed in aggravation. "I want the security with the freedom to create my own stuff!"

Henry chuckled softly while Mom shook her head, her lips tipped into an amused smile.

"Well, Beth," Henry said, one eyebrow cocked high, "the only way I see clear for that is if you continue doing both your own artwork *and* meet the demands of this construction company. To be honest, I'm not so sure you could handle all that on your own."

Beth sighed. "So what do I do?"

Henry shrugged. "If you want it all, hire a full-time staff."

Slumping back in her chair, Beth swallowed the groan that pressed at her throat. A full-time staff. As if workers were lining up for jobs in this little Mennonite farming community! She knew of only one person willing to dedicate time to the art studio.

It was back to Andrew.

Andrew unplugged the soldering iron and rotated his head, trying to work loose the tense kinks in his neck. The acrid taste from the solder lingered on the back of his tongue, making him wish he had one of those bottles of water Beth liked to carry around with her. Placing the soldering iron on the concrete floor to cool, he turned back to the worktable.

Satisfaction welled, bringing a tired smile to his face. It had been a hard eight hours of steady work, but seeing the suncatchers lined up, ready for the craft show, made it worthwhile. Hopefully this would make up for this afternoon, when he'd fiddled with Beth's drawing instead of doing what she'd asked him to do.

"You let me down."

Her remembered words stung on a variety of levels. He'd been taught to honor his commitments, and it created a sense of disappointment in himself that he hadn't followed through on what had been expected. Deeper than that, though, was Beth's lack of understanding that he wasn't trying to let her down—he was trying to help. There had been something wrong with her design, and he had discovered the needed element to bring out the dimension.

He wished she'd at least looked at what he'd done before flinging out an accusation and storming off. Hadn't she figured out by now that he wanted what was best for her? For them? Sighing, Andrew picked up a little whisk broom and began cleaning up the work area.

Sometimes he wondered if his fascination with Beth was unhealthy. She was so different from the other girls in the community. And it was much more than the way she dressed. She was self-reliant, a freethinker. She didn't let anybody tell her what to do. Some perceived this as pigheaded, but Andrew preferred to think of it as independent. He admired it.

And at the same time, he resented it. An independent person didn't need anybody else. Andrew wanted Beth to need him. One thing was certain: He needed her if he wanted to use his artistic abilities full-time.

His cleanup finished, he yawned and reached for his coat. Outside, full dark had fallen, letting him know without looking at a clock that it was well past his normal bedtime. But before heading out the door, he glanced once more at the worktable. Returning to the table, he took a moment to arrange the suncatchers in a neat line.

When Beth came in tomorrow morning, she would see he had honored his commitment. She'd teasingly told him to make half a dozen. He'd done it. She would see she needed him as much as he needed her.

SEVEN

A dull ache throbbed at the base of Beth's skull as she brushed her teeth. Straightening from bending over the sink, a wave of dizziness hit, and she grabbed the porcelain basin to steady herself.

"Whew, I hope I'm not coming down with something."

Her equilibrium restored, she headed to the bedroom to dress. It was early for her to be up—especially for a Saturday—but she didn't know when Sean McCauley would be stopping by, and she needed to be ready.

Her hands trembled slightly as she slipped on a fuzzy sweater, and again she wondered if she was getting sick. But then she shook her head, reminding herself of her restless night. Of course she felt wimpy this morning. It had been well after two when she looked at the clock last, which meant she'd had fewer than five hours of sleep.

"Once I get some coffee in me, I'll be fine," she encouraged herself as she sat on the edge of the bed to tie her sneakers. Bending down that way made her head spin, and she added through gritted teeth, "And I better eat something, too."

She considered going to the café for breakfast. The new owner, Henry's sister Deborah, baked the most delectable cinnamon buns.

But Saturday mornings were always busy at the café, and Beth might have to wait to be seated. She didn't want to waste time this morning. Instead, she visited her own kitchen, frowning at the limited choices.

With a sigh, she plunked a mug of coffee left over from yesterday's pot in the microwave and dropped two frozen waffles in the toaster. The microwave dinged just as the toaster tossed the waffles into the air. Leaning against the counter, she munched the dry, blueberry-flavored waffles and sipped the bitter liquid. Although it couldn't compete with Deborah's cinnamon buns and freshly brewed coffee, it filled her belly and revived her enough to go to the studio. Tucking the drawing pad containing both hers and Andrew's designs and the thick contract beneath her arm, she headed to her vehicle for the short drive.

Cars—plain ones and "worldly" ones—lined Main Street, providing evidence of the café's patronage of both Mennonite and non-Mennonite customers. Lisbeth's Café had brought in the highway traffic for more than four decades. The café was as popular now as it had been when Beth's great-aunt had operated it. Beth had chosen to build her studio on the south side of the café partly because the land had been bequeathed to her and partly because it was a great opportunity to pull in café customers when she finally built the showroom addition.

Her heart pounded as it always did when she thought of her dreams for the studio. Although she'd lain awake last night, mulling things over and over in her mind, she still wasn't 100 percent certain about signing on the dotted line with McCauley Church Construction. *God, You're going to have to clunk me hard with an answer before Sean McCauley gets to the studio. I want to do the right thing.*

She pulled her car into its usual spot behind the studio and entered through the back door. Tugging off her coat, she flipped on the fluorescent lights and then dropped her coat onto the end of the display bench. She pulled a work apron from a box beneath the bench and tied it over her clothes. Finally, she turned toward the cabinet to retrieve the copper foil and soldering iron so she could get those cut pieces turned into suncatchers.

But as she shifted, her gaze drifted across the worktable, and she froze, her eyes widening. Six suncatchers lay in a row across the tabletop, glittering beneath the bright overhead lights. She moved slowly toward the table, shaking her head. "It's like 'The Elves and the Shoemaker,' " she muttered, remembering her favorite of the Grimms' fairy tales her mother had read to her when she was small.

One by one, she touched the completed projects. She then lifted a pink cross to the light to admire the change in colors. Placing the piece back on the table with the others, she drew in a slow breath through her nose. Apparently Andrew hadn't gotten much sleep last night, either. Guilt pricked when she recalled how she had berated him for spending his time drawing instead of completing projects. He'd followed through after all.

Different emotions warred in her breast. When she saw him next, she'd thank him and apologize for being so snappy, but she would also need to talk to him about his position in the studio. He was her employee, not her partner. His job was to follow her directions. Period. No more of this acting on his own.

After retrieving cardboard and foam, she made a careful stack, sandwiching the suncatchers between protective layers, and put them in a box labeled "Salina—2/22." That done, she slid the box beneath the display bench next to the box containing butterfly designs. Recalling Sean McCauley telling her the company's interest in her stemmed from the purchase of a simple purple butterfly, her heart doubled its rate.

How quickly life can change, she thought, moving to the clean work-table and staring out the window across the snow-dusted landscape. Lost in thought, the sound of the back door opening startled her, and she whirled toward it in time to spot Andrew stepping through. He yawned as he slipped out of his coat, and she couldn't help but smile at his droopy expression.

"Rough night last night?" She deliberately affected a teasing tone.

He shrugged and didn't reply, sending her a sheepish look.

His silence told her clearly he felt uncomfortable after their last heated, one-sided exchange. Taking a breath, she formed an apology. "Andrew, I'm sorry I jumped on you like I did yesterday."

He responded with a silent nod, his lips pulled to the side.

Puffing her cheeks, Beth blew an exasperated breath that ruffled her bangs across her forehead. She shoved the strands aside and said, "Look, I got testy because I know how much I have to get accomplished and I can't"—she gritted her teeth for a moment, reality creating a knot in her stomach—"do it all alone. I need to know I can depend on you."

"You can." He finally spoke, his tone carrying a hint of defensiveness.

"Really?" She tipped her head, her eyebrows high. "To do what I ask you to do, rather than what you want to do?"

Andrew's lips formed a grim line. His dark eyes narrowed, and for a moment Beth wondered if he was going to spew angry words. She'd never witnessed him being anything but mild mannered, but she'd never pushed him quite so hard, either.

Finally, he gave a brusque nod. "You're the boss."

She fought a grin. "Don't make it sound so painful."

An answering grin, albeit a weak one, found its way to his face. "Sorry."

Beth's stomach fluttered. Remembering Henry's comment that

she would need help were she to meet the demands of the new opportunity as well as continuing to create her own artwork, she pressed. "Andrew, you realize if I sign this initial contract with McCauley, it could mean big changes around here. Can you deal with that?"

Andrew stood for a moment, his gaze aimed somewhere to her left, his jaw working back and forth as if in deep thought. She waited, wondering if she was about to be left to handle things on her own and trying to decide if it would be for the best if she was. At last, he looked at her and shoved his hands into his pockets, hunching his shoulders.

"Honestly? I'm hoping for big changes. I'd like to work here full-time, year-round. To do that, you've got to make this studio a raving success. All that craft-fair stuff, it's fun, but it won't take you places." He nodded toward the worktable, where she'd placed the contract. "That opportunity from McCauley—that's the big time. That's where I want to go. So I'll do what it takes to get there."

Beth fought a frown. While his words were spoken with conviction and he offered his assistance without hesitation, something didn't set quite right. She couldn't put her finger on it. While she processed his reply, seeking the reason for the discomfort that wiggled through her chest, a tap at the front door captured her attention.

Andrew charged past her and opened the door. Sean McCauley, his face wearing a broad grin, stepped into the studio.

"Good morning." Sean unbuttoned his jacket, swinging his smile from Andrew Braun to Beth Quinn. He let it linger on Beth. Once again, her attractiveness took him by surprise. Working with her would be a pleasure in more ways than one.

"Good morning." She walked toward him, the stiff apron crackling with the movement, and held out her hand. "I trust you had a good night's rest?"

"Yes, I did. Thanks for asking." He observed the tired lines around her eyes and refrained from asking her the same question. "And did you have a chance to look over the contract thoroughly?"

She nodded, her gaze shifting briefly toward her employee. "Yes. Andrew and I were just discussing how my signing it could alter our focus."

Sean raised one brow. "Alter your focus in a positive light, I hope."

Beth didn't answer. Instead, she turned toward the worktable, moving to the opposite side and climbing onto a stool. She pointed to another stool. "Please join me."

Sean accepted her invitation while Andrew remained rooted in the middle of the floor.

Beth seemed to wait for Andrew to make a move on his own. When he didn't, she sent a tense smile in his direction and said, "Andrew, I doubt I'll be doing any real work this morning, so you can feel free to go if you'd like."

For a brief moment, Andrew's face clouded. Then his expression relaxed, he gave a nod, and he moved toward the back door. "Fine." Sean suspected there was more the man wanted to say, but Andrew clamped his jaw and tugged on a coat. "I'll see you Monday then." He headed out the door.

Beth turned her attention to Sean. "Okay, let's talk shop."

Sean rested his elbows on the tabletop. "Before we get into the contract, would you mind telling me how you got involved in stained-glass art?" Jerking his thumb toward the outside, he commented, "Seems a rather unusual business for this area. Stained glass is pretty ostentatious. You sure won't have customers from the community."

Beth's light laugh made Sean smile. "Oh, no, I'm certain the

Sommerfeld residents won't purchase my goods. But we get quite a bit of traffic through here. The café brings in customers, and we also get an unbelievable number of gawkers."

Sean raised his brows.

Another laugh rang. "Curiosity satisfiers. People interested in the simpler lifestyle of the Mennonites and Amish who live around here."

"And that's why you built your studio here? To capture the business of the gawking curiosity satisfiers?"

"Partly." She took a deep breath, as if seeking fortification. "You see, my mom grew up in Sommerfeld, on a farm east of town. She left the community to marry my dad, and we lived in Wyoming until about a year and a half ago. Mom's favorite aunt passed away and left the café and her house to me."

"Why you?" Sean was genuinely intrigued.

A slight shrug accompanied her reply. "Mom named me Lisbeth after her aunt. I guess since Great-Aunt Lisbeth never had children of her own, she chose me to be her inheritor."

Sean got the impression there was more to the story than Beth was sharing. He waited a few beats to see if she would continue, but when she didn't, he said, "That was nice."

"Nice. . ." Beth licked her lips. "And unexpected. So, Mom and I found ourselves in Sommerfeld. I had land to build on and, with the sale of the café, funds to put up the building. Mom says it was God's way of meeting my need before I knew I had one."

Again Sean suspected he was getting the *Reader's Digest* version, but he didn't push her to give more details. For whatever reason, she was guarding herself. There would be time to get the full story when their relationship had developed further. "I see. So you always planned to have a studio?" He was puzzled by the pain that flashed through her blue eyes.

"No. Stained-glass art is something I learned when I came to Sommerfeld. But it grew on me quickly."

Her light tone made him wonder if he'd imagined the earlier signs of discomfort. He smiled. "I'm glad it did. My company can certainly benefit from your newly acquired ability."

She swallowed, her gaze jerking away for a moment before lighting on the contract. Her fingers trembled slightly as she gently flipped the corners of the pages. "Yes, well, let's hope this will be mutually beneficial."

"There's no doubt," Sean said, leaning forward. "My biggest concern at this point is whether you truly have the space to create the kinds of windows we'd need." He patted the top of the four-foot square worktable. "This won't be big enough."

She lifted her gaze to meet his. "I know. But my stepfather and Andrew could build a work surface in that open area—a platform to get the design up off the floor a bit but low to the ground to make it easier to work on larger designs."

Sean chuckled. "You've been doing your homework."

Her smile turned timid, making his heart skip a beat. "Eventually, I'd need a larger studio if I plan to construct more than one window at a time and especially if I add more equipment so I can stain and fire my own glass and have more than one cutter going, but I don't want to go to too much expense until I know for sure things will work out."

Sean smoothed his mustache with one finger, nodding with approval. Her caution impressed him. She had business savvy. From his conversation with her yesterday, he already knew she had the desire to expand her business. All necessary elements for success were in place: the drive, the talent, and the means. She was the perfect choice.

"So do you have any concerns about the contract itself?" He maintained the same light, interested tone he'd used earlier when questioning her about her interest in stained-glass art. It made for a smooth transition into business talk.

"For the most part, I'm fine with the contract. The financial compensation is fair considering the number of hours that will go into each window, and your past experience in dealing with the purchase of windows shows me you understand how much time is needed to create the artwork."

Sean nodded, smiling. *So far, so good.*

Beth flipped the contract open, her gaze scanning the printed pages. When she located what she wanted, she turned the pages around and pointed to a block of text. "But I am concerned about the clause that gives you the right to refuse the windows once completed. That leaves me holding a piece that would, in all likelihood, be unsuitable for any other purpose. The amount of time and expense going into creating it would then be lost."

"That's unlikely to happen if you meet the requirements on the first piece," he reminded her. "You're new in this line of business, so we're taking a chance on you. We need to be certain you can do what we're asking you to do."

"I understand that. It's a protective clause." Her eyes bored into his, not so much as a hint of a smile lighting her eyes. "But all the protection is at your end. How can we even the scale?"

Sean assumed the same businesslike attitude she had adopted. "We *can't* even the scale until we know for sure you can produce. Once the first window is completed to our satisfaction, you'll have proven yourself. At that point, you become an employee of McCauley Church Construction with the same rights and privileges of all other workers."

Beth sucked in her lips, observing him with narrowed eyes. "So you're asking me to purchase glass, set aside all other projects—which equates to no other means of income—until I have completed this single piece of artwork. And then it's possible you can reject it, which would leave me holding the tab."

"You make it sound so cutthroat." Sean offered a light laugh. She didn't respond in kind. He linked his fingers together, his arms on the table, and dropped all flippancy. "Look, Beth, if you're concerned your abilities won't meet our expectation, you don't have to sign that contract. I'm not going to force you. I admit this first window puts a lot of pressure on you. But when"—he purposely chose to avoid the word *if*—"you prove yourself, you stand to gain the means to turn this place into a full-blown studio. I gathered from your comments yesterday that that's what you'd like."

Her nod told him she was listening.

"If things go well, you could be the designer, hire a staff of workers to construct the windows, and turn more of your attention to being the artist behind the projects rather than the producer. That would free you up to work on your own projects in addition to ours."

Slipping a pen from the pocket of his shirt, he held it out. "We're willing to give you a chance. Sure, it might mean the loss of a few weeks and a portion of your bank account, but it can lead to financial freedom, the expansion of your studio, and your name becoming synonymous with stained-glass art. So. . .is it worth the risk?"

For a moment, he feared he'd lost her. Her brow furrowed, her chin quivered, and she blinked rapidly while holding her breath. He offered a quick silent prayer for her to push past her fears. They both stood to gain tremendously if she would just take the chance.

Beth released her breath in a *whoosh* and shook her head, her blond tresses tumbling across her shoulders. Then she jerked the contract around, flipped the pages back to reveal the last page, and picked up the pen.

EIGHT

As soon as Sean McCauley left with the signed contract in his hand, Beth paced the studio. The opportunities made available by the contract loomed in front of her. Sean's comment about her being able to hire people to put the projects for his company together while she worked on her own projects had been the deciding factor. It was the best of both worlds, and the excitement of being able to fulfill all of her dreams concerning the studio set her heart pounding in her throat.

According to the contract, she had exactly two months to complete the first project—the kaleidoscope pattern must be finished by April 1. Charging to the worktable, she flipped open her sketch pad and removed the preliminary drawing she'd made. The pad open, she glimpsed Andrew's rendition, as well. She started to put it aside, but her breath caught. She held his design at arm's length.

Her gaze jerked between the drawing in her hand and the one lying on the table. The two designs were identical through the center, but at a middle row, a circle of diamonds, the similarity ended. Andrew had modified her diamond by lowering the apex and stretching the bottom half. The simple change added a breathtaking shift in the overall pattern, making it appear that the center portion of the design stood out from the background.

Dimension. Andrew had brought the dimension to the pattern, just as he had said.

She slapped his drawing on top of hers and closed the cover on the pad. His words rushed back. *"The big time. . .that's where I want to go."* Suddenly the discomfort she'd experienced earlier found a basis. Fear struck hard, making her break out in a cold sweat. Would Andrew's desire for success lead him to undermine her as Mitch had? She shook her head, trying to set aside the worry, yet it niggled.

"Once bitten, twice shy," she murmured. Turning her face toward the tiled ceiling, she prayed aloud. "Dear God, I'm going to need help, and Andrew is the only one who has any training around here. I need to depend on him, but now I'm afraid to."

When she was a little girl, Beth had always been able to run to her mother in times of fear or doubt. Although she was hardly a child anymore, the solace of her mother's attention became a pressing need. She glanced at the wall clock. Henry would be in his shop; Mom would be home alone. It gave her the perfect opportunity to spend some one-on-one time with her mother. Something that would be extremely rare once those twins made their appearance.

A wave akin to fear hit Beth, bringing the sting of tears. The desire to see Mom increased. Grabbing up her coat, she locked the studio and headed for her car. When she knocked on the back door of Henry's house, however, no one answered. Cupping her hands beside her eyes, she peered through the window. No lights on, no movement. With a frustrated sigh, she returned to her vehicle. Where could Mom be? She rarely ventured outside of Sommerfeld on Saturdays.

Beth considered going to her own home but decided against it. She didn't want to be alone right now. Even if she couldn't be with her mother, she wanted to be with someone. *The café,* she decided, putting the car into DRIVE and turning in that direction. Although it would be less busy now than it had been during the breakfast rush, she could sit in a corner booth, eat a leftover roll, and maybe visit with one of her cousins who served tables. Not the same as being with her mother, but it beat sitting at home by herself.

The Main Street parking areas were still filled with the plain-colored, Sommerfeld vehicles of citizens doing their weekend shopping, as Beth had learned was typical for the community. She parked behind her studio and walked to the café. Only two tables were filled, both with Sommerfeld citizens. The occupants sent lazy glances in her direction, then went back to visiting with each other. But Henry's niece, who waited tables and ran the dishwasher, skipped across the floor and held out her arms for a hug.

"Hi, Trina," Beth greeted, appreciating the quick embrace. Trina had been the first person to befriend her when she arrived in town, and Beth held a fondness for the bubbly teenager.

"Hi! Haven't seen you for a while, although Andrew keeps me up on what you're doing."

Beth's eyebrows rose. Andrew spoke of her to his family? Her stomach did a funny somersault with that news. "I do stay busy," she commented briefly as she followed Trina to an empty booth.

"And it promises to get busier, huh?" Trina's eyes sparkled. "Did you sign the contract with the big construction company that builds churches?"

Beth stifled a sigh. Although she knew she should appreciate the interest expressed by her stepfather's family, at times she wished the little community wasn't quite so knowledgeable. There were no secrets in Sommerfeld. With a forced smile, she nodded.

Trina clapped her hands. "Oh, good!"

Despite the reservations that had struck when she had replayed

Andrew's comment, Beth's spirits lifted with Trina's unbridled enthusiasm. Folding her arms on the tabletop, she said, "So do you want to give up your waitressing and come put windows together for me instead?"

For a moment, Trina's sunny disposition faded. "I'd like to give up the waitressing, but. . ."

Beth waited for Trina to finish her sentence, curiosity striking at the girl's serious expression.

The girl shook her head, making the little ribbons on her cap dance, and she winked. "I'll let Andrew be your helper. He's much better at it than I would be."

A frown pinched Beth's forehead. Before she could form a reply, Trina started backing away from the table.

"I'll go tell Aunt Marie you're here.".

"Mom's here?" Beth's heart leaped. She'd get to talk to Mom after all.

"In the kitchen with Mama. Do you want to come back, or should I send her out?"

Henry's sister Deborah, who now owned the café, was also in the kitchen. Although Deborah had warmed up considerably toward Beth in the months she'd lived in Sommerfeld, Beth still sensed the woman's disapproval of her worldly attire and mussy hairstyle. She made a quick choice.

"Send Mom out, please." She waited, her gaze on the doorway that led to the kitchen. When her mother appeared, Beth stood up and met her halfway across the room. Giving her a hug, she said, "I went by your house to see you. I didn't think to look here."

Mom grimaced as she walked with Beth to the booth. "I decided I could benefit from some exercise, but the brief walk has me all swollen again."

Beth glanced at her mother's feet and gasped. "Mom! You don't even have ankles!"

Mom's chuckle sounded as she peered at her own feet. "Oh, I'm sure my ankles are under there somewhere."

Beth huffed. "You know what I mean. What does the doctor say about this?"

Her mother's sheepish shrug as she slid into the booth provided the answer.

"You haven't mentioned it?" Beth's tone rose in volume, drawing the attention of nearby patrons.

Mom patted her hand. "Honey, please, it's nothing to be concerned about. Most women experience some foot swelling during pregnancy."

"But how do you even wear shoes?" It looked as though Mom's flesh spilled over the top of her simple oxfords. Beth released a shudder.

"I put them on before my feet swell. And then I don't dare take them off." Mom gave a little laugh that Beth didn't echo. "Now stop looking at me like that. I'll be fine. But I admit I'm glad to see you. You can drive me home."

"Of course I will." Beth drew in a deep breath, ready to question her mother about other discomforts related to pregnancy.

"Why were you looking for me?"

Mom's question shifted Beth's attention. "Oh, I wanted to let you know I signed the contract."

"Are you excited?"

Beth forced a short laugh. "Yes—and nervous. A lot rests on the success of this first project."

"You can do it, honey." Mom's warm hand on Beth's arm offered assurance. "You have wonderful ideas, lots of talent, and the gumption to see it through."

"And you aren't at all biased," Beth teased, pleasure spiraling through her chest at her mother's praise.

A light laugh crinkled Mom's eyes. "Of course not! I just know genius when I see it."

"Genius. Right." Beth shook her head, but she couldn't stop smiling.

"Besides, you aren't doing this alone."

Beth's heart skipped a beat. How much responsibility would everyone give to Andrew?

"Remember Philippians 4:13? 'I can do all things through Christ. . .' "

Beth finished, " 'Which strengtheneth me.' " She swallowed, pushing aside the prickle of guilt that pressed upward at her mother's reminder of Beth's ever-present help. She wondered how long it would be before thinking of God came before thinking of people.

The café door opened, allowing in a gust of cool air. Beth glanced toward the door and recognized her stepfather. She waved him over. When he reached the booth, he leaned down and gave his wife a kiss on her cheek before greeting Beth. "Hello! Andrew says the man from the construction company was by already. What did you decide?"

Beth released a snort. "News travels fast."

Henry sat beside Mom and stretched his arm along the back of the booth, his fingers grazing Mom's shoulder. "You can't blame Andrew for being excited. This affects him, too, you know."

Yes, Beth knew. Resisting the urge to scowl, she said, "I signed. So now I have until April 1 to put together a window that will knock McCauley Church Construction's socks off."

"You can do it," Henry said, but he smiled into Mom's face rather than looking at Beth. Mom whispered something that didn't reach Beth's ears.

Beth cleared her throat. "I may need your assistance. My worktable isn't large enough to accommodate a project of that size. Do you suppose you could build a platform in the open corner of the studio?"

Henry glanced in her direction. "A platform? Oh, sure, I don't know why not. When will you need it?" Immediately his attention returned to Mom's upturned face.

"I have lots of glass to order and cut first, so not right away." Beth watched her parents, unease tickling her spine. She looked away from them toward the other two filled tables. Conversations at the tables went on, oblivious to the three people in her booth.

Beth suddenly felt completely alone despite the fact that eight other people sat in the room with her. Would she ever feel as though she belonged in this community? Lowering her eyes, she stared at her jeans-covered legs draped with the tails of her flannel shirt. In her attire, she stuck out like a sore thumb from the Mennonite women in their simple, home-sewn dresses and neat caps.

Shifting her gaze slightly, she observed Mom and Henry's quiet exchange. Despite sitting directly across from her, they seemed to have forgotten she was there. Henry rested his broad hand on Mom's rounded abdomen, and she laughed softly into his face. Once again, Beth was struck by how complete her parents appeared. Unmindful of her. Unneedful of her. . .

She jumped from the booth, causing both Mom and Henry to look in her direction. "Listen, I'd better scoot. I have lots of planning to do if I'm going to get that project finished for McCauley. Henry can drive you home, right, Mom? I'll. . .I'll talk to you both later." She dashed from the café before either of them could answer.

Beth spent Saturday afternoon and evening reworking her drawing to scale until she was satisfied. Using Andrew's twist on the center row of diamonds changed her original idea, but she discovered she liked the new design much better. Using her all-in-one printer, she made several copies of the design, then set to work with colored pencils. She skipped supper to continue working, ignoring the growl of her stomach. When she was so tired her eyes no longer focused, blurring the colors together, she put the drawings aside and crawled into bed.

Her sleep that night was fitful, her dreams disconcerting. Images from the town blended with images from the city of her upbringing. Faces from Sommerfeld and others from Cheyenne kept coming and going until confusion jerked her out of sleep. Twice she awakened, her face damp, but she wasn't sure if sweat or tears were responsible for the moisture she felt on her skin.

When the morning sun crept between the cracks of the window blinds, she swung from the bed, relieved to be able to face reality instead of battling the odd, disjointed images of her dreams. With a yawn, she padded to the bathroom, then stood, staring at her reflection in the mirror. Her tangled hair stuck out in all directions, giving evidence of restless shifting on her pillow. Blue circles underscored her eyes, and her face looked pale.

"I'm a sight," she snorted. After running cold water on a washcloth, she mopped her face and then looked again at her reflection. The tiredness remained despite the thorough scrubbing.

"If I go to the meetinghouse looking like this," she spoke aloud to her dismal face in the mirror, "Mom will think I'm sick." With the thought of her mother came the remembrance of Henry and Mom in the booth yesterday, absorbed in one another. Swinging from the mirror, Beth charged to her bedroom and sank onto the edge of the mattress.

Her head slung low, she moaned, "Dear God, where do I fit in?"

She wasn't a member of the church, so she didn't belong there. Having been raised far away from the cousins who resided in this little town, she didn't blend in with them. Grown and out of her mother's house, she no longer fit there. She released a humorless huff of laughter as a childhood memory struck.

Every Christmas season, she and Mom had curled together on the sofa to watch the television version of *Rudolph, the Red-Nosed Reindeer*. She had loved to sing along with the characters. Now the lyrical question "Why am I such a misfit?" drifted through her mind, bringing both a rush of fond remembrance and a stab of pain. The words were too close to the truth.

Beth simply didn't fit in—not in Sommerfeld, not in her mother's house, not back in Cheyenne.

But she had her business, her art. Pushing to her feet, Beth straightened her shoulders with resolve. Hadn't Mom said God gave her the gift of creating beauty from bits of colored glass? Well, then, that's where Beth belonged: in her studio, creating beauty. And if the next few weeks went well, she'd have enough business to keep her too busy to worry about needing to fit in anywhere else. Her misfit days were nearing their end, thanks to the contract offered by McCauley Church Construction.

Knowing her mother would worry if she didn't show up at the meetinghouse for services, Beth laid out a modest skirt and blouse and headed for the shower. But when the service was over, she'd come home, get out her pencils again, and finish planning the window for McCauley's. By the end of the day, she'd shoot several color options to him via e-mail, and she hoped that by the end of tomorrow she'd be able to order glass.

She had one chance to carve her niche in the stained-glass world, and she wouldn't let it escape her.

NINE

Andrew shut off the cutting wheel. His ears buzzed as if the carbide wheel still screeched. He removed his goggles and peered toward the newly constructed platform where Beth sat cross-legged, scissors snipping a steady rhythm. Her shining ponytail captured the light, and as always, he found himself wondering if those strands felt as silky as they looked.

She turned and caught him staring.

Heat built in his ears, and he gestured clumsily toward the stack of glass he'd scored. "Got enough here for six more crosses and six butterflies."

A nod bounced her ponytail. "Good. I'm glad you're ahead of the game there, since my order of glass for this one"—she tipped her head toward the paper pieces scattered across the platform—"should be arriving this afternoon. That frees up the wheel for me to get to cutting."

Andrew fought a frown. She had hoarded each step of the process in creating the window for McCauley, spending every minute of the past week finalizing the colors, putting a rush order on glass, drawing the design to scale on butcher paper, and now cutting the pattern into pieces. He had hoped to at least help by cutting and fitting the glass pieces together, but apparently she intended to see this project through as a solo artist. He supposed he should be grateful she'd allowed him to help build the platform where she planned to construct her window.

Her brows pulled down in a brief scowl of worry. "I hope the glass will arrive as promised. I've got a pretty tight schedule to keep in order to meet McCauley's deadline."

Andrew considered telling her if she'd allow him to help, they could speed up the process, but instead, he glanced out the window at the sunshine-bright February day and said, "Can't see any reason why they'd be delayed."

Beth turned back to the paper spread across her lap and began snipping once more. "I sure hope not." Without looking at him, she said, "Go ahead and snap those pieces apart and then grind the edges. Hopefully by tomorrow, you'll be ready to put them together. And maybe you can ask Trina to go to Salina with you for the show so you'll have some company."

Andrew, reaching into the drawer for the pliers, jerked to attention. "You aren't going?"

She paused again to stare at him over her shoulder. "Of course not. I can't take a whole day away from here—at least not until this first project for McCauley is done. So from now until April 1, whatever shows we do are yours."

Andrew rounded the worktable to stand beside the platform and gawk down at her. "Trina can't take a Saturday off from the café." It was the only argument he could compose on short notice. He knew he shouldn't say what he was thinking: *But I look forward to those times when we go away together.* Away from Sommerfeld, Beth was more open, animated, and relaxed, which made him more open, animated, and relaxed. He relished those snatches of time.

Beth made a sour face. "Oh, I didn't think about that. Of course she couldn't." A graceful shrug bunched the blond ponytail that lay on her shoulder. "Well, you should be able to handle it on your own."

Her unconcerned comment set his teeth on edge. Andrew clomped back to the storage cabinet and snatched up the pliers.

"You could ask someone else if you prefer not to go alone."

Andrew preferred not to go alone, yet he didn't want anyone else's company. Besides, who else would be interested? His family either ignored or made sport of his art-related pursuits. Beth waited for an answer, the scissors motionless in her hand. He finally grunted, "We'll see."

She shot him a speculative look before offering another shrug and bending over the paper once more. They worked without speaking, with only the *snap* of the pliers, the muffled *clink* of glass pieces being placed on the table's surface, and the *snip-snip* of the scissors breaking the tomblike quiet. After a long while, Beth released a noisy breath and spun on her seat to face Andrew.

"What's your problem?"

Andrew, startled, raised one brow and pointed to his own chest.

A second huff split the air. "Yes, you."

"I don't have a problem." He'd lied. His chest constricted with the knowledge, yet he couldn't retract the words.

Beth crunched her lips into a scowl. "Oh, yes, you do, or you wouldn't be so sullen." Plopping the scissors onto the wooden platform with a solid *thunk*, she folded her arms and glared at him. "Come on, spit it out. Neither of us will be able to focus until you do."

Andrew's heart set up a thudding he feared could be heard. He disliked conflict. How often had he held his tongue at home, even at his age, when his father forced his opinions on him? He'd been raised to honor his father and mother, so he did. He'd been raised to believe confrontation dishonored God, so he avoided it. Now he looked at

Beth, who sat waiting, her pretty face pinched with frustration. She gave him an opportunity to speak his mind, to share his thoughts, but words failed him. All he could do was give a helpless, wordless shrug.

Throwing her hands outward, she filled the silence. "Andrew, things are changing here. For the better, I hope. I realize we've done most everything together, but right now, I have a huge task I have to tackle on my own, proving to Sean McCauley and his father that I am capable of putting together a window that will meet their expectations. What that means is I have to concentrate solely on this project."

She gave the platform a slap with her palm that sent a few cut pieces scooting across the wooden surface like ducks skidding across a pond. "But I can't afford to just ignore the other commitments I've made—namely, the second cardinal piece for Fox's studio and the two craft fairs between now and McCauley's April 1 deadline. People are waiting for those stained-glass projects. And I can't do it all without your help."

Andrew swallowed and managed to give a nod. He would help. That wasn't the issue. He wished he could get his tongue to express the issue, which was his desire to be needed for more than someone to work on her secondary projects.

She went on, her tone rising in intensity. "Once this project is completed and McCauley extends the contract beyond the conditional one I signed, I intend to be the designer rather than the producer. At that point, I'll want you to put together the windows I design for the churches. I'll probably even hire a couple more people to work with you, which will free me up to focus on one-of-a-kind pieces for galleries. I can really broaden the scope of the studio that way.

"But"—for the first time, her fire seemed to flicker—"none of this is going to happen if you aren't going to be around. So. . .what's the plan, Andrew?"

To become so indispensable you lean on me at work and home. But of course he couldn't say the words out loud. He sat stupidly, perched on the stool like a crow on a fence post, but unlike a crow, he couldn't manage to release so much as a squawk. Looking at her with his lips clamped shut and his thoughts racing, he carefully processed everything she'd said.

Her choice of the word *I* rang too prominently in his mind for him to feel completely secure, yet he replayed her comment about him eventually putting together the windows for McCauley. His heart sped up, making his breath come in spurts. That meant full-time work. Which meant supporting himself with art. His hands quivering, he rubbed the underside of his nose and swallowed.

She had asked him the plan. It seemed she already had one mapped out, but he wouldn't oppose it if it meant the fulfillment of his dreams. He opened his mouth and forced a reply past his dry throat. "My plan is to help you get this studio going."

Her eyes narrowed to slits as she seemed to consider his brief response. "Even if it means doing all the little stuff on your own until April?"

He felt as though his tongue stuck to the roof of his mouth. Dad might have different ideas about his time in another few weeks. He'd be needed to help in the fields by the first of March for sure. But somehow he'd make time for Beth's "little stuff," as she put it, and bide his time until he could prove to his father this art studio had the capability of supporting a family.

"Whatever it takes," he said with conviction.

Beth nodded. A smile curved her lips. "Thank you. That's what I hoped you'd say. Now"—she pointed to the idle pliers in his hand—"finish snapping, and get to grinding. We've got work to do."

Andrew followed her direction, and at noon, she suggested he go to the café and pick up sandwiches. By the time he returned, she had finished cutting the design apart and was reconstructing it on the platform. Slender coils of butcher paper—the pieces removed by the scissors to allow for the width of the lead came—lay in tumbled heaps around the wooden platform, giving the illusion that someone had thrown confetti. He supposed that was apt, considering the party that would take place when the project had served its purpose in securing future contracts with McCauley.

For a moment, he stood, paper sack in hand, and watched her carefully secure each labeled pattern piece with a roll of masking tape. The look of concentration on her face made him hesitate to interrupt her. Always zealous when it came to her work, she'd been almost obsessed this past week. He admired her hardworking attitude, and he wondered if she would be as fervent in other aspects of her life. . . such as relationships.

A lump formed in his throat with that thought, and he cleared it, making Beth jump. She whirled on her knees and stared at him with wide, blue eyes, a strand of hair framing her cheek.

"Oh! You're back." She pushed off from the platform and stood, brushing off the knees of her jeans with both palms. "You should have said something."

He grinned. "You were busy."

She glanced at the array of snipped paper and frowned. "Yeah." Turning her gaze to the window, she sighed. "But I'll be out of things to do in another hour if that glass doesn't arrive."

"Here." Andrew reached into the bag and retrieved a sandwich. Holding it out, he said, "Take a break and eat. It will take your mind off the missing glass."

She flashed a quick smile, took the sandwich, and sat down on the edge of the platform. After a moment's hesitation, Andrew perched next to her, even though she hadn't offered an invitation. Her smile told him it was okay, and heat once more built in his ears. He blurted, "Should I pray?"

She gave a wordless nod, and he bowed his head and asked a brief blessing for the food. He ended, "And let the glass come, please." When he raised his head, he found Beth's smiling face aimed at him, which only increased the warmth in his ears. He turned his attention to his sandwich.

He finished before her and stood, stretching his tense muscles. Accustomed to hard work, he always found it interesting that his muscles complained more about sitting still than they did from a long day in the fields. The hunching over, he decided, made things tighten up. If he was going to be an artist, though, he'd need to get used to it.

The kinks worked loose, he sat back on the stool and picked up a carborundum stone. Just as he began grinding, Beth set aside the remainder of her sandwich and picked up the roll of tape.

"You should at least finish eating," he admonished. While he admired her slender figure, she needed the energy to keep working.

"I'll finish it later." Swinging her ponytail over her shoulder, she sent a quick grin across the room. "When this project is done."

He snorted. "You'll waste away by then."

She imitated his snort. "Not likely. It's only until April."

"That's two whole months," he reminded her, warming up to the teasing and surprising himself with the ease he found in playfully sparring with her.

"You mean *only* two months." A slight frown marred her brow. "That's really not much time at all." Slapping her knees, she stomped to the window and peered outside. "Oh, where is that glass?"

Andrew set aside the carborundum stone and crossed to stand behind her, looking past her head to the road outside. "My mother always said a watched pot never boils."

If he thought his lighthearted comment would bring a laugh, he was wrong. "It's got to get here soon." She rested her hands on the windowsill and strained forward, her shoulders tense. "I've got limited time, and I must meet that deadline."

His hands twitched with desire to squeeze her shoulders and offer comfort. He put his hands in his pockets. "I could help."

She spun to face him, shaking her head adamantly. "Huh-uh. I told you. This project is mine. After I've proven myself, then I'll let you work on windows for McCauley. But this one. . ." Her gaze drifted to the paper pieces forming the design. "This one is all mine."

"Then work on your cardinal piece," he suggested. "It'll occupy your time."

She stared at him for a moment, her brows low and lips tucked between her teeth. He wondered if she would start spewing frustration. Her mood swings reminded him of a mule he'd had when he was a boy. Old Pokey nosed you with affection one minute, then bruised you with a nip the next. Despite the animal's sometimes irascible nature, Andrew had always been fond of Old Pokey. He'd felt as though he'd accomplished something when the mule greeted him with a happy bray.

"I suppose I could. . . ." Her musing tone was cut short by the sound of an engine's roar. She jerked toward the window, once more nearly pressing her nose to the glass.

Andrew tipped sideways to look, too. A shipping truck bearing the logo HALE'S SHIPPING AND TRANSPORT came to a groaning halt in front of the studio.

Beth grinned at him, her nose crinkling impishly. "I guess sometimes a watched pot does boil!"

With a chuckle, he headed across the room and grabbed up his coat. "I'll help the driver unload."

TEN

Sean McCauley leaned back in his desk chair, wincing at the *squeak* of the springs. As a kid, he had never cared for high-pitched noises. His brother, Patrick, had teased him by stretching the mouth of a balloon and releasing its air in ear-piercing squeals. He had played basketball in high school, but the squeak of sneakers on the polished floor jarred his concentration. Even as an adult, the screech of a saw or the squeal of brakes was enough to set his teeth on edge. He supposed that was why he'd chosen the architectural side of construction rather than being part of the assembly crew.

Sean glanced at his computer screen, smiling at the most recent e-mail from Patrick.

> *Hey, little bro! Had some awesome tamales in a café on the border this evening. Thought about you and wondered if you were eating a cold bologna sandwich—ha! Tell Dad things are on schedule and that glitch with the plumber is all fixed now so he doesn't need to worry. I'll touch base again tomorrow.*

As an assembly crew foreman, Patrick traveled all over the United

States. Each day since he'd arrived in Columbus, New Mexico, he had sent Sean an e-mail raving about some unique feature from landscape to customs to food. Patrick, the older of the McCauley brothers, had always loved to pester and tease, and his daily e-mails were his way of letting Sean know exactly what he was missing by being stuck in the little office he'd set up in the smallest bedroom of his 1960s unpretentious ranch-style home.

What Patrick didn't realize, however, was that Sean was perfectly happy in his office. He loved the planning side of construction—meeting with church committees, drawing blueprints, finalizing dreams. His prayer was that the churches he designed would be attractive, inviting, usable buildings, but mostly that they would serve as places of growth and worship for the members of the community in which they were built.

His gaze shifted to the blueprint that lay on the drafting table in the corner. A small town outside of Salina, Kansas, had requested his services in planning a church building. Their original building, erected in the early 1900s, had burned to the ground nearly a year ago, and the congregation currently met in the high school gymnasium. They were eager to build, but the congregation was split between re-creating the chapel they'd lost and building a more modern facility.

Sean viewed this as his biggest challenge thus far, and he had an idea for a compromise he believed might meet the desire of the entire congregation. But it involved Beth Quinn, and he wasn't sure he could ethically involve her until he knew for sure she would be working long-term with McCauley Church Construction. He reached back to massage his neck, bringing another complaining *squeak* from his chair's springs.

Grimacing, he pushed himself out of the chair and crossed to the office closet, where he kept a can of lubricant. A few well-placed squirts insured the chair's noise-making days were over for the time being. He put the lubricant away, then crossed to the drafting table and looked down at the drawings.

The congregation had limited funds—they hoped to keep the cost equivalent to the insurance settlement—and building costs had increased since the policy had been purchased. Extravagance wasn't possible, but Sean hoped he could squeeze in one small splash of ostentation.

"And when it comes to splashes of ostentation. . ." He could use an artist's input on whether his idea would work or not. Only one artist came to mind. Moving from the table to his desk, he clicked a few buttons on the computer keyboard, bringing an address book into view. He gave a one-fingered *click* on Q, and Beth Quinn's telephone number popped onto the screen. In short order, he punched in the series of numbers on his cell phone and then waited, rubbing his lips together in anticipation of hearing her voice.

"Quinn's Stained-Glass Art Studio."

That was not Beth's voice, and a horrible racket came from the background. Sean frowned. It sounded as if a dentist were drilling a mastodon's teeth. The fine hairs on the back of his neck prickled. He raised his voice to block the unpleasant sound. "Is this Andrew?"

"Yes. May I help you?"

"This is Sean McCauley. Is Miss Quinn available?"

"Oh." The tone took a turn, a bit of cold air seeming to whisk through the line. "Yes. Just a moment, please." A slight *thunk* was followed by a wheeze as the grinding sound came to a halt. Muffled voices let Sean know Beth was on her way. Finally, the voice of the person who had filled too many of his thoughts lately came through. "Hello, this is Beth."

"Good morning, Beth. Sean McCauley here. How are you today?"

"Busy," she replied with a light laugh. "I have a lot of glass to cut for a large stained-glass window."

He smiled. "Glad to know it's coming along. Listen, I need to be in your area early next week. I wondered if I could swing by, check on your progress, and discuss a different project with you."

"A different project?"

Did he detect a slight note of panic? "I'd like your input as an artist," he said. "This is a window that might not come to pass for reasons too complicated to explain over the phone, but if it's a possibility, I'd like to be able to present the idea to a church planning committee."

"Oh, I see." A slight pause, then, "Sure. You can stop by. I'm here pretty much around the clock these days, so feel free to just pop in."

"Great. I'm guessing it would be around nine in the morning on Monday. I have a meeting in Carlton at noon. Will that give me time to get there?"

"Let me ask Andrew. He's more familiar with the towns around here." Her voice became muffled, as if she had shifted the receiver away from her mouth. "Andrew, how far is Carlton from here?" A mumbled tone answered, and then her voice came clearly through the line once more. "Andrew says it's less than forty minutes from here, so that should give you plenty of time."

"Okay. Nine it is then."

"Fine. I'll see you Monday." The *click* indicated she had disconnected.

Sean stared in surprise at his telephone for a moment before bursting into laughter. Beth Quinn was all business. Placing the cell phone on the corner of his desk, he tapped his lips with one finger, his laughter fading. He needed her to take her business seriously if he was going to be able to use her services regularly. So why did her abrupt departure leave him feeling slightly disappointed?

Beth moved directly back to the cutting wheel, slipped her goggles into place, and reached for the switch.

"So he's coming to check up on you?"

Andrew's voice, carrying a hint of something—rebellion, maybe?—gave her pause. She moved the goggles to the top of her head and gave him her full attention.

"He's coming because he has a meeting with some people in Carlton and needs my advice before he goes."

Andrew's eyebrows rose. She'd seen that look before when Sean McCauley's name had come up in conversation. If she didn't know better, she'd think Andrew was jealous of Sean. But how ridiculous would that be? Her relationships with both men were business only. An odd sensation wiggled down her spine. At least from her end, they were business only, weren't they?

Giving a shake of her head to dislodge that thought, she pulled her goggles down and suggested, "If he is checking up on me, I want to have progress to show him, so I'm going to finish cutting. How are the butterflies coming?"

Andrew held up the soldering iron. "Almost done."

"Good." Beth flipped the switch on the cutting wheel and focused on her task. The *whir* of the spinning wheel changed to a high-pitched *squeal* when she pushed the heavy glass beneath the carbide wheel. Brow pinched, lower lip tucked between her teeth, Beth concentrated on following the lines she'd drawn on the glass.

Making straight cuts was simple; the curved ones required complete concentration. But as she guided the glass with glove-covered fingers, she found her thoughts wandering. Andrew's behavior over the past few days had begun to concern her. He remained his usual helpful and hardworking self, but at times he exhibited a protectiveness—an almost territorial attitude—that created a niggle of discomfort. This studio was hers and hers alone. He was an employee. But his actions made her feel as though he saw himself as much more than mere employee.

Sliding the blue glass free, she reached for a second piece, and her gaze drifted across to Andrew. He sat at the worktable, guiding the soldering iron along the lines of copper foil. She felt a little better seeing him engrossed in his task. Maybe she'd only imagined his change in demeanor. Yet something told her she hadn't. Still, worrying about it wouldn't get the glass cut.

Keep me focused, she prayed silently and aligned the mark on the glass with the wheel. For the next two hours, she repeated that simple prayer a dozen times. It helped. By the time noon rolled around and she let the wheel wheeze to a stop, she had the glass scored for at least a third of the McCauley window.

"A good morning's work."

She almost didn't hear Andrew's approving voice over the whine in her ears. It always took awhile before the sound of the saw ceased its echo in her head. Mom had suggested earplugs. Beth was beginning to think that was a good idea. Crossing to the worktable, she fingered the line of butterfly suncatchers with the tip of a gloved finger.

"You, too. Thanks for finishing these up."

"That's my job."

The words were glib, yet Beth once again sensed an odd undercurrent. Dropping her gloves on the worktable next to her goggles, she pushed aside the twinge of worry. "When we get back from lunch, I'll help you pack these; then we can snap and grind the pieces I scored this morning."

Andrew, whisking a small broom over the surface of the worktable, shot her a startled look. Before she had a chance to question him about it, he said, "Do you want to go to the café for lunch? Trina told me Aunt Deborah planned chili and cinnamon rolls for today's special."

Beth's stomach growled on cue, and she laughed. "I'll never pass up Deborah's homemade rolls, but I need to run by the house and check my mail. Marilyn Fox e-mailed me—"

"Is she checking up on the lilac piece?"

Now Beth was certain she'd heard an edge in Andrew's tone. The "checking up" comment had been made earlier in reference to Sean. Apparently, Sean McCauley brought out a rather unattractive side to Andrew. With a pointed look, she said, "No, she only wanted to let me know the cardinal-and-dogwood piece sold and she'd be sending a check." She gentled her voice as she concluded, "I don't want to leave something like that in my box for long."

Andrew nodded. "That's fine. Grab your jacket. We'll take my truck."

For a moment, Beth hesitated. What had happened to asking what she preferred? Although his words weren't exactly a directive, she sensed a command in the tone that made her want to dig in her heels. Then she gave herself a mental shake. What was wrong with her these days, reading more into everything Andrew said and did?

"Okay. That sounds fine." She followed him out, and he opened the passenger door for her. She had to admit it was nice having a man perform little courtesies for her. Mitch had never been one to, as he put it, "pamper" her. He said she was capable of opening her own doors, carrying her own packages, and filling her own gas tank.

During the months of their relationship, she had never questioned it. She'd seen it as his confirmation of her strength and independence, and she found no fault in it. She had rather liked having Mitch treat her as an equal rather than someone weak and in need of looking after. Since coming to Sommerfeld, though, she'd seen a different relationship between men and women. Henry's tender care of her mother, almost a doting now that she expected his babies, often raised a desire in Beth to be treated in a like manner by a man.

At other times, she feared that much attention would smother her.

Risking a glance at Andrew as he drove slowly toward her house, she wondered if he would emulate his uncle in how he treated his wife. In all likelihood, yes. Most of the Mennonite men were more like Henry than like Mitch. Certainly that would include Andrew.

He pulled up beside the mailbox, put the truck in PARK, and opened his door.

"I can get it!" Beth's voice burst out more loudly than she intended. He sent her a puzzled look. "I mean," she added lamely, twiddling with the door handle, "there's no need for you to run around the truck when the mailbox is on my side."

Slowly he closed his door, offering a nod. "All right."

She popped the door open, dashed to the corrugated metal box, and peeked inside. Three envelopes, including the one from the Fox Gallery, waited. She snatched them out and slid back into the warmth of the truck's cab. "Got it."

She slipped the envelopes into her purse as Andrew turned the truck around and headed back to the studio. After parking behind the studio, they walked together to the café. Even though Beth was in the lead, Andrew reached past her and opened the door, gesturing her through. She offered a wavering smile of thanks as she unzipped her coat.

Trina bounced over the moment they slid into a booth, her smile bright. "Two specials?"

"Yes, please, and two coffees with cream and sugar." Andrew answered for both of them, giving Beth a rush of frustration. She could place her own order!

"Be right back," Trina promised and dashed to the counter, which held coffee mugs and a brown plastic carafe.

"Coffee okay?" Andrew's quirked brow and hesitant tone smoothed Beth's ruffled feathers. He meant well.

"Sure, it's fine." Leaning back, she sighed. "It always smells so good in here."

Andrew sniffed deeply, his nostrils flaring. "Deborah's a good cook. As good as your great-aunt was, I'd say." He gave a quick glance around. "At least, it's just as busy in here as it always was when Miss Koeppler ran it."

Beth glanced around, too. Deborah had made no changes in decor. The same simple tables, plain walls, and tiled floor that Great-Aunt Lisbeth had installed when she opened the café in the mid-1960s gave the feeling of stepping back in time when one entered the café. If Beth had chosen to keep the café, she would have updated everything. But apparently the decor didn't put anyone off, because the café maintained a steady flow of business.

Trina bustled over with two steaming mugs and a little silver pitcher of creamy white liquid. "There you go. Chili and cinnamon rolls coming right up." She zipped off before either Andrew or Beth could thank her.

Beth chuckled fondly. "That Trina is a real go-getter."

Andrew frowned slightly as he gazed after Trina's departing back. "Yes, she is. . . ." He looked at Beth, and his expression cleared. "You were real smart to build your studio next to the café. When you finally get your showroom up and running, the business from here should just trickle over."

Beth smiled. "That's the plan." She leaned forward, propping her chin in her hands. "But in the meantime, the craft fairs will get my name out there and bring in money."

Andrew's brow crunched into a curious scowl. "You pay me a wage for helping, and I know you have other expenses. Those craft fairs don't make that much. So how are you keeping things afloat right now?"

Beth straightened in her seat, setting her lips in a firm line as she contemplated not answering at all. Since when did an employee stick his nose into an employer's business? The feeling that Andrew was becoming too territorial returned, flooding her with indignation. She formed a response. "As long as you're getting paid, you shouldn't need to worry about it."

His face blotched with color.

At his obvious embarrassment, Beth experienced a pang of remorse. He'd been a good friend, and without his help, she probably wouldn't be enjoying her current success. She forced a casual shrug and said, "I have a couple of credit cards I've been using to get things going."

Andrew's expression told her clearly he disapproved of her means of staying afloat.

The fine hairs on her neck bristled at his silent, condemning look. "But I'll be able to pay them in full and still be ahead financially when I finish the window, so it's not a big deal."

"Using credit cards is borrowing trouble," he said, chin tucked low and brows pinched.

"Well, it isn't your trouble," she snapped, "so don't let it worry you."

He jerked upright, his ears glowing bright red, and he shifted to peer across the café rather than looking at her. Regret flooded her. To be honest, the growing amount on her card concerned her, too, and his comments only increased her worries. But she shouldn't take her anxieties out on him, even if his comments were unwarranted.

She opened her mouth to apologize, but Trina interrupted, delivering crock bowls filled with thick, aromatic chili and a plate of cinnamon rolls. By the time she'd asked a silent blessing, Beth decided it was less awkward to leave the topic of finances closed.

She couldn't, however, set aside the feeling that Andrew was assuming a bigger interest in her affairs than was prudent. For either of them. She would need to find a way to communicate where he fit in Quinn's Stained-Glass Art Studio.

ELEVEN

Andrew placed the paper pattern on a piece of mottled lavender glass and slowly drew around it with a marker. His gaze was fixed on the tip on the pen by necessity—multicolored, textured glass was twice the cost of smooth, single-colored, and he didn't dare make an error in marking—but his ears were tuned to the quiet conversation taking place at the platform.

Beth sat on the edge of the raised wooden box with Sean McCauley beside her. At least the man kept a respectable distance, although he tended to lean his head close to hers occasionally to peek at the sketch pad she held in her lap. Every time his reddish hair drew near Beth's shining blond locks, a band seemed to clamp tighter around Andrew's heart. That's why he'd stopped looking. But he couldn't ignore the mumbled voices, the soft laughter, the sound of two people talking as if completely at ease with one another. The way he wished he and Beth would talk.

His chest tightened another notch.

How did a man get completely comfortable with a woman? The only woman with whom Andrew was able to communicate easily on a consistent basis was his cousin Trina. Of course, at seventeen, she was barely a woman, and she'd always been like a little sister. It was hardly the same thing. He hated how he got tongue-tied and hot in the ears when conversing with a woman.

It had taken weeks for him to grow comfortable enough to talk to Beth without her speaking first. He had even been able to tease with her a little. He liked it—the playful sparring. It reminded him of Uncle Henry with his wife, Marie. Even though they were old already— entering their forties—they acted like young teenagers and bantered good-naturedly. Every now and then, he'd been able to do that with Beth. Until McCauley came along. That had changed things between them.

Setting aside the piece of lavender glass, he risked a quick, sidelong glance at the pair at the platform. Beth's attentive expression, the slight curve of her rosy lips as she listened to whatever McCauley was telling her, brought a rush of jealousy so strong Andrew's hands quivered. When he picked up a piece of green glass, the thick square slipped from his grasp and clanked against the worktable.

Beth's gaze swung in his direction, her brows high.

He held up both hands as if under arrest. "Nothing broken. It's okay."

She offered a brief nod, then returned her attention to McCauley without a word. The band around Andrew's chest nearly cut off his breath. Sucking air through his nose, he forced his hands to cease their quivering and picked up the pen. *Don't look at them, don't listen to them, just focus.* But a burst of laughter sent the pen squiggling across the square of glass. Quickly, he snatched up a dry erase marker from beneath the worktable and scribbled it over the errant mark. A firm scrub with a paper towel removed every trace of the black line, and he blew out a relieved breath.

A glance in the direction of the platform confirmed Beth had witnessed his error. His ears burned. He wished McCauley would hurry up and leave so things could return to normal! But, Andrew realized as he bent over the table to move the marker slowly around the paper pattern, things would be forever changed with this new contract of Beth's. McCauley would be a permanent fixture.

He felt as though he stood in the middle of a seesaw, with the board waffling up and down and carrying his thoughts with it. Having McCauley as a permanent fixture meant the success of the studio, but it also meant having Beth's attention claimed by the other man. So did Andrew want success, or did he want Beth?

His hands stilled and he turned to examine his boss. The internal seesaw froze in place perfectly parallel to the ground. He wanted both. And his father would not approve of either.

Sean sensed Andrew's gaze boring a hole through him. It took Herculean effort not to shift his head to meet it and send the man a glowering frown. Andrew's protective act, while perhaps endearing to Beth, made it difficult for Sean to focus on Beth. And Sean was discovering a deep desire to focus solely on Beth.

"Do you mind if I take this sketch with me?" Sean pointed to the pad in her lap.

She wrinkled her nose as if uncertain. "It's just preliminary based on your description. I can't imagine it would be very impressive. If I had a photograph of the old church, though, I could make a much better drawing."

Sean battled a grin. He admired her perfectionism—it would serve him and his company well. "And if they like the idea, I'll bring you a photograph. But I need something to show them the potential. So. . . may I?"

Only inches from her, he could see his reflection in her irises. As he stared into the deep blue depths of her eyes, some emotion flitted through—mistrust? Confusion? Before he could fully process it, she lowered her gaze, ripped the drawing from the pad, and thrust it at him.

He took it, his forehead creasing into a slight frown at her abrupt action, but then he offered a smile. "Thank you." Slipping it into the leather folder that rested against his leg, he said, "I know this will help the committee see what I envision. We can worry about a detailed, accurate sketch after we've gotten their approval to proceed."

Beth nodded, swinging a quick glance in Andrew's direction. Sean turned his head in time to see Andrew give a nod of approval. He voiced what he assumed the pair were thinking: "If this committee approves you creating a window that resembles the original church building, you'll have two major projects to complete. Pretty exciting, isn't it?"

Beth's wide-eyed expression didn't appear as much excited as terrified. She chuckled softly, rubbing her finger beneath her nose. "Andrew and I will have to burn the midnight oil to stay on top of everything."

Andrew's grin let Sean know he wouldn't mind burning the midnight oil with Beth. A stab of jealousy pinched Sean's chest, but he forced a smile and pushed to his feet, bouncing the leather folder against his trouser-covered thigh. "I have confidence you'll be able to handle it."

Beth rose, too, holding her hand toward Sean. He took it, her palm cool and smooth, and gave her fingers a gentle squeeze. "Thanks again for spending your morning with me, Beth. I know you have things to do, so I appreciate the time you took to help get this idea solidified in my head."

Her hand still in his, her gaze flitted toward the mess on the platform that would eventually turn into a stained-glass window. Another soft laugh tripped out, almost nervous in its delivery. "The hour I spent with you means I have to make it up this evening."

That wasn't exactly the response he hoped for. "I'm sorry."

Her startled gaze met his. "Oh! I didn't mean—" Her face flooded with pink, and she jerked her hand free from his grasp. "I wasn't complaining. Really. This time we spent—it's an investment in my future, so it's worth it."

"Good." He remained rooted in place, peering into her eyes and gaining courage. There was something more he wanted to ask. Nibbling his mustache, he wished Andrew would leave the studio.

Beth stood silently, too, her hands tangled in the tails of her sloppy work shirt.

Finally, Sean blurted, "I wondered. . ."

She tipped her head. "Yes?"

"Well, after I meet with the committee in Carlton, I might need to meet with you again. If they like this stained-glass window idea, I'll ask for a photograph right away, and I could drop it by so you'd have it to work from. And maybe we could. . ."

Her eyes shot briefly toward Andrew. Sean looked sideways to find Andrew staring boldly in their direction. Simultaneously, he and Beth shifted, their shoulders coming together with Andrew at their backs. He was certain she smirked. Maybe she didn't find the Mennonite man's protectiveness as much endearing as annoying.

In a whisper, she said, "We could. . . ?"

Sean cleared his throat. "We could talk over dinner. I've heard the little café here in Sommerfeld is good. Could we meet there at, maybe, six thirty?"

Sean was certain that disappointment twisted Beth's lips, giving him a rush of satisfaction despite her negative response. "I'm sorry.

The café is always closed on Mondays." From behind them, Andrew coughed. A contrived cough, Sean was sure. He resisted looking at the man.

"Oh." Sean smoothed his mustache with two fingers, observing Beth's attention on his motion. "Well, then, I could take you into Newton. I'm sure something will be open there." He winked. "Unless you really do need to stay here this evening and make up the hour I stole from your day."

They laughed softly together. Beth answered quickly. "Dinner out sounds great."

"Good. Will you be here or at your house?"

Andrew cleared his throat loudly. "Beth, is dinner out a good idea?"

Both Sean and Beth turned to face Andrew. Although his face appeared deeper in hue, he spoke in a bold, authoritative tone. "If you go out, you'll end up leaving earlier than usual to. . .gussy up." The man's neck blotched purple. "That's even more lost time. Can you afford it?"

Sean fought a laugh as Beth glared at Andrew, her jaw set in a stubborn angle. Without responding to her employee, she turned her face to Sean. "I'll be at my house. When you come back into town, just turn left off of Main Street onto First. I'm on the corner of First and Cottonwood, one block west of Main. The white bungalow. I'll have the porch light on."

A "harrumph" actually came from the worktable. "All the porch lights will be on by then," Andrew said. He swung a pair of goggles in his hand, a silent message that he had work to do.

Beth drew a deep breath, her eyes spitting fire. But when she looked back at Sean, a smile washed away the fury. "It'll be the white bungalow with the wraparound front porch, spirea bushes under the front window, *and* a porch light on. Does that help?"

Sean chose to ignore Andrew's second, softer snort. "I'm sure I can find you. Sommerfeld isn't that large."

"True enough."

They shared an amused grin, and Sean found himself tempted to lean forward and place a kiss on her softly curving lips. The sound of the cutting wheel split the air. Beth gave a start, and Sean jerked backward, bumping his heels on the platform. He caught his balance, swung a wide-eyed look toward Andrew, then took a stumbling step toward the door.

"Six thirty," he hollered over the sound of the cutter. His jacket draped over his arm, he headed out the door.

Beth paced the living room floor, the heels of her black dress boots clumping against the carpet. Despite her efforts to set aside the aggravation, she still stewed about Andrew's rudeness hours ago. She wondered if Sean would show up after his abrupt departure from the studio. Recalling how he practically ran for the door without bothering to put on his jacket made her blood boil. She and Andrew really needed to have a talk.

Mom had always told her to think before she spoke, especially when she was upset or angry. That advice had kept her silent over the past week. Whenever the urge to confront Andrew arose, it came with a wave of frustration or anger, and she didn't want to dishonor God by being unkind. So she'd wait, and then she'd forget. Until the next time he irritated her. She felt caught in a merry-go-round and didn't care for the sensation.

What had gotten into him, anyway? His first weeks in the studio, he'd been the model employee, following her directions, working meticulously and quietly, showing up early and expressing a willingness to stay late, and offering her endless support. But lately? It seemed he was trying to rise to the top and wanted to use her as the stepping stool to get there. What had brought about the change?

Her pacing ceased, her heart firing into her throat as realization struck. Andrew's attitude change coincided with Sean McCauley's visit to her studio. But why? Before she had a chance to explore the reasoning behind Andrew's behavior, a tap at her door signaled the arrival of a visitor. Charging to the front door, she swung it open and returned the smile Sean McCauley offered.

"Right on time," she said, glancing at the silver watch that circled her wrist.

"And you're ready to go." His eyes glowed with approval.

"Yes, well, punctuality has been drilled into me from an early age." She underscored her words with a light laugh, reaching for her coat, which hung on a hall tree beside the front door. "My mother always said—"

Sean plucked the coat from her hands and held it open. For a moment, she stared at the coat, her heart tripping through her chest at a pace far above normal. Then turning her back to him, she slipped her arms into the sleeves and finished her thought in a reedy tone. "Being late is disrespectful. Respectfulness has always been one of her favorite virtues."

"I think our mothers would get along well then."

She faced him, sliding her hands behind her neck to release her hair from the coat's collar. His gaze seemed to follow the tumble of her curls across her shoulder, and a surprising warmth filled her cheeks. "So, have you decided on a restaurant?"

He shrugged, grinning. "I'm the new one around these parts, so you choose."

"A place called the Apple Barrel is right off the highway on the outskirts of Newton, and they have a good variety of menu choices."

"That'll do. Let's go." He held the door open for her, and as she passed through, she felt his hand lightly press the small of her back. The whisper touch sent a shiver of pleasure up her spine and a wave of heat to her face. The chill evening air whisked across her, cooling her cheeks. She hugged herself and danced in place while waiting for him to unlock the car door.

His smile as he popped the car door open for her sent a second rush of fire through her face. While she waited for him to round the car and get behind the wheel, she reminded herself this was a business dinner, not a date. But her jumbled nerves didn't settle down until midway through the meal.

Sean carried a seasoned french fry to his mouth, bit off the end, and chewed, the movement of his mustache oddly fascinating. Beth wasn't unfamiliar with facial hair—Mitch had deliberately waited days between shaving to give himself a rugged Indiana Jones appearance— but Sean's neatly groomed, red-gold mustache was a far cry from Mitch's dark shadow.

An image of Andrew's clean-shaven face with its square chin and firm jaw popped into her mind, competing with the mental pictures of Mitch and the real-life view of Sean across the table. To rid herself of the parade of images, she approached the purpose of their time together.

"You haven't told me whether the church committee was interested in your idea."

Sean's face lit up. "Ah, my idea. . ." He used his napkin to wipe his mouth and hands, set the wadded paper square aside, and leaned forward, eagerness in his bearing. "They liked my idea very much and would like to see an official sketch of the proposed window."

Two major projects in quick succession! Beth caught her breath. "Wow!"

Sean laughed, his teeth flashing. "Wow, indeed. They gave me a copy of their church directory, which has photographs of the church building for you to use in creating your sketch. The photos are black and white, so I also have a description of the building to help you decide on appropriate colors."

Beth put down her fork. "You must be a great salesman."

Sean shrugged, grinning. "I know my business." The statement, while confident, didn't sound cocky. He placed his elbows on the table edge and linked his fingers together. "I've been praying for quite a while about this particular project. The committee was so firmly divided into two ranks, I knew I'd need to find a way to bridge their different goals. Having a modern building with a beautifully crafted Beth Quinn window serving as a reminder of the original building turned out to be a compromise they could accept."

"I'm so glad." Beth realized she was pleased for two different reasons. First, it offered her another opportunity to build her business. And second, Sean indicated he had prayed about the project. His easy acknowledgment of consulting God gave her a feeling of security and increased her admiration for him.

Sean reached across the table to cup his hand over hers. "And I'm so glad we're in this together. I think you are going to be a wonderful asset to McCauley Church Construction. Making use of your skills is one of the smartest moves I've made."

The feeling of security instantly fled.

TWELVE

Sean observed Beth's smile fade, her eyes taking on a wariness she'd witnessed on earlier occasions. But he had no idea what had caused the change. Removing his hand from hers, he reached for another french fry and a different topic.

"So, tell me about your family. You mentioned you grew up in Wyoming even though your mom was raised in Sommerfeld. Do you have any brothers or sisters?"

Beth's gaze narrowed, as if she were trying to read more into his question than what existed, but after a moment, her expression relaxed and a slight smile teased the corners of her lips. "Not quite yet."

Her cryptic reply raised Sean's eyebrows. "Not quite yet?"

Her grin grew. "My mother is expecting twins in mid-May."

Sean whistled through his teeth. "Wow! Why'd she wait so long to have more children?" He realized how abrupt the question sounded, but to his relief, Beth didn't appear insulted.

She took a sip of her cola and shrugged. "My father died in an accident before I was born. It was just Mom and me during all of my growing-up years. Then when we returned to Sommerfeld, Mom's childhood sweetheart started courting her again. They married a little over a year ago. Henry had never married, so having a family was important to him. They were both thrilled when they found out Mom was pregnant."

"I bet." Sean tried to imagine being in his early twenties and becoming a big brother. The picture wouldn't gel. He observed, "She must have been pretty young when she had you."

Another casual shrug lifted Beth's shoulders. "Eighteen when she married my dad, nineteen when she had me."

"And widowed at nineteen." Sean felt a rush of sympathy toward this woman he didn't know. "She must be very strong."

"She is." Beth's eyes glimmered briefly. "She's a wonderful mom."

Sean nodded. She must have been a good mother to have raised such a strong, capable daughter. His admiration for Beth grew with the knowledge of what must have been a difficult childhood. "And now she'll be a mom again." He shook his head, chuckling. "Twins, huh? That'll keep her busy."

Beth offered a silent nod, lifting a bite of salad to her mouth.

Gesturing with a french fry, Sean said, "It's good you're close by. You'll be able to help her."

"Oh, she's got lots of family around for that. I'll be busy in my studio."

The glib tone seemed to carry an undercurrent Sean was tempted to explore, but he decided their relationship was too new to go digging below the surface. So he threw out another question. "Have you ever thought about relocating your studio?"

Beth's fork froze between her plate and her mouth. "Why do you ask that?"

There was no denying the challenge in her tone. He frowned slightly. "Curiosity. I know you said you hoped to garner some of the café's business when you open a showroom, but I would imagine in a small town like that, you're still limiting yourself. A larger city might hold more opportunities for you."

Beth put her fork down without taking the bite. "Did you have a city in mind?"

Sean's frown deepened. The defensiveness she presented at times seemed so alien to her soft appearance. What brought about these mercurial mood swings? "Not particularly. Although remaining in Kansas would be good if you plan to ship projects throughout the United States. It's centrally located."

"Well"—she picked up the fork again—"Sommerfeld is in central Kansas, so I think I'll just stay put." She chewed the bite of lettuce, swallowed, and then continued. "Besides, you haven't been around in the warmer seasons. Between the farmers' market, carriage rides, and café, plus the demonstrations for wheat-weaving, quilting, and harness-making, Sommerfeld teems with activity on the weekends. And all of those tourists are prime candidates for exploring my showroom."

He swallowed a chuckle. Her fervent defense of Sommerfeld was almost amusing in its intensity. He wondered briefly whom she tried to convince: him or herself. Biting off the end of a french fry, he raised his brows to indicate interest. "Harness-making demonstrations and carriage rides? I thought the Mennonites had converted to using automobiles."

"Most in Sommerfeld have," Beth said, "but their Amish neighbors have not. They combine forces for these weekend events, since the visitors are mutually beneficial."

"I see." Sean chewed and swallowed thoughtfully while Beth pushed the remainder of her salad around on her plate with the prongs of her fork. Something struck him. "You don't claim to be Amish or Mennonite. You must feel like an odd duck in that community."

She dropped her fork with a clatter against the plate. Fixing him with a steady look, she took in a deep breath through her nose. "Sean, I'm not moving my studio. My mother is settled in Sommerfeld, and she's my only family. I've told you several reasons why my location works for me. Please do not continue to try to influence me to go somewhere else even if it's more convenient for you. 'Odd duck' or not, I won't disrupt my life again for any man."

Ah. Suddenly the wariness, the defensiveness, the mood swings all made sense. Setting the french fry down, Sean pushed his plate aside and said softly, "So what was his name?"

Beth's cheeks streaked with pink. She fiddled with her napkin, her eyes downcast. "Whose name?"

He released a low, light chuckle. "The man who disrupted your life."

The red stain in her cheeks deepened. She shot him a stern look. "That isn't important." Flopping her napkin over her plate with one hand, she lifted her glass with the other and took a long draw that helped return her face to its natural color. She put down the glass, jiggled it to make the ice clink, then set her chin at a proud angle. "I believe the purpose of this evening was to discuss the church window. So let's get to it, huh?"

Her meaning was clear. Her personal life was *her* personal life, and he would need to keep his distance. Well, he'd follow her lead. . .for the moment. He could stick to business for now. But as their business relationship grew, he fully intended to pursue her on a more intimate level. Beth Quinn was far too intriguing for him to remain forever distanced.

Beth yanked open the drawer containing goggles and snatched up a pair. The rubber headband caught on something, and when she gave a hard jerk to free the goggles, the band snapped against the side of her thumb.

"Ouch!" She sucked the stinging spot. The back door swung open, and Andrew stepped through, catching her with her thumb in her mouth. She swung her hand abruptly downward and slammed her wrist on the edge of the open drawer. With another yelp, she thumped the drawer shut with her hip. The tail of her shirt caught in the drawer, holding her captive.

Releasing a loud "Uh!" of aggravation, she grabbed her shirt and tried to jerk it free, only to hear the flannel tear. She puffed her cheeks and blew a noisy breath toward the ceiling.

Andrew's laughter rang, filling the room.

For one brief moment, she glared at him. Then she felt a grin twitch her cheeks. How ridiculous she must have looked first with her thumb in her mouth and then attached to a drawer by her own shirttail. Imagining it from his viewpoint, her frustration evaporated, and she couldn't help but laugh, too.

He strode forward, pulled the drawer open a few inches, and removed the tattered tail of her shirt. He stuck his fingers through the tear, chuckling. "And how is your morning?" Dropping the fabric, he grinned at her.

"I think you already know the answer to that," she retorted in a saucy tone, but she smirked. His easy laughter and teasing comment gave her heart a lift. With an exaggerated sigh, she added, "I hope this start isn't an indication of how the whole day will go."

"Stay away from the drawers, and you should be okay," he advised.

She teasingly held up her hands and took one giant sidestep away from the storage unit.

Andrew grinned at her, but then his brow pulled down. He

crossed his arms. "Did you get any sleep last night?"

"That obvious, huh?" She moved toward the worktable, forcing him to shift back a few feet. The truth was, she'd gotten little sleep. Her mind had kept replaying bits of her dinner conversation with Sean McCauley. Even after prayer, she felt troubled by his seeming overzealous interest in her studio and subtle attempts to convince her to relocate.

If only he weren't such a handsome package, it might be easier to set thoughts of him aside. Unfortunately, the feminine side of her felt drawn to his boyish charm and obvious intelligence. But, she told herself firmly, he wasn't worth losing sleep over!

Andrew leaned against the opposite side of the worktable and watched her slide the goggles into place. "Did McCauley keep you out all night?"

The easy camaraderie she'd felt only moments before now swept away. "No!" She slapped the goggles onto the tabletop and pointed at him. "And don't even think of mentioning something like that to anyone in your family! My mother doesn't need to be worrying about me."

Andrew drew back, his eyes wide. "I—I don't talk about you to—"

"Oh yes, you do. But not this time, Andrew." Her anger grew, tiredness and frustration welling up to spew like steam from a boiling pot. "In fact, not ever again, for any reason. Do you know how tiresome it is to have everyone knowing my business? To go to the café for a cup of coffee and have people mention things that don't concern them at all? I don't like being the topic of gossip. If you're going to continue working here, I've got to be able to trust you. And that means *you— don't—talk.*"

She glared into Andrew's stricken face. Guilt smacked her. What was she doing, haranguing him in such an unprofessional manner?

Her mother's admonition to think before she spoke came back to haunt her, but it came too late. She couldn't take back the words she'd just poured out.

The expression on Andrew's face, however, made her wish she could.

She closed her eyes, asking God to calm her racing heart and tumbling thoughts. When she opened her eyes, she found Andrew still leaning on the worktable, seeming to examine his hands. She reached across the table and tapped his wrist. When he raised his gaze to meet hers, she spoke.

"Andrew, I'm sorry I snapped at you. I am tired. It's not because I was out all night—I was home by nine o'clock." Why she felt the need for him to know that, she wasn't sure. She only knew she felt compelled to assure him. "But I had a lot on my mind, so I didn't sleep well, and I guess I'm grumpy."

His expression didn't change.

She sighed, fluttering her eyelashes and peeking at him out of the corners of her eyes. "I'm grumpy a lot?"

He sucked in his lips—an obvious attempt to stop a grin from growing.

Now that he'd lost the hurt look, she stopped goofing around and faced him squarely. "I really am sorry. I do get aggravated when Trina or Henry mention things they could know only if you told them. It makes me feel like people are talking behind my back."

Andrew straightened and placed one hand against his chest. "I don't talk about you out of maliciousness. It's because I'm excited for the things happening here for us."

Beth's antenna went up. She carefully tempered her tone. "You mean for *me*. It's my studio, Andrew, not ours."

His ears glowed. "That's what I meant."

She nodded slowly. "I hope so. I need your help on projects, and I need McCauley's contracts to get everything up and running around here, but both of you are going to have to understand that the studio is *my* business. It's going to stay that way."

Andrew remained silent, his narrowed gaze pinned to hers. She held her breath, waiting for him to tell her she was out of line in her expectation.

"Okay. You're the boss."

At his flat comment, she nearly sagged with relief. Although his words were pushed past a tense jaw, she hoped she'd made herself clear about where he fit in the studio. She also hoped it would be the end of his possessiveness concerning the studio. And her.

"Great." She slid the goggles back in place. "I've got to sand the edges of these pieces for the McCauley window. With the number of pieces involved, I speculate I'll be sanding all week."

"And you need me to. . . ?"

She nodded toward the cutting wheel as she picked up the carborundum stone and began whisking it across the edge of a piece of cornflower blue glass. "It wouldn't hurt to make up a few more crosses and butterflies. The e-mail I got from the organizer of the President's Day Extravaganza said they expect a great turnout. I'd rather have too many than not enough."

Andrew's jaw dropped. "The craft show—it's this Saturday."

Beth's hand paused. "Yes. We've had it on the calendar for months."

He slapped his forehead. "I didn't make the connection."

Beth put the stone down. "What's the problem?"

"The men are meeting at Uncle Henry's on Saturday to put up the walls and roof for his addition. They want to get it going before the farmers need to be out in the fields. I had hoped. . ."

Beth didn't need to hear the remainder of his sentence to know what he'd hoped. But she'd already lost time this week with the meetings with Sean. She couldn't take Saturday off to man her booth, yet she counted on those sales to cover the expense of having made the suncatchers plus expenses involved with keeping the studio open. Andrew already knew all of that; she wouldn't spell it out for him. She simply waited for him to decide what to do.

With a sigh, he gave a nod. "There will be plenty of men around to help with the addition. I'll go to Salina like we'd planned."

"Good."

Andrew turned toward the drawer that contained the patterns, and Beth leaned over her pieces of glass. As she whisked the stone along the edge of the diamond-shaped piece, her thoughts skipped ahead to Saturday. She had fully intended to work all day in the studio. But after the community—organized by Henry—had rallied around her in erecting the building that housed her business, didn't she have an obligation to help in the construction of the room addition?

Once more the question stabbed her heart: *Where do I fit in?*

THIRTEEN

Beth and Andrew worked in quiet amity the remainder of the week—Beth grinding until her fingers ached from gripping the glass and stone, and Andrew constructing another dozen suncatchers. Sean McCauley called twice to check on progress and forward a couple of questions from the church in Carlton. Each time, Beth sensed Andrew's disapproval, which gave her a slight feeling of unrest, but she managed to sweep it away. On the Saturday morning of the craft show, she watched him load the boxes of foam-cushioned suncatchers into the back of his pickup truck.

As usual, he'd dressed in his Sunday suit for the fair. In his workday clothes of dark trousers, solid button-up shirt, and suspenders, he could blend in with farmers outside of Sommerfeld. But the black homemade suit with no lapels on the jacket, a light blue shirt buttoned to the collar, and the black, flat-brimmed felt hat marked him as Mennonite. Each time they'd attended a fair, his attire had drawn curious gazes and a few bold questions. She'd recognized his unease in fielding queries about his "Amish" clothing in the past, and she had frequently explained the differences between the Amish and Mennonites who lived in Sommerfeld. Today he'd have to answer questions himself, and his silence told her he wasn't keen on going alone.

"It's too bad Trina can't go with you." Beth knew Trina was the favorite of many of her cousins, Andrew included. Her bubbly personality added a healthy dose of fun wherever she went.

Andrew grunted. "Yeah, I'd like that, but Aunt Deborah would never let her loose from the café. Especially today, with half the town turning out to help Uncle Henry. Aunt Deborah plans to take lunch over for all the workers, and she'll need Trina to get it accomplished."

"Sure seems like Kyra or someone might have been willing to take Trina's place," Beth mused. Kyra, one of Beth's many cousins, often helped out in the café.

"She *is* helping," Andrew said, giving the hatch of his pickup a firm slam. "Aunt Deborah needs both Trina and Kyra today."

"Oh." The crisp air tugged strands of her hair free of her ponytail and whipped them beneath her chin, tickling her. She shoved the errant strands behind her ear and squinted up at Andrew. Beneath the brim of his hat, his shadowed eyes appeared uneasy. "Well, I'm sorry you have to go alone, but you look very handsome."

The instant the word *handsome* slipped from Beth's tongue, embarrassment washed over her. It increased when she saw his ears turn bright red before he ducked his head, pulling his hat brim lower. But it was true. Andrew, with his close-cropped hair, dark eyes, and solid frame, was a handsome man. The unpretentious clothes in some odd way seemed to accentuate his rugged attractiveness rather than detract from it. Maybe if he realized it, he would set aside some of his insecurities and feel more confident.

So she ignored the awkwardness of the moment and added, "I am positive you will single-handedly sell out of suncatchers and bring back orders for more."

He chuckled, a low, throaty sound that made Beth smile. "Whatever you say, boss."

She laughed out loud, then waved as he climbed into his pickup and drove out of the alley. Turning toward the door of the studio, she heard a sound, an echoing, sharp ring. A hammer hitting a nail. Then came another, followed rapidly by two more. The rings came in closer succession, taking on the semblance of off-pitch bells, and Beth realized it was a chorus of hammers.

The men were already at work on Henry's addition. She quickly stepped into the studio and closed the door, but even behind the steel door, the sound of clanging came through. Guilt hit hard. She should be helping like everyone else was. The rooms were for her new siblings. What would people think if she didn't come?

She walked to the platform and looked down at the array of glass pieces waiting to have their edges ground. The grinding was taking much longer than she had anticipated given the weight of the glass and the number of pieces. She rubbed the calluses on her thumbs, grimacing at the roughness of her hands.

Maybe she'd wear gloves today, even though it was harder to control the carborundum stone with the bulky leather. Or maybe she'd use her credit card and purchase an electric grinder, even though she worried she'd ruin some pieces while learning to operate it.

Clang! Clang—clang—ring!

The hammer sound called to her. She drew a deep breath, debating with herself. Her gaze went from the scattered pieces of the glass to the window then back to the glass. With a disgruntled huff, she marched to the radio in the corner and snapped it on. Music covered the hammer rings. Returning to the platform with carborundum stone in hand, she plunked down and lifted a red diamond.

But the moment the stone touched the glass, the image of a

hammer connecting with the head of a nail intruded. She knew she would not be able to focus unless she at least made an appearance at the house.

After bundling up in her heavy jacket and scarf, she decided to leave the car and walk. It was only six blocks, and the late February morning was crisp but not unbearably cold. The clear sky seemed to echo the choir of nail strikes, making Beth's ears ring. Halfway there, she picked up the sounds of voices and muffled laughter in addition to the ringing of hammers. For some reason, the mingling sounds made her chest feel tight.

When she rounded the final corner and glimpsed the clusters of townspeople, the tightness in her chest increased. The women, with their skirts showing beneath the hems of plain wool coats and their heads covered with simple white caps, made Beth feel slovenly in her faded blue jeans and short suede jacket with her ponytail tumbling over her shoulder. Her steps slowed, and she considered returning to her shop.

But a masculine voice called out, "Beth!" Heads turned. She'd been spotted. Lifting her hand to wave at Henry, who smiled from his perch on a roof rafter, she closed the remaining distance between herself and the group where her mother stood.

"Hi, honey!" Mom greeted her with a hug and a press of her cold nose to Beth's cheek. "I'm glad you came by. Look at that!" Mom's breath, released on a sigh, hung in the morning air. "It never ceases to amaze me how well they work together."

Beth's gaze followed her mother's to the addition. Already the studs clearly marked the peripheries of the room, and the rafters connected with the existing roof. At least a dozen men swarmed over the skeleton, adding crossbars and securing the rafters to the wall studs. More applied saws to lengths of wood laid across sawhorses or unloaded Sheetrock and plywood from the backs of pickup trucks.

"By noon," Mom continued, her arm around Beth's waist, "they'll probably have the roof sheathed and ready for shingles."

A woman on Mom's right released a snort. "Not if Nort Borntrager has anything to do with it. Look at him over there, leaning on the Mullers' car hood as if he's already earned a break."

"And I saw him eating buns instead of unloading lumber," another contributed.

As they watched, the man pushed himself free and ambled toward the sawhorses. He stood, hands in pockets, watching the wielder of the saw. A yawn nearly divided his face.

The cluster of women clucked their disapproval. One said with no small measure of sarcasm, "That Nort, he's so slow you have to look twice to see him move."

The women all chuckled, and even Beth fought a grin. Someone like Nort, who watched rather than worked, was the exception rather than the rule when it came to the hardworking attitude the Mennonites possessed. But then she swallowed her grin, her hands clenching within the pockets of her trendy jacket. What might these women say about her when she wasn't in earshot?

She ducked her head, taking in the sea of skirts surrounding her denim-clad legs. Discomfort pressed harder. Just as Nort's laziness set him apart, her attire set her apart. Once more, the feeling of being a misfit washed over Beth. Her heart pounding, she raised her gaze to her stepfather, who straddled a rafter and swung his hammer with precision. A glance to the side confirmed her mother also watched Henry.

By joining the church and marrying Henry, Mom had reestablished her place in the community. Beth knew her mother had never been more content than she was in her role as Mrs. Henry Braun, accepted resident of Sommerfeld, Kansas. Jealousy hit, surprising Beth with its intensity. As much as she wanted to feel as though she belonged, did she want everything else that would be required to be accepted here?

She tried to envision herself in the head covering and simple dress of the Mennonite women, and she nearly laughed out loud. No doubt she'd look ridiculous! She squirmed within the confines of her jacket and ducked her gaze once more. The sight of her mother's legs next to hers gave her a jolt of concern.

"Mom, you're all swollen again."

The hand at Beth's waist slipped away, and Mom tucked her coat beneath her belly to look at her feet. She grimaced. "Oh, goodness, and I've hardly been up. Well"—she flipped her hands outward in a nonchalant gesture—"at least I'm consistent. This puffiness has become the norm."

"But it isn't normal, is it?" Beth pressed, worry making her heart thud in tempo with the hammers that continued to pound.

One of the other ladies in the group shook her head and pursed her lips at Beth. "Now, young lady, don't fuss at your mother. We check on her every day, and she always says she feels fine. A little swelling isn't uncommon."

Beth bristled at the implication that she didn't check on her mother as frequently as she should. She also didn't believe one would call what she was seeing a "little" swelling. Mom's legs looked puffy from the knees down, and the flesh extended over the tops of her brown oxfords. It looked painful and worthy of great concern.

She clamped her jaw and didn't answer. These women already saw her as an oddity who was too headstrong for good sense. She wouldn't argue and give them fuel for gossip about her. Instead, she offered a brief nod and looked back toward the workers.

She easily located Henry. From the back, his dark hair and broad shoulders reminded her of Andrew. How much Andrew resembled his uncle. Along with the thought of Andrew, a recurring idea teased the back of her mind. If she were to marry into the community, as her mother did, she would belong. *Really* belong. Remembering his formal bearing this morning and her comment on his handsomeness, she felt color flood her cheeks.

"Mom," she blurted out, jerking sideways two steps, "I'm going to head back to the studio. I have work to do."

The disapproving raised brows and pinched lips of the women standing nearby made Beth's face grow hotter.

"But I'll go to the café at noon and help Deborah carry lunch over, so I'll see you then, okay?"

Some of the women gave small nods of approval, their expressions softening. Beth wasn't sure if this pleased or aggravated her.

Mom moved forward on her swollen feet to offer a quick hug. "All right, honey. Enjoy your day."

Beth turned and fled.

Sean hung up the phone and stifled a frustrated groan. He replayed his father's parting comment: *"You're sidetracked, son. Focus. We've got deadlines to meet."*

He'd like to argue with his father. He'd like to say he was just as on top of things as he'd always been, but he knew it wouldn't be the truth. And he admitted only to himself, *sidetracked* wasn't a strong enough word to describe what had happened. He'd been completely derailed. By a blond-haired, blue-eyed, cleft-chinned artist whose sole focus was her art. Ever since their "business dinner" a week ago, he'd had a harder time setting aside thoughts of Beth. Despite the original intention, it hadn't been a business meeting, and Sean knew it.

Shaking his head, he looked toward the ceiling. "God, I prayed we'd find a dependable artist with a heart for You who would be willing to use his talents in our company. Did You have to send me to a woman too pretty and independent for her own good?"

He didn't get a reply. But he didn't expect to. God worked in mysterious ways, as Sean well knew, and he'd learned long ago to simply trust His judgment. But that was easier when it didn't affect every aspect of his life. He could not get Beth Quinn out of his mind.

Their relationship—such as it was—was only weeks old. They'd had little face-to-face contact, although he communicated with her daily by e-mail and weekly by telephone. How had such minimal connections managed to keep her in the forefront of his thoughts? He saw the checkout girl at the local grocery store more regularly than Beth. But the checkout girl didn't have that endearing cleft in her chin.

He pushed away from the drafting table and stormed to the kitchen, where he yanked open the refrigerator and grabbed a can of cherry-flavored cola. Popping the top, he stared at the silver ring and for the first time contemplated placing a gold ring on a woman's finger.

Without taking a sip, he plunked the can on the counter and spun toward the window. Looking across his neatly trimmed backyard, he tried to imagine working side by side with someone under the sun, putting in a garden—tomatoes, cucumbers, and green beans, like his parents did every year. Turning a slow circle, he envisioned sharing the cooking duties, sitting down with someone and holding hands to pray, loading the dishwasher after someone else rinsed the pots and plates.

In each case, the someone had a face. Beth.

He shook his head, grabbing up the can to take a long draw that did little to cool his racing thoughts. Hadn't she made it clear she had no interest in leaving that little town called Sommerfeld? Imagining her in his yard, his house—his *life*—was a waste of time.

"An exercise in futility," he said aloud, then drained the can. He dropped it into the recycling bin before returning to his office. Sliding into the chair at his tall drafting table, he picked up his pencil and T square and bent once more over the drawing pad. Although the final drawing would be done on computer, he always did hand sketches first. Applying the pencil to paper somehow made the building more real to him than when he created it on a computer screen. As his eyes followed his line of lead on the page, he suddenly pictured Beth's hand forming the peak of the little chapel from Carlton.

He sat straight up and slapped the pencil against the pad. "What will cure me of thinking of that girl?" he exclaimed to the empty room.

Oddly enough, a voice from his past offered a solution. His grandfather, for whom he'd been named, had once proclaimed, "The best cure for any ill is the hair of the dog that bit ya." Sean remembered how his mother had shaken her head in disapproval, and he'd learned later that often that statement was used in reference to imbibing. While neither of Sean's parents ever partook of alcoholic beverages, nor had Sean, that saying now seemed to offer a solution to his dilemma with Beth.

Perhaps a quick phone call. Hearing her voice, being reminded of how focused she was on her own work, would help him put his attention back where it belonged. Yes. He slid his cell phone from his pocket and flipped it open. Just a few minutes of conversation would certainly get him back on track.

He scrolled to Beth's number, pushed the TALK button, and lifted the phone to his ear.

FOURTEEN

Andrew glanced up as Beth placed the telephone earpiece on its cradle. The slight frown on her face captured his attention.

"Everything okay?" The question formed without effort. He knew she'd been talking to Sean McCauley—she used a different tone when she spoke to that man, a tone that always ruffled Andrew's feathers as much as he tried not to let it.

"Yes." Beth walked slowly to the platform, where she stopped, staring down at the pieces of glass that would form McCauley's window. But she didn't crouch to resume working.

Concerned, Andrew stepped beside her. He resisted touching her arm. "Are you sure? You don't look too happy."

Beth sighed and tipped her head to look at him. Andrew was struck by the circles under her eyes. Doing this window on her own was taking a tremendous toll. When would she realize she didn't need to carry this project alone? He waited for her to say something, but she remained silent, simply looking at him as if she expected him to do something, say something. But he stood motionless and silent, as well.

A second sigh escaped, and her attention returned to the window. Then, in a matter-of-fact tone that took him by surprise, she said, "Do you suppose you could take a break and go after another two dozen horseshoe nails?"

Andrew gave his head a quick shake. He felt as though he'd missed something between the phone call and now. "Horseshoe nails?"

"Yes." Still with her eyes aimed downward, she added, "I'll be needing them before too long."

He stared at her profile, trying to read beneath her bland expression, but he wasn't well enough versed in females to figure out what she was thinking.

She laughed lightly. Not a humorous laugh, but one that had a frightened ring to it. "Sean plans to drive over in the middle of next week to talk to the Carlton committee. He said he'd stop by and take a few pictures of the progress here." Crossing her arms, she sent Andrew a brief sidelong look. "Think he'll be pleased or disappointed?"

Andrew looked down at the makeshift design on the platform. Even though the pieces weren't connected and lay in a haphazard display of shapes and color, he could imagine the finished product. The window would be beautiful when completed. "Why would he be disappointed?"

"Because I'm not far enough along." The tinge of frustration came through. "I've got to pick up the pace."

Andrew took her arm and turned her to face him. Boldly, he brushed her cheek with his thumb right below her eye where the pale skin showed a hint of purple. The slight contact with her skin catapulted his heart into his throat. "The pace you've set now is doing you in. Have you looked in a mirror lately?"

Jerking her arm free, she stepped away from him and glared upward. "Thanks a lot."

Andrew realized how insulting his words must have been. He'd only meant to express concern for her obvious tiredness. Why couldn't he ever say the right thing when it came to Beth? "I didn't mean it that way."

He would have explained, but she shook her head, her bright hair swinging across her shoulders. "Forget it. I'm tired and testy, and I'm worried that this window isn't going to be done. I've used half my time already, and I'm not halfway there."

It was on the tip of Andrew's tongue to say, "Let me help," but he knew she would only rebuff him. Instead, he said, "You're on the downhill slide. The cutting and grinding always takes longer than soldering."

"But with lead came?" Panic underscored her question. "I'm so used to the smaller projects. I've only used lead came once—on the cardinal piece."

"And you did great." Andrew was relieved when the furrows in her brows relaxed. He straightened his shoulders, determined to make up for his previous comment. "You will this time, too."

The furrows returned. "But on time?"

Andrew gave a firm nod. "On time. I'll pray about it."

To his puzzlement, her cheeks flooded with pink, and she lowered her gaze. She sat back on the edge of the platform and reached into the box of cut glass pieces near her feet. Andrew knew her focus was fully on the project. He'd been forgotten. He cleared his throat as he backed away from the platform. "I–I'll go get those nails now."

Her nod provided her approval. He headed out, leaving his jacket on the hook. The ground was mushy from the end-of-February snow that had fallen two days ago followed by the beginning-of-March sun. He crossed the ground with wide strides, reaching his truck quickly, and slid into the cab. It felt good to close the door on the wind, which carried a bite despite the clear sky and bright yellow sun beaming overhead.

The sight of that sun sent a stab of worry through Andrew's chest. March had arrived, and Dad was pressuring him to use his hours on the farm instead of in the studio. It was hard to convince Dad that making suncatchers was more important than tending to a money crop. He jammed the key into the ignition and started the engine with a firm press of his foot against the foot pedal. The rev of the engine vibrated away thoughts of Dad and winter wheat.

The drive to Doug Ortmann's farm took him past Uncle Henry's shop and house. He felt a stab of regret when he saw the neat addition on the side of the house. Taking care of Beth's business had kept him from helping, but the walls had gone up without him. His father hadn't been any happier than Andrew had been about missing the workday, and Dad hadn't minded saying so. He'd also made a suggestion Andrew approved—helping to spackle and paint the inside walls to make up for not being around on construction day. On the way back to the studio, Andrew would stop at the shop and let Uncle Henry know he would do that.

He left the town and turned left at the first country road. The Ortmann farm waited at the end of a mile-long lane that was nearly impassable thanks to the soft ground. Andrew kept a steady, slow speed, gritting his teeth when the tires slipped in the mud. When he reached the graveled area in front of the house, he released a whoosh of breath.

As he stepped around the hood of the truck, the door to the house opened and Livvy Ortmann stood framed in the doorway. Andrew had known Livvy since they were toddlers, but between him being tongue-tied and her being shy, he didn't think they'd exchanged more than a dozen words in all their growing-up years. He wished briefly that her dad or one of her brothers had opened the door. But he couldn't just walk out to the barn now that she'd seen him. He headed for the porch and stopped at the base of the steps.

"Are you looking for Dad?" She wore a flowered apron over her blue dress, and she tangled her hands in the square flap of cloth, wrinkling it.

Andrew nodded. "Beth Quinn needs some more horseshoe nails."

Livvy lowered her face for a moment, her lips puckering in an odd way. "Dad went to Hillsboro to look at a trailer, but he keeps the nails in the tack room. I can get some for you."

Andrew backed up one step. "No. That's okay. I know where he keeps them, and you'll get yourself all muddy if you come out. It's a mess."

A soft warmth lit her eyes at his comment, but he didn't understand why. She moved forward, allowing the screen door to close behind her. "How many do you need? So I can tell Dad what you took."

Andrew pushed his hands into his pockets. "I'm getting twice as many as last time, a couple dozen. Think that'll be okay?" The question wasn't necessary. Hadn't Doug Ortmann told him he could come back for more?

"Sure. Get what you need. Do you need a little sack?"

Andrew grimaced. He hadn't brought anything along in which to carry the nails. But an unexplained desire not to detain Livvy made him give a shrug. "Nope. I'm okay. Thank you."

"Sure. Good-bye, Andrew."

He felt certain she sounded sad when she offered the farewell. But she slipped so quickly back into the house, he couldn't see her face to confirm it. With another shrug, he headed for the tack room at the back of Ortmann's horse barn. As he passed the stalls, a soft mewling complaint captured his attention. He glanced to the side and spotted a gray and white cat, half grown, crouched in the hay.

He stopped and looked closer. One of the kitten's eyes was crusted over. As he watched, it raised its back paw and scratched at the eye.

"Hey, now, don't do that," he chided. "You'll only make it worse."

The little cat rolled to its side, pressing its face into the hay.

Sympathy rose in Andrew's chest. The poor thing must be suffering. Immediately, he thought of his cousin Trina and her love for small creatures. The last time he'd talked with his young cousin, she'd expressed the desire to have something to do besides work at the café all the time. Trina would want to doctor this little kitty back to health.

Andrew hurried on to the tack room, jammed his shirt pocket full of nails, and headed back to the house and banged on the door. Livvy answered again, her lips tipped into a bashful yet welcoming smile.

The smile unnerved him. "Is anybody else here?"

Her face fell. "No. The boys are at school, and Mom's visiting the Erlichs. What do you need? W-weren't you able to find the nails?"

Andrew touched his bulging pocket. "I found them. But I also found a cat with a bad eye."

Livvy nodded. The white ribbon trailing from the right side of her cap caught on her shoulder. She flicked it loose before replying. "Yes. One of Ginger's kittens. We don't know what he got into."

"Trina could probably cure it," he said, "but I don't want to take it without permission."

He was certain Livvy looked at him with approval. His ears grew hot.

"You can take him. Dad won't care—he thinks cats are more of a nuisance than they're worth, but they keep the mouse population down in the barn."

It was the lengthiest speech Livvy had ever delivered directly to him. He wasn't sure what had brought out this talkative side, but it increased his feeling of unease. He didn't want to stay and chat more, but he needed something from her. "I'll take him, but do you have a box to put him in so he won't get under my feet in the cab?"

Without a word, Livvy stepped back into the house, closing the door behind her. Andrew wasn't sure if she would come back or not, but he waited, hoping. In a few minutes, just as he was deciding to let the cat run loose in the cab, she returned.

"Here." She thrust a square box marked with black-and-white bottles of ketchup at him. "I had to empty it. It had Johnny's rock collection in it."

Andrew peered inside. Small bits of grit peppered the bottom. He moved to the edge of the porch and shook the bits onto the ground. Looking over his shoulder, he asked, "Will he mind me taking it?"

Another grin lit her face. "I just put the rocks in another box in his room. My brother has dozens. I doubt he'll even notice it's missing."

"Okay, then. Thanks." Andrew bounced the box against his knee as he headed back through the muck to the barn. To his relief, the gray and white cat was still stretched out in the hay and didn't resist as he lifted it. It took some doing to get it into the box and fold the flaps down over it, though, and he worried all the way back to town that the scrabbling paws would manage to pop the top loose before he reached the café. The cat yowled as if its tail was on fire, and Andrew wondered at the wisdom of carting it back.

He drove straight past Uncle Henry's, deciding that getting the cat into Trina's hands took precedence. After pulling behind the café, he put the truck in PARK and left the engine running. "You stay in there," he told the cat, then slammed the door and headed to the café's back door. He spotted Trina at the dishwasher. Aunt Deborah was nowhere in sight.

Opening the door just enough to be seen, he called, "Can you come here?"

Without questioning him, Trina wiped her hands on her apron

and skipped to the door.

He crooked his finger at her. With a quick look over her shoulder, she followed him to the truck. The moment he peeled back the lid, the little cat shot straight in the air and into Trina's waiting arms.

"Oh!" Trina cradled the frightened cat. "You poor little thing. What happened to you?"

"It belongs to the Doug Ortmanns. They don't know what happened to it."

Andrew watched Trina put the cat in the crook of one arm and gingerly examine its eye with her free hand. To his surprise, the animal didn't fight to free itself, although it did try to turn its head away from her prying fingers.

"It looks like he's got an infected scratch," Trina said. "Probably from some sort of wire." Lifting the kitten beneath her chin, she let it nuzzle her. A purr sounded, and Trina laughed softly. "Oh, you're a sweetie." Smiling at Andrew, she said, "Thank you for bringing him to me. I'll clean out that sore and put some ointment on it. Hopefully his eye will be okay."

Andrew nodded, smiling, too. He enjoyed Trina's pleasure. Just then, the back door opened and a cranky voice interrupted.

"Trina! What are you doing?"

Trina sent Andrew a guilty look before facing her mother. "Andrew found a kitten with a sore eye."

Deborah stepped carefully across the muddy expanse to look at the kitten. "Well, I'd say it's sore." She shook her head, her arms folded. "You and these animals." Although her tone gave the impression of disgust, Andrew glimpsed sympathy in Aunt Deborah's eyes. "Where do you plan to keep it?"

Trina's brows went up in an innocent expression. "In the storage shed?"

Andrew glanced at the shed, which once had housed the original owner's buggy. The building had stood empty for years, and the wood had weathered to a dull gray, but it would make an acceptable home for an injured kitten.

"That's fine. Put it in there now, and you can see to it after the supper rush." Aunt Deborah headed back toward the café, calling, "And mind you wash well when you come back in! I don't want cat hair in any food!"

"Yes, Mama!" Trina reached with one arm to give Andrew a hug. "Thank you, Andrew. I'll take good care of him, I promise!" She headed to the storage shed, the kitten held against her shoulder.

Andrew paused for a moment, watching until she sealed herself inside with the cat. It gave his heart a lift to see Trina's happiness at the prospect of nursing the kitten. He'd managed to please one female today. Giving his shirt pocket a pat, he remembered he had a way to please Beth, too. He climbed back into his truck and drove behind the studio.

He found Beth just where he'd left her, leaning over the platform, arranging glass squares, diamonds, and triangles. The moment he closed the door, she pushed herself to her feet and released a huge yawn. But she broke into a smile when he offered the nails.

"Oh, good." She counted them, then twisted her lips into a funny pout. "I hope I'll have enough nails to hold things in place. It's a big window." Her gaze returned to the glass-scattered platform.

Andrew stepped forward, hands in pockets, and looked down at the unconstructed window, too. "You have a month," he reminded her, but he knew the amount of time it took to put the pieces together for a small work. This window was not a small work.

"A month. . ." Her voice quavered, mute evidence of her uncertainty. "And that lilac-and-cardinal piece still needs completion."

"I'll do the lilac-and-cardinal piece. I can follow the drawing as well as you. You keep going." Andrew wondered when he had finally let go of the idea of working on McCauley's window. He also wondered at the wisdom of making such a promise when Dad was pressuring him to be at the farm. Then an idea hit. An idea for striking a deal. But not with Beth—with Albert Braun, his father.

FIFTEEN

Sean held the digital camera over his head, hoping the angle would capture the entire platform. He prayed his face hadn't reflected the dismay he felt when he'd seen how little of the project was put together. For a few moments, he had considered not taking pictures at all, but Dad and Patrick expected to see evidence of Beth's work. Besides, he'd told Beth he would be taking pictures, so he felt trapped. He just hoped Dad's reaction wouldn't be negative.

He snapped twice, checked the screen, and sucked in a satisfied breath—he'd caught the whole thing. But a frown formed as he examined the image and anticipated his father's concern. Didn't Beth understand speed was as important as quality? McCauley Church Construction was known for keeping its schedule—late-arriving windows could slow construction and cast a bad light on the entire company.

"I know it doesn't look like much now because it's just the border. I started with that to be certain the dimensions would fit the window casing exactly." Beth's voice pulled his attention away from the camera. She wove her fingers together and pressed them to her stomach. "But it *will* come together."

"Oh, I know." Sean chose his words carefully. "I've seen your completed works, so I know you have the *ability* to finish this one." He forced a soft chuckle. "But I bet you didn't realize how time-consuming a piece of this size could be."

Her nod bounced her shining ponytail. "You're right. It is a major project." She drew a deep breath that raised her shoulders. "But I'll be done on time. I made a commitment—I'll keep it."

The fervency in her tone encouraged Sean and increased his admiration. Her determination to be successful must equal his. They were a perfect match in so many ways.

Placing his hand on her shoulder, he gave a slight squeeze. "I know you will. I trust you. But"—he felt her tense—"it does seem to be moving more slowly than we had expected."

Sean waited, giving her an opportunity to explain delays, but Beth remained silent, her lips clamped tightly together. He offered another squeeze of her shoulder before lowering his hand, pleased that she hadn't rattled off excuses.

"If you're going to need an extension, now is the time to ask so we can modify the construction schedule. That isn't something we do in the middle of a project, but it can be done before we send out a crew."

Beth shook her head. Her ponytail swung so hard it slapped her on the side of the neck. "No. Don't modify your schedule. I said I'd have it done, and I will."

The stubborn set to her jaw made Sean want to smile, but he swallowed and managed to maintain a businesslike demeanor. "Thank you for your diligent attitude. That's exactly what McCauley Church Construction desires." He paused, hoping his next words would be accepted in the manner intended. "And expects."

Beth looked at him, her brow puckering momentarily. Then she gave a small nod, biting down on her lower lip. "I understand. Don't worry."

Although he hated to admit it, Sean was worried. He knew the demands that would be placed on Beth should she end up being McCauley's designated designer. He also recognized his own desire to spend time with her, to get to know her as a woman rather than an employee. If she didn't meet this first deadline, his father wouldn't trust her with a second, and Sean's time with her would be over.

Mixed emotions warred inside of him as he said, "I'll try not to worry, but you try to pick up the pace a bit, huh? We want this to work out—for all of us."

"Then I'd better get busy." Turning her back on him, she knelt on the platform and picked up a piece of glass.

He watched for a few moments, intrigued by her focus despite the fact he stood behind her. It didn't take long for him to feel uncomfortable and neglected. He cleared his throat.

She looked over her shoulder, her ponytail cupping her cheek. "I'm sorry. Did you need something else?"

"Um, I guess not." He released one brief huff of laughter, then lifted his shoulders in a shrug. "And I am expected in Carlton in. . ." He glanced at this wristwatch. He had plenty of time, but he realized diverting her attention would only slow her work. "Soon." Backing toward the door, he held up the camera. "Thank you for the pictures. I'll be in touch."

A nod gave her only reply, and he stepped out the door. He knew he should appreciate her focus and dedication to the project. After all, he'd meant to convey the importance of meeting the deadline, and her actions only proved he'd succeeded. Yet a regret he didn't fully understand hovered over him the remainder of the day.

Thursday morning, Andrew's truck followed Beth into the parking area behind the studio. He swung out of his cab and jogged across the uneven ground to open her door for her.

"Good morning," she greeted. "Thanks." They walked side by side to the stoop where she unlocked the back door. "How did your day go in the fields yesterday?" She asked as they stepped into the studio.

Andrew didn't smile. "It went fine."

She shot him a curious look. "Wasn't your father pleased to have you back?"

Andrew chuckled, but it lacked his usual enthusiasm. He tugged at his smooth-shaven cheek with one finger. "Yes, but he's still grumbling about only having me two days a week."

Beth leaned against the worktable, crossing her arms. "I'm sorry working here has created so many problems for you." Henry had informed Beth that Andrew's father opposed his son dabbling in art. Andrew paid a price to be here, and she knew she didn't show him enough appreciation for his choice. Somehow she needed to rectify that.

Andrew crossed to the cabinet and removed goggles and gloves. "It isn't your fault. My dad and me. . .we haven't seen eye to eye on much since I was pretty young. He's always gotten along better with my brothers."

Beth considered his words. Oddly, some of Sean's comments from yesterday replayed through her mind. Both men hinted at difficult relationships with their fathers. Even so, she experienced a stab of envy. At least they each had a relationship with a father—something she'd never known.

She opened her mouth, intending to encourage him to try to work things out, but she realized if Andrew were to satisfy his father, it would mean the end of his working here. Confused over which choice was right, she chose silence.

Pushing off from the worktable, she crossed the floor to retrieve her own gloves. "Well, just wait until this window is finished and the contracts with McCauley come rolling in," she found herself saying. "Your father will be glad you had a part in that."

"That's what I'm counting on."

His growling tone gave Beth a chill. She shrugged it off and said with a forced nonchalance, "Well, let's get busy, huh?"

As Beth worked, meticulously fitting the pieces within their lead came framing, her mind tripped over Sean's visit yesterday and his obvious concerns about her ability to complete the project. She understood; she held the same concerns. Glancing up at the calendar on the wall, she felt her heart skip a beat. Even if she continued working Monday through Saturday, that left only twenty-two days to finish.

She looked back at the wooden platform. Its expanse seemed endless, emphasized by the colorful border of glass held in place with dull, silver horseshoe nails. *How will I get this done, Lord? Help me!* her heart begged. So many of her prayers recently had centered around this project. Her business. Gaining new contracts.

Fitting another wedge of glass into place, she defended that focus to herself. What else did she have besides her business? She didn't have a husband. Or children. Or even a church family like the rest of the community. Her studio was her life. God surely understood that and would honor her prayers to build it. After all, hadn't He given her this ability and paved the way for her to discover it? Surely He would now bless it with the means to keep it going, to build it, to be successful. Why else would He have brought Sean McCauley to her doorstep?

Sean McCauley. A picture of his face appeared in her memory. Not the image from yesterday, with worry creasing his brow, but the first time—the open, eager, interested expression that lit his blue-green eyes and brought a curving smile to his lips beneath the neat mustache.

Although their contact hadn't been excessive and had been largely limited to e-mails and telephone calls, she felt as though she knew him well. She recognized in him the same drive to succeed that existed in her own heart, and it both impressed and terrified her. What if his drive to succeed ending up forcing her off the road?

She sat up and rubbed her lower back, working loose the kinks that always formed from leaning over the platform. While she worked the tight muscles, her thoughts pressed on, constricting her chest. Would she ever be able to trust a man to have her interests at heart rather than his own?

Behind her, the scraping of the stool's legs against the concrete floor reminded her of Andrew's presence. Although he had been faithful in his commitment to helping her, she still couldn't fully trust that his diligence wasn't selfishly motivated.

She remembered his shining eyes when he'd explained the compromise he'd worked out with his father. Originally, he had only planned to work at her studio until it was time to cut the winter wheat. That was happening now all around Sommerfeld. But he had gained approval to work in the fields two days a week—Wednesday and Saturday—and continue in the studio the remaining weekdays. She frowned as she recalled his exact words when he had explained the details of his arrangement: *"But once you prove this studio can support us full-time, my father is willing to let me pursue art as my job instead of farming. So let's do it!"*

That seemed to prove that his desire to get her business up and going had more to do with his own desires to pursue art than with a genuine interest in seeing her dreams come true. And it also made her wonder if he would try to undermine her in order to become the artist rather than the employee.

Bolting to her feet, she spun to face him. "Andrew."

He jumped, dislodging the piece of glass he'd been placing. With a grunt, he slid the piece back where it belonged and then looked at her.

"I was counting the days I have left to meet the McCauley deadline."

Andrew's gaze drifted briefly to the calendar. He turned back to her and nodded.

"I'm not sure I can do it, even working Saturdays. I'm thinking about working Sundays, too—just the afternoons. I'd still go to the meetinghouse in the morning." Her mother would have choice words if Beth skipped Sunday services, and she also knew she shouldn't expect God to make time for her if she didn't carve out time for Him. "What do you think?"

"You would dishonor God's third commandment?"

Beth blinked twice. He both looked and sounded flabbergasted. "What do you mean?"

"We are commanded to keep the Sabbath day holy. That means following God's example to rest."

Suddenly Beth understood. He referred to one of the Ten Commandments Moses brought to the people—she had read about it in one of the earliest Old Testament books, although she couldn't remember if it was Genesis or Exodus. "So the people of Sommerfeld wouldn't take kindly to my working then, huh?"

Andrew shook his head, sadness in his eyes. "Beth, when I say *we*, I don't mean Mennonites only. I mean Christians. That includes you. Your God takes seriously His teachings. Rest is important. You wear down and get sick if you never rest. God knows this. That's why He gave us the instruction."

Well, her mind argued, *God understands I have a deadline hanging over my head!* But she didn't voice the thought. Andrew's serious expression held her too-often-flippant tongue. "Okay." She sighed. "I won't work on Sundays. I'll just work a few more hours every other day."

When Andrew's brows pinched, she laughed. "I know what you're thinking. I already look awful." She tipped her head and smirked. "Yes, I *do* look in the mirror on occasion."

His ears turned bright red, and she knew he remembered his uncomplimentary comment from Monday.

"But it won't be for much longer. Twenty-two more days, *excluding* Sundays, to be exact. Then, with contract in hand, I will advertise for two or three more employees. I will instruct you and those additional employees to put together stained-glass windows. And I will be the creative force behind the windows!" She threw her arms outward and exploded in an exaggerated laugh of glee. "And I will have it all!"

If she thought Andrew would join her in laughter, she was mistaken. Instead, when she looked at him, she found him wearing a smug, almost conniving grin that erased the momentary playfulness from her heart.

She recounted Andrew's response to her attempts at teasing that evening when she stopped by to see her mother and check on the progress of the addition. They stood in the second of the two bedrooms. The unpainted walls and ceiling and uncovered wooden floors gave the impression of standing in a tomb.

"I just wish," Beth said, her soft voice echoing in the empty space, "I could set aside my worries that Andrew is going to somehow take over or destroy what I'm trying to do."

Mom's arm slipped around Beth's shoulders. "I understand why you're worried, honey, after what you went through with Mitch. But you have to remember Mitch isn't a Christian. He doesn't have the same moral values that Andrew has. Don't you believe Andrew's

Christianity is important to him?"

Beth remembered his shocked response to her question about working on Sunday. She also recalled his devotion to a father who seemed bent on destroying his dreams. Yes, Andrew's Christianity was important to him. Still. . .

"Not only that," Mom continued, her eyes crinkling, "I happen to have it on good authority that Andrew likes you."

"And I don't know if that makes it better or worse!" Beth stepped away from her mother and stormed several feet away. Turning back, she said, "I like Andrew, too. He's one of my few friends around here. But liking him as more than a friend? I don't think I could ever do that."

Mom crossed her arms over her stomach, her fine eyebrows crunching together. "Because?"

Beth sighed. "Because he's Mennonite. And if I end up liking him as more than a friend, the only way our relationship could work is if he leaves the Mennonite faith or I join it."

"And you don't see that happening?"

Beth examined her mother's face. A hint of pain existed in her eyes, creating an ache in Beth's heart as she admitted, "I don't think so. At least not for me. I–I'm sorry if that hurts you."

Mom moved forward, her steps stiff. "No, Beth, I understand. You weren't raised in the faith of my family. For me, it was coming home. For you, it's something completely different. You only see the constraints, and it doesn't offer a feeling of security for you as much as a feeling of being stifled."

Beth nodded. Her mother had managed to put into words exactly the way Beth viewed the lifestyle "rules" of the Old Order Mennonite sect's teaching.

Mom continued. "It's enough for me to know you've accepted

Jesus as your Savior. Being a church member won't secure your place at His side in heaven, but asking Him into your heart did. That's what is important."

Beth nearly expelled a breath of relief. But then she shook her head. "Still, it doesn't solve my issues with Andrew. There just seems to be. . .something more. . .he wants from me. If it's a relationship, I can't give it. And if it's equal footing in my studio, I *won't* give it. But I don't know how to make that understood."

Mom's gaze suddenly jerked somewhere behind Beth. Her face turned white. Puzzled, Beth turned to look. Her heart fell to her stomach. Henry and Andrew stood right outside the door.

SIXTEEN

Uncle Henry moved into the bedroom, but Andrew's feet remained glued to the floor. Beth's comments rang in his head. She didn't want a relationship with him—either working or personal. He couldn't face her, so he stayed beside the unfinished door frame, staring at the toes of his boots.

"Andrew stopped by to offer his help in mudding, sanding, and painting the new rooms." Uncle Henry spoke softly, sympathy underscoring his tone.

Andrew held his breath, waiting for Beth's reply, explanation, or apology, but she said nothing. He jerked his chin up. "I meant to come by earlier this week, but I got busy with a cat." He realized how stupid his excuse sounded, but he didn't know what else to say.

Aunt Marie sent a weak smile in his direction. "That's kind of you. Henry will appreciate the help. Our time is running short, isn't it?"

Beth's time on the window was running short. And Andrew's time to convince her he was needed in all aspects of her life had apparently run out.

"Marie?" The concern in his uncle's tone caught Andrew's attention. "Is your stomach bothering you again?"

Andrew peered through the doorway in time to see Uncle Henry take his wife's chin and tip her face so their eyes could meet.

Aunt Marie laughed softly. "Now, you know an upset stomach isn't anything to worry about." The words were meant to appease fear, but even Andrew could see the white lines around Marie's mouth and the way she held herself in an odd position, as if standing straight was too painful.

"I'm not convinced it's your stomach." Henry put his arm around Marie's waist and guided her from the room.

Andrew stepped back to allow their passage, then followed them to the front room. He stood beside the couch where Marie sat on the edge of the cushion. Beth stood at his elbow, but he was careful not to look at her.

Marie peered up at the trio and shook her head. "It's nothing. Just a pulled muscle, probably, from carrying this extra weight. At my age, it's harder than it would have been twenty years ago."

Henry looked at Beth, his brows low. "She's been throwing up. Should a woman be throwing up at six months pregnant?"

Andrew flitted a glance at Beth's face. Her wide blue eyes blinked in confusion.

"I don't know. I've never had a baby. But it does seem odd. I always thought women just got sick in the first trimester."

"That's what I thought, too."

Andrew's ears felt hot, and he wanted to leave the personal conversation, but he didn't know how to gracefully walk away. So he clasped his hands behind his back and stared at the black ribbons dangling from his aunt's cap. They emphasized the pale pallor of her skin.

Marie caught Henry's hand. "Stop talking about me like I'm not here."

Henry bent down on one knee, still holding his wife's hand. "Marie, I'm worried."

Andrew caught Beth's eye. Despite the hurt she'd caused with her comments a few minutes earlier, he sensed her distress and wanted to help. Like he always wanted to help. She stared at him helplessly, and he reached out to brush her shoulder, just a light graze with his fingertips. A nothing touch. But she offered a small smile of thanks before facing her mother again.

"I'm fine, Henry. Really. Just old and tired." Marie released a light laugh, convincing Andrew there was no need to fear. "There are two of them in here." She cupped her stomach with both hands, shaking her head. "They're probably putting pressure on a nerve or something, which is why I hurt."

"I don't know. . ."

Marie shook her head, her expression tender. "Poor first-time daddy. You're overprotective, and I love you for it, but you don't need to fuss so. I'm sure it's nothing."

Henry rose, but his frown remained. "First it's pulled muscles, then pressure on nerves. And I don't like it."

Marie stretched her hand up, pressing it to her husband's chest. "Don't worry. In another few months they'll be here, and I'll be back to normal. Or"—another laugh sounded—"as normal as it can possibly get with two infants vying for my attention. Believe me, you may want to return to these days when my only complaint is a stitch in my side that upsets my stomach."

Andrew chuckled, and Beth echoed it. He looked at her again, but her gaze was on Marie.

"I'll come by and help with housework, Mom," Beth offered.

Marie shook her head. "Oh, no. You have a studio to run, and you need to concentrate on that. I'll be fine. But if you want to do something to help"—she raised her brows—"you could cut Andrew loose for a day or two so those rooms can be finished on the inside."

"I can do that." Beth's answer came quickly.

Too quickly. Andrew frowned. Did she see this as a way to get him out of her studio, to distance herself from him? "What about the cardinal piece?"

Beth barely glanced at him. "You're ahead of schedule on it. We can spare a few days off from that. Take tomorrow and Monday to work here, Andrew. It's fine."

"I'm ahead at the shop, too," Henry inserted. "With everyone working their fields, this is a good time for me to take a couple of days and finish those rooms."

Andrew looked from person to person. It appeared plans had been settled. He gave a brusque nod. "Okay. I'll be here tomorrow morning then, and I'll bring my own trowel."

"Dress in old clothes," Henry warned, a grin finally finding its way to his face. "It gets messy."

Andrew didn't need to be told that. He'd done more than his share of mudding when other community members had built extra rooms onto their houses. Since there seemed little to add, he inched toward the door. "I'll see you tomorrow then. Good night, Uncle Henry and Aunt Marie. . .Beth." He ducked out the door before anyone answered.

Since Uncle Henry was also a man of few words, Andrew and he worked mostly in silence Friday. Aunt Marie popped in periodically to check on their progress, but Uncle Henry always chased her out, scolding her about breathing in the fumes from the spackle. Her teasing replies made Andrew smile. Beth definitely inherited her spunk from her mother.

Each thought of Beth brought a stab of pain. Not since he had started working at the studio several months ago had he gone more than a day without seeing her. Now he was facing four days with only a brief contact at the meetinghouse Sunday. Days had never seemed so long.

At the same time, he welcomed the break. What he'd overheard her tell her mother was hard to swallow and even harder to digest. Maybe these days away would help him find his peace with her statement. But he doubted it. Uncle Henry had carried a torch for Marie more than two decades, and it had never flickered. People always told him he looked and acted like Henry. What if he proved to be like his uncle in that regard, too? What if he was never able to let go of his desire for Beth?

That question plagued Andrew over the next two days. It wiggled through his brain during Sunday service, stealing his attention from the minister. He was contemplating it again in the churchyard, when someone slapped him on the back and nearly startled him out of his hat.

Doug Ortmann stood beside Andrew. His daughter Livvy held on to his arm and peeked around his shoulder at Andrew. "Livvy said you came by when I was out. Did you find what you needed?"

Andrew nodded, centering his hat back over his ears. "Yes, sir. A couple dozen horseshoe nails."

"She said you also took a cat."

Andrew noticed Livvy's grin. He turned his gaze to Mr. Ortmann. "Yes, but I'll probably bring the cat back."

Trina bounced over, her white ribbons dancing beneath her chin. She caught Andrew's elbow and clung to him, much the way Livvy clung to her father. "Mr. Ortmann, the kitten's eye is looking better already. A thorough washing and application of ointment made a big difference. He could probably go home this afternoon, if you like."

Mr. Ortmann shrugged. "It doesn't really matter, Trina. I was about to tell Andrew that we have plenty of cats. He can just let it go somewhere as far as I'm concerned."

Trina's gasp made Andrew press his elbow to his ribs, giving her fingers a comforting squeeze. "I think Trina's gotten attached to it," he said, "so maybe you could let her keep it?"

Ortmann smiled. "Sure. And if you need any more of those nails, just come on out." He gave Andrew another hearty clap on the back and strode away. Livvy waved over her shoulder as they moved to speak with someone else.

Trina beamed up at him. "Thank you, Andrew! How could anyone just abandon a poor little kitten that way?" Her face clouded. "But Daddy will never let me keep it. He doesn't mind my nursing hurt animals, but he always says no when I ask if we can have a pet."

Andrew scratched his chin, thinking. Out of the corner of his eye, he saw Beth with her mother and her aunt Joanna Dick. Beth's straight brown skirt and fuzzy sweater, although much more conservative than her normal tight-fitting jeans and bright T-shirts, still marked her as non-Mennonite. His heart ached as he remembered her saying she could never be Mennonite.

"Andrew?"

Trina's plaintive voice reminded him he'd drifted away again. Looking back at his cousin, he gave her hand on his arm a light pat. "Don't worry. I'll help you find a home for it. I rescued him, remember?"

Her smile returned, lighting her freckled face. Stretching up on her tiptoes, she planted a quick kiss on his cheek. "Thank you, Andrew. You're the best!"

She scampered off, and Andrew stood alone, thinking. Who would take a small cat with one damaged eye? Someone who could use the company. . .

One person came to mind. The same person he'd been trying to forget. But maybe a little gift like a pet would help her look at him differently. It was worth a try.

Beth said good-bye to Aunt Joanna and her mother and turned toward her car. Her gaze swept across the churchyard and landed on Andrew, who stood alone in the middle of a patch of brown grass. He seemed lonely. The past two days, she'd been lonely, working by herself in the studio. She'd discovered she missed his company, and for a moment she considered lifting her hand in a wave.

But she reminded herself that part of the reason she'd insisted he work at Henry's was to give them some time apart, to reevaluate their relationship. Waving would only encourage him. She stuck her hand into her purse and fished for her car keys while she crossed quickly to her car. Her sporty red car with its shiny silver bumpers and white pinstripes, even though it was several years old, stood out among the Mennonites' plain black or blue sedans. It looked especially modern next to the few horse-drawn buggies on the edge of the parking area.

Once more, she was reminded of her ill fit in this community, and she felt the urge to hurry from the churchyard. Aunt Joanna had invited her to join her family for lunch, but she had declined. Despite Andrew's warning, she had considered sneaking to the studio, but the more she thought about a day of rest, the better it sounded.

A nap. A long nap. A refreshing nap. That's all she wanted right now. She'd eat a quick sandwich and jump into bed for the afternoon. The decision made, she drove home. After dressing in her pajamas, she leaned against the kitchen counter and ate a peanut butter sandwich. The sandwich, followed by a glass of milk, filled her, and she headed for the bedroom. Snuggled beneath the covers, she closed her eyes and was drifting off when her telephone rang.

Her eyes popped open. For a moment she considered letting it ring itself out, but concerned it might be her mother or Henry, she threw back the covers and dashed to the kitchen. Snatching up the receiver, she said, "Hello? Beth here."

"Beth."

The masculine voice—not Henry's—threw her for a moment. She rubbed her eyes. "Sean?"

"Yes. I'm sorry to bother you on Sunday."

"Oh, that's all right." She stifled a yawn. "What did you need?"

"I'm going to be out of town for the next ten days. I'm flying to Denver and then driving into the mountains to finalize the building plans with a committee in Blue River."

Beth didn't reply, uncertain why he found it necessary to share his plans with her.

"Sometimes at that elevation my cell phone doesn't work, and I'm not sure if I'll have Internet access, so I wanted to let you know if you couldn't reach me, you could call the home office and leave a message with the receptionist. She'll forward it on to me eventually."

For what reason would she need to contact him? Her fuzzy brain tried to process the reason for this unexpected update on his itinerary. She had only called him once. Every other conversation had been initiated by him.

"I'll let you get back to what you were doing—"

She yawned again, slumping against the wall.

"And I'll talk to you when I get back, if not before."

"Okay. Have a good trip." She put the receiver on the cradle and stumbled back to bed. She dropped across the mattress, but when her head hit the pillow, she came fully awake. Popping back up, she blinked in rapid succession, her mouth open in surprise.

Sean wanted her to know where he would be.

He wanted her to know she didn't need to worry.

He wanted her to be able to contact him.

Flopping backward with her arms out to the side, she stared at the ceiling. That was not a business call. That was personal. Very personal.

She couldn't decide if she found the realization flattering. . .or troubling.

SEVENTEEN

Beth marked an X in the calendar box, then stood back and frowned. She had hoped having a visual reminder of the days left to complete the McCauley window might motivate her. All it managed to do was scare her.

Flipping the pencil around, she forcefully applied the eraser to remove the X. Despite herself, she felt a chuckle building. The last time she had marked Xs on a calendar, she had been counting down the days before she would be allowed to leave Sommerfeld. When Great-Aunt Lisbeth had left her the house and café, it hadn't come without its stipulation—live on the property for three months before dispensing of it. Who would have thought she'd end up living permanently in this little, religiously based community?

Beth tipped her head, staring at the remnants of the X, and considered her aunt's motivation for the requirement. Great-Aunt Lisbeth had wanted Beth to stay, to become a part of Sommerfeld and the Koeppler family. And she had. But not completely. She lived here. She worked here. She even worshipped here. But still. . .underneath. . . she didn't belong here.

"And I hate always being reminded of that!"

She nearly shouted the words, slapping the wall beside the calendar and spinning away from it. Her gaze landed on the platform. The window awaited her attention. This was her last day to work alone—Andrew would return tomorrow—so she might as well make good use of the lack of distraction.

Kneeling beside the platform, she reached for the glass pieces. Not even Sean would bother her today since he was on his way to Denver. A full day of uninterrupted work. "So, how much do I think I can accomplish?" she murmured, then shook her head. Was she going to resort to talking to *herself*? How ridiculous would that be!

Her tongue between her teeth, she leaned forward and carefully fitted a red diamond into place. An odd noise—not a knock, but more of a muffled scratch—came from outside the door. Puzzled, Beth turned her head in that direction. Had she imagined it? But no, there it came again.

Curiosity drove her to her feet. She opened the door slowly, peering out left and right. No one was there. The scratching sound came again, louder, and she looked down. A box with a line of Sunshine ketchup bottles printed on the side sat on the stoop. The scratching came from inside the box.

"What's this?" Beth crouched down and stuck her fingers between the folded-down flaps. Something furry batted her hand. She jerked back for a moment, startled, then grabbed the flap again and pulled it open.

A gray and white whiskered face with round yellow eyes peered at her. It seemed to wink with one eye.

"A cat!" Beth laughed, delighted when the little thing raised one paw toward her as if to shake hands. "Where did you come from?"

Of course, she got no answer, but it leaped from the box and ran past her directly into the studio.

"Hey!" Beth jumped to her feet and followed. She watched the little cat walk around the periphery of the studio, stopping to examine anything that remotely resembled a threat. Threats included the legs of the display bench and Beth's shoes, which she'd kicked off and left beside the door. She chuckled softly at the little thing's ruffled fur, twitching tail, and lowered ears.

Its survey apparently complete, it stuck its tail straight in the air and dashed to her. Rubbing against her legs, it sent out a loud purr.

Beth knelt down. "Well, you are a nice. . ." She peeked. "Boy. Do you have a name?"

The kitten placed one paw on her knee and stretched the other toward her face, his whiskers twitching.

"No? Well, if you're going to stick around, you'll need a name." She offered her hand, and the cat rubbed his chin against her fingers, his motor increasing in volume. He continued to hold his left eye at half-mast, as if caught in the middle of a wink. She chuckled again. "Maybe I'll call you Winky, since you seem to enjoy doing it."

At closer examination, Beth could see the winking eye had recently sustained some kind of injury. A scab, partially hidden by his fur, showed beneath the eye. Her heart stirred with sympathy. "You poor little guy." She scooped him up and was delighted when he allowed her to hold him. He bumped his head on the underside of her chin and kneaded her shoulder with his little paws.

"I've never had a pet before, besides goldfish. And I have to admit, they weren't nearly as friendly as you," she informed the cat, "but I've always lived in apartments. I have my own house now, and I get to make the rules. So I suppose it's okay if you stay."

The telephone rang, and Beth got to her feet without relinquishing the cat. He grabbed the receiver with both front paws and bit it when she pressed it to her head. "Good morning, Quinn's Stained-Glass Art Studio."

"Good morning, honey." Mom's voice came through in a cheerful tone. "I called the house, but you must have left early."

Beth lifted her chin, trying to avoid Winky's swinging paws. "Yes. I've got to make use of every available hour these days."

"I understand. Henry and Andrew are painting today, and they promise me the rooms will be ready for inspection by suppertime."

"Really?" Winky caught her ponytail and chewed on the strands, his motor rising several decibels. She put him on the floor, where he wove around her feet, his tail whipping the air. "They've made good progress then."

"Oh, yes." Mom's light chuckle sounded. "And they demand a celebration. So I'm fixing pot roast, potatoes, carrots. . .the whole shebang. Want to join us?"

"Why me? I didn't have anything to do with it."

"Yes, you did. You let Andrew have a couple days off so he could work here. So you're included."

Beth chewed her lower lip and watched Winky attack a piece of string he found under the display bench. Did she want to spend an evening with Andrew? It might give him ideas. Then again, it might give her an opportunity to ease back into their working relationship. Thinking about being alone with him tomorrow gave her an uneasy feeling in the pit of her stomach. But an evening with Mom and Henry in attendance might provide a nice transition to once again being alone with Andrew.

"That sounds fine. Want me to bring something?"

"Well, if the café were open, I'd call Deborah and ask her to set aside some rolls and dessert, maybe a coconut cream pie. Henry loves it. But since it's Monday, we can't do that."

Beth swallowed a hoot of laughter as Winky rolled onto his back, holding the string between his front paws and kicking at it with his back ones. *He must think it's a vicious string.*

"Beth? Are you there?"

Beth gave a start and turned her back on the cat so she could focus on what her mother was saying. "Yes. Sorry. How 'bout I pick up some rolls and a prebaked pie at the grocer? They won't be as good as Deborah's, but they'll be better than anything I could cook."

Mom's laughter sounded. "Okay, that sounds fine. Be here by six. We'll tour the bedrooms first and then eat."

Beth nodded. Perfect. After dinner she could return to the studio for a couple more hours of work if need be. "Okay. Thanks, Mom. See you then."

After hanging up the receiver, she put her hands on her hips and shook her head at the cat. "You are entirely too cute, Mr. Winky. I don't know how you got here, but I think I'm going to enjoy having you around."

Andrew prolonged the last few sips of his coffee as he listened to the one-sided telephone conversation. His heart thumped. Had Beth opened the back door and found the cat yet? Her early arrival had spoiled his initial plan of having the box waiting for her when she got to the studio. He'd had to be extra quiet placing the box on the stoop and sneaking away.

But now worries struck. What if the cat managed to escape and all she found was an empty box? Should he have stuck around and made sure the cat made it safely into the studio?

He wanted to ask Aunt Marie, yet he wanted to keep the surprise gift a secret. He wished she'd say something to give him some clue about whether or not Beth had found the cat.

Marie moved to the stove with a swaying gait and picked up the coffeepot. She sent a smile in his direction as she held out the pot. "More?"

Andrew swallowed the last drops and shook his head. "No. I better get my paint roller out. Uncle Henry's already hard at it. Did Beth"—he searched for a question that might lead Aunt Marie to offer what he sought—"say anything. . .about. . . ?"

Aunt Marie raised one brow. "About coming to dinner? Yes, she'll be here. And I promised her a tour before we eat."

Her smile encouraged Andrew to go get busy. He gave a nod. "It'll be ready."

Midmorning, Beth took a break and walked to her uncle Art's place of business, Koeppler Feed and Seed. Although he dealt mostly in farm implements, she knew a small selection of pet supplies was stored in the back corner of the store. She hoped she'd be able to find cat litter and one of those scooper things in addition to food and perhaps a collar with a little bell on it. She smiled. Winky was a sneaky beast—her feet had been attacked numerous times in their short time together. If a bell signaled his presence, maybe she wouldn't be caught off guard anymore.

Entering the shop, she headed straight to the counter, where an old-fashioned cash register took up one full corner. No digital readouts or computers in Sommerfeld. This store, like so many others in town, still held the feel of its early 1920s beginning. The wide planked floor and simple shelving, lit by bare bulbs hanging from twisted wire from the stamped tin ceiling, gave Beth the impression of stepping back in time. The smells—leather and sawdust and grain—added to that sensation.

Art's wife, Doris, stood behind the counter, shifting items around in a box. She looked up and, probably without even realizing it, swept her gaze from Beth's head to her feet and up again. The seconds-long examination complete, a small smile formed on her lips.

"Why, hello, Beth."

"Good morning," Beth greeted, forcing a cheerful tone. Doris's perusal and the hesitant warmth in her eyes once more reminded Beth of her worldly—in the town's opinion—appearance. She tugged at the tails of her flannel shirt and fidgeted.

"What brings you here this morning? Surely you don't need a plow."

"Oh, no." Beth gave the expected laugh. "But I do need some cat food, a collar with a bell, if you have one, and a litter box."

Doris's eyebrows shot high. "Marie didn't mention you were planning to get a kitten."

Beth shrugged. "She didn't know." Beth didn't bother to mention she herself hadn't known.

"Well, we do have clay litter. Lots of our farmers use it to absorb oil spills from their farm equipment." The rubber soles of Doris's sensible oxfords squeaked against the wood-planked floor as she stepped from behind the counter. "But we don't carry litter boxes." She led Beth past aisles of knotty pine shelves holding tools, boxes of boots, and stacks of work pants to the area where pet supplies were kept. "However, you could probably go next door to the variety store and buy a dishpan. It would work just as well."

"Thanks. I'll do that."

Doris returned to the counter while Beth looked at the small selection of cat collars. She chose a pale blue one with felt underlining. Its little bell sent out a low-toned jingle. "That'll keep you from creeping up on me," she mumbled. And, she decided, Winky would look quite jaunty with the blue collar against his gray fur.

She looped the collar over her wrist, then scooped up a ten-pound bag of litter and a five-pound bag of cat food and waddled to the counter. For a moment, she wished she'd brought her car; the three-block walk to the studio might seem longer carrying her burden.

Doris punched the amounts into the register and gave a blunt total. When she put the collar in a little bag, she commented, "This is a ten-inch. Are you sure you don't want a nine-inch?"

Beth frowned. "What's the difference?"

"A ten-inch might not stay around a kitten's neck; it could be too long."

"Well, he's not quite a cat, but he's not a kitten anymore." She smiled at Doris's puzzled expression. "I'm guessing he's halfway to grown up."

"Oh." Doris rolled the bag closed. "Then this will probably be okay if you hook it on the inside notch. Getting the bell is a good idea. It will keep him from catching birds." She grimaced. "Nasty thing to do."

Beth agreed. But she intended to make Winky a studio cat, and the only birds he could chase in there were ones formed from bits of colored glass. She thanked Doris once more, then headed out. As she aimed her feet toward the variety store, she released a chuckle. It wouldn't be long before the entire town knew she was the proud owner of a half-grown cat. Word spread amazingly fast in this little town.

Winky seemed pleased to scratch around in his dishpan-turned-litter box, which relieved Beth mightily. He also gave no indication of being offended by the plastic cereal bowls that held his food and water since she'd been unable to find an official pet dish at the variety store. However, he turned into a real stinker when she tried to fasten the collar around his neck.

"Now, behave yourself," she scolded as he backed up between her

451

legs, eluding her grasp. "This is for your own good!" She spent at least five minutes chasing him around the studio before she finally conceded defeat. Smacking the collar onto the worktable, she warned, "You've got to sleep sometime, and I'll get you then."

From across the room, Winky washed one paw and fixed her with a heavy-lidded stare. She laughed. "Whoever left you on my doorstep is going to get the biggest thank-you. You really are precious." She sighed. "But now I've got to get back to work. Leave my feet alone, huh?"

Winky simply winked.

Eighteen

And there it was, right on my doorstep." Beth buttered another roll and took a bite of it. "But unlike the movies where there's always a note attached saying, 'Take care of my baby,' there was no communication."

"Hmm. . ." Henry stabbed a forkful of green beans. "A cat, you say?" He sent a speculative look across the table to Marie. "Didn't Trina say something Sunday evening about needing to find a home for a cat?"

Andrew cleared his throat loudly and pointed to the saltshaker. "Could someone pass the salt, please?"

Henry obliged, and Andrew grabbed it with a mumbled "Thank you." Beth hoped her mother wasn't insulted. In her opinion, everything tasted great, but judging by Andrew's zealous application, the food was flavorless.

"You said Trina?" Beth chewed thoughtfully. Yes, she could see Trina giving her a kitten. But she couldn't imagine why the girl would be so secretive about it.

"Yes." Mom sat back, most of her plate untouched. "Something about it having been hurt, but—"

453

"This is all really good, Aunt Marie."

Andrew's ears turned as red as the plum jelly in the middle of the table as everyone stopped eating and stared at him. Gesturing with his fork, he added, "All of it. Really good."

Mom offered a slow nod. "Thank you." Her tone indicated puzzlement.

"Yes." He cleared his throat again. "Did you. . .use any special kind of seasonings on the meat?"

Henry burst out laughing. "Don't tell me you're collecting recipes."

Beth didn't think Andrew's ears could get any redder. But he was only embarrassing himself by butting in and inserting topics that were clearly outside of his area of interest. What was he. . . ? Her thoughts were interrupted by the theme song from *Looney Tunes* coming from her purse. She leaped from the table.

"Sorry," she said as she snatched it from the floor beside the door, "but I'm expecting a call from the owner of the Salina mall about my commission check from the craft fair." She flipped open the phone and looked at the number. Her brows pinched. She didn't recognize it. After clicking the TALK button, she held the phone to her ear. "Hello?"

"Hello, Beth. It's Sean."

"Sean! Are you in Denver?" Eating came to a standstill at the table. Three faces aimed in her direction. She pointed to the hallway and mouthed, "I won't be long." Then she moved around the corner, out of sight of her parents and Andrew.

"Yes. I'm calling from the hotel. I wanted to give you the number."

Beth shook her head. "Thanks, but if I needed something, I could've just contacted the office."

"I know, but. . .I wanted you to have it."

"Oka-a-ay." Beth drew out the word, uncertain how to respond.

"That way," his soft voice continued, "I can stay up-to-date on your progress, and you can check on mine."

A self-conscious giggle spilled out. "Why do I need to check on yours?"

"Because if this committee signs with McCauley, they've already indicated they want seventeen stained-glass windows. A large one of a rainbow with a dove behind the lectern; and eight on each side of the sanctuary, nine representing the different fruits of the Spirit and the remaining seven showing symbols of Christianity. That should challenge your artistic side."

Beth leaned against the wall. "S–seventeen? The fruits of the Spirit?"

Sean's chuckle sounded. She pictured his crinkled eyes, his warm smile. Funny how given the few times they'd been face-to-face he could appear so easily in her memory. "Yes. That should keep you busy, I'd think."

"Oh, yes, I'd think. . ."

Another chuckle. "So get that one finished and out of the way so we can get moving on these fruits."

Already her mind was spinning. "Yes." Fruits of the Spirit: gentleness, mercy. . .what else? "I will. Well, the number of the hotel will be in my phone's memory bank, so I've got it."

"Oh. Good. Then. . .I'll let you go. I've got an early meeting tomorrow."

"Thanks for calling." She snapped the phone shut and dashed around the corner.

"Mom! Guess what!"

Andrew lowered his fork and looked up, his heart leaping at Beth's glowing face.

"What?" Marie asked, tipping her head.

"That was Sean—Sean McCauley—and he says their next project includes seventeen stained-glass windows. Seventeen!" She nearly danced to the table, her fingers in her hair. "They want each to be a depiction of a Christian symbol or one of the fruits of the Spirit."

Marie's jaw dropped. "W—what?"

Henry leaned his elbows on the table. "That sounds like quite the challenge."

"I know." Beth shook her head, her eyes wide. She faced Andrew and clasped her hands beneath her chin. "Andrew, I know I've said you need to work on other things and let me do the McCauley window, but I've changed my mind. You know, woman's prerogative and all that. . ." Her giggle filled the room. "Starting tomorrow, you're going to work with me. I want to finish early—beat the deadline."

Andrew put down his fork. "But what about the Fox Gallery? You have a deadline there, too."

"I know, but it's commissioned; there's no set customer waiting for that one, so a delay won't really hurt anything. This McCauley project is absolute top priority."

The way she emphasized the last words set Andrew's teeth on edge. Although all along he'd wanted to help with the window, now resentment smacked hard. Since when should McCauley be the only customer who mattered?

"Why?" He nearly barked the word, startling himself as much as Beth.

She moved slowly to the table and put her hands on the back of her chair. "Why?" She crunched her mouth into a scowl. "I should think it would be obvious. I want the chance to design those windows."

Suddenly the room faded away. All that existed for Andrew was he and Beth facing off. He folded his paint-speckled arms across his chest. "I understand you want to win the contract. But that can be done without setting everything else aside if you keep up the pace you've been doing lately. Are you sure it's only the contract you're after?"

Beth's scowl deepened as her fingers curled tight on the chair's top rail. "What is that supposed to mean?"

"Are you sure you're not trying to win"—Andrew's bravado briefly flickered, but a jealous wave drove the final word from his heart— "Sean?"

Beth yanked out the chair and plunked into it, her jaw dropping. "I can't believe you just said that."

Andrew couldn't either. But he was glad he had. The way she'd lit up when she realized who was on the telephone. Her willingness to set aside everything—everything!—to please that man. Her defensiveness now. In his eyes, it all pointed to one thing: Beth liked Sean. And even though he recognized it, he wouldn't say it aloud and give it credence.

"Honestly, Andrew, you're just out of line." Beth angled her head with her chin jutting to the side. "I thought we'd come to the understanding that you are my employee, not a co-boss. It isn't your business to presume on my motives. You're just to do what you're told. So plan on helping with the McCauley window starting tomorrow morning."

"Whatever you say, *boss*." What was he doing? He'd never spoken to Beth this way before. In the back of his mind, the biblical reminder to be angry yet sin not raised a flag, but he refused to acknowledge it. He clamped his jaw, holding back the apology for which she was certainly waiting. She could just wait, the stubborn, bossy girl!

They sat glaring at each other across the table for long seconds until a strangled sound—not quite a snort, not quite a cough—came from Henry's side of the table. Andrew shifted his gaze to his uncle. Uncle Henry's lips were pursed as if trying to hold something back, and his eyes were watering. Had something gone down the wrong pipe? Andrew lifted his hand to give his uncle a whack on the back, but before he could do it, Henry's mouth popped open, and a loud burst of laughter broke out.

"Henry. . ." Aunt Marie's voice held a warning, but a sparkle lit her eyes, as well.

Uncle Henry covered his mouth with his fist and coughed, bringing himself under control. "I apologize. I really do. But if you two could see yourselves." Another guffaw blasted, and Aunt Marie followed it with a giggle muffled by her hand.

"I don't see anything funny," Beth inserted, her blue eyes sparking dangerously.

Neither did Andrew. Conflict held no humor for him, even when it was necessary. And this time it was necessary.

Uncle Henry held up both hands in defeat. "As I said, I apologize. But after just having talked about Beth getting a cat, it was like watching two tomcats square off for battle."

Aunt Marie added, "Or watching siblings squabble."

Andrew jerked his gaze in her direction. Siblings? He nibbled the inside of his cheek. The only other people with whom he'd ever openly argued were his brothers. He'd never felt comfortable enough to be boldly forceful with anyone else. Yet right then, he'd held nothing back from Beth.

But surely he didn't look at Beth the way he looked at his brothers. That was ridiculous! He faced her again, taking in her jutted chin with its delicate cleft, her narrowed eyes still snapping fire, and her tightly crossed arms. He'd manage to rile her as much as he'd ever riled his brothers. And he wasn't any sorrier about it than he'd ever been when he'd argued with either Ted or Joe. Confused, he looked down at his empty plate.

A lengthy silence hung over the table, broken by Aunt Marie clearing her throat.

"Well, I believe I'm ready for dessert. How about you?"

The bright note in her voice did little to ease Andrew's discomfort, but he lifted his gaze and nodded. "Sure. Sounds good." He glanced at Beth. Would she be willing to set aside her aggravation and try to end the evening pleasantly?

She unfolded her arms and placed her hands in her lap. Her lips curved up in a tight smile. "Just a small piece, please. Thanks." Her tone was light, giving no indication of lingering anger, but when Andrew met her gaze, the spark in her eyes let him know they'd address this topic again. Soon.

Well, he decided, maintaining eye contact and lifting his brows, that was fine with him. Maybe it was time he and Beth defined their relationship. This time, though, it would be defined to his satisfaction. Maybe it was time to stop letting Miss Beth Quinn have the upper hand in everything.

Beth opened the plastic sack of goodies she'd gathered from the house and grinned down at Winky, who stood at her feet with his whiskers and tail tip twitching in synchronization. "Yes, I brought you some entertainment. You need something besides my feet to play with around here."

The kitten stretched up on his back feet and pawed her leg, releasing a mournful meow.

"Don't be so impatient," she scolded with a light laugh. "Just like a male. Wants everything right now."

Even though she had made the determination to keep her mind on finishing the window and not allowing thoughts of either Sean or Andrew to distract her, her own comment immediately had the opposite effect.

Sean wanted the window done *right now*.

Andrew wanted to be in the middle of everything *right now*.

And she didn't know what she wanted.

With a sigh, she pulled a mateless sock—with every trip to the Laundromat, she seemed to lose one half of a pair—from the bag and began rolling it at the toe. "Let me turn it into a ball for you. It'll be more fun."

But Winky jumped up, eager to explore this new item. With a chuckle, Beth dropped the sock across the kitten's back. He leaped in a circle, dislodging the sock, then dove on it. She watched him scoop the sock between his front paws and give it a thorough kicking with his back claws while emitting dangerous growls.

"You are something else." She emptied the remainder of the bag onto the worktable. When he tired of the sock, she'd offer a new toy—a ball of tinfoil, a shoestring, or an empty matchbox. Anything to keep him occupied so she could work.

She glanced at the wall clock, her chest constricting. Andrew would be arriving soon. They needed to have their chat concerning yesterday's dinner fiasco. For some odd reason, she felt hesitant to reopen the discussion. Maybe, she acknowledged, because she feared there might be some truth to what he'd said.

Why else had her heart fired into her throat when she realized Sean was on the other end of the telephone connection?

She shoved that thought aside. It didn't matter if Andrew's comment had merit. What mattered is that she needed him to focus on work instead of her personal life. And if that meant fighting like siblings or—she glanced at Winky, who crouched in preparation for a mighty pounce on the unwitting sock—two tomcats, then so be it.

460

The back door opened, startling Winky from completing his intended attack. Instead, he scuttled across the room and cowered behind the platform, peering out with round, yellow eyes.

Beth knelt down and stretched her hand toward the kitten, grateful for the opportunity to avoid eye contact with Andrew for a few minutes. "Hey, it's okay. Come back here."

Although she didn't look, she knew from the silence he remained by the door rather than stepping into the room. Obviously, he was as uncertain about how to proceed as she was.

"So that's the cat, huh?"

She didn't turn around, but she nodded and picked up the sock, jiggling it to entice the kitten out of hiding.

"What did you name him?"

The cat's tail waved above the platform like a flag. Beth snickered. "Winky."

"That'll make sense until his eye heals. But he probably won't wink so much after that."

Beth slowly straightened to her feet, the sock forgotten in her hand. "How did you know he had a bad eye?"

Andrew stared at her for a moment; then he scratched his head and shrugged. "Uncle Henry said it last night."

Beth replayed the conversation concerning the kitten that had taken place at the dinner table. "No, he didn't. Mom said if it was the same kitten Trina had, it had been hurt somehow, but nothing was said about a hurt eye."

As she'd come to expect in moments of uncertainty, Andrew's ears changed to a rosy hue. Suddenly she remembered another comment he'd made about being busy with a cat. She pointed at him. "You."

He looked at her and gulped—one mighty up and down of his

Adam's apple. He jabbed his thumb against his chest, his eyebrows high.

"*You* gave me Winky!" The deepening color in his ears was the only confirmation she needed. "But why?"

NINETEEN

A ndrew watched the cat dash from behind the platform and leap at the sock that dangled from Beth's hand. The moment the furry streak smacked the sock with his paw, Beth released it, and cat and sock tumbled in a tangle at her feet.

"I love the cat," she said softly. At the tenderness in her expression, he felt as though his heart tumbled in his chest as erratically as the cat tumbled on the floor with its toy.

"Good," he managed.

Tipping her head, she lowered her brows in puzzlement. "But why leave it on the doorstep? Why not just give him to me?"

Even though his motivation for gifting her with the kitten had been to gain favor, he hadn't anticipated her finding out so soon. He found himself at a loss for words, so he simply stood stupidly in front of the door with enough heat in his ears to replace the furnace.

Beth's face fell. "You meant it to be a secret, didn't you? I'm sorry I guessed."

Andrew had heard an apology from Beth only once before, and that time she'd followed it up with a *but*. This time, no excuse or explanation followed. His lips wobbled into a smile. "That's okay. I'm surprised you didn't figure it out last night when I kept pouring salt on my food to get Uncle Henry to stop talking about it."

Beth giggled. "How could you even eat after emptying the salt-shaker on it? Mom has always seasoned her food well enough. It must have tasted awful!"

He rubbed the underside of his chin, grimacing. "It was pretty bad. I drank lots of water after I went home."

They laughed together. When the laughter faded, Beth crouched down and petted the cat, which had finally given up its fight with the sock and lay washing its feet.

"Andrew, about last night. . .and my reaction to your comment about Sean. . ."

Andrew took a deep breath and moved forward several feet. He bent down, too, his elbows on his bent knees. "I might have been out of line, but I'm not going to say I'm sorry. Because that would be lying."

Her forehead creased. A warning sign.

He continued. "I do have some concerns."

To his surprise, rather than bristling, she sat on the floor with her legs criss-crossed. She tugged the cat into her lap and scratched his chin. His purr rumbled. "Okay. What?"

"Okay. . ." He paused, organizing his thoughts. Beth had so often insinuated he couldn't separate business from personal, he wanted to be sure he kept this conversation on a business level. Personal could wait. "First of all, this idea of asking for an extension on the consigned piece so we can finish the McCauley window early. I don't think that makes good sense."

Her fingers continued stroking the cat's neck, but her gaze didn't waver. "Go ahead."

"I thought your goal was to have your own gallery, make pieces of art available to the public, *and* work for McCauley." His knees complained, so he shifted, moving to sit on the edge of the platform. Beth's eyes followed him. "But if you forgo everything and just focus on McCauley, you risk running off the very people who can bring in business to the gallery or online."

Beth surprised him by smirking.

"What?"

"You said 'online.' "

Andrew frowned. "What's wrong with that?"

She shrugged. "Nothing, I guess. It's just you're the first Mennonite I've heard use a word that referenced the Internet."

Andrew snorted. "We might not use it, but we're aware of it, Beth."

"Don't get defensive," she said, but her tone remained friendly, open. The kitten had fallen asleep. She planted her palms on the floor behind her and leaned back. "How can focusing on McCauley run off other business?"

Her return to the topic caught Andrew by surprise, and it took a moment to get his thoughts back together. "Think about it. What if Uncle Henry, when a particular person came into his shop with a mechanical problem, set everyone else's needs aside and took care of that person exclusively? How would those who had tractors or cars waiting feel, being treated as though their vehicle didn't matter as much?"

Beth's shoulders rose and fell in a slow-motion shrug. "They probably wouldn't like it."

"Do you think they'd bring their business to Uncle Henry again, or go elsewhere?"

The impish smirk returned. "Well, seeing how there's only one mechanic in the whole town of Sommerfeld, they'd probably grumble and wait their turn."

Andrew refused to be caught up in teasing. "And that works as long as you're the only one providing the service. But you aren't the only stained-glass artist in the state, are you? The Fox Gallery can go elsewhere. Customers can go elsewhere. You have more to lose."

Even as he spoke, he recognized Beth had a rare talent, something that set her apart from other stained-glass artists. He waited for her to point out her unique ability to create depth. To argue that her work was worth waiting for. But she surprised him again.

"Maybe you're right. Maybe I shouldn't put one ahead of the other but recognize that each client, each project, has equal value. But. . ." Her brows pinched; her tongue sneaked out to lick her lips. "But if I don't get the McCauley contract, so many of my other desires won't be fulfilled. I need the money from the McCauley contract to expand the studio, buy equipment, hire more—"

"If you want it all, you have to do it all." Andrew leaned forward, increasing his volume and fervor. "You can't let anything slide. You've got to satisfy Fox, you've got to satisfy McCauley, and you've got to prepare for the customers who will be coming to your door."

She had to listen to him. Only if everything she had planned—the showroom, the Web site, the church windows—came to pass could she hope to support more than one person with this studio. He couldn't let her drop one for the other. She needed them all to see her dream come true. *He* needed them all for *his* dreams to come true. He wouldn't let her back off now.

Beth sat staring at him, her lips clenched together, for several long seconds. Finally, she drew in a breath through her nose, her gaze narrowing. "Andrew, will you answer one question for me as honestly as you can?"

Although he knew he might set himself up for an uncomfortable situation, he could do little else but nod.

"Are you sure you don't want me putting everything else except the McCauley project aside to keep me from having a long-term relationship with Sean McCauley?"

Andrew stifled a groan. He'd agreed to answer, but now he wasn't sure he could form one. Yes, he was jealous of the attention she paid Sean McCauley. Yes, he wished she would pay more attention to him—and not as an employee. That was why he'd given her the cat, which she clearly loved. But never having said anything remotely personal to a girl before, he had no words. He stared at his linked hands in his lap.

After a few silent seconds, Beth released a sigh. "It's okay. You don't have to answer. It's enough that you think about it and realize that if this studio is to take off, Sean McCauley is going to be a part of the picture around here. You'll need to accept it eventually. And sooner would be better than later."

After their lengthy talk that morning, Beth had put conversation on hold so she could concentrate on the window. Despite Andrew's arguments, she had instructed him to stop working on the second cardinal piece after lunch and help with the McCauley project instead. He'd scowled but followed her instruction, working in from the opposite corner of the platform.

The work was painstakingly slow, each piece requiring a tight fit with no gaps if the window was to hold its shape without buckling when lifted to a vertical position. Twice Beth had stopped and applied the carborundum stone to small bumps on the edge of a piece to insure a better fit. The meticulous task, while satisfying, was also stress-inducing, given the need for accuracy.

Winky did his best to add moments of levity by pouncing on their feet or leaping onto the platform to curl into a ball and turn on his motor. He always managed to land right where she needed to place the next piece of glass, bringing a laugh that eased her taut muscles and refreshed her.

As suppertime approached, Beth found herself glancing at the clock at closer intervals, eager for the excuse to stop, stretch her legs, and rest her eyes and fingers. She suspected Andrew felt the same way by the number of times he sat straight up on his knees and twisted his back. She understood. Leaning over the platform was much more difficult than leaning over the worktable. The angle was different, putting more pressure on the lower spine, and one had to avoid the horseshoe nails that kept the project square on the wooden base. But if he was going to be working on other big projects, he might as well become accustomed to using the platform.

She was scooping the cat out of the way for the umpteenth time when the telephone on the wall jangled. "I'll get it," she said as Andrew started to stand. Lifting the receiver, she offered her standard, "Quinn's Stained-Glass Art Studio. May I help you?"

"Hello, Beth. I hope you're ready to design like crazy."

Sean's greeting made her heart double its tempo. "They signed?"

"They signed."

Her smile stretched across her tired cheeks. "Congratulations!"

"To you, too. The stained-glass windows are part of the contract."

"Yes, if I meet your stipulation for this first one." Beth looked at the partially completed window, which would determine whether or not the stained-glass windows for the Colorado church would truly be her projects. Her stomach turned a somersault. She still had so much to do! And those windows in Denver wouldn't be hers if this one wasn't completed.

"So how are you coming along over there?"

Beth clenched her teeth for a moment, holding back the grunt of frustration. "It's coming," she said. "I've got Andrew working on it, too."

Andrew glanced up, meeting her eyes. She smiled and pointed at the platform—a silent reminder to keep working. His brows tipped together briefly, but he picked up another piece of glass.

"Well, good. He needs to learn how to do the larger pieces."

"That's what I thought." Beth smiled when the distinct sound of a yawn met her ear. "I didn't realize meetings were such exhausting work."

At his laughter, her smile grew. "I think it's the elevation. Whenever I get up in the mountains, I feel sleepy."

Beth couldn't confirm that. She'd never spent time in the mountains. She'd done little traveling, although she'd always wanted to. But Mom's limited income hadn't allowed for long vacations in faraway places. Now her focus was on getting her studio running. She frowned. If the studio became the success she hoped, would there be time for travel in her future?

A brief wave of panic struck. Did she want her work to be *everything?*

"Well," Sean's voice carried through the line, "I know you're hard at it, so I'll let you go. I just wanted to share the good news. By the end of the week I'll have dimensions for the windows and a construction schedule. You'll need that information before you can proceed, but be thinking about the designs and how you can bring in that wonderful depth."

Beth swallowed. "Yes. Yes, I will. 'Bye, Sean. Thanks for calling. And congratulations again." She hung up and looked at Andrew, who settled back on his haunches and pressed his hands to his knees. "You ready for a break?"

He answered with a shrug.

"Let's walk next door, work some kinks out. I need to. . ." She paused. Did she want to involve Andrew in her worries? If she shared her concerns with him, she would be leaning on him. More than she already was in letting him help with the window. Mitch's face appeared in her memory—his smiling, beguiling, devious face—followed by the remembered pain of his betrayal.

Waiting beside the platform, Andrew prompted, "You need to. . . ?"

"Walk." She gave a single, empathic nod. "I need to walk. And I'm hungry for one of Deborah's greasy burgers. So let's go."

They slid in on opposite sides of an open booth, where they could look out on the peaceful street. Since it wasn't the weekend, not many tourists were around, but Beth easily recognized the patrons who were not citizens of Sommerfeld.

The two tables closest to the booth she and Andrew shared were each occupied by a young family—mother, father, and preschool-age child. Beth's gaze flicked back and forth between the tables, her mind unconsciously recording the similarities and disparities.

One family was Old Order Mennonite—the man's closely trimmed hair, the woman's cap, and the little girl's tiny braids serving as calling cards. The second family was obviously not. Even their daughter, who couldn't be more than four, had pierced ears and designer-brand blue jeans.

At each table conversation took place, the adults leaning forward now and then to speak in lowered tones, the mothers occasionally pausing to offer instruction to use the napkin or be careful with the cup of milk.

Beth examined their faces, searching for evidence that one family might be happier, more contented, more complete than the other. But she couldn't make a determination. They both seemed like normal, involved, satisfied families. Her heart begged for an answer to the question plaguing her mind: In which of those families—Old Order or worldly—would *she* have the best chance to find fulfillment and contentment?

Swinging her gaze away from the families, she found Andrew openly examining her. Heat rose from her neck to her cheeks as she got the distinct impression he knew what she had been trying to discover.

TWENTY

Leaning her elbows on the table, Beth brought her face closer to Andrew's. "Are you happy here?"

Andrew raised one brow.

"In Sommerfeld, in the fellowship. Do you ever wonder what it's like 'out there'?"

Andrew glanced out the window, then at the worldly couple seated nearby. His lips twitched, and he rubbed his hand over his mouth. "I guess all of us wonder. Outsiders come in driving fancy cars and wearing their fancy clothes and talking about the things they do. So, yes, I've wondered."

She nodded. "I can see why. Everything here is so. . .regimented. Controlled." With a grimace, she added, "I don't know how you stand it."

Sorrow filled Andrew's eyes. "I don't just *stand* it, Beth. I embrace it."

The word *embrace* wrapped around Beth's chest in a breath-stealing hold. "How?" The word came out in a strangled whisper. She gestured to the café. "What is it that you find so. . .desirable here? I see the smiles, the contentment, the acceptance of the simplicity, but I don't

472

understand. Help me understand, Andrew." *So I can find out whether or not it can one day be mine.*

Andrew's brow furrowed, and for long moments he looked out the window. His jaw worked back and forth, letting Beth know how deeply he sought the right answer to her question. Although impatience tugged at her like Winky at her pant leg, she managed to stay silent and allow him the opportunity to collect his thoughts.

Finally, he looked at her, and his eyes held a variety of emotions she couldn't define. "There's security, Beth, in knowing what applied to my parents' world at my age also applied to my grandparents and great-grandparents and now applies to me. The history, the generations-long tradition, feels stable in a world that—out there—isn't always stable. There's security in having a firm boundary around me, a fence that keeps me safe."

She opened her mouth to protest, but he held up his hand.

"I know you see it as hemming you in and holding you back. But I see it as keeping potentially dangerous things away and giving me freedom within the boundaries of my beliefs."

Beth leaned back, sucking in her lips as she processed his answer. The words sounded good in theory, but there was a problem. "Then why are you bucking so hard to break free of your father's plans for you?"

He jerked as if her words had impaled him.

"Your family's history is farming, right? Your father, your brothers, probably your grandfathers, too—all farmers. But you? You're trying to be something else."

His ears filled with the familiar red. Although his mouth opened, no words came out.

She nodded. "See? You don't like the boundaries, either, or you'd just farm and not say anything." Sitting forward, she allowed a small smile to form on her lips. "But I have to tell you, Andrew, I admire you for going after what you want. I might get aggravated with you sometimes because I feel like you're stepping on my toes, but I still admire you." Lowering her eyes, she fought a feeling of sadness. "At least you know what you want."

"You know, too." The fervency brought Beth's head up. "You know. You want success." He pointed to the table beside them where the worldly family prepared to leave the café—the mother helping the little girl into her pink denim jacket and the father digging in his wallet for a tip. "I saw the look on your face when you were watching the families. You think being a wife and mother will hold you back. That's why you don't want to be Mennonite. A Mennonite wife wouldn't spend all her day in an art studio. You don't think you can fit the role."

He gave the saddest smile Beth had ever seen. "I heard you when you told your mother you could never be Mennonite. I tried not to hear, but I heard. And I've been thinking about it."

Beth wasn't sure she wanted to know what he thought, but she couldn't deny a fierce interest in hearing his opinion. In the past days, a side of Andrew—a strong, confident, openly knowledgeable side—had come into view, piquing her interest as much as it surprised her. It gave a new, attractive dimension to him worthy of further exploration.

"So what do you think?" Her breath came in little puffs as her heart pounded, waiting, hoping for some nugget of insight that might help her find her place in this community.

Andrew squared his shoulders. "I think you were raised in the world, and that's where you belong. You found God here, and maybe that's what you came for, to become part of His family. But what you told your mom is right. You'll never be a Mennonite. It isn't who you are." His back slumped as if his honesty had cost him his strength.

"And maybe, since you'll never fit unless you are Mennonite, you'd be better off somewhere else."

"You'd be better off somewhere else."

Andrew's words haunted Beth the remainder of the week. Each morning as she opened her Bible for her devotions, those words tried to steal her focus and interfered with her ability to pray.

Hadn't Sean told her she should relocate her studio away from this quiet town? And now Andrew had indicated the same thing.

"You'd be better off somewhere else."

Fear held her captive. These two men, in whom she needed to be able to place her confidence and trust to build her studio and fulfill her dreams, each seemed to have agendas that would benefit themselves if she followed their advice.

Sean suggested Kansas City, closer to his home, where undoubtedly he could keep a close eye on her projects and have some control. Could his increased, more personal contacts be a means of drawing her closer?

And Andrew suggesting she go somewhere else would leave an empty studio in Sommerfeld for someone else's use. His use? Is that why he said she would never be happy here?

God, please help me set the fears aside! she begged each time the worry rose, yet it continued. Each glimpse of Andrew across the platform increased the feelings of uncertainty, and finally on Friday morning, she sent him back to the cardinal piece with the instruction to see it through to completion and then work on suncatchers.

"I'll need a stash ready for when I get the Internet store up and running," she said in response to his questioning look. To her relief, he didn't argue. But sending him away from the platform didn't solve the problem. Just having him in the room was a constant reminder, and she came close to telling him to go work in the fields.

When he left for the noon break, the telephone rang. Wearily, Beth answered it to find Sean on the other end. He would be back in Kansas by Saturday, and he had a final meeting with the Carlton church committee next week on Wednesday. He asked if could swing by the studio, take another peek at the window, and perhaps treat her to supper to celebrate the Colorado contract.

"No." The word burst out much more forcefully than she intended.

Sean's shocked silence on the other end filled Beth with embarrassed shame, and she struggled to explain herself.

"I mean, I'd like that, and you can certainly stop in if you want to, but"—her gaze fell on the wall calendar, the few squares remaining in the month sending a new jolt of panic through her chest—"I really can't afford to be away from the studio right now. I have less than three weeks to finish this project."

"And you and Andrew can't get it done?" He sounded more puzzled than worried.

"Yes, I can if I stay here and see it through!" Once more, against her will, her tone reflected her anxiety.

"Beth. . ." Sean's voice lowered, and she pictured him pressing the receiver closer to his face. "If this window is too much for you, then maybe—"

No more suggestions! "It's not too much for me," she insisted, forcing a levity to her voice she didn't feel, "I just prefer to commit my time to work right now. When the work is done, there will be time for play."

But not much time, she realized, since two more churches were already lined up and waiting for Beth Quinn stained-glass windows. She felt dizzy and slid down the wall to sit on the floor.

"Okay then." Sean sounded resigned. "I'll pop in on my way back from my meeting at Carlton. It will be late afternoon or early evening, so hopefully I won't disrupt your routine too much. I look forward to seeing. . .your progress."

Beth was certain he had intended to say he looked forward to seeing her and had changed it at the last minute. The thought brought mingled emotions of relief and regret.

"Wednesday then. Thanks, Sean. Have a safe trip home." She hung up before he could create more conflict in her heart.

Winky pranced over and batted her pant leg in his typical bid for attention. She scooped him into her arms and rubbed her chin on his head. His purr expressed his appreciation. She petted him for a few minutes, letting the cat's soft fur and gentle motor soothe the frayed edges of her nerves.

"You are quite the gift," she whispered, giving him a kiss between his ears and setting him back on the floor. "Thank you for your sweet attention. At least I don't have to second-guess your motives."

Winky padded beside her as she returned to the platform and picked up a green triangle. "Okay, now, no pouncing. I have to focus," she warned the kitten. He licked one paw and stared at her with an innocent expression she had learned never to trust. Maybe she should locate one of his toys to keep him occupied.

He shifted positions, holding down his tail with one paw and beginning a thorough wash of the tip. She smiled. The cat was too cute for his own good. Convinced he was duly occupied, she turned her attention to the window.

Leaning forward between two horseshoe nails, she rested her weight on one hand and positioned the triangle on the wooden surface, centered below two red diamonds. She held her breath, prepared to slip the triangle into its location, when four paws hit smack between her shoulder blades.

With a yelp of surprise, she jerked forward, cramming the point of the triangle into the existing design and banging her knee on a horseshoe nail. The worn denim tore. Pain shot up her leg as the head of the nail gouged her flesh.

"Winky!"

The cat shot away from the platform, his fur on end. He huddled beneath the display bench, his wide eyes peering back at her in fear.

Stumbling to her feet, Beth stretched the slit in her jeans to examine the cut. It bled freely—a good thing, she thought, considering what caused it. She limped to the supply cabinet and opened a bottom drawer, withdrawing a small first-aid kit. Winky watched her progress with interest, his tail twitching. She glared at the cat as she rummaged for a Band-Aid.

"Didn't I tell you to leave me alone? What was that all about? Do you think you're a mountain lion or something? Really!" Still grumbling, she applied the bandage, wincing as the pad came in contact with the cut. "I'll have to leave you at the house instead of bringing you here with me if you can't behave."

The cat tipped his head sideways as if to question the sincerity of her threat.

"Yeah, yeah, you know I couldn't do that," she muttered, shaking her head. As aggravated as she felt at the moment, she knew she wouldn't leave the kitten alone all day. It would be too lonely for him. And, she admitted, she would miss him too much. Shaking her finger at him, she added firmly, "But no more jumping on me!"

She took a minute to locate the empty matchbox he enjoyed batting across the floor and skidded it under the bench with him. He slapped his paw on it, tail swishing back and forth, then rolled onto his side and closed his eyes.

"*Now* you nap." Beth sighed, shaking her head. Her knee stung as she walked back to the platform, and she sucked air through her teeth when she knelt down.

But the real pain struck when she looked at the window. "Oh, no!" She ran her fingers along the border, which no longer formed a straight line. Apparently when she had kicked the nail loose, she had also bumped the squares forming the boundary of the project. Her panic increased when she picked up the green triangle and realized she'd nicked its tip when she'd shoved it across the platform.

She sank onto her bottom, her knee throbbing with each pounding beat of her heart. "I don't have time to redo anything," she moaned aloud. "Oh, why did this have to happen now?"

A furry head bumped her hip, and she lifted the cat into her arms, cradling him against her shoulder. "Winky, you naughty cat. Look what you made me do." His purr offered an apology, but it didn't fix the problem.

Pressing her face to the cat's neck, Beth dissolved into tears.

TWENTY-ONE

"Trina." Andrew waved his cousin over.

"Ready for your check?" She removed the little order pad from her pocket.

"I'm done, but I think I want to take a sandwich over for Beth." He fidgeted under Trina's speculative look. "She didn't take a lunch break, but she needs something to eat."

"That's nice of you," Trina mused, one eyebrow rising higher than the other. "What's her favorite?"

"Turkey on wheat with lettuce, tomato, and honey mustard." The answer came so promptly, even Andrew had to laugh. Trina grinned and scampered off, disappearing into the kitchen.

Yes, he'd gotten to know his boss pretty well. And most of it came from observation, because even though she wasn't one to mince words, most of her spouting had little to do with Beth-the-Person. Beth-the-Person tried to remain aloof. But Andrew had finally peeked beneath the surface.

This had been a rough week. He'd seen it in the tense set of her shoulders, the creases in her forehead, and the tightness of her voice. The only smiles had been aimed at the cat, and at times Andrew had felt envious of the furry critter. At the same time, he felt grateful she had something in her life that seemed to bring her happiness.

It had pained him to be so honest with her last Tuesday when they'd come to the café for supper. But knowing Beth, seeing how she fought against the dictates of the fellowship and the community, he couldn't imagine her making Sommerfeld her permanent home. Thinking of her leaving brought pain on a different level, but not so much as he would have expected a few weeks ago.

Maybe, he mused, accepting the unlikelihood of her becoming Mennonite had begun the process of releasing his fascination with her. He still admired her, still was intrigued by her, but he was beginning to understand their backgrounds would never mesh. What he wanted in a wife, Beth surely wouldn't give. How could he be happy with that?

And she would never be happy living in a box. That's how she viewed the simple rules of the Mennonite community. Beth was a free spirit, an untamed wind. Even—he nodded to himself—a rebel. It suited her. But a Mennonite? No, she would never be that.

He glanced up and spotted Trina trotting toward him with a paper bag in her hand. He stood and tugged his money clip from his pocket.

"There you go, and Mama put in some chips and a pickle, too." Trina took his money. "I'll get your change."

"Keep it," he said, picking up the sack.

With a grin, she returned to work, and he headed out the door. He weaved between the café and the studio so he could enter through the back door. Pushing it open, he called, "Beth, I brought you a—"

His voice died when he spotted her sitting on the floor with the cat in her arms. The sound of her sobs filled the air.

Dropping the sack, he rushed to her and bent on one knee, touching her shoulder. "Beth, what is it?"

She lifted her tearstained face. "I ruined the window."

He scowled, shifting his gaze to the window. At first glance, everything appeared fine. But when he looked closer, he noticed a slight bend along the closest edge. Though not more than two or three centimeters, it was enough to guarantee the window wouldn't fit the intended frame unless repair work took place.

"What happened?"

"Winky." At the mention of his name, the cat pushed against Beth's shoulder with his front paws. She released him, and he dashed away with his ears back. "He was playing, and he startled me. I. . .I fell onto the platform. I cut myself"—she pointed to a tear in her jeans, which exposed a Band-Aid on the side of her knee—"and messed up the window."

Andrew puffed his cheeks and blew out a noisy breath. "I should have known we needed more nails to hold something this big. And I shouldn't have brought that kitten here."

She sat sniffling. He settled back on his haunches and scratched his head. "Well, I can go out to Ortmanns', buy some more nails, and we can press this back into position. Hopefully, with no further than it's been moved, it'll go back without affecting the strength of the joints. We'll double up the nails so there won't be the chance to move it again."

Without a word, she held up a thick green triangle.

Even without taking it, Andrew could see the shattered tip. It wouldn't fit tightly that way. He pulled his lips to the side in a pucker. "Do you have more green?"

Her shoulders slumped dismally. "Scraps. I didn't order much excess because of the cost."

He gave her back a pat and pushed to his feet. He located a piece in the scrap box just large enough to replace the chipped triangle.

Showing it to her, he said, "I'll have to be extra careful when I cut it, but I think this will work."

Beth took both pieces of glass and lay the triangle on top of the odd-shaped scrap. She nodded. "Yes, it's big enough, barely. I like to have more space around the cut to insure a crisp corner."

"Me, too," Andrew said, "but beggars can't be choosers. We don't have time to wait for an order of a new sheet."

She held her hand to him, and he gave a tug that brought her to her feet. When she grimaced, his heart gave a lurch.

"Are you sure that leg is okay?"

"It's fine," she insisted. Still holding the glass in one hand, she said, "Go on out to Ortmanns' and get those nails. While you're gone, I'll score this glass and get it cut."

Andrew swallowed a grin. She sounded like the old bossy Beth again. "Do you want me take the cat with me and leave him at the farm?"

Her gaze flitted sideways, and a soft smile grew on her face when she found the kitten lying on his side with both front paws over his eyes. "No. That was his first major offense. I think I can forgive him. Besides. . ." She turned back with a chuckle. "I'll get even when I start the grinder. I'm sure his nap will be seriously disturbed."

Andrew grinned. He turned toward the door and spotted the discarded lunch sack. After picking it up, he dumped its contents onto the worktable. "Here. Deborah made you a sandwich—your favorite. Eat it. It'll help you feel better."

It gave his heart a lift to see her smile of thanks. He took the empty bag with him and drove as quickly as possible to Ortmanns'. Dust rolled behind his pickup and sneaked between window cracks, making him sneeze. When he reached the farm, he pulled his pickup right up to the barn. Since Mr. Ortmann had told him he was welcome to as many nails as he needed, he let himself into the tack room and loaded the paper bag with several handfuls of pewter-colored nails, not even bothering to count. He'd count them as he used them and make sure he reported it later.

His mission complete, he returned to the pickup. Just as he opened the door to the cab, someone called his name. He looked over his shoulder and saw Livvy Ortmann stepping off the back stoop. She balanced a basket of wet clothes on her hip.

Andrew held up the bag. "I came for more nails. I'll settle with your dad later."

"That's fine," she said, a smile tipping up the corners of her lips. "I heard Beth might be doing even more of those big windows."

Andrew chuckled. Beth often complained about everyone knowing her business. But this time he hadn't told, so she couldn't blame him for blabbing.

"I bet it's fun, putting the pieces together. Like working on a big puzzle." Livvy's voice sounded wistful.

"Yes, it's fun," Andrew confirmed, "but it's also work. And I'd better get back to it. We have a lot to do."

Livvy stepped forward, prolonging his leave-taking. "How many windows do you have to do?"

Andrew pulled himself into the cab. "None, if she can't finish this first one on time." Then, realizing he probably shouldn't be sharing something so personal, he stammered, "B–but I'm sure she will."

Livvy's smile drooped. "Well, I won't keep you. But maybe. . . maybe I could come by the studio and see how the pieces go together sometime?"

"Sure, Livvy. Sometime." Eager to return to the studio and help Beth set things to right, Andrew slammed the door. He put the pickup in REVERSE, made a quick turnaround, and headed out of the Ortmann yard with a wave of his hand. When he reached the end of the drive, he glanced in his rearview mirror.

Oddly, Livvy still stood where he'd left her, staring after the truck.

Sean turned off the engine and sat, staring at the front of Beth's simple, metal-sided studio. For reasons he couldn't fully explain, he hesitated approaching the front door. He was impatient to see her—he'd missed her more than he understood. Yet given their last stilted conversation, he felt as though his friendship with Beth had faded before it had had a chance to bloom.

He snorted in derision. Hadn't he made fun, not too long ago, of a man from the recreation center where he worked out who'd met some woman online and fallen head over heels after a few brief e-mail messages? He'd thought it ridiculous, the man desperate to feel such intense emotion for someone he hardly knew. Yet sitting here, staring at the studio and trying to summon up the courage to go in, he understood that man's feelings.

After only a few face-to-face meetings, a mere dozen less-than-meaningful conversations, and a spattering of e-mail communications, he was. . .smitten.

Another snort blasted. Since when did he use old-fashioned words like *smitten*? He shook his head, grasping the door handle. It must be the simple setting that inspired the use of a word from time past. But the truth remained. Sean was attracted to Beth.

Taking in a great breath, he opened the door and stepped out. A mild breeze tousled his hair as he followed the smooth white sidewalk to the front door. Since his last visit, the grass had started to green up, showing the promise of spring around the corner.

Spring meant new life in so many ways. In nature, of course, but also in business. Most new contracts came in the spring, when people were ready to build. And this year, it seemed that spring had opened his heart to the idea of leaving his bachelor days behind.

He stopped in the middle of the sidewalk, the bold thought taking him by surprise. *Marriage?* His dad would certainly tell him it was premature to be thinking marriage. Yet in his twenty-five years of life, Sean couldn't remember ever coming close to coupling the M word with any other female.

"Smitten for sure," he mumbled, and he raised his hand to knock on the door.

Beth herself opened it, and he felt his shoulders tense as if she could read on his face what he had been thinking only moments before. Well, he decided, if she was able to ascertain his thoughts, she didn't find them repulsive, because she offered a smile.

"Come on in. Is it good to be back in Kansas?"

Sean closed the door behind him and unzipped his light jacket. "It's always good to be home." He faltered, seeking a topic of conversation that hadn't been covered in their brief telephone conversations and didn't relate to the window. Suddenly one was provided without warning.

A gray and white furball zipped across the floor and dove on the shoelaces of his right shoe.

"Hey! What's this?" The cat rolled on its back, all four feet in the air, batting at the loop that formed the bow.

Beth chuckled and picked up the cat. "This is Winky, the newest addition to Quinn's Stained-Glass Art Studio. He thinks he owns the place, so don't tell him otherwise."

Sean scratched behind the cat's ear. "Winky, huh? He's pretty cute."

The cat allowed Sean to make one more sweep with his fingers before it struggled in Beth's arms, and she put him down. Straightening, she shrugged. "I guess it's silly to have an animal running loose in here, but he's good entertainment."

"Not silly at all." Sean watched the kitten crouch, its tail sweeping madly, before bouncing on a splash of sunshine on the concrete floor. "I bet he's good company, too."

"That he is."

Sean looked around. "Speaking of company. . ." He glanced at his watch. "Has Andrew gone home already?"

Beth turned and moved toward the platform. "Our schedule has changed a bit. I don't have Andrew on Wednesdays or Saturdays anymore. He works for his dad then."

"Oh?" Sean trailed Beth, his gaze on the colorful array of glass on the wooden platform. "Is he easing back into farming?"

Beth released a short, humorless laugh. "No, actually he's trying to ease *out* of farming." She slipped her hands into the pockets of her apron and looked at Sean. "He's worked a deal with his dad that if the studio picks up the contracts from your company, which means it can support a full-time staff of workers, he'll be an artist instead of a farmer. So. . ." She raised her brows and quirked her lips.

Sean completed her thought. "A lot rests on this project."

"It always has."

Her voice sounded tight, and for a moment Sean regretted the pressure he'd put on her to meet this initial obligation. He knew the time had been short, yet he and his father had needed to see how well she stood up to pressure. The construction business was one requiring speed and accuracy. If Beth was going to be part of the team, they had to know she could meet the requirements.

"Well, let's see how it's going." He tempered the words with a grin, then stepped beside her and made no pretense of doing anything but thoroughly examining every minute inch of the design.

He whistled through his teeth. The completed sections were amazing. The play of color, the illusion of some sections standing out from others, the perfect balance of lights and darks. . .it was a work of art, there was no doubt.

"It looked great on paper, but in reality. . .wow."

Beth shot him a worried look. "But it isn't done."

"No, but I can see how much progress you've made since I was here last." He pulled a camera from his jacket pocket. "I'll take a couple of updated shots. Dad will want to see this."

Beth stood back and allowed him to take the pictures. In the last one, her cat leaped onto the platform at the last minute. He put the camera away, laughing. "So he's entertainment, company, and a nuisance."

"He can be," she agreed, shooing the cat from the platform.

Sean noticed something. "You've really barricaded this thing in with tacks." He pointed to the line of nails surrounding the project. "Afraid it's going to fall off or something?"

Beth grimaced. "No, just wanting to make sure it stays square. I want it to fit the opening you've got waiting for it."

He sensed there was another reason for the number of nails. It looked as though she and Andrew had built a miniature picket fence around the window. Shaking his head, he shrugged. "It certainly looks secure."

"Good." Beth now sounded grim. "If it's secure, then my future is secure."

TWENTY-TWO

Sean, his meetings completed and a signed contract tucked securely in his leather portfolio, turned his car onto the highway and headed west. He would have rather gone south, back to Sommerfeld, to spend a pleasant evening with Beth. But she'd made it clear she needed to work.

Dad would be thrilled. Her dedication to the task was exactly what Evan McCauley wanted in employees. Sean had always seconded Dad's opinion on that and had adopted the work ethic for himself. Even though his office was in his own home with no time card to punch or boss close by to check up on him, he'd kept the same working hours as any other businessman, even spending many Saturdays and Sunday afternoons in his office, as well. With no family of his own demanding his time, Sean's sole focus had been McCauley Church Construction. Just like it was for Dad.

And now, it seemed, pleasing McCauley Church Construction was Beth's focus, too. Yes, that would certainly please Dad. Sean realized he should also feel pleased. But something other than *pleased* flitted through his mind when he considered Beth's response to his invitation to dinner.

The midafternoon sun glared off the hood of his car, causing him to squint. Frowning, he groped for his sunglasses in the pocket on the side of the door, slipped them into place, and rested his arm on the window ledge. He drove past a wheat field, where a plainly dressed man with a beard used a tractor with metal wheels to pull an implement that looked like it came straight from an antique store. Yet the outdated equipment seemed to be getting the job done, as the wheat fell in a neat swath.

The sight of the farmer—although Sean was sure this man was Amish rather than Mennonite, judging by the beard—reminded him of Beth's comment about Andrew trying to ease out of farming. What an awkward position for the man—answering to a woman in a workplace. Sean couldn't imagine that being the norm in the Old Order community.

Although he hadn't spent a great deal of time in Sommerfeld, he surmised the religious group would discourage women from being in positions of leadership over men. Yet there was Andrew, contentedly following Beth's instructions in the hopes of never planting another crop.

Or was there a deeper hope existing in the tall man's heart?

Sean snorted. No sense in creating problems where none existed. Even though Sean suspected Andrew's protectiveness of Beth went beyond mere employee to employer, he knew Beth held no interest in Andrew outside of his assistance in the studio. Neither her words nor her actions even hinted at a personal interest in Andrew. Sean had no competition there.

Competition. Shaking his head, he hit the button to roll down the window and let the rushing air cool his warm face. He'd be better off focusing on the competitors for his business. Although McCauley held its own in the world of construction, it still took considerable time and attention to stay in the game. Juggling three projects while planning six more was Dad's goal, and that took time. Sean didn't have time to be dwelling on a relationship with a pretty artist. Especially when the relationship must be handled long-distance.

Still, thoughts of Beth—wisps of hair slipping free of her ever-present ponytail to frame her heart-shaped face, the little cleft in her delicate chin, and the determination in her bright blue eyes—teased him all the way home.

"Amen."

Beth cupped her hand beneath her mother's elbow and helped her rise from a kneeling position. Although she'd gotten over the initial embarrassment of kneeling in a room full of people for the closing prayer at service, she wished they would set aside the tradition for the sake of her mother. As Mom's pregnancy progressed, she could hardly get back to her feet. And since Henry sat on the opposite side of the church in the men's section, it was up to Beth to assist her.

Beth's aunt Joanna offered help on the other side, and between the two of them, they helped Mom settle on the bench.

"Whew," Mom huffed, as if she'd done the work alone. "It's a good thing the end is in sight, because I don't know how many more times I'll be able to do this."

Joanna sat down and took her sister's hand, giving it several pats. "How many more weeks?"

"Seven weeks and two days," Mom answered promptly, "but who's counting?"

The two women laughed.

"I'm counting." Beth made the firm assertion. "I have enough to worry about at the studio without worrying about Mom's swollen feet and stomachaches."

Joanna tipped her head back and stared at Beth in surprise. "Why, you don't need to worry about those things, Beth. Those are very typical for expectant mothers." Her smile didn't quite convince Beth. "You'll see when you get married and carry your first child. It's all just part of the price we pay for the privilege of creating new life."

Beth arched one brow. "Maybe. . ."

"No 'maybe' about it," Mom insisted as she planted her hands against the backless bench and pushed to her feet. "These babies are worth every bit of trouble." She cupped her expanded girth, chuckling softly. "And truthfully? They are probably less trouble in here than they will be after they're born."

She and Joanna shared more smiles. Beth had little to offer in the way of experience. But like her mother, she was ready to see the pregnancy over and these babies born so things could settle down.

Henry wove his way through little clusters of congregants who gathered to talk before heading home for a good dinner. He stopped beside Beth and put his hand on her shoulder. Although the touch was not inappropriate and although there were times Beth longed for a closer relationship, she still squirmed a bit under the familiar gesture. When would her prayers to finally feel completely at ease with her stepfather be answered?

"Did you invite Beth to dinner?" Henry asked.

"She knows she has a standing invitation," Mom replied, sending Beth a quick grin. "I invited my parents today, so it would be nice if you would join us."

It had taken a long time for Beth to develop a relationship with the grandfather who had refused to acknowledge her existence for the first two decades of her life. But both Grandpa and Grandma Koeppler had gone overboard in the past year to make up for their earlier neglect. In fact, Grandpa Koeppler was convinced her talent in art came from him since he enjoyed creating works of art from wood. He had been her biggest supporter when the studio was constructed.

It had been awhile, though—since the McCauley project started, to be exact—since she'd spent an afternoon with her grandparents. So she eagerly accepted her mother's invitation.

"I'll come on one condition." Beth shook her finger at her mother. "You let me serve and clean up afterward."

Mom laughed lightly, but she nodded. "I'll take you up on that, honey. Thank you."

Mom had put pork chops with cranberry sauce, sliced onions, and green peppers in the oven to slow bake. Henry insisted Mom sit with Grandpa Koeppler in the front room while Grandma sliced home-baked bread, Beth boiled water for instant rice, and he placed the plates and silverware on the table.

The smells teased Beth's senses, and her stomach growled, reminding her how her eating schedule had gone haywire in the past weeks. She could hardly wait until they sat down to eat. With five chairs around the kitchen's round table, their elbows touched, but no one seemed to mind. Grandpa asked the blessing, and they chatted as they enjoyed the meal.

Well, Beth acknowledged with a small stab of discomfort, Mom and Grandma chatted, and Henry and Grandpa chatted, but she ended up being left out of most of the conversation. It wasn't intentional—she knew that—but the odd number simply left her without a conversation partner. For a brief moment, she wished her parents had asked someone—Andrew? Trina?—to join them so she wouldn't feel so. . .ignored. Then Grandpa accidentally bumped her elbow, and she realized that even if they had asked someone else, there wouldn't be room for another person at this table.

In fact, she thought as her scowling gaze swept around the periphery of the table, once those twins were born, there wouldn't really be room for her here. The thought ruined what was left of her appetite, and she put down her fork.

Mom glanced over at the *clink* of the silverware against the plate. "Are you finished?"

Beth glanced at her plate. She hated to waste food, especially food that had only moments ago given her taste buds great pleasure. But she knew she wouldn't be able to swallow another bite. "Yes." She pushed away from the table. "Do you want me to cut the pie and put it on dessert plates?"

Mom started to rise, too. "Let me get the ice cream out of—"

"I'll do it," Beth said, rising quickly. "You stay put."

She listened to the continued conversation as she sliced the apple pie purchased at Deborah's café. Once each slice had been topped with a healthy scoop of vanilla ice cream, she carried the plates to the table and refilled the coffee cups for her grandparents and stepfather. Mom had sworn off coffee for the duration of her pregnancy, claiming the caffeine created water retention. Beth didn't think Mom could possible retain any more fluid than she already had.

Even though she didn't cut a piece of pie for herself, she did sit down and sip coffee while the others ate.

Grandpa slurped at his cup, then gave her a speculative look, his bushy gray brows high. "So I hear you have lots of windows to build."

Beth resisted shaking her head. Word sure got around if it made it all the way out to Grandpa's farm! "Yes, they're waiting for me. But I have to finish the first project McCauley gave me to their satisfaction before they'll trust me with anything else."

"Well, that Andrew is helping you, isn't he? At least, his dad was fussing that the boy is always at your studio." Grandpa's voice held a note of teasing.

Beth chose to ignore the insinuation that Andrew hung around the studio for reasons other than working. "He's there quite a bit, but he's helping his dad, too. I know he wants to work at the studio full-time, though."

Grandma nodded slowly. "He's always been different from his brothers, not interested in farming and such. It's good there's something he likes to do that is close by."

"He's a big help to me at the studio." Beth drew a thoughtful sip of the hot liquid before continuing. "But even with his help, we've had some trouble finishing this *one* large project. I'm pushing mighty close to that deadline. It makes me a little nervous, thinking about the big windows waiting for me."

"Maybe I can come in and help," Grandpa said.

Beth imagined her elderly grandfather bending over the high worktable or on his knees beside the platform. Neither picture would gel. But she wouldn't tell him that. "If you want to spend a day at the studio, you're more than welcome, Grandpa."

He nudged her with his elbow and grinned, his lips twitching. "I build things, too, you know. In my woodshop. It's pretty much the same thing." Suddenly his face lit. "Say, I have an idea. We could work together. I could build cabinets, and you could make stained-glass windows to put in the door panels."

Without intending to, Beth groaned.

Grandpa reared back, his forehead creasing. "You don't like the idea?"

"Oh, no, it's a great idea. I love it, actually!" She touched his arm. "It would be an honor, considering the furniture making that's been done in the family throughout generations. Then I'd have a part in that, too." She sighed. "No, it's just the idea of one more project. Right now it's a little overwhelming."

"So hire workers," Henry said. He pushed his empty pie plate aside and draped his arm across the back of Mom's chair. "You know McCauley plans to use you. You've seen a contract to know how much they will pay, so we could sit down and figure out the hourly wage you could offer."

"Workers? Plural?" Beth propped her elbows on the table.

"Certainly plural." Henry's fingers drew a circle on Mom's shoulder—Beth was certain he wasn't even aware he was doing it. "You've had Andrew with you for several months now, and sometimes it's still hard to keep up. If your workload is going to increase, it makes sense to add a few more employees to the studio. They could start with the little things—the suncatchers—and work up to the larger projects, just as Andrew has. On-the-job training."

Beth considered what it would be like to have more than one person in the studio. She frowned. "I like the idea of extra hands, but right now with just Andrew and me, it can feel crowded. I don't know how we'd fit more people in there."

"So expand." The enthusiasm in Henry's voice stirred excitement in Beth's chest. "You've got enough land to build on three of the four sides if you need to. Start interviewing people now who would like to learn stained-glass art. Then, when it's time to start working on those multiwindow contracts, you'll have people in place ready to go."

"But how will I pay for a bigger studio?" Beth threw her hands outward. "I don't have any money from these contracts yet."

"Take out a small-business loan," Henry said.

"A loan?" Grandma sounded horrified.

"An investment," Henry countered, his tone gentle. "If Beth is going to build her business, a loan may be necessary."

"No loans. I don't trust banks." Grandpa shook his head adamantly and wrapped his hand around Beth's forearm. "You don't go to any bank. If you want to expand the business, I'll give you your portion of your inheritance early."

Grandma immediately sat up straight, her face lighting. "Yes! Much better."

"In-inheritance?" Beth looked from one grandparent to the other. "But I already got an inheritance from Aunt Lisbeth. Her café and house. That's enough." It was much more than she could have anticipated, having grown up far away from this community and her mother's relatives.

"That was from Lisbeth," Grandpa said. "But I always planned to divide my holdings between my children and grandchildren. Already one of Art's boys claimed his portion when he took a wife and needed to purchase land for a house. Now you can do the same. There should be enough to add on to your studio."

Beth's heart raced. "If I add workers, I'll need more equipment, too."

"If the community puts up the building for you, like they did last time, you'll have money for equipment."

Beth stared at her grandfather. "You'd really let me do that? Take my inheritance early?"

Grandpa looked steadily into her eyes. "Do you believe this studio is what God planned for your future?"

The seriousness in his expression and tone made Beth think carefully before she answered. She had prayed about the studio, and she did believe she'd been given the talent and desire by God to create beauty with stained glass. She nodded. "I do believe it's what He intended for me."

"Then I will give you the money. Tomorrow."

TWENTY-THREE

"Grandpa Koeppler is quite the go-getter." Beth and Andrew sat on opposite sides of the worktable and sipped lemonade from tall paper cups. There wasn't anything from Deborah's café that Beth didn't like. The sweet, cool liquid revived her after a long day. Her work had been interrupted several times to confer with her grandfather on the addition to the studio. "He's done more in one day than most people would accomplish in a full week."

"Because he wants to see you happy," Andrew said, his smile crinkling his eyes. "And he knows the studio makes you happy."

"Well. . ." Beth bit down on her lower lip for a moment. "I'm wondering how you feel about all of this. The expansion is moving pretty fast." Grandpa had already placed the order for materials to build toward the alley. Tomorrow a small crew of men would pour the concrete foundation so it would be dry and ready for construction when the steel beams and siding arrived by truck next week. Beth's head spun with the idea that by the beginning of April she could have a staff of three under her supervision!

"You need to expand if the studio is to be all you've envisioned." Andrew raised his broad shoulders in a shrug. "Your success is my success, so I'm not arguing."

Beth could have reminded him of his comment that she shouldn't stay in Sommerfeld, that she didn't belong. But she chose instead to ask a question. "Since we'll have the space for a full crew in here, do you have any suggestions for employees? I have no real preference for male or female, but I do think I'd like the workers to be at least eighteen years old."

It wasn't uncommon for youth as young as fourteen to begin working full-time, whether on their own family farms or in other positions in and around Sommerfeld. But given the potential danger of some of the equipment used in the studio, Beth preferred workers with a little more maturity than the normal fourteen-year-old.

"Hmm. . ." Andrew's furrowed brow and thoughtful tap of his finger against his lips told Beth he took her question seriously. "If you want to hire young people from here in town, I would start with your uncle Ben Koeppler's older girl, Catherine. She is eighteen but not yet married, and I heard she was looking to be hired at the big discount store in McPherson. Her parents would rather she wasn't driving."

Beth nodded. She'd met Catherine at family gatherings. She was a sweet, quiet girl who would likely prefer staying close to home. "Anybody else?"

"Maybe. . ." Suddenly Andrew's ears began filling with pink. "She's another of your relatives, although not so close—a cousin from your maternal grandmother's side. Doug Ortmann's daughter Livvy asked me not long ago if she could come by and see what we do. Maybe she would be interested."

Beth, observing his flaming ears, resisted making a teasing remark. "I had thought about Trina. She'll be eighteen next month, right? And I know she's said she'd rather not work at the restaurant."

"Working here would be the same as working there to Trina."

Andrew's voice held a touch of sadness. "She wouldn't be any happier. And asking her would only create problems with her mother."

Beth agreed with that. Although she didn't find Deborah as intimidating as she first had when she'd come to Sommerfeld, she still tried to keep her distance from the forceful woman. The last thing she wanted was to cause conflict in Trina's relationship with her mother.

"Okay, then. My cousin Catherine and. . .Livvy, you said?" At his nod, he shifted his gaze to the side. A curious reaction. Beth pressed her lips together to keep from grinning. "Well, here's what I suggest. We might as well find out now whether they're interested. That way, if they aren't, we can look for someone else. We also need to know if they can learn the process. Do you suppose they could come in tomorrow and watch you make a suncatcher from start to finish? Maybe even start one themselves."

Andrew's head whipped around. "Tomorrow?"

Beth flipped her hands outward. "Why not? If they get some training, they'll be ready to step into full-time slots when the addition is finished. I can't pay them a wage until they actually start working, so I'd need to make that clear, but if they're interested and can prove their ability, I could put them on the payroll when they start constructing projects."

"Or maybe pay them per project to get started?"

"Not a bad idea. . ." Beth leaned her chin on her hand, thinking out loud. "To start with, I had thought of paying minimum wage. But I kind of like the idea of paying per project. Then, as their skills grow and they work on the bigger projects, the pay could increase. I'll probably also start them out part-time—maybe just mornings. Ease into it. What do you think?"

Andrew's lips curved into a lopsided grin. His brown eyes glowed. "I think we are going to have a real art studio right here in Sommerfeld."

He released a hoot that surprised Beth. She'd never seen him so animated. He reached across the table and gave her hand one quick squeeze. "It's going to happen, isn't it?"

Beth couldn't stop her own smile from growing. "It's going to happen." She looked over at the platform. The kaleidoscope of color sparkled beneath the overhead lights, and her heart rate increased as her gaze skimmed around the circle of glistening shapes. "And to think it all rests on one window. . . ."

"Both Ben Koeppler and Doug Ortmann have telephones. Do you want to call the girls' fathers now and make arrangements for them to come in tomorrow morning?"

Beth jerked to face Andrew, blinking in confusion. "Ask their fathers?"

"Well, of course. The girls still reside beneath the roof of their fathers' homes. They must have permission for the job."

Beth hadn't considered having to ask permission for employees to join her workforce. Her stomach churned. She was still considered an outsider. Even though the men were related to her, they could say no.

"You know them better than I do." She clasped her hands in her lap, almost holding her breath. "Would you mind making the calls? You'll be pretty much in charge of their training anyway, as my top assistant."

Andrew sat up straighter, his smile wide. "I can do that. Should I call now?"

"Please do." Beth slipped from the stool. "And I'll get busy on the McCauley window. The last thing we want to do now is miss the deadline!"

Beth listened with half an ear as Andrew made telephone calls. In both cases, the men were working away from the house, but he elicited promises for them to call him at the studio when they returned home for the evening. It occurred to her as she listened to the calm surety in Andrew's voice how much he had changed in the months at the studio. His self-confidence had grown by leaps and bounds, and she realized with a small rush of pride that she had shared in his growth.

A warmth spread through her middle, and she lifted her face to send him a smile of approval. When he smiled back, his ears didn't even turn red.

By ten o'clock Tuesday morning, Beth wished she had a pair of head-phones to block out the noise that stole her concentration, yet she didn't complain. She would show nothing but appreciation for the four men who'd graciously come to block and pour the floor for her addition no matter how raucous their laughter and noisy their hammers.

Inside the studio wasn't much better with Andrew running the cutting wheel to ready pieces for two pink butterfly suncatchers. Beth glanced up and swallowed the giggle that tried to form. Both Livvy and Catherine in their dresses, white caps, and neat anklets seemed so unsuited to this setting. Yet they stood side by side, aprons and goggles in place, and watched each step of the process with concentration. The hammering and voices from behind the studio didn't seem to distract them at all, and for a moment, Beth envied them their complete attentiveness to their task.

If only she could be so single-minded today! Last night she'd lain awake, her mind refusing to shut down. So many things to think about. If she hired workers, she needed to file paperwork with the Social Security Administration, be sure she talked to an accountant about tax laws, and update the record-keeping system in her computer so if she was ever audited, she'd be prepared. She needed to browse catalogs for the best prices in new equipment—another cutting wheel;

more gloves and pliers and nippers; and an oven for staining and firing her own glass.

Her heart tripped at the idea of coloring glass. Creating her own hues and shades rather than relying on a little block of color from an online store or paper catalog to match the hue and shade in her imagination. Her dreams were rapidly becoming reality, and Beth alternated between wanting to dance and shout and sing. . .and wishing she could hide and cower and cry.

Lord, thank You for the progress being made, for the people willing to help me. Let my studio be a reflection of what You have planted in me—let these projects bring glory to You.

The prayer formed effortlessly, and the fear shrank. Surely, as she'd told her grandfather, this studio was God's plan for her life. "If God is for me, who can be against me?" She murmured the words, paraphrasing a verse she'd encountered in her devotional reading. The thought washed her in peace, the fear melting away. It would be fine. Everything would be fine.

Andrew and his two observers moved to the worktable, where he demonstrated and then allowed each of them to snap the glass. Soon the three of them each held a carborundum stone and applied it to the edges of the wedges of pink glass. Beth, watching out of the corner of her eye, developed an even greater admiration for Andrew. He would be a wonderful foreman.

She sat upright, wondering when she'd finally released her worry over depending on him too much. God must be working on her, too. Humming to herself, she bent back over the platform.

With all the hammering outside, she almost missed the sound of the telephone ringing. Andrew stepped away from the worktable to answer it, then held it out to Beth. "It's Sean McCauley."

Beth rose, brushed off her knees, and took the phone. She plugged her opposite ear with her finger. "Good morning, Sean."

"Good morning. It's noisy over there!" His chuckle softened the complaint.

"I know." Beth paused, suddenly unwilling to divulge everything taking place. She couldn't explain why, but she didn't want Sean to know about all of the changes. . .yet. She sought a way to tell the truth without divulging specifics. "There's some construction nearby. It gets loud."

"I guess so." He seemed to accept her explanation. "Listen, I won't keep you because I know you're busy, but I needed to let you know Dad will be accompanying me to Sommerfeld next Wednesday. Although he's stayed up on the progress of the window through my reports and has seen pictures, he wants to meet you in person and see the window himself before we finalize McCauley's working relationship with you. Will that work?"

Beth's heart set up a patter. One more week, and everything would be final! "That sounds fine."

"And Dad would like to take you to dinner. We'll discuss all the details while we eat."

Beth frowned. "Well, the café here in town closes early on Wednesday since that's Bible study night, so we'll have to drive in to one of the bigger towns."

Sean's laughter came through the line, giving Beth a lift. "Not a problem, although one of these days I do want to sample the cooking at that café. I've heard good things about it."

"Someday," Beth promised, then fell silent. How many times would she and Sean meet face-to-face once her employment was set? Wouldn't they just communicate through e-mail, fax, and phone calls? The thought depressed her. She shook her head, throwing off the sadness. "Do you know what time you'll get here Wednesday?"

"We'll probably leave K.C. at noon. It generally takes me a little over three hours, so look for us around three, three thirty. Is that okay?"

Beth licked her lips. "Sure. That'll leave me most of the day to finish things up."

"Sounds good." A pause, and then his voice returned, lower, husky. "I'm looking forward to seeing you again."

Beth's mouth went dry. "Me—" She swallowed. "Me, too, Sean. See you then." She hung up the phone before anything else could be said.

As she returned to the platform, she glanced at Andrew. He smirked and winked. Heat rose in her face, and she turned away to get busy.

Sean pushed the disconnect button on his telephone, then released it and punched in his father's number. When he heard his father answer, he spoke without preamble. "Next Wednesday afternoon will be fine. Do you want me to swing by and pick you up?"

"I'll pick you up. I want to drive."

"Okay. Noon then. Anything else you want me to do in preparation for the final contract?"

"No." Dad's authoritative voice boomed through the line. "You've done the legwork. I'll do the paperwork. But do bring all the dimensions for the windows for that Denver church, as well as the one in Carlton. Even though we'd have time to get that to her later, given the construction schedule, I'd prefer she have them so she can fit the planning into her schedule."

Sean fingered the neat paper on his desk. It already bore the dimensions of each window and its location in the finished buildings. "Not a problem."

"Does she plan to continue doing her own work, as well?"

Sean frowned. "I'm not sure. I know initially she hoped to, but I'm not sure how she could handle all we're throwing at her plus her own stuff." For a moment Sean felt guilt press at him. He hoped Beth wasn't setting her own dreams aside for the sake of fulfilling McCauley contracts.

"Where there's a will, there's a way," his father stated emphatically. "Let her work it out. What matters is being able to brand that young lady as the McCauley stained-glass window artist. No other churches will sport windows with the kind of design we can offer. It'll give us yet another edge in the construction world. So how are the mock-ups for that annex in South Carolina coming?"

It took Sean a moment to catch up with Dad's abrupt change of topic, but he answered several questions about the potential recreational facility on the East Coast. They discussed the project in Mexico, which was nearing its completion, and argued about the best supplier for cross beams before hanging up.

As Sean put the phone back in the cradle, he felt as though something had been lacking in their conversation. He pressed his mind, and when the answer came, it surprised him. Because it had nothing to do with business.

When, he wondered, was the last time he and Dad had talked about anything that didn't directly involve McCauley Church Construction? He couldn't remember. But why did that bother him?

TWENTY-FOUR

Beth whistled, enjoying the quiet inside the studio. She'd come early to beat the crew, who planned to pour concrete into the frame they'd constructed yesterday. Mixing and pouring concrete was much less noisy, yet knowing they were out there might still provide too much of a distraction. She hoped that by getting a jumpstart, she'd be so focused she wouldn't even notice when the men arrived.

Knowing she'd be the only one inside the studio since Andrew spent Wednesdays with his father, she had told the two girls to come back on Thursday. She came close to taking Winky with her. She'd left him home yesterday out of worry the confusion outside would frighten him. In the end, though, she'd decided a day of no distractions also meant a day of no Winky. As much as she loved the kitten, he did tend to demand attention.

He was also turning into a real jumper. His back legs must have springs in them. In the middle of the night, a mighty crash had signaled his naughtiness. She hadn't been too happy when she'd discovered her answering machine on the floor instead of on the corner of her desk where it belonged. That had finalized her decision to leave the kitten at home. She intended to make full use of this totally-to-herself day and finish the McCauley window before the deadline.

Taking stock of the remaining unfinished area, Beth calculated how many more hours would be needed before she could solder and glaze the entire panel. The last step would be soldering metal crossbars in place to give the window additional strength—the last thing she wanted was to have this window buckle! But attaching crossbars would be the simplest task of the entire project. If she worked hard today and there were no more errors—unlikely, she chuckled, with the pouncing Winky at home—she should be able to finish just under deadline.

Oh, please, Lord! I want this studio to be everything You planned it to be!

She organized the next section of glass on the floor, then knelt down and picked up the first piece and slid it into the left-hand side of the H formed by lead came. Just as she wiggled it firmly against the lead border, the back door opened. Assuming it was one of the men ready to start pouring concrete, she kept her eyes on her work and called, "I'll be right with you."

"Beth."

Andrew's voice—and the serious note held in the single word—brought Beth's head up. When she saw his face, her heart fired into her throat. The piece of glass forgotten, she pushed to her feet. "What is it? What's wrong?"

"You haven't answered your phone." Andrew took a step forward. He twisted his hands at his waist, the nervous gesture heightening Beth's worry with each passing moment.

"It hasn't rung this morning."

"Last night, Henry tried to call."

"H-Henry?" Beth stumbled around the platform. Why wouldn't she have heard the phone? Then she remembered. She'd had a headache, probably from the additional activity at the studio, so she'd turned off her cell phone and the ringer on her home phone. She had been in such a hurry this morning to get to the studio, she hadn't bothered to turn either of them back on.

Grabbing Andrew's hand, she begged, "What did Henry need?"

Andrew shook his head, his eyes sorrowful. "Last night, a little after midnight, Aunt Marie woke up and felt as though something was wrong. She woke Uncle Henry, and he took her to the McPherson hospital. They transferred her by ambulance to Wichita."

Beth's heart pounded so hard her ears rang. "Mom? Is she okay? The. . .the babies?" A cold chill broke out over her body. She tugged Andrew's hands. "Tell me! What happened?"

Andrew shrugged. "That's all I know. My folks followed Uncle Henry to McPherson, then followed the ambulance to Wichita. Your grandparents went, too. But I haven't heard anything this morning. Uncle Henry asked me to let you know what was going on."

Beth dashed to the door. "Which hospital?"

"Wesley Medical Center." Andrew stepped toward her, his hand outstretched. "Uncle Henry would have called if something. . .bad. . . happened. I think you can assume no news is good news."

Beth pushed that comment aside. "I've only been to Wichita a couple of times since I moved to Kansas. I'm not sure I can find the hospital on my own. Do you know where it is?"

Andrew nodded slowly, his delayed reactions infuriating Beth. "Yes. My grandpa had surgery there once."

"Good. Then you can take me. Let's go." She pushed the door wide and started to step through. But a glance at Andrew's face stopped her. "What's wrong?"

"I can't go. Dad needs me to work today, especially since he isn't here." He shifted his gaze toward the platform. "And you have the window to finish."

She stared at him, her jaw hanging open. How could he even

suggest she work on the window while her mother lay in a hospital bed, and the babies. . .

Beth couldn't complete the thought.

He turned back to face her. "Will you be able to meet the deadline if you don't work today?"

The full impact of his question nearly buckled her knees. If she missed the deadline, she wouldn't have the contract for more windows. If she didn't have the contract, how many people would be affected? She ticked them off one by one.

The McCauleys, who were planning on her meeting their needs for windows.

Andrew, Catherine, and Livvy, who were planning on the studio providing jobs for them.

Her grandfather, who had willingly given her the money to expand the studio.

Even the men who were now arriving, preparing to pour concrete. They had postponed their own work in order to help her. Would they resent the time spent away from their own pursuits if she didn't follow through on the expansion?

Beth's head spun, and she clutched the door frame. How could she let all of those people down? But how could she stay here, knowing her mother or her unborn brother and sister might at this very moment be slipping away? Tears spurted into her eyes.

"Andrew, I have to go!"

Andrew's brows formed a fierce V. "But what about the studio? All the plans?"

Suddenly Beth knew the answer. "If the studio is God's will, it will happen with or without the McCauley contract."

Andrew gestured toward the platform. "And what if the McCauley contract is God's way of making everything available to you, and you throw it away? What will God think?"

"What will God think if I turn my back on my mother for some. . . some window?" Even she knew that was a simplification—the window was merely the representation of the whole of her dreams. Still, she shook her head wildly, her ponytail slapping her shoulder. "If you think God can't make it happen without my help, without that window, then you're underestimating Him." She smacked the doorframe with her open palm, creating a sharp sting that shot to her fingers. She grimaced, coiling the hand into a fist. "There's no way I'm staying here today, Andrew. I'm going to Wichita."

She didn't wait for him to respond. Charging out of the building and past the two men who stood, silent and watchful, at the edge of the wooden frame for the footing, she called, "Thank you for coming today. You can work without me here, right?" They each gave a nod, and she headed straight to the café. She bolted through the dining area to the kitchen, where she found Deborah at the stove.

"Deborah, can you tell me how to get to Wesley Medical Center?"

Deborah put down the spatula to offer a quick, brusque hug. "Of course I can. Trina, get something to write on and a pencil so I can put down directions for Beth." She scribbled a coarse map on a strip of paper towel, then handed it to Beth. "Tell Henry I'm praying for him, for all of you."

"I will, Deborah. Thank you." Beth forced the words past a lump in her throat. She accepted a hug from Trina before racing back through the café and out the door. The mumble of voices from the patrons told her everyone knew of the situation. She hoped they, like Deborah, were praying.

Oh, Father—Beth added her pleas as she slammed herself into her car and revved the engine—*please don't let anything happen to Mom or the babies! They're all I have.*

Andrew watched from the window of the studio as Beth zipped down the alley, creating a mighty cloud of dust that drifted across the frame awaiting concrete. The men began working, their movements automatic, but no banter was heard. Apparently they, too, knew of Uncle Henry and Aunt Marie's midnight run to the hospital.

Stepping away from the window, Andrew crossed to the platform and looked down at the stained-glass project. So close. They were so close. He knew what his dad would say if the contract didn't come through.

"Art isn't something you can count on. People will always need bread, so wheat is a secure future. I tried to tell you, didn't I?"

Andrew resisted putting his hands over his ears, knowing he wouldn't be able to stop the voice in his head with such a childish action. But his father didn't always have to be right, did he? The dream was here, right within reach, and it could be realized if this single project was finished on time.

Temptation teased. He had the pattern, the materials, the know-how. He could work on the window. Finish it, if need be. But Beth hadn't given him permission to work on it. Being a man who followed the rules, as much as he twitched to pick up the next piece of glass and get busy, he couldn't bring himself to do it. Not without her approval.

Besides, Dad had given him instructions for today. Since he and Mom were in Wichita with Uncle Henry, Andrew was expected to fill Dad's spot in the fields. If he didn't go, Dad would be furious. With a sigh, he locked the studio. He spent a moment visiting with the men and apologizing for not being able to help them; then he climbed into his truck.

As he aimed his vehicle toward the farm, he wondered what was happening in the hospital at Wichita. Belatedly, he remembered to offer a prayer.

Following Deborah's map, Beth managed to locate the medical center. After circling the campus and reading the names on the buildings, she pulled into the parking area off of Murdoch, next to the Birth Care Center. She jogged across the parking lot and entered the building, searching for someone—anyone—who could direct her.

A blue-haired lady sat at a desk with a little placard reading INFORMATION hanging over her head. Breathlessly, Beth dashed to the desk.

"Marie Koeppler," she said shortly.

The woman consulted her computer screen, her face crunched into a scowl. "Mrs. Koeppler is in High Risk Obstetrics, which is on the third floor of Building Three."

Beth stared at her in confusion. The woman must have read her expression.

"Here." She picked up a piece of paper, drew a zigzagging line, circled something, then handed it to Beth.

Beth looked at it, a campus map. "Thank you." Paper in hand, she exited the Birth Care Center, jogged through a parking garage, and entered Building Three. She located an elevator, punched the UP button, and bounced in place until a beep signaled a car's arrival. A jab of her finger on the three brought the doors closed, and she continued her anxious bouncing during the brief ride.

Once in the hallway, she wheeled around a corner and glanced through a plate-glass window. She spotted an elderly couple side by side, the man's gray head close to the white cap covering the woman's equally white hair, their hands linked. Her heart leaped in her chest.

"Grandpa! Grandma!" She dashed to them, dropping her purse on the way. Leaning forward, she shared a three-way hug, then sank to her haunches in front of them. "How is Mom? Where's Henry?"

Grandma's faded eyes looked glazed from the presence of tears. "He and Al and Maura walked down to the garden. . .to pray."

Beth realized Grandma hadn't addressed the first question. Fearful, she squeezed her grandmother's hand. "And Mom?"

"All we know is she has HELLP." Grandpa's voice, usually so strong, came out soft and broken.

Beth frowned, confused. "Yes, of course she has help. But what's wrong with her?"

Grandpa shook his head. "No. She has some condition called HELLP syndrome: H-E-L-L-P. I forget what it stands for. Her blood pressure is too high. And the babies. . ." Grandpa's chin quivered. "This morning. . ."

Beth thought her chest might pound clear out of her chest. She wrapped her arms around her grandfather's neck. "It's okay, Grandpa. It's okay."

The sound of footsteps intruded, and Grandpa gently pushed her away to wipe at his eyes with his sleeve. He leaned into Grandma as Beth rose and turned. Henry, followed by Andrew's parents, entered the room.

When Henry spotted her, he stopped and simply held out his arms. She raced across the floor and threw herself against his chest. Immediately, his arms closed around her, and she pressed her cheek to his collarbone. Never had a hug felt as good as the one she now experienced. She tightened her arms around Henry's middle, tears stinging her closed eyes, as she wondered why it had taken something so extreme to finally lead her to this moment with her stepfather.

Somewhere behind her, she heard Al quietly telling her grandparents the surgeon had located Henry. His voice dropped to a mumble, and she couldn't understand what he was saying. Then Henry spoke, covering Al's voice.

"You came."

She heard relief and wonder in his tone. "I came," she reiterated unnecessarily. Where else would she be? Her throat constricted with the realization that she had surprised Henry by coming. How out of touch with the family had she become that he would think she would stay away?

"I'm so sorry you couldn't reach me last night. I. . .I turned off my phone because I had a headache. If I'd known—"

"Shh." Henry rocked her gently back and forth. "Your knowing wouldn't have changed anything. The doctor said this condition, this HELLP, has been bothering your mother for several weeks. We didn't pay enough attention because we didn't know. But don't blame yourself for anything, Beth. You're here now. That's all that matters."

She felt him rest his cheek on her head. His rough hand caught in her ponytail as he stroked its length. His tender words, his sensitive attention to her needs touched Beth on a deeper level than anything she'd known with any other person besides her mother. *This then,* she thought, *is what it is to have a father.* She allowed herself a few minutes of comfort, safe within the circle of Henry's arms. Eventually, the questions that had plagued her all the way from Sommerfeld to Wichita pressed upward again.

Swallowing her tears, she pulled back enough to study his face. He looked as though he'd aged ten years since last Sunday's dinner. Although she feared the answer, she had to know.

"Henry, the babies—are they. . . ?"

"The babies were delivered early this morning. They did it

surgically, a cesarean section. They had to, to save them. Both were in distress—their heart rates dropping too low. So the doctors took them from your mother's womb."

She searched his face. A gentle smile curved his lips.

"A boy and a girl, just as the ultrasound predicted. Both not much bigger than my hand." He held up one hand and examined it.

Beth looked at it, too, trying to imagine her little brother and sister near the size of the broad hand only inches from her face.

With a disbelieving shake of his head, Henry added, "Such tiny miracles."

Beth zipped her gaze back to his face. "Then they're. . .alive?" She whispered the last word.

"Alive." Henry swallowed, cupping her cheek. "But critical. We won't know for several hours, maybe days, whether they will be. . . healthy."

Beth read a great deal into the simple statement. She would worry about the babies later. Right now she needed to know something else. "And. . .and Mom?"

Henry's face crumpled, and he crushed Beth to his chest. She clung, her hands convulsing on his back as she felt him shudder. *Oh, no, God. Please, no. Not my mother.*

TWENTY-FIVE

A s if in answer to her silent prayer, Beth heard Henry's rasping voice whisper, "She lives. Praise our Lord, your mother lives."

The relief was so great, Beth nearly collapsed. Henry guided her, with a firm arm around her waist, to the row of plastic chairs. She sank into the one next to Maura, and Andrew's mother put a steadying hand on her knee. Beth clasped it, drawing strength from the simple touch.

"Can I see her?"

Henry shook his head. "No. The surgeon just now said we have to wait until she's stabilized. She lost a lot of blood in the surgery to deliver the babies. The doctor said this HELLP made it so her blood won't clot. They're keeping her sedated so she won't move around and start the bleeding again. He explained to me that the high blood pressure can cause damage to her liver and other organs."

Beth gasped, but Henry offered a reassuring squeeze on her shoulder. "They're running tests to make sure everything is all right. Her body needs a chance to recuperate." A small, hopeful smile played on the corners of his lips. "We can go peek at the babies, though, one at a time, as long as we stay quiet and don't try to touch them yet."

"Why not?" Beth looked at the other two women in the room. "Isn't it harmful to just leave babies without any contact? Doesn't someone need to. . .to *bond* with them?"

Maura squeezed Beth's knee. "Honey, these babies are fragile. It's more important not to cause any distress. Touching them could overexcite them, which would do more harm than good. We need to let them rest and gain strength. Then we can all stroke their little backs and sing lullabies to them."

Beth wasn't sure she agreed, but she decided arguing would only cause more stress for Henry. "When are you going to go see them?"

Henry glanced at his wristwatch. "The surgeon said we could start visiting the special nursery at one o'clock. So. . ." He held out his hands in a helpless gesture. "Until then, we wait."

Over the remainder of the morning, more people arrived, turning the waiting room into a somber family reunion. The room rapidly filled with Henry's brothers and their wives, each of Beth's aunts and uncles, and many of her cousins. Even Deborah, her husband, and their children showed up unexpectedly shortly before one.

When Henry sent Deborah a questioning look, she snapped, "Yes, I closed the café." Her voice broke as she added, "Don't you know you, Marie, and those babies are more important than any café could be?" Then she spun toward Beth, held out her arms, and said, "I see you made it. Come here and thank me for that map."

Without exception, the new arrivals greeted Beth first, offering hugs and words of support, before giving the same to Henry or to Beth's grandparents. Beth thought her chest might burst from the warmth of their acceptance. How could she have waited so long to embrace these people as her family? Looking back, she realized she had held them at arm's length, distancing herself from gatherings out of fear of rejection. Now her fears seemed foolish.

Trina sat close, her capped head on Beth's shoulder, and a thought struck Beth. She was not a member of their church, but she was a member of their family. Apparently in their opinion, she *did* belong. Their actions today clearly expressed that. Now it was up to her to accept it. Beth felt as though she matured at least five years in those moments of reckoning.

The instant the clock on the wall read one o'clock, Henry bounded for the door. Before leaving the room, he paused and looked back at Beth. "You'll be next," he promised. Then he clipped past the window and disappeared.

Trina lifted her head and smiled at Beth. "Are you excited?"

Beth released a short, humorless laugh. "I'm more nervous than anything. I've never been around babies. And for them to be born so early, and to be sick. . ." Tears stung again.

"They'll be okay," Trina said with such certainty Beth almost believed it. "Wait and see."

"I'd feel better if I could see them for myself." Beth looked longingly toward the door. But Henry had only been gone a few minutes. She shouldn't be selfish and hurry him back with her thoughts.

Trina touched her arm. "Beth? Was it hard for you to come, knowing you have work to do?"

Beth looked at the younger woman. Trina's spattering of freckles stood out like copper pennies in her pale face. She seemed to hold her breath as she waited for Beth's reply, but Beth couldn't imagine why it held such importance.

"It wasn't hard at all," Beth answered honestly.

Trina's eyes widened. "Really?"

"Really. Suddenly the studio, the artwork—all of it—seemed secondary." Shaking her head, she gave a soft, rueful chuckle. She glanced around the room at the gathered family members. "This is first: family." With a sigh, she admitted, "The studio is still there. It might take me longer to do all the things I've planned—the expansion, the new equipment, the big projects—but I believe God led me to open the studio, so I'll just trust Him to open the door to me when the time is right. Apparently the time wasn't right yet."

Trina shook her head, the white ribbons of her cap swaying gently with the movement. "Oh, yes, Beth. The right time. Thank you."

Beth wanted to discover the reason behind Trina's reaction, but Henry returned.

"Beth? Come on. I'll walk you down."

Beth eagerly joined her stepfather.

Sean hung up the phone, an unexplained concern weighting his chest. He glanced at his wristwatch. Where could she be? She'd said she would be working at the studio, yet she didn't answer the phone there. Nor did she answer her cell phone, and last night when he'd called her home phone, it had also gone unanswered.

Dad was waiting for a reply to his questions concerning the weight of the glass she'd chosen for the window they'd assigned. Sean assumed she had used tempered glass, which was thicker and more durable, but he couldn't remember her ever stating that for sure. He wanted to verify it before reporting to his father.

But he couldn't do that if he couldn't reach her. He picked up the phone and dialed again, then allowed the telephone to ring a dozen times before hanging up again.

He pressed his memory. He knew she'd had an answering machine at one time, yet no recording message had invited him to leave a call-back number. Maybe she'd turned off the machine, although he couldn't imagine why she would choose to do that. He had no idea if

Sommerfeld offered caller ID. But if she had it, could she possibly be choosing not to answer his calls?

He didn't like that thought. If Beth wasn't answering the telephone, there had to be a logical reason. She was straightforward enough to simply tell him she didn't have time to talk; she'd done it before. He chuckled. Beth was honest. Sometimes painfully so. But that honesty was something he'd come to appreciate, even it meant being put off. At least she didn't play games.

Sean's computer beeped, indicating the arrival of an e-mail. He gave his office chair a push that slid him to the computer. A click of the mouse brought his mailbox into view. His heart sank. The message wasn't from Beth. But it was from a pastor in Texas, asking questions about the electrician they had subcontracted to wire the new Sunday school classrooms McCauley Church Construction had added to their existing church. It took a few minutes to address the concerns.

The moment he hit SEND, his fingers itched to write another e-mail. This one to Beth. If he couldn't get through via the telephone lines, perhaps e-mail would reach her. He brought up a message box and quickly typed his father's question. He finished the brief message with, "Give me a call, if you would, please. I'm concerned that I haven't been able to reach you."

He reread the last line, his heart thudding. Should he leave it or not? It didn't sound like something a business associate would say. It sounded more like a friend. After a few moments of contemplation, he decided a friendly comment wasn't inappropriate. His finger trembled slightly as he connected with the SEND button, but he didn't reverse his decision.

Once more he glanced at his wristwatch. One fifteen in the afternoon. She could possibly have run home for a late lunch. He'd try her house again. *Ring. . .ring. . .ring. . .*

Holding the receiver to his ear, he leaned back in his chair and ran his fingers through his hair. "C'mon, Beth, where are you? Answer, huh? You're starting to scare me."

Monitors emitting soft beeps and flashing dots of light stood sentinel over the clear Plexiglas boxes where Beth's new baby brother and sister lay. The enclosed beds were necessary to maintain their oxygen levels and body temperature, the nurse had said, but it made her sad to see them separated after they'd shared a single womb. She wondered if they felt lonely being apart from each other. Standing between the two Isolettes, Beth fought tears as she looked back and forth at the tiny babies. Completely naked on stark white sheets, they looked so helpless and vulnerable.

On the way to the neonatal intensive care unit, Henry had done his best to prepare Beth for the myriad tubes inserted in each baby's arms, nose, and stomach, but seeing it was still a shock. He explained the babies had IVs to receive fluids, withdraw blood, and administer antibiotics. The little boy had a tube that appeared to be inserted through his throat—a gentle *whoosh* indicated it sent oxygen to his lungs. Beth cringed at the sight of the tiny wrinkled neck with the crisscross of tape holding the tube in place. She bit back a sob. Poor little guy. . .

Both babies required feeding tubes since they were born too early to have developed the ability to suck. Looking at the green tubes in the impossibly small nostrils, Beth felt another stab of sadness. Mom had so looked forward to breastfeeding the babies. Would that be possible later, when they were bigger?

Before sending her in, Henry had shared, "Their names are Theodore and Dorothea. Both names mean 'gift from God.' That's what they are, Beth—gifts. Children are His, only loaned to us for a time."

Beth hadn't been sure if he was preparing her for the possibility of God taking them back or was sharing the Mennonite viewpoint. Either way, she hadn't questioned him but had merely nodded and repeated the names, trying them out: "Theodore and Dorothea."

Now, examining the miniscule infants, she thought the names were far too big for such tiny babes. She leaned over Dorothea's Isolette and whispered, "I'm your sister Lisbeth, but everyone calls me Beth. I'll have to come up with a nickname to call you. I'm sure I'll think of something special for you, little girl."

Turning toward the baby's twin, she added, "You, too. Theodore is for someone big and brawny, and you will be, someday. But for now, I need something that fits you better." She smiled as the baby curled fingers no bigger than a pigeon's toes into a pearl-sized fist. "How about Teddy, huh? Do you like that?"

She got no response, but it didn't matter. Just looking down at the baby, taking in the downy tufts of hair on his perfectly shaped head and the pucker of his sweet mouth was enough for now. There would be time for Teddy to respond to her later. She'd be around.

Turning back to her sister's Isolette, she continued in a voice as soft as a sigh. "And you, Dorothea, maybe I'll just call you Dori. I had a friend in kindergarten named Dori. She was sweet. She shared her raisins with me at snack time. We'll have time to share things, too, little girl. Maybe not makeup tips or clothing styles, but secrets. Lots of secrets, the way sisters do."

Little Dorothea shifted her fuzzy head slightly, and tears spurted into Beth's eyes. The baby's tiny chin had a clearly discernible cleft. Just like Mom's. Just like Beth's.

A rush of emotion swept over Beth, a love so intense it nearly toppled her. She put her hand on the top of each Isolette and closed her eyes for a moment, willing what she felt to somehow transfer through the plastic case to the babies inside.

"Miss Quinn?"

Beth opened her eyes and blinked, clearing her tears. A nurse wearing a scrub shirt printed with pink and blue hippos stood nearby.

"I'm sorry, but it's time to change the babies' IV fluids. I'll have to ask you to return to the waiting room."

Although Beth considered begging to be allowed to stay, she remembered Maura saying the babies were fragile and shouldn't suffer undue disruptions. Doing what was best for the babies took precedence over her own desires. She nodded. But she took one more second to place her fingers against her lips and then press a kiss on the top of each plastic box.

"I'll be back, Teddy and Dori. Sister loves you."

TWENTY-SIX

Sean clinked the ice cubes in his glass and stared at the clock ticking above the sink in the kitchen. Raising the glass, he tipped a cube into his mouth and chewed, his gaze never wavering from the clock and its slow-moving second hand.

Six thirty-one. Six thirty-two. Six thirty-three. . . Would he stand here forever, waiting for the telephone to ring?

Plunking the glass onto the counter, he whirled back down the hallway to his office and slumped into his desk chair, his chin in his hand. Another minute-measurer in the lower right-hand corner of his computer screen captured his attention. He watched three more minutes click by before releasing a sigh.

She was working late. That's why she hadn't answered his e-mail. It didn't explain why the telephone rang unheeded in the shop, unless she was so focused on her work she chose to ignore it. It didn't explain why her cell phone went unanswered. He'd stopped calling it, embarrassed by the number of times she'd be greeted with "missed call" when she finally picked it up.

He wished he could avoid picking up his telephone. Dad had called three times today, and his impatience at having his question unaddressed was creating a knot of tension between Sean's shoulder blades.

He lowered his head and closed his eyes for a moment, offering a silent prayer. *Dear Lord, is everything okay over there in Sommerfeld?* The nervous twinge in the center of his chest made him want to suspect something was wrong, but he also wondered if it was just his imagination running wild. In this day of increased communication, he wasn't accustomed to waiting to reach someone. It could be his own impatience causing this feeling of dread.

He looked at the little clock on his computer screen again. Six forty-four.

C'mon, Beth, where are you?

Beth looked up as Henry slapped his knees and rose, his gaze sweeping the room.

"It's past suppertime. Would anyone like to walk to the hospital cafeteria and get something to eat?"

Although Beth wasn't hungry—the weight of worry sufficiently filled her stomach—she knew Henry could use the company. She offered a nod. "I'd eat a little something." She looked at Grandpa and Grandma, who sat close to her in the corner. "Do you want to come along, or would you rather I bring you something back?"

Grandpa answered. "Someone should stay here in case the surgeon comes to tell us about our Marie. You go ahead. Bring us a sandwich." He looked at his wife. "A sandwich, Mother?"

Grandma gave a halfhearted shrug.

Grandpa touched Beth's hand. "See if they have ham. Your grandmother likes ham."

Beth nodded and looked at the others. "Anyone else?"

Al, Maura, and Deborah got up and joined Henry in the doorway. The others said they would eat when they went home, which they planned to do as soon as they received word on Marie's condition. Henry turned toward the hallway with Al at his side, and Maura and Deborah fell in step with Beth as they followed the two men.

There was a slump to Henry's shoulders that told of his fatigue, yet not once had he complained. Beth's respect for her stepfather raised another notch as she thought of his steadfast positive attitude and calm assurances to everyone else over the course of the long day. Without conscious thought, she skipped forward two steps and slipped her arm around Henry's waist.

Surprise registered on his face, but he quickly replaced it with a warm smile and a tired wink. He draped his arm over her shoulders, and they made their way down the elevator to the first floor, then through long hallways, their feet in step with one another as if they'd done this dozens of times.

The cafeteria smells greeted them before they turned the final corner. Although the food odors were much more pleasant than the antiseptic odor that had filled Beth's nostrils since she had arrived, her stomach still churned. Henry's hand slipped away as he gestured for her to enter the cafeteria first.

Deborah, Maura, and Al followed Beth, with Henry at the rear, and they loaded a tray with sandwiches, fruit, plastic-wrapped cookies, and small cartons of milk and juice. When they reached the register, Henry withdrew his wallet, but Al stepped forward.

"No, Henry. I'll take care of this."

Henry hesitated, his fingers already grasping a few bills. But when Deborah touched his arm and shook her head, he said, "Thank you, Al," and slipped the wallet back in his pocket.

The cashier put everything in two brown paper bags, and the little group made its way back to the waiting room, this time with Henry and Beth in front and Al walking with the other two women. The moment they stepped back into the room, Henry asked, "Has anyone come about Marie?"

"Not yet, Henry," Deborah's husband, Troy, answered.

Henry released a sigh, rubbing the back of his neck. "When will they come?"

Beth wrapped both hands around his upper arm and gave a comforting squeeze. "Surely it won't be much longer. Sit down, eat something. You'll feel better."

He gave her a dubious look.

She forced a light chuckle. "Okay, then, it'll make the time pass more quickly."

His smile thanked her, and he sat down and took the sandwich and cookie offered by Deborah.

The group ate in silence, each pair of eyes flitting to the clock on the wall periodically. At seven thirty, people began leaving. One by one, they gave Henry and Beth hugs, whispered words of encouragement, and promised to continue to pray for Marie and the babies. Eventually only Henry, Beth, Al and Maura, and Beth's grandparents remained.

Al turned to Grandpa, who sat slumped forward so far his chin nearly touched his chest. "JD, how about Maura and I take you and Erma home?"

Grandpa sat up, his jaw jutting forward. "I don't want to go until I've seen Marie."

"I can tell you're tired." Al spoke softly yet evenly, more matter-of-fact than persuasive. "It's been a long day"—he yawned—"for all of us. I'm ready to go."

"I'm not."

Al sent Henry a look that communicated he needed assistance.

Henry leaned forward and put his hand over Grandpa's knee. "JD, there's no sense in waiting here. It could be hours. Go ahead and go home. Sleep in your own bed. As soon as I hear something, I'll call."

Grandpa shot Henry a sharp look. "I don't have a telephone."

"But I do," Al inserted, "and I'll drive out and share the news with you as soon as Henry calls me. Come on." He stood up, looking expectantly at Grandpa. "Let's go on home and get some rest. We can all come back tomorrow."

Grandpa and Grandma exchanged a long, silent look, during which Beth was certain they expressed their thoughts clearly to the other without the need for words. Observing them, Beth felt the prick of tears behind her eyelids.

Grandma sighed and gave a tired nod. "We'll go. Thank you."

Both of her grandparents took the time to embrace Beth, Grandpa planting a kiss on the top of her head and Grandma kissing both of her cheeks before talking quietly with Henry and hugging him, too. When they left with Al and Maura leading the way, Beth and Henry were alone.

The first time she'd ever been completely alone with her stepfather.

Although she would have expected the situation to be uncomfortable, it wasn't. Despite the location, despite the worry that must still be pressing on him as much as it pressed on her, she discovered she was glad she was there. Glad that she could offer a bit of support to Henry during this time of mixed emotions.

She watched as he paced the periphery of the room, his hands in his pockets and his head low as if measuring his steps. He stopped in the center of the room and looked at the wall clock. Sighed. Paced the room in the opposite direction.

Beth started to suggest they turn on the television but remembered in time the inappropriateness of the idea. She sat back in the two-person settee she'd occupied earlier with her grandmother and picked up the magazine from the small table tucked in the corner.

Just as she placed the magazine in her lap, Henry spun and faced her. "I'm tired of sitting. Do you want to take a walk?"

Beth set the magazine aside, rising. "What if the doctor comes looking for us?"

Henry chewed the inside of his lower lip for a moment. "We can stop by the nurses' station and tell someone we're out in the garden area. I could use some fresh air." He pinched his nose, his dark eyes twinkling.

Beth couldn't help it. She laughed. "I couldn't agree more."

Her purse strap looped over her shoulder, she walked with Henry to the nurses' station, and he informed the woman on duty where they could be located. Then, his wide palm resting gently between her shoulder blades, he guided her to the elevator and, once on the first floor, to glass doors that led into a grassy area surrounded by towering buildings.

A concrete bench invited one to relax, but Henry passed it, instead ushering Beth along the sidewalk. Although dusk had fallen, the area was well lit with light from the buildings' windows, as well as lampposts standing sentinel all along the sidewalk. Beth inhaled deeply, enjoying the tangy scent of freshly cut grass. The antiseptic taste that had lingered on the back of her tongue all day washed away, and she sighed, lifting her face to the brief expanse of pinkish sky glimpsed overhead between the towers.

"I'm glad you came." Henry's deep, quiet voice fit the peacefulness of the surroundings.

"Me, too." Beth looked at her feet, matching her stride to his. "The babies. . .wow. They're amazing. So small but so perfect." She looked into Henry's face. "Dori even has little stubby eyelashes already. I think she's going to be a beauty."

Henry's lips curved into a lopsided, questioning grin. "Dori?"

Heat filled Beth's face, but she didn't look away. "Yes. Dorothea. . . well, it's pretty, but it's too much name right now. So I've been thinking of her as Dori."

"I see."

They reached the turn in the sidewalk, and Beth slowed her steps so Henry could make the outside curve without leaving her side. She searched his face for any sign of disapproval. "Do you mind?"

"Of course not. I kind of like it." He clasped his hands behind his back and pursed his lips as if in deep thought. "What about Theodore? Did you shorten his name, too?"

"Mmm-hmm. Teddy."

"Teddy?"

Beth laughed at his doubtful expression. "Yes, Teddy. Someone small and cuddly and warm."

Henry tipped his head to the side. "I suppose that's okay. For now. But it's not something I'd want attached to him at, say, sixteen."

"I agree. But Theodore. . .it's pretty stuffy for an infant."

Henry chuckled. "Point taken."

They walked on in silence until they'd made a full circle. Henry paused, looking toward the double doors that led back inside.

Beth, sensing his thoughts, said, "I'm not ready to go back in. Want to make another loop?"

Henry's smile expressed his answer, and once more they set out. Beth glanced over her shoulder at the doors and blew out a noisy breath. "I keep wishing somebody would chase us down and tell us something."

"I know." Henry raised his hand to grip her shoulder for a moment.

"But your mother is in good hands. We have to trust." He lowered his hand and sent her a worried look. "But you probably need to get back. You have that window to finish."

Several faces paraded through Beth's mind: Sean's, Andrew's, Catherine's and Livvy's, her grandfather's, the workers', people who depended on her to follow through on her plans. Plans that depended on the signing of the contract with McCauley. Without intending to, she grimaced. She came to a stop.

"Henry, I'm torn. I want to be here with you and Mom and the babies, but I'm worried about what will happen if I don't get the McCauley window done. I don't want to let anyone down."

"If you need to go, your mother will understand. She knows how much the studio means to you," Henry said, his voice warm and assuring.

Beth knew Mom would understand. Mom had always put Beth first. And Beth had always allowed Mom to take second place, never considering her mother might have needs and wants that weren't addressed. But over the past year and half, Beth had tried to change her selfish mind-set. Right now, however, she didn't know which was less selfish: allowing the contract to slip away, which meant hurting a number of people she'd come to care about, or honoring the deadline, which meant leaving Henry to handle this heartache without her support.

She opened her mouth, prepared to ask Henry what he would do if it were his decision. A siren blasted, making conversation impossible. Even before the siren faded into the distance, a man and woman charged from one of the other buildings and immediately broke into a fierce argument about who would get Milt's matching sofa and loveseat.

Henry swallowed and glanced down at Beth, his brows raised in silent query. She gave a brisk nod, and the two of them crossed the center of the courtyard, right across the grass, and ducked back into Building Three.

Beth decided she'd go back to the little waiting room that had been assigned to the family and talk to Henry there, where they'd have more privacy. They rode the elevator to the third floor without speaking. The silver doors slid open, and Henry gestured her through. As they turned toward the waiting room, a nurse hurried up to them.

"Mr. Braun, Dr. Mulligan needs to see you."

Henry stopped, and his hand reached outward, as if in need of support. Beth clasped it. He squeezed her fingers as he asked in a surprisingly calm tone, "Whom does it concern: my wife or my children?"

The nurse spun around, beckoning them to follow with a glance over her shoulder. "Your wife."

Twenty-seven

Andrew heard the back door open, and he set aside the book he'd been reading and rose. His parents' voices pulled him to the kitchen, where he found them beside the door engaged in quiet conversation.

"How is Aunt Marie?" He interrupted them to ask the question, but he'd been waiting for hours for word. Courtesy didn't seem as important as being informed.

His father turned to him, slipping off his hat. "Has your uncle called?"

Andrew shook his head. "No one's called. What's going on?"

Briefly, his father recounted the details of Marie's surgery to deliver the babies, the possible consequences of the syndrome that created the need for early delivery, and what they knew of the babies' conditions.

Andrew drew in a slow breath. "Will they be okay?"

"We don't know yet." His mother bore dark circles beneath her eyes. "But Henry said he would call with any news. So we'll have to wait."

Andrew followed his parents as they moved toward their bedroom.

"What about Beth? Did she come back, too?"

"She was still at the hospital when we left." His father paused at the bedroom door, while his mother went on in and sat on the bed, her shoulders slumped. "I think she plans to stay there with Henry."

"For how long?" Andrew's heart caught. If it were only for tonight—if she planned to be back midday tomorrow, or even the morning after that—then if they worked together, maybe they could still finish the window.

Dad shrugged, his face twisting in a displeased scowl. "I don't know, Andrew. She didn't say."

Andrew wanted to ask other questions, but his father's foul mood stifled them. "Get some rest," he said, "and I'll listen for the telephone."

"Thank you," his mother called.

Dad closed the door.

Andrew moved slowly back to the front room, sat down with his elbows on his knees, and stared unseeingly at the patch of carpet between his feet. Surely she would come back. They were so close to being finished. Surely she wouldn't let the opportunity go when only a few dozen shapes of glass stood between a successful launch of a fully operating studio, or continuing to do craft fairs until another opportunity came along. *If* it ever came along.

"Andrew?"

He jumped and sat up.

Dad stood in the opening of the hallway. "Your mother is worried about Beth's cat. It hasn't been attended to all day."

Rising, Andrew said, "She keeps a key under the mat on the back porch, just like her great-aunt always did. I could go over and check on it."

Dad released a grunt of frustration. "Please do. Your mother won't rest until she knows the poor animal is all right."

Andrew was already moving toward the back door. "Tell Mom not to worry. I'll take care of Winky." As he passed his father, he added, "Get some sleep. You look like you need it."

Dad nodded, rubbing his hand over his whiskery cheek. "Yes. Thanks, son."

Andrew headed out the back door. Less than ten minutes later, he let himself into the utility porch of Beth's bungalow. Winky wrapped himself around his ankles before he could get the back door closed. The cat's yowls pierced Andrew's eardrums.

"Hey, hey," he chided, slapping the light switch and scooping up the cat in one smooth motion, "stop yelling. I'm here now."

Winky continued to emit strangled mewls between loud purrs as he bumped his head on the underside of Andrew's chin and worked his paws against Andrew's shirt front.

"You sure know how to make a guy feel welcome." Andrew held the cat for several minutes, stroking his fur. Finally, the little critter struggled to get down.

Winky headed for the kitchen, his tail straight in the air, yelping out a series of meows Andrew interpreted as a command to follow. He found the cat weaving back and forth between the stove and his empty pet dish, which had been turned onto its side.

"Sure, I'll feed you," he said, picking up the dish. "But where does Beth keep your food?" He spent a few frustrating minutes opening every cupboard door in the kitchen, all without success. Winky's meows became more insistent, and Andrew muttered soothing words while he considered where else cat food might be kept.

Suddenly he slapped his forehead. "Oh, the basement!"

Winky trotted along as he headed back through the utility porch to the basement door. Just inside the door, on the second step, waited a half-full bag of dry cat food. Andrew grabbed it and had to high step his way back to the kitchen to avoid Winky, who darted in and out between his feet in eagerness.

Andrew filled the dish on the counter, thinking it would keep Winky out of his way, but to his surprise the cat leaped up beside the bowl and stuck his head under the flow of small brown squares, sending a flurry of cat food across the countertop and floor.

"Winky!" He pushed the cat to the floor, but before he could even take a breath, Winky was back on the counter, in his way again. Finally, out of desperation, he closed the cat in the bathroom while he finished filling the food dish and cleaned up the mess on the floor. Winky's indignant yowls spurred him to work quickly. Once released, the cat pattered right to the bowl and buried his face in Kitty Krunchies.

While Winky ate, Andrew wandered to the front room, scanning for any messes the cat might have made while Beth was away. Other than a rug all askew by the front door and a tennis shoe dragged beneath the dining room table, it appeared the cat had behaved pretty well. As he turned to head back to the kitchen, his gaze fell on Beth's cell phone, which lay on the desk in the corner of the dining room.

A little red light next to the stubby antenna flashed on and off. Curious, he moved to the desk and touched the slim silver phone with one finger. What did the flashing light mean—that the phone was going dead or that someone was calling? Uncertain what to do, he simply stared, watching the repeated blinks until he realized he was becoming mesmerized.

Shifting his gaze, he encountered the desk telephone. A small red button beneath the word "ringer" glowed as brightly as the flashing light on the cell phone. He touched the button and the color changed to green. He raised his eyebrows, realizing he must have turned it on. He reached to punch it back to off when, ri–i–ing! He jumped, jerking his hand away from the offending noise.

Ri–i–ing!

Should he answer it? It might be Henry. But no, Beth was with Henry. He had no need to call her.

Ri–i–ing!

Maybe it was Dad, calling to find out what was keeping him. He'd better hurry on home.

Ri–i–ing!

He came to a halt. Dad would probably worry more if Andrew didn't answer, since he'd said this was where he would be.

Ri–i–ing!

No, he should just ignore it and go home. Andrew took two steps toward the kitchen, but then he whirled back and snatched the receiver from the cradle. "Hello?"

A dial tone greeted him. He'd waited too long. With a muffled groan, he slammed the receiver back in place. A glance in the kitchen showed Winky still hunkered over his food dish. Obviously the cat would need attention again in the morning, but for now Andrew had better go home.

While the cat was occupied, he slipped out the back door.

Sean whirled his chair away from the desk and rose, heading for the hallway. If he remained in his office, he'd only continue trying to call Beth. And she obviously wasn't able—or willing—to answer.

He stopped in the kitchen to remove a bottle of carbonated water from the refrigerator, then passed into the small family room that had been added on to the back of the house. Settling into his recliner, he propped up the footrest and pointed the remote at the large-screen television that filled the middle of the entertainment center on the opposite wall. A detective show of some kind exploded onto the screen. He sipped his fizzy water and watched.

Having come in midway through the program, much of the story-line didn't make sense, but it filled the time. He remained in the recliner until the water bottle was empty, the backyard was fully dark, and the ten o'clock news came on. Only then did he shut off the TV, slam down the footrest, and head for his bedroom.

As he passed his office, he felt the urge to go in and try Beth's number one more time. But unwilling to face another series of unanswered rings, he pushed himself past the door.

He lay beneath the solid blue sheet on his bed and stared at the shadowed ceiling, trying not to envision unpleasant scenarios that would keep Beth from having access to her telephone. Closing his eyes, he prayed for God to shut down the images that only created needless worry. He prayed for Beth to be safe, wherever she was. And he asked, pleaded, that he would be able to reach her tomorrow.

Beth, her legs feeling like rubber, made it to the corner to the chair she'd occupied earlier, and collapsed. She covered her face with her hands, determined to keep dammed the tears that pressed behind her lids. All through the doctor's explanation, the visit to her mother's room, and the long walk down the hallway, she had maintained a calm facade. But now in the privacy of the waiting room, her resolve faded. With a broken sob, the tears broke loose in a torrent that doubled her forward and convulsed her shoulders in uncontrolled heaves.

In moments, strong arms surrounded her, pulling her firmly against a solid shoulder. Henry. For a moment, she clung, welcoming the consoling embrace, but then she realized how selfish she was being. She shouldn't expect him to offer comfort when he was so in need of it himself. She pushed against his chest even as she continued to sob, and his arms loosened, allowing her to pull free.

Crunching into the corner of the vinyl-covered settee, she tried, unsuccessfully, to bring her weeping under control.

"Beth, Beth, shh now. . ." The low-toned voice filtered through Beth's sobs. "Come here. Let's pray together. You'll feel better."

"I. . .I can't!" Beth heard the recalcitrant note in her own voice, but she couldn't seem to stop it. How could she possibly find a way to convey the depth of her concern and worry? Her prayers would be senseless groaning.

"Beth, please, you're breaking my heart."

The words sounded strangled, and Beth shifted to meet Henry's gaze. His eyes, shimmering with empathetic tears, brought another rush of tears to her own. With a little cry, she forgot her resolve not to be selfish and threw herself into his arms. Her face buried against his chest, she choked out, "I'm just s–so scared, Henry. Mom's. . .Mom's all I've got. W–what if. . ."

His chin pressed against her head, the day's growth of whiskers catching her hair. "Your mother will be fine. The doctor didn't say we would lose her, did he?"

Snuffling, she admitted, "No, but. . .but he said she was w–weak from the babies' delivery, and that a second surgery could b–be risky." Beth pictured her mother on the hospital bed, her face nearly as white as the pillowcase beneath her head. The tousled curls scattered across the pillow took Beth by surprise. How long had it been since she'd seen Mom's hair free of her cap? Mom had looked young, fragile, defenseless.

"Risky, yes." His sigh stirred the fine strands of hair that had slipped loose of her ponytail. "But I trust she'll come through the surgery. She's a strong woman, and she's in good hands—the best hands, the nurse said, in all of Kansas. We must trust, Beth."

"It-it's so *hard*." She whispered the words against Henry's front, wishing they weren't true.

His soft chuckle vibrated against her ear. "Ah, Beth, if trust were easy, it wouldn't be worth having." Gently, he pushed her away and handed her a handkerchief from his shirt pocket. While she dried her eyes, he added, "And something else. Don't ever think your mother is all you have."

He paused for a moment, pulling his upper lip between his teeth and looking steadily into her eyes. She sensed he was gathering courage, and she held her breath, wondering what he might say.

Finally he spoke, his voice low and gravelly with emotion. "I've never said it because I didn't want to presume that you. . .you would accept me for something more than your mother's husband. But I love your mother, Beth, and you are a part of her. I love you, too."

Beth's breaths came in little spurts as she fought the need to weep again but not from anguish. No, not from anguish.

"You're a young woman already, and I know you don't need a dad, but—"

"Yes, I do." She blurted out the words, then lowered her gaze, abashed by the admission. She did need a dad—she'd always needed a dad. Her hands convulsed on the soggy handkerchief. Her words tumbled out in a harsh whisper. "But Mom got pregnant, and she has Dori and Teddy now, and you. . .you're. . ."

She didn't complete the thought. Right now, in an operating room, the surgeon was cutting into her mother, taking away the chance for her to ever bear another child. He'd said they had to, to stop her from bleeding. But the thought knifed through Beth's chest, stealing her words. How could she express a jealousy for the two tiny infants lying in Isolettes, knowing they would be Henry's only children? How could she

541

expect him to want her—flesh of another man—when he had them?

"Yes," Henry said, his voice as tender as she'd ever heard it, and Henry was the most tender man she had ever known. "Your mother *and I* have Dori and Teddy. . .and *we* also have you."

She jerked her chin up to meet Henry's gaze. The subtly emphasized words delivered a message that reached Beth's heart and expanded it in a way she hadn't expected.

"Having Theodore and Dorothea doesn't change anything for your mother. You will always be her child. And just because I now have Dorothea and Theodore doesn't mean I won't have time for you. If you need a dad, I'm here. If you don't want me as a dad, I accept that, too. We're friends, aren't we?"

He waited, and she gave a slight nod. Yes, they were friends. Henry had never betrayed her, never hurt her, never ignored her, even though she had held him at bay. He had always shown her unconditional acceptance. . .and love.

He went on softly, his hand resting on her clasped fists. "Whatever you choose for our future relationship, Beth—whether a friendship or a father-daughter relationship—just know you are loved, by your mother *and* me. You can trust that."

Overwhelmed by emotion, Beth couldn't find her voice. For long minutes she sat looking into Henry's face, absorbing the sincerity reflected in his eyes. A part of her wanted very much to say, "Thank you." To say, "Thank you, Dad." But the words caught in her throat. The time wasn't appropriate, not in this needy moment. It would be as though she only wanted him for what he could give.

The time to call him by the name she now accepted in her heart would come later, when Mom was well, the twins were home, and they were all together under Henry's roof like a family. She could wait. Looking into his unwavering, accepting eyes, she knew he could wait, too.

She pushed her lips into a quavering smile.

"Are you ready to pray now?"

Beth gave an eager nod and closed her eyes. Henry petitioned God, speaking to the heavenly Father as easily and comfortably as he would speak to a friend. He thanked God for the precious gift of life in his children; he expressed gratitude for the care his wife was receiving and asked for divine help for the surgeon now operating; and he asked God to calm Beth's fears and remind her of His presence.

Beth swallowed hard at those words. Only a dad would think of her before he thought of himself.

He concluded the prayer by telling God he trusted Him for the outcome, whatever it would be. When Beth opened her eyes and met Henry's gaze, the calm peace she saw in his face gave her peace, too. Her mother would be okay. She trusted that implicitly.

Henry slapped his knees and pushed to his feet. "Now, the doctor said it would be morning before we'd be able to see your mother. I'm going to go call Al and have him share what's happening with those in Sommerfeld. Then I'll stop by the nurses' station to ask for pillows and blankets. Do you think you can get comfortable on this little thing?"

Beth gave the settee a pat. "I've always liked a firm mattress."

"Good girl." Henry gave her cheek a quick caress; then he headed out of the room.

TWENTY-EIGHT

B eth? Beth, wake up."

The soft voice, the gentle hand on her shoulder drew Beth from a deep, dreamless sleep. She opened her eyes in increments, blinking against the glare of fluorescent lights, and finally focused on a face only inches from hers.

Henry's face, darkly shadowed by whiskers.

Frowning, she sat up, grimacing as her back complained. It took a moment for her to remember why she was folded into a small settee in an unfamiliar room. But then memories from yesterday—Andrew's announcement, her mad dash to Wichita, the visits to the nursery, and her mother's second surgery—rushed over her, and she jerked stiffly upright and grasped Henry's hand.

"Mom? Is she okay?"

Henry's tired smile gave the answer before he spoke. "Your mother rested well last night. The worry about bleeding is over. We'll be able to see her after breakfast."

Beth felt as though someone had taken the air out of her. She collapsed against the back of the settee and peered up at Henry. "Thank the Lord."

His eyes crinkled. "I already did."

With a yawn, Beth pushed to her feet.

Henry pressed a clear resealable bag into her hand. "The nurse said we could use the shower in the bathrooms on the lower level. She gave us these."

Beth looked into the bag. A toothbrush, comb, and sample-sized containers of toothpaste, soap, shampoo, conditioner, and deodorant awaited her use. "That sounds like a great idea." Looking down the length of her wrinkled clothes, she made a face.

Yesterday she'd been too concerned about Mom to worry about her clothes. But now she realized how slovenly she must look in her normal work attire of faded jeans, T-shirt, and oversized flannel shirt.

"I wish they had some clothes in here, too." She gave her armpit a sniff, wrinkled her nose, and said with a rueful chuckle, "I could use a change."

Henry shook his head, his eyes twinkling. "You'll be fine. People understand. Why don't you go down first? I'll stay here in case someone needs us. When you get back, I'll go clean up, and then we'll visit your new brother and sister before we see your mother."

Beth admitted it felt wonderful to be clean even if she did have to put on clothes that were wrinkly and slightly musty from yesterday's wearing. Her wet hair pulled up in a ponytail, she returned to the waiting room to find Henry finishing a simple breakfast of cereal and fruit. On the tray, a second box of cornflakes, a banana, and small carton of milk were untouched.

He pointed. "Look here. If you open the box on these dotted lines, you can pour the milk right inside and use the box like a cereal bowl."

His boyish amazement at using the box for a bowl tickled Beth, and she couldn't stop a giggle from forming. But when Henry sent her a questioning look, she said simply, "Pretty ingenious," and sat down.

He left for his shower. She turned on the television and watched a morning talk show while she ate her breakfast. Surprisingly, she was hungry. The food tasted better than she would have thought.

When Henry returned, she clicked off the TV, loaded the remains of their breakfast onto the tray, and stood up, tray in hand.

"The nurse said to leave it on the table there. A janitor will pick it up." He ran his hand over his smooth chin. "I think I'm presentable enough now to peek at the babies. Let's go."

As they walked toward the NICU, Beth said, "I wish I'd remembered to grab my cell phone yesterday. It would make calling people easier."

"The nurse said we could use the telephone downstairs as much as we need to."

"I know, but"—Beth sent him a sheepish look—"I need to call Sean McCauley and let him know the project has been delayed, and I don't have the number memorized. It's in my cell phone's memory bank."

Henry slowed his steps, his expression thoughtful. "Can't you ask an operator for help?"

Beth came to a halt and slapped her forehead. "Oh, duh! Information. . ."

Henry laughed. Throwing his arm around her shoulders, he got her moving again. "You can make your call after we've had our visits."

This time when Beth entered the nursery set aside for the babies in need of critical care, she didn't look at her brother or sister. She watched Henry. Frequently she had to blink to clear her vision as the man leaned over one Isolette, then the other, his broad hand pressed to the clear cover, his nose mere inches from the Plexiglas top that kept him from being able to touch his children.

BEGINNINGS

The tenderness in his eyes, the gentle curve on his lips, the deep breaths he took while his eyes slid closed—Beth was sure in those moments he prayed—created a rise of emotion in her breast that was nearly impossible to contain. If she had hand-selected a father, she wouldn't have been able to find a better one. For the babies, or for herself.

Henry straightened and looked at her. "They look good, don't they?" He kept his voice whisper-soft so as not to disturb any of the tiny patients. "Small, yes. So small. . . But good. Strong." His gaze dropped to Teddy's bed. "Look at Theodore there, making those fists. He's a fighter." Turning to the second bed, his smile gentled. "And Dorothea. . .with that little dent in her chin. . .how much she looks like her mother."

Henry looked toward Beth. "All of my girls have dented chins."

Beth shook her head, emitting a quiet laugh. "That dent is called a cleft."

He shrugged, his face creased with a grin. "Okay. Clefted chins." He looked back at the sleeping baby. "I like it."

In those moments, Beth liked it more than she ever had before. She allowed Henry several more minutes of silent examination as she crouched between the two beds and prayed for each baby in turn. When she straightened to her feet, Henry took her hand.

"Come. I've memorized their faces so I can share. Let's go see your mother now."

It occurred to Beth as she and Henry headed toward the surgical ICU where her mother recovered that Mom had yet to see or hold her babies. Beth's heart twisted in sympathy. If she itched to reach through that Plexiglas and cradle Dori and Teddy, how much more must Mom's heart ache with desire to have them in her arms.

She and Henry stopped at the station briefly to make sure it was okay for them to go into Mom's room, and with the nurse's approval, Henry ushered Beth in. To her surprise, Mom was propped up on pillows rather than lying flat. A tray with a half-eaten piece of dry toast and a plastic tumbler with a bent straw sticking out of it sat on a tall cart beside the bed.

When Mom spotted them, she offered a weak smile and held out the arm that had no tubes running from it. Beth hesitated, but Henry gave her a gentle nudge, and she dashed forward to press her cheek to her mother's—a full hug would probably hurt her.

"Good morning." Mom's voice sounded dry and raspy. "You were here all night?"

Tears pricked Beth's eyes again at her mother's obvious surprise. Maybe it was a blessing she wouldn't get that McCauley contract. She had obviously spent far too much time being Beth, business owner, instead of Beth, daughter. Closing her eyes for a moment, she made a silent vow of doing a better job of balancing her priorities—and moving family higher on her list.

"Yes. All night. And I probably smell as bad as I look."

Mom laughed softly, shaking her head. "You look fine, honey." She turned to Henry. "Have you held the babies yet?"

Beth watched Henry lean forward to place a kiss on his wife's lips. "Not yet. But I've seen them, and they're beautiful. Perfect."

Sensing her parents' need to have some time alone, Beth inched toward the door. "I'll be back a little later. I need to go make some phone calls."

Henry sat gingerly on the edge of the bed and took his wife's hand. "All right. I plan to stay here until they kick me out."

Beth nodded. "I understand. I'll see you soon. I love you." When she spoke the words, she looked at her mother, but then allowed her gaze to flit over Henry, too.

His smile followed her from the room. A request from Information garnered the telephone number for McCauley Church Construction. Beth pressed her finger against the telephone's number pad. After only one ring, a friendly female voice chirped, "McCauley Church Construction. How may I direct your call?"

Beth licked her lips. "I need to speak to Sean McCauley, please."

"Mr. Sean McCauley is at a different location. This is the main office."

Beth sucked in her breath. Of course, she should have asked specifically for Sean's number rather than the construction company's.

"But," the voice went on, "Mr. Evan McCauley is in. Would you like to speak to him?"

Beth pressed her memory. Was Evan the father or the brother? She supposed it didn't matter. She just needed to let someone know she would be unable to meet the deadline. "Evan McCauley is fine."

"Your name, please?"

"Beth Quinn of Quinn's Stained-Glass Art Studio."

There was a brief, startled silence, then, "Oh! Miss Quinn—yes. Mr. McCauley has been trying to contact you. I'll put you right through. Please hold."

Beth tapped her fingers against the desktop while she waited. Seconds later a deep, almost brusque voice came on.

"Evan McCauley here."

"Mr. McCauley, this is—"

"Beth Quinn. The *elusive* Beth Quinn."

Although the words could be construed as teasing, Beth couldn't determine by his tone whether he intended to tease or berate.

"My son," he continued without giving her a chance to speak, "tried several times yesterday to reach you."

This time she was sure she heard a hint of accusation in his tone.

She chose her reply carefully. "Yes, sir. I apologize for being unavailable. You see, my mother was rushed to the hospital early yesterday morning. I left in such a hurry, I neglected to carry my cell phone with me. I'm sorry if I caused Sean worry." Picturing Sean repeatedly dialing her number, getting no response, created a tightness in her chest. She realized she truly did regret any concern she may have caused.

"And how is your mother?" The man's tone didn't gentle at all, but the lowered volume let Beth know the question was sincere.

"She had complications from a pregnancy and required an emergency C-section, followed by a second surgery late last night. She came through both surgeries well, and she's recovering. But it will be several days before she's released. Longer still"—she swallowed—"for my premature brother and sister. But we trust they'll be fine, too." When had she decided to simply trust? Of its own volition, a smile formed on her face. "However, it does create a problem for me. . .and you."

When he made no response, she continued. "I would like to stay at the hospital with my stepfather until my mother is released. Which means I'm not in my studio. I'm afraid, with these delays, the window I'm constructing for you won't be completed by April 1."

"You realize your failure to meet that deadline results in a termination of our agreement." It wasn't a question. Beth wasn't sure she would classify it as a statement, either. It sounded almost like a threat.

She licked her dry lips and formed a calm response. "Yes, sir, I am aware of that."

A lengthy pause followed, during which time Beth could feel the prickle of tension from nearly three hundred miles away. "Very well, Miss Quinn. I appreciate your honesty. Sean and I will pursue another artist for our company. My best wishes to your mother and her babies. Take care." The line went dead.

Beth slowly placed the receiver on the hook. She waited for regret, sorrow, self-recrimination to strike. But they didn't. Yes, there was a slight hollowness in her chest, a realization that a dream would go unfulfilled. She supposed eventually she would need to mourn that loss. But for now, she only felt a sense of calm, a realization that she'd done the right thing for her family and for herself.

Closing her eyes, she offered a silent prayer. *Thank You, Lord, for putting me where I should be for Mom right now. I said I trusted that she and the babies would be fine, and I meant it. I also trust that, somehow, things will work out for the best for the people involved in my studio.*

Heading back toward the maternity wing, Beth heaved a sigh. She might be at peace with her decision, but that peace may be shattered when she shared the loss of the contract with Andrew.

TWENTY-NINE

She declined the contract?" Sean's knees turned to rubber. He sank into the chair facing his father's massive oak desk. "I can't believe she'd do that."

"Yes." Dad drummed his fingers on the desktop, his lips twitching. "I was surprised, too. And it certainly leaves us in a lurch."

Sean wasn't as concerned about their "lurch" at the moment as he was about Beth. Knowing how many plans she had for the studio, he couldn't imagine her turning down the very means to seeing those plans through. "But why? Did she give a reason?"

Dad nodded. "Apparently, her mother had a complicated delivery and required surgery. She is staying at the hospital until her mother recovers. That equates to not meeting the deadline, so. . ." Dad raised one brow. "No contract."

Sean leaned forward, his heart pounding with alarm. "Did she say whether her mother was all right?" Beth adored her mother. She would be devastated if anything happened to her.

"She indicated her mother was recovering nicely. I waited for her to make the determination that, with her mother being cared for, she should return to her obligations, but she chose to stay at the hospital.

So that's that." Dad lifted a file from the corner of his desk, opened it, and began to peruse its contents.

Sean stared in amazement for several stunned seconds. "That's it?"

Dad didn't even look up. "Yes. She made her choice. The contract must not have been that important to her. If she isn't able to make honoring contracts a priority, then it's best we know that now. Obviously the girl isn't as dependable as we'd hoped she would be."

He flicked a quick glance at Sean. "Why don't you look up the number for the stained-glass studio we used for the Cincinnati project? See if they're available." He clicked his tongue, shaking his graying head. "Their work doesn't have the depth I hoped we'd be able to corner, but—"

"Is that all you can think about? The *depth?*" The only time he'd heard regret enter his father's tone was concerning what he'd wanted and couldn't have. What had happened to his Christian compassion? Didn't Beth and her family's difficulty make an impact at all?

Dad's brows lowered into a fierce scowl. "Watch your tone with me, Sean. You may be an adult and copartner of this business, but I am still your father and your boss, and—"

"And you're being a fool."

"What?" The word was growled.

Sean faced his father squarely and repeated in the same firm yet respectful tone, "You're being a fool. You're allowing an emergency that is completely out of Beth's control to dictate your assessment of whether or not she's dependable. It's hardly a fair measuring tool."

Slapping the file closed, his father roared, "She chose not to finish the window!"

"No, Dad. She chose to be with her mother in a time of need." Leaning forward, Sean lowered his voice. "What if Mom were in the hospital, recovering, and a church team was waiting for final blueprints on a project? Whose needs would you meet—your wife's or the team's?"

Dad scowled. "Sean, you're treading on dangerous ground."

"Just answer me, please."

After a long moment, during which Sean was forced to suffer a low-lidded glare, Dad forced his answer between stiff lips. "I would honor my commitment to the church team—"

Sean slumped back in his chair, shaking his head.

Dad came out of his chair, hands on his desk, to bring his face near Sean's. "Because as a Christian businessman, I lose my credibility if I don't deliver what I've promised. Remember what Paul told Timothy—to be a '*workman* that needeth not to be ashamed.' I can't do that if I dishonor my commitments."

Sean rose to his feet and looked into his father's eyes. "But what about commitment to family, Dad? Doesn't that count for anything?"

Slowly Dad straightened his spine.

Pressing his palms to the desktop, Sean said quietly, "Jesus, on the cross, expressed concern for His mother's care. While He was taking the penalty for the sins of mankind—what greater task was there, ever?—He still thought of His mother. To me, that says family should come first."

Sean faced off with his father over the distance of the desk's width. Neither man spoke for several minutes that felt like an eternity. When it became clear Dad wasn't going to respond, Sean took a step back and released a sad sigh.

"Okay, Dad, you're right." He lowered his gaze to the floor. "You're the boss, and it is your decision who we hire to design the windows for our churches. But would you think about one more thing?" He lifted his head.

Dad was staring out the window, the muscles in his jaw quivering. He didn't turn his head.

Facing his father's stern profile, Sean went on. "McCauley Church Construction has touted itself as a family business determined to bring glory to God. You chose to focus solely on church construction, because, as you've told countless committees over the years, the church is God's family in the flesh. It seems to me that by placing her family's needs above her job, Beth has demonstrated the very dedication you desire. What a sacrifice she made for her mother. Personally, I think that kind of dedication should be honored and trusted."

Dad didn't move.

Sean drew a deep breath and released it slowly, giving his father an opportunity to reply. "Well," he finally concluded, "I've got work to do. I'll touch base with you later about locating a stained-glass window designer."

Sean opened the door and stepped through. As he turned to close it behind him, he glanced once more at his father. Evan McCauley remained standing behind his desk, his gaze aimed out the window, his fists clenched at his sides. Sean shook his head, regret filling him. Then he closed the door and left his father alone.

"You go through Beth's things and pick out some clothes." Andrew ushered Trina to Beth's bedroom while Winky danced around their feet. "I'll take care of the cat."

Two days ago, he and Trina had made a similar visit to Beth's house to retrieve a couple of changes of clothes and her toiletries. Since Beth and Uncle Henry had taken up residence at the hospital, remaining there day and night, they appreciated the fresh clothing, books, puzzles, and snacks delivered by various townspeople.

Although Andrew's parents had driven to Wichita each day of Aunt Marie's hospitalization, Andrew had yet to make the trek. His job, he had decided, was to guard the home front, which included Beth's house, her cat, and the studio.

Trina, watching Winky, giggled. "He likes you, doesn't he?" She crouched down to capture the furry critter, but Winky eluded her, wrapping himself around Andrew's left leg.

"He should," Andrew groused. "I've been the only one feeding him for the past four days. I think he's decided I'm his mother." He plucked the cat from the floor.

Trina tipped her head and puckered her lips into an exaggerated scowl. "You've been really grumpy lately. What's wrong with you?"

"I'm not grumpy." When she raised her eyebrows, he admitted, "Okay, you're right. I am grumpy. But who can blame me?" Winky's tail swished in his face, and he pushed it down. "For the past two months, all we've done is look forward to the day Beth would sign that contract with McCauley so we'd have the funds to really get her studio going. Now, because Beth's spending all her time at the hospital, the window isn't getting done. No window, no contract, no money. . .no studio." Andrew gritted his teeth. "So it's back to the fields for me."

"Why?"

Hadn't she listened to anything he'd said? "Trina, no studio, no job for me. Dad will expect me to work for him if I'm not working for Beth. So everything's ruined."

The girl shrugged. "Not everything. Even if she's not doing those big windows for churches, Beth will still have her studio. So you can still work there."

"Not full-time."

"Stop being so grouchy! Not everybody gets to do what they want to all the time."

Andrew knew Trina spoke from experience. She harbored desires that extended beyond the café, yet she went in with a cheerful attitude every day. A prick of guilt made him squirm.

"Besides that, Beth is very talented. If that McCauley from clear in Kansas City saw it, somebody else will, too. So it didn't happen this time. It doesn't mean it will *never* happen. Have faith, Andrew."

Despite himself, Andrew felt a grin twitching. "When did you get so smart?"

Trina giggled. "Just born that way."

Andrew snorted.

Another giggle rolled before Trina stepped into Beth's bedroom.

Andrew, with Winky squirming under his arm, headed for the basement staircase. "Let's get you fed, huh? Maybe if you're eating, you'll leave people alone."

He fed the cat, then sat on his haunches, idly stroking Winky's back and considering what Trina had said. He wondered if, underneath, he'd thought as Trina did—that the studio would still one day be as big and successful as Beth envisioned it. Because despite his dad's report that Beth had informed McCauley she wouldn't be able to meet his deadline, Andrew had still gone to the studio each day. He'd overseen the completion of the addition and had continued training Livvy and Catherine, just as if nothing had changed.

Trina was right. If McCauley had taken note of Beth's unique talent, someone else would, too. It was only a matter of time. Lowering his head, he offered a silent prayer. *Forgive me, Lord, for my shortsightedness. Beth dedicated the studio to You, and her goal is to glorify You through her artwork. Let me also bring glory to You in whatever tasks I do, whether in the studio or on the farm. Help me to wait patiently for Your plan to unfold.* Perhaps he'd have to do farm work for a while yet, but God hadn't given him an interest in art for nothing. God wouldn't leave him on the farm forever.

"Nope, Winky, not forever." He muttered the thought aloud.

"Not forever what?"

Andrew looked up and found Trina in the doorway between the kitchen and dining room. He straightened. "I won't pet him forever." He looked at the neatly folded clothes in his cousin's arms. "You have everything she'll need for one more night?" His folks had indicated Marie would be released tomorrow, but the twins would remain in the hospital nursery for at least another month, if not longer. Beth, however, intended to return home once her mother's hospitalization was over.

"Yes, but I should have brought a sack."

"I can get you one." Andrew had seen a pile of empty grocery sacks under the sink when he'd come the first time and searched through every cupboard for the cat food. He pulled one out and handed it to Trina.

"You sure know your way around," Trina remarked as she stuffed the clothes into the sack. "But you've pretty much given up on living here, haven't you?"

Andrew jumped as if pricked by a pitchfork. "What do you mean by that?"

Trina blinked in innocence, her dark eyes wide. "Your crush on Beth. You wanted to court her, didn't you?"

Andrew frowned. "Who have you been talking to?"

Shrugging, Trina placed the bag on the counter and then rested her hands on top of it. "Nobody. I could tell by watching you watch her. But you're over it."

It seemed his little cousin had grown up when he wasn't looking. He fought a grin. "Are you so sure?"

Her emphatic nod made her ribbons dance. "Oh, yes. Now you're watching Livvy Ortmann."

Andrew's ears went hot. "Trina. . ." A warning growl.

She giggled and snatched up the bag, swinging it from her hand. "It's okay. I won't tell anyone." She pranced by him, heading for the back door. "And just so you know, she watches you, too."

"Trina!"

The girl laughed and skipped out the door.

Beth's hand trembled as she reached inside the Isolette and ran her finger gingerly down the length of her baby brother's spindly arm. Little Teddy bent his elbow and drew up his knees. Beth murmured, "Yes, it's me, your big sister. Don't worry. I won't hurt you." Slowly she retraced the path upward, then transferred her attention to his leg. She followed the curve of his tiny knee and the inside of his ankle, ending with his impossibly small toes.

The baby blinked and shifted his head on the sheet. Beth laughed, a controlled, whispered laugh. "Are you ticklish?"

Next to her, Mom gave Dorothea the same treatment—a one-fingered, gentle massage. Beth flashed her a grin over the tops of the Isolettes. Although the babies were five days old, they had yet to be held and rocked by their parents or doting big sister. But touching them, Beth decided, was the next best thing. She hoped the powdered latex glove didn't feel rough on the delicate, wrinkled skin. The nurse had explained many preemies were sensory intolerant, so it was important to use the gentlest of touches.

"Are his eyes open?" Mom whispered.

Beth nodded. It was rare to see either of the twins awake. The nurse had assured them sleep was good medicine, and each rest allowed the babies to gain strength. Still, Beth relished the opportunity to peer into Teddy's eyes and pretend he peered back.

"Dorothea's are, too." Mom's voice purred, rising and falling as gently as if wafting on an early morning breeze. "As deep and blue as the sea, but I think they have a brown rim. I'd like it if they turned brown like her daddy's. Pretty girl. Pretty baby. Mama loves you."

Beth marveled at how the babies, even separated, still seemed to be in sync with one another. The few times she'd seen them awake, they were both awake. And when one became agitated, immediately the second showed signs of distress, although Teddy had proven easier to calm than his stormy sister.

Already hints of personality could be read in their reactions and precious facial expressions. Despite the fact her relationship with them was just a few days old, Beth loved them so much there were times her eyes welled with tears just thinking about them. It would be hard for her to leave tomorrow, but now that Mom was up and moving around, it was time for her to go.

Only two family members could enter the nursery at the same time. With her going in, either Mom or Henry had to stay out. As much as she loved visiting the babies, Beth knew it was better for their parents to be with them. So tomorrow morning, she would return to Sommerfeld.

"But I'll be back every weekend," she promised little Teddy, caressing his downy head, "and we'll have lots to catch up on."

A nurse stepped near, clipboard in hand, and recorded the numbers flashing on the monitors. Her recording done, she smiled at each baby in turn. "They seem to be enjoying their massages."

"Oh yes. Attention," Mom singsonged. "They like attention."

"Just remember not to overdo," the nurse cautioned. "Overstimulation can be detrimental."

Mom offered a smile and nod. She spoke to the nurse but kept the same sweet, singsong tone she used with the babies. "I've learned their signs of 'too much,' and I won't overdo. Thank you for the reminder."

Beth enjoyed another few minutes of singing softly to Teddy before she and Mom traded places. Beth continued the whisper-soft strokes and low-toned crooning, this time with Dori. Looking down at the tiny replica of her own baby pictures, Beth couldn't help but envision the future two years, ten years, sixteen years down the road and wonder how Dori's childhood and teen years would differ from her own.

Dori would be raised Old Order Mennonite. Her friendships and relationships would be limited by the restraints of the community. Would this little girl, whose personality already seemed to indicate feistiness, blossom or wither within those restraints? Beth couldn't know for sure what lay ahead for Dori, but she silently vowed to pray every day for Dori's contentment. She also vowed never to be a stumbling block in her little sister's life. Somehow, even though she knew she wouldn't adopt the Old Order lifestyle, she would be supportive of it.

Beth shifted her position slightly to relieve a mild cramp in her wrist, and as she did, she glimpsed her own reflection in the Isolette's Plexiglas top. No makeup, hair slicked away from her face in a tight tail, simple silver studs in her ears—as plain as she'd ever seen herself. Yet in her eyes lay a peace and maturity that took her by surprise.

In the past days in this hospital, filling the role of big sister, attentive daughter, and full-fledged member of the Braun and Koeppler families, Beth had found her niche. She closed her eyes for a moment, sending a silent thank-you heavenward to God for opening her heart to the place He had planned for her to call home.

Mom cleared her throat, capturing Beth's attention. Beth raised her gaze, and Mom gestured with her chin toward the large, plate-glass windows that faced the nursery. Turning her head, Beth located Henry standing outside the glass.

Certain he wanted to trade places with her, she offered him a quick smile and nod and slipped her hand from the Isolette. When she looked again toward the window, Henry was gone. In his place stood a tall man with red-gold hair and a neatly trimmed mustache. She clutched her hand to her chest, her jaw dropping.

Sean?

THIRTY

Beth rounded the corner from the nursery. Henry stood right outside, and he briefly touched her hand as she passed him. She paused long enough to give him a smile and nod, then crossed on quivery legs to stop several feet from Sean. Only then did she see that he held a huge cluster of flowers, daisies in every color of the rainbow tied with an abundance of lavender ribbon.

Her gaze bounced from the bouquet to his eyes.

The blue-green eyes crinkled into a self-conscious smile, and he lifted the bouquet. "These are for your mother when she comes out."

"Oh." To her surprise, she was more touched than disappointed. "That's sweet." Although she'd left the nursery, she still whispered. She took two steps forward, closing half the distance between them. "But how did you know where to find us?"

Sean's boyish shrug made Beth's lips twitch with a grin. "I called the studio. Andrew was there, and he told me which hospital. Then I just went online and did some hunting for directions. And here I am."

Here you are. Beth's heart pounded as if she'd just run a race. She pressed her hand to her chest once more, willing things to settle down.

"I—I brought some things for the babies, too. But your dad told me you weren't allowed to have stuff in the nursery, so they're in the waiting room."

"*Your dad*". . ."*dad*". . . ."*dad*". . . The word echoed in Beth's head. She liked the way it sounded.

"Teddy bears."

It took a moment to process the meaning of Sean's simple sentence. "You brought teddy bears?" She tried to picture him in a store, picking up stuffed toys. It was easier to envision him behind a desk or a computer.

"Yes. I figured. . .babies. . .toys. . .something soft." He swallowed, the gulp audible in the quiet hallway. "I brought one for you, too."

Beth's eyes flew wide. "For me?"

"It only seemed fair. Everybody else got something, so. . ." His voice trailed off.

They stood in silence, staring at each other, with Sean clutching the bouquet of flowers against his thigh and Beth clasping her hands against her rib cage. The flowers seemed to tremble, capturing Beth's attention.

"Should we go find some water to put those in?"

"What?" Sean appeared startled; then he jerked the bouquet up as if he'd just noticed it. "Yes. That would be great."

"There's a gift shop on the main floor." Beth pointed toward the elevators. "Shall we?"

Sean followed her, and once inside the elevator, he said, "Beth, after we get the vase, can you take some time and. . .visit. . .with my father and me. . .in the lobby?"

"Your father is here, too?" Beth couldn't believe the two men would travel all the way from Kansas City to deliver flowers and teddy bears to a woman they'd never met and her newborn children.

The doors slid open, and they stepped into a bustling hallway.

"Yes. I'll explain later, okay? Right now, let's take care of these."

It didn't take long to choose a clear, fat vase that would hold the bouquet. After paying for it, Sean said, "Why don't you take it up to the waiting room? I'll stay down here and wait for you. My father"—he pointed—"is over there."

Beth spotted a man sitting with his elbows on his knees and his fingers interlocked, who appeared to be five or six years older than Henry. She could see a resemblance to Sean in the square jaw and unusual eyes, but the older man's hair had faded to a dusty peach. Beth wondered briefly if Sean's hair would do the same given time. Embarrassed by her thoughts, she gave a brusque nod and backed toward the elevator.

"I'll be right back."

To her relief, her parents hadn't returned, so she could slip in and out quickly. She left the flowers on the table in the corner and hurried back to the elevator. Her heart hammered, but she couldn't decide if it was excitement at seeing Sean, nervousness about what his father might say to her since she hadn't finished the project, or uncertainty about what lay ahead.

When she approached the two men, they both stood up.

Sean said, "Beth, I'd like you to meet my father, Evan McCauley. Dad, this is Beth Quinn."

Sean's father held his hand out to her. "Miss Quinn, it's nice to meet you." His grip was firm and warm, his expression serious but not intimidating.

"Likewise, but please call me Beth."

The older man gestured to a chair that he had apparently pulled near to create a triangle of seats in the corner. Beth sat, and the two men followed suit. Mr. McCauley assumed the same position she'd seen earlier—hunched forward, resting his weight on his elbows. It made him seem tired and somehow sad, and Beth felt her heart lurch in a sympathy she didn't quite understand.

"Miss Quinn, as you know, we had planned to meet with you today at your studio and complete our arrangements to utilize your skills for future projects."

Beth's chin jerked into a brief nod. "Yes, sir, I know." She didn't apologize. She had done that on the telephone with him, and she didn't see the need. Another apology would sound like an excuse, and she wouldn't excuse her choice. She knew—as difficult as it had been—her choice had been the right one.

The man fitted his fingers together and stared at his thumbs as he continued. "Before driving to Wichita, we stopped by Sommerfeld. Your employee—tall man, dark hair. . ."

"Andrew," Sean and Beth supplied at the same time. They exchanged a quick glance.

"Andrew," Mr. McCauley repeated, "let us look at the incomplete project. It was. . ."

Beth held her breath.

"Amazingly done."

Her breath whooshed out.

Mr. McCauley sat upright. "Even unfinished, the elements of depth were in place. When the piece is complete, it will be magnificent."

"Thank you, sir." Beth glanced quickly at Sean before facing his father again. "Even though you won't be using it, I plan to finish it. It will go into storage for a while, and then I'd like to use it as the front window for my gallery when I'm finally able to open it."

"No."

The blunt response took Beth by surprise. "Sir?"

He shook his head, his brow low. "No, it won't be available for that purpose. Because we will be purchasing it from you."

Beth hadn't thought her heart could race any faster, but it proved her wrong. It was now a steady hum. "B–but I didn't meet the contingency. So the contract with you is void. You aren't obligated to purchase it."

"Obligated, no. But interested? Yes." His heavy brows hooded his eyes, but Beth could see a slight twinkle in their depths. "And it won't be the last window we purchase from you."

Beth looked back and forth between the men, her mouth open in a silent plea for an explanation. Both men held grins that told of a secret yet to be divulged. She turned toward Sean—the one with whom she felt comfortable—and said, "What are you trying to say?"

Although Sean offered no verbal reply, she was certain she read an answer in his steady gaze. The hum in her chest changed to a booming Sousa march.

"Miss Quinn—Beth." Mr. McCauley's deep voice pulled her attention from the son. "Sean and I had a lengthy conversation about. . . dedication. . .and commitment. It has always been my policy to meet—every—deadline." He slapped the backs of his fingers into his palm to emphasize each word. "I saw it as good business sense, and I haven't changed my stance on that one iota. But. . ."

His eyes shifted to Sean, and his expression softened. In his warm look, Beth read a silent thank-you that raised her curiosity.

"I've also come to realize there is something more important than honoring business commitments, and that is honoring one's commitment to faith and family." He leaned forward, bringing his face closer to hers. "We've seen the evidence of your skill. We know you have the ability to do the job. And your choosing to put the needs of your family above all else tells me you have the dedication we're seeking when adding to the McCauley team.

"So, Beth, if you are still interested in signing a long-term contract and designing windows for churches, starting with the ones in Carlton and Denver, then we are very interested and eager to finalize those plans."

Beth's hand shot out. "I'm interested, sir. And thank you."

He sandwiched her hand between his. "Thank *you*." He rose, his hands slipping away. "I have the paperwork drawn up. We took a room at the hotel across from the hospital. Sean can bring you over later and we'll make it official, hmm? But for now. . ." He looked at his son, and Beth was certain she saw him wink. "I believe I'll go over and lie down for a bit. The long drive has worn me out. Sean, I assume you'll want to stay here and visit with Beth?"

"Yes." But Sean looked at Beth when he answered.

"In about an hour then." The man strode away.

Beth watched until Mr. McCauley's broad back disappeared through the wide double doors leading outside, then she turned to face Sean. "Do you want to—"

"Should we—" he said at the same time.

They both laughed, and he held out his hand, giving her the floor.

"Do you want to go outside? There's a small bench where we could sit and talk."

"Clouds were gathering in the west as we drove over. We could get wet."

"I'm willing to take the chance," Beth said. "I could really use the fresh air."

Sean nodded his agreement. He followed as she led him toward the outside doors. "I would imagine you're tired of being cooped up here."

Beth shrugged. "I'm used to being cooped up in the studio, but you're right that it's different here." She pulled in a deep breath of the crisp, scented air as she seated herself on the bench. Sean gave his pant legs a little tug before sitting on the other end. When he was settled just a few inches from her, Beth continued. "Still, I wouldn't have traded my time here for anything. It has helped me develop a much deeper appreciation for my family and helped me put things into perspective. I guess you could say this has been a growing time."

"For my dad and me, too," Sean said, looking to the side. She sensed there was more he was thinking, but he didn't divulge it.

"It has also," she continued, watching his gaze come back around to meet hers, "convinced me without a doubt that my studio—and I—belong in Sommerfeld." She searched his face for signs of disappointment. Since he'd previously indicated the wisdom of relocating, she hoped he and his father hadn't made that a part of her contract. She wouldn't be able to sign if that stipulation was added.

Sean nodded, seemingly unconcerned. "I assumed that when I saw the addition."

Beth slapped her hands to her face. With her focus on Mom and the babies, she'd completely forgotten about the addition. "You saw it? The men finished it?"

"All but the shingles, from the looks of things." Sean smiled, seeming to find humor in her amazement. "Of course, the wall separating the two halves is still in place, so you could hardly consider it a finished job, but I could see the potential. You'll have quite the work area, plus room for an office, if need be."

Beth nodded in slow motion, picturing it. Although she hadn't originally considered including an office space, the idea held merit. Especially if there were several workers on a daily basis, she might need a quiet spot to get away and think.

"If I were you," Sean went on, his forehead creased thoughtfully, "I would put the office in the southeast corner. That way when you get your showroom up, the office will be close enough for you to be available to customers."

Beth bit down on her lip, but she couldn't stop a smile from growing. "Are you planning my studio for me now?"

A boyish grin made her heart skip a beat. "Just a suggestion. . . from someone who plans buildings for a living."

She assumed a high-chinned, formal posture, her lips still twitching. "I'll take that under advisement, Mr. McCauley." Dropping the playful pose, she said, "So it won't be a problem, having my studio so far away from the main office?"

Sean crossed one leg over the other and grasped his knee with both hands, staring at the horizon. "It won't be a problem at all. My reason for wanting you to consider moving was. . .selfish." He flicked a glance in her direction.

She offered a warm smile, which she hoped would encourage him to continue.

He faced her fully. "I admit from the first time we met I've had a difficult time separating our business relationship from a personal one. I wanted you closer. So I could get to know you. . .better."

Beth swallowed. She stretched out her hand and touched his elbow. "I've had the same thoughts, Sean. But I don't know how it could work. Long-distance relationships are pretty hard to maintain. I. . .I can't leave Sommerfeld. It's where God has planted me, and I won't step outside of His will. But your office is in Kansas City." She stopped, the ramifications of the statement bringing a crush of sorrow to her chest.

So slowly she almost thought she imagined movement, his hand slid across the bench until his fingers found her hand. He didn't squeeze, just held her fingers loosely within his. "You know, Beth, my job—drawing blueprints and planning—can be done wherever I choose."

He paused, his gaze seeming to seek her face for silent messages. "With the Internet and fax machines, I can communicate with anyone, anywhere in the world. I'm not limited to working in Kansas City."

Beth's booming heart nearly stole her breath. She understood what he was saying. But things were moving so rapidly she couldn't form a reply.

His lips tipped into a warm smile, and his hand gave hers a squeeze. "But we can talk about that another time. There will be time, since we'll need to be in communication concerning our business relationship. The other? We'll wait for God's leading."

"Can we pray about it now?" Beth blurted out the question, then felt her cheeks fill with heat at her impatience.

Sean didn't laugh. He nodded and bowed his head, and Beth followed suit. She listened as he thanked God for the opportunity to work together to create houses of worship that would meet the needs of congregations both spiritually and aesthetically. Her breath tripped raggedly as he requested guidance concerning their future together. "Lord, whatever You have planned, we are open to Your will. Lead us on Your pathway, please, and may we always bring glory to You as we journey, whether together or individually. Amen."

A distant rumble sounded, alerting them that Sean's prediction of rain could certainly prove true. But they remained on the bench, fingers linked, enjoying the moment of communion they had shared. Beth's chest filled with gratitude for God's hand bringing her to the point of belonging—with Him, with her family, with the community that she now considered her own, and with Sean. Giving Sean's hand a gentle squeeze, she offered a smile she was certain he understood.

A plop of something wet smacked the top of her head. Two more drops landed on her shoulder and lap.

"Here it comes!" Sean said with a laugh.

And come it did! Raindrops pelted them, warm and redolent and renewing. They jumped to their feet, their hands still clasped, and dashed toward the safety of the building. Beneath the brief overhang, they came to a laughing stop. Beth's back pressed securely to Sean's side with her head on his shoulder, and his arms loosely circled her waist.

Together they watched the rain gently bless the earth with moisture. With each patter, Beth envisioned a new blessing from God. Her lips formed the words without effort. "Thank You, Father, for everything."

And Sean's tender voice echoed, "Amen."

Discussion Questions

1. Beth is a new Christian in the beginning of the story, trying to find her "fit" in God's family. What practices did she employ to strengthen her relationship with God? What things could she have done differently?

2. Andrew views the success of Beth's studio as his means of deliverance. How does this viewpoint color his behavior?

3. Beth desires to use her talent to bring glory to God. In what ways do her actions support that desire? In what ways does she stumble?

4. Despite remaining in the community, Beth continues to feel like a misfit. Why does she harbor those feelings? What could she have done differently to help herself "fit in"?

5. Because Beth has never known a father's love, she feels as though she carries a hole in her heart. She tried to fill that empty place by throwing herself into her studio. Was she successful?

6. Considering the void in Beth's life, what relationship could help her fill the emptiness—with God, with Henry, with her grandfather, or with Andrew or Sean? How do we try to fill the empty places in our lives? What advice would God offer to help us feel complete?

7. Sean's company goal is to glorify God. Did his actions substantiate that goal? Was he following God's lead or his father's lead in his business relationships? Which should be more important?

8. Due to Mitch's choices, Beth has a difficult time trusting. What choices made by others influence how you react to people today? How can we overcome the impact of the past so it doesn't negatively affect our present?

9. It took an emergency for Beth to realize she had Henry's love and the extended family's acceptance. Why does it sometimes take an extreme situation to awaken us to truth?

10. Andrew pressured Beth to put the studio commitment ahead of familial commitment. Was he right in advising her to honor the contract? What was his motivation for the advice he offered?

11. What changes can you see in Beth's spiritual life from the beginning of the story to the end? What was the source of these changes?

12. Beth's life in Sommerfeld is completely different from the life she had planned in Cheyenne. She believed God orchestrated the events that led her to establishing the studio in Sommerfeld. Does God open doors, or do doors open by happenstance? How can we know whether we are in God's will or simply responding to "opportunity"?

13. When facing the uncertainty of the future, Beth suggests she and Sean pray for guidance. What does this show about Beth's spiritual maturity? Do you seek God's guidance before moving forward? Does it make a difference?

BLESSINGS

DEDICATION

For Jacob Dean,
the unexpected blessing added to our family.
I know God has something special planned for you,
little one—seek His face and heed His voice.
Joy will surely follow.

ACKNOWLEDGMENTS

When I count the blessings in my life, family tops the list: Mom, Daddy, Don, my dear daughters and precious grandsons. . . . Walking this pathway with your encouragement is a joy beyond description. Thanks, too, to my wonderful parents-in-law and the whole Sawyer clan—I'm so blessed to be a part of your family.

They say old friends are gold, and I am rich in the decades-long blessing of friendship with Kathy Henson, Phil Zielke, and Vicki Johansen. Thank you for your steadfast presence in my life.

Prayer support is crucial in any ministry, and so many lift my writing to the Father: Connie, Rose, Carla, Cynthia, Ramona, Kathy A., Don and Ann, Ernie, Ginny, Brother Ray, my "posse" members. . . . May God bless you as abundantly as you have blessed me.

Becky and the staff at Barbour: Thank you for the opportunity to bring Sommerfeld and its citizens to life. What a pleasure it has been!

Finally, and most importantly, thanks be to God, who blesses me beyond my deserving and uses me even in my failings. May any praise or glory be reflected directly back to You.

The blessing of the LORD, it maketh rich,
and he addeth no sorrow with it.

PROVERBS 10:22

ONE

Trina Muller set the plates of hamburgers, grilled onions, and french fries in front of the booth's occupants. Straightening, she flipped the white ribbons of her cap behind her shoulders and formed an automatic smile. "Can I get you anything else?"

Even though she used her cheerful, attentive, I'm-here-to-meet-your-needs tone, her gaze drifted out the window. A row of cars drove by the café, headed south toward the highway. She stifled the sigh that rose in her chest.

"Ketchup and mustard, please," the man said.

With a nod, Trina turned from the table. Her tennis shoes squeaked against the tile floor—a familiar sound. She retrieved red and yellow squirt bottles from a small refrigerator in the corner of the dining room then carried them to the table. A glance out the window confirmed the last car had departed for Newton. The sigh escaped.

Forcing herself to look at the couple seated in the window booth, she said, "Enjoy your meal."

Trina made the rounds, coffeepot in hand. She carried on her normal banter, smiling, meeting the needs of the café's patrons, treating Mennonites and non-Mennonites with equal affability. But her feet felt leaden and her smile stiff. Her heart simply was not in the task.

Right now her friends—including Graham—were on their way to the skating rink for an evening of fun and relaxation. But as usual, Trina was stuck in the café. Waiting tables. Washing dishes. Honoring Mama and Dad like the good girl she'd always been—the good girl she had always wanted to be. When had this uncomfortable resentment started? And how could she set it aside and go back to being the cheerful, obedient Trina?

Or did she really want to be that Trina anymore?

She wrung out a soapy cloth and used it to scrub a table clean, pocketing the single bill and coins left behind to thank her for her service. She fingered the coins in her apron pocket, thinking about the growing savings account at the bank in McPherson. In the six years she'd worked at the café—first for the original owner, Lisbeth Koeppler, then for Lisbeth's heirs, and now for her own mother—she had rarely spent the money she earned.

Since she and Graham began openly courting, he paid for the occasional dinners out and their skating expeditions. According to Mama, a girl needed only so many dresses—an overstuffed wardrobe was prideful. Books, her main source of amusement, were reasonable when purchased from the used-books shelf at the bookstore she and her friends patronized in Newton. Of course, her parents might disapprove of a few of the titles she'd chosen, but she had reasons for buying what she did. And even with the number of book purchases, the account steadily grew.

Her hand paused on the table's glossy surface; her lips sucked in. Surely, she had enough for one year. Maybe a year and a half. A good start, certainly. If only—

"Trina?"

Her mother's voice jarred her out of her thoughts. She trotted to the doorway between the kitchen and dining room where Mama stood. "Yes?"

"I see some empty plates on tables. Have you asked if people want their checks?" Although Mama kept her voice low, disapproval came through the tone.

Trina felt heat fill her cheeks. "I'll do it now."

"Good." Mama pursed her lips, her brows low. "This daydreaming must stop, Trina. Stay focused on your work."

Trina nodded. A shoddy workman displeased the Lord—Trina knew this well. Guilt propelled her across the tiled floor to a table Mama had pointed out. "I'm sorry for the delay. Did you save room for pie this evening? We have a lovely lemon meringue made from scratch."

She went through the normal routine of slipping the check onto the table and clearing the dishes, but despite her efforts to remain on task, her thoughts drifted again. Maybe she knew these tasks too well. The familiar routine offered no challenge, no true problem-solving. Not like—

The door to the café burst open, bringing in a flow of warm evening air. Her cousin Andrew Braun rushed toward her. He left his bill cap in place over his dark hair, a clue that something was amiss. The fine hairs on the back of Trina's neck prickled.

"Trina, can you come out to the house? It's Regen—his leg. I tried calling Dr. Groening, but his wife said he's out. She'll give him the message, but I don't know how long he'll be."

Trina untied her apron and slipped it over her head, careful to avoid dislodging her cap. "Of course I'll come." Regen, the sorrel quarter horse Andrew had purchased for his wife's wedding gift, was more pet than working animal, since Andrew didn't farm. But they relied on him to pull the vintage carriage Livvy's grandparents had bequeathed

581

to her, giving rides to visitors to Sommerfeld every Saturday afternoon and many summer evenings. "Livvy must be beside herself."

"She's worried," Andrew confirmed, his expression grim. He lowered his voice. "Trina, it doesn't look good."

Trina's heart pounded. Throwing the apron behind the counter that held the cash register, she darted into the kitchen. "Mama, Andrew is here. He needs me to go with him—Livvy's horse was hurt."

Trina watched her mother's gaze lift to the clock on the wall before giving a nod of approval. "Go ahead. It's only an hour to closing time. I'll call Tony and have him come help me clean up."

Even before her mother had finished speaking, Trina caught Andrew's arm and hurried him out of the café. They climbed into his pickup, which waited at the curb with its engine rumbling. Andrew pulled into the street and headed east.

"What happened?" Trina asked. Wind coursed through the open window, tossing the string ties of her cap. She caught the ribbons and held them beneath her chin.

He snatched off his cap, threw it onto the seat between them, and ran his hand over his short hair. "Livvy went into the corral to throw Regen some hay. She leaned the pitchfork against the fence while she went to drag the hose out to the corral and fill the water tank, and somehow the horse caught his foot between the tines of the fork. She heard a pop, and he wouldn't put his weight on the leg." He grimaced. "She stayed out with him until I came home rather than calling the vet, and by the time I got there, the cannon on the injured leg had swelled up like a balloon. It looks bad."

A pop could mean tendon or ligament damage or a misplaced knee. Trina immediately began running through a list of possible treatments. "How long ago did he injure himself?"

"At least two hours." He shot her a brief, grateful glance. "I'm glad you were there. I was afraid you might have gone skating."

Her mother had insisted Trina stay at the café and work rather than going to the skating rink with the other community young people. Sometimes on skating nights, a teenage member of the fellowship, Kelly Dick, came in to help so Trina could have the evening off, but this time Mama had said no. Although both Graham and Trina had experienced frustration at her refusal to let Trina go, now relief washed over Trina. *Thank You, Lord, that I was here. . . .*

Andrew barely slowed to make the final turn into his long driveway. Trina grabbed the dash to keep from tipping sideways. Dust swirled alongside the truck and wafted through the window, making her sneeze. He pulled up beside the barn and killed the engine.

Trina hopped out, ducked between the crossbars of the fence, and ran to where Livvy stood, petting the length of Regen's nose. Tears of grief and worry rained down Livvy's pale cheeks. Her work dress and apron looked sodden and soiled, giving evidence of her long vigil in the summer sun and gusting wind. The horse tapped the shoe of his injured leg in the dirt and released soft snorts of distress, but he made no effort to move away from his mistress. Trina dropped to her knees in front of the powerful animal and ran her hands down his leg. She didn't need to feel the swelling to know it was there. The horse's leg bulged midway between his knee and pastern on his right foreleg.

"Must've torn a ligament," she muttered. Rising, she glanced at Livvy's frantic face and turned to Andrew. "Get me some burlap, two or three bags of frozen corn, and about three yards of elastic."

Without a question, Andrew spun on his boot heel and jogged toward the house.

"Livvy, can you lead Regen to the barn?" Trina gentled her voice when speaking to her cousin's wife. "He'll be more comfortable in there."

"Are you sure we should let him walk on it?"

Trina drew in a slow breath and held it. She wasn't sure putting pressure on it was a good idea, but she knew they couldn't leave the poor animal outside. The summer heat was sweltering during the day—he'd be better off in the barn, where he'd have shade and protection. Her breath whooshed out with her emphatic nod. "I think it's best."

Livvy nodded. Her arm curled around the underside of Regen's jaw, she crooned, "C'mon, pretty boy. Come with me. . . ." Slowly, she led the limping animal into the barn. Trina trailed behind, watching Regen's legs.

Inside the barn, Livvy led Regen to his stall. "Should I let him lie down?"

"No. I need him up to—"

Andrew trotted in, his arms full. He plopped two clear plastic bags of homegrown frozen corn and a snarl of one-inch-wide elastic at Trina's feet. "Here you go, Trina—corn and elastic." Pressing a soft bundle of worn cloth into her hands, he added, "And one of Livvy's aprons so you don't get your dress all dirty. I've got burlap in the storeroom. Hang on." He dashed toward the back of the barn.

Trina tied the apron in place while Livvy sent her a puzzled look. "What are you going to do with the corn?"

Trina knelt and began to untangle the elastic. "It'll stay cold, which makes it a good compress. But I need to protect his leg with the burlap first so it isn't too cold against his skin. The elastic will hold it in place, and as the swelling goes down, it will continue to hold the compress against his leg."

Livvy shook her head, stroking Regen's neck and forehead. "I hope it works."

"Me, too."

Andrew trotted to Trina's side, a bulky, rolled burlap bag in his hands. She squinted up at him. "Can you help me?"

Andrew crouched on the other side of Regen's leg. "What do you want me to do?"

"Wrap the burlap around his leg first, to provide some protection from the cold corn, but don't make it too tight." Andrew held the coarse fabric in place while Trina grabbed the bags of corn. Although Regen nosed the back of Trina's head, blowing air down the back of her neck, he remained still under their ministrations. She placed one bag on either side of Regen's leg. "Okay, wrap the burlap around the corn now." As Andrew followed her directions, she slipped her hands free. "Hold it." Andrew kept the burlap and corn from slipping. Trina wrapped the elastic around several times and then tied it in place.

Andrew moved out of the way as she felt around the bulky compress, frowning. It needed to be tight enough to hold but not so tight it cut off circulation. Satisfied the compress would hold without hurting the animal, she sank back in the hay and looked up at Livvy. "You've been standing in the corral for quite a while. Why don't you go in and get a drink?"

Livvy's arms crept around the horse's neck. "I don't want to leave him."

"I'll stay right here, and so will Andrew," Trina promised. "If you'd call the café and let Mama know I'll be out here the rest of the evening, I'd appreciate it, too."

Livvy pursed her lips, her brow furrowing, but she nodded. "All right. But I'll be back soon." She gave Regen another loving stroke from his forehead to his nose before turning away.

Andrew watched his wife until she exited the barn. Then he faced Trina. "Do you think the horse will be all right? I don't know how she'd take it if we had to—"

"You won't have to put him down." Trina squeezed her cousin's arm. "It isn't bad enough for that. But. . ." She paused, swallowing. "It'll be a long time before he can do any work, Andrew. If he's torn a ligament, it'll take months of healing."

"Well, even though we'll miss the income those carriage rides bring in, I won't complain. Not as long as he'll be okay again." A slight smile curved his lips. "I'll never forget when I brought him home. It was raining cats and dogs, and Livvy got drenched to the skin, but she stood outside in the downpour and kept stroking his nose and talking to him. That's why she chose *Regensturm* for his name, you know—in honor of the rainstorm." Andrew sighed. "Liv looks at this horse like a child."

Trina smiled, smoothing her skirt over her knees to protect her bare skin from the scratchy hay. "She'll quit that once you have children to spoil." She knew Livvy was seeing a special doctor in Wichita for the purpose of having a baby.

"I suppose. . ."

"In the meantime, we'll take good care of Regen so there won't be permanent damage." She pushed to her feet. "While we wait for Dr. Groening, let's get some rigging set up to get the weight off Regen's leg."

Andrew rose. "What do you suggest? Rope would cut into his skin, I would think."

After a brief discussion, they decided a loop of sturdy gabardine, which Livvy had purchased for quilt backing, slung beneath the horse's belly and over the crossbeam, would provide enough support without chafing his skin. When Andrew returned with the fabric, Livvy trailed him back to the barn. Trina gave her the task of talking to Regen and rubbing his nose to keep him calm.

After a half hour of trial and error, experimenting with fabric, rope, and pulleys, they finally managed to provide a means of support for Regen. They stood back, hands on hips, looking at the animal to see if he'd be okay. He whickered softly, but he stopped tapping the sore leg against the ground.

Trina smiled. "I think that's done the trick." She pointed. "He's not trying to stamp, so it must not be bothering him as much."

"Good." Andrew wiped his brow, whistling through his teeth. "That was a chore!"

"But worth it," Livvy said, stepping forward to caress the horse's jaw. "I can tell it's helped him." The woman and horse rubbed noses.

Trina, watching Livvy with Regen, felt a rush of satisfaction. Her hour with Regen had given her more pleasure than her years of waitress work. If only she could spend all of her days helping animals.

The sound of a vehicle pulling into the yard captured their attention. Andrew headed for the barn's wide door. "That's probably Dr. Groening. I'll bring him in."

Trina linked her fingers together and waited anxiously as Dr. Groening examined Regen's leg and ran his hand under the cloth loop. Finally, he turned and put his hand on Trina's shoulder. "You've done everything exactly right here. Bringing the swelling down and getting the pressure off the leg is just what I would have prescribed."

Trina nearly wilted with relief. "Oh, thank you! I'd never want to do anything harmful to an animal."

His fingers squeezed gently before slipping away. "I know." The older man's thick gray brows lowered. "You have an innate ability, young lady."

"Well. . ." Trina crunched her lips into a grimace. "I got the idea from a book I bought on horse care." It had been one of the pricier of her purchases, but the book, with its veterinary guide, was a wealth of information.

"So you're still studying," the doctor said, lowering his tone to a near whisper.

Trina nodded. The string ties of her cap tickled her chin, reminding her of the futility of her study. Never, never, never would Mama and Dad allow her to get the schooling she'd need to be a veterinarian. Not as long as she wore her Mennonite cap.

Two

The sympathy in Dr. Groening's eyes communicated his understanding of Trina's dilemma. Three years ago, she had confided her interest in animal care to the kindly veterinarian from Lehigh and asked how she could become an animal doctor. His brief explanation—a college degree—had crushed her.

Attending college was out of the question. She knew that. But she had finally decided she could study on her own, learn for her own interest, and maybe do some good in her community. What she'd just done for Regen proved to her that all her reading hadn't been a waste of time.

Offering the doctor a weak smile, she nodded. "I buy as many books as I can find at the store in Newton."

"And study on your own. . ." Dr. Groening shook his head, his eyes sad.

"It's better than nothing." Trina forced a light tone, but resentment pressed at her breast. Why couldn't she go to college and become a veterinarian? It wasn't fair!

"Well," Dr. Groening said, clapping his palms together and turning to Andrew and Livvy, "the work you started here won't end soon. You'll have to keep applying cold compresses to the leg—probably through the night—and then each time the swelling comes up again." He stepped forward and patted the horse's neck. "This big boy won't be doing any work for a while, either. You'll need to keep him still for at least two weeks, then only gentle exercise—walking, no trotting or running—for another two to three months."

"It's that bad?" Livvy clasped Andrew's hand. Her wide eyes brimmed with tears.

"It could be worse," the doctor said. "But the treatment you started here helped a lot. Be grateful." He gave the horse's broad neck one more pat and turned to Trina. "Will you be staying?"

Trina nodded. Her parents would have to understand.

"Then he's in good hands," Dr. Groening said to Andrew and Livvy. "I'll be back tomorrow afternoon to check on him. Call if something changes. In the meantime, Trina, I'll leave you some reusable cold packs you can use in place of the corn." He grinned. "You'll clear out the freezer in no time using corn, but it was a perfect choice in a pinch."

Trina followed the doctor to his pickup.

He opened a metal box in the truck's bed and pulled out four rectangular, plastic-covered cold packs. "Alternate these between the freezer and Regen's leg. They're good for three hours before they need to be traded out."

"I will. And thanks again, Dr. Groening."

"You're welcome, Trina." He opened his truck door then paused and sent her a speculative look. "You still work in your mother's café?"

"Yes, sir."

"Do you ever think about doing something else?"

All the time. She lifted her shoulders in a shrug.

He smiled, seeming to understand her silence. "Well, if you ever decide on a change, I could use an assistant at the clinic. My helper heads off to college this fall, and he's decided to take the summer off to play. I need to replace him. You'd learn a lot."

Trina's heart pounded. She licked her lips. "Thanks, Dr. Groening. I'll–I'll give it some thought."

"Good." He hopped into his pickup and closed the door. With a wave of his hand out the open window, he pulled away.

Trina watched the truck head down the driveway, her heart thudding with desire to run, jump into the bed of that truck, and learn everything she could from the aging doctor.

Graham Ortmann slammed the car's back door closed and leaned against his friend's blue sedan. Laughter floated across the calm, late-evening breeze as the other young people from Sommerfeld stepped out of their vehicles to say good-bye to the group before heading to their respective homes.

"You want me to drop you off at your place, Graham?" Walt asked.

Graham shook his head, gesturing with his thumb toward the café, where lights still glowed behind the windows even though it was past closing time. "Looks to me like Mrs. Muller and Trina are still cleaning up. I'll head over there and see if Mrs. Muller will let me walk Trina home."

Walt snorted. "Good luck. The Mullers keep Trina tied to her mother's apron strings."

"I know." Most of the Old Order Mennonite parents were protective, but Troy and Deborah Muller carried it to the extreme.

"Might be easier to walk Susan or Darcy home instead," Walt

suggested, a grin creasing his face. "They'd be willing, I'm sure."

Graham glanced across the car's hood. The two young women Walt referenced stood on the sidewalk in front of Koeppler's Feed and Seed, their capped heads close together. Even with the evening shadows limiting his sight, he knew they were watching him. He sighed and turned back to Walt.

"It might be easier to court another girl, but I don't want another girl. Trina's the only one for me." He'd spent more than a year getting up his nerve to ask Trina's parents for permission to spend time with her. Their six months of visits, walks, singings at local homes, and skating parties convinced him that he and Trina were a perfect match. As soon as she turned twenty—only six more months—they would publish their relationship and plan a wedding. Or maybe they could be published now. Nineteen wasn't too young. His heart picked up its tempo at the thought.

"Well, good luck to you." Walt gave Graham's shoulder a hearty smack. He chuckled softly. "I think you'll need it."

Graham pushed off from the car and headed down the sidewalk toward the café. He frowned as he thought of Walt's words. He didn't need luck. Luck was for worldly people—people who lacked faith. Graham had prayed about seeking a wife, and he knew Trina was the right choice.

Easily the cutest girl in the fellowship with her spattering of freckles and sweetly upturned nose, she exuded an innocence and spark for life that made a person happy just to be near her. He'd never met anyone with a more positive attitude. His feet sped up of their own volition as eagerness to see her, talk to her, steal a few minutes of her time urged him forward.

The café door was locked, but when he tapped on the glass, Trina's younger brother, Tony, trotted from the kitchen and unlocked it. "Hi,

Graham. How was the skating?"

"Fun." Graham limited his reply. Tony, at fifteen, was too young for the skating parties, but in another couple of years, he'd be able to join the group. No sense in getting the boy stirred up at what he was missing. He followed Tony to the kitchen. "I came to see if I could walk Trina home."

Mrs. Muller turned from the stove, a dripping cloth in her hand. "Trina isn't here, Graham. Andrew stopped by a couple of hours ago and took her to the farm. Livvy's horse was injured somehow. Livvy called again about an hour ago and said Trina would be staying all night."

Even though disappointment struck, Graham's heart swelled with pride. Of course, Trina would go if an animal needed her. Trina's compassionate concern for all creatures was just another reason he loved her so much. "I hope the horse will be all right."

Mrs. Muller turned back to the stove. "I don't know. Livvy said it was a bad injury, but they were doing what they could."

Graham scratched his chin, wondering if he should drive out and check on Trina. Her cousin would be there to provide chaperonage, so it wouldn't be indecent. He lifted his gaze and found Mrs. Muller watching him with narrowed eyes. He felt a blush building, certain she read his thoughts.

He backed toward the kitchen door. "Well, I'll let you finish up, then. Tell Trina I stopped by, please."

"I will." Mrs. Muller put the scrub rag to work.

Graham waved to Tony then headed out of the café. Outside, he stood for a moment, looking at the glittering stars and debating with himself. He'd had very little time with Trina this week, and he missed her. At the other end of the block, two cars remained in front of Koeppler's Feed and Seed—Walt was still there. Walt could drive Graham home, where he could get his own car and head out to Andrew and Livvy's place. Just to say hi and make sure the horse was doing okay.

Decision made, he broke into a jog. "Walt! Hey—I need a ride!"

The slam of a car door jolted Trina from dozing. She blinked, looking around the dusky barn. The lantern Andrew had hung from a nail on the stall post glowed softly, but outside the window, stars twinkled in a velvety sky. It was much too late for visitors. Maybe she'd imagined the car door—maybe she'd been dreaming.

Regen bounced his head, snorting softly. Livvy sat up from her nest in the hay and nudged Andrew. "Somebody's here." He yawned and pushed to his feet.

While Andrew went to check, Trina tossed aside the light blanket she'd used to cover herself. She crawled forward a few feet and pressed the compress on Regen's leg. The horse blew, but he didn't try to move his foot. "Good boy, Regen," she praised, gently pressing the compress. Certain it was still cold enough and well secured, she straightened to her feet and nuzzled the horse.

"Trina?" Andrew stood at the edge of the stall. Someone stood behind him—a man, judging by his attire—but he stood in Andrew's shadow, making it impossible to identify him.

"Dr. Groening?" she asked.

"No, it's me, Trina."

Trina's heart did a little somersault. She stumbled forward a few steps, squinting until she made out Graham's crooked smile. "How did you know I was out here?" She longed to reach for him, take his hands, but instead she tangled her hands in the folds of her borrowed apron.

"I stopped by the café. Your mom said you were here."

"Why did you come out?"

"I wanted to make sure the horse was okay."

Andrew took a sideways step away from the couple and held his hand to Livvy. "Let's go in and see if there's any more coffee in the pot."

Livvy flicked a quick glance at Trina and Graham. An understanding smile curved her lips, and she nodded.

Trina watched her cousin and his wife stride from the barn, gratitude filling her. Rarely did she and Graham have an uninterrupted minute alone. Andrew and Livvy had just given them a gift. She skipped forward, closing the distance between her and Graham. She was close enough for him to touch her if he wanted to.

His hands remained appropriately in his pants pockets, but his smile caressed her. "So is the horse going to be okay?" The question was completely impersonal, yet his tone managed to convey deep feeling.

"I hope so." Her words came out on a breathy sigh. "It'll be a long time before he's able to work, but we're praying the damage will heal."

Graham's swallow sounded loud in the peaceful barn. "But you need to stay all night?"

"Yes. The cold compresses must be changed every three hours. So Andrew and I are taking turns."

Graham nodded. For long moments neither spoke. Then Graham cleared his throat. "I missed you at the skating tonight."

Trina's heart twisted. "I know. I'm sorry. Mama insisted I work. But it's probably best since Regen needed me." She moved to the horse and stroked his neck, her gaze on Graham. "Dr. Groening said I did everything right for him." Although she knew pride was a sin, she couldn't stop the swell of satisfaction that filled her when she remembered the doctor's praise for her ministrations to the animal. She blurted, "He said I could work for him, if I wanted to."

Graham stepped forward and cupped the horse's nose. "Instead of the café?"

Trina nodded. "I could learn so much, spending time with him! And maybe—" She lowered her gaze. There was no sense in getting her hopes up. "Of course, Mama probably wouldn't let me."

Graham spoke, his breath brushing her cheek. "Talk to your folks. Maybe they'd say yes. You won't know until you try."

Raising her head slowly, she met Graham's tender gaze. She wished she possessed hope, but she knew her parents too well. They'd never approve it. Lehigh, although less than ten miles down the road, was too far away. "They'd say no. Mama would say she needs me in the café. And Dad would have to drive me to Lehigh every day since I haven't got my license."

"Well, maybe it's time for you to learn to drive," Graham said, "and for your mom to think about getting some other help. Because you won't be available to her at the café forever."

Her heart lurched. Although Graham had never uttered the word *marriage*, she knew his attentiveness indicated his interest. She also knew she wasn't averse to the idea. No other boy in the fellowship made her heart clop harder than the hooves of a runaway horse. She jerked her gaze downward and watched Graham's hands gently stroke Regen's soft nose. Her throat felt dry, and she swallowed hard. She chose an innocuous subject. "But Dad says he doesn't have time to teach me to drive."

"I can teach you."

"And Mama. . .she depends on me."

"There are other dependable girls in town."

His soft rebuttals to her arguments made something flutter through her middle. She peeked at him out of the corner of her eye. "You'd really teach me to drive?" *Dad would never approve it.*

He shrugged, grinning. "Sure. And I'll take you to Lehigh myself until you learn, if you start working for the vet."

Mama will never let me leave the café. "But I don't have a car." She waited for his response.

He opened his mouth, but Andrew and Livvy came in. Andrew carried a thermos jug, and Livvy held up four mugs. Andrew said, "Livvy fixed a fresh pot, so we can all have some."

Graham stepped well away from the horse, and Trina took the mug Livvy offered. Trina locked gazes with Graham, offering a smile she hoped communicated her regret for their interruption. His slow wink let her know he felt the same way. Trina experienced a prick of conscience—desiring to be alone with Graham was sinful. It could lead to trouble. Just as pursuing her desire to gain a license to treat animals would create problems.

She stifled a groan that pressed at the back of her throat. *God, why does everything I want seem to be wrong?*

THREE

Bright, early morning sun streaming through the barn's window wakened Trina. She stretched and yawned, opening her eyes by increments. When she could focus, her first sight was Regen, staring at her with wide, unblinking brown eyes.

She laughed. "Good morning, pretty boy." Crawling across the hay, she removed the compress and checked his leg. A smile grew on her face. "The swelling's way down." She stood and gave the horse a pat. "You'll be okay, big fella. It will just take time."

The barn door opened, and Andrew strode in with a cup of coffee in his hand. "Oh, you're awake. I was just going to get you up and take you into town." His gaze dropped to Regen's leg. "It looks a lot better, doesn't it?"

"Better, yes, but there's still some swelling. Dr. Groening said to keep the compresses on there until it was completely gone." She leaned over and scooped up the compress she'd removed. "I'll get a fresh one for him and put this one in the freezer."

Andrew caught her arm as she went to pass him. "Trina, your mom called. She needs you in the café."

Trina resisted rolling her eyes, knowing it was a disrespectful response, but it took great control. "I'll call her and tell her to get Kelly."

"She said Kelly is already there, helping her open up, but she needs you, too. With the farmers' market opening this weekend, she's overrun with customers."

Trina thrust out her jaw. "I need to take care of Regen."

Andrew's fingers pressed gently on her arm. "Livvy and I can put compresses on Regen's leg as well as you can, and I promise to call the café if something changes." Although his tone carried no reprimand, Trina knew he wanted her to obey Mama's direction.

She sighed. Her night with little sleep had left her droopy and out of sorts. Working in the café—especially on Saturday, the busiest day of the week even without the additional customers brought in by the farmers' market—would be less than pleasant. But she didn't have a choice. She must honor her parents. "All right. But take me home, not to the café—I've got to clean up."

He grinned. "I agree with that. You smell like the barn."

While he drove her back to town, she slurped the coffee he'd brought out. The hot, strong brew helped bring her to life. The drive was short—Andrew and Livvy lived little more than a mile outside of Sommerfeld on a small, four-acre plot surrounded by corn and alfalfa fields. In no time, Andrew pulled up in front of her parents' home. She set the empty coffee cup on the seat and leaned over to bestow a hug.

"Thanks for coming to get me when Regen got hurt." Her throat felt tight, and she swallowed. "It meant a lot to me, that you trusted me with him."

Andrew gave her back a pat before setting her aside. "There's no one I'd trust more."

Trina ducked her head, a huge sigh lifting her shoulders.

"Go get cleaned up," Andrew ordered in a gruff, big-brother tone, a mock scowl creasing his face. "Then march yourself down to that café and let your mother know you want to make a job change."

Trina stared at him.

His scowl turned into an impish grin. "I heard Dr. Groening mention the job at his clinic. You want to do it, don't you?"

Trina blew out a long breath. "More than anything. I wish—"

Andrew pinched her chin, his familiar gesture of affection. "Don't wish. Pray. If it's God's will, your parents will come around."

Trina knew Andrew spoke from experience. Although his father and brothers were farmers, Andrew spent his days working in the stained-glass art studio owned by Beth Quinn McCauley. At first, his father had opposed Andrew's desire to be an artist, but over time, he had released his antagonism and instead offered his blessing.

If only Mama and Dad would give in, like Uncle Al.

Andrew interrupted her thoughts. "Talk to your mother, Trina, and *pray.*" He gave her chin one more gentle pinch. "God can work things out."

"Thanks, Andrew." Trina bounded out of the truck and headed inside. After a bath and change of clothes, she felt more prepared to face the day. But by the time she reached the café, things were bustling, and she had no opportunity to talk to her mother. As the day dragged on, with an abundance of out-of-town patrons as well as the usual Sommerfeld residents taking advantage of Deborah Muller's Saturday specials, Trina's energy lagged, and her frustration grew. Even with her brother, Tony, and Kelly Dick helping, there was never a minute to sit and relax, let alone tell her mother about Dr. Groening's job opening.

She thought the last customers would never leave, but when they finally did, she still faced a mountain of work. Heaving a sigh, she filled the mop bucket and grabbed the mop, but then she stood, leaning on it, her eyes closed. Someone tapped her shoulder. Opening her eyes, she found Kelly grinning at her.

"Do you want me to mop?"

Trina chuckled, keeping her hands wrapped around the handle and her cheek pressed to her fist. "If you take the mop, I'll probably fall down."

Kelly laughed. "You've been dragging all day."

From the stove, Mama snorted. "Because she was out all night instead of sleeping."

Kelly's eyebrows shot up.

"My cousin's horse got hurt. I spent the night putting cold compresses on his leg." Trina maintained an even tone, although she wanted to snap at her mother. "So I didn't get much sleep, but the horse was much better this morning."

"That's good." Kelly glanced back and forth between the two Muller women, who glared across the floor at each other. She took a hesitant step toward the dishwasher. "Well, if you're going to mop, I guess I'll. . ." She waved her hand, indicating the stack of dishes.

"That's fine, Kelly. You've put in a good day already," Mama said. "You go ahead and go home." She turned toward the dining-room doorway and called, "Tony?"

Tony immediately appeared in the opening between the dining room and kitchen.

"Are you finished out there?"

"The money is in the bank envelope, the menus are stacked, the tables are clean," Tony listed, holding up his fingers and ticking off the accomplished tasks, "and the salt and pepper shakers are full. I haven't checked the napkin dispensers, though."

Mama nodded. "I'll take care of that. You walk Kelly home; then you can go home, too."

Trina nearly wilted, tiredness bringing the sting of tears behind her nose. How she wished to be released of the duties! But of course Mama would let the youngsters go. Since Trina was considered an adult, more was expected of her than of Tony and Kelly.

The moment the two younger teenagers headed out the back door, Mama pointed at the mop. "Let's finish up so we can leave, too." She began transferring dirty dishes from the cart to a washing tray.

With a sigh, Trina pushed the mop across the floor. Normally she took pleasure in watching the mop strings bunch and straighten with each push and pull, seeing the grime replaced by a shiny clean surface. But today, she just wanted to finish and be done. For good.

Her mind drifted to the edge of town, to Andrew's barn, where Regen rested his injured leg. She wondered what Dr. Groening had said when he visited as he'd promised. She hoped he was pleased with the decrease in swelling and had given Livvy encouraging words concerning Regen's future ability to pull the carriage. She'd heard a few café patrons mention their disappointment that no rides were available today. Andrew might need to borrow a horse from one of his brothers so they could still offer the carriage rides.

With the thought of Andrew came the reminder of his advice to talk to her mother about her desire to work for Dr. Groening. She glanced across the kitchen at her mother, whose hands moved steadily between the cart and tray. Busy hands. Mama had always had busy hands. Idle hands were the devil's workshop, she always said, which is why Trina and Tony had been encouraged to find jobs when their school years were complete.

Trina stifled a snort of frustration. As soon as Tony had finished the ninth grade, he chose to work for an Amish farmer who lived a few miles outside of Sommerfeld, and he drove himself there each day in an old pickup truck their Uncle Henry had fixed up. But Trina hadn't been given a choice. The day after her thirteenth birthday, Mama had marched her into the café and asked Miss Lisbeth Koeppler if she could use Trina's help after school and on weekends. Then when she finished her schooling, she automatically began working full-time at the café. Trina had grown to love Miss Koeppler, and she didn't regret the time she'd spent with the dear old woman, but now that Mama owned the café, Trina's help seemed to be expected.

Giving the mop bucket a firm push with the mop head, she propelled it across the floor to the utility sink. She watched the dirty water go down the drain, feeling as though her dreams went with it. She was nineteen already. Her folks—and Graham—would expect her to become a wife and a mother before too long. When would she be allowed to do what she wanted to do rather than what everyone else wanted her to do? The unfulfilled desires rose up strong enough to choke her.

Spinning from the sink, she raised her voice and called, "Mama? Can we talk?"

Mama shoved the last tray into the dishwasher, closed the door, and flipped the switch. The roar of running water echoed throughout the kitchen. "At home, Trina. Let's finish up here without delays, please."

Trina clamped her lips together and nodded. Might be better to wait until she was home and could talk to both parents at once, anyway. Even though Dad was strict, he was usually more reasonable than Mama. She headed to the dining room to refill the napkin dispensers.

When Trina and her mother reached their home, the sky was fully dark. Dad sat in the living room in an overstuffed chair shaped like his bulky form, a newspaper in his hands. He set the paper aside when they entered. "Ah, you're home."

Trina glanced at the ticking clock on the wall. With worship service in the morning, normally the family went to bed early on Saturday nights. Trina fully expected her mother to give her customary order—"Off to bed now. Service tomorrow." But she surprised Trina by sinking onto the sofa and patting the seat beside her. "All right. What did you want to talk about?"

Encouraged by her mother's apparent openness, Trina scurried to the sofa and sat, turning her body slightly to face both parents. They looked at her expectantly, and Trina offered a quick, silent prayer. *Let them say yes, Lord, please. . . .*

"Yesterday when I went out to Andrew's to help with Regen—"

"Oh, Trina," Mama cut in, sighing, "if it's about the horse, can it wait until tomorrow? I'm tired."

Trina released a little grunt of displeasure. "Mama, please, let me finish. It isn't about the horse."

Mama's eyebrows came together briefly, but she remained silent.

Turning her gaze to her father, Trina continued. "When I was helping with Regen, Dr. Groening came out. He said I did a good job getting the horse stabilized. He said I have an innate ability with animal care, and"—she took a deep breath, her gaze flitting briefly to her mother's stern face—"he offered me a job at his clinic."

Mama said, "You already have a job." She started to rise.

Dad leaned forward, putting out his hand. "Wait, Deborah." He looked at his daughter. "What kind of job?"

Trina faced Dad, ignoring Mama's pursed lips. "He didn't exactly say, but I would imagine I'd be helping with the animals—cleaning up after surgery and assisting during exams. Really learning how to help them when they're hurt."

Dad frowned at her. "And you'd like that?"

To her embarrassment, tears sprang into her eyes. The desire to follow her childhood dream of caring for animals welled up and filled her, and it was all she could do to keep from begging her parents for this chance. But she swallowed hard and nodded.

Dad's stern countenance softened with a gentle smile. "Ever since you were a little girl, you've brought home hurt animals and nursed them. I understand why you want to work with Dr. Groening." He propped his elbow on the chair arm, cupping his chin. "But Lehigh is too far to walk, Trina, and you don't drive."

"I could learn. Graham said he'd teach me."

Mama and Dad exchanged quick glances. "You've asked Graham to teach you to drive?" Mama's voice was sharp.

Trina felt heat rush to her cheeks. "I didn't ask. He just offered."

"A kind gesture, but it isn't his responsibility," Dad said.

Mama cut in. "I've never learned to drive, and I do just fine."

"But you work right here in town, Mama—just blocks from home. If I—"

"I depend on you to help in the café." Mama glared at Trina, daring her to contradict her.

Trina clasped her hands together in her lap. "I know you depend on me to help in the café, Mama, but now that it's summer, there are other girls who could work there. Some, like Kelly Dick, are finished with school now for good, so maybe they'd like an every-day job. Someone else could wait tables and mop the floors. It doesn't have to be me."

Mama opened her mouth, but Dad put his hand on her knee, silencing her. He looked at Trina. "Your mother and I will discuss this, Trina. I've known Josiah Groening most of my life, and I trust him as an employer for one of my children. But there are several things that would need to be worked out for you to work in Lehigh."

"But, Troy—" Mama started.

Dad hushed her with a look. "The girl is nineteen already, Deborah.

She'll be on her own before long. She might as well explore a little bit before becoming responsible for her own home. And better she explore under the supervision of someone we approve."

Mama's lips nearly disappeared, she pinched them so tightly together.

Trina gave her father a brief hug. "Thank you, Dad."

"We'll talk more tomorrow. To bed now. We have service in the morning."

Trina hurried off, but sleep didn't come quickly. Through the bedroom wall, the mumble of her parents' voices—Mama's angry, Dad's frustrated—kept her from drifting off. Two emotions warred within Trina's heart—guilt for creating conflict between her parents and hope that they would say yes to her request.

FOUR

After Sunday morning service, the members of the fellowship mingled in the churchyard beneath the summer sun, visiting. Graham scanned the grounds, seeking Trina. When he spotted her with Andrew and Livvy, he jogged over and joined them.

Trina's smile of welcome lit her eyes. The tawny specks of gold in her brown irises picked up a hint of lavender from her dress of bold purple—a royal color that suited her somehow. Graham wished he could slip his arm around her waist and draw her near, the way Andrew did with Livvy. But that would certainly start the tongues wagging! Instead, he greeted Andrew and Livvy first then turned to Trina. "Do you have plans for lunch?"

Trina raised her hand to shield her eyes from the sun. Her squint wrinkled her nose. "Mama invited Uncle Henry and Aunt Marie and their twins for lunch."

Graham stifled a groan. Trina would probably be expected to help serve at her own table. Henry and Marie Braun had twins a little over two years old, so Marie would be taking care of the toddlers and wouldn't be much help.

"Why do you ask?"

Graham quirked his lips into a grin. "Mom said you could join us, if you were free."

Trina's mouth formed a perfect O. "I'd like that! Let me ask Mama." She scampered off.

Graham visited with Andrew while he waited for Trina to return, but he didn't hold out much hope for a positive answer. In all his months of courting Trina, she had only been allowed to come to his home without her parents one time, and that was on his twenty-first birthday. When Trina returned, however, she wore a huge smile that sent his heart to thumping.

"Mama says that's fine. Thank you for the invitation."

"She said *yes*?"

Trina's grin turned impish. "She probably wants me out of the way so she and Dad can talk freely." She turned to look at Andrew. "I talked to Mama and Dad last night, and Dad said they'd discuss it."

Andrew reached out and squeezed Trina's shoulder. "Good. I'll be praying for God's will."

"Thank you."

Graham watched the exchange with interest. "Something important going on?"

Trina peeked at him, her smile secretive. "I hope so."

"Will you tell me about it?"

"Later." She slipped her hand through his elbow, creating a mighty caroming in his chest. "We'd better go before your mother thinks we're not coming."

Graham escorted Trina across the grassy yard to his vehicle, opened the door for her, then ran around to his side. He sighed with satisfaction. Just having her in his car, sitting primly on the opposite side of the bench seat, felt wonderful. How much better it would be when they were published and she could slide into the middle of the seat.

Lunch seemed to drag on forever. Graham enjoyed every bite of the baked ham, scalloped potatoes, last year's canned beans, and gooey chocolate cake, but when the meal was over, he and Trina would be able to sit on the front porch and talk. The handmade swing was visible to his family through the large picture window in the living room, so they would be properly chaperoned without having to be around the others. Graham relished his moments alone with Trina. Those scarce snatches of time made him eager for the day when she would be his wife, when they would share their own little house and he would have hours of time every day with her.

When the meal was finished, Trina rose and began clearing dishes.

"Now you stop that," Graham's mother scolded. "You're a guest."

"Nonsense." Trina sent a smile across the table that softened the word. "If I were home, I'd be helping with cleanup. I want to help."

"No, no. You do enough cleaning up at your mother's café." To Graham's relief, his mother shooed Trina away from the table. "I'm accustomed to doing my dishes. You young people go enjoy your time."

Before Trina could launch another argument, Graham caught her elbow and ushered her through the living room and out the front door. The early June sunshine raised the temperature, but the porch was shaded by thick spirea bushes, and a slight breeze pushed from the west, making it bearable. He pointed to the swing, and they seated themselves on opposite sides of the wood-slatted hanging bench. At least a foot and a half of distance separated them. That would be considered acceptable.

All through lunch, Graham had held his curiosity about Trina and Andrew's brief conversation in the churchyard, but now that he had her alone, he let the question come out. "So what's this important topic your parents are covering while you're over here sitting on my porch swing?"

Trina's eyes danced, and she pushed her feet against the porch floor, setting the swing in motion. The white ribbons of her cap swayed beneath her chin. A silken strand of deep brown hair slipped along her cheek. Graham wondered what she'd look like with her hair down. He focused on her sweet face as she finally answered his question.

"They're considering allowing me to work for Dr. Groening."

Ah, he should have known. The look on her face Friday night had clearly indicated her interest. "I'm surprised your mom is even thinking about it."

For a moment, Trina's expression dimmed. But then her smile returned. "I know, but Dad can be persuasive. Of course"—she shrugged, bunching the ribbon on her left shoulder—"he said there would be a lot to work out for it to happen, but. . ."

"But you're still hopeful," he completed.

She nodded. "Oh yes. Working with Dr. Groening, learning how to doctor animals, would be so wonderful!"

He smiled, enjoying her animated voice and face.

"Spending the night out at Andrew's with Regen, I had such a feeling of contentment when the swelling in the horse's leg went down. I love animals, and I want so much to help them." She closed her eyes, tipping her head back and drawing in a deep breath. "There's so much I don't know, Graham, and I want to learn it. I want to learn *everything*." She threw her arms wide and giggled, peeking at him.

Graham resisted taking her hand. Her enthusiasm toward life always lifted his spirits. He could imagine coming home to her after a long day at the lumberyard, letting her smile and cheerful chatter lift him from tiredness. His chest tightened with desire to make her his as soon as possible.

Suddenly an impish grin creased her cheeks. "I told them you offered to teach me to drive."

Graham chuckled to cover his embarrassment. He fiddled with the buttons on his shirt. "Oh? And what did they say?"

Trina sighed. "Dad said it wasn't your responsibility."

Graham nodded. "No, probably not. But in a few months. . .it could be."

She turned a puzzled look in his direction. "What do you mean?"

Graham glanced through the window. His father dozed in his chair, and his mother was nowhere in sight—probably still in the kitchen. His younger brother—usually the one to spy—appeared caught up in the *Mennonite Weekly*. Graham looked at Trina and shifted a few inches closer to her. He lowered his voice, just in case it might carry through the window's screened opening into the house.

"If we were published, no one would think it wrong for me to teach you to drive."

Her eyes widened. "Published?" She licked her lips. "But—but it's summer."

"The wedding would have to wait until the winter months, when the harvest is over." He substantiated her unspoken thought. "But we could publish our engagement now."

She fell silent, only the creaking of the swing's chains intruding. He waited, nearly holding his breath. He knew they couldn't be published without her parents' permission, but he wanted to know what she thought—if she were as agreeable to the idea as he hoped she would be. When the silence lengthened, he released his breath in a noisy rush.

"Would you be opposed to that?" He feared her reply. Maybe he had misread their relationship.

But she shook her head firmly. "No, I'm not opposed. I—I like you a lot." She looked straight ahead, her cheeks flooding with pink. The color gave her an innocent appearance that sent Graham's heart thudding in the top of his head. "But. . ."

Graham leaned closer. "Then what?" His whisper stirred the ribbon hanging from the left side of her cap.

Still facing ahead, she whispered in reply. "I'm not sure I'm ready for it. . .now."

He frowned, sitting upright. "Not ready? But you're nineteen—that's old enough. You know how to keep a house. You've been baptized, so the bishop would have no reason to decline our request to be published. So what's wrong, Trina?"

Slowly she shifted her head to meet his gaze. "After I'm married, I won't work anymore."

He laughed lightly. "Of course not. You'll be taking care of a house, raising children." Warmth filled his face at his statement. He cleared his throat and rushed on. "There won't be any reason for you to work. I'll take care of you."

Trina lowered her gaze, toying with a loose thread in the waistband of her purple dress. "But I *want* to work. . .with Dr. Groening."

Graham planted his feet, stopping the swing's gentle motion. He waited for Trina to look up at him again. He deliberately kept a frown from forming. "Trina, you realize that your job will be caring for the home once you're a wife."

"But why can't I work, too?" Her tone turned pleading. "Mama runs a café, and she's married."

"Yes, but she waited until you and your brother finished school before she bought the café. If she had tried working when you and Tony were younger, your dad would have said no."

Trina scowled. "Beth McCauley works at the art studio every day, and her husband doesn't mind."

Graham harrumphed. "Beth McCauley is worldly. She isn't Mennonite. She doesn't understand our ways." He stared at her, appalled. "You surely don't want to be like her!"

Trina turned her gaze sharply away, worrying her lower lip between her teeth.

Graham clamped his jaw and brought his racing thoughts under control. The last thing he wanted to do was push Trina away. She was young, easily influenced. He knew Trina had befriended the young woman whose mother had abandoned the Mennonite faith when still a teenager. Beth's mother—Marie—was now an accepted member of the fellowship, having returned to her faith as an adult, but Beth remained separate.

He gentled his voice and touched her arm. "Trina."

She looked at him, her expression wary.

"I admire your tender heart, wanting to be friends with everyone. But Beth—she can lead you astray. When the Bible speaks of not being unequally yoked, it mostly means marriage, but we need to be cautious in all of our relationships."

"This isn't about Beth." Tears winked in her dark eyes. "This is about me and what I feel. . .called to do."

Graham frowned. What calling would a woman have beyond being a wife and mother? Fear fluttered through his chest. "Exactly what do you want to do, Trina?"

At that moment, a pickup pulled up to the curb. Graham slid back to the corner of the swing as Trina's younger brother, Tony, bounded up the porch steps two at a time. He started for the front door, but when he spotted them in the corner of the porch, he turned toward his sister.

"Trina, Mom and Dad want you to come home now." Tony shrugged, his face pulled into an apologetic grimace. "Mom says you've been here long enough."

When Trina pushed from the swing, Graham felt certain she looked relieved to be leaving their topic behind. He rose, as well, a feeling of dread settling in his middle.

Trina followed Tony to the edge of the porch; then she turned and looked at Graham. "Please tell your parents thank you for the invitation to lunch. Everything was very good." Such a prim, impersonal statement.

Graham forced a smile. "Sure. I'll see you Wednesday for the singing, right? It's at Walt's this time."

Trina nodded, her ribbons bouncing. "Yes. I want to go."

Graham nearly wilted with relief. He hadn't scared her away if she was still willing to go to the singing with him. "I'll pick you up at six thirty."

She flashed a quick smile then grabbed Tony's arm, hurrying him off the porch. "Did Mama and Dad say anything about. . ." Her voice drifted away as she slammed herself into the pickup.

Graham watched Tony drive down the street. Even though he knew it was selfish, he hoped her parents wouldn't allow her to work at Dr. Groening's. He feared too many changes would take place if they did.

"So if your mother can find two dependable young people to work in the café and your brother agrees to drive you to Lehigh, then we will allow you to work for Dr. Groening."

Trina grabbed the couch cushion with both hands to keep herself in the seat. She smiled at her father and nodded. "Okay. Good. Thank you."

"But"—Dad scowled, pointing his finger at her—"we will expect you to conduct yourself appropriately. Limit your communication with the non-Mennonites who bring animals to the clinic, and be respectful at all times of your employer."

"Of course!" Trina looked back and forth between her parents, meeting their stern gazes with her most convincing look.

"But I must replace you first, Trina," Mama said in a firm voice. "And I'll expect you to help the new employees learn the routine before I allow you to go to your new job."

Trina stifled a frustrated sigh. It might be weeks before Mama was satisfied with the new employees. But she knew better than to argue. She gave another quick nod.

Dad released a sigh and leaned back in his chair. "I'll drive over to Lehigh tomorrow and talk with Dr. Groening about this job, just to be certain we are clear on his expectations and the hours."

"May I go, too?"

Mama shook her head. "No. Let your father do it."

"But the café is closed on Mondays—I won't be working." Trina used a reasonable rather than argumentative tone.

"No, Trina," Dad said, a scowl marring his forehead. "I will let you know everything Dr. Groening says."

Trina stood. "All right." Although she would have preferred to go along—see the clinic, talk to Dr. Groening herself—she knew neither Dad nor Mama would budge once their minds were made up. She also realized they had made a huge concession, allowing her to work for the veterinarian. It took no effort to offer a smile of thanks. "Mom and Dad, thank you. I appreciate your permission."

Mama sighed. "You're welcome, Trina. I just hope we don't regret it."

Trina didn't explore Mama's meaning. She gave each of her

parents a hug then headed to her bedroom. After closing the door, she threw herself facedown across the bed, propped her chin in her hands, and closed her eyes, imagining the glorious days to come.

Working with Dr. Groening, caring for animals. No more cleaning floors, washing dishes, and placing plates of food in front of customers. She focused on every positive aspect of the change and carefully avoided reflecting on the worry in her mother's eyes or recalling Graham's statement about her "calling."

FIVE

Monday morning, Trina rose early, prepared breakfast for the family, waited impatiently for everyone to finish eating, then cleaned the table and washed the dishes without a word of complaint. When the final dish was placed in the cabinet, she interrupted her mother at her sewing machine.

"Mama? May I go to town?"

Mama looked up from pinning the zipper into a pair of brown twill trousers. "Where are you going?"

Trina battled the frustration that wiggled in her stomach. When would she be allowed to simply do what she desired without having to ask permission of her parents? She knew the answer—when she married and moved out from under their roof. But then she'd answer to her husband. The frustration grew.

She took a breath and released it, bringing her rambling emotions under control. "I want to go by the art studio and ask Andrew about Regen's leg."

Mama nodded. "Go ahead."

Trina spun to leave.

"Trina, wait."

Stifling a sigh, Trina turned back.

"Take some money out of my purse, stop by the grocer, and buy two pounds of link sausage. We'll fry it for supper tonight."

"Okay." She slipped away before her mother could give her any more directions. The summer sun beat down, warming her head and shoulders. She walked the familiar streets toward town, just as she had every day for the past six years on her way to the café and her parent-chosen job. Her heart skipped a beat, a smile growing on her face without effort. But soon her routine would change. She'd be climbing into Tony's pickup, riding down the highway the few miles to Lehigh and Dr. Groening's clinic to the Trina-chosen job.

Oh, please hurry and hire those workers, Mama! her heart begged. She could hardly wait to start a new routine—a routine she'd dreamed of since she was a little girl. She hurried her steps, eager to move into the future.

Even though it was still morning—not even nine o'clock yet—by the time she reached the studio on the west end of Main Street, her hair felt sweaty, and perspiration dampened her skin. Stepping into the air-conditioned interior of the studio was a welcome relief. The smells of the studio were so different from the café's—burnt metal and something that left an acidic taste on the back of her tongue as opposed to grease and baking bread. She wondered briefly what the animal clinic would smell like.

The moment she closed the door, Andrew looked up from the worktable in the middle of the floor and broke into a smile. "Good morning, Trina."

Beth Quinn McCauley, Andrew's employer, turned from the large platform on the floor where she and her cousin Catherine Koeppler arranged cut pieces of colored glass into a rose pattern. "Well, good morning, Miss Katrinka."

Trina grinned at the silly nickname her grandfather had chosen. No one used it except Grandpa Muller and Beth.

Beth asked, "What brings you here? Checking up on Winky?"

At the cat's name, he sprang from beneath the worktable and attacked the laces on Trina's tennis shoes.

Andrew muttered, "The cat's the same as always—ornery."

With a giggle, Trina leaned over and scooped the furry critter into her arms. She always enjoyed playing with Winky. She had nursed his injured eye when he was a lanky kitten. The cat still bore a small scar below his left eye, but he was beautiful with thick gray fur and white markings. He set up a loud *purr* as she scratched his chin, and she laughed again.

"As much as I enjoy seeing Winky, I actually came to see Andrew." Still holding the cat, she turned toward her cousin. "How is Regen?"

"Still in the sling," Andrew reported, scraping a small stone over the edge of a piece of blue glass. "Dr. Groening said we need to keep him from putting his full weight on the leg for at least another five days. Then we'll let him stand in the stall. But the leg's looking good. Livvy keeps a close eye on it."

"Good." She filed Andrew's comments away for future reference, in case she ever needed to treat another horse with a torn ligament. She skipped forward, lowering her voice to avoid disturbing Beth and Catherine. "Guess what? Mama and Dad said I can go to work for Dr. Groening."

Andrew's eyebrows shot upward, and a smile broke across his face. "Wonderful!"

Trina nodded happily then grimaced. "Of course, Mama has to find some workers to replace me in the café, and I have to work out transportation with Tony, but when that's all done, I get to be an assistant in a veterinary clinic!"

Andrew put down his stone and glass long enough to throw his arm around her shoulder for a quick hug. "Congratulations! I'm sure you'll enjoy it."

"I know I will, too." Winky wriggled in Trina's arms, so she set the cat down and leaned her elbows on the worktable. She frowned slightly. "I wish I knew more about veterinary science. I read every book I can find on animal care, but most of the books I buy are used, so they don't have the most recent information."

"Hmm." Andrew pursed his lips. "You'll learn a lot from watching Dr. Groening, won't you?"

"Yes, but I'd still like to know things in advance. I can be more help that way." Her hunger for knowledge ate at her, creating a hollow ache in her chest.

"Trina?" At Beth's voice, Trina turned and faced the young woman. "You're welcome to use the computer in here to search the Internet for articles on veterinary science."

Trina's mouth went dry. Would Mama approve? She licked her lips. "The Internet?"

"Sure." Beth slid a slice of pink glass next to one of deeper rose. "The Internet is a great source of information. You can do a Google search for veterinary science or animal care. All kinds of Web sites and articles will come up."

"Google?" Trina laughed. "That's a silly name."

Beth grinned. "I suppose, but it's a very useful search engine."

Trina shook her head, awareness of her limited education smacking hard.

Beth continued in a thoughtful tone. "You know, there is very little that can't be accomplished online these days. I conduct three-fourths of my stained-glass business over the Internet—and Sean and I can communicate with each other through e-mail no matter where he's traveling."

For a moment, Beth's brow pinched, and Trina's heart turned over. She knew Beth missed her husband when he was away on his travels, meeting with church committees about building projects. They had been married less than a year, and Beth often bemoaned how much of that year had been spent apart. Trina wondered if Beth would ever hand the operation of the studio over to Andrew and travel with Sean instead of staying behind.

"Not only that," Beth continued, "but I took an online course through an art institute in Maryland to learn how to color my own glass." She raised one brow and sent Trina a speculative look. "The Internet is a handy tool." Then she shrugged. "Like I said, you're welcome to do some searching for articles on animal care, if you want to."

"I want to." Trina clasped her hands beneath her chin. "Could I do it right now?"

"Sure." Beth got up and crossed the floor, linking her hand through Trina's elbow and guiding her to the desk in the corner where a computer waited. "I'll get you online and show you how to use Google; then you can search as long as you want to."

Trina caught on much more quickly than she had expected, which gave her a rush of self-satisfaction. She chose to explore "veterinary science," and she released a surprised "Whew!" when she spotted the number of hits on the topic. "Three million four hundred and thirty thousand sites!" She stared at Beth. "I'll never get through all of those!"

Beth laughed. "You don't have to. Look at the descriptions. A lot of those are Web sites for different veterinary clinics. You can avoid those and just find the sites that offer information about veterinary science itself. Choose ones that seem the most interesting." She patted Trina's shoulder. "Have fun, Katrinka."

While Andrew, Beth, and Catherine worked on the stained-glass projects, Trina scanned articles on everything from animal reproduction to the latest techniques in animal surgery. The vocabulary used frustrated her from time to time, but she plowed through, absorbing as much as she could. She wished she'd brought paper and pencil to make notes.

She was amazed at the number of educational institutions that specialized in training people for the field of veterinary medicine. At first, she avoided those sites, focusing instead on information concerning the care of animals, but eventually, curiosity drove her to click on a site titled "TO BE A VET."

The Web site was geared toward children, she realized, but a quick glance showed a variety of interesting topics. She leaned forward, propped her chin in her hand, and began to read. "*Getting into veterinary school is harder than getting into medical school. . . . High school subjects you must have mastered include English, biology, chemistry, physics, and several math classes. You need to pass the ACT in those subjects, as well.*"

Trina's chest constricted. She hadn't even attended high school beyond grade nine! She didn't know what physics was or what ACT stood for. Tears pricked her eyes. She blinked rapidly, clearing her vision, and forced herself to continue.

"*To earn your Bachelor of Veterinary Science degree takes five years of full-time study in an approved university.*"

Five years! Full-time? Trina jerked upright in the chair. Although she had harbored a glimmer of hope that perhaps one day her parents would relent and allow her to seek a degree, that hope now plummeted. College cost money, and she couldn't possibly have enough saved for five years. That was if she could get into a college. Tears stung again. She rubbed her eyes, erasing the tears, and leaned closer to the screen to reread the information. Maybe she'd missed something—some other way to become a veterinarian.

The telephone blared, and Trina jumped.

"Trina," Beth called from the platform, "would you mind answering that?"

Reluctantly, Trina moved away from the computer and picked up the telephone. "Quinn's Stained-Glass Art Studio. May I help you?"

"Trina?" Mama's voice.

Trina glanced at the clock on the wall. It was nearly noon! Her hands began to tremble. "Yes, Mama?"

"What are you still doing there? I've been waiting for you to come home."

"I'm sorry, Mama. I—" But she didn't want to tell her mother what she'd been doing. "I'll get that sausage and come straight home."

"No, just go to the café." Mama sounded completely exasperated. "I made a couple of calls this morning, and Janina Ensz is interested in working in the café. I want you to show her how to run the dishwasher and to figure tabs for customers."

"Yes, ma'am! I'll be right there."

The phone line went dead. Trina faced Beth. "It was for me. Mama needs me at the café." Spinning to include Andrew, she said, "Janina Ensz wants to work at the café. If Kelly Dick will work full-time, too, then I'll be free to go to Dr. Groening's."

Andrew winked. "Sounds like it's working out well, Trina."

Catherine pushed to her feet, her hands on the small of her back. "Trina, if Kelly doesn't want to work full-time, have your mother call my house. My sister Audra finished school this past term, and she's looking for a job, too. Maybe she and Kelly could split the time."

Trina squealed. "Oh! I'll tell her! Thank you!"

Beth waved at her. "I'll shut down the computer for you, but anytime you want to use it, just come by."

Trina bit down on her lower lip, sending a pleading look in Beth's direction. "Anytime? Even an evening?" If she worked days at Dr. Groening's, her only free time would be after supper.

Beth shrugged. "I don't know why not. When Sean isn't home, the evenings get long. I'd enjoy the company, even if you are so wrapped up in reading that you don't talk to me." The teasing note in her voice made Trina laugh.

"I'll read out loud to you," she suggested.

Beth grinned. "Deal. See you later."

Yes, Trina would certainly see Beth later. She needed to finish reading the information on the Web site. Surely there was a way to see her dreams come true without going through five years of college.

At supper, Trina wanted to ask her father how his meeting with Dr. Groening had gone. But Mama, still upset about her spending the entire morning at Beth's studio, glared across the table, and Trina decided it was better to wait until she could talk to Dad alone.

Not until the dishes were cleared, washed, and put away did she find a minute to join her father in the yard, where he tinkered under the hood of his car. When she spoke his name, he jumped, nearly banging the back of his head on the metal hood. "Trina." The single word held a hint of exasperation.

She leaned sideways, peeking beneath the hood. "What are you doing?"

"Adjusting the carburetor."

"Why don't you let Uncle Henry do it? That's his job."

He sent her an impatient look. "Because I'm capable of doing it myself. What do you need? I'm busy."

Trina clasped her hands at her apron waist. "I wondered. . .what Dr. Groening said. About me taking a job at his clinic. But if you'd rather wait. . ." She held her breath, hoping he wouldn't send her away.

He heaved a mighty sigh and rested his elbows on the car's fender, angling his head to look at her from beneath the hood. "Well, the job doesn't sound all that good to me, Trina. You'll be cleaning up: cleaning up cages and kennels, cleaning up the exam room, cleaning up after surgery. Are you sure that's what you want to do?"

Trina met her father's steady gaze. "Yes, sir. I know I don't have an education"—her thoughts added the word *yet*—"but I can learn a lot from watching. And maybe I'll be able to help people around town if their animals get sick or hurt."

He shook his head. "You are determined to see this through, aren't you?"

"Yes, sir."

His gaze narrowed, a hint of sympathy showing around the edges of his unsmiling face. "Is it really that bad, working at the café?"

"Oh, Daddy. . ." Trina paused, gathering her thoughts. "It isn't that I dislike my work at the café. It's fun to be around the people, and I know it serves a purpose. But it isn't. . ." She furrowed her brow, seeking an appropriate word. "Fulfilling."

"And cleaning up after animals would be?"

Her father's incredulous expression made Trina want to giggle. But she kept a serious face and nodded. "Yes, sir." Cleaning up after animals was just the start. She'd do more. Someday.

He shook his head, slapped the fender, and leaned back over the engine. "Well, all right, then, daughter. The job will be from nine in the morning until five o'clock each evening. With the distance, you won't be able to come home for lunch, so you'll need to pack yourself a sandwich each day." He glanced at her. "I hope you know what you're doing."

Trina gave him a bright, beaming smile. "I know what I'm doing, Dad. Don't worry."

Six

Trina stuck her arm out the open window of Tony's truck, her hand angled to catch the warm, coursing wind. The pressure against her palm and cupped fingers created a tickling sensation, and she laughed.

From behind the steering wheel, Tony sent her a grin. "You're really happy to be out of the café, aren't you?"

The wind threatened to pull her cap loose, so she shifted a little closer to her brother and caught the dancing strings of her cap, holding them together beneath her chin. "I'm happy to be on my way to the vet clinic," she said. After two weeks of training, Mama had finally deemed Janina Ensz and Kelly Dick capable of handling the tasks of taking orders, serving, and cleaning up at the café. Trina wished Tony would drive faster so she could get to Dr. Groening's as quickly as possible.

The Groening Animal Clinic, located off Highway 56 between Sommerfeld and Lehigh, was housed in a red brick building that had previously served as a country school. Trina had visited it once before when she rode along with Beth McCauley to get Winky's vaccinations. She admired the way Dr. Groening had divided the one-room classroom into a small reception area, two examination rooms, and an operating room. Most of his supplies were stored in the storm shelter beneath the clinic. Although small and unpretentious, the clinic met the needs of those who brought their pets to him. And now Trina would be learning to meet those needs, as well, through firsthand experience. Her heart twanged crazily at the thought.

"I hope taking you doesn't make me late to my job." A hint of worry underscored her brother's comment.

Trina shot him a concerned look. "Will Mr. Bruner be terribly upset if you're a few minutes late?"

Tony hunched his shoulders, his eyes on the road. "He's pretty particular. Suzanna"—he glanced briefly in Trina's direction, his cheeks splotching with pink—"that's his daughter—she warned me to follow his directions carefully if I wanted to keep my job. He's older and set in his ways, and he expects things to go just so. Suzanna can't wait until she's old enough to have her own family so she doesn't have to live with him anymore."

"Where's her mother?"

"Remember? Mrs. Bruner died several years ago."

Trina nodded. "Oh, now I remember." She patted his arm. "We left plenty early. You should be okay." Then she grinned. "Or are you more worried about missing time with Suzanna than you are about being late for your job?"

"Trina!" Tony jerked his arm free of her hand. "She's Amish."

Trina shrugged. "Stranger things have happened."

Tony gritted his teeth. "Her dad would never allow it."

Trina considered pursuing the subject a little further, but then she spotted the clinic up ahead. "There it is!" She pointed out the window, leaning forward to grab the dash. "Oh, look! He's added kennels in the back. Those weren't there when I came over with Beth. I wonder if he keeps dogs overnight." Maybe she could help with their care, too.

Tony slowed down to pull into the graveled driveway. "I don't know. I don't see any dogs out there now."

She craned her neck, disappointment striking. "Neither do I." Then she brightened. "But I'm sure there will be animals inside. Oh! Hurry, Tony!"

He laughed as he brought the truck to a stop in front of the building. "We're here. Get out so I can go to my job."

She flashed him a grin, snatched up her lunch bag, and jumped out of the pickup. Giving the door a slam, she called, "See you at five!"

"Or a little after," he replied. "It'll take me awhile to get over here from the Bruners'."

"I'll wait outside for you. See you later!"

"Have a good day, sis."

She waved as he pulled away; then she turned and dashed up the three steps leading to the clinic's door. She stepped into the room, stopped, and drew in a lengthy, lingering breath, processing the smell. Clean, a little bit like a hospital, but with an underlying essence of wet dog. She laughed out loud. At the sound, Dr. Groening stepped from the far examination room.

He grinned, his gray eyebrows high. "You find my clinic amusing?"

Trina tangled her hands in her apron and gasped. "Oh no! Not at all! That was a happy laugh, that's all."

His grin grew, twitching his mustache. "Well, we'll see how happy you are by the end of the day. It gets pretty messy around here."

Trina swung her lunch bag. "Don't worry. I'm used to messy."

She discovered by the end of the day, however, that messy in the café couldn't compare to messy in the vet clinic. Nervous dogs often emptied their bladders—or worse—on the floor before they made it to an examination table. One poor dog, a golden retriever named Mo, threw up three times in the reception room and twice on the exam table. While Trina's sympathy was roused, it was the least pleasant scrub job she'd ever encountered. And cats shed terribly, their hair clinging to everything.

By lunchtime, she was ready for a break, but when she lifted her sandwich, she suddenly thought about all the other things her hands had touched during the morning. Even though she'd worn latex gloves for the cleanup tasks and washed her hands with an antiseptic soap afterward, she couldn't make herself take a bite of the sandwich. Instead, she drank the milk from her little thermos and put the sandwich back in the bag.

Dr. Groening made visits to local farms during the afternoon. Trina would have loved to ride along with him, but he left her behind to hose out the kennels and wash all the dog dishes—even though they weren't being used at the moment—and dust the shelves in the storm shelter. It was hardly the day of animal treatment she'd been anticipating, and her spirits flagged as the day wore on.

At five o'clock, she wrote her time on a little card Dr. Groening had given her in the morning and went to sit on the front stoop to wait for Tony. Chin in hands, she contemplated the day of cleaning, cleaning, cleaning, and she realized it was exactly what her father had told her to expect. Still, considering her conversation with Dr. Groening, she had hoped for something. . .more.

A vehicle approached, and Trina shielded her eyes from the late-afternoon sun, squinting. When she recognized Graham's sedan, she trotted to the driver's window.

"What are you doing here?" She bent forward and peered into the backseat. "You don't have an animal with you."

Graham grinned. "I came for you."

Trina stood upright. "But Tony is supposed to pick me up."

Graham's grin turned impish, and he raised one eyebrow higher than the other. "I talked to Tony about an hour ago when he came into the lumberyard to pick up some nails. I told him I'd get you instead."

"And Mama cleared it?" Despite the disappointing day, Trina didn't want to do anything to jeopardize this opportunity. Getting Mama riled was the best way to lose her new job.

Graham shrugged. "I don't know why she would protest. I've driven you places before."

"With other people along, too," Trina pointed out. Boys and girls spending time alone together was discouraged in their fellowship. Others who had disregarded the dictate of group activities had received reprimands from the minister. Trina had no desire to be disciplined— not by the minister or by her parents.

Graham tipped his head to the side and fixed her with a steady look. "Well, Tony isn't coming, so unless you want to walk, you'd better hop in."

Trina bit down on her lower lip for a moment, but finally she sighed and slid into the passenger side of the front seat. "All right. But I'll need to check with Mama and make sure it's okay for you to do this another time."

Graham turned the car around and aimed it toward the highway. "How about I come in and ask your parents if I can pick you up each day? And while I'm talking to them, I'll make another request."

Trina stared at his honed profile and waited.

"I'd like to ask if they'd allow us to be published, Trina."

She jerked her gaze to the ribbon of highway. The white dashes zipped by, one after another, as mixed emotions zipped back and forth in her chest.

Graham's hand started to reach toward her, but then he wrapped his fingers around the steering wheel again. Eyes ahead, he asked, "Is that all right with you?"

A part of Trina wanted to exult, "Yes!" But another part of her wanted to exclaim, "Not yet!" She examined her heart, trying to understand the confusion. She cared a great deal about Graham. Of all the young men in Sommerfeld, he was the only one she could imagine spending her life with. She did hope to marry him. . .someday. But now? Was she ready for it now?

She had to say something. "I—I—"

The car began to slow, and Graham eased it onto the shoulder of the road. Leaving the engine on, he put the vehicle in PARK and turned to face her. "Trina, I love you. I've loved you for over a year now. I want you to be my wife. But I need to know: Do you love me?"

Trina stared into his dear, stricken face. Something inside of her melted. A feeling of longing rose up, putting a mighty lump in her throat. She swallowed and formed a sincere answer. "I do love you, Graham."

"Then what's wrong? Why won't you let us be published?"

"I want to be published, too! It's just—" How would Graham feel, knowing she was putting the opportunity to work with animals ahead of him? Yet if he truly loved her, wouldn't he support her desire to be more than a wife and mother? Wouldn't he encourage her to fulfill her dreams? Maybe he wouldn't mind being the first husband in Sommerfeld to have a veterinarian for a wife.

Graham took her hand. He didn't curl his fingers around it but just placed his palm over her hand on the seat. The simple touch ignited feelings inside of Trina that took her by surprise. She stared at their hands—his much larger one, with blond hairs on the backs of his lumpy knuckles, covering hers. Only the tips of her fingers with their uneven, broken fingernails showed. Suddenly the gesture made her feel smothered, and she jerked her hand away, fearful of where the feelings might lead.

Graham's forehead creased, and for long moments, he remained with his hand lying in the middle of the seat, the fingers curling into a fist.

Trina said, "We'd better go, or Mama will worry."

He grabbed the gearshift and gave it a quick jerk, then pulled the car back into traffic. Neither spoke the rest of the way to Sommerfeld. But when he pulled up in front of her house, Trina didn't get out.

"Graham?"

Several seconds ticked by before he finally looked at her. His stern expression didn't offer much encouragement, but she knew if they were to have a relationship, she needed to be completely honest with him.

"I want to be your wife."

His expression softened.

"But just not yet. There are. . .other things. . .I want to accomplish first. Things that"—she pressed both palms to her heart—"that live in here. I have to let them come out before I can be a good wife to you."

Graham shook his head. "Trina, you are the most confusing girl. What things can a woman need besides being a good wife and mother? That's your God-ordained purpose."

"And I'll want to be a good wife and mother. Someday." Without conscious thought, she leaned slightly toward him. "But don't you think God gives us other tasks, too? Why would He plant the interest in animal care in my heart if I wasn't supposed to use it?"

"You do use it," Graham argued. "You helped with Livvy's horse the other night. You're always taking care of sick animals. I wouldn't stop you from helping animals. Of course, once our children start arriving, then you wouldn't be able to run off all night like you did with Regen, but—"

"But I want to do more!" Trina implored him with her eyes, begging him to see how much this dream meant to her. She needed someone to understand, to support her, to encourage her. She wanted desperately for that someone to be Graham.

He ran his hand over his short-cropped hair—the hair that reminded Trina of the sandstone posts surrounding Uncle Al's cornfields. Even though Graham worked mostly inside at the lumberyard rather than outdoors as a farmer, there was so much about him that reminded her of the outdoors. His sandstone-colored hair, his sky-colored eyes, his lips as full and deeply hued as a pink rosebud ready to burst. But now his eyes bore into hers with a hurt that tore at her heart, and his lips pressed into a firm, stubborn line.

"Exactly what do you want, Trina?"

It was the question she'd wanted him to ask so she could share her deepest desire, but now that the opportunity lay before her, she hesitated. She hated her hesitation. Shouldn't she feel free to share with the man who would one day be her husband?

Taking a deep breath, she whispered her dream aloud. "I want to be real."

He stared at her, confusion evident in the rapid blinking of his eyes.

She rushed on. "A real animal doctor. Someone trained in the field."

"You mean attend college?"

Trina wasn't sure whether he was astounded or agitated. "It will probably take that. Yes."

Graham threw himself against the seat, his head back, his hands on the steering wheel, and his arms straight as if bracing himself against a fast downhill ride. "I can't believe it."

"I've talked about my interest in animals, Graham."

"Interest, yes." He slumped, twisting his head to meet her gaze. "But you're talking about having a *career*, Trina."

She had never applied that word to her dream. Suddenly the barrier between her and school seemed to double in size. Who was she fooling? They'd never let her have a career.

"But. . ." The word squeaked. She cleared her throat and tried again. "It would be worthwhile to the community. There isn't anybody in town who can doctor animals. We have to go clear to Lehigh, and Dr. Groening is getting older. He'll retire before too much longer. Surely—"

The look on Graham's face silenced her. She pushed the car door open. "Thank you for the ride, Graham. If you—if you want to get me tomorrow, make sure you check with Mama first."

His eyebrows rose, and even she realized the ridiculousness of her statement. She was planning to attend an institution of higher education, which was unquestionably against her parents' desires. Accepting a ride home from work carried significantly less importance than enrolling in college. He didn't respond, and she slammed the door. He drove off without a backward glance.

Heart aching, Trina stared at the house. She didn't want to go in. Turning, she headed for town, but she passed the café and went around to the back door of the stained-glass studio instead. Andrew's truck still stood in the alley. Relief flooded her. Of all the people she knew, Andrew should be the most sympathetic to her desire for something more.

She reached for the door handle, but the door swung open before she could connect with the silver knob. Andrew stepped onto the small concrete slab. When he spotted her, a smile lit his face, and he gave her an affectionate little pinch on the chin.

"Hey, Trina! How did your first day at Dr. Groening's go?"

To Trina's chagrin, she burst into tears.

SEVEN

Graham pulled his car into the shed behind his house and shut off the ignition, but he didn't get out. He sat behind the steering wheel, images of Trina filling his vision. Her expectant, hopeful face as she shared her desires crushed him. She didn't want him. She didn't want a home and family. She wanted. . . He couldn't bring himself to finish the thought. It was wrong what Trina wanted! He wouldn't give credence to it by letting it invade his mind.

He got out of the car and slammed the door hard—harder than necessary. It didn't help. He stomped across the grass to his own back door. Once inside the house, he stood in the little mudroom and peered through the open doorway into the kitchen. How many times had he stepped through his back door and imagined Trina in his kitchen. At his stove, stirring a pot. At his sink, her hands submerged in sudsy water. At his table, serving a meal.

Shaking his head, he forced himself to walk through the kitchen to the living room. He sank onto the sofa and closed his eyes. The silence of the house pressed around him. The house was less than four months old. He and the men of the community had built it. The ladies—including Trina—had provided meals to keep the men going during the working hours.

The house still smelled new. New wood, new paint, new rubber from the purchased throw rugs he'd dropped here and there on the floor. Even some new furniture. What there was of furniture. Only a sofa in the living room. The bedroom he'd claimed had the familiar full-size bed, bureau, and bedside table from his old bedroom at his parents' home. He'd deliberately put off purchasing furniture, knowing his wife would want a say in what to buy.

Trina would want a say in what to buy.

Now he'd heard Trina's say, and he wasn't sure whether she'd ever choose furniture to fill his house. The house he'd meant to be theirs. He groaned, covering his face with his hands. When he'd fallen in love with Trina Muller, he'd never imagined she would hurt him like she had today.

"Dear Lord, why does she want something else instead of me?"

Trina covered her face with her hands, clamping her lips together to silence the sobs that jerked her shoulders in uncontrolled spasms.

Warm, broad hands curled around her upper arms, drawing her forward, into the shop. Then those hands slipped to her wrists, pulling her hands away from her face. She peered into Andrew's concerned eyes.

"Trina, what's wrong? Didn't your day go well?"

"Oh, Andrew!" For a few minutes, she gave vent to the frustration that bubbled upward. As she'd learned to appreciate over the years, he didn't tell her to stop crying but just stood by and let the tears run their course. When she finally sniffed hard, bringing the raining tears to a halt, he gave her a tissue.

"Here. Clean up."

She rubbed her face clean. "I'm sorry. I didn't mean to do that."

"Don't apologize to me. Sometimes a person just needs to cry." He put his hand on her back, guiding her to the tall stools beside the worktable. She climbed onto one, and he leaned against a second one, resting his elbow on the tabletop. "You aren't one to cry over nothing. Do you want to talk about it?"

The sweet concern in his voice nearly sent her into another bout of weeping, but she took a few deep breaths and kept control. While Andrew's attentive gaze remained on her face, she poured out every event of the day, from cleaning up doggy doo and dusting shelves to the car ride home and facing Graham's disapproval.

"I want him to understand, but he doesn't. I know my parents won't, either." She twisted the soggy tissue in her hands. "Why is it wrong for me to want to go to school and learn how to take care of animals? Why would God give me this desire if I wasn't meant to pursue it? Why can't Mama and Dad and Graham let me be the person I want to be?"

To her surprise, Andrew didn't immediately validate her questions. Instead, he walked slowly around to the opposite side of the table and braced both palms against it. "Why are you asking me these questions, Trina?"

She blinked in confusion. "Who else would understand? Your father wanted you to be a farmer like the rest of your family. But you wanted something else. Surely you know how I feel!"

"But I didn't break any fellowship rules to become a stained-glass artist, Trina. What you're talking about—going to college—that's different."

Trina stared at him in amazement. The one person she felt would be completely, 100 percent on her side seemed to distance himself from her. Tears threatened again.

Andrew went on quietly, his gaze lowered. "Being a wife. . .and mother. . .is the highest calling for any woman. If you didn't have Graham wanting to marry you, I'd probably say keep learning what you can about animal care from the Internet or books and help out the way you did with Regen. But not at the expense of a family."

Trina slammed her fist against the tabletop. "Oh, this is so aggravating! Why can't anyone understand?"

"And why can't you understand what you're throwing away?"

At Andrew's angry tone, Trina drew back, gawking at her cousin. "Th–throwing away?"

"Yes." He glared at her, his lips quivering. "You have a man—a good man—who wants to marry you. You could become a wife and then a mother, but you'd rather take care of sick kittens. What's wrong with you, Trina?"

Of all the people she'd feared might attack her, Andrew was at the bottom of the list. She sat in silence, too hurt to respond.

"Don't be selfish." He held himself stiffly erect, his chin high. "You have an opportunity Livvy would kill to have—the opportunity to be a mother. And if you throw it away over some ridiculous idea about—" The last words came out in a growl; then he seemed to crumble. He spun, leaning his hips against the table with his back to her.

Trina slipped from the stool and rounded the table. She touched Andrew's arm. "Andrew? Is something wrong with Livvy?"

Tears winked in her cousin's dark eyes. His chin quivered. "All the trouble she's been having with. . .female issues?"

Trina nodded. The family had been praying for Livvy's difficulties.

"She got her tests back today. The doctor says she won't be able to. . ."

Although he didn't finish the statement, Trina needed no more explanation. She tightened her fingers on his arm. "I'm sorry."

"Me, too." His voice had lost its hard edge, but it still lacked his usual warmth. He placed his hand over hers and looked directly into her eyes. "Trina, think carefully about what you want. Going to school, getting a degree—people do it every day. But not everybody has the opportunity to build a family. Don't throw something so valuable away over a childish dream."

Trina pulled her hand back, stung by his simplification of her desires. But she didn't argue. She nodded. "I'll think about it. And pray about it."

"Do that." He headed for the door, cupping her elbow and pulling her along with him. "I need to get home to Liv. I'll talk to you later, Trina."

After he drove off, Trina started for the café. But she didn't want to face her mother after the two emotionally exhausting conversations she'd just had. But where to go? Since Andrew's opinion was now colored by his personal conflict, who else might be able to offer support and sympathy?

"Beth," Trina whispered. Beth wasn't Mennonite. She would have a different viewpoint from everyone else in town. Trina would ask Beth. She set off in the direction of the little bungalow on Cottonwood Street.

The door opened to Trina's knock, and Sean McCauley stood framed in the doorway. He smiled, his mouth half hidden by his mustache. "Well, hello. It's Trina, right? Come on in."

Trina stepped over the threshold and stood on the little square of linoleum in front of the door. A television set blared from the corner, the screen showing a close-up image of a man holding a microphone and pointing to a building behind him. Sean quickly shut off the noisy box then headed toward the back of the house, still talking. "Beth and I were just getting ready to sit down to dinner. Come on back and have a bite."

Trina shrank against the door. "Oh, I'm so sorry! I didn't think about the time. I'll come back later." She grabbed the doorknob.

"Trina, wait." Beth hustled into the room and caught Trina's hand, pulling her away from the door. "Don't run off. Tell me about your first day at the vet clinic. Andrew said you were very excited to finally get to work with Dr. Groening."

"But your dinner. . ." Trina flapped her hand in the direction of the kitchen, where Sean disappeared around the corner. "It'll get cold."

"Sandwiches don't get cold." Beth grinned. "Sandwiches and canned fruit—that's what we're having, and it'll keep. Fill me in."

Trina couldn't imagine her mother putting such a simple meal on the table for supper. Beth was so different. She twisted a ribbon tie around her finger. "Well, it was nice to finally be there, but it wasn't what I expected. I mostly just cleaned up."

Beth tipped her head. "Cleaned up?"

"Yes. Floors, cages, exam tables, kennels, shelves." Trina made a face. "I knew I wouldn't be doing surgery, but I had hoped to at least work with the animals a little bit."

"Oh, Trina, I'm sorry." Beth offered a brief hug. Trina savored the touch of sympathy she'd been seeking. Beth continued. "But surely it's just because you're new. Don't you think, after you've been there awhile and have proven yourself capable of handling the little tasks, he'll give you something more challenging to do?"

Trina considered the question. When she'd started at the café with Miss Koeppler, she'd run the dishwasher and mopped floors. Gradually, the owner had increased Trina's responsibilities until she finally became a waitress and handled the cash register. "Maybe you're right." Her heart leaped with hope. "Maybe I just need to prove myself."

"I'm sure that's it," Beth said, her smile encouraging. "Hang in there. You've wanted this for too long to give up now."

"Oh, I'm not giving up!" Trina heard the determination in her own voice. No matter what Graham or Andrew or Mama said, working with animals was in her heart. She wouldn't set it aside.

"Good for you." Beth gave Trina another hug. "Come see me again on Friday and let me know what you're doing by then, okay?"

"Thanks, Beth." Trina glimpsed Sean peeking out from the kitchen doorway. Beth might not be in a hurry to eat, but it appeared he was. She backed up to the door, her positive spirit restored. "I'll see you Friday with a great report!"

Trina's optimism waned as the week progressed with the same duties assigned each day. On Friday, Dr. Groening remained at the clinic all afternoon, and he called Trina to his messy desk in the corner of the reception area at closing time.

"I'll plan to pay you each Friday, if that works for you."

"That's fine." She was accustomed to Mama paying her once a month, which worked okay since she rarely went to the bigger towns more often than that. Tony went into McPherson frequently, though, sometimes giving rides to their Amish neighbors who didn't own vehicles. He could take her pay to the bank for her.

Dr. Groening placed a check in her hand. "You've done well, Trina. I appreciate your efforts."

Trina folded the check without looking at it and slipped it in her apron pocket. "Thank you."

The doctor crossed his arms and peered down his nose at her.

"Are you satisfied with the job?"

Trina raised her shoulders in a slow shrug. She didn't want to complain, but she did want to know when she would finally be doing something besides cleaning up. "I appreciate being able to work here, but I wonder when I might actually get to work *with* the animals."

Dr. Groening's gray eyebrows twitched. "With the animals?"

"Yes. Like I did out at Andrew's with Regen."

The man stared at her in silence for several seconds, and then he drew back, shaking his head. "Oh, Trina, we have a misunderstanding."

Trina waited, her heart pounding.

"Without any kind of veterinary training, licensure, or certification, you can't work with the animals. It's against the law. I'm sorry if I wasn't clear on that."

Trina's heart sank. "You mean, until I get something from a school that says I have training, I'll never get to help with the animals?"

"You'll be able to bathe them and feed and water any boarders I might keep, but doctoring? No, I'm afraid not." His face and voice reflected sympathy. "If you want to quit, I'll understand."

"I'm not quitting." Trina set her chin in a determined angle. "I want to stay, because I can watch you and learn from you even if I'm just cleaning up after you."

The doctor smiled, his eyes warm.

"But I won't always be cleaning up," she said. "I'm going to get the schooling I need."

Dr. Groening's brows rose. "Your parents are letting you—"

"I'm taking classes online." The moment the words were out, Trina knew she would follow through. Beth had said a person could do nearly everything online these days. Beth had taken a class, and she had offered Trina the use of her computer. If Beth could do it, Trina could do it.

"That's very admirable," Dr. Groening said. "I knew you had an interest in animal care, but I had no idea you were working toward a certificate."

"Well, I am." Trina felt a small prick of conscience. She hadn't actually started the work yet, but she knew she would. Her words would prove true. A *beep-beep* from a vehicle horn outside the clinic interrupted. "That must be Tony. I've got to go. I'll see you Monday morning."

"Good-bye, Trina. And let me know if I can help you with your studies."

"Thank you, Dr. Groening. I will." She ran outside, climbed into Tony's pickup, and slumped into the seat.

"Rough day?" her brother asked with a smirk. "What was it this time?"

Each evening she'd shared one of her messy cleanup tasks with him. It kept her mind off the hurtful remembrance that Graham hadn't asked Mama if he could pick her up from work. Instead of answering Tony's question, she removed the check from her pocket and held it up. "Dr. Groening said he'd pay me every Friday, so could you take this with you when you go to McPherson tomorrow?"

"Sure. Don't you want to go with me?"

Although normally Trina would jump at the chance to go into the big discount store in McPherson, she shook her head. "No, I have something to do in Sommerfeld."

"What's that?"

Trina couldn't tell Tony about her plan to take college classes online. He'd tell their parents, and she needed to wait until the right time to share it with them. She said, "Nothing you need to worry about. Will you take my check to the bank or not?"

He shrugged. "Sure." He glanced at her. "How much did he pay you?"

Trina unfolded the check and released a little gasp. It was nearly double what she would have made in a week at the café working for Mama. She held it out to Tony, and he whistled appreciatively.

"That'll add up quick." He winked. "I can help you spend it."

"Oh no," Trina shot back, giving him a playful punch on the arm. "I can spend it all by myself." She slipped the check back into her pocket then kept her hand pressed over it. Hadn't she just been worrying about how she would pay for college? And now God was providing. She knew exactly how she would spend this money.

EIGHT

S o the first thing we have to do," Beth said, her fingers tapping rapidly on the keys of the computer keyboard, "is help you get your GED." Behind her, the dining-room table held the dirty plates and nearly empty pans from supper. Trina had offered to help clean up, but Beth had laughingly said Trina had done enough cleaning up this week.

Trina propped the heels of her hands on the edge of the huge computer desk that took up an entire wall in Beth's dining room. She was cautious not to bump any of the machines that stood in a neat line along the desktop. "What is that exactly—a GED?"

Beth rocked back and forth in her leather chair. "It's short for General Education Development. You didn't attend high school, so you don't have a diploma, which is required in order to enter college. The GED is just like having a high school diploma without going to school."

"How do I get it?"

"You have to take a test to show your knowledge of the general education subjects."

Trina sucked in a worried breath. Would that include physics?

"Can I take the test on the computer?" She peered over Beth's shoulder at the Web site sponsored by the Kansas Board of Regents.

"No, I'm afraid not." Beth pointed to the screen. "You have to go to one of the testing sites. It looks like the closest one for you would be Hutchinson."

Trina cringed. "Hutchinson? But we hardly ever go there."

Beth continued tapping buttons, leaning close to the screen. "Looks like you'll need to plan a trip. And you'll need some sort of identification." She scowled at Trina briefly. "Do you have a Kansas ID card or a driver's license?"

Trina drew back. "No. I've just worked here in town, so I've never needed an ID. And I haven't learned to drive yet, so I don't have a license."

Beth shook her head, her long, blond ponytail swishing back and forth over her shoulders. "Well, you'll need an accepted form of identification to prove you live in Kansas, so you'd better plan to get one or the other." She clicked a few more keys, adding, "In addition to the GED, you'll also need to take the ACT—nearly every college requires the scores from that test, as well."

"Another test?" Trina yanked a chair from the dining table and flopped into it. "There are so many steps! This is going to take forever!"

Beth swiveled again to look at Trina. Her serious expression held Trina's attention. "Is it worth it?"

Trina gulped.

"Is it what you're supposed to do?"

Trina hung her head.

"If so, then don't see the steps as roadblocks but as stepping-stones to your goal." Beth touched Trina's arm. "Anything worth having is worth working for."

Tears pricked Trina's eyes. Head still down, she said, "Do you know you're the only person who is encouraging me instead of telling me I'm doing the wrong thing?"

"Even Andrew?"

Trina sighed. In the past, she and Andrew had been each other's cheerleaders. She'd always encouraged him to pursue his dream of art despite his family's misgivings. It hurt that he didn't reciprocate now. "Livvy's problems have changed his focus. He thinks I'm foolish to put aside marrying Graham and having children just to. . ." She cringed, remembering the sting of his words. "To take care of sick kittens."

"Aw, Trina. . ." Beth leaned back and nibbled her lower lip. "Well, it is kind of odd, isn't it, for someone from your religious group to want to go to college?"

Trina shrugged. "I'm sure I'm not the only one who's thought about it, but as far as I know, I'm the only one from Sommerfeld who's ever tried to follow through." Wrinkling her nose, she admitted, "They'll probably kick me out."

"Out of what?"

Trina released a dramatic sigh. "Out of my family, out of the fellowship, out of *town*."

Beth started to laugh, and despite herself, Trina joined in. The laughter relieved some of her tension. Little wonder the Bible said laughter was good for the soul.

Beth tipped her head, her expression thoughtful. "Trina, why is your sect so opposed to higher education? What does college hurt?"

Trina shrugged. "Mostly there's a fear of young people losing their sense of self and their faith if they get caught up in the world out there." She swung her hand in the direction of the window. "The more things you're exposed to, the less satisfied you become with simplicity, so by limiting our experiences, we remain content where we are."

Beth nodded slowly. "I suppose that makes sense. It's the main reason Sean and I attend the church in Carston rather than joining the fellowship here. We're Christians, but we've lived our lives with stuff." She gave the computer monitor a pat. "And having sampled all of that, it's hard to let it go. Besides"—she shrugged—"I believe I can follow God without wearing a certain kind of clothes or doing without the world's conveniences."

Trina slid her fingers down the length of her cap's ribbons. "I understand. And truly, I don't want to leave the fellowship. I love my faith and how we express it. When I put on my dress and cap, it reminds me where I belong, and there's a security I wouldn't trade. I just want to be allowed to follow my heart." Releasing the ribbons, she wove her fingers together and pressed her hands to her apron. "Do you know in Pennsylvania, some Old Order Mennonite youth have been allowed to attend college? Their bishop approved it because it was training that would benefit the community as a whole."

"Having a real veterinarian in the community would be good for Sommerfeld," Beth observed in a thoughtful tone.

"I think so, too."

"So maybe your bishop will approve it."

Trina grimaced. "The bishop might, eventually, but my dad? When Dad read about those youth going to college, he was very upset. He said it would lead to trouble." She shuddered. "He'll be very upset with me when he finds out what I'm doing."

Beth sat quietly, looking hard into Trina's face. "Should you tell your parents what you're planning before you get too far into it?"

Trina's chest constricted. "I want it to be a. . .surprise."

Beth crunched her forehead. "Well, sometimes surprises aren't all that pleasant. I kept secret where I was and what I was doing when I was learning the art of stained glass in order to surprise my mom, and it turned out to be pretty hurtful before the truth came out. Remember everybody in town thought I was stealing from them because I wouldn't tell anybody where I really was? Maybe it would be better to tell your mom and dad up front and—"

"No." The word came out more forcefully than Trina intended. She took a breath to calm her racing heart and spoke in an even tone. "I'll tell them after I've gotten enrolled in a college. If they see how much it means to me, it should make it easier for them to accept."

"I suppose you know best." Beth sounded uncertain.

Trina gave an emphatic nod. "Yes, I do."

"All right, then." Beth swung around to face the computer, pointing to the screen. "This says there's a fee to take the test. You can retake it if you don't pass, but you have to pay again each time. There's also a practice test." Beth sent Trina a speculative look. "I think that sounds like a good idea. For your peace of mind, if nothing else."

Trina squinted at the screen's small print. "How much does the practice test cost?"

"Twenty-five dollars."

Trina sat back, thinking about her bank account. "A small price to pay for peace of mind."

"So. . ." Beth tapped her lips with her finger. "Before you can sign up to take the practice test, you've got to be able to identify yourself. Should we download the test booklet for a Kansas driver's license so you can start studying?"

Trina thought about Graham's offer to teach her to drive. Would he still be willing? He hadn't come by to see her since Monday. Maybe asking him would give them some time together to mend their torn relationship. "Yes." She bobbed her head in one quick nod. "Please do."

"Tuh–ree–na!" Graham held to the dashboard of the car as it bucked like an untamed colt. "Let out on the clutch!"

Trina's knee left the seat, and the car died. A whirl of dust from the county road drifted through the open window, and she coughed.

"But not that fast." Graham wiped his forehead with an already-soggy bandanna. When Trina had called yesterday evening and asked so sweetly if he would teach her to drive, he'd had no idea what he was getting himself into. He hadn't been opposed to spending time with her—he'd missed her tremendously over the week—but she was aging him fast with her mistakes. He just hoped she wasn't damaging the car's gears.

She peeked at him with a contrite expression. "I'm sorry. I'm not doing it on purpose. I just can't seem to get my feet to work together."

Looking into her brown eyes, Graham melted. "You'll get it. It just takes some practice to get the out-and-down right. Remember, out on the clutch, down on the gas. The secret is to let up at the same rate you push down. Try it again."

Trina thrust her jaw into an adorable stubborn set, pushed down on the clutch, turned the ignition key, and tapped the gas pedal until the engine caught. "Okay, here we go." And go they did! The car lurched forward.

Trina screeched, "Whoa!" And the car died.

Graham laughed uncontrollably, holding his belly. After several moments, Trina bumped him on the shoulder with the heel of her hand.

"Stop laughing at me!"

He coughed to bring himself under control, but when he looked into her stern face, he erupted again. Her scowl deepened. He held up both hands in surrender. "Okay, I'm sorry. No more. But you said 'Whoa,' and the car stopped. Don't you think that's funny?"

"No." Then she giggled, hunching her shoulders. "Well, didn't you tell me there was horsepower in the engine? It probably recognizes 'Whoa.' "

They laughed together. When the mirth died away, they sat looking across the seat at each other. Graham felt a pressure build in his chest. He would have no difficulty looking into her face for the rest of his life. How he hated the disagreement that had kept them apart this past week.

"Trina, I want—," he said.

"I'll never—," she said at the same time.

He waved his hand. "Go ahead."

She sighed. "I'll never learn to drive at this rate."

Graham grinned, giving the ribbon on her cap a gentle tug. "But the longer it takes, the longer we get to be out here together. That's a good thing, right?"

Her shy smile made him want to lean across the seat and kiss her lips. But if someone saw them, the consequences would be severe. He threw his car door open and stepped out of the vehicle. They were parked in the middle of the road, but he didn't expect traffic. He'd deliberately chosen a seldom-used dirt road for her practice. "Come out here."

With a puzzled look, Trina obeyed, following him to the front of the car.

"Sit on the hood." he directed. As soon as she was settled, he knelt in front of her and held up the palms of his hands. "Okay, now let's pretend my hands are the clutch and the gas pedal."

Trina giggled, crossing her ankles and pressing her heels to the painted black bumper.

He clapped his hands twice then angled his palms outward again. "C'mon. Feet right here."

She stared at him, her eyes wide. "You're kidding!"

"No, I'm not. You said you were having trouble getting your feet to work together, so we'll just practice. Put your feet against my hands." With another self-conscious giggle, she lifted her feet and placed them gingerly against his palms. He curled his fingers around the soles of her tennis shoes. "Okay, up on the clutch"—he tilted her left foot back—"and down on the gas." At the same time, he pulled her right toes forward. "See how it feels?" He repeated the motions several times.

Trina scowled with concentration, one fist in the air as if holding onto a steering wheel, the other gripping an imaginary gearshift. Graham swallowed his chuckle. If she only knew how cute she looked. He let her practice until the discomfort of the hard ground biting into his knees made him grimace.

"I gotta get up." He pushed to his feet, brushed off his trousers, then rubbed his knees, bent forward like an old man.

Her fingers grazed his shoulder. "I'm sorry."

He tipped his chin to give her a smile. "It's okay. You're worth it."

Pink flooded her cheeks, and she hopped from the hood. She twisted her apron around her hands. "Do you trust me to try it now with the car?"

"That's why we're out here." But suddenly teaching her to drive was secondary. Just *being* with her out on the open landscape with the wind whispering through the cornfields and the Kansas sun warming their heads was a pleasure beyond compare. He stifled a groan. Would he be able to make Trina his in every sense of the word?

She bustled around the hood and climbed back into the driver's seat. Graham followed more slowly, and when she reached for the ignition, he caught her hand. She sent him a look that was half puzzled, half scared.

"Trina, this week was the longest of my life. Know why?"

The breeze through the open window caught her ribbons, making them twirl beneath her chin. She licked her lips, shaking her head slightly.

"Because I didn't see you."

"You could have if you'd taken me to the singing like we'd planned."

He cringed at the slight accusation in her tone. He regretted not going after her, yet the hurt had still been too deep. Meeting her gaze, he hoped his eyes reflected an apology. "I don't want to go another week like that." He hesitated then braved a question: "Do you?"

A smile trembled on her lips. "I missed you, too, Graham." She swallowed. "I really don't want to displease you."

Her innocent expression, the sweet words, gave Graham the courage to slip his fingers between hers, linking their hands. "I know you don't."

She removed her hand from his grasp, curling it over the gearshift. "And I appreciate your teaching me to drive, even though we had a falling-out."

"It's easy to forgive you, Trina."

She shot him a quick look, her brows low, but she didn't say anything.

Graham went on. "And I'm willing to wait while you get your animal-care whim worked out of your system." He released a chuckle and said teasingly, "Tony told me you're doing a lot of scrubbing. I figure it won't take you too long to get tired of that."

The answering smile he expected didn't come. A weight pressed on his chest. "What's wrong?"

"Graham, I've tried to tell you. This isn't a whim." She closed her eyes for a moment, drawing in a slow breath. When she faced him again, the seriousness in her expression made him hold his breath. "Do you really love me?"

He leaned toward her. "You know I do."

"Then can I trust you to keep a secret?"

Graham glanced out the window, scanning the empty landscape. He lifted his shoulders in a shrug and met her gaze. "Yes."

She looked hard into his face, seemingly deciding whether or not she truly could trust him. He resisted fidgeting, frustration building. Finally, she gave a little nod, as if giving herself a private message, and then she spoke. "Learning to drive is just the first step in becoming a real animal doctor. I've been using Beth McCauley's computer, and I figured out how I can get the equivalent of a high school diploma. After that, I plan to enroll in online classes. It will probably take me several years, and I might even have to leave Sommerfeld for a little while, but eventually I'll be a real veterinarian."

"College." Graham tried to hold his temper, but he knew the word barked out. "You're really going to do it." He had hoped the long week of distance between them had awakened her to what really mattered—namely, becoming a wife. *His* wife.

She nodded. "That's what I'm working toward. Maybe it won't happen, but I have to try. This. . .this tug on my heart is too strong to ignore. I *have* to try."

Her pleading expression tore at him. He faced forward, away from the silent entreaty for understanding. "College, Trina, is against the fellowship." He didn't say it was against what he wanted. She already knew that.

She ducked her head. "I know. And it's hard to think of going against the rules of the fellowship, but—" Her head came up, her hand grasping his arm. "Why would God give me these desires if I wasn't meant to follow through with them? That would be cruel! Don't you see?"

Graham carefully removed her hand from his arm. "All I see is you are foolishly chasing a dream that will lead to nothing but heartache for—" He started to say "me." Realizing how selfish it would sound, he amended, "Your parents. Have they approved this?"

Her quivering chin gave the answer. Suddenly, he wondered about something else. "Do they know I'm teaching you to drive?"

She pulled in her lower lip and slowly shook her head.

"Then you're sneaking around behind their backs. That's a sin, Trina!"

"I don't want to sneak, but if I tell them now, they'll say no. They need time to think about it. Once they see how much it means to me, they'll come around."

Graham considered her statement. Did she think he, too, would come around? He'd just told her he was willing to wait for her, but now, looking down the road to years of college classes and her using the earned degree, he feared he may have told a lie.

Slamming out of the car, he stomped around the hood and yanked open the driver's door. "Scoot over."

She blinked at him, her mouth open in surprise.

"I'm driving you back to town," he said, his voice grim. "I won't help you deceive your parents."

Tears trembled on Trina's lashes, but she worked her way over the gearshift to the opposite side of the seat. Graham sat behind the steering wheel and gave the ignition a vicious twist that brought the engine to life. He jammed the car into first gear, revving the engine. Not until he had shifted into third and they were traveling at fifty-five miles per hour with a cloud of dust whirling behind them did Trina speak.

"Graham?"

He grunted, his eyes aimed ahead.

"Even if you won't teach me to drive, you–you'll keep my secret, won't you?"

His jaw clenched, the back teeth clamping down so hard it hurt. But he gave a brusque nod.

He heard her sigh. "Thank you, Graham."

He wouldn't need to tell. There were no secrets in Sommerfeld. It wouldn't be long. Her folks would get wind of her plans, and they'd bring an end to this nonsense. Then maybe she'd listen to reason and accept his marriage proposal.

NINE

"Hi, sweetheart." Beth set the paper bag she was carrying onto the kitchen table and opened her arms for Sean's hug. "I didn't expect to see you until late this evening." He had left before dawn that morning for Kansas City to meet his father and representatives from a church in Olathe.

"The meeting ended early."

"Did they like your plans?" Beth knew Sean had worried over the drawings of the church addition, mixed messages from various committee members making it difficult to pinpoint their exact needs.

He sighed, his breath stirring her hair. "Back to the drawing board."

"Oh, hon, I'm sorry." She burrowed closer. "And then you come home to no wife and no dinner started."

"That's okay." Sean nuzzled her ear, his hands roaming up and down her spine. "If nothing else, we'll walk to the café and grab something there."

"It's Wednesday—they close at three, remember?" With a gentle push against his chest, she freed herself, reaching up to tousle his thick red-blond hair. "But I can throw together some grilled cheese sandwiches and open a bagged salad." She didn't pretend to be a good homemaker, and so far Sean hadn't complained. Of course, they were still in their honeymoon period. Sometimes she wondered how he could bear to leave her as often as he did with his business travels, and other times she savored the privacy.

Sean crossed his arms and yawned. "So where've you been? I called the studio to let you know I was on my way. Andrew said you'd left early, but you didn't answer the cell."

Beth crinkled her nose. "I left it at home—sorry." She moved to the sack and reached inside. "I went to an auction in Carston this afternoon. They'd advertised a Depression-era bedroom suite. I thought if I could get it reasonably, I'd fill up the second bedroom."

Sean came up behind her and curled his hands over her shoulders. "I take it you didn't get it?"

"Nope. Went higher than I wanted to spend. But"—she lifted a stack of books from the sack—"I got all of these for a dollar." She laid the books across the table, brushing the covers with her fingertips. "Look—high school textbooks. They're outdated, but they're better than nothing." Trina would be delighted with her find.

Sean reached to pick one up, a frown on his face. "Algebra." He looked at the others on the table. "American history, geometry, and earth science? What are you going to do with these?"

Beth laughed, rising on tiptoe to deliver a quick smack on his lips. "They're for Trina so she can prepare for her GED."

Sean's frown deepened. "So you're helping her, huh?"

She shot him a sharp look. "Is there some reason I shouldn't?"

He sighed, plopping the book back onto the table. "You know how the Old Order Mennonite feel about higher education. Letting Trina explore on the Internet is one thing, but buying her books so she can prepare for a GED? That's overstepping some pretty big boundaries, Beth."

Beth took a step back and gawked at her husband. "So I should leave her floundering alone? The poor kid is getting trampled from every direction—her parents, her boyfriend, even Andrew, who should know better than to stomp on somebody's dream. *Someone* needs to offer a helping hand."

"Now don't get all defensive on me." Sean reached out and tucked a stray strand of hair behind her ear. She jerked her head away from his touch. He clamped his jaw for a moment then dropped his hand. "Stop and think about it, Beth. We already have trouble fitting in around here since we aren't Mennonite or Amish. Do you want to give the community another reason to distrust us?"

"I'm not going to let their attitudes dictate what I do," Beth protested. "Trina's a smart girl with a lot of ambition. It isn't fair that she can't pursue veterinary school if she wants to."

"It might not be fair," Sean countered, "but we don't write the rules. And I'm afraid you're going to open a can of worms if you get involved."

Beth opened her mouth to argue, but Sean placed his fingers over her lips.

"No, let's don't fight about this." He slipped his arms around her again, drawing her close. She allowed his embrace but held her body stiff, still disgruntled with him. He murmured into her ear. "I'm tired and hungry. Let's drive into McPherson or Newton and get some supper, relax, and talk about nothing, okay?"

Sean's hands roved gently over her back, reminding her how much she had missed him during his absence. Beth relented, relaxing into Sean's embrace. "All right. That sounds good. Let me change my shirt, though—I got really sweaty out in the sun." She lifted her face for his kiss then headed to their bedroom to change.

"I'll put these books back in the bag," Sean called after her, "and put them on the utility porch."

She sighed. "Fine." *Out of sight, out of mind,* she supposed. She didn't want to fight with her husband, but Trina was the first person in Sommerfeld to befriend her. She owed the girl something. If that something turned out to be assistance in seeing her dreams become reality, then Sean would just have to accept it.

Trina slammed the book shut and released a strangled groan. From the computer, Beth looked over her shoulder.

"What's the problem?"

"Algebra. Rational expressions, factoring, complex numbers. All I had in school was add, subtract, divide, and multiply. None of this stuff makes sense to me!" She put her forehead on the books. The musty smell of the old textbook filled her nostrils, reminding her of the generations-long rules of the Old Order community. Who did she think she was, trying to change the traditions? "Maybe I should just forget it."

A hand grabbed her shoulder and pulled her upright. She looked up into Beth's stern face.

"Trina Muller, I never took you for a quitter."

"But, Beth," Trina said, "it's pointless! Even if Mama and Dad do say it's okay, I'll never pass the test." Flopping the book open, she pointed to a problem. "Look at this! If $x-y = 1$, and $2x-y = 5$, then what are x and y?" She clenched her fists. "I don't know!"

Beth sat down next to Trina and looked at the problems in the book. She sighed, sending Trina an apologetic look. "I took algebra in high school, but it was a long time ago. I'm afraid I don't remember a lot about the formal steps involved in resolving algebraic equations, but I know with this we can do a little simple problem-solving and find the answer."

"How?" The feeling of hopelessness made Trina want to cry. For the past week, she'd spent her late evenings holed up in her room reading the history and science books Beth had purchased. Those subjects were interesting, almost like reading stories or taking a walk through nature, and she'd enjoyed them. But neither algebra nor geometry was enjoyable. Certainly both mathematics areas would be on the GED test, and Trina would have to master them in order to pass. She blinked back tears. "Can you show me?"

Beth picked up Trina's pencil. "Look. You know in each of the equations, x and y have to be the same number. So let's just explore. Start with 2–1, which equals 1. Put the 2 for x and the 1 for y in the second equation. Does it work?"

Trina frowned at the problem. "No."

"Okay, then go to the next two sets of numbers that will equal one—3–2."

Trina worked her way through Beth's system. When she tried 4 for x and 3 for y, both problems worked. She clapped her hands and crowed, "Success!" Her euphoria lasted only moments, however; an entire page of problems—more complex than the one she'd just solved—waited. She wilted again. Looking at Beth, she implored, "Tell me again I can do this."

Beth caught one of Trina's string ties and tickled her nose with it. "You can do this! I believe in you!"

Tears of gratitude flooded Trina's eyes. "Thank you, Beth. It means so much to have you encouraging me. I just wish I had a private teacher—what is that called?"

"A tutor."

"Yes, a tutor. But I don't know anyone in town who's had this kind of math."

Beth flicked a glance into the front room, where her husband sat watching television. Trina's heart skipped a beat. Sean McCauley drew blueprints for elaborate buildings. Surely he was familiar with these different types of mathematics. She waited for Beth to ask him to help, but instead she turned back to Trina.

"Well, it isn't as if you have to know the whole book to pass the test," Beth said. "There will be basic math and a spattering of the higher-level mathematics. If you do well on the other parts, then a so-so score on the math part should still let you pass."

"Do you really think so?" Trina pressed both palms to her stomach. "When I think about taking that test, I start to feel queasy."

"And how do you feel when you consider not taking the test and giving up?"

Trina's lips trembled into a weak smile. "Queasy."

Beth laughed. "So you might as well feel queasy and forge forward, huh?" She tapped the book. "Study. Do at least five of these." She got up and returned to the computer.

With a sigh, Trina got back to work. It took nearly half an hour to work five problems, and she was almost relieved when the telephone rang and Beth held it out to her.

"It's your brother."

Trina took the phone. "Hello?"

"Mom said to call and have you come home." His voice dropped to a whisper. "I think she's upset about all the time you've been spending over at the McCauleys' lately. Might want to step careful when you get here."

Trina stifled a sigh. Never demonstrative, Mama had been down-right cold to her ever since she started working with Dr. Groening. Between Mama's chilly treatment and Graham's avoidance, Trina carried a constant heartache. She said, "Maybe I'll swing by the park and pick her a few daisies. That usually cheers her up."

"Okay." Tony brought his voice back to full volume. "See you in a few minutes."

Trina handed the telephone back to Beth. "I have to go—Mama's missing me."

Beth smiled. "Well, you have been spending a lot of time here. She's used to seeing you all day, every day. I imagine she does miss you."

Trina forced a light chuckle as she gathered up her papers and pencils. "Probably mostly she just wonders what I'm up to over here."

Sean pushed off from the sofa and walked to the wide doorway between the front room and dining room. "You haven't told your parents yet?"

Trina glanced up and caught Beth and Sean exchanging a quick, tense look. She shook her head slowly. "No. I'm going to wait until I've passed the GED and have been accepted into a college program."

Sean leaned against the doorjamb and folded his arms across his chest. "Was that Beth's advice?"

Beth shot Sean a look that made Trina gulp.

"Um, no. Actually, Beth advised the opposite—to just come right out and tell them what I'm doing. But I want to wait." She observed Sean's expression change to approving, and Beth's mouth unpursed. Uncomfortable with the silent messages being sent back and forth between the pair, Trina snatched up her things and bustled toward the door. "Thanks again for the help, Beth. I'll see you tomorrow. . . maybe." She closed the door behind her and stepped into the humid air of midevening.

Instead of going directly home, Trina headed for the area dubbed "the park" by Sommerfeld's young people. Just an empty lot where a livery barn had burned down almost twenty years ago, the area now sported halfhearted grass, a spattering of wildflowers, and a crude picnic table and benches constructed out of scrap lumber by a couple of boys learning to use their fathers' tools.

The farmers' market sellers used the area, as did young people on pleasant evenings for a place to gather and talk. Trina hoped a handful of daisies, her mother's favorite flower, might stave off an unpleasant series of questions concerning her frequent evenings spent with Beth McCauley. Mama had warmed considerably toward Beth since Uncle Henry, Mama's younger brother, had married Beth's mother, but she still didn't approve of Beth's non-Mennonite lifestyle. Anyone who wasn't Mennonite was suspect, as far as Mama was concerned.

Trina rounded the corner toward the park and heard laughter. She slowed her steps, turning her ear toward the various voices drifting across the warm summer breeze. The high-pitched giggle belonged to Darcy Kauffman. Wherever one found Darcy, Michelle Lapp was nearby. Michelle had acted sweet on Graham's best friend, Walt Martin, for quite some time, and Walt had recently begun responding, so that masculine rumble no doubt came from Walt's throat.

Previously the café had kept Trina too busy in the evenings to spend much time with friends. Now, studying for her GED had curtailed her social time. The thought of catching a few minutes of chatting with Michelle, Darcy, and Walt sped her feet, and she headed around the side of the general merchandise store with a smile on her face.

"Hello!" she called, and the group at the picnic table turned. Her smile faltered when she realized Graham was with the others.

He leaped up from the table, where he'd been sitting next to Darcy. "Trina. . ." The word sputtered on his tongue. Then, seeming to pull himself together, he gestured toward the table. "Come join us. Michelle was telling us about her cousin's trip to the Kansas City zoo and the antics of the chimpanzees."

Trina stopped several feet away from the table. She hugged the book and stack of crumpled papers tight to her pounding heart. "No,

I—I can't. Mama's expecting me. I just wanted to pick a few daisies."

"I'll help you." Graham strode toward her, his hands outstretched. "Let me take those so you can pick flowers."

She shook her head, backing away from him. "No. That's okay."

Darcy turned around on the bench, peering at the items in Trina's arms. "What have you got there? A new book?"

Reading was a favorite pastime of the Old Order young people, and they often shared new purchases with one another. But Trina knew she wouldn't share this one. She shouldn't have come this way. "Yes, but it's not—not anything you'd enjoy." She hoped Darcy would take her word for it and not ask to see the math textbook.

Graham looked down at her, his expression unreadable. Trina begged him with her eyes to keep silent. He offered a barely discernible nod. Turning back to the group at the table, he said, "Daisies are thickest over against the Feed and Seed's west wall. Hope your mother enjoys the bouquet."

Trina swallowed, called a good-bye, and hurried off. As she picked a handful of the cheerful flowers, she listened to the laughing conversation at the table. Beth's question replayed in her mind: *Is it worth it?* Her heart heavy, she discovered the answer didn't come as easily as she would have preferred.

TEN

O ut of the corner of his eye, Graham watched Trina head down the sidewalk toward her house. Just seeing her created a lonely ache in his chest. Darcy and Michelle jabbered away, unaware how little he cared about their endless prattle. The only voice he wanted to hear was Trina's, but she'd just told him his assistance wasn't needed.

In other words, *Go away.*

He never would have thought anything would come between him and Trina, but something had. *Lord, why'd I have to fall in love with her? It's not supposed to be this hard.* He sighed.

Walt clapped him on the shoulder. "Hey, didn't you hear her?"

Graham jerked his gaze to Walt. "What?"

Walt laughed. "Michelle just said her mom's got a key lime pie in the refrigerator. We're heading over there to have a piece. You coming?"

Graham's favorite, and Mrs. Lapp took no shortcuts when it came to cooking. At fellowship gatherings, good-natured arguments broke out between people vying for the last slice of her pie or a second piece of her cornmeal-coated fried chicken. Graham waited for his mouth to water, but instead he felt as though cotton filled his throat. He shook his head. "That sounds good, but I need to get home."

BLESSINGS

Darcy caught his arm. "Are you sure?"

Graham looked into Darcy's hopeful face. She was a pretty girl with large blue eyes, thick lashes, and sunshiny hair. And she was interested in him—she let him know without being forward. He half wished some sort of feeling would rise up—even a hint of a desire to spend more time with her. But nothing happened. Pulling his lips into a rueful smile, he said, "I'm sure. Thanks anyway."

Darcy's hand slipped away. She ducked her head, the white ribbons of her cap bunching against her shoulders. "If you hurry, you could still catch her."

Graham wasn't sure he heard correctly. He leaned forward slightly. "What?"

Head still downcast, she shifted her eyes to peer at him through her lashes. "I said, you could still catch her."

Graham jolted to his feet. Heat filled his face. "I—I—"

Across the table, Michelle tipped her head. "Yes. What happened between you and Trina? I thought for sure you two would be getting published soon, but lately you're never together."

Graham grimaced. Darcy at least tried to be tactful. Michelle had always been one to boldly state her opinions—there were times when he thought she belonged more with Trina's mother than Trina did. Michelle and Darcy waited, their gazes fixed on Graham's face. He formed an answer. "She's just. . .busy." Even to his ears, the excuse was lame, but it was the only thing he could think of.

Darcy and Michelle exchanged looks. Michelle asked, "With what? I understood it when she worked at the café—her mother hardly gave her a moment's rest. But now? She works in Lehigh and has every evening off. And we still don't see her. How is she staying so busy?"

Graham couldn't answer that question truthfully without betraying a confidence. As much as he resented Trina's choice to pursue a career in veterinary care, he couldn't bring himself to divulge her secret. He shrugged, forcing a light laugh. "You know Trina. . .always up to something." He realized his statement pertained more to the old Trina. The girl he fell in love with had been bubbly, full of life. This new one was slowly losing the sparkle. Sadness struck with the thought.

He stepped away from the table, lifting his hand in a wave. "You all enjoy your pie. I'll see you Sunday in service."

Before they could say anything else, he hurried down the sidewalk, his heels thudding against the red bricks. Darcy's comment about catching Trina if he hurried ran through his mind, and of their own volition, his feet sped up. Did he want to catch Trina?

He knew he did. Despite her crazy ideas of going to college and becoming some sort of animal doctor, he still wanted her. Still loved her. He wished he could set the feelings aside, but how did a person turn off love? The whole community still talked about how Henry Braun had remained a bachelor for over twenty years when the girl he loved married someone else. Henry didn't marry until that girl, widowed, returned to Sommerfeld. Now they were happily married and the proud parents of twins.

Henry Braun had waited two decades to marry the girl of his heart. Wouldn't Henry say his wife, Marie, had been worth the wait? But Graham was ready to be married now. Waiting for Trina to go to college, get a degree, and spend some time working as a veterinarian seemed interminable. He sucked in a breath of hot air then blew it out with a snort. Henry Braun was a much more patient man than Graham professed to be.

Somehow he needed to get Trina's focus turned around. Now that she wasn't working at the café, there shouldn't be any barriers to spending evenings with her. Maybe he should do what Darcy said— catch up to her, walk her the rest of the way home, go on into the house, and ask permission to take her to the barn party planned at the Kreider farm on Saturday night.

His heart pounded with the thought of having an evening with Trina. Surrounded by their friends, being seen as a couple—the time was just what Trina needed to remember there were other things in life besides taking care of animals. The decision made, he broke into a jog. He caught Trina just as she was walking up her sidewalk.

"Trina!"

She paused at the bottom of the porch steps and turned. Her face didn't light with pleasure when she saw him, giving him momentary pause, but he refused to let her lack of warmth deter him.

"I didn't get a chance to tell you about the party tomorrow night at Kreiders'."

She tipped her head, bringing her cheek near the bedraggled cluster of daisies in her fist. "What kind of party?"

"Shucking." Graham laughed at her grimace. "But the girls will probably do more watching than working."

"Yes, you boys will want to show off."

The hint of teasing in her tone encouraged him. "So do you want to go and watch me show off?"

She released a brief giggle then turned her head toward the house. "I'll need to ask permission."

"Here." He took the book and papers from her arms. "Take those flowers in to your mom, ask, and then come let me know the answer." By taking her belongings, he solved two issues—first, her parents wouldn't see them; and second, she would have to come back out to get them.

"All right." She skipped up the steps and entered the house. He heard the mutter of voices through the screened door. The voices drifted away to the back of the house, and still he waited. Finally, Trina returned, her mother on her heels.

Mrs. Muller remained in the doorway. "Graham, what time will the party be over?"

"Early, ma'am. I'd have Trina home by ten o'clock for sure." With service in the morning, Saturday evening activities never went late.

"Who else is riding with you?"

Graham recognized the woman's underlying concern—would he and Trina be alone at any time? "I plan to ride out with Walt Martin and Michelle Lapp."

Trina stood on the edge of the porch, her gaze on her mother. It appeared she held her breath, but Graham wasn't sure if she was hoping for a positive or a negative response.

Finally, Mrs. Muller gave a brusque nod. "All right. She can go since she'll be home early and you'll be in a group. Does she need to bring anything?"

"A snack, if she wants to."

"She wants to."

For a moment, sympathy swelled for Trina. Small wonder she kept secrets from her parents. Deborah Muller tended to think for her children, controlling every part of their lives. Another brief thought struck—wasn't he, too, trying to control Trina? He pushed the thought away and looked at Trina.

"Trina, shall I pick you up at six o'clock?"

Still looking at her mother, Trina replied, "Yes. Six would be fine." Trina moved back one step from the door. "Mama, I'm going to sit out here with Graham for a little bit."

Graham's gaze jerked from Trina to Mrs. Muller. He'd never heard Trina state her intentions before—she always asked. From the look on Deborah Muller's face, she was as surprised as Graham. For a moment, he feared the woman would yank Trina into the house.

But to his surprise, she bobbed her head in one quick nod, her black ribbons jerking with the stiff movement.

"Very well. But you've been gone all day. Make it a short visit." She closed the door before Trina could respond.

Trina sat on the top step of the porch stairs. With a triumphant grin, she patted the spot beside her. "We won't have much time. Better sit."

A few uninterrupted minutes with Trina had always been a gift. But for some reason, Graham hesitated. Her sudden change in demeanor made him think of the young woman who ran the stained-glass studio on the edge of town—Beth McCauley. Beth told people what to do rather than asking.

"Or do you need to hurry off?"

The quaver in her voice pulled him forward two feet, but he couldn't make himself sit. Instead, he held out the math book and stack of lined papers. "I'd like to, but it's been a long day. And I have to work tomorrow, so I'd better head home." He put the items into her arms. "I'll pick you up a little before six tomorrow, okay?"

Her brown eyes looked sad, yet he felt the need to step back and process the subtle change he'd just witnessed. He couldn't do that sitting beside her—he needed some distance. He almost snorted. For the past two weeks, he'd had nearly constant distance from Trina and had begrudged the time apart. Now he was choosing to separate himself? It didn't make much sense, yet he still moved backward down the sidewalk.

Still perched on the porch floor with her feet on the bottom riser, she offered a meek nod. "I'll see you tomorrow, Graham. Have a good day at work."

He glanced back before turning the corner toward his own house. She was still sitting there, staring into the gloaming.

"So tell me about your new job, Trina."

Darcy Kauffman pulled Trina into the corner of the barn, away from the raucous young men who tried to outdo one another in the number of ears shucked per minute. The cheers from the girls added to the din.

Trina normally enjoyed watching Graham—although he worked inside at the lumberyard, he could hold his own against the farmers' sons, and her heart had always thrilled to his success. Tonight, however, she sensed his displeasure, although no one else would have recognized it, and she welcomed a few moments away from the crowd.

"I like Dr. Groening a lot," Trina said, leaning against the barn wall and running her fingers along the attached modesty cape of her dress. "He's very patient, and he lets me watch all of the examinations."

"Your mother told my mother you're basically Dr. Groening's cleaning service."

Darcy's words were uttered without a hint of malice, but Trina still cringed. "I suppose that's true. But I still like it."

Darcy smiled, leaning closer. "I also heard Graham is teaching you to drive."

Trina's jaw dropped. They'd only had one lesson. One unsuccessful lesson ending with a disagreement that had yet to be resolved. "Who told you that?"

Darcy giggled, hunching her shoulders. "Is it true?"

Trina shrugged. "He tried. It didn't work out very well."

"Oh." Darcy sighed, her lips twisting into a pout. "I'm sorry."

A mighty cheer rose from the group in the center of the barn. Both girls looked toward the gathered group. Walt stood up and waved a red ear over his head. Darcy and Trina shared a snicker—Michelle would be given a kiss before the night was over.

Darcy caught Trina's hand. "Don't you wish Graham had found the red ear? Then you and he. . ." Her voice trailed off, her cheeks glowing bright red.

Trina felt heat fill her face, and she was certain she blushed crimson. Many times she'd fantasized about Graham kissing her. But she knew she didn't want their first kiss to be the result of a chance find in a corn-shucking contest. "No!" She hissed the single word.

Darcy's eyes widened. "You don't want him to kiss you?"

Oh, Trina wanted Graham's kiss. Sometimes she wanted it so badly it frightened her. She closed her eyes and imagined it—a sweet, tender joining of lips. But in her dreams, it always took place on the day they became officially published. Her eyes popped open, her heart skipping a beat. Would they become published if she continued to pursue a degree in veterinary science?

She planned to take the GED test at the end of August. If she passed, she would immediately begin trying to enroll in the community college in El Dorado. A two-year college didn't require ACT scores, so she could get several classes out of the way before transferring to a bigger college. She and Beth had worked everything out. But now a fear struck. Graham might decide to pursue some other girl—maybe even Darcy—if she persisted in her pursuit of education. A stinging behind her nose let her know tears threatened. She quickly turned her back on Darcy.

"Trina?" Darcy's worried voice came from directly behind Trina's ear. "Is something wrong?"

Yes, many things were wrong. But Trina didn't have the slightest idea how to fix them. *Lord, I'm so confused. I believe I'm meant to care for animals. But I love Graham, too. How can we make this all work?*

She sniffed hard and turned to face her friend. "It looks like the girls have started bundling the shucks for fodder. Should we help?"

Darcy's brows pulled down briefly, but then she offered a smile and nod. "Sure."

They moved toward the group just as another whoop rose. Walt pounded Graham on the back, and the other young men laughed and hollered. Trina's feet came to a stumbling halt as people began turning, aiming their laughing gazes in her direction. Behind her, Darcy grabbed her shoulders and murmured, "Uh-oh." Trina knew without even looking.

Graham, too, had found a red ear of corn.

ELEVEN

Graham held his prize with a mixture of elation and regret. A month ago he would have presented Trina with the red ear then given her a possessive kiss that would make clear to everyone his intentions regarding her. But now? He held the ear against his thigh while whistles and cheers sounded, and Trina stood twelve feet away on the straw-covered barn floor, her brown eyes wide in her pale face.

She didn't know what to do, either.

A feeling akin to anger welled up inside of Graham. This ridiculous notion of hers had changed everything. He couldn't put his stamp of possession on a woman who might not be his someday. But how could he save face with his friends? He had to kiss her. Yet, looking into her apprehensive face, he hesitated. His mind raced through the options, and he decided there was only one thing he could do.

With deliberately slow steps for the benefit of their audience, he advanced on Trina. Her cheeks flamed brighter with every inch that closed between them. He stopped less than a foot and a half in front of her. Between his buddies' encouragement and the girls' giggles, he hoped she'd be able to hear him. Leaning forward, he let his lips brush her temple, which would satisfy the gawkers, as he whispered, "Don't worry—I won't kiss you in front of everyone."

The look of relief she gave him sent another rush of mixed emotions through his chest, but he squeezed her arm, straightened, and called over his shoulder, "Okay, I won that round. Who's going to top me this time?"

By nine thirty, the corncrib overflowed with stripped ears, and the bundled shucked leaves lay in neat rows in the loft to dry. Everyone began climbing into their vehicles to return to their homes.

Graham couldn't help but notice Trina's reticence during the good-bye process. In the past, she would have bounced from car to car, offering private farewells to each person in attendance. Tonight, however, she stayed close to Walt's vehicle, waving and smiling, but clearly eager to be done with the formalities and on their way.

He and Walt got into the front seat, and Michelle and Trina shared the back. Michelle chattered away, leaning forward occasionally to tap Walt's shoulder and whisper comments that made him laugh. Trina responded to questions but did very little talking. That, too, was different.

Graham faced forward, his chest tight, as he compared the Trina he had begun courting six months ago to the one sitting in the backseat of Walt's car. He missed the old Trina. Ever since she got the idea of pursuing a career, she hadn't been the same. Why couldn't she see it? Surely if she set the notion aside, her old bubbly self would return.

Wouldn't it?

Walt pulled up in front of Trina's house. "Here you go. See you at service tomorrow."

"Thank you for the ride, Walt. Bye, Michelle." Her gaze flitted to Graham, her eyes questioning. "Bye, Graham."

She expected him to just ride off with Walt and not have a private good-bye? He popped his door open. "Thanks for the ride, but I'll walk from here." He knew Michelle and Walt would want a few minutes alone, too. Based on the silent messages flowing between the two of them following their kiss tonight, it wouldn't be long before they were published. He envied his friend.

Walt nodded. "See you, buddy."

Graham slammed the door and remained on the road until Walt drove off. Trina stood on the sidewalk, her gaze on him. The same reserve he'd seen during the leave-taking at the party was still very much in existence. How he wished she'd warm up a little. Was it only a month and a half ago she'd nearly danced into his arms when he visited her in Andrew's barn?

He walked toward her, watching her suck in her lower lip. She tipped her head back to look into his face when he stepped onto the sidewalk. Her brown eyes appeared darker in hue with the evening around them.

"You could have let Walt take you home," she said. "It's late—Mama will expect me to come in right away."

He shrugged. "Walt will want some time alone with Michelle." He should have said he wanted some time alone with Trina.

"I suppose." She turned toward the porch and took tiny steps along the walkway. He wished she'd say she wanted some time alone with him.

Although she didn't offer an invitation for conversation, he fell in step with her. The porch light cast a golden path for them to follow, and he touched her back lightly as they neared the steps. She scurried forward, away from his fingers, and stepped onto the first riser. But then she turned to face him.

The eight-inch riser put her at an equal height with him. How simple it would be to lean forward and place a kiss on her lips. But if he did it now, she'd think it was because of the red ear. Besides, her mother was probably watching.

He slid his hands into his trouser pockets. "Did you enjoy this evening at all, Trina?" He heard the resignation in his tone and did nothing to mask it.

Her eyes widened. "W–why, of course I did. The shucking parties are always fun." She licked her lips. "And it's been ages since I had an evening with everyone."

He wanted to ask, *And whose fault is that?* But he didn't want a fight. He wanted things to go back to the way they were before that night Andrew called her out to work on Regen's leg. So he said, "I'm glad you came. I wish we had more evenings together."

"I know." But she didn't say, "Me, too," or "We will," or anything else that would have been encouraging.

Graham blew out a noisy breath. "Well, you'd better go in."

Her eyes seemed sad as she nodded. But she remained on the step, her hands clasped girlishly behind her back, her white ribbons trailing down her cheeks. "I don't want to go in with you mad at me."

Graham took a stumbling step backward. "I'm not mad at you."

"Yes, you are." She looked at him, unsmiling. "You invited me to go to the party, but I can tell you're mad. You've been mad at me for a long time."

He knew exactly how long, too. "Trina, I'm not mad, I'm—" But what could he say? If he was honest, he was mad. Mad at her for heading in a direction she shouldn't. Mad at her for being stubborn. Mad at her for disrupting his life. With a rueful snort, he admitted, "Okay, I'm mad."

"Tell me why."

In her expression, he saw a hint of the old Trina—the spunky, I-can-handle-whatever-comes-my-way Trina who had captured his heart. Yet the firmly held posture, the tension in her brow spoke of the new

Trina—the one he didn't want to know.

"Because you've changed. All your plans to go to school, to become some kind of animal doctor—it's taken something away from you. I miss that something."

For long moments, Trina stared into his eyes without moving, without changing expression, without speaking. When he felt as though she'd turned to stone, she finally raised her shoulders in a tiny shrug and turned her face slightly to the side. She sighed. Without looking at him, she said, "It isn't the planning for school that's taken something away from me."

Without offering further explanation, she climbed the remaining two risers and entered her house. Despite the sultry evening air, Graham experienced a chill. He got the distinct impression he'd just been told good-bye.

Trina followed her mother from the cloakroom. On the benches across the worship room, Graham sat beside the other unmarried men in the last row in the men's section. Her heart ached when she saw him. Not that long ago, he would have met her gaze and sneaked a wink or sent her a secretive smile. But today he didn't even glance in her direction.

He was still mad.

She slid onto the bench next to Mama and blinked rapidly to control the sting of tears. She missed Graham. She missed his laughter, his teasing, the way he could make her tummy tremble with a simple look. How it hurt that he now held himself aloof. She had hoped better of him.

Her gaze drifted to Andrew, sitting stoic and serious two benches ahead of Graham. She had expected more from her favorite cousin, too. Fulfilling her heart's desire meant so much to her, but everywhere she turned she met resistance. Why had so many people let her down lately?

Trina had no time to process that question. The deacons and minister marched in, and the congregation knelt for the opening prayer. Head bowed and eyes closed, Trina added her own prayer to that of the minister—*Please, Lord, bring our hearts together so I can walk where You lead.*

After the service, as people mingled in front of the simple clapboard building before going to homes for meals, Trina moved to the center of the grassy yard and waited. Graham came out the front doors with Walt. The two slapped their black hats on their heads in unison then paused at the foot of the steps to chat. She watched, waiting, hoping, her hands clasped at the waist of her purple dress and her breath coming in short spurts of anticipation.

Look at me, Graham. Look at me. If he would only look—just once—then she could send him a silent message. *I still care. I still love you. Please, we can work this out.*

Someone touched her arm, and she jumped. She turned to find Michelle Lapp. "He won't be coming over here anytime soon."

Trina frowned. Was she that transparent? Denying she was waiting for Graham would be pointless as well as untruthful. "Why not?"

"Walt is talking to him about..." Michelle glanced around, her lips pursed tightly. Then she leaned forward and whispered, "Our plans to be published. He talked to my folks last night after the shucking." Michelle's eyes danced with excitement.

Trina squeezed her friend's hands. "Oh, Michelle, how wonderful for you." She tried to truly mean it, but she recognized a wave of jealousy underscoring her words.

"Yes." Michelle smoothed her hair beneath her pristine cap then ran her fingers along the white ribbons. "All along I thought you and Graham would beat us to it, but we'll be first, after all."

Trina's brows pulled down. Did Michelle see marriage as a competition to be won?

Apparently reading Trina's mind, Michelle laughed and threw her arm across Trina's shoulders. "Oh, don't be silly. I know we aren't in a footrace. I'm just surprised, that's all. Graham's had eyes for no one but you for over a year now, and we all finally saw you looking back with the same interest. Graham's a year older than Walt, so we just figured. . ."

Trina didn't care for the use of the word *we*, implying others had been talking about her behind her back. She also wondered what else had been discussed. As Andrew had often joked, there were no secrets in Sommerfeld. Did they know the deepest secret in her heart, too? While she sought a way to ask without giving herself away, her mother's voice carried across the yard.

"Trina! It's time to go—come along."

With a sigh, Trina sent one more look toward the men's doors. To her surprise, Graham was no longer there. She spun around, seeking his car. It was gone. Her heart fell. He'd left without saying a word to her.

"Trina!"

Michelle gave her arm a little nudge. "I think your mother is getting impatient. I'll see you later, Trina. Don't tell anybody about me getting published yet, okay?"

Trina looked directly into Michelle's eyes. "I don't tell secrets."

Michelle's blush let Trina know she understood the hidden meaning. Of all their friends, Michelle had the biggest tendency to talk too much. "Bye." She scurried away.

"Trina, are you coming?"

The irritated note in Mama's voice set Trina's feet in motion. "Yes, Mama, I'm coming."

TWELVE

Tuesday after work, Tony dropped Trina off at the stained-glass art studio. Before she closed the door of the truck, he said, "Be sure to be at the café by six thirty to eat supper."

Trina caught the warning note. Mama's disgruntlement at the amount of time Trina had spent with Beth McCauley—and the number of times she'd missed the supper hour since she'd started working with Dr. Groening—made everyone walk on eggshells. Trina felt bad that Tony sometimes got caught in the crossfire of Mama's ill temper when he'd done nothing to deserve it. The family's caution around Mama reminded Trina of a comical plaque she'd seen in a discount store that read IF MAMA AIN'T HAPPY, AIN'T NOBODY HAPPY. At the time, she'd laughed. It wasn't funny, however, when it proved true.

"I'll be there. Maybe I'll stick around and help with cleanup, too."

Tony nodded in approval. "Good idea." He glanced at the clock in the truck's dash. "It's almost five thirty already—you'd better hurry."

Trina gave the door a slam and scurried up the short sidewalk to the front door of the studio. Stepping inside, she called, "I came to use the Internet, if that's okay." Too late she noticed Beth seated at the computer. She moved past the workstations to the desk and looked at the screen. The complex design, half colored, let Trina know Beth was in the middle of planning a new stained-glass art window.

Beth offered a sympathetic smile. "I'm sorry, Trina. I know I told you the computer was available to you anytime, but I've got to have this preliminary window ready for Sean to show to a committee tomorrow. I really need to work."

Trina backed up, aware of Andrew at the worktable behind her. "That's okay."

"You wanted to go back to that math site, didn't you?"

Beth had located a tutorial site with basic math plus algebra, geometry, and trigonometry. Trina had spent at least an hour each evening on it for the past week. She nodded. "Yes. But I can wait—it'll keep." However, she knew what she needed to do wouldn't keep for long. In just two weeks, Beth would drive her to McPherson to get her Kansas ID, then to Hutchinson to take the GED test.

Beth dug in her pocket and withdrew a key ring. She held it out to Trina. "Here. I'll work on this at home this evening, which will free up the studio's computer. You can let yourself in the back door after supper and go online."

Trina pressed her hands to her dirty apron. "Are you sure? I don't want to infringe."

"It's fine." Beth pressed the key into Trina's hands. "No one will be here to distract you. Just leave the key on the desk and remember to lock up when you're done."

"Thank you, Beth." Trina's heart swelled with gratitude. Aware of Andrew's silence behind her, she appreciated more fully the support she had from one person in town. "I guess I'll go over to the café and give Mama a hand with the supper rush."

"Good idea," Andrew said. Trina turned to face him as he continued in a mild tone that still sounded accusatory to Trina. "I'm sure your mother will appreciate your company. She told my folks Sunday she feels like you're a stranger."

Trina felt sometimes like a stranger to herself, so far removed from the girl she'd been before the desire to become a veterinarian took control of her thoughts. In the past, she would have shared these odd feelings with her favorite cousin, but given the distant way he'd treated her of late, she shrugged and said, "Some unplanned time with her should cure that. I'll see you later. Thank you again, Beth."

Back in the sunshine of the sidewalk, she felt a chill. Once again the question Beth had asked her—"*Is it worth it?*"—winged through her mind. She nearly stomped her foot. Yes, it was worth it! Being a veterinarian was her dream, and dreams were worth sacrifice!

But the sacrifice of family and friends? Is it truly worth that? With a grunt of frustration, Trina pushed the question aside. Of course she wasn't sacrificing her family and friends. Not permanently, anyway. They would come around eventually. Andrew's family came to accept his desire to work as an artist. Aunt Marie, the prodigal daughter, had been accepted into the community after a twenty-year absence. It just took time, and Trina had time.

Turning toward the café, she forced the troublesome thoughts out of her head. It all depended on whether or not she passed the GED in two weeks. If she didn't have a high school diploma, she couldn't enroll in the community college. So why worry about losing her family and Graham until she knew for sure what would happen? The decision made to put worry on hold, Trina marched through the busy dining room to the kitchen and gave her mother a huge smile.

"Hi, Mama. I'm here to help."

Graham hung his canvas work apron on a nail, plopped his cap on his head, and waved good-bye to his boss. Stepping from the lumberyard's dim storage barn onto the sunny sidewalk, he squinted and tugged the hat brim a little lower.

He heaved a tired sigh and turned toward home, but a smell wafting from down the block brought him to a halt. Cabbage, onions, and bread. If his nose was correct—and he had no reason to doubt it—Deborah Muller had prepared *bierocks* at the café today. His mouth watered as he considered biting into one of the beef-and-vegetable-filled bread pockets. She probably had pie, too. If he was lucky, lemon with meringue inches high. Nothing in his cupboards at home would compete with home-baked bierocks and lemon meringue pie.

He changed direction and entered the café. The overhead fans whirled, providing a stir of air that felt good after he'd been in the heat all day. A quick glance at plates in front of other diners confirmed he had gotten a whiff of bierocks. He licked his lips in anticipation, slid into an open booth, and inhaled deeply, enjoying the mingle of mouth-watering aromas. Two bierocks, he decided, a wedge of pie, and a tall glass of milk.

Tapping his fingers on the tabletop, his gaze on the doorway that led to the kitchen, he waited eagerly for someone to come take his order. Someone zipped through the opening, hands filled with plates of bierocks and thick french fries, and he blinked twice, rearing back in surprise. Trina! His heart leaped with hope—she was working at the café again! She must have quit her job with Dr. Groening.

She buzzed by his booth, glancing sideways as she went. "I'll be with you in—" Her steps slowed, her eyes widening as recognition dawned. She gulped. "In a minute," she finished in a hoarse whisper then hurried off with the plates.

Graham resisted craning his neck around to watch for her return. Before she made it back, Kelly Dick trotted to his booth. She offered a big smile. "Hi, Graham. Mrs. Muller made bierocks, so that's the special. Want some?"

"That's what I came in for. I could smell them clear down the block," he said, resisting the urge to send her away so Trina would take his order. "I'd like two, with fries. And is there any lemon meringue pie?"

Kelly pulled her lips to the side. "Um. . .there was a little bit ago. Let me go check." She zinged off toward the kitchen.

As soon as Kelly left, Trina stopped beside the table. "Did Kelly get your order?"

"Yes."

"Okay."

Graham caught her arm before she could escape. "Wait a minute."

Trina shot him an impatient look. "Graham, I can't stop to chat right now. We're bringing in the highway traffic from the softball tournament in McPherson—we probably won't even get our own supper break. Mama needs me to get a load of dishes run so we'll have silverware for the next customers. I'm sorry. I don't have a minute."

He released her arm. "Okay. But when you're done, can we talk?"

For a moment he held his breath, certain she'd refuse. But she gave a quick nod. "Later." She hurried off as Kelly returned, carrying a plate heaped with two bierocks bigger than his fist and a pile of french fries.

Kelly placed the plate in front of Graham. "There was one piece of lemon meringue pie left, so I set it aside for you."

Graham sighed, smiling. "You're a sweetie."

Kelly blushed crimson and fled. Graham ate slowly, savoring every bite. While he ate, he watched other diners come and go; watched Trina, Kelly, and another teenage girl, Janina Ensz, scurry around meeting needs; and watched the hands on his wristwatch. Eight o'clock—closing time for the café—couldn't come quickly enough to suit him.

He knew from past experience that Trina would be busy an hour past closing, and he hoped Mrs. Muller wouldn't mind his sticking around and waiting until she was free to go. Or maybe she'd let Trina leave early since both Kelly and Janina were working, too. Curiosity burned in his full belly. Had his final comment to her the night of shucking awakened her to her need to let go of the foolish notion about going to college? Was she back in the café? Was she back to normal?

At a little after eight, the last diners left and Mrs. Muller turned over the sign from OPEN to CLOSED. Then she turned and put her hands on her hips, glaring at Graham. "I suppose you're waiting for Trina."

Graham remained in the booth and offered a grin. "Is that all right?"

The older woman sighed. She ran the back of her hand over her forehead, removing a sheen of perspiration. "I suppose, as long as you leave her alone while she cleans up."

"Or I can help."

Mrs. Muller's scowl deepened at Graham's hesitant suggestion. "Just stay out of the way." She charged back into the kitchen and began issuing orders.

Graham remained in the booth and watched the workers restore neatness to the café. Time crept slowly, and he wished he had something to read besides the menu. Twice he almost nodded off, but he straightened in the seat and forced himself to stay awake. His heart pounded in anticipation of asking Trina the question that filled him with hope: Had she returned to the café for good?

Trina put the mop in the closet, wiped her forehead with her apron, and turned in a slow circle. Dishes on the shelves, tomorrow's breakfast items stacked and waiting on the back of the stove, floor clean and shiny, condiment bottles refilled, and dispensers plump with brown paper napkins. Everything was done.

With a sigh, she removed her apron and dropped it in the wash basket beside the back door. As she did so, she glanced through the doorway to the dining room where Graham sat in a booth, his gaze straight ahead, his hands clasped on the clean tabletop. Another sigh escaped. She hated the dread that filled her when considering talking to Graham. How she longed for the days when uncontrolled eagerness carried her to his side at every opportunity for a moment of time with him.

Kelly and Janina tossed their soiled aprons into the basket. The two teenagers looked first at Trina then at Graham, and giggles erupted. Without a word, they each sent smirking grins in Trina's direction before slipping out the back door, their high-pitched laughter following them as they left the café.

Trina shook her head. Although only three years older than the other two girls, she felt decades older. When was the last time she had giggled with such carefree abandon? She blew out a breath, squared her shoulders, and crossed the floor to Mama, who sat at the desk in the corner, counting the evening's receipts.

"Mama? Do you mind if Graham and I take a walk?"

Mama's gaze jerked upward, her brows low. "A walk? Where to?"

Trina shrugged. "I don't know—just around town. Maybe the park."

Mama glanced at the wall clock. "Be home by ten." She turned her attention back to the tabs on the desk.

Trina turned and headed for the dining room. She jumped when she discovered Graham standing right inside the door that led to the kitchen. Hands clasped against her ribs, she said, "I have to be home by ten."

Graham nodded, his blue eyes solemn yet holding a hopeful spark Trina didn't understand. "I heard. Let's hurry, then, huh?" Cupping her elbow, he guided her to the front door, pushed it open, and ushered her through.

Once on the sidewalk, his fingers slipped away. Despite the balmy evening, a shiver shook Trina's frame. The release of her arm seemed indicative of all the pulling away people had been doing for the past several weeks. She hung her head, staring at the brick sidewalk beneath her feet.

"Trina?"

She looked up, meeting Graham's gaze. That same odd emotion in his eyes set her heart to pattering. "Yes?"

"We don't have much time. Let's walk. And talk. Okay?"

His hand returned to her elbow, and another slight shiver struck. "Okay."

Still loosely holding her arm, he set his feet in motion, and she followed suit. Yet he didn't speak until they reached the corner on the opposite end of the block from the café. Then his fingers tightened, he drew her to a halt, and he angled his body to face her. His warm hand framed her cheek, and he leaned forward slightly. She feared he might kiss her, and her gaze darted back and forth in search of prying eyes, but instead he whispered, his breath touching her forehead.

"You were in the café tonight, working. Does that mean you're back?"

She read the multitude of meanings in the simple question. And the answer to every meaning was no. Taking a step away from his fingers, she shook her head. "I was just helping out. Mama was very busy tonight."

Graham seemed to deflate before her eyes. "Oh." The single word was uttered in a low, flat tone that spoke volumes.

Although she had distanced herself from him only seconds ago, she now found the need to connect with him. Her hand shot out to grasp his wrist. "Graham, please. Can't you try to understand how important this is to me?"

Graham twisted his wrist free and clamped his hands over her shoulders. His fingers didn't bite into her skin, but she sensed the anger coursing from his fingertips. "And can't you understand how wrong you are being?"

Trina blinked rapidly. "Why is it wrong to want something more than what other women in the community have? It takes nothing from you, Graham, for me to become a veterinarian. I can still be a wife. I can still be a mother someday. It will be a challenge, yes, but why is it wrong?"

Graham raised his chin, blew a noisy breath heavenward, and then looked directly into her eyes. His stern, unyielding, critical gaze made her heart skip a beat. "It's wrong because you're breaking the ninth commandment."

Trina released a squawk of protest. "I haven't been lying! I've been very open with you!"

"And with your parents?" His harsh tone bruised her conscience. "You've been honest with them?"

"Well. . ." She licked her lips, her chin quivering. "I will be. Soon."

"That's not good enough, Trina." Graham withdrew his hands and shoved them into his trouser pockets. "All this sneaking around behind their backs makes me feel as though I can't trust you, either. How can we have any kind of relationship if you knowingly go against the teachings of the fellowship and are dishonest with your own family?"

Trina sniffed, the truth of his words piercing her more deeply than she cared to admit. Since she'd started pursuing the idea of becoming a veterinarian, she knew she'd put aside several lifelong practices, and being open and honest was only a part of it. With all of her studying, she hadn't read her Bible in weeks. During prayer at worship, instead of praying for others, she'd prayed for herself—for her dream to become reality.

Her heart constricted painfully as she recognized how these changes must be grieving her heavenly Father. She hung her head, shame striking hard. But how could she be honest with her parents and still proceed? "I—I don't know what to say. . . ."

Graham's sigh carried to her ears. "I don't, either." The sad resignation in his tone sent another shaft of hurt through Trina's chest.

Lifting her gaze, she said softly, "I am sorry, Graham, that so much has changed. I wish—I wish I knew how to fix it so everyone could be happy."

He twisted his lips into the semblance of a grin. It fell short of any warmth or amusement. "Yeah. Me, too. But it isn't going to happen, is it?"

Trina had no answer to that question. To say yes would mean giving up her dreams; to say no would mean letting go of Graham. She wasn't ready to do either.

After several long seconds, with only the strident chorus of locusts breaking the silence between them, Graham gave a jerk of his head. "Come on. I'll take you home before you're late. Might as well honor your mother's wish in that regard, at least."

THIRTEEN

Trina stared at the gray ceiling of her bedroom. The rustle of her curtains, lifted by the night breeze, and the ticking of her bedside clock seemed loud in the otherwise quiet room. Now and then the squeak of a mattress on the other side of the wall told her Tony tossed and turned, but she lay perfectly still, eyes wide open, mind racing.

How she hated to concede that Graham's words had hit their mark. But her conscience ached with the knowledge of her sins. She must tell Mama and Dad what she'd been doing when she visited Beth McCauley. Sweat broke out over her body as she considered their reaction. Dad would be disappointed, Mama so angry. They might even make her talk to the minister. Not for forgiveness—only God could forgive—but because her actions went against the fellowship's teachings.

A fierce gust sent her curtains sailing into the air and twisted them into a knot. Then, as the breeze lessened, they settled back into the gentle, nonthreatening swish. Trina watched them, feeling as though her heart were twisted into a tight knot. She wished her conscience could be as easily settled.

She squeezed her eyes closed, willing sleep to come, but after counting off a series of steady clicks—the passing of minutes—she knew she wouldn't be able to sleep until she'd cleared her conscience.

Throwing back the light sheet, she snatched up her robe, which lay across the foot of her bed, and slipped her arms into it. The sash firmly tied, she tiptoed down the hallway to avoid disturbing Tony and stopped outside her parents' closed door.

Trina could count on one hand the number of times she had entered her parents' bedroom. The room was off-limits, and it felt strange now to tap lightly on the solid wood door. At her first tap, she heard a snuffle, but no one replied. So she tapped again, a little harder, cringing as she glanced over her shoulder in hopes the noise wouldn't bother her brother.

This time, she heard her father's cough, followed by, "Who's out there?"

Without touching the doorknob, Trina whispered, "It's me, Dad. May—may I come in?"

"Trina?" Dad's voice sounded croaky.

"Yes."

"Just a minute." A scrabbling could be heard, underscored by her parents' muttered voices, and then the door opened. Dad blinked at her in confusion. "What are you doing up in the middle of the night?"

"I couldn't sleep." Trina linked her fingers together beneath her chin. "I need to talk to you and Mama."

Mama snapped on the bedside lamp. Her hair, usually slicked back in a smooth roll, lay tumbled across her shoulders in shimmering waves. With a start, Trina thought, *Mama's pretty.* How strange to see her formal mother in such an informal setting—propped up on bed pillows, a cotton nightgown buttoned to her throat, hair loose and flowing. She appeared approachable and. . .kind.

Mama lifted her hand, gesturing. "Come in, Trina."

On bare feet, Trina crossed the threshold and stood at the foot of the bed. The polished wood floor felt cool and satiny against her feet, and she twitched her toes, waiting until Dad sat back on the bed next to Mama.

"I'm sorry to wake you up, but there's something I need to tell you, and I couldn't wait any longer."

Mama and Dad looked at her expectantly, their expressions curious but open.

Trina took a deep breath. "All these evenings I've been in my room or over at Beth's, I've been—" Her mouth went dry, and she swallowed. "I've been studying."

Neither expression changed.

Trina's heart pounded so hard she was surprised her parents didn't hear it. She took a deep breath and finished. "I've been preparing to take a test that would give me a high school diploma."

Mama gasped, and Dad's brows came together. "Why?" Dad growled the query.

"If I have a diploma, I can get into college." Trina held her breath, waiting for the explosion. She didn't wait long.

"College!" Dad leaped from the bed and stood glowering. "Where did you get the idea you could go to college?"

Mama folded her arms across her chest. "I know where. From Marie's daughter, that's where. I knew letting Trina spend time with Beth would serve no good purpose."

"But, Mama, it wasn't Beth's idea!" Trina held out her hands in entreaty. "It was all my idea. She just helped me because no one else would."

"Of course no one else would!" Dad paced between the bed and dresser, his hands clenched into fists. "My child. . .college!" He spun around, fixing his squinted gaze on Trina. "And what did you plan to do with a college degree?"

Although Trina quivered from head to toe, she wouldn't withhold any information. "Become a veterinarian like Dr. Groening."

Mama dropped back against the pillows, shaking her head. Dad brought his fist down on the dresser top with a resounding *thud*. "So that's why you wanted to work for him—so you could take his place. Not because you like animals, the way you led me to believe."

"It *is* because I like animals!" Trina scurried around the edge of the bed to stand in front of her father. Fury emanated from him, and she trembled in her nightclothes, but she stood tall and refused to cower before him. "I like them so much I want to be able to do all I can to help them. If I'm an animal doctor, then I can—"

"You deceived us, Trina." Mama's strangled voice captured Trina's attention. The hurt in her mother's eyes brought a sting of tears. The anger Trina had expected was nowhere in sight—only pain of betrayal showed in her mother's pinched face. "You know our feelings about higher education, yet you went behind our backs and pursued the notion." Mama thrust out her jaw, stopping the quiver in her chin.

"Dad? What's going on?" Tony stood in the bedroom doorway, rubbing his eyes.

"Get back to bed!" Dad roared. "This doesn't concern you!"

Tony's eyes flew wide, and he scuttled off without another word.

Dad wheeled on Trina. "Go back to your room, young lady. Your mother and I will deal with you in the morning. But you will not be going to Dr. Groening's again. You're done."

Trina's jaw fell open. "But—but, Dad! He depends on me!"

"That isn't my problem." Dad's hard tone sent a chill down Trina's spine. "You should have thought about that before you lied to me."

Trina stood on wooden legs, unable to believe her father would be so cold.

"Go to your room!"

At his thundering command, Trina fled. She threw herself across the bed, hiding her face in the rumpled sheets. Had she really thought telling her parents the truth would make her feel better? When she was little, confessing her infrequent crimes had led to swift punishment followed by forgiveness—a cleansing absolution. But this confession had only led to hurt, anger, and despair. Where was the release?

Her misery welled up, bringing a rush of tears. "Oh Lord, I don't know what to do. . . ."

Trina moved through the remainder of the week as if walking in her sleep. Dad and Mama made it clear she was in disgrace. They forbade her to go to the stained-glass art studio or to Beth's home. Her mother walked her to the café each morning, and they walked home together each evening. She spent her afternoon break in a corner of the café's kitchen under her mother's watchful eye.

Her request to attend a Wednesday night singing was met with a stern, silent stare that communicated denial. The only place she found freedom from a chaperone was the bathroom or her bedroom. Her schoolbooks mysteriously disappeared, so she sat alone in the evenings, staring out the window or at her ceiling, mourning the opportunity that had been lost and wondering if things would be different had she been up front with her parents from the beginning. She doubted it, yet she wondered.

Adding to her humiliation and heartache, Dad insisted she be the one to tell Janina Ensz and Audra Koeppler their part-time services were no longer needed since Trina would be working at the café full-time again. Seeing the disappointment in the teens' faces increased Trina's pain. Now they were left hunting for jobs. She hadn't meant for these innocent girls to be hurt by her decisions.

Graham came into the café each day for lunch, and Trina waited on him, but she didn't give him any more attention than the other diners. He seemed hurt by her aloof behavior, but she couldn't garner enough desire to change it. Her lips felt incapable of smiling, her tongue unable to form conversation, her soul dead. She had nothing to give, and she made no effort to pretend otherwise.

The emptiness inside frightened her, but she had no idea how to regain a sense of purpose. So she moved through the day as her parents expected, waiting tables, cleaning up, being obedient, saying "Yes, ma'am," and "Yes, sir" without complaint or argument. And a constant, pervasive sadness blanketed her world.

Midmorning on Saturday, Beth McCauley entered the café and slid into a booth. The breakfast rush was over, and the lunch rush hadn't begun, so the dining room was empty except for Beth. Trina clinked ice in a glass, filled it with water, and brought it over with a menu.

But Beth pushed both items aside and pointed to the seat across from her. "Join me."

Trina glanced around.

Beth glanced around, too, her eyebrows high. "Nobody's here who needs you. Have a seat."

Trina looked toward the kitchen. Although she couldn't see Mama, she knew she was there. Mama would frown plenty if she saw Trina sitting with Beth. With a sigh, she shook her head. "I can't. I'm not on break."

Beth sighed, too, tipping her head to the side. Her shiny ponytail fell across her shoulder, reminding Trina of her mother's hair falling over her shoulders the night she chose to be truthful. Trina jerked her gaze away.

A soft *swish* indicated Beth had slid the menu across the table. Trina peeked. Beth sat with the open menu propped up on the table like a shield, but she looked over the top of it to Trina. "So. . .haven't seen you in quite a while. Are the rumors true—have your parents shut you down?"

Trina sent a worried glance toward the kitchen, holding her breath. But Mama didn't appear in the doorway, so she braved a quick reply. "Yes."

"So I won't be driving you to Hutchinson to take the GED test?"

Trina clenched her jaw for a moment. "No."

Beth's lips puckered in sympathy. "I hate to hear that, Katrinka. I wish it were different."

Trina wished it were different, too, but she should have known better than to try. Why had she thought God would call an Old Order Mennonite girl to be something more than wife and mother? All she'd managed to do with all of her dreaming and scheming was make a fool of herself and let everybody down.

She said the words aloud in an attempt to convince herself of that truth. "It was a dumb idea. Graham is right—the highest calling for a woman is being a wife and mother. That's all I need to be."

Beth smacked the menu closed. She leaned forward, her eyes flashing. "Listen to yourself! If it's such a high calling, where's the passion? Where's the excitement? You might as well be discussing how many cups of flour go into the recipe for buttermilk pancakes— that's how *blah* you sound. Trina, there's no life left in you!"

Trina backed away from the table. Her hands trembled as she fumbled with the little order pad in her apron pocket. "You—you decide what you want to eat. I'll be back." She turned with a squeak of her tennis shoe on the tile floor and hurried into the kitchen, her heart in her throat. What if Mama had heard Beth? To her relief, her mother was in the storeroom measuring navy beans into a large colander and seemed oblivious to the brief conversation.

Trina cleared her throat. "Beth McCauley is in the dining room. I thought you might want to take her order." It occurred to Trina she could put a bite in her tone and deliver a secondary message to her mother, but years of practicing respectful behavior removed the temptation.

Mama turned to face Trina. "Yes, I suppose I should." She looked at Trina for long moments, her gaze narrow and her lips unsmiling. Yet she didn't appear as much disapproving as sad. She put the colander in Trina's hands. "Rinse these well and sort out the stones, will you? I'm going to make ham and beans for tomorrow's lunch." She moved past Trina and headed into the dining room.

Trina walked to the stainless steel sink and began the task of sorting beans. The mumble of Beth's and Mama's voices drifted through the open doorway, but she didn't try to hear the words. The comment Beth had made kept replaying through her head—*"There's no life left in you!"* Trina knew her friend was right.

Closing her eyes, Trina hung her head. *Father in heaven, help me. Help me want to be the person Mama and Dad and Graham want me to be. Change me. Please change me. Because I don't want to live like I'm already dead.*

Fourteen

A men."

At the minister's rumbling closure to silent prayers, Graham rose from his knees and slid back onto the bench. During the prayer time, he'd found himself unable to pray. He couldn't remember a time since he'd been baptized that his thoughts had remained empty during silent prayer. What was happening to him?

A deacon stepped behind the wooden podium, opened his Bible, and began to read. " 'Who can find a virtuous woman? For her price is far above rubies. . . .' "

Graham's heart thudded in double time as the deacon read from chapter 31 of Proverbs. The words pelted him like grit from a windstorm—" 'The heart of her husband doth safely trust in her. . . . She will do him good and not evil. . . .' " Despite his efforts to keep his gaze aimed forward, his head jerked toward Trina. He'd told her he couldn't trust her. She'd hurt him immeasurably with her plans to attend college.

The deacon read on, describing all the duties the virtuous wife performed. Graham had heard these verses preached before—he knew the list was long. But for some reason, this morning certain pieces seemed to stand out from the others.

" 'She perceiveth that her merchandise is good. . . . She reacheth forth her hands to the needy. . . . She maketh fine linen, and selleth it. . . . A woman that feareth the Lord, she shall be praised. Give her of the fruit of her hands; and let her own works praise her in the gates.' "

The deacon sat down and the minister rose to begin the main sermon, but Graham's focus turned inward. Why had he never noticed references to selling before? Selling indicated a business. That meant a woman would be involved in a business other than managing a household. And reaching forth her hands to the needy—could that include animals in need of care?

He shook his head hard, trying to clear the thoughts. What was he thinking? That Trina *should* go to school? *Should* become a veterinarian? It was ridiculous! Trina's own words returned to replay in his mind— how God had given her the desire to treat animals with a doctor's care. If this idea had truly come from God, should Graham consider it ridiculous?

His stomach churned as he realized where his thoughts were taking him. Outside of the dictates of the fellowship. Outside of the borders established for his community. Outside of his own personal ideals and beliefs.

Once more, his gaze drifted to Trina. She sat, spine straight, hair neatly tucked beneath her cap, her attention unwavering. His heart turned over in his chest. She was everything he wanted in a wife— lovely, gentle, hardworking, God-fearing.

Virtuous? He considered the word carefully. Could he still consider her virtuous despite the changes he'd seen in her over the past several weeks? And then another thought came—*To whom should Trina ultimately answer: to God or to man?*

The sermon continued, the minister's droning voice addressing the congregation, and Graham finally found words to pray. *Father God, help me understand Your will for Trina and me. I believe we're to be married, yet she believes she is meant to be more than a wife and mother. Reveal Your will to us, and give us the courage to follow it, whatever it may be.*

As he closed the silent thought, an image of Trina the night of the shucking flashed through his mind. She'd stood on the edge of the porch riser, her face sad, as she'd told him it wasn't the pursuit of education that had changed her. Now he pondered the statement. If it wasn't studying that had changed her, then what?

Before he could find the answer, the minister instructed the worshippers to kneel for prayer. Graham knelt, rested his linked hands on the hard bench, and lowered his head. As the minister prayed aloud, Graham formed his own prayer: *Help me help Trina find her way back to the way she used to be. Help me help her find her happiness again.*

Beth stood beside the car and waited for Sean to open her door. Before sliding into the seat, she rose up on tiptoe and gave him a kiss on the jaw to say thank you for the courtesy. Fastening her seat belt, she smiled, enjoying the way Sean made her feel like a lady with his gentlemanly gestures. She'd married a jewel.

Sean plopped in behind the wheel and started the engine. He glanced at her and grinned. "What're you smiling about over there?"

"Oh, just thinking about how lucky I am to have you for a husband." She reached across the console to take his hand. "I love you, Sean." Having been raised by a single mother, Beth hadn't witnessed the give-and-take relationship between a husband and wife during her growing-up years. Yet she sensed what she and Sean had was better than many. Maybe better than most, despite the frequent separations due to his job obligations. She gave his hand a squeeze.

He lifted her hand to kiss her knuckles and angled the car onto the highway. "I love you, too, darlin'. But what brought that on?"

Beth shrugged, squinting against the high sun. "Nothing special, I suppose. It's just been awhile since I said it, so I figured it was time."

His low-toned chuckle made her smile. "Well, I never get tired of hearing it."

With a grin, she singsonged, "I love you, I love you, I love you, I—"

His laughter covered the words. "You're a nut." But he said it affectionately. "So what are we doing for lunch today? Want to drive to McPherson?"

"No. Remember? Mom invited us over." Beth frowned. "I think she also invited Troy and Deborah and their kids. So things could get a little tense."

Sean shot her a sympathetic look. "They still mad about Trina using our computer?"

Beth nodded grimly.

"Well," Sean said in an I-told-you-so voice, "it shouldn't surprise you. It isn't as if you don't know the rules of the sect."

Pursing her lips, Beth refused to respond. Yes, she knew the rules. She also thought they were silly. Her mother had explained the reasoning behind the restrictions of the Old Order Mennonite group, but Beth still couldn't see the harm in wearing up-to-date clothes, driving a sporty vehicle, or getting a college education.

Sean's fingers tightened on her hand. "They'll get over it eventually. Don't let it bother you."

Beth sighed, shifting in the seat to face her husband. "I really don't care that they're mad at me. We don't have any kind of relationship anyway, so I'm not losing anything with their anger. I am concerned about how it will affect Mom, and I'm mostly concerned about Trina.

She's just so. . .so sad all the time."

Sean nodded. "But don't you think she'll get over it, too, in time? I mean, you wanted to open a big boutique and it didn't work out. You're still happy, aren't you?"

"Well, of course I am. But I'm doing what God designed me to do—I believe the art studio is His will for me." Beth released a huff of aggravation. "Trina isn't being given a choice to find God's will. She's just being forced to do her parents' will. That isn't right."

"Well. . ." Sean nibbled the lower edge of his mustache as he turned the vehicle onto Highway 56.

Beth yanked her hand from his and folded her arms across her chest. "What do you mean, 'Well. . .'?"

"Honey, don't get testy. Don't you think we've argued enough over Trina?"

At his reasonable tone, Beth melted a bit. "I don't want to argue. But she's my friend. I care about her. I want to see the bubbly, cheerful, full-of-life Trina return. And as long as people are trying to force her into a role she isn't meant to fill, we might never see that side of her again."

Sean shook his head. "I don't know, Beth. I understand what you're saying, but you have to remember these people have a lot of rules to live by, and those rules are important to them. I don't see how Trina would have been completely happy going through with her plans if it meant censure from the community and her family."

Beth sat in silence, digesting Sean's statement. All the years her mother had spent away from Sommerfeld were years of censure. She knew there were times her mother had been sad, even though she had tried to hide it. Now that she was back in Sommerfeld, living as an accepted member of the fellowship, her contentment was evident. Maybe Sean was right, and it was best that Trina didn't pursue veterinary training without her family's approval.

Sean patted her hand. "Beth, I admire your concern for Trina. But what you're suggesting means breaking a generations-long rule. I don't see that happening."

"I don't, either," Beth said, sorrow rising with the recognition. "But it just seems to me that people should be more important than rules."

Sean brought the car to a stop in front of Henry and Marie Braun's bungalow. Beth looked out the window and released a sigh. Troy Muller's car was parked along the curb.

"We don't have to go in, you know," Sean said.

Beth grimaced. "Yes, we do. Mom's expecting us. And I want to see Theo and Dori. I don't get enough time with them." Just thinking about spending time with her twin siblings gave her heart a lift.

"Then let's go."

Beth met Sean by the hood of the car, and they linked hands as they walked up to the porch. Without bothering to knock, Beth pushed the screen door open and called, "Hey, where are the munchkins?"

The patter of feet on hardwood floors told of the twins' approach, and Beth laughed as she crouched down to catch the giggling toddlers.

"Whiz-beff! Whiz-beff!" the dark-haired pair chorused, clinging to Beth's neck and trying to climb onto her knees. Their childish attempts to pronounce her given name of Lisbeth made Beth laugh.

"What about me?" Sean asked, and the two immediately abandoned Beth to reach chubby hands to Sean.

Beth straightened as her mother approached, arms outstretched. "Hi, Mom." Beth returned Mom's hug then smiled at Henry, who entered the room. "Hi, Dad." She released her mother to accept her stepfather's hug, relishing the freedom of stepping into his embrace without embarrassment. "Are we late?"

Henry captured Theo, and Mom scooped up a wriggling Dori. On the way to the kitchen, Henry spoke over his shoulder. "We were ready to strap the twins into their highchairs when they heard you, so you're just in time."

Mom added, "Troy and Deborah are already here with Tony and Trina."

Beth shot Sean a quick look, and he slung his arm across her shoulders. They entered the kitchen, and Beth pasted on a smile as she let her gaze drift over each member of the Muller family. None of them smiled back. Not even Trina. Beth's stomach clenched.

Henry had put an extra leaf in the table to accommodate the guests. Beth and Sean sat next to Trina on one side of the table, with Troy, Deborah, and Tony on the opposite side. Mom and Henry each swung a twin into a waiting highchair; then they sat down, and everyone joined hands for Henry's prayer. Beth noticed Trina's hand felt moist, and it trembled. Her heart lurched in sympathy. Why couldn't her family see the harm they were inflicting?

Henry ended the prayer with "Amen," and Theo immediately began pounding on his highchair tray. Henry caught the little boy's hands. "Patience, son." Theo obediently clasped his hands and waited.

Serving bowls circled the table, and spoons clacked food onto plates. The smell of roast beef, carrots, and potatoes was tantalizing, but Beth had a hard time swallowing, aware of the steely glares coming from Troy and Deborah.

Trina, on her left, pushed the food around her plate rather than eating, her head downcast, her voice silent as conversation took place between the older adults. Sean contributed occasionally, but the cotton in Beth's mouth kept her silent, as well.

"So, Beth," Henry said as he buttered a crusty roll, "when do you plan to add the showroom to the studio?"

Beth put down her fork. "We had hoped to get the construction started next spring, but we may put it off a bit longer. I need to have two more employees in place to help with the windows before I can even think about additional projects for the showroom."

"But the Internet sales are going well on the suncatchers, aren't they?" Henry took a bite, his attentive gaze on Beth's face.

"They're going great," Sean answered for Beth, giving her hand a squeeze. The pride in his voice made Beth smile. "Not to mention the consigned pieces she ships all over the United States."

"Sounds to me like you're overly busy." Troy's stern voice carried over the twins' cheerful jabber. "What with making fancy church windows, too."

Beth forced herself to meet the man's gaze. She didn't really care if she offended Troy, but she wanted to avoid conflict for her mother's sake, so she tempered her voice when she replied. "I am busy, but if I want to have a successful business, it means meeting demands. I don't begrudge the time it takes."

Sean inserted, "She's incredibly talented, and people are recognizing it more and more. It's been a joy to see how God is using her abilities."

Troy harrumphed.

"I think she also serves a purpose in the community," Sean continued.

Beth stared at him. Not one to seek confrontation, Sean almost seemed to be goading Troy.

"How so?" Troy barked the question.

Sean shrugged. "She employs four people from Sommerfeld now. As the studio grows, she'll be able to offer employment to more young people. I would think that would be preferable to having them drive out of town to find work."

Troy lifted his water glass and took a sip. He thumped the glass onto the table. "Maybe, but how long can she keep it going?"

Sean opened his mouth to reply, but Beth put her hand on his knee under the table. "The studio is my life's calling. I have no plans to close it or do anything else. Unless, of course, God opens a different door to me."

"Like motherhood?"

Beth heard Trina's sharp intake of breath at her father's brusque question. Suddenly Beth felt as though she was being used as a bad example to Trina, and heat filled her face. "I don't see how one affects the other."

Mom stood, lifting the almost-empty roast platter, and cleared her throat. "I'll get these serving bowls out of the way, and we can have dessert. I made cherry pie. Who would like ice cream with it?"

Troy acted as though Mom hadn't spoken. "If you have a child, you'll still work every day at the studio, just as you've been doing?"

"Of course I will." Beth raised her shoulders in a shrug. "My mother worked all during my growing-up years. I learned to be independent and responsible as a result. That's not to say every mother should take a job outside of the home, but I don't see anything wrong with it." She gestured toward Deborah. "Even Mrs. Muller has the café, and she has children. It's worked out all right for you, hasn't it?"

Deborah flapped her jaw, surprising Beth with her lack of response. When had she ever seen Deborah Muller speechless?

"But my wife stayed at home with her children until they were grown," Troy argued. "She now has the café so our Trina would have a safe place to work, and she also hires other Sommerfeld young people. Her café serves a purpose in the community."

"As does my studio," Beth said. "And as would. . ." Her gaze drifted sideways briefly to Trina, who sat staring at Beth with wide, disbelieving eyes. She faced Troy Muller again. "As would having a certified veterinarian right here in town."

FIFTEEN

Trina gasped at Beth's boldness. Dad's face blazed red. Mama looked as though she'd swallowed something bitter. Tony stared at his empty plate, his lips twitching. Uncle Henry and Aunt Marie gawked at each other across the table as if uncertain what to do. Only the twins seemed oblivious to the tension in the room, pushing against their highchair trays and complaining to be released. Uncle Henry lifted them in turn from their chairs, and they scampered around the corner, giggling. An apprehensive silence fell in their wake.

Oh, Beth, please don't say anything else, Trina's thoughts begged, but a glance at her friend confirmed her worst fears—Beth had only gotten started.

Aunt Marie also must have suspected Beth had more to say, because she leaned forward and spoke loudly. "So are we ready for that pie now?"

Everyone around the table jumped and stared at Aunt Marie. Beth stood up, and all heads swiveled to look at her. Had the moment been less stressful, Trina might have laughed—everyone moved as if their heads were attached to a single string, being pulled here and then there in unison.

"Thank you, Mom, but I think I'll pass on the dessert. Sean and I will go. But before I do, I have to say something to Mr. and Mrs. Muller."

Trina held her breath, her fists balled so tightly her fingernails dug into the tender flesh of her palms. Beth's hand clamped over her shoulder, and Trina looked up. Tears glittered in her friend's eyes.

"Trina is special. I've known that from the first time I met her. She had a joy that was contagious—she lit a room. I know you all saw it, too." She met Trina's gaze for a moment, her lips turned down sadly. "And I know you also see that now. . .the joy is gone." Beth's sigh brought a sting of tears to Trina's eyes. "I miss it. I miss the real Trina—the bouncy, cheerful girl she used to be."

Trina dared a quick glance across the table. Dad's jaw muscles twitched, and Mama's chin quivered. Were those tears in Mama's eyes?

"You've taken it out of her with your inability to see beyond your narrow views. We were talking earlier about service to the community. A veterinarian in Sommerfeld would be a tremendous service. Half of your residents depend on livestock for their livelihoods. Think what good it would do them to have someone close at hand to take care of their animals as needed."

Beth's voice, although low in tone, trembled with fervor. "That in itself should be reason enough to give Trina a chance to become a veterinarian. But there's a deeper reason. She believes God has placed that calling on her heart. Who are we to say He didn't?"

"A woman's calling is to be a wife and a mother." Dad spoke in a firm, flat tone.

"And," Beth said, "sometimes something else, too. Like an artist. Or a terrific cook, like Mrs. Muller. Or. . ." Once more she looked tenderly into Trina's face. "A caregiver for God's lowly creatures."

Turning to face Dad, Beth said, "Being a wife and mother is a very important calling, Mr. Muller, but it doesn't have to be a woman's *only* calling."

Beth took hold of Trina's chin and aimed her face toward Dad. "Look at your daughter. It breaks my heart to see her in so much pain, and she's just my friend. She's your child. How can you look at her and not respond to her heartache?"

Trina pulled loose and ducked her head. She didn't want to look at Dad right now, to see anger instead of compassion, condemnation instead of understanding. Beth's fingers on her shoulder tightened for a moment and then slipped away, leaving Trina feeling cold and alone.

"Mr. Muller, I know you think I'm impudent." Beth released a light, humorless chuckle. "Maybe I am. But what I've said has been out of love for Trina."

Dad came out of his seat, pointing a finger at Beth. "Trina was just fine before you came along and opened your studio and put crazy ideas in her head. Well, she won't be spending time with you anymore, so your influence will fade away. *Then* our Trina will come back. She will honor her father and mother just as the Bible commands her to, and she will be happy in the decision."

Dad grabbed Mama's arm and pulled her up. He shot a look from Uncle Henry to Aunt Marie. "I thank you for the good dinner, but we need to go home. Come on, Tony, Trina. Let's go."

"Thanks for dinner, Mom. Everything was good." Graham pushed away from the table.

His brother, Chuck, shoved his last bite of cake into his mouth and spoke around it. "Want to play some checkers?"

Normally Graham would jump at the chance to trample Chuck in a checker match, but today his heart wasn't in games. He felt burdened from the thoughts that had attacked during worship service, and he needed time to be alone and process all of the emotions warring for release.

"Sorry, Chuck. I'm going to head on home."

Mom looked up, disappointment on her face. "You aren't staying to visit?"

Graham fiddled with the buttons on his shirt. "Not today."

"And you're going to *your* house?"

Mom's sharp tone caught Graham's full attention. "Yes. Why?"

Mom sighed, her shoulders slumping. "I hoped you might be going to visit Trina. She's looked so forlorn the last couple of weeks. Makes me feel sad for her." Mom tipped her head, one black ribbon slipping along her cheek. "You're still courting, aren't you?"

Graham clutched the back of his chair, his head low. He knew how much his family liked Trina—Mom especially—and he didn't want to upset her by saying he was no longer courting Trina. Yet saying yes might give her false hope that things were okay between them. He wasn't sure what would happen as far as Trina was concerned, despite how his heart still ached with loving her.

"Graham?"

He lifted his head and met his mother's concerned gaze. He forced a smile. "Don't worry, Mom. Things'll work out for the best."

An ambiguous answer, but it seemed to satisfy his mother. She nodded and began clearing dishes. "Well, you run on, then, and get some rest." A scowl marred her brow. "You look haggard, son."

Graham waved good-bye and headed outside. Shoving his hands into his pockets, he made his way slowly toward his own little house. His empty little house. His mother's parting comment followed him.

He looked haggard? Well, he supposed it was possible. Worry and sadness could do that to a person.

He let the screen door slam behind him; then he crossed to the sofa and threw himself onto the center cushion. Head back, eyes closed, his mind drifted over the morning's sermon and all the strange feelings that had coursed through him when the Bible passage was read.

Something pressed at the fringes of his mind, trying to clarify itself. He squeezed his eyes tight, pinching his lips. *What is it, Lord?* Unable to grasp the elusive message, he got up and retrieved his Bible. Flopping it open to Proverbs, he located the text and read it himself. Slowly. Finger underlining each word. Face pursed in fierce concentration. Heart begging for understanding.

When he reached the final verse, a jolt as powerful as a lightning bolt straightened him in the seat. He lurched backward and then forward as he bent over the Bible and read the verse again.

" 'Give her of the fruit of her hands; and let her own works praise her in the gates.' " He closed the Bible and aimed his gaze unseeingly across the room. His mind raced to comprehend his strange reaction to the words. Like layers being peeled away to reveal a hidden treasure, understanding dawned bit by bit until a clear picture emerged.

Graham leaped from the sofa and charged to the door. He hoped Trina was home. He needed to talk to her.

A light tap roused Trina from an uneasy sleep. She rolled over on the bed, her cap coming loose. Still reclining on the mattress, she said, "Yes?"

The door squeaked open a few inches. Mama peered in. "Trina, Graham is here and would like to see you." A frown creased her face. "But before you come out, straighten your hair and cap."

Graham. Trina sighed. She wasn't up to Graham's disapproval after the awful lunch scene at Uncle Henry's. Beth meant well, but she'd gotten Dad so upset he wouldn't even speak on the way home. Trina couldn't face another angry man.

Her heart heavy, she shook her head. "I'd rather not visit today, Mama. Would you tell him, please?"

Mama's lips pursed so tightly they nearly disappeared. But then her face relaxed, her expression showing sympathy. "All right, daughter. I'll tell him."

Trina lay, her heart booming as she held her breath, and listened to the mumble of voices. Graham's raised slightly, the words indiscernible but the tone insistent. Mama's firm reply came, then a brief rebuttal from Graham, Mama's voice again, and finally Graham's resigned farewell. The click of the screen door signaled his departure.

Her breath whooshed out in relief. She rolled to her side, closing her eyes once more, but another tap at the door intruded. Without moving, she called, "What is it?"

"Trina?"

Tony's whisper. Trina peeked over her shoulder. "What?"

"Can I come in?"

Trina released a loud huff. "All right." Her tone wasn't welcoming, but Tony tiptoed in anyway. When he sat on the edge of the bed, she snapped, "What do you want?"

"I think you should've talked to Graham." Tony's youthful face puckered in concern. "He looked really disappointed when Mom sent him away."

Trina tried to conjure sympathy, but none would come. Graham had been sending her away, figuratively, for weeks. Why should she care about his disappointment? It certainly couldn't equal hers. She shrugged.

Tony shook his head, staring at her in confusion. "You and Graham've been seeing each other for a long time. I thought you liked each other. I thought when you really like somebody you try to work things out."

"Tony, how is this your business?" Trina's words came out in a harsh hiss.

Tony's face blotched red. He picked at a hangnail, his eyes downcast. "Dunno. Just. . .makes me feel bad, having everybody upset with everybody else."

Trina shifted her gaze to the ceiling. "Everybody's not upset with *everybody*. Everybody's just upset with *me*. So don't let it bother you."

"But it does bother me!" Tony nudged Trina on the leg, capturing her attention. "I–I've been thinking. . .about what Beth said at lunch today."

Trina groaned. "Tony, let's not talk about lunch, please?" An image of her father's furious face flashed through her memory. She threw her arm across her eyes to block the sight, but it replayed behind her closed lids.

Tony yanked her arm down. "I have to. She's right. And—and I know I bug you a lot, but I miss my happy sister."

Trina opened her eyes and looked at Tony. Tears pricked her eyes at the sorrow reflected in his dark eyes. She swallowed hard.

"Are you going to be unhappy forever if you don't get to be a veterinarian?"

The whispered question hung in the air for several long seconds. Tony waited, silent, his unblinking gaze pinned to her face. Finally, Trina heaved a sigh. Running her fingers up and down the length of her dress's modesty cape, she shook her head. "I wish I knew. It sure feels like it right now. But I hope not."

Tony hung his head. "Me, too."

Trina touched his shoulder. "I'm sorry you're feeling bad, Tony. I don't mean to make everyone feel bad. I just—" But what could she say? Tony wouldn't understand the hollow ache that left her feeling dull and empty. How could he understand when she couldn't understand it herself? Why, she wondered again, had God given her a desire He knew she couldn't fulfill?

Giving her brother's shoulder a pat, she swung her legs over the edge of the bed. "I'll be okay, Tony. Don't worry."

He sent her a dubious look.

She forced her lips into a smile, although she was certain it lacked its former spark. "You know how girls are. Moody."

He snorted. "Yeah." He interjected disdain into the word while grinning.

She punched him on the arm, as she knew he expected, then pushed to her feet. "I think I'll go ask Mama and Dad if I can take a walk."

"Want me to go with you?"

Trina crinkled her nose. "If I say no, will you be offended?"

Tony rose, shrugging. "Who wants to walk with a moody girl anyway?"

A light chuckle found its way from Trina's throat. A rush of love swept over her, and she impulsively threw her arms around her brother. "Thanks, Tony."

He gave her back a few awkward pats and pulled away. "Yeah. Okay." His cheeks blazed red. He backed up toward the door. "I hope the walk helps."

"I'm sure it will." But when he stepped out of the room, Trina felt her shoulders collapse. A walk wouldn't cure anything even if she walked all the way to Alaska and back. She feared she would carry the weight of unfulfilled dreams forever.

Sixteen

W here are you going?" Dad nearly growled the question.

Trina shrugged. "Just around town. Maybe to the cemetery and back."

"Not to McCauleys'?"

It took effort not to sigh. "No, Dad."

Mama, seated on the opposite side of the sofa, stretched her hand out to touch Dad's knee. "Let her go. Sometimes a girl just needs to. . . get off alone."

Trina nearly jolted in surprise. Never had Mama been so understanding. She looked at Dad—would he heed Mama's words?

Dad smacked his newspaper against his knee a couple of times, peering at Trina with narrowed eyes. Finally he let out a huff. "All right. But be back before supper so you can help your mother."

Trina nodded and headed for the door. She stepped onto the porch, breathing in the heavy, hot air of midafternoon. Knowing her parents were probably watching through the big front-room window, she moved down the sidewalk toward the cemetery. It had been a snap decision to name the community resting place as her destination, but now that she thought about it, it seemed a likely choice. One buried the dead in a cemetery. She needed to bury her dream.

Sweat broke out across her brow and trickled between her shoulder blades despite the thick shade offered by the towering elms and maples lining the street. In another week it would be August—and probably even hotter. Then September, when college classes traditionally began. She kicked a pebble, a feeble attempt to dislodge the thought.

Determinedly, she turned her attention outward. As she passed neat houses, she named off the families. And their pets. Funny how she might forget the name of a child residing under the roof, but she knew the names of every cat, dog, rabbit, and parakeet. Didn't that mean something?

Puffing out her cheeks, she blew out a frustrated breath. Then she clenched her fists and picked up speed. Her feet smacked the brick walkway. Her arms pumped, stirring the air. Her nose stung with the desire to cry. By the time she reached the cemetery, her back was covered in sweat, and fine strands of hair, loosened from the roll on the back of her head, clung to her sticky neck. She scanned the grounds, seeking the tallest stone to crouch behind and give vent to the tears that longed for release.

Most of the headstones were uniform in size and shape, but the Braun family stone loomed higher and wider. The sun glinted off the back of the massive sandstone marker. Surely a large slice of shade waited on the other side. Trina moved briskly across the short grass to the stone, prepared to crumple behind it. But when she rounded the chiseled edge, she came to a surprised halt. Someone was already leaning against the stone, picking apart a blade of grass.

"Graham?" She blinked twice, shielding her eyes with her hand.

He leaped to his feet, snatching off his ball cap at the same time. "Trina."

"What are you doing here?" they asked at the same time.

Trina clamped her jaw shut, taking a hesitant step backward. Two longings filled her—to run away as quickly as she could and to throw herself into his arms. But she did neither. She simply stood with clasped hands at her waist, staring into his unsmiling face.

"I come here a lot." Graham held his cap against his thigh, his fingers convulsing on the brim. "It's a good place to think. . .and pray."

Trina nodded. Hadn't she come here to think? But praying. . . she hadn't considered that. Guilt struck. She took another slow step backward. "Well, I'll leave you alone, then."

"No!" His hand shot out, not quite touching her.

She jumped, and he lowered his hand.

"I mean, please don't leave. I—I came by your house to see you, but your mother said you were asleep."

Mama fibbed? Trina could scarcely believe it. She stood stupidly, trying to make sense of her mother's strange behavior.

"But I'm glad you're here. I have something I want to tell you."

Trina brought her focus back to Graham. Her heart began to pound. If anyone saw her out here with Graham and told her dad, he'd be madder yet. She shook her head. "Please. I don't think—"

"Just for a few minutes."

"But if my folks find out I met you here. . ." She licked her lips.

Graham looked around, seeming to scan every inch of their surroundings. "There's no one nearby, Trina. And we aren't doing anything wrong." He caught her elbow and pulled her into the shade of the headstone. "Just let me say this, okay?"

Holding her arm stiffly while he grasped her elbow, she debated jerking free and dashing away. But she was tired. With a sigh, she offered a meek nod.

He sat, tugging her down next to him. Trina tucked her legs to the side, smoothing her skirt over her knees. Graham shifted over slightly, putting a few inches of space between them. The sandstone felt rough but cool against her back, and she leaned a little more heavily against it, her head angled sharply to meet Graham's gaze.

"Trina, this morning's sermon. . .I can't get the Bible reading out of my head."

Trina nodded miserably. The "virtuous woman" had been preached before, always as a means of encouraging women to be godly, industrious wives and mothers. The reading of those verses this morning had been like rubbing salt in an open wound.

"Especially the last verse—the one about giving her the fruit of her hands and letting her works praise her."

Trina's brow furrowed as Graham's face contorted with emotion.

"Trina, I fear I've been wrong."

She tipped her head, her heart skipping a beat. Had she heard him correctly?

"I fear. . .we've all been wrong."

Trina swallowed. "W–what do you mean?"

Graham shifted slightly, resting one shoulder against the grave-stone, his face turned toward her. "Tell me again why you want to become a veterinarian."

She had no difficulty finding the answer to his question. "Because for as along as I can remember, I've always loved caring for animals."

"And you think—no, you *believe*—God put that desire in your heart?"

"Yes, I do."

"Trina, you said it wasn't the desire to become a veterinarian that changed you." Graham's hand moved forward, his fingertips brushing against hers. "I didn't understand at the time, but I think I do now. The reason you've changed—the reason you never smile anymore—is because. . .because we're holding you back."

She sucked in a sharp breath.

"We're keeping you from answering God's call, and it's crushing you inside."

Trina nearly wilted. Finally, someone understood! So great was her relief, tears spurted into her eyes.

Graham leaned forward slightly, bringing his face closer. "Am I right?"

With a choked sob, Trina nodded. "Yes. And—and it's hurt *so much*, Graham."

He cupped her cheek with his broad hand. "I'm sorry."

She searched his face, seeing sincerity in his eyes. The comfort of his simple touch lessened the pain in her chest. She nodded, accepting his apology.

With a sigh, he dropped his hand. "I can't change what's past, Trina, and I'm not sure that things will change for you in the future. Your parents may never grant permission; the fellowship may say it can't be done. So you might not be able to follow through on what you want, but I want you to know I understand. And I won't stand in your way if you want to try."

Trina stared, her mouth open. "Do you really mean that?"

His solemn nod offered a response.

"But what about—what about getting published?" She hardly dared to breathe, waiting for his answer.

"I love you, Trina."

The beautiful words swept Trina from despair to delight. She had asked God to bring their hearts together so she could walk where He led, and God had answered. Despite her neglect of Him in the past days, He'd still heard and answered. A genuine smile broke across her face, bringing with it the rush of happy tears. She clasped Graham's hand between both of hers. "Oh, Graham, I love you, too."

Graham rose, helping her up at the same time. "Then let's go talk to your parents. Let's tell them we want to be published. And let's tell them we want to talk to the bishop about the possibility of you going to college."

Trina's knees buckled, and had it not been for Graham's strong hands holding tight, she might have collapsed onto the grass. "Are—are you sure?"

"I'm sure." Graham slid his finger along Trina's cheek. "I know I love you. And if you believe God is calling you to this service, then I must give you the fruit of your hands."

"Oh, Graham. . ." Tears distorted her vision.

He gave her hand a squeeze. "They might say no, Trina."

She blinked rapidly, peering into his serious face.

"But we'll try."

Trina took in a deep breath and released it slowly. "We'll try."

"And if it doesn't work?"

Now it seemed Graham held his breath.

Trina shifted her hand to link her fingers with his. "Then I'll be grateful that I at least had your support. And I'll try to accept it."

"Okay." Graham put his hand on her back, aiming her toward the cemetery gate. "Then let's go try."

Graham perched in a straight-backed chair transplanted from the dining room to the living room and faced Trina's father. The man sat in his overstuffed chair like a king on a throne, his presence stern yet attentive. Graham hoped he maintained a calm appearance. Underneath, he felt as though he might quiver to pieces. Yet a potential father-in-law should see only conviction and courage when being asked for his daughter's hand in marriage. So Graham squared his shoulders, clamped his hands over his knees, and met Troy Muller's stern gaze without squirming.

"I have a good job at the lumberyard—as you know, the business will be mine someday. My dad has promised that. My house is already built, so I have a home waiting."

Mr. Muller waved his hand. "All superficial." He leaned forward, resting his elbows on his knees. "You know what's important to me."

Graham flicked a quick glance at Trina. She sat beside her mother on the end of the sofa. The soft expression in her eyes gave him the courage to continue.

"I love your daughter, sir, and I commit to being a godly husband to her. If God sees fit to bless us with children, they'll be raised in the fellowship. Trina will not be left wanting physically, emotionally, or spiritually."

Mr. Muller gave a brusque nod and leaned back. "That's what I was waiting to hear." He shifted to pin a serious look on Trina. "Trina, Graham is asking permission for you to be published. Do you have any opposition to his request?"

A smile quavered on Trina's lips. She shook her head. "No, sir."

The man slapped his knees. "Very well. I'll speak to the bishop, and when he gives his approval, your intentions will be published." He started to rise.

Graham held out his hand. "There's something else we need to discuss."

Mr. Muller sank back into his chair.

Graham rose and took two steps to stand at the end of the sofa. He put his hand on Trina's shoulder. Although he didn't look at her, he sensed her turning her face upward. Her muscles felt tight beneath his hand, and he gave a gentle squeeze of assurance before speaking.

"As you know, Trina has spent time studying—"

"Behind our backs," Mr. Muller inserted, his brows coming down into a sharp *V*.

Graham nodded. "Behind your backs. But I was aware of her actions. She shared them with me."

Mr. and Mrs. Muller exchanged a quick glance.

"You're aware she had plans to take a test to get a high school diploma and then attend college."

Mr. Muller's cheeks became streaked with banners of temper. "And you're aware we've forbidden her from further pursuit."

Graham nodded. "Yes, I know. But I'd like to humbly ask you to reconsider."

Mr. Muller gaped at Graham as if he'd suddenly broken out in purple polka dots.

Trina's mother leaned forward to peer into Graham's face. "Why would you ask such a thing?"

Graham offered a quick, silent prayer for guidance before replying. "Trina believes God has called her to this task. And the Bible verses read in service only this morning say that a woman should be allowed the fruit of her hand. I believe God is telling me this is His will for Trina."

Trina's father came out of his chair. "You speak nonsense! We have always followed the belief that a woman's place is in the home." He whirled on Trina. "Not in a barn!"

Trina recoiled, her shoulder connecting with Graham's side. He curled both hands over her shoulders. She trembled beneath his touch, stirring his ire. He opened his mouth to respectfully request the older man to calm himself, but Mrs. Muller bolted to her feet and stepped in front of her husband.

"Troy, please do not raise your voice. The neighbors needn't be aware of our business." She spoke reasonably, as a wife should, yet an undercurrent of tension carried through.

Mr. Muller's lower jaw jutted forward. "If my voice is raised, it's because of great frustration. They've both lost their senses!"

Trina's mother lowered her head for a moment, her shoulders lifting and falling as if she took mighty breaths. Finally, she returned to the sofa and sat next to Trina. Her face was white, but her eyes flashed with a fire Graham had often seen in Trina's eyes.

Taking Trina's hand, she spoke directly to her daughter. "Trina, you know I've always been strict with you." She paused, and Trina offered a small nod that seemed to encourage her mother to continue. "We've never told you this, but. . .before you were born, your father and I lost three babies. I couldn't carry them to term."

Graham took a step back. The subject matter was personal—something reserved for families. "Maybe I should leave. . . ."

But she held her hand to him. "No, Graham. If you're to marry Trina, you need to know this, too."

Mr. Muller moved to his wife and sat beside her, putting his hand on her knee. His expression softened. Graham returned to his spot at Trina's back and once more placed his hands over her shoulders.

Mrs. Muller continued. "When I found out I was expecting you, I told God if He let me have this baby, I would raise it right. The child would learn early to respect and follow His teachings. I would make no mistakes, and He wouldn't regret allowing me the privilege of motherhood." Tears spilled from the woman's eyes. "I've taken that promise seriously, Trina, but I fear in my attempts to teach you respect, I didn't give you freedom to grow into your own person."

"Oh, Mama. . ." Trina raised her arms to embrace her mother. "You've been a good mother to me. You did raise me right. I'm sorry I've disappointed you."

Pulling free, Mrs. Muller shook her head fiercely. "You haven't disappointed me. You've always been obedient, always meeting your father's and my expectations, never giving us a reason to distrust you. Until. . ."

Graham finished the sentence in his mind. *Until now.* Silence fell—a heavy, uncomfortable silence. Trina hung her head, and her mother sniffled while her father sat stern and stoic. Graham stared over their heads, wondering if he should speak in Trina's defense. What she'd done—sneaking behind her parents' back—was wrong, yet her reasons were good. How to reconcile the wrong with the right? Before he found an answer, Mrs. Muller turned to face her husband.

"Troy, has Trina ever defied us before. . .before this time?"

Mr. Muller shook his head.

"No, never. Not until now." Spinning, she faced Trina again. "Trina, I don't agree that you should have misled us. That was wrong. But. . .I think. . .maybe. . .you should go ahead and take that test."

SEVENTEEN

Trina held her breath, anticipating her father's explosion. Graham's warm hands on her shoulders gave her strength to face the tirade, but she still wished it could be avoided.

But instead of jumping up and spouting in frustration, Dad shook his head, narrowed his gaze, and stared at Mama. "Has everyone in this house gone crazy?"

He nearly whispered the words, and Trina resisted the urge to giggle. He must be remembering Mama's admonition about the neighbors hearing. It was the only logical explanation. But all other logic seemed to have fled the room. Was it logical that Graham would ask her parents to allow her to go to college? Was it logical that Mama would agree? Was it logical that Dad, after exhibiting his temper, would respond calmly? Trina felt as though she were caught in a dream, where nothing made sense.

"Please listen to me, Troy." Rarely had her outspoken Mama seemed so hesitant. Trina listened, spellbound. "The very fact that our daughter has always abided by our wishes tells me she wouldn't do this thing without having solid reasons—without having solid beliefs that it is right. She isn't rebellious. She isn't thoughtless. Yes, she made a mistake in going ahead without our permission. She's young, and the young can be impetuous. Even us, once. . ."

For a moment, Mama and Dad locked gazes, and Trina suspected they were both reliving some youthful activity known to no one but them. She tried to imagine her parents young and foolishly impetuous, but the picture wouldn't gel. Dad broke away to stare at his clenched fists in his lap.

"Of course, Trina's wish to attend a college could be denied by the bishop." Mama went on softly, thoughtfully. "Our sect, unlike some others, has never allowed our young people to go beyond grade nine. But I think, given the usefulness of the profession, and her strong conviction that it's God's will, we should let her ask." In an uncharacteristic display of affection, Mama placed her hand over Dad's fists. "Please, Troy?"

Graham slipped to one knee beside Trina. "Mr. Muller, as Trina's intended husband, I should have the greatest reasons to object. Trina knows how much I have objected when she's spoken to me of her desire. I fought her, telling her she needed to be a wife and mother only. I was afraid I would lose her to this dream."

Trina looked at Graham's chiseled profile, her heart expanding with love for him. To hear him openly support her ideas gave her more joy than she could have imagined.

He continued in a steady, courteous voice. "But God has softened my heart. I would like to pray with you and your wife for God's will to be done. If Trina is meant to become a veterinarian, then surely the leaders will grant permission."

"And if they say no?"

Trina chose to answer her father's question. "If they say no, I will accept it as God's will."

Dad looked at her for a long time, his thick brows pulled down, his lips pressed tightly together. No one spoke, waiting for him to make a decision. Trina's heart pounded with hope. Although she inwardly begged for a positive response, she knew a part of her had been restored with Graham's and Mama's understanding and acceptance of her longing. Even if Dad said no—even if the leaders said no—there would always be the knowledge that someone believed in her.

Finally, Dad shook his head and pushed to his feet. "I still don't understand, Trina. I'm still very disappointed in your deceptions. But I am willing to allow you to speak to the minister and deacons for permission to ask the bishop. Whatever they deem acceptable, I will also accept."

Trina leaped from the sofa and threw her arms around her father's neck. He stood with his arms at his side, allowing her embrace, but he didn't hug her back. Trina understood that, too—she had hurt and displeased him. It would take time to regain his trust and affection. Arms still tight around his neck, she whispered, "Thank you."

He caught her shoulders, set her aside, and left the room without another word.

Trina hung her head. Tears stung behind her nose at her father's abrupt dismissal. Arms embraced her—Mama, offering a rare hug. Trina rested her head on Mama's shoulder, savoring the comfort provided. In time, Mama pulled away and cupped Trina's cheeks.

"You and Graham go sit on the porch, talk about your plans. You have much to consider if you're to be married. I'll. . .I'll go speak with your father."

Trina grasped Mama's wrists. "He'll be okay, won't he?"

Mama sighed. "His father was a deacon, Trina. He feels very accountable to the fellowship and its teachings. But he'll be okay. You go on now." Her gaze lifted to include Graham, who stood behind Trina. "I want you to know I approve of your relationship. I haven't openly welcomed you—just as you feared Trina's dream would rob you of her presence in your life, I've feared you would take her from us. But children grow up and make their own lives—that's the way it should be. You're a fine young man, and I trust you to take good care of my daughter."

"Thank you, ma'am."

With tears distorting her vision, Trina watched Mama leave the room. She had received more warmth from her mother in the past few minutes than she could remember in all of her growing-up years. She marveled at the change.

Graham took her hand. "Come, let's go sit as your mother said." They went to the porch and sat side by side on the top riser, their legs in the sun. Graham asked Trina about the GED test and what would happen next. She shared all she had learned from the Internet searches.

"Before I can train as a veterinarian, I have to take two years of basic courses. Beth says a community college will be less expensive, and Barton County Community College in El Dorado allows online classes," Trina said. "So I will take as many classes from Beth's computer as I can. But eventually, I'll need to go to a college campus and finish."

Graham nodded solemnly. "That means moving away from Sommerfeld." He chewed his lower lip, his brows pulled down, but the expression was thoughtful rather than stern. "Do you want to wait to be married until after you've finished your schooling?"

Trina tipped her head and toyed with one white ribbon. "If I become a licensed veterinarian, it will take at least five years, Graham. That's a long time for us to wait."

He drew in a deep breath, his blue eyes narrowing. "A very long time. . ."

"No one knows that you've asked Mama and Dad for us to be published. If. . ." Trina swallowed. "If you want to court someone else, I'll—"

"I don't want to court anyone else." His firm tone convinced her of his sincerity. "I love you. I want to marry you."

Trina sagged with relief. "I want to marry you, too."

"Do you want to wait five years?"

"I want to marry you tomorrow," Trina said. The warmth of his smile nearly melted her. "But I'll do what you want. I know your dad relies on your help at the lumberyard. Being away from Sommerfeld would create a hardship for him."

"There are others who could work there if I needed to be away for a while." Graham looked outward, his hands on his knees. "And I could find a job in a city, I'm sure." He chuckled, shaking his head. "I just can't imagine living anywhere else."

Trina sighed. "Me neither. I truly love Sommerfeld."

Graham looked at her. "So you're sure, if you go away to college, you'll want to come back here?"

She blinked at him in surprise. "I've never wanted to leave Sommerfeld. Or the fellowship."

"But being away might give you other ideas."

Trina thought about her friendship with Beth McCauley, and how Mama and Dad had worried Beth might pull her away from the fellowship. Now it seemed Graham was worried time away from Sommerfeld might keep her away. But in her heart, she knew where she belonged—here, with her family and friends and fellowship. God might be opening a door to learning, but she was certain it was a door that wouldn't close behind her as she went through.

"I'll be back." She said it with conviction, and Graham's shoulders seemed to wilt. She placed her hand over his. "I know where I belong.

I want to use the skills I learn to help the people in my own community. I know it's right."

"Well, then," Graham said, turning his hand over to link his fingers with hers, "we need to make arrangements to speak with the deacons and minister. But for now. . ." Rising, he pulled her to her feet and aimed her toward the house. "Go find your schoolbooks and study. You have a test to pass."

"So how do you think you did?"

Beth adjusted the dial on the car's air-conditioning system, and a blast of cool air twirled the ribbons on Trina's cap. Trina caught the dancing tails of the ribbons between her fingers and toyed with the ends. "I'm really not sure. It was hard! But I know I did my best."

"That's all a person can do." Beth's warm tone offered Trina some reassurance. "And remember, if you don't pass the first time, you can always retake it."

Trina sighed. "I know. But the next date is three weeks away, and the longer it takes to get my GED in hand, the longer I prolong enrolling in a college. Waiting for the fellowship's approval took up almost two weeks. We're already near the end of August! I don't have much time to spare."

Beth glanced in her rearview mirror before switching lanes. "Well, no sense in worrying over it. Just proceed as if you already have the certificate in hand. Then, when you do have it, you'll be ready."

Trina looked out the window at the passing landscape, eager to return to town and tell Graham how things had gone. Although Graham had wanted to take her to Hutchinson for the test, his father had insisted he stay in Sommerfeld and work. Trina suspected Mr. Ortmann, like many others in Sommerfeld, wasn't in favor of Trina's plans to be a college graduate. But the deacons, minister, and bishop, after long discussion, had granted permission. The others in the community would eventually have to accept the decision.

"Do you realize"—Beth's voice cut into Trina's thoughts—"you are being a trendsetter?"

Trina faced Beth and released a light, puzzled laugh. "What?"

Beth grinned, her eyes sparkling. "A trendsetter. You're paving the way for change. Just like the Mennonites before you who wanted to use electricity or wanted to drive a car." With an impish smirk, she smacked the car's horn. "Now, because of you, other young people from Sommerfeld will be able to get an education if they want to."

Trina stared at Beth. "But I didn't want to change rules. I just wanted to be a vet."

Beth laughed. "I know that, silly. But don't you see? Now that you've been given permission, they'll have to give permission to others, too. You've opened the door of opportunity to every person in Sommerfeld! I'm really proud of you, Katrinka."

Trina shook her head wildly, her ribbons slapping against her shoulders. "Don't give me too much credit. The deacons made it clear this is experimental and conditional. *If* I can attend college without jeopardizing my personal faith or becoming a stumbling block to others, *then* I'll be allowed to continue. But they're watching, believe me."

Beth snorted. "Oh, I believe you." Then she flashed Trina a smile. "But if there's anyone who could do it—who could attend college without losing one inch of her belief system—I think it would be you."

Trina's heart thumped in appreciation of Beth's support, but curiosity drove her to ask a hesitant question. "Why me?" She hoped Beth wouldn't assume she was fishing for compliments. Mama would certainly frown at that activity!

"Because of what you told me when we first started exploring on the Internet." Beth tucked a strand of hair behind her ear. "Do you remember? You said you loved living in Sommerfeld and loved your fellowship. You didn't want to leave it; you just wanted to help the residents by being able to treat animals. So I believe, even if you have to live somewhere else for a while, you'll come back to Sommerfeld, still wearing your cap and modest dress, still firmly entrenched in your faith."

Tears pricked Trina's eyes. "Thank you for believing in me, Beth."

Beth shrugged. "Believing in *you* was easy. Believing *they* would actually let you do it—that's another thing entirely."

Trina understood Beth's doubts. Although Beth and Sean lived in Sommerfeld and socialized occasionally with Beth's cousins, she knew the worldly couple still felt like outsiders. Beth, although rarely openly disdainful, didn't pretend to support the community's restraints, which created conflict in relationships with residents. Trina wished everyone would recognize the good Beth's business did for the community—not only providing jobs for a handful of people, but also bringing business to town. Shoppers who visited her stained-glass art studio also visited other Sommerfeld businesses.

In Trina's opinion, Beth's presence was a positive thing for the community, but others still looked at her blue jeans and T-shirts and kept their distance. Why, Trina wondered, was it so hard for people to look on the heart instead of the exterior? But then, she mused, worldly people had a difficult time looking past her simple attire and seeing the person underneath the cap, so Mennonites weren't the only ones who struggled with looking on the heart.

Beth curled her hands around the steering wheel and straightened her arms, pushing herself into the seat and releasing a yawn. "But I'm sure glad the leaders surprised me with their decision to let you try college. God answered our prayers, and you're able to forge ahead into your dream."

"Oh, He sure did." Trina propped her chin in her hand and peered out the window. Having Beth's wholehearted support from the beginning had given her courage to pursue her dream. Now she had support from Graham and her mother, too. If only Dad would be more encouraging. Even though Dad had said he'd go along with whatever the leaders decided, he still held himself aloof from Trina, almost as if punishing her for stepping outside the generational boundary limiting education.

"But there's still a lot to pray about." Trina shifted to face Beth. "Graham and I aren't sure whether we should get married before or after I finish college."

Beth sucked in her lower lip, her gaze ahead on the road. "That's not a question I can answer, Trina. Once you're married, you'll probably start a family, and that would sure make it harder to go to school."

"Or to be a veterinarian," Trina concurred. She felt a small prick of conscience. Was it fair to set Graham and their future family aside for the sake of a college degree? She felt the strong tug on her heart to care for animals, but she also felt a tug toward Graham. Which tug should be honored first?

"What does Graham want?"

Trina sighed. "Graham says he's willing to wait if that's what I think is best, but I know he's eager to be married. He has a house built and waiting. He's older than me, you know, and he's ready for a family."

"I see." Beth ran her fingernails over the curve of the plastic steering wheel, her brow furrowed in thought.

Even though Beth wasn't Mennonite, Trina respected her opinions.

Beth was older, and because she'd been raised in the secular world, she often had insights beyond the limited scope of Trina's experience. Now that Beth was a Christian, Trina trusted her not to lead her astray. "How do you and Sean make decisions?"

"We argue."

Trina raised her eyebrows.

Beth nodded, smirking. "Oh yes, we argue. All my fault. I'm pretty stubborn, and I always want my way."

"Beth!" Trina couldn't believe her friend would openly admit to arguing and demanding her way with her husband. Dad had always had the final word in their household. Even though Mama was strong willed, she bowed to Dad's leadership in the home. Albeit reluctantly at times, Trina suspected.

Beth's laughter rang. "Sean's headstrong, too, so he doesn't cave in to me when he believes he's in the right. And eventually we find a compromise that works for both of us." Suddenly she frowned. "At least, most of the time."

Trina thought she understood. "Except on his being gone so much?"

Beth shrugged and flipped a strand of hair over her shoulder. "Except that. But I do okay on my own. That's where my independent spirit comes in handy. I don't *need* Sean to be around. I just *want* him. There's a huge difference."

Trina nodded thoughtfully. As a single person living at home, she followed her parents' lead. As a married woman, she'd follow her husband's. She sent up a silent prayer of gratitude for Graham's change of heart concerning her desire to become a vet. Having come to a compromise on that huge issue, Trina had every confidence they could find a solution to any problem—including whether to get married before or after her graduation from college.

Eighteen

G raham! Graham!"

Graham dropped the length of lumber with a clatter and spun around, his heart in his throat. Trina raced toward him, tears staining her cheeks, the ribbons of her cap streaming over her shoulders. He held out his arms, and she plowed into him, setting him back two stumbling steps. Catching her shoulders, he regained his balance and held her to his chest.

"What is it? What's wrong?" Her panicked voice and the tears sent a shaft of fear through his belly.

"My test. . . .I got the letter. . . ." Trina blubbered against his shirtfront, and suddenly he understood.

"Aw, Trina." He rubbed her shoulders, resting his cheek on the top of her head. The cap felt abrasive against his skin, but he didn't move, hoping his embrace would soothe her bruised heart. The weeklong wait for the test results had been excruciating for both of them, and it hurt him to have it end this way. "I'm sorry."

"No!" She pulled away, shoving a folded piece of paper beneath his chin. Only then did he notice the smile behind the tears. "I passed! Just barely—my score isn't all that good, but I passed. I really passed!"

"You passed? Let me see." He opened the letter and scanned the contents. Sure enough—there it was, in black and white, that all-important word: *Passed*. "Trina, you're a high school graduate. Congratulations."

She beamed up at him. "Thank you." Taking the letter back, she stared at it with awe lighting her eyes. "I can't believe it. I really didn't think I would pass. It was a hard test, Graham."

"Well, you studied hard. You deserved to pass." When the leaders had given their approval for Trina to take her GED with the intention of applying to a college, Graham had offered his support. Yet as much as he hated to admit it, a sense of foreboding now pricked as he realized it wasn't just a dream. Trina's attending college would be a reality.

"Now I've got to let Barton County Community College know I have the GED. If they approve my application, I'll be a college student!"

Her unbridled glee chased away the hint of melancholy. Graham gave a genuine smile and squeezed her upper arm. "I'm proud of you."

"Oh, thank you! I can't wait to tell Beth and Mama and Dad and. . ." Suddenly her face clouded. "But probably only Beth will really be happy with me. Mama wants to be, I know, but with Dad so upset, she can't be."

Graham slipped his thumb up and down on her arm. "No one said it would be easy to do what God calls us to do. But you know you won't be happy unless you keep trying." He reminded himself of the truth of his words, battling the urge to worry.

She nodded, blinking rapidly. A smile trembled on her lips. "I'm so glad you're happy. Having you celebrate with me means so much."

He brushed her cheek with his knuckles then pushed his hand into the pocket of his work apron. "You're impossible to resist. You know that."

Trina giggled, hunching her shoulders. The gesture reminded

him of the old Trina—the one who'd been too long absent. His heart thumped in double beats. *Thank You, Lord, that Trina is back.* He jerked his chin toward the lumberyard doors. "Now scoot on over to the café and show your mom. I'll come by after work, and we'll talk more, okay?"

She nodded, her face wreathed with a smile. "Okay. See you later!" She skipped away, carefree as a young girl, cradling the letter against her chest.

Graham watched her, chuckling. She really was impossible to resist. A groan replaced the chuckle. Could he wait five years to make her his wife? They had a serious discussion coming. *Give us guidance, Father.* With that prayer hovering in his heart, he returned to work.

Graham considered having supper at the café. Thinking about the Thursday night special of German sausage, kraut, and fried potatoes made his mouth water. But in the end, he decided he'd rather go home, clean up, and have some quiet time alone before speaking with Trina about when they should be married.

The short walk seemed longer in the stifling heat of late August. As a boy, he'd once commented that summer did its best to get as much heat as possible in before it closed, making August unbearable. His father had berated him for complaining and told him to appreciate his indoor job—he didn't have to be outside under the sun, like the farmers. Graham kept his thoughts to himself after that, but he still believed August to be the most uncomfortable month of the year.

After scrubbing himself clean in a bath and eating two bologna and cheese sandwiches, he felt ready to face Trina. But a glance at the clock told him he'd better wait awhile. Trina's responsibilities at the café wouldn't end until after eight. Now that she'd passed her test, she would probably return to her job at Dr. Groening's, if he hadn't filled it with someone else. He'd have to ask her about providing transport to work—that would give them time alone each day. The thought appealed to him.

He glanced at the clock again. Only two minutes had passed. Blowing out a noisy breath, he looked around the neat living room for something to do to fill time. His gaze fell on his Bible, which sat on the end of the sofa, still open from his morning's reading. He sank down beside it and flicked a few pages, until he reached Proverbs. Bending forward over the book, he reread chapter 31, seeking further illumination as to how to proceed in his relationship with Trina. Finding no real answers, he idly turned pages, scanned brief passages, and allowed his mind to wander.

When he came upon Proverbs 10:22, he read the words out loud. " 'The blessing of the Lord, it maketh rich. . . .' " He counted Trina as one of his blessings. Her spark for life, her openness to everyone around her raised his spirits and made him want to be more openly cheerful himself. She added a richness to his life that had nothing to do with monetary gain—he couldn't put a value on what she meant to him. A smile tugged at his cheeks as he thought about her sweet laugh, her dancing eyes, her joyous spirit.

But his smile faded when he focused on the final words. " 'And he addeth no sorrow with it.' " There had been a great deal of sorrow lately in his relationship with Trina. Even if he and the fellowship leaders endorsed her desire to attend college, others murmured in opposition to the decision, just as there were those who still murmured about the use of electricity or the driving of automobiles. Those unpleasant, demeaning voices would surely bring a touch of sorrow to the situation.

Then, of course, her own father and some other family members who stated their objections openly or made known their disapproval with firmly pressed lips created sorrow, too.

"How can we keep the sorrow away, Lord?" He asked the question to the empty room, his face tipped upward, seeking a reply. "Even I struggle with all of the changes it will mean for me. As much as I want Trina to follow Your will, there are things I may have to give up, and the thought of them makes me sorrowful, too."

For some reason, saying the words out loud offered a release Graham didn't realize he needed. So he said them again. "I support Trina. I'm happy for her, but I feel sad for me at the same time." With that admission, something struck him. The verse said *He* added no sorrow to it. That meant the Lord wouldn't add sorrow to His blessing. But *man* certainly could—and probably would.

With a sigh, Graham closed his eyes. "Lord, help me not to add sorrow to Trina's blessing. Let me support her sincerely and without reserve. Let my support ease the sting of sorrow inflicted by others in the community. Open my heart to the blessing You have in store for us as a couple dedicated to Your service. Amen."

Revived by the prayer, he looked at the clock, eager to meet with Trina and discuss plans. Not quite seven o'clock. With a shrug, he rose and headed for the door. He'd have some dessert and wait for her at the café. His steps felt light despite the sluggish weight of humidity in the air. *"The blessing of the Lord, it maketh rich."* *It won't be easy to do what's right, but I'll do it because I trust in Your promise, Lord.*

Trina caught Graham's eye as she closed the door behind the final patrons. Something in his expression—a tenderness, a warmth, a secret promise of good to come—made her chest feel like a bell holding a raucously clanging clapper. She pressed her hands to her apron bodice, the thud of her heart pounding against her trembling palms.

A grin crept up his cheek. "You're staring at me like you've seen a ghost."

She stepped to the edge of the table and shook her head. "No, not a ghost. A glimpse of. . .the future."

He tipped his head, his forehead crinkling even while the smile still curved his lips.

She laughed at his puzzlement. "Don't ask me to explain, because I can't. But if you'll give me a half hour to help Mama with cleanup, maybe we'll be able to make sense of it together."

"I can wait."

The words took on a much broader meaning, and an impatience filled Trina. He'd said he could wait for her to finish her schooling, too, but did she want to wait? Peering into his handsome, open, adoring face, she wanted everything right now—Graham, her degree, her own home. Taking a step backward, she waved her hand in the direction of the kitchen. "Let me get that cleanup going. I'll go fast."

He nodded, and she scurried away. She banged things together getting the mop and mop bucket out. Just as she set the bucket in the sink to fill it, Mama came over and put her hand on Trina's arm.

"Go ahead and leave. Tony is coming in to help, so between Kelly, him, and me, we'll get it covered."

Trina raised her eyebrows. "Are you sure? Graham said he'd wait."

A smile softened Mama's normally stern expression. "Graham's been waiting long enough. Go ahead."

"Thank you, Mama!" Trina shut off the stream of water and reached to remove her apron.

Mama grabbed her arm again. "And, Trina? This is your last day. I called Janina and Audra, and both of them are willing to come back here. I know you want to work for Dr. Groening, but even if he's filled the position, you won't be needed here. You'll want to use your time to study."

Tears filled Trina's eyes, making Mama's image swim. Even though Mama hadn't offered congratulations for passing the GED, her words now spoke of her pride in Trina's accomplishment. "Thank you, Mama." Trina gave her mother a quick hug. "I'll see you later tonight. Ten o'clock?"

"That'll be fine." Mama turned her attention to the mop bucket.

Trina scampered out to the dining room and captured Graham's hand. "Mama says I don't need to stay."

Outside the café, Graham lifted his shoulders in a shrug and smiled down at her. "Where should we go?"

Someplace private was preferable, yet Trina knew the community would frown on it. "How about the cemetery?" The open location, in sight of anyone who happened by, would be considered acceptable and still be without an audience.

"That's fine." Graham held Trina's hand as they walked the distance to the cemetery. In the treetops, cicadas sang their buzzing chorus, but neither Trina nor Graham spoke. For Trina, just walking with Graham, her hand held loosely within the confines of his firm calloused fingers, was pleasure enough. Conversation would come when they reached their destination.

Instead of crouching behind a tombstone, they chose a bench beneath a towering elm at the corner of the cemetery. The concrete bench felt cool despite the warmth of the night air, and Trina released a satisfied sigh.

"It's nice to be alone with you this way."

Graham nodded, keeping his face attentively turned to her.

"And right now I can't imagine waiting five years to get married."

Graham ducked his head for a moment, his eyes closed. When he raised his gaze to meet hers again, she glimpsed a maturity and strength beyond what she'd seen before. She swallowed, waiting quietly for him to share his thoughts.

"Trina, my desire would be to marry you this winter. My home is ready; my heart is ready to make you my wife. But I don't want to be selfish."

"Selfish?"

He nodded. "Think how much time you took studying to pass the GED. Don't you think college will be even harder than that? I want you to have the time you need to do your best. If you're working for Dr. Groening *and* running a household, you aren't going to have time to focus on studies. Maybe. . ." Suddenly the conviction in his tone faltered. He cleared his throat and started again. "Maybe it would be best for us to wait so you can give this dream the time and attention it deserves to be fully born."

Trina stared at him in amazement. "You really want to wait?"

He chuckled softly, placing his hand over hers in the center of the bench. "No, my precious Trina, I don't *want* to wait. But I wonder if it's best to wait." He drew in a deep breath and released it, his gaze heavenward where a few stars glittered softly against the fading evening sky. "I read a verse in Proverbs about the Lord giving us rich blessings without adding any sorrow to it. It seems to me that stressing over finding time to study and not being able to apply yourself fully to this task is going to lead to sorrow for you. That isn't right."

"Oh, Graham. . ." Trina knew what it cost him to make this concession. His readiness for a home and family hadn't been kept secret, yet he was willing to set aside his desires for the sake of hers. If she'd harbored any question about whether he truly loved her, the unease now whisked away like a cottonwood seed on a stiff Kansas breeze.

"We could still be published but just put off the wedding until you have college finished. I would like to take you to Lehigh to work each day so we'd have some time together. I'm not saying it will be easy." His voice dropped to a low growl. "But I do think it will be for the best."

Trina nodded slowly, absorbing the wisdom of his words. Looking back on the number of hours she had spent in preparation for the GED, she knew taking college classes would tax her time and energy. But five years. . .

She groaned. "How did Uncle Henry live for twenty years without Aunt Marie?"

Graham laughed—a low, throaty sound. "I've wondered that myself. I guess when I get to feeling impatient, I can always go talk to him. He should be able to give good advice."

Suddenly something occurred to Trina. "If we wait until I'm finished, then. . .when it comes time for me to take classes on a campus instead of over the Internet, I'll be moving away from Sommerfeld all alone." Uncertainty washed over her. Could she manage by herself in a strange town, hours away from her family and Graham?

His warm fingers tightened on her hand. "That isn't something you need to worry about yet. It's at least two years away, since you'll be taking your first classes online. By the time you need to go away, God will give you the strength you need." Another chuckle sounded, this one rueful in tone. "And He'll give me the strength to let you go."

"Or maybe. . ." Trina licked her lips, peering at him hopefully. "I won't have to go alone?"

He smiled, shaking his head. "As I said, we'll worry about it when the time comes. But until then, you need to learn what you can from Dr. Groening, you need to study hard, and you need to prove to everyone in Sommerfeld that becoming a veterinarian will not be damaging to your faith."

Trina threw her hands outward, releasing a snort of laughter. "Oh, that's nothing! Anyone could do it!" Then she sobered, taking Graham's hand again. Amazing how the feel of his strong fingers gave her courage. "I'm sorry I'm making you wait, but thank you for being willing to wait for me."

"Oh, my Trina. . ." Graham sighed, raising his free hand to cup her cheek. "I've told you before: You are worth the wait. God will get us through this time of waiting, and when we are finally together as husband and wife, I'll feel like the richest man in the world."

NINETEEN

Trina closed her Bible and slipped to her knees beside her bed. She'd made a commitment to God not to give studying more importance than fellowship with Him, so her early mornings were committed to Bible reading and prayer.

While her books waited on the table she'd set up in the corner of her bedroom, she spent long minutes talking to God, offering praises for His work in her life, acknowledging her weaknesses, and petitioning Him for assistance and strength. She was careful to ask for His help for others before ending with her daily request: "And help me do well in my classes so I can honor You."

Rising, she crossed to the table and smoothed her hand across the cover of the top book. Despite the fact that she'd been following a study routine for two weeks now, there were still moments when it all seemed like a dream. She really didn't own college textbooks; she really wasn't a college student. But the stack of books beneath her hand was solid; the pages contained words and pictures and graphs. Not a dream but a certainty.

Suddenly, as had happened frequently in the two weeks she'd studied on her own and submitted assignments through Beth's computer, a feeling of impatience struck. Her first two years of study would be basic subjects—nothing directly related to animal care—and she longed to dive into the classes that would benefit her the most. Yet the college adviser had said every student was required to pass the basic subjects first.

Closing her eyes, she whispered, "Make these first two years go quickly, please." The addendum to her formal prayer time brought a smile to her face. During her weeks of preparing for the GED, she'd nearly put aside conversation with her heavenly Father. But now it came naturally again, making her even more certain she was doing exactly what He'd called her to do.

She slid onto the wooden chair Dad had grudgingly hauled in from the car's shed and opened the English composition book. Since she would be returning to work at Dr. Groening's clinic on Monday, this would be her last full day of study—she intended to make the most of it. But despite her best efforts to keep her attention on past and present verb tenses, her mind kept drifting a few miles east to Lehigh and the clinic.

With a sigh, she allowed herself to replay the telephone conversation with the aging doctor.

"Trina! Of course, I'd be delighted to hire you again. My receptionist has been filling in for you since I haven't been able to find anyone else. She'll be very willing to let you have those duties again."

Trina had smiled then stated adamantly, "But I won't be doing only cleanup forever, you know. I'm now enrolled in college. I will be a veterinarian one day."

"The fellowship approved it?"

The shock in the man's tone hadn't surprised Trina. It gave her great pleasure to repeat his words as a statement. "The fellowship approved it."

"Well, congratulations, Trina."

"And, Dr. Groening, I'd appreciate it if you would consider selling me your practice when the time comes."

At that point there had been a lengthy pause, during which Trina feared the connection might have been terminated. But finally his voice had returned, hesitant in its delivery. "You know, Trina, I'm already past the age of retirement. I've continued because I'm the only veterinarian nearby for many of the area farmers. But another five years of practice? I'm not sure I want to continue that long."

Trina's heart pounded with trepidation. She couldn't possibly complete the necessary coursework and practicum in fewer than five years. Given the expenses involved, she feared the time might be extended while she worked to save up enough money to finish. "Will you at least consider it?" she had managed to squeak.

Finally Dr. Groening's tired voice had said, "I'll consider it. We can talk more when you come into work, all right?"

That promised conversation was just around the corner, and Trina was both eager and reluctant to finalize her plans with the doctor. Sighing, she rested her chin in her hand and stared out the open window. Although September had arrived, bringing a change in color to the trees, the daytime weather still held the feel of summer. Evenings were somewhat less stuffy, however, and she and Graham spent at least an hour together on the porch before sundown each day.

Closing her eyes, she deliberately conjured Graham's face—his handsome, honed, adoring face. He had a way of looking at her that made her feel treasured and special. Just thinking of him now increased her pulse while a flutter of something pleasant coiled in her chest. A smile played on the corners of her lips. Her intended husband. . .

How fortunate she was to have a man willing to listen to God's voice rather than remaining trapped in the traditions of man. Based on the reaction of many of the community members, she felt certain no other young man in Sommerfeld would have supported her desire to further her education. God had certainly chosen the perfect mate for her. Each evening, as he bestowed a chaste kiss on her forehead, Graham whispered, "Do a little reading before you turn in. Keep your grades up."

With the remembered gentle admonition, Trina gave a start. How long had she been sitting here daydreaming? She had work to do! Determinedly, she turned her attention back to the English book. When she met Graham for lunch at the café, she wanted to give him a good report on her morning's progress.

"So I got three English assignments done—one that isn't even due for another week—and a science paper written. I'll need to type it, and then I can send it. Beth taught me how to e-mail attachments. It sure makes things simple." Trina pushed her empty plate aside and rested her elbows on the table edge. Despite the busyness of the café's noon traffic, she and Graham were secluded in a corner booth, giving them a small amount of privacy.

Graham took a bite of grape pie, his gaze never leaving Trina's face. How he loved to watch her dark eyes sparkle and her animated face beam with pride in her accomplishments. "That's good to get ahead. So the typing is going better?"

At the mention of typing, her cheery expression turned sour. "Oh, I hate it! My fingers are so clumsy. It takes forever." She sighed then straightened her shoulders and tipped up her chin. "But I'll get better the more I do it. Beth got me a tutorial that shows me the right way to put my hands on the keys so I'm not pecking around like this." With a laugh, she demonstrated by jabbing her pointer fingers against the tabletop in a wild dance. She laced her fingers together and shrugged. "She says I'll enjoy typing more when I'm not having to stare at the keys and poke them."

Graham winked. "I'm sure you can do whatever you set your mind to. But doesn't the tutorial eat up your study time?"

Once more, Trina crinkled her face into a scowl. "Yes. It hasn't put me behind because I've had the whole day to commit to studies since classes started, but when Monday comes and I go back to work. . ." She sent him a mournful look. "How will I fit everything in, Graham?"

"Well. . ." He scratched his chin. "Don't work full-time."

"I have to!" She leaned forward, her palms flat on the table. "I thought I had a lot in savings, but college is very expensive. I didn't get any scholarships, partly because I enrolled so late but mostly because all I had was the GED, and my score wasn't very good. I don't know how I'll pay to finish if I don't work full-time."

Graham put down his fork and slid the dessert plate to the edge of the table. He placed his hands over hers. "Do you think you might be able to get a scholarship next year?"

Trina shrugged, turning her hands to twine her fingers with his. He sensed she wasn't even aware of the action, but it had a serious affect on his heart rate. "Maybe. . .if I get really good grades in all my classes. But according to what I read online, most scholarships are for activities like music or sports." She released a regretful chuckle, shaking her head. "I'll never get any of those."

"God will pave the way." Graham gave her hands a quick squeeze. "If you have to work full-time, then it means you'll just have to budget your study time wisely."

She bit down on her lower lip, sending him a repentant look. "But what if it means no evening time with you?" Her face puckered into a pout. "I've gotten spoiled the last couple of weeks, seeing you every day. I don't want to give it up, but—"

"Are you going to the skating tonight?" At the intruding voice, both Trina and Graham jumped, their hands jolting apart. Graham met Kelly Dick's smiling face. The girl's gaze bounced back and forth between them. "I get to go—Mom and Dad said I could. Are you going?"

"I don't know." Graham looked at Trina. "I had forgotten they scheduled the rink for tonight."

Trina tipped her face up to Kelly. "Is this your first time to go skating?"

Graham already knew the answer, but Trina's mother had kept her home so often, he wasn't surprised Trina didn't know who regularly attended the skating parties.

Kelly's eager nod exhibited her enthusiasm. "Yes. They made Kyra wait until she was seventeen, but Mom said I could go if Dad said it was all right, and Dad said it was okay if Mom approved it." She laughed. "So I'm going a full year earlier than Kyra!"

Graham couldn't imagine the significance of Kelly's statement, but by Trina's laughing eyes, he sensed she understood.

"Well, don't tell Tony," Trina said, "because I'm sure Mama and Dad will make him wait until he's seventeen, just like they did me."

Kelly teasingly ran her fingers over her closed lips then snatched up their plates and scampered away.

As soon as she left, Graham said, "Well? Do you want to go to the skating party? Especially if our time together is going to be limited when you go back to work, maybe we should have a fun evening together with our friends."

Trina licked her lips, her eyebrows rising in speculation. "Would you rather do something. . .quiet? Just the two of us?"

Could she possibly know how tempting he found her question?

He loved their together time, yet he realized the more time they spent one-on-one, the harder it was to put off their wedding. At times it was tortuous not being able to exhibit the affection his heart longed to release. Although he told himself it was best to wait, he knew it wasn't going to be easy.

Leaning forward, he grasped her hands again. "Trina, I would love nothing more than to have an entire, uninterrupted evening with you. But you've spent all of your free time just with me lately. Wouldn't you like to have time with your other friends? You must miss them. I know they miss you."

Her smile turned impish, and she bobbed her head in a firm nod. "It's hard for me to have time alone with you without wanting more, too."

He burst out laughing then coughed to cover the sound. "How did you know that's what I was thinking?"

She shrugged, still grinning. "I just know."

"Well, you're right. Being alone with you makes it a lot harder to leave you afterward. I'm starting to think that's how your uncle Henry managed to wait so long for Marie—he didn't *see* her every day, which would have let him know exactly what he was missing. So being in a crowd is probably best—for both of us." He gave her hand a slight tug. "Do you want to go? If so, go check with your mom and make sure it's okay."

Without another word, Trina slipped from the booth and disappeared into the kitchen. Moments later she returned, a smile on her face. "Mama says to go. She says I've been holed up in my room too much lately and getting out will do me good." Shaking her head, she stared at him in wide-eyed wonder. "I can't believe how much Mama has changed."

Graham agreed Mrs. Muller seemed like a different person than the one who used to watch him with a scowl on her face. Although she still didn't greet him with huge smiles or cheerful banter, she did acknowledge him with a nod of hello and conversed with him. Most noticeable, however, was her willingness to allow him time with Trina. He wasn't sure what had precipitated the change, but he was thankful for it.

"Dad's changed, too." Trina's melancholy tone captured Graham's attention.

"I know." Graham had witnessed the man's drawing away from Trina since she started the college classes. He prayed daily for Mr. Muller's acceptance of Trina's choice. Although in the past her father had been strict, he'd also been warm. Graham knew how much Trina missed the dad she used to know. "Give him time. He'll come around."

Trina nodded, her gaze to the side, seemingly lost in thought.

Squeezing her hands, he said, "I'll pick you up at six o'clock." He waited until she looked at him. "We can eat at McDonald's before we go to the rink."

Trina finally rewarded him with a slight smile. "That sounds good."

He affected a stern look and pointed at her. "But now you go home and use the afternoon to study. Or go to Beth's and type that science paper. But get some work done, okay? Earn your evening out."

Trina giggled, not at all put off by his mock dictatorial attitude. "Yes, sir!" Bounding from the seat, she said, "Thank you for lunch. I'll see you this evening."

He watched her leave the café, her steps light and head held high. How he wished he had the money to give her for school so she wouldn't have to work. But it wouldn't be seemly, considering they weren't married. And he didn't have it anyway. He'd used his savings to build his—their—house. Then an idea struck with such force he sat upright, banging his head on the high back of the booth.

Withdrawing his wallet, he dropped enough bills on the table to cover the lunch tab plus a tip for Kelly. Then he hurried out of the café, eager to locate his father. He had something important to discuss.

TWENTY

Watching Michelle and Walt huddle in a corner of the rink sent a shaft of jealousy through Trina's middle. Since they were officially published, expressing affection was acceptable. How she'd love to rest her head on Graham's shoulder, to have his arm slip around her waist, to feel his breath on her cheek as he whispered in her ear.

But she couldn't.

She turned her attention away from the benches and watched the skaters. She'd removed her borrowed skates early, offering the excuse of a blister on her toe. In truth, she simply needed to separate herself from the giggling and teasing and roughhousing going on. Why, she wondered, did the childish displays—displays that only a few months ago she would have cheerfully joined—now set her teeth on edge?

Propping her elbows on the wooden ledge of the rink's surrounding wall, she observed Kelly laughing into the face of Paul Lantz as she held on to his arm. Paul appeared quite content to move slowly around the rink with Kelly attached to her elbow. Smiling, Trina remembered her first attempts and the repeated falls before Graham had offered his elbow to keep her upright. Would romance bloom for Kelly and Paul as it had for her and Graham?

Automatically her head raised, her gaze seeking, until she spotted Graham's familiar sandy head of hair. He skated like an expert, his body angled forward, arms swinging in rhythm with the smooth movement of his feet. Her heart caromed at his display of athletic prowess. As she watched, he whizzed between two slower skaters and came alongside Darcy Kauffman. With a huge grin, he tapped her opposite shoulder, then zoomed on while Darcy glanced back with a puzzled look. His laughter brought Darcy's gaze forward, and she shook her fist at him, skating faster to catch up. But of course she couldn't catch him.

Trina scowled. Graham was still laughing when he careened to a halt on the other side of the wall, but his expression changed quickly when he met her gaze.

"What's wrong?"

With effort, Trina pushed aside the rush of envy that made her want to snap at him for tapping Darcy's shoulder. He and Darcy were friends—he should be able to tease a friend. But she couldn't quite manufacture a smile.

"Nothing."

He placed his hands over hers and leaned closer. She had to strain to hear his voice over the noise of the skaters. "Do you want to leave now?"

She thought about the fun he'd been having only moments before. It would be selfish to pull him away just because she didn't want to skate. With an adamant shake of her head, she said, "No."

"Are you sure? Can't be much fun just standing there watching."

He was right—it wasn't as much fun as being a participant. But tonight she had no desire to participate. "I'm okay, really. Go ahead and skate. See if you can make it around faster than Lester."

Graham snorted, his grin returning. "Lester, huh? Oh, that's easy." He whizzed back to the floor and in moments caught up to Lester Hess. After a whispered consultation in the corner of the rink, the two lined up for a race. An excited wave of laughter carried the other skaters to the edges to watch the contest. Several heads blocked Trina's view, and she rose up on tiptoe to peek out just in time to see Graham zing by a few seconds ahead of Lester.

A cheer rose, and someone grabbed Trina's hand.

"Did you see him? He's the fastest skater ever, I think." Darcy's blue eyes shone with admiration. "I wish I could skate that fast, but never in a dress." She giggled, and Trina couldn't help but join in, imagining Darcy trying to keep up with Graham's long-legged stride.

The crowd headed back to the floor, except for Darcy, who remained next to Trina and waited for Graham's smiling approach.

"Well, I guess I showed him, huh?"

Before Trina could answer, Darcy said, "You sure did! That was exciting!" She crinkled her nose. "Lester is always bragging, so it's good to see him bested now and then."

"I guess so." Graham wiped the sweat from his brow. "But that wore me out. I'm ready to go now, Trina, if you want to leave."

Darcy grabbed Graham's sleeve. "Oh no! Don't go yet! A bunch of us are going for ice cream afterward. You'll want to come." She turned to include Trina. "Won't you?"

Seeing Darcy and Graham side by side on the other side of the wall left Trina feeling strangely distanced from her friends. She swallowed. "I'm not really hungry." She looked at Graham. "But if you want ice cream, I don't mind staying."

To her relief Graham shook his head. "It sounds fun, Darcy, but I worked today, and I'm worn out. I think Trina and I will go on home." He skated around Darcy and left the rink.

Darcy's lips slipped into a brief pout, but then she shrugged and shot Trina a grin. "Well, I'll see you at service tomorrow." Her smile turned impish. "Maybe I'll go console Lester on his loss in that race." With a laugh, she skated off.

Graham approached, skates dangling from his hand. He pointed to his gray-stockinged feet. "I'll get my boots on, and then we can go."

She nodded, shifting her gaze to watch the skaters for a few more minutes. A part of her longed to rush onto the rink and laugh and chase with abandon, but another part of her only wanted to go home. With a sigh, she turned from the wall and stood beside the bench where Graham pulled his boots over his socks. When he'd tugged his pant legs back over the boots, he looked up at her. A sad smile played around the corners of his mouth.

"This wasn't much fun for you, was it?"

Trina's chin trembled as she fought tears.

He rose, taking her hand. "Come on. We can talk in the car."

When the door closed behind them, sealing away the noise of the other skaters, Trina heaved a sigh of relief. She shook her head. "I never realized how loud we were. Was it always so. . .uncontrolled?"

Graham laughed, swinging her hand as he led her to his waiting vehicle. "Yes, and you were usually in the middle of the ruckus."

Did she detect a note of regret in his tone? He opened the car door for her, but she stood beside the car and peered up at him. "Are you upset about leaving early?"

"No." The answer came quickly. "Time alone with you is precious, so I don't mind heading out." He put his hand on her back, giving a gentle nudge. "Slide in there."

When he was behind the steering wheel, he sent her a sympathetic look. "I noticed most people avoided you tonight. I'm sorry. I guess they're not comfortable with the direction you're taking, and they don't know what to say. So they say nothing."

Trina nodded. Her friends, with the exception of Darcy, had been distant. But, she acknowledged, she'd distanced herself, too. She couldn't blame them entirely. "I know. I understand them. I just wish I understood *me*." Shifting her gaze, she stared at the building that housed the skating rink. All the times Mama made her stay behind, she'd longed for the opportunity to go. Now she could go, and she longed to be away. With a soft laugh, she added, "I must be going through one of those 'stages' Mama used to complain about. I don't know what I want."

"Yes, you do." Graham gave her hand a tug, bringing her focus to him. "You want to serve God by taking care of animals. And you want me to be your support system." His smile grew. "Well, you're getting what you want. So let's see a smile on your face."

Obediently, Trina offered a smile, but she suspected it lacked luster.

Her suspicion was confirmed when Graham snorted. "That's a pretty poor excuse for a smile. I guess I'll just have to buy you a double-dip chocolate ice cream cone. That always perks you up."

After Graham purchased two double-dip chocolate cones at a dairy store's drive-through window, he aimed the car toward the highway and home. Trina kept her window up while she ate her cone to keep the dancing tails of her cap from landing in the chocolate, but the moment she finished, she rolled it all the way down and put one hand out.

The pressure of the cooling evening air against her palm sent a tremor clear to her shoulder. She experienced a sense of strength, keeping her hand braced while the coursing wind tried to push it back. If she could hold that wind at bay, surely she could overcome the difficulties facing her as she moved toward her dream.

"Trina?"

She pulled her arm inside and turned to face Graham.

"I'm glad we have this time alone. I need to talk to you about something."

His serious tone sent her heart pattering. She scooted to the center of the seat, away from the wind's whistle, so she could hear clearly. "Okay."

"You were talking about not having enough money to finish your degree."

She nodded. In her daily prayers, she had petitioned God to help make a way to cover all of the expenses.

"I think I know how you can do it."

Trina's eyes flew wide. "You do?"

"Mm-hmm." His gaze flitted sideways, a twinkle in his blue eyes. "You've never been upstairs in my folks' house, but when Dad built it, he made the second floor kind of like an apartment. My grandmother was living with them when he and Mom got married, and he wanted her to have her own space that felt like a separate house."

Trina nodded to let him know she was paying attention, but she couldn't figure out why he was telling her about his parents' house.

"Well, Grandmother died when I was still small, so Mom and Dad moved me up there after Chuck was born. Chuck has those rooms now, but there's the second bedroom downstairs still, which he could move into again." Graham removed one hand from the steering wheel and placed it over hers. "Which leaves the upstairs open."

Trina shook her head. "But what does that have to do with paying for college?"

His hand tightened. "Just listen, okay?" Another quick glance combined with a wink held her silent. "I built my house for us to live in when we got married, but we don't have to have our own house if we live in the upstairs at my folks'. If I sell my house, then—"

"No!" Trina jerked her hand free, pressing it to her chest. "I can't let you do that!"

Graham's lips turned downward. "Why not? As your husband, it should be my responsibility to help pay for your needs. And education is one of your needs."

"But, Graham! I—" And then it occurred to her that he'd referred to himself as her husband. She gulped. "Are you wanting to be married right away, then? Even before I finish school?"

He shrugged with one shoulder, the gesture boyishly appealing. "Well, if you don't have a whole house to care for—if we live with my folks—it would eliminate one responsibility, giving you more time to study. And it would also mean you wouldn't need to go off to college by yourself. I would go with you, get a job, and support you while you finished your schooling."

Trina's mind whirled. She had worried about going off alone, had fretted over putting off their wedding for so long, but now that another option was available, she didn't know what to think.

"Your parents said it would be all right for us to live with them?"

Graham smiled. "Mom's never had a daughter, so she was especially thrilled to think you might live with them for a while."

"And your dad? He didn't mind, either?"

Graham chuckled softly. "Well, to be honest, Dad thinks I'm a little nutty, building a house and then selling it, but he didn't say I couldn't do it. He said if it was what we wanted, he'd be okay with the decision."

"And Chuck isn't unhappy about losing his room?" Trina thought about how Tony would feel if he were kicked out of his bedroom. There would certainly be resentment. She didn't want to live with that.

"Chuck is fine. He's only been up there a year or so—and he's young enough to think it'd be neat to have me home again." He shot her a serious look. "It wouldn't be permanent—just until you have your degree. Then I'd build us another house."

Trina chewed her lower lip, her mind racing. "But would anyone buy your house?"

"There is someone interested." For a moment Graham didn't answer, his fingers curling briefly around her hand before slipping away to grasp the steering wheel. "Walt. For him and Michelle. They're getting married in early February, you know."

Although the words were delivered on a light note, Trina sensed an element of sorrow. She imagined Michelle working in the kitchen Graham had designed for her, and she understood the undertone. A lump filled her throat. "Oh, Graham. . ."

"It'll be all right." The glib tone didn't fool her. "After all, it's just a house. Not really a home until a family lives in it, and we haven't had that chance yet. So after you've finished school, we'll build another house, and we'll move in, and it'll be home. It'll be fine."

Tears welled in Trina's eyes, and she turned her face to the window to allow the wind to dry them. Her face aimed away from Graham, she said on a sigh, "You're giving up so much for me."

His fingers cupped her chin, bringing her face around. "I'm not giving up anything I don't want to—nothing I can't live without. You're more important than ten houses—you know that."

His hand found hers, and she clung to it, welcoming the contact. "Thank you, Graham."

"So. . .if you agree. . .then we need to talk to the deacons. Get published. And start planning a wedding."

"A wedding. . ." Trina shook her head, wonder filling her. Soon she'd be Mrs. Graham Ortmann *and* a veterinarian. How could her heart hold so much happiness at once?

TWENTY-ONE

The first Sunday in October, the acting minister published Graham and Trina to the congregation, making known their intention to become husband and wife. Although Trina noted the well-wishing didn't seem quite as exuberant for her as it had for Michelle only a few weeks earlier, she managed to swallow the prick of disappointment. Changes were hard for many in the fellowship, and she would need to be patient until they accepted this new road on which she was embarking.

Mama, in preparation for the announcement, had invited Graham's immediate family plus Trina's grandparents, aunts, uncles, and cousins to dinner at the café. Dad had grumbled a bit about opening the café on a Sunday, but Mama pointed out there wasn't enough room at the house. Plus she wasn't serving paying customers—she was treating the family to a celebration. So Dad nodded and agreed.

Nearly all of the tables and booths were filled, and when Trina tried to help serve, the ladies shooed her from the kitchen. "Go sit," Aunt Marie said, taking her by the shoulders and giving a gentle shove. "Soon enough you'll be serving Sunday dinner to your own family.

For now, let us spoil you a little bit."

So Trina joined Graham's family, Dad, and Tony at the table in the middle of the dining room and allowed the others to wait on her. Mama had prepared all of Trina's favorites—meat loaf, mashed potatoes with lots of butter and fresh chives, steamed whole green beans flavored with slivered almonds, crusty rolls, and lime Jell-O holding together chopped apples, pecans, and celery. Filling her plate, Trina wondered if she'd have room for the German chocolate cake Mama had baked for dessert.

Conversation around the many tables and booths filled the café with happy noise, and Trina missed Mrs. Ortmann's comment. Trina leaned closer, raising her eyebrows in a silent query for her to repeat the words.

"Has Dr. Groening agreed to sell you the clinic when he retires?"

Trina stifled a sigh. "No, but he hasn't come right out and said he won't, either." Trina recalled the lengthy discussion concerning the future of the clinic. While she understood the doctor's reluctance to commit to another five years of work, she still wished for the security of knowing the clinic would be there waiting for her. "He's sixty-eight years old already, and he isn't sure he wants to continue for five more years."

Mrs. Ortmann nodded, sympathy softening her expression. "I don't suppose a person can blame him. He's taken care of animals in our community for many, many years. He's earned a break."

Trina agreed wholeheartedly. Dr. Groening had been a dedicated servant and was well liked by all of the area residents—Amish, Mennonite, and worldly. She would have some big shoes to fill when she took over the clinic.

Graham's father inserted, "I can't imagine there's anyone else around here who would buy the place. I haven't heard of any young people in the nearby communities planning to go to veterinary school."

Trina's heart tripped hopefully. "I haven't, either. Even though I'd prefer a commitment from him to let me take over the clinic, I have to trust God will work things out. After all"—she flashed Graham a smile—"He's worked everything else out."

Tony reached to the middle of the table for another roll. "And who knows? If Trina makes good, maybe the bishop will say it's okay for others of us to go to school. I think it might be fun to go to college, too."

Trina put her hand on Tony's arm. "I'm not doing this for fun, Tony. If God hadn't put the desire in my heart, I wouldn't be pursuing it." Her brother's cheeks flushed even though Trina kept her voice gentle. "You need to pray about your future and follow the plan God has for you instead of looking for fun."

Dad harrumphed under his breath, the sound barely discernible.

Trina hung her head, battling tears. The celebratory mood darkened with her father's reaction. Why couldn't he see she hadn't set out to hurt him by following her heart? Why couldn't he allow her to follow God's leading without making her feel guilty?

Graham's warm hand on her shoulder brought her head up. Graham leaned forward to address her father. "Mr. Muller, I know you still harbor concerns about Trina going to college."

Dad's brow furrowed into a scowl. "You're right."

"I want you to know I was very concerned, too, but prayer gave my heart peace. I will continue to pray for your peace."

Silence fell around the table, although talking went on animatedly at the other tables. Everyone looked at Dad, who kept his gaze on his plate. Suddenly he pushed his chair back and dropped his napkin on top of his uneaten food. "If you'll excuse me." He strode from the restaurant. Mama jumped up and followed him.

A knot formed in Trina's throat, and she swallowed hard, willing herself not to cry. Too frequently tears had been her companion of late. She did not want to cry today—not on the day she was published to the man she loved. With effort, she lifted her chin and forced a bright smile. "Tony, pass the green beans, please. Mama outdid herself today—everything is so yummy!"

To her gratitude, the others followed suit by talking again, filling the uncomfortable silence with cheerful chatter. In minutes, Mama returned, sat down, and sent Trina an apologetic look. Trina shrugged, offering a silent reply, and they finished their meal without commenting on her father's absence.

When everyone had finished, Tony and their cousins Andrew and Jacob and their wives volunteered to wash dishes and put the café back in order. Graham gave Trina a gentle hug good-bye at the door.

"Do you want me to come over to the house with you?"

She knew he was asking if she would need support in facing her father, and her heart swelled with gratefulness for this understanding man. But she shook her head. "No. I'm going to have a talk with Dad—somehow I must make him understand why I have to follow my heart—but it needs to be between the two of us. In fact. . ." She scowled, glancing past Graham to her mother, where she chatted with Uncle Henry and Aunt Marie. "I'm going to see if Mama will leave us alone and let us work this out for ourselves. She means well, but she tends to interfere."

Graham smiled, releasing a light chuckle. "Your mother interfering? I can't imagine that."

Trina laughed, recognizing the teasing. "Yes, we all know her well! But I love her anyway. And since this whole thing started, she's become such a surprising support. I feel as though I finally have the mother I always wanted. I'll never complain about her again."

Graham quirked one brow.

She laughed again. "And someday you'll probably need to remind me I said that. But for now. . ." With a quick glance around, she rose up on tiptoe and planted a quick kiss on Graham's smooth cheek. "I'll go talk to Dad. Pray for me?"

"Of course." He squeezed her hand.

Mama willingly agreed to give Trina and her father some alone time, and she went to Uncle Henry's. Trina headed home, praying all the way for a reconciliation of her relationship with her father. When she entered the house, she found Dad in the living room on the sofa. A newspaper lay in his lap, but his eyes were closed, his head back.

Trina cleared her throat, and Dad jumped. He opened his eyes and peered around, focusing on her. Immediately a frown formed on his face.

"Trina." The single word managed to convey disapproval.

"Dad." Trina sat down at the other end of the sofa.

He straightened in the seat, lifting the paper. "Is the party over?"

"Yes."

"Where are your brother and mother?"

"Tony's cleaning up the café, and Mama went over to Uncle Henry's."

Dad's eyebrows rose. "Oh?"

"I asked her to."

His brows came down. "Oh."

Trina scooted a little closer. "Dad, can we talk?"

Dad shook the paper, turning his frowning gaze to the printed pages. "About what?"

Trina reached out and pushed the newspaper back into his lap. "About me. And college. And you." Despite her determination not to let emotion get in the way, tears pricked her eyes. "Please, Dad. You're tearing me in two."

Dad set his jaw, his eyes straight ahead. "You obviously don't need my approval, Trina. You're going on without it, so I don't see why—"

"Because I love you." Trina spoke quietly, her gaze never wavering from her father's face even if he refused to return it. "Because your approval is important to me. You were so supportive when I asked to work for Dr. Groening. I know I should have been completely honest about why I wanted to work for him, but I've asked you to forgive me for that. I guess I'm asking again, because until you truly forgive me, I don't think we'll ever be able to get past your anger."

"I'm not angry!"

In spite of herself, Trina smiled. "Your tone says otherwise."

"Trina. . ." Dad sighed, dropping his head as if he carried a great burden. "It comes out as anger, but I'm not as much angry as worried. Worried for you. Worried for Tony. Worried for the fellowship as a whole."

Trina tipped her head. "Why?" Finally Dad looked at her. She saw the concern in his eyes, and her heart melted, her frustration with him washing away. "Please tell me why."

"You're young, Trina. You haven't seen what change can do to the community. When I was just a young boy and my father was a deacon, the fellowship split when the deacons agreed to allow members to have electricity in their homes. Those who disagreed with the decision moved to southeast Kansas—among them, some cousins I miss to this day. My life was never the same. Relationships were never the same."

Dad flipped one hand outward, grimacing. "Oh, over time, the furor settled down, but there was always a hole where those people used to be. And that hole has never been filled." He snorted. "The benefit of electricity can't take the place of *people* in a person's heart."

Trina nodded. Being able to pursue her dream had created a rift in several relationships. Even though she hadn't been separated from those people physically, there was an emotional separation that was just as wide. "I understand."

"I don't think you do." Dad leaned his elbows on his knees. He linked his fingers then stared at his joined hands. "What you're doing—going to college—has the potential to divide the fellowship again. Already I've heard rumblings that one of our members plans to leave with his children. Others could follow. Even if it doesn't divide the entire fellowship, it's dividing our family. Things haven't been the same under this roof ever since you woke your mother and me up in the middle of the night."

Trina could have argued it was her father's choice to divide the family—with his acceptance, things could return to normal. But she kept her thought to herself, allowing him to fully express his views without interruption.

"Now your brother is talking about college." He blew out a noisy breath. "What would he do in college? He wants to be a farmer, like me. Like his grandfathers. All college would do for him is to take him away from the fellowship and put him with worldly people who could distort his faith. No good could come of that."

Dad angled his head to peer at her. His lowered brows turned his eyes into slits of distrust. "By giving you permission to attend college, the deacons have opened the door for all of our young people to leave the community. Some will do it just because they can, not because—as you've claimed—God put a desire in their hearts. And some will get caught up in the world and never come back. Leaving holes, Trina."

Trina swallowed, seeking words to offer reassurance. She wanted to promise that what her father feared wouldn't come to pass, yet she knew words would be futile. And she couldn't make promises that might not be able to be kept. How could she predict what might happen in the future?

"I wish I could say you're wrong, Dad, and that only good will come of my being allowed to become a veterinarian. But I don't know what others will do. I keep praying things will be okay, that everyone will accept it as God's will. Some will, eventually, and others may not. All I know for sure is I can't ignore it. When I wasn't preparing to walk where God called, I was miserable."

Dad's head slowly bobbed in a single nod.

"I sure don't want to make others feel miserable—especially you, because I love you so much—and a part of me still aches because of the unhappiness I've created. But now that I'm studying again, I feel. . ." She sought a word to describe what following her dream meant, and she settled on one: "Whole. I *have* to do what God asks me to do. Can you try to understand that?"

Dad drew in a deep, slow breath and held it for several long seconds. The breath expelled in a rush, and he puckered his lips into a thoughtful scowl, staring straight ahead. Finally he looked at her and shook his head. "No guarantees, Trina, but I'll try to understand. And I'll try not to let my worries turn into anger."

Trina squeezed his knee. "Thank you. I can promise one thing, Dad. I won't be pulled into the world permanently. When I'm done with college, I'm coming back. I want to be a veterinarian right here in Sommerfeld. My heart is in this community, in this fellowship, in this family. That won't change."

Dad pushed to his feet. He looked down at her, his face resigned. "All right." He glanced toward the window. "It's a pretty day. I think I'll take a walk."

"Do you want me to come with you?"

"No." He softened the negative reply with a sad smile. "Sometimes it's good for a man to be alone with his thoughts."

"Okay." Trina rose and stepped up to hug her father, wrapping her arms around his middle and pressing her face into the familiar curve of his shoulder. "I love you, Dad."

His hands chafed her upper arms, and then he set her aside. "I love you, too, daughter."

Trina's heart thrilled to the words. She watched him stride out the door with his hands in his pockets and his head hanging low. His dejected pose brought a rush of pity to the surface, and she closed her eyes. *Lord, please give Dad the same peace You gave me. Not so I can do what I want to, but so he can rest in You.*

Although Dad never mentioned where he'd gone or what he'd done on his walk, the next week was peaceful in the house. The blanket of anger was gone, replaced by a respectful if resigned acceptance far preferable to the gloom of previous days. Trina rejoiced constantly in the change and trusted full acceptance would one day come when her father realized she intended to keep her promise of remaining rooted in the fellowship.

She missed Graham tremendously in the evenings, since she had to spend her after-work hours studying. But she consoled herself with the knowledge that soon she would be his wife. They would reside together in the upstairs of his parents' home, and she would study at a table in the kitchen, where Graham would sit on the opposite side and read a book each evening. Even if they were quiet together, they would be together.

They enjoyed their brief minutes when Graham transported her to and from Dr. Groening's clinic each day. Graham began stealing kisses as he let her out of the car, and those tender moments made her long for the day when they could express their affection openly within the privacy of their own rooms.

On Friday, Graham's kiss lengthened, and Trina giggled as she gently pushed him away. "I have to go in."

He groaned, grinning. "I know. How many more days?"

"One hundred and twenty." They had chosen the second Saturday in February as their wedding day, one week after Walt and Michelle's.

"Then I need one more kiss to make it that long."

She laughed but obliged, then scooted across the seat. "I'll see you after work."

"I love you! Have a good day!" he called as he pulled away.

Still smiling, basking in the warmth of Graham's love, Trina bounded up the stairs and entered the clinic. "Good morning, Mrs. Penner. Do you have—" She stopped when she noticed a tall, well-dressed man leaning on the counter. As she spoke, he straightened and turned to face her, a smile lighting his narrow face.

"Oh!" Trina smoothed her hands over her work apron. "I'm sorry. I didn't realize anyone else was here already. I'll just go get started—"

"Trina, wait." Mrs. Penner's voice stopped Trina from dashing to the back room. "I want you to meet Marc Royer."

Trina offered a shy nod at the tall stranger. He held out his hand, and Trina took it, giving it a slight shake. Then she grabbed her apron again. She couldn't explain why, but the man intimidated her.

Mrs. Penner went on. "Marc was born in Hillsboro, but his family moved away when he was in junior high."

Trina finally found her voice. "Are you visiting friends?"

Marc Royer flicked his smile to Mrs. Penner then back to Trina. "Not exactly. I'm here to shadow Dr. Groening."

Confused, Trina looked from one to the other. " 'Shadow'?"

"Follow him around today." Mrs. Penner beamed. "Marc graduated last May as a doctor of veterinary medicine and has come back to his hometown in the hopes of opening a practice."

Trina's dreams crumbled at her feet.

TWENTY-TWO

Trina stumbled through the day, hardly able to function. If that man—Marc Royer—already had his degree, then surely Dr. Groening would choose to let him purchase the clinic. He would have no need to wait five years for Trina.

Oh God, her thoughts groaned, *what am I to do? Why did he have to come now?*

She managed to complete her tasks with efficiency, keeping her fears to herself until Graham showed up at the end of the day. The moment she slammed the passenger door closed, she covered her face with her hands and let loose a torrent of confused tears.

"Trina!" Graham slid across the seat and embraced her, pulling her head into the curve of his neck. "What is it? What's wrong?" Trina took great, shuddering breaths to bring herself under control. But when she looked into his worried face, she fell apart again.

He gently set her in her seat and said, "I'll get you home."

All the way, Trina stared at the landscape, tears continuing to fall in torrents down her cheeks. Why, why, why did it have to be so hard for her to achieve her dream? She tortured herself with the question that had no answer.

When Graham pulled in front of her house, he put the car in PARK, turned off the ignition, and shifted on the seat to face her. "Ready to tell me what happened today?"

Trina sniffed hard and nodded. She shared, haltingly, about Marc Royer's arrival at the clinic, his educational background, his goals. On a sob, she finished, "So where does that leave me? The clinic won't be available to me when I finish my schooling."

Graham pulled his lips to the side, looking at her in silence. Finally, he asked, "Do you have to take over Dr. Groening's clinic?"

Trina huffed, throwing her hands outward. "Graham! It makes so much sense! He has the building, the equipment. People are used to going there. It would have been so perfect! But now. . ."

"But now maybe God has something else in mind." Graham caught her hand and carried it to his lips, pressing a kiss to her knuckles. "When God closes a door, there's usually a reason. Can't you trust Him with this?"

"That's easy for you to say." Trina's voice sounded hollow from her stuffed-up nose. She snuffled again and shook her head, turning to stare out the window. "You didn't just get the rug pulled out from under your feet. All my plans. . ."

"All *your* plans?"

Trina recognized the emphasis. She clamped her teeth together and refused to answer.

Graham lowered their joined hands to the seat. "Trina, you haven't been in charge of this from the beginning. Why did you choose to pursue becoming a vet? Because God led you to. Don't turn it into *your* plans now, or nothing will work right. You know that."

Shamed, she knew he was right. But the pain of finding a degreed doctor ready and able to assume responsibility for the clinic was still too fresh. She stared out the window and refused to answer.

After a long while, Graham spoke in a reasonable tone. "Look at the obstacles you've had to overcome to get this far. You had to convince me and your family that it was right, you had to convince the fellowship leaders it was right, you had to prepare to be accepted into a college. Look at everything you've accomplished so far."

"Look at how many mountains I had to climb already," she shot back.

"All of which God helped you climb," he returned calmly.

Her frustration grew. Why did he have to be sensible? "Maybe I'm *tired* of climbing, Graham!"

"Then maybe you aren't cut out to be a veterinarian."

At his soft statement, Trina whirled to face him, her mouth dropping open. "What?"

He met her gaze squarely. No hint of a smile showed on his lips. "If you get a case with an animal that's hard to solve—an illness you can't figure out at first—will you just quit and let the animal die?"

"Of course not!" How dare he even suggest something like that?

"What you're facing right now isn't much different, Trina. It's a challenge. So this Marc somebody—"

"Royer."

"—Royer is here, ready to take over. Sure, it works better for Dr. Groening, so he'll probably let him take over. But that doesn't mean there will never be room for you. It just means you've got some competition. A challenge. The question is, are you going to meet it or be defeated by it?"

Trina thought about Graham's words. She wanted to rise to the challenge, to let everyone know nothing or nobody would hold her back from walking where God directed her to walk, but at the moment she felt spent. She didn't have the energy to form a response, let alone rise to a challenge.

And then her greatest fear struck—the one that had festered in the far corner of her mind all day. The one she hadn't wanted to bring out and examine but knew must be addressed. She swallowed, took a breath, and whispered, "But. . .what if this is God's way of telling me I've been going the wrong way?"

Graham lowered his brows, his expression thoughtful. "Are you thinking He doesn't want you to be a veterinarian, after all?"

"Do you think it might be possible?" Trina held her breath, thoughts tumbling through her mind. What if this whole idea was her own fanciful flight rather than God's will? If she gave up the dream, things would be much simpler. Her father could relax, the fellowship would return to normal, Graham wouldn't have to sell his house. . . .

She stared at him, waiting, while her heart beat in fear—or hope?— that he would agree with her statement.

Suddenly he shook his head, his fingers clamping hard around her hand. "I don't believe that, Trina. I've had too much peace about it to think it's wrong. And I've seen too much evidence of growth and peace in you to think it's wrong. You're meant to be given the work of your hands as a caregiver for animals."

Trina released her breath on a lengthy sigh. Having his confirmation helped eliminate the mighty worry. Yet another one remained, nearly as sizable as the first. "But do you think I'll still be able to be a veterinarian in Sommerfeld? In all the years Dr. Groening has practiced veterinary medicine, he's handled it alone. If Marc Royer takes his place, then—"

"Then we'll figure something out." Graham rested his head briefly against the seat. When he looked at her again, conviction burned in his eyes. "God never said we wouldn't face hardship in life. He only promised to walk with us. He's been your companion along this journey so far. He's even managed to convince several people to walk along beside you as your encouragers. I don't know why this other man has shown up now, but I do know you can't quit. You *can't* quit, Trina."

"You can't quit, Trina." Those words carried Trina through the week. She deliberately called upon them as she studied and completed assignments. She pulled them out and let them be her encouragement when faced with an unpleasant task at the clinic. She whispered them to herself when Marc Royer returned for a second day of shadowing Dr. Groening. And she nearly chanted them aloud when Dr. Groening took her aside on Friday to talk.

By the look on his face, she knew what he was going to say before he opened his mouth. "Trina, I know you hoped to be able to take over the clinic when you get through school, and it pains me to disappoint you, but—"

Trina nodded. "You're going to sell it to Marc Royer."

Dr. Groening sighed, sympathy in his lined eyes. "Yes. After the first of the year, we'll make it official. In the meantime, he'll be working with me, familiarizing himself with the area and gaining the trust of the folks who live around here."

Trina crossed her arms, trying to press away the ache that filled her middle. "But there must be other places he could work—other cities. Why here?" *Why my town?*

"Since he lived in Hillsboro when he was a youngster, he feels at home in this area. He's eager to stay."

Trina blinked hard, determined not to cry. But the doctor must have seen the presence of tears, because he put his warm hand on her shoulder.

"Your job is secure. Even Marc acknowledges your assistance is needed. As long as you want to, you can still help out here. And when you have your degree, maybe you and Marc can work together—a partnership."

Heat flooded Trina's face. She couldn't imagine joining in a partnership with a man. Especially a man who was not Mennonite. She didn't answer.

The older doctor sighed, lowering his gaze for a moment. "But if you decide you don't want to work here—"

"I need the job." If she was to pay for college, she had to work. Graham was giving up his house for her education—the least she could do was contribute.

"Good. Well, then. . ." Dr. Groening stepped back and slipped his hands into the pockets of his faded blue scrub top. "I just hope you understand this has nothing to do with a lack of confidence in you. I've seen you with animals, Trina. You'll make a fine doctor one day. I only wish you were further along in your studies. Maybe then. . ."

Trina nodded, forcing a smile. "It's all right, Dr. Groening. I understand. And I appreciate your kind words. Whether I end up practicing in Sommerfeld or not, I will still be a veterinarian. Graham and I agree it's what I'm supposed to do."

But, God, her thoughts continued as she headed for the door to meet Graham for the ride home, *I wish You'd let me know where I'm meant to serve as a veterinarian. I don't think Dad will ever forgive me if I leave another hole where a person used to be.*

Graham flicked the edges of the Louis L'Amour western he'd brought along to keep himself occupied while Trina took her midsemester exams. He wished he'd brought a second book, too. Next time he'd know to plan for more than two hours of waiting.

The chair, although padded, boasted a straight back that kept him uncomfortably upright. If he slouched, the slickness of the vinyl cover made him feel as though he might slide right off onto the tiled floor. An action like that would certainly capture attention. And he was conspicuous enough already.

Perched in a seating area where two bustling hallways converged, he was in a prime location to be noticed. Normally when he ventured away from Sommerfeld, he was in a group. Being alone in worldly surroundings was new and, he decided with a tug at his collar, less than pleasant. No one was rude to him, but he was painfully aware of the curious glances, the muffled giggles, the whispered comments—"What's up with that?" and "Dude, call the fashion police." When with his friends, he could focus on them and ignore gawkers. But today he didn't have that privilege.

A door down the left hallway opened, and people spilled out. Graham glanced up, his heart leaping with anticipation—was Trina coming? But to his dismay, he realized the classroom door through which she had disappeared was farther down. Stifling a frustrated huff of breath, he opened the novel and began reading it for the second time.

He was just starting the fourth chapter when another *click* and several voices pulled his attention away from the book. This time, he spotted Trina among the group milling in the hallway. The other students made a berth around her, making it easy for her to rush toward him. He rose, reaching for her sweater, which she'd left on the chair beside him, and smiled as she approached.

"All done?" he asked as he draped the sweater over her shoulders. Two girls in shirts that didn't quite meet the waistlines of their very tight blue jeans walked by, their heads swiveling to stare. Graham kept his gaze pinned to Trina's face.

"All done. We can go."

Graham almost gave an exultant shout. He deliberately ignored the other people who moved around them as they made their way to the parking lot. "So how do you think you did?"

Trina hunched her shoulders with a nervous giggle. "I hope okay, but I won't know for sure until they post the grades online." She stopped, gave a quick glance around, then rose up on tiptoe to whisper, "It felt funny to be in there. I've never been with so many worldly people by myself."

Graham nodded. He understood exactly. "But you did it," he praised. And he had, too. If they were going to have to live out on their own, away from Sommerfeld, while she finished college, they might as well get used to it.

She sighed, swinging their joined hands as they began moving again. "People are so funny. They look at my clothes and my cap. They look and look, but they don't say anything. They look, but I don't think they really see *me*." She frowned. "Maybe that's why I like animals so much. They don't much care what you look like—they just respond to how you treat them."

Graham searched for words to encourage her and make her feel less uncomfortable, but none came. They reached his car, and he opened the door for her. On his own side of the vehicle, he took care not to let his door bump the side of the fancy red sports car parked very close to his car.

Once behind the steering wheel, he finally responded to her statement. "I think, once they get used to seeing you on campus, they'll look beyond your clothes to Trina." Wondering how he would cope, he asked, "But what about you? Will you get used to being around them?"

She chewed her lower lip, her thoughtful gaze aimed in his direction. "I suppose over time you can get used to anything."

At that moment, a young man in baggy jeans, an untucked plaid shirt, and flat rubber shoes that whacked against his bare soles approached the car. The man halted at the hood of Graham's car, lifted silver-lensed sunglasses to the top of his head, and let his gaze rove over every inch of Graham's fellowship-approved dark blue sedan. Graham felt his face grow hot as the man's face twisted into a smirk.

Giving the hood a pat, the man called, "Nice wheels, dude. Did you inherit this from your gramma?"

Graham pinched his lips tight and started the engine, backing out of the space. The other man laughingly slipped his sunglasses into place, aimed a little black box at his car, then climbed behind the wheel. Graham's face continued to burn as he left the parking lot, watching carefully for traffic. There seemed to be more drivers on this campus than on Main Street in Sommerfeld on its busiest shopping day.

When they were finally away from the campus and heading toward the highway, Graham puffed his cheeks and blew out a breath, relaxing his tense shoulders. "Tell me again how a person can get used to anything given time."

Trina slid her hand across the seat, and he grabbed it. The squeeze of her fingers let him know she felt bad about how the college student had behaved. He glanced at her and saw apprehension in her expression. He couldn't let her worry about his feelings—she needed assurance they would make it just fine in the world while she finished her schooling. So he pushed his lips into a smile and forced a light laugh.

"I think next time I'll just wear my work clothes instead of my Sunday suit. The students don't seem to wear formal attire." He knew his statement would let her know he was willing to go there again.

A smile lit her eyes. "Thank you, Graham."

Graham winked in reply then turned his attention to driving. He would go out again. And again. He would continue going until the stares and comments didn't bother him anymore. *Lord, let that day come quickly!*

TWENTY-THREE

Over the next two weeks, as October slowly melted away, Graham took every opportunity he could find to drive into one of the larger towns nearby—Newton or McPherson and once all the way to Hutchinson. Always by himself. Always wearing his distinctive Mennonite suit. He chose the busiest stores and walked around, sometimes pushing a cart, always meeting others' gazes, forcing a smile and nod if someone maintained eye contact long enough to see it.

These excursions used up a lot of gasoline, time, and energy, but Graham decided it was his form of education. Trina was learning to be a veterinarian; he was learning to feel comfortable outside of Sommerfeld. The time would come when the two of them—just them, no crowd of friends—would leave their secure Mennonite community. He would work among the worldly. Shop among the worldly. Reside in an apartment next door to the worldly. And he refused to spend that time feeling misplaced and uncomfortable.

It was simply a matter of adjusting, he told himself as he pushed a squeaky metal cart around a large discount store on the outside edge of McPherson. And he would adjust. For Trina's sake. If he was comfortable, then she would be comfortable. He was determined she *would* be comfortable. Because if she wasn't, she wouldn't be able to focus on her studies. So he would make sure everything flowed smoothly for his Trina.

He dropped two cans of honey-roasted peanuts—his favorite snack—into the cart, his heart lifting with the thought of Trina. Fewer than fifteen weeks and she would be *his Trina* in every way. Already they were best friends, but soon they would be husband and wife. Nothing could be better, he decided. He envied his friend Walt, who had seven fewer days than Graham to wait.

Mom couldn't wait, either. In her delight at having another woman under her roof, she had been busy in the upstairs of his childhood home, cleaning and hanging new curtains and repairing the rag rugs that had become torn from energetic boys using them to slide across the linoleum floor. Which reminded him, Mom wanted him to pick up a spool of upholstery thread since she'd used hers up on those rugs.

He turned the cart toward the fabric department, and when he rounded a display of bolts of cloth, his cart banged into someone else's. "Please excuse me!"

The woman gave a start, dropping the bolt she'd just pulled from the shelf. To Graham's surprise, he knew the woman—Dr. Groening's wife. He rushed around the cart and retrieved the dropped bolt.

"Thank you," she said as she took the cloth from his hands. Then her expression turned puzzled. "Do I know you?"

Graham nodded. "We've seen each other before at the café in Sommerfeld. I'm Graham Ortmann. My fiancée, Trina Muller, works at the clinic with your husband."

"Of course! Trina!" The woman smiled broadly, her eyes twinkling. "What a sweet girl. But engaged. . . I didn't realize she was engaged."

Graham offered another shy nod.

"Well, congratulations." Mrs. Groening extended her hand, and Graham shook it. "Josiah thinks the world of Trina. He felt so bad about not being able to let her buy the clinic."

Graham swallowed. "I know. And she understands. We don't hold a grudge."

The woman pressed a wrinkled hand to the bodice of her sweater. "That's a great relief. Even Marc was concerned about taking over, knowing of Trina's interest." She tipped her head. "Isn't it odd that two people would want to establish themselves as veterinarians in the same small circle of communities? I would think it would be more likely to have to hunt for someone, yet two step up, ready and willing to take Josiah's place."

With a shake of her head, she smiled again. "It has certainly made things easier for us. Joe was ready to retire two years ago, but he couldn't because he wouldn't leave people without care for their animals. Now it isn't a concern. We're very grateful."

"I'm glad it's worked out for you."

"Well!" The woman released another light laugh. "I've kept you here too long already. I'm sure you have other things to do than visit with me. It was nice seeing you, Graham, and please give Trina my sincerest congratulations. I wish you both much happiness."

"Thank you, ma'am." Graham moved on, but his thoughts lingered over Mrs. Groening's comment about two people interested in taking over the veterinary clinic. Trina's keen disappointment in not being able to assume the Groening Clinic made his heart ache, but he couldn't help but believe God had something special planned in its stead. *Lord*, he silently prayed as he pushed the cart down another long aisle, *thank You for the opportunities You've already given Trina. Guide her in where to use her degree. And, Lord, please, if it be Your will, let us remain in Sommerfeld.*

Beth leaned over Trina's shoulder and moved the mouse on the pad, bringing the cursor on top of a word underlined with a red squiggle. "See that funny line? That means you've spelled the word wrong. Now look. If you right-click on the mouse, the correct spelling will come up, and you can change it."

Trina shook her head, tossing her ribbons over her shoulders. "Well, why didn't you tell me that before now? I wouldn't have gotten so many poor marks on the English papers!"

Beth laughed, bumping Trina's shoulder. "You didn't ask. Let me show you something else." She dropped to one knee beside Trina's chair and brought up an options box. Clicking inside one small square, she activated the grammar check. "This will even tell you if you've made grammatical errors in your sentences. I usually don't use it, but I'll keep it on for you, if you would like."

"I would like that!" Trina sighed as Beth saved the change. Suddenly she grabbed Beth's hand, her face pinched into a worried scowl. "This isn't considered cheating, is it? I don't want to use something the other students don't have."

Beth snorted. Trina's naïveté was endearing, but she needed to learn the wiles of the world if she was going to venture into it. "Believe me, Katrinka, nearly all of the other students have had computers from grade school on up. They're familiar with the use of these tools. I'd be willing to bet a lot of them just surf the Net, find an essay, download it, tweak it a bit, and then turn it in as their own."

Trina's brown eyes grew round. "That's dishonest!"

"Of course it's dishonest. And if they got caught, they'd be punished—hopefully. But quite a few still take the chance."

Trina shook her head, her eyes snapping with indignation. "Well,

I don't see how anyone could do that. Letting someone else do the work for you does nothing more than cheat yourself. How do you learn if you don't do the work on your own?"

"Aw, Trina. . ." Beth sat back on her haunches, warmth filling her middle. "It is so refreshing to know there are still honest, hardworking people in the world. I suspect you are going to be a terrific influence on your co-students when you're finally sitting in a classroom instead of all alone in front of a computer screen."

The indignation faded, replaced by an expression of apprehension. "Beth, can I tell you something?"

"Sure you can."

For a moment, Trina bit down on her lower lip, her gaze averted. "Sometimes I get really scared about going to those classes." She lifted her head, her dark gaze meeting Beth's. "It's so much easier here—all alone, like you said. I don't feel like anybody's watching me or judging me. I can just work and feel at peace. But when I went to El Dorado to take my tests, it was *hard*. Not just because of what was on the tests, but because I had to be with so many people who are different from me."

Beth released a short, rueful chuckle. "You aren't telling me anything I can't understand. Look at me!" She held her hands to her sides, glancing down at her blue jeans and long-sleeved T-shirt. "Don't you think I feel different when I walk down the streets of Sommerfeld? I don't exactly fit, you know."

Trina stared at Beth, her eyes wide. "I hadn't thought of that. When I look at you, I don't worry about your clothes. You're just Beth, my friend. That's all that matters."

"And how did that happen?" Beth tipped her head, smiling at Trina.

Trina shrugged, bunching the white ribbons on her shoulders. "I don't know."

"I do." With a smirk, Beth bounced to her feet and put her hands on her hips. "You got to know me as a person. That's how we became friends. Between friends, the outside doesn't matter nearly as much as the inside, Katrinka." She gave one of Trina's ribbons a gentle tug. "It will feel strange at first—it did for me—but you'll get acquainted with others in your classes, and pretty soon you won't feel out of place anymore."

Beth frowned, hearing her own words. Was she being completely honest with Trina? There were still times she and Sean felt out of place in Sommerfeld. They'd found a measure of acceptance, for which she was grateful, but a segment of the community either acted resigned to their presence or held them at bay, barely tolerating them.

Yet she sensed if she shared this whole truth with Trina, it would only discourage her, so she offered another smile and said, "Give it time. It'll all work out eventually."

Trina sighed. "I hope so. I know a lot of things have already worked out, but there's still so much that must be done. Sometimes it's scary."

"New things always are." Beth caught the back of the computer chair and turned Trina to face the computer. She assumed a teasing voice as she instructed, "But you now have a new thing at your disposal that is going to make writing these papers easier, so get to it. Sean is due home this evening around nine, and I'll want you out of here by then so he and I can be alone."

Trina's cheeks flooded with pink.

Beth laughed. "There's something else you'll learn, Katrinka. It's wonderful to have all-alone time with your husband."

For a moment, Trina pressed her lips together, peering at Beth out of the corner of her eye. Then an impish grin climbed her cheeks. With a smug look, she said, "That's one lesson I don't need to learn.

I already know it well."

Beth laughed again, gave Trina a quick hug, and backed away from the computer to let her work. Settling into Sean's recliner, Beth picked up a book and opened it, but Trina's comment—*"I already know it well"*—ran through her mind, and she couldn't stop a chuckle from rumbling. That Trina. . .full of surprises. She sincerely hoped the world wouldn't squelch Trina's joyful spirit. Just to be on the safe side, she closed her eyes and handed that concern to her heavenly Father.

At a quarter to nine, Trina closed down the computer, gathered up her papers, and headed for home. Beth watched her through the front window until she turned the corner. Then she watched for Sean's return. The days were shorter, and full dark let her see the car headlights when they turned the corner a block away. She stepped out onto the porch, dancing a bit as the cold floor seeped through her socks, and waved when he turned into the driveway.

He rolled down the window and called, "Hello, beautiful!"

She danced across the grass to lean in and give him a welcome-home kiss. She missed him tremendously when he spent days away, but she had to admit the homecomings were nice.

"Mmm." He pulled back, still smiling. "Let me get this car put away, and we can continue in the house."

With a giggle, she slipped into the backseat then accompanied him as he walked across the yard to the back door. Once inside, he wrapped his arms around her and lowered his head to meet her lips. They enjoyed a lengthy welcome-home kiss before he finally pulled back, sighed, and said, "Wow, I'm hungry."

Beth created a mock scowl. "That's all you have to say?"

He tipped his head, his eyes teasing. "I'm hungry, *darling?*"

She laughed. "Okay. Supper first." She turned toward the re-frigerator. "I have some leftover goulash, which I can heat up, or there's a bagged salad, or I can fix you a sandwich. Which sounds the best?" Her hand on the fridge door, she peeked at him over her shoulder.

He sat at the table, one elbow propped on its edge with his chin in his hand. He grinned. "Come here." He patted his knee.

Without hesitation, she sat. He buried his face against her hair and sighed. "I hate these days apart."

Beth coiled her arms around his neck, holding back the comment that the days apart were his choice, not hers. He could draw blueprints from here and let his father travel to the different areas to present the plans, but instead, he packed his bags and headed out at least once every other week. She wondered sometimes if he did it just to escape to places where he didn't feel as odd as a licorice whip in a jar of jelly beans. He'd never completely adjusted to Sommerfeld.

She kissed his ear and pushed off his lap, crossing to the refrigerator to remove the tub of goulash. Dumping the macaroni and ground beef into a bowl, she asked, "Did the meeting go well?"

He nodded, yawning. "Oh yeah. And if they sign, it'll mean more stained-glass work. Just across the front, but four windows at least."

Beth nodded, popping the saucer into the microwave. Just before hitting ON, she remembered to throw a napkin over the bowl. She leaned against the counter while the microwave zapped Sean's supper. "When will you know?"

"They want me to make an adjustment in the dimensions of the Sunday school classroom wing. I had made the classrooms all of comparable sizes, but they want the children's rooms larger than those for adults, so I'll need to move a few walls around. Once they get that in hand, they should make a decision." He yawned again. "And they want to see the final drawings by the end of next week."

The microwave dinged, and Beth carried the bowl to Sean. She waited while he offered his silent prayer. When he grabbed a fork from the cup in the center of the table, she said, "So you'll probably be using the computer quite a bit in the next couple of days."

"No doubt." He took a bite, chewed, and swallowed. "Why? Do you need it?"

Beth sank into the chair across from him and shrugged. "I can use the laptop. I just want to make sure there's one available for Trina to do her schoolwork."

Sean, his head lowered over his bowl, peered at her with a thoughtful expression.

"What are you thinking?"

He set down the fork for a moment. "I just wondered how long Trina will continue to make use of our computer. It isn't terribly convenient."

Beth blustered, "Well, what do you want me to do? She doesn't have any other way of completing her assignments."

Sean shook his head, his eyes twinkling. "My combatant, Beth. Must you always jump to conclusions?"

"But you made it sound like you want to take our computer away from Trina."

A grin twitched his cheek, and he smoothed his fingers over his mustache, removing the smirk. "I do."

Beth started to jump up, but Sean's hand around her wrist kept her in place.

"Stay put, my bristling beauty." His chuckle did little to alleviate Beth's frustration. "Let me finish eating, and then I'll propose a compromise I think you, Trina, and I can all accept."

Beth folded her arms across her chest and scowled. "I'll listen, but it better be good."

TWENTY-FOUR

"Trina?"

Trina jumped, clanking together the clean test tubes cradled in her apron. She spun around from the surgery's wash sink. "Y–yes, Dr. Royer?" His very presence made her stomach quake. Even after nearly a month of working with the man, she still found him intimidating. His height, his superior manner of looking down his nose when he addressed her, and his enviable knowledge—proven by the certificates that now hung on the wall of the reception area above Dr. Groening's—left her feeling very young, very backward, and hopelessly ignorant.

"Would you please explain the condition of the poodle in exam room one?"

Hope leaped in her breast. Was he asking her opinion? She licked her dry lips and formed an answer. "He hurt his leg—cut it on something. It was quite jagged in appearance and obviously requires stitches."

She waited for him to affirm her assessment, but the man folded his arms across his chest, his expression severe. "I am well aware of the injury and its required treatment, Trina. My question concerns the bandage on his leg. A bandage, his owner tells me, *you* applied."

Her heart pounded like a bass drum as trepidation made her knees go weak. "Yes, I—I applied a bandage. You were busy in another room, and the dog was bleeding badly. His owner was very upset. So I cleaned the wound with an antibacterial wash and bandaged it in readiness for your attention." She swallowed, fear rising as he continued to glare at her. Had she injured the dog somehow? Her hands pressed to her heart, she rasped, "The dog. . .did I do something wrong?"

Dr. Royer took a step forward. His great height coupled with his look of fury made Trina shrink backward. "Yes, you did something wrong. You have no business providing medical attention to any animal."

Trina opened her mouth to explain she had performed a similar treatment for numerous animals in Sommerfeld, but Dr. Royer forged on in a scathing tone.

"You crossed the line, Trina, and I won't tolerate it. You are not a veterinarian or even a certified assistant. I will not be held liable for your rash actions. You are never—I repeat, *never*—to put your hands on an animal in this clinic for the purpose of providing medical care."

"But I only wanted to help the little dog," Trina protested weakly.

"Help all the dogs you want to in your neighborhood at home, if people are willing to bring their pets to you." He pointed his finger at her, his brows low. "But at the clinic, you will leave the care of the animals to me. Do you understand?"

Too stunned to do anything else, Trina nodded.

"Good." He took a step back, his gaze sweeping the operating room. "Finish your cleaning in here, and then shelve the shipment of pet food that arrived this morning. As soon as I've stitched the poodle's leg, I'm going in to Hillsboro. Mrs. Penner knows to contact Dr. Groening if there is an emergency." His voice rose, carrying, she was sure, to the examination room where the lady and her poodle awaited his attention. "Should someone come in requiring attention, you are *not* to try to handle it."

"A–all right," she replied, blinking back tears of humiliation.

He strode out of the small laboratory on long legs that covered twice the distance in half the time as those of most people Trina knew. She sank against the sink's edge, her chest aching with the desire to cry. How Dr. Royer's attack stung. She'd only wanted to help. Dr. Groening never would have spoken to her so harshly, even if it was deserved. But since his decision to sell the clinic to Dr. Royer, the elderly vet had spent less time at the clinic.

Unwilling to suffer another rebuke, she focused on completing her assigned tasks to the best of her ability. When the last bag of cat food was neatly on the shelf, she wandered to the reception area and leaned her elbows on the counter, peering over its top to Mrs. Penner. "What is Dr. Royer doing in Hillsboro?" She supposed it wasn't her business, yet she couldn't deny being curious.

"I'm not sure. He doesn't tell me things the way Dr. Groening always has."

Trina wondered if that bothered the receptionist. It must be different for her to work for this new young doctor after spending so many years with the gentle, laid-back Dr. Groening.

Mrs. Penner tapped her lips with one finger, looking hard at Trina. "You don't like him much, do you?"

Trina jerked upright. "Who?"

"Dr. Royer."

Heat filled Trina's face. "What—what makes you say that?"

The older woman laughed softly. "How much do you think you hide with those big eyes of yours?"

Trina hid her cheeks with her hands. "I'm so sorry. . ."

Mrs. Penner offered a flippant wave. "Oh, honey, don't apologize.

He hasn't given you much reason to like him, has he? Waltzes in, takes over, talks to you as if you don't have a brain in your head. . .and the way he hollered at you today. . ." She shook her head, sympathy in her eyes. "You have every reason to dislike him."

Trina stared in silence at the older woman.

Mrs. Penner went on in a thoughtful tone. "I think because he's newly graduated he feels pretty full of himself—conceited. He had a tendency toward that when he was a boy because he stood a good six inches taller than any of his classmates." Her eyebrows flew high. "That's not an excuse, mind you, but it's a reason. In his mind, I suppose, 'bigger' equated with 'better.' " With a rueful sigh, she added, "All that being said, don't let him bother you, Trina. You're a smart girl—Dr. Groening thinks so, and I do, too—and you do a good job. You keep doing that job. The people here appreciate you."

Trina's face still felt hot, but now pleasure rather than embarrassment created the warmth. She couldn't remember the last time anyone had complimented her so blatantly. She swallowed hard and managed to reply. "Thank you, Mrs. Penner. I—I appreciate your kind words."

Another wave of her hand dismissed Trina's words. Propping her chin in her hands, Mrs. Penner grinned up at Trina. "So. . .tell me about your wedding plans. How are you balancing preparing for a wedding with your work here and all your studying?"

Trina laughed. Mrs. Penner obviously didn't know Mama. "I don't have to do a thing in preparing for my wedding—my mother has it under control. The ceremony will be at the café since our house isn't big enough to accommodate all of the guests. She already has one of my aunts sewing my dress, another aunt making and freezing cookies, and Mama will prepare the fine dinner for afterward." She laughed, shaking her head. "She won't let anyone else bring anything for the dinner—she says she'll do it all herself."

"What colors are you using?"

Trina blinked twice. "Colors?"

"Yes. Don't you have a color theme, like lavender and mint, and particular flowers picked out to go with the theme?"

Trina remembered peeking in a bride's magazine once in Mc-Pherson. Those pictures were nothing like a Mennonite service. With a shake of her head, she explained, "No, ma'am. Weddings are pretty simple affairs. People come dressed in their Sunday worship clothing, and only the bride has a special dress."

She closed her eyes for a moment, imagining the moment she would stand beside Graham in her pale blue dress, holding a white Bible. Her heart picked up its tempo at the thought of Graham in his black suit and tie, his blue eyes shining with love for her.

"And why aren't you getting married in the church?"

Trina popped her eyes open. "We only use the meetinghouse for worship, although I've heard some Mennonite groups elsewhere have begun holding weddings in their meetinghouse. But mostly weddings are in the bride's home or a community building. Since Sommerfeld doesn't have a community building, Mama says the café will do."

"I see." The woman pursed her lips thoughtfully. "I guess I didn't realize a Mennonite wedding would be different from those performed in my home church. Do you have bridal showers? A party where people bring you gifts?"

Trina shook her head, smiling. "That sounds nice, but no. But people will bring gifts for our new home to the wedding. Mama doesn't know I know, but my cousins are working on a quilt for our . .bed." Heat flamed her cheeks again. She hurried on. "My cousin Andrew's wife, Livvy, is especially talented with quilting, and she's helping, so I'm eager to see it."

"And where are you and Graham planning to live? Do you have a house in Sommerfeld all picked out?"

Guilt pricked Trina's conscience. She still felt bad about Graham selling his house to Walt, yet she knew he wouldn't have done it had he not prayed about it and believed it was the right thing to do. "No. We'll live with Graham's parents—until I go away to finish my college. While I finish up, I imagine we'll rent an apartment near the campus, and Graham will find a job. Then we'll probably live with his parents again until we can save enough money to pay for another house." She realized she was sharing plans that would take her several years down the road. Drawing a deep breath, she admitted, "It's all a little frightening but exciting, too."

"Starting out always is," Mrs. Penner agreed, sounding like Beth. "But you know something, Trina? You are a very blessed young lady. Just from listening to you now, I can tell you have family and friends who think a great deal of you and want to help you out. You have a young man willing to help you pursue an education beyond what I've heard the Mennonites usually allow. And you are going to have knowledge that will benefit you as well as give you an opportunity to bless the community wherever you and Graham decide to settle down. You have much for which to be thankful."

Trina nodded, her chest expanding with gratitude for each of the things Mrs. Penner had mentioned. "You're right." She needed to do a better job of thanking God for all of the doors He was making available to her, including working here at the clinic. Even if Dr. Royer was difficult, she could still learn from him if she set aside her personal antagonism toward the man. She made a private vow to give God His deserved appreciation the next time she prayed.

The crunch of tires on gravel intruded, and Trina dashed to the window to peek out. "There's Graham! Five o'clock already." She hurried to her time card and scribbled the time then flashed Mrs. Penner a smile. "I'll see you on Monday. Have a good weekend."

"You, too, Trina. Good-bye."

Trina trotted out the door and down the steps to Graham's car. The moment she slid into her seat, she leaned over and placed a kiss on Graham's cheek.

He drew back in surprise, a smile on his face. "What was that for?"

"A thank-you kiss," she said with a grin, "for being such a wonderful, supportive blessing in my life."

He chuckled as he put the car in DRIVE and aimed it toward the highway. "Well, you must have had a good day."

Trina thought about her encounter with Dr. Royer and how he made her feel inept. She wouldn't call all of it a good day, but Mrs. Penner's comments had changed her attitude. Her focus needed to be on the positive things happening rather than the negative. "It has been a good day. And the best part is right now because I'm with you."

Graham reached his arm out to capture Trina's shoulders and pull her close. He glanced down at her, smiling, and she smiled right back, tipping her chin upward to graze the underside of his jaw with her lips. He chuckled, and she shifted to rest her head on his shoulder. But when she looked forward, her heart leaped into her throat.

A truck, its driver appearing to dig under the dash for something, crossed the center line, the grill aiming directly at Graham's car. Trina screamed, "Graham!"

Graham jerked his gaze forward, and his elbow slammed into Trina's head as he flung his arm free to jam the heel of his hand against the horn. A discordant *ho-o-onk!* sounded. The other driver looked up, and Trina clearly saw his panicked face. But instead of turning away from them, the truck lurched directly into their path.

"God, help us!" Graham cried out. He yanked the wheel to

the right then threw himself across Trina. The impact of the truck slamming into the driver's side brought Trina out of the seat. The sickening crunch of metal against metal echoed through her head, and she opened her mouth to scream again as the car spun around.

Trina's stomach turned inside out as the car slid into the ditch then flipped onto its side. She felt herself being tossed like a tumbleweed as the car turned again, rolling to its top, and she closed her eyes, battling nausea. Another wild turn, and finally the car stopped, bouncing on its tires, with Trina crumpled onto the floorboard.

For a moment she simply lay, stunned, but then she realized Graham was no longer in the vehicle with her. She pushed to her knees, calling, "Graham! Graham!" She continued screaming his name as she banged her hands uselessly against the passenger's door.

Frantic, she grabbed the dash and pulled herself upright, peering through the shattered windshield. A strong odor permeated the area, burning her throat. She buried her face against her shoulder for a moment and coughed. Then she forced her gaze back to the window. The shattered glass distorted her vision, turning the world into tiny pieces, like a jigsaw puzzle with its parts lined up but not connected. She squinted, her heart pounding, her dry throat rasping one word over and over: "Graham. . .Graham. . ."

And finally she spotted him—lying in a heap in the ditch just a few feet away from the car. "Graham!" She pounded her fists, desperate to get to him. "Graham! Graham! Graham!"

The world became a sickening, disjointed dream. Cars stopping. People running from every direction. Voices calling.

"Has anyone called 911?"

"There's a girl in that car! We need to get her out in case the gas tank catches fire!"

"Is the man in the pickup okay?"

"Don't try to move anybody—wait for an ambulance!"

Frantic, bustling activity everywhere. And Trina, her heart pounding, shut it all out. With her bleeding hands curled over the dash, she stared, grunting with displeasure when milling people temporarily blocked her vision. Trapped like a bug in a jar, she kept her gaze pinned to Graham, praying silently, *Please, oh, please be all right.*

But not once did she see him move.

TWENTY-FIVE

Around, and around, and around. Trina spun like the clothes in a washer drum. She reached out to grab something. . .anything. . . to make the spinning stop, and her hand connected with something solid.

Pain stabbed, bringing her eyes open. She blinked, uncertain, peering into a dim, unfamiliar room. She lay in a tall, narrow bed. Something trailed from one hand, and the other—the one she'd flung outward—was wrapped in a bandage. It throbbed. She cradled it against her chest. Soft beeps interrupted the silence. A lump shifted in the chair beside the bed, and Trina squinted, trying to make sense of the strange surroundings.

By increments, remembrance dawned. She was in a hospital room. An ambulance had brought her here after the emergency workers had extracted her from Graham's car. The doctor—young, with kind eyes— had insisted she stay overnight for observation. Mama was in the chair because she refused to leave with Dad.

Now, her gaze on her mother, she whispered, "Mama?"

Mama shifted again, groaning slightly. Then she sat straight up, twisting around to face Trina. "Trina, you're awake? The doctor said the sedative would make you sleep all night."

So that's why she felt so groggy. It took great effort to hold her eyelids open. But her memory only retained bits and pieces. She needed the whole picture. "What happened to Graham?" Her tongue felt thick, clumsy, and her words sounded slurred. For a moment, she wasn't sure Mama understood.

But then Mama answered. "Graham. . .isn't here."

Trina's heart leaped in her chest. "Where—where is he? He isn't—" A picture of him sprawled on the ground, unmoving, filled Trina's head. She squeezed her eyes shut. *Oh, please don't say it. Don't say it!*

A warm hand smoothed Trina's tangled hair away from her face, and Trina opened her eyes. Mama leaned over the bed, her tired face sad. "He's in Wichita, Trina. They needed him to be where there were surgeons who could better take care of him. They think he fractured his spine."

Trina swallowed, her mind scrabbling to grasp the possible consequences of such an injury. The most severe lodged in her brain and refused to leave. "Oh, Mama. . ."

"Now, it's too soon to worry," Mama soothed, her hand stroking, the touch comforting. "You just sleep and let the doctors take care of Graham. Trust, Trina. Just trust."

Despite the fear that pressed upward, her eyelids were too heavy to hold open. They drifted shut, sending Trina back into the dark world of sleep.

"She's going to be fine." The doctor sent Trina a smile then turned to face Mama, who hovered on the opposite side of the bed. "She does have some bruised ribs, and her wrist is sprained, but fortunately there are no broken bones. Over the next few days, you'll probably see lots of black and blue places pop up, but considering the way she was thrown around, that's to be expected. It's miraculous, really, that her injuries aren't more severe."

Like Graham's, Trina's thoughts continued. "So I can go?" she asked.

"Yes, I'll prepare your release papers right now." The doctor put his hand on Trina's shoulder. "But I want you to take it easy for a few days. Take a week off from work. Don't just lie around—your muscles will stiffen up if you do that—but don't overdo, either." He shifted his gaze to Mama. "I'll want to see her again in a week, just as a follow-up. I ordered a prescription painkiller to help her sleep. You can pick it up in the pharmacy on your way out, as well as a list of dos and don'ts to follow while she's recovering."

"Thank you," Mama said, and the doctor left.

Trina immediately grabbed the rail of the bed and pulled herself upright, throwing her legs over the side. A sharp pain stabbed her left side, but she ignored it and rose to her feet. "Help me dress, please."

Dizziness struck, and she clung to the bed rail while Mama retrieved her dress from a small cubby in the corner. She helped Trina remove the hospital gown and slip back into her clothes. Her dress was dirty and torn, but Trina didn't care. She sat on a chair and let Mama put her socks and shoes on her feet. Then, fully dressed, she said, "I want to go see Graham."

Mama, still on her knee in front of Trina, shook her head. "No. You heard the doctor. He said—"

"He said to take it easy, but he didn't say I couldn't ride in a car." Memories of her last car ride struck, and for a moment, her resolve faltered. Then she thought of everything Graham had done to make her dream of becoming a veterinarian come true. She shook her head, dispelling the unpleasant memories. "I need to see him, Mama. I need to talk to him—to find out for myself how he's doing."

"His mother promised to call and leave word with your dad," Mama said. "We'll get all the information we need from Mrs. Ortmann. Besides, you can't do him any good in Wichita."

"But it will do *me* good," Trina insisted, imploring her mother with her eyes. When she was growing up, she never begged her parents—she always accepted their no. But Graham was worth begging for. Graham was worth everything.

Mama grimaced. "Trina, we're both filthy."

For the first time, Trina noticed Mama's scraggly hair and rumpled clothing. Dark circles rimmed her eyes, sending a silent message of Mama's restless night. Tears welled in Trina's eyes as she realized the selfishness of her request, yet she couldn't set the desire aside. "Mama, *please.*"

Mama turned stubborn, setting her mouth in a firm line. "Not today, Trina. We'll go home, talk to your dad—find out the news on Graham. But we won't be traveling to Wichita."

It was all Trina could do to keep from dissolving into a tantrum, but she managed a stiff nod. "Tomorrow, then?" Tomorrow was Sunday, a day of rest.

Mama sighed, her head sagging as if her neck muscles were incapable of holding it up. "We'll see."

Not a promise, but not an outright denial, either. Trina could accept it. For now.

Mama headed for the door. "I'm going to go call your father and tell him to come pick us up. You stay there in the chair and rest. I'll be right back."

Dad joined ranks with Mama in keeping Trina home to recover rather than taking her to Wichita to see Graham. Beth, Andrew, and Uncle Henry all volunteered to make the drive, and her parents still said no. Dad insisted Mrs. Ortmann could keep them apprised of Graham's progress without their visiting. Trina resented the decision, but she could do little but obey since she had no vehicle of her own and no driver's license.

Sunday after service, many people approached Trina to let her know they were praying for both her and Graham and to express their happiness that the couple had survived the accident. Trina's family went to Uncle Henry and Aunt Marie's house for lunch. When they'd finished eating, Trina and Tony walked next door to Uncle Henry's repair garage to see Graham's car. A tow truck had hauled it there, but looking at it, Trina had to wonder why it hadn't been taken straight to a junkyard. She was no expert on vehicles, but even she could see the car wasn't salvageable.

Another thing Graham had to give up.

Tony ran his hand over the crumpled hood. "Whew, Trina. It's hard to believe you were in that thing and walked away from it." He stared at her with wide brown eyes. "You could have been killed!"

"That's what the doctor said," Trina said. She walked to the driver's door and placed her uninjured hand on the window frame. The firemen had broken all the glass out when they pried the door open to rescue her, and bits of glass sparkled on the seat. Trina shivered, remembering the fear of the moments when the car went rolling from top to bottom. She pushed the memory away and said, "I don't know how Graham will buy another car."

Tony perked up. "I do. I heard the folks and Uncle Henry talking. This one is going to be claimed as totaled, and the insurance company will give him a check for its value. It should be enough to buy another used car."

Trina was pleased it would be replaced, yet she knew it wouldn't be the same. Graham's grandparents had given him this car as a gift—it meant a great deal to him. Something else occurred to her. "But won't he need to use the money from the car insurance to pay for his doctor bills?"

Tony shook his head. "That pickup driver—the one who hit you? The police said the accident was his fault, so his insurance is covering all the hospital expenses. Even yours."

Trina nodded slowly. At least there would be no concerns about paying the bills. Almost three years ago, when Aunt Marie's twins had come early, requiring surgery for Aunt Marie and a long hospital stay for the babies, the community had rallied around to help pay the bills. Even with the contributions, Aunt Marie and Uncle Henry still made monthly payments to the hospital and probably would for many more years. If Graham needed surgery and a long stay in the hospital, his bills would probably be just as big as Aunt Marie's had been.

"I wish I could see him."

Somehow Tony understood she meant Graham and not the truck driver. He nodded, his eyes sad. "I know."

"It was all my fault." She whispered the worry that had plagued her ever since she'd glimpsed Graham lying in the ditch.

Tony's brows came down. "No, it wasn't."

"It was." Trina gulped. "Graham only had one hand on the steering wheel because I—I was snuggling up to his side, and he put his arm around me. If I'd stayed on my own side of the seat, then—"

"Trina, that's dumb." Tony's voice sounded like Dad's, although Dad never used the word *dumb*. "The police said the pickup truck driver was messing around with the CD player in his cab and not paying attention. That's why he crossed into your lane. Then, instead of hitting his brakes, he panicked and pushed down on the gas pedal. He made a mistake and ran into you."

Trina considered Tony's words. She remembered seeing that the driver's head was down, as if looking at something below the dash. But still, if Graham would have had both hands free, maybe he could have gotten out of the way. If only she could see him and apologize to him! If she knew he was going to be all right, maybe she could set this worry and guilt aside.

"Trina," Tony said, his voice fervent, "it wasn't your fault. It's just something that happened—an accident. Don't feel bad, huh?"

Suddenly she realized she didn't know whether the truck's driver was injured, and a different sort of guilt struck. "Was the other driver hurt?"

Tony made a face. "According to Dad, he had some bumps and bruises—kind of like you. But nothing serious."

A part of Trina was relieved by the news but a tiny bit rankled at the unfairness of the situation. Graham hadn't been in the wrong. She and the pickup truck driver had been in the wrong. They were the ones who should be suffering. Pressing her forehead to the top of the window frame, she closed her eyes and prayed again for forgiveness for her part in the accident.

"Let's go back over to Uncle Henry's," Tony suggested, touching her arm. "You've been up long enough now."

Trina wanted to snap at her brother that she already had enough people telling her what she should and shouldn't do—he didn't need to add to it! But she knew her brother only wanted to help, so she held the words inside and nodded.

That evening, after supper, Trina asked, "Will someone drive me to Wichita tomorrow so I can see Graham?"

Mama and Dad exchanged looks across the table.

Before they could refuse, Trina spoke again. "He's going to wonder why I haven't come. He may worry that I'm really hurt and I'm not able to come. Worrying can't be good for him—not if he's seriously injured." She looked at her mother. "You aren't working tomorrow, Mama. Please, won't you find someone to drive us to Wichita?"

Mama sighed. "Trina, there isn't anything we can do for Graham right now except pray, and praying can be done from home. Remember how crowded the waiting room got when we all spent time at the hospital with your aunt Marie? We'd only be in the way over there."

"But I promise not to bother anyone. I just want to see him, to talk to him, to make sure he's okay and let him know I'm okay."

Another lengthy silence followed while Mama and Dad poked at their nearly empty plates and refused to answer.

Trina bounced her gaze back and forth between her parents, taking in their firm, unmoving faces. A fierce fear struck, and she dropped her fork with a clatter. "What are you trying to keep from me? Why don't you want me to see Graham?"

"That isn't it at all, Trina," Dad blustered. "Of course we want you to be able to see Graham, but—"

Mama interrupted. "We've told you everything we know about Graham."

"Tell me again." Surely she'd missed something. There had to be some reason her parents wouldn't take her—some tidbit of information that would explain everything.

Dad lifted his face to the ceiling for a moment, as if gathering strength, then faced Trina. "Graham's spine was fractured. When he's stabilized and they are certain he has no internal bleeding, they plan to operate. Until then, they are keeping him in a drug-induced coma so he doesn't move around and cause further injury to the spine. That's all we know, Trina."

"If he's not awake, he won't know you aren't there," Mama added, putting her hand over Trina's.

Trina jerked her hand free. "But *I'll* know! And I need to see him.

For myself—I need to see for myself that he is alive. Why won't you let me see him?"

Tony, normally silent during family discussions, cleared his throat. "I think you should let her go. She's really worrying about him. It would do her good."

Much to Trina's surprise, neither parent reprimanded Tony for interfering. For long moments Mama and Dad looked at each other, and Trina sensed they were silently communicating with each other. Hoping they were deciding to let her go to Wichita, she remained quiet, too, her breath coming in little spurts while she waited for them to reach the conclusion.

Finally, Dad put both hands flat on the tabletop and faced Trina. "Daughter, we didn't want to tell you this because we feared it would hurt you. But you don't leave us much choice." His voice sounded low, gruff, heavy with pain.

Trina's heart turned a somersault in her chest. "W–what is it?"

Dad pinched his lips together, his forehead creasing into a knot. "When Graham's mother called the first time—when they'd just gotten Graham settled in the room at Wichita—she had a message for you from Graham."

"Well?" Trina thought she might explode from impatience. "What? What did he say?"

Her father's head lowered, giving her a view of his thinning scalp. His shoulders heaved in a sigh. Then, his face still aimed downward, he said, "She said that Graham said to tell you not to come."

TWENTY-SIX

Wednesday morning after breakfast, Dad and Tony headed to their jobs as usual, and Mama walked to the café. She had chosen to keep it closed Tuesday and spend the day with Trina, but she said people needed a return to normalcy, so she'd better go back. However, right before leaving, she instructed Trina to take it easy. Trina couldn't remember her mother ever leaving her alone without a list of chores to occupy her time. At first, it seemed like freedom. But in short order, restlessness struck. Sitting and doing nothing made the time crawl by.

Her schoolbooks sat on the table in her room, yet she couldn't open them. Her focus was too far away—one hundred and ten miles away, to be exact. She knew whatever assignments on which she tried to work would only be done poorly. *Why would Graham ask me to stay away?* The question plagued her constantly, but she could find no answer.

She tried reading her Bible and praying, seeking peace, but even talking to God turned into a frustrating question session without answers. So with nothing else to do, she paced the living room, pausing at the window at each turn to stare out at the late October morning.

It almost surprised her to see the multicolored leaves on the trees. Fall had sneaked up on her this year.

Staring unseeingly across the yard, she thought about the hours she'd spent in her bedroom or at Beth's computer, working on her college classes. Even though she knew it was God's call on her heart and something Graham encouraged, she now discovered a small prick of resentment. She'd missed watching summer give way to fall. She'd missed hours and hours of time with Graham. Those lost hours multiplied in value when faced with the prospect of not having time with him again.

She thumped the window casing with her fist. "I've got to think about something else!" Stewing over the strange message wouldn't change it. She'd not be able to make sense of it until she talked to Graham, and she might not be able to talk to Graham for several more days. According to his mother, the doctors would keep him in the drug-induced sleep until the swelling completely subsided. Then they would try to repair the damaged vertebrae.

How she wished the doctors could say for sure what the end result would be after the surgery. Whether Graham would have full use of his legs. If he couldn't, it would change everything.

But what would it matter if he no longer wanted her around?

Turning from the window, she flumped onto the sofa and ran her fingers over the elastic bandage that held the splint on her left wrist. Typing would be even more of a challenge now that she was one-handed. How would she keep up with her classes? Or should she even continue her classes?

"Oh, dear heavenly Father," Trina groaned, rubbing her hand down her cheek and discovering tears, "what am I supposed to do now? I'm so confused. Why does it seem there's always something in the way of my becoming a doctor for animals?"

Just as she finished the thought, a knock at the door sounded. She quickly wiped away the remainder of tears and opened the door. Andrew stood on the porch, a serious look on his face.

"Hi. Can I come in?"

"Sure." Trina stepped back as he moved through the opening then closed the door behind him. "Aren't you working today?"

"Beth is sending me on an errand."

Trina sat back on the sofa, peering up at her cousin. Andrew had been very honest in his feelings about her pursuing veterinary science. Even though he had stopped openly discouraging her, his silence on the subject had spoken loudly about his continued disapproval. They hadn't had time alone for several weeks, and to Trina's regret, she realized she felt uncomfortable in his presence. The discomfort held her tongue.

"I'm taking a couple of stained-glass projects for consignment to the Fox Gallery in Wichita. The drive gets long all by myself, so I thought I'd see if you might want to go to give me some company."

Trina's heart skipped a beat. *Wichita.* Then maybe she could go by the hospital and see Graham. Immediately the anticipation plunged. Graham had said not to come. She sighed. "Mama and Dad probably won't let me."

Andrew worked the toe of his boot against the carpet, his brow furrowed. "I stopped by the café before coming over here. Aunt Deborah said it was okay."

Trina's jaw dropped. "Really?" But then, Mama had given permission to go to the gallery, not the hospital.

"And while I'm in town, I plan to go by St. Francis and take some cards and food to the Ortmanns. I figured you'd probably like to check on them, too."

Trina bounced to her feet, cringing as pain caught her ribs. "Did you tell Mama all of this?"

"I wouldn't be asking you otherwise. I don't want to sneak behind her back."

Recognizing the hidden message, Trina nodded. "I wouldn't ask you to. That's why I wanted to make sure."

A slight smile finally tipped up the corners of Andrew's mouth. "So do you want to go or not?"

"I want to go!" She started for the bedroom then turned back. Tipping her head, she sent him a curious look. "How did you convince her? She and Dad told me I couldn't go."

Andrew raised his shoulders in a slow shrug. "I just told her being kept away from Graham when he needs you most isn't fair to you or to Graham."

Trina stared, amazed that Mama had listened. "Thank you."

Andrew nodded then pointed at her feet. "Go put your shoes on, and we can go."

Trina scampered for her bedroom.

Trina greeted Graham's mother with a hug that turned lengthy. The older woman clung, pressing her cheek to Trina's.

"Oh, Trina, it's good to see you. I've been so worried about you." Mrs. Ortmann pulled back and grasped Trina's shoulders. "How are you? Are you recovered from the accident?"

"I'm all right. Just bruises, that's all."

"Good. I'm so grateful." She gave Trina another gentle hug before guiding her to a vinyl settee. It squeaked with their weight when they sat down. The waiting room was small, with windows that looked out on a courtyard. Crumpled candy wrappers, empty soda bottles, and fast-food cartons gave mute evidence of a long stay.

"Are you comfortable here?" Trina wiggled on the stiff cushion. "Is there anything else you need?"

"The hospital staff has been wonderful," Mrs. Ortmann said. "They bring us blankets and pillows each night, and of course we have visitors from Sommerfeld who bring us food. We're doing okay."

Trina gestured toward Andrew, who stood in the crack of space between the window and a small table. "Andrew brought a box of snack things—crackers, fruit, candy, and granola bars."

"That's kind of you," the older woman said, flashing a tired smile in Andrew's direction. "Ed and Chuck went down to the cafeteria to get some lunch a few minutes ago, but we try to stay here in the room as much as possible. Just in case someone comes with news. We aren't allowed much time with Graham—not while he remains in the intensive care unit."

Trina took Mrs. Ortmann's hands. "What is the latest news? Mama said they're still keeping him in a coma."

"That's right." The woman's chin quivered. "He looks so pale and weak, but I suppose that's to be expected. The not knowing is the hardest part. Until they do the surgery, we won't know for sure the severity of the injury. It could be that they'll be able to fix his spine and everything will be all right. It could be that there was spinal cord damage, and he won't be all right. It's nearly driven me mad, wondering."

Trina swallowed hard. "I'm so sorry."

Mrs. Ortmann pressed her lips together tightly and lifted her chin. "Well, if they follow through as planned, they'll do surgery tomorrow. Then we should know what we're facing. That will help."

Trina nodded, her head down. Several minutes ticked by before Mrs. Ortmann drew in a deep breath and tugged Trina's hands.

"So have you been doing what Graham said?"

Trina jerked her gaze up, her brow crunching. What a funny question. Obviously she'd stayed away. Trina didn't know how to answer.

Mrs. Ortmann's expression turned puzzled. "Your father did give you the message, didn't he?"

A band of hurt wrapped around Trina's chest. "Yes. He told me."

"Good." A smile quavered on the woman's face. "Graham was so worried you'd fall behind because of him."

That statement made no sense. Trina shook her head, her ribbons grazing the underside of her jaw. "Mrs. Ortmann, I'm sorry, but—"

She squeezed Trina's hands hard. "You were the last thing he thought about before they put him under." Tears appeared in the corners of her eyes. "I'm so glad you're studying. Graham will feel so bad if this accident has kept you from doing your work."

Trina's heart thudded hard in her chest. Studying? Dad hadn't mentioned studying—only staying away. "Mrs. Ortmann, I don't know what you're talking about. My father told me Graham said I shouldn't come here."

The woman's eyes flew wide. "Well, he did—but somehow you only got part of the message." She clapped her hand over her mouth. "Oh my! I hope. . ." Capturing Trina's hand again, she leaned close, her face pursing into a look of worry. "I was so upset that night, Trina—there were people coming and going, so much activity, so much concern. I may have mixed up my words and left your father with the idea that Graham didn't want you here.

"It is true that's what he wanted, but not because he didn't want to see you." She shook her head. "He only wanted you to keep studying—not to let the accident interfere with your work. Do you understand?"

Trina understood. And she'd let Graham down by not picking up her books this week. She would make it up, though. Then she looked at her bandaged wrist and groaned. She held up the injured hand. "I want to study, Mrs. Ortmann, but I don't know how I'll submit my assignments. I can barely type with two *good* hands. I don't know how I'll do it with one."

"Oh, honey." Mrs. Ortmann offered a brief, sympathetic hug. "Can you contact your teachers? Let them know you've been hurt and ask if they'll let you turn things in late? Or maybe you could talk into one of those machines. . .what are they called?"

Andrew inserted, "A tape recorder?"

"Yes!" The older woman turned to Trina, eagerness lighting her eyes. "You could *say* your assignments and send them in."

"I don't know." Trina had never operated a tape recorder. But then, until she'd started college, she'd never used a computer, either. Yet she'd managed to master it well enough to keep up. "I—I guess I could try, though."

"Of course you can!" Mrs. Ortmann beamed. "And as soon as Graham comes out of surgery, I'll let him know how you're doing and that you aren't falling behind. If he knows you're moving forward just like you two planned, it will give his heart a lift. It will give him a reason—" Her chin crumpled, tears spurting into her eyes. "A reason to try to get well."

"I'll do my best," Trina promised.

The door to the little room opened. Mr. Ortmann and Chuck came in, carrying a tray of food.

Trina rose, looking at Andrew. "We should get out of the way so you can eat." She gave Mrs. Ortmann another hug, shook Mr. Ortmann's hand, and tweaked Chuck's ear. After their good-byes, she and Andrew headed back to the lobby.

"I'm sorry you didn't get to see Graham," Andrew said.

"Me, too." Trina's heart felt heavy with desire to see him, talk to him, touch him, and assure herself he was alive. "But maybe Mama and Dad will let me come back after he's had his surgery and he's no longer in the coma."

"I'll bring you if they can't," Andrew offered.

Trina held his elbow as they crossed the parking lot. "Thank you. But won't Beth need you at the gallery?"

"Beth knows I'll make up the hours." Andrew opened the car door for her. "Besides, Graham is practically family. She'll understand."

When Andrew started the car and headed into traffic, Trina said, "What do you think of Mrs. Ortmann's suggestion about doing my assignments on a tape recorder?"

"I think it's better than not doing them." Andrew glanced at her. "What would be easier—typing with one hand or speaking into a tape recorder?"

Trina laughed. "I don't know. I haven't tried either one of those things."

Andrew grinned. "Well, I guess you won't know until you try."

Trina sighed, her laughter fading. "Andrew, I'm worried about how things will be when Graham gets out of the hospital." It felt good to share her concern with Andrew, the way she would have before he got so angry with her. She let all of the fears of the past days spill out in a rush. "If he can't walk, how will we live in the upstairs of his parents' house? Will he need me to stay home and take care of him? Will he still want to marry me? What kind of job will he be able to do? I could provide for him if I become a veterinarian, but how can I leave him to go to school if he needs me to care for him?"

Andrew held up his hand, shaking his head. "Slow down, Trina. Seems to me you're borrowing trouble."

Despite herself, she smiled. He sounded just like the old, patient, big-brother Andrew she knew and loved.

He went on. "We don't even know yet how severely he's injured. Sure, it will take him awhile to recover—he'll be having major surgery. But he could very well walk out of the hospital. I say put off all those questions until we get word from the doctor concerning how badly Graham is injured. You'll make yourself sick worrying."

Trina sighed. "I know you're right, but it's hard."

"Put it in God's hands, Trina. Just like you've done with everything you needed to accomplish to become a college student." Andrew bumped her elbow, winking. "He took care of you, right? Now trust Him to take care of Graham."

TWENTY-SEVEN

Y ou have to push RECORD and PLAY at the same time, Katrinka, remember?" Beth pointed to the two side-by-side buttons on the 1980s cassette tape recorder. "If you don't push them both, it doesn't record."

Trina's face fell. "You mean this whole morning's work didn't record?"

Beth shook her head. When Andrew had returned Wednesday and mentioned the possibility of Trina's using a tape recorder, Beth had taken it upon herself to locate one. She'd visited three pawn-shops before finding one in good working condition with a built-in microphone. But finding it proved to be easier than teaching Trina to use it.

Twice now, Trina had neglected to push the right buttons to re-cord, and once she'd accidentally overwritten everything by hitting both buttons when she meant to listen to what she'd recorded pre-viously. Although they'd both laughed at the puzzled "Why am I not hearing anything? Where's the assignment? Oh, what did I do wrong *now?*" that took the place of the work intended to be there, Beth didn't want a repeat. It took too much time to replace the errors, and Trina was already playing catch-up thanks to the accident.

"I'm sorry, but no. Look carefully and make sure both buttons are all the way down before you start talking."

Tears glittered briefly in Trina's eyes; then she blinked them away. "All right. So before I start working on my history paper, I'll try again to record the grammar assignments."

Beth smiled at the determined set to Trina's jaw. "Both buttons!" she said before turning back to the computer. She listened to Trina go through the grammar exercises, her voice steady and enunciation precise. It was good to keep Trina busy today—Graham's surgery had been scheduled for eight o'clock that morning. His mother had promised to call as soon as he was out. Beth intended to keep Trina too occupied to watch the clock, even if it meant spending the whole day away from the studio. Andrew was capable of running things over there, and she could do whatever planning she needed to do on her home computer.

Computer. She smiled, sending a secretive glance over her shoulder at Trina. Wouldn't Trina be surprised when she found out what Beth had hidden in the bedroom? The shipment had arrived late yesterday afternoon, and Beth's eyes had filled with tears when she realized how perfect the timing was of its arrival. God had met a need before Trina knew it would exist.

Regardless of how the surgery turned out, Graham would need attention for several weeks. If she knew Trina, the girl wouldn't want to leave him alone in the evenings. Thanks to Sean's "compromise," it wouldn't be necessary for her to come to Beth's or the studio to use a computer again.

Although Beth suggested a desktop, Sean insisted on purchasing a laptop—something Trina could carry to class with her, if need be. It wasn't a top-of-the-line model, but it had adequate memory, wireless

Internet capabilities, and several programs including word processing, budget helps, and spreadsheet templates that could come in handy when Trina was charting the care given to furry critters later down the line. When Sean returned from his latest trip, they would present the laptop to Trina together. Although Beth itched to do it now, it had been Sean's idea in the first place, so he should be involved.

Beth suspected Trina would argue about taking the gift, but Beth could be stubborn, too. She'd make Trina understand how much she'd need that computer, especially when she and Graham left Sommerfeld. Suddenly a wave of sadness struck. Of all the people in Sommerfeld—other than Mom and Henry, of course—Trina was her favorite. The town wouldn't be the same without her.

But she'd be back, Beth reminded herself, turning her attention to the computer screen. With that new veterinarian taking over Dr. Groening's clinic, maybe Trina could establish her own clinic right here in Sommerfeld. It would be harder starting from scratch, but she had a rapport with the community that would encourage people to come to her. Beth suspected Trina had the gumption it would take to make a brand-new veterinary clinic run successfully, and it would be fun to watch it all happen.

Trina's voice stopped, and a *click* signaled she'd turned off the machine. Beth swiveled in her seat. "All done?"

"With the English," Trina reported with a sigh. "Now on to the—"

The telephone rang, and both women jumped, spinning toward the sound.

"It's probably about Graham." Trina rose from the table, straining toward the telephone.

Beth snatched it up on the second ring. "Hello?"

"Hello, Beth." Deborah Muller's voice. "We just got the call from Mrs. Ortmann. May I talk to Trina?"

Beth's hand trembled as she held the phone to Trina. "It's your mom. She has news on Graham."

Trina dashed around the table and snatched the receiver from Beth's hand. Beth leaned close to listen, too. Trina rasped, "Yes? How is he?"

"The doctor said they successfully replaced the damaged vertebrae with a piece of cadaver bone." Relief carried clearly through the line. "There was a bone sliver dangerously close to the spinal cord, but it didn't appear to have punctured the cord. The doctor felt confident Graham will eventually regain use of his legs."

Beth let out a war whoop, and Trina burst into tears. Trina shoved the receiver into Beth's hands and sank down at the table, burying her face in her arms. Beth asked all the questions she knew Trina would want answered: How long would Graham be in the hospital? Would he require rehabilitation? When might he be able to return to work? Would they be able to proceed as planned for their wedding?

To Beth's surprise, Deborah responded to each question without a hint of impatience. And when Beth ran out of questions, Deborah said, "Thank you, Beth, for helping Trina and keeping her busy this morning. We appreciate you." The line went dead before Beth could reply.

She placed the receiver back in its cradle, shaking her head in wonder. Funny how conflict brought people together. . .

Sitting next to Trina, she put her arm around the younger woman's heaving shoulders.

"I–I'm so sorry." Her face still hidden against her arms, Trina's voice came out muffled and broken. "I d–don't know w–why I'm crying now."

Beth chuckled, rubbing Trina's shoulders. "Go ahead and cry. I would imagine there's a lot of pent-up worry behind the tears. When you're done, I'll tell you everything your mom said about Graham, and then we'll walk over to the café and have some lunch to celebrate a successful surgery."

A half hour later, Trina splashed her face with cold water, and the two women headed to the café. The dining room was full of excited, chattering Sommerfeld residents, all seeming to discuss Graham's surgery. Trina got pulled into the conversations, so Beth sneaked into the kitchen to find Deborah.

"It's wonderful news about Graham's legs," Beth said by way of greeting.

Deborah used her apron to wipe her brow and nodded. "An answer to prayer."

Beth agreed. "But I've been wondering. Rehabilitation could take several months. Who knows how long it will be before Graham is able to work? I know Trina is going back to Groening's clinic on Monday, so she'll have a little income, but how will they get by?"

Deborah smiled, the lines around her eyes tired. "Beth, haven't you figured out by now that Mennonites take care of the needs of their people?" Not a hint of sarcasm colored her tone. "It's kind of you to be concerned, but rest assured Graham and Trina will be all right."

Beth's shoulders sagged with relief. "Okay. Thanks. I realize I'm not Mennonite, but I do care a lot about Trina."

Deborah gave Beth's cheek a quick pat and turned back to the stove. Beth took that as her hint to leave. She returned to the dining area and sat down in a booth next to Trina, joining in the conversation. But at the back of her mind, a question hovered: How would the community take care of Graham and Trina?

Something poked the sole of his left foot. Graham grunted in frustration. "Chuck," he rasped through a throat that felt as gritty as sandpaper, "quit it."

A low chuckle sounded, and then his right foot got the same treatment.

With a snort, Graham opened his eyes and focused blearily toward the end of the bed. "What're you—" Then he realized Chuck wasn't in the room. A tall man in a white shirt and rainbow-colored tie stood smiling down at him. "Who're you?"

The man moved closer. "I'm Dr. Howey. How are you feeling?"

"Like I got hit by a truck."

The doctor chuckled again. "Are you in pain?"

Graham considered the question. He wasn't comfortable—a pressure in his back made him wonder if someone had stuffed something under the mattress, and his head felt twice its normal size, but he couldn't honestly say he was hurting. "No. Not really."

The doctor moved back to the foot of the bed and grasped Graham's feet, squeezing his toes. "Are you able to feel this?"

Graham scowled. "Yes. Never have cared much for people messing with my feet."

Dr. Howey let go and returned to the side of the bed to pinch Graham's wrist and frown at his own wristwatch for several seconds. While the doctor did his checking, Graham twisted his head and found a clock on the wall. Three fifteen. But morning or afternoon? With the window shades drawn and the lights in the room on low, he couldn't be sure. The uncertainty left him feeling unsettled.

And something else occurred to him. "What day is it?"

Dr. Howey released his wrist with a pat. "Friday."

The accident had been on a Friday. Had an entire week passed? Graham pressed his memory, trying to account for the time. He recalled riding in an ambulance, telling his folks to make sure Trina stayed home and studied, but after that. . .nothing.

"Have I really slept away an entire week?" It hurt his throat to talk.

The doctor put his hand on Graham's shoulder. "It was important for your body's recovery for you to remain perfectly still. So we used drugs to keep you in a coma, Graham. Keeping you still brought the inflammation down enough that we could do surgery. So early this morning, we replaced your crushed vertebrae. The fact that you can feel me touching your feet is a good sign, but I need you to try to do something for me." He moved back to the foot of the bed. "Can you wiggle your toes?"

It took great concentration, and sweat broke out across Graham's forehead, but he waggled the toes of both feet up and down.

"Wonderful!"

Graham closed his eyes, exhausted from the effort. Sleep claimed him. When he opened his eyes again, instead of the doctor, he found his parents and brother lounging in plastic chairs. The clock read seven forty-five. He swallowed against his sore throat and managed a weak greeting. "Have you been here the whole time?"

His parents leaped from the seats and rushed to the bed, leaning over him. His mother stroked his hair. "And where else would we be with you here?" Her scolding tone let Graham know the depth of her concern.

"But a whole week. . ." Guilt struck as Graham realized how worried his parents must have been. "I'm sorry."

"You don't have anything to apologize for, son," his dad said. "You didn't do anything wrong."

Graham hoped that was true. The details of the accident were fuzzy, other than trying to get out of the way of the truck and praying Trina wouldn't be hurt. He hoped there wasn't something more he could have done. Fear made his heart pound, but he managed to ask, "Is Trina. . . ?"

His mother squeezed his shoulder. "Trina is right as rain. A sprained wrist, some bruises, but nothing serious."

"Thank the Lord." Graham released a heavy sigh. "She hasn't been here, has she?" He wasn't sure what answer he wanted.

"In and out a couple of times," Mom said. "She's been studying, just like you wanted her to."

Relief flooded Graham that the accident wasn't putting her behind on her course work, yet he admitted to a prick of disappointment that she wasn't here when he opened his eyes. "Good." The word grated out without much enthusiasm.

"Lots of people have been in and out," Dad reported, his hand on Graham's arm. "We kept a book and had them write their names down so you'd know. Your uncle John and cousins have kept the lumberyard going, and they said they'd work as long as we need them to. The doctor said we'll spend at least a couple of weeks in Nebraska at a rehabilitation clinic to help you get on your feet, but then your job will be waiting for you."

Graham processed everything his father had said. He focused in on one thing: rehabilitation clinic in Nebraska? He'd never been out of Kansas, and he wasn't sure he wanted to go. But if it meant walking again, he'd go. He had to walk. He had to work. He couldn't allow this accident to keep Trina from finishing college. She depended on him.

The pressure in his back increased, turning into a dull ache. He grimaced, squinting his eyes closed.

"Are you hurting, son?" His mother's anxious voice carried to his ear.

"A little."

"I'll get a nurse."

Graham decided he would avoid asking for painkillers as much as possible. The medication instantly put him to sleep, and he'd already lost too many days of his life. From this point on, he needed to be awake and alert. He had work to do.

The doctor came in Saturday morning with a chart of a spine to explain Graham's injury. Graham found the terms *cervical, thoracic,* and *lumbar* confusing, but he managed to comprehend that his injury—which the doctor called a T-11—affected his legs but not his arms. The doctor explained that many people with lower thoracic injuries regained the full use of their legs over time, and he encouraged Graham to make walking his goal.

"Of course," Graham retorted with vehemence.

But when the doctor indicated months of therapy, Graham's resolve wavered. Months? He didn't have months. He'd sold his house—he would be living in Mom and Dad's upstairs. He needed to work to support Trina—how could he cut and haul lumber from a wheelchair? And would it be fair to Trina to saddle her with a husband who couldn't take care of her? Of himself? He didn't want *her* taking care of *him!*

After the doctor left, Graham closed his eyes so his parents would think he was sleeping, but inwardly he raged at the unfairness of the situation. He might as well be an invalid. He would only hold Trina back. Her studies would be set aside so she could see to his needs. Instead of caring for animals, as she'd planned, she'd be stuck caring for him—a grown man.

He stifled the anguished groan that longed for release. *Oh Lord, I don't understand. Why did You allow this to happen?* Graham had been taught that all things worked together for good for those who were called to God's purpose, but he couldn't see any good in being stuck in a wheelchair while Trina set aside her own dreams to wipe his chin and help him change his socks.

His back throbbed. His legs ached. Temptation to ask for more pain medication to give him blessed escape pressed hard. But he knew the moment he awakened from the drug-induced rest, the worst pain would still be with him. How could he set aside the sharp agony of disappointment?

TWENTY-EIGHT

H ere you are, Trina." Dr. Groening placed a paycheck into Trina's waiting hand. "It includes a small bonus."

Trina's eyes widened. "Oh, Dr. Groening, that isn't necessary!"

The older man smiled, his eyes crinkling. "You let me decide what is and isn't necessary. I appreciate your hard work, and I know you have a heavy load to carry between working here and keeping up with your studies." He frowned, crossing his arms. "When are finals?"

"Another four weeks," Trina said. She didn't know who would take her—Graham was still in Nebraska with his mother, although his dad was home running the lumberyard. No one seemed to know when Graham's time in rehabilitation would end. Her chest held a constant deep ache from missing him.

"Being able to use both hands must make things easier," he said.

Trina rubbed her left wrist. The splint had come off only three days ago, and it felt odd not to have it there. A twinge reminded her not to overuse the wrist, but typing shouldn't tax it too much. "Yes. It will be better to send files by e-mail instead of cassette tapes through the mail." She released a light laugh. "Easier for me and for my instructors, I'm sure."

Dr. Groening chuckled. "Well, it's good you have this Thanksgiving break, then—a couple of free days to concentrate on studies, hmm?"

Trina managed a smile.

The doctor went on. "Has Marc talked to you at all about his plans?"

Trina shook her head. Even though she spent every day at the clinic, her path rarely crossed Dr. Royer's. He preferred to spend his time at farms, going to the animals rather than remaining at the clinic and letting the animals come to him. Trina admitted the arrangement suited her fine—something about the man continued to intimidate her.

"Well, I'm sure he will when the time is right. He has some ideas for expanding the clinic, and he indicated you would be instrumental in seeing those plans through."

Trina pinched her face into a puzzled scowl. "Expanding the clinic?"

Dr. Groening rubbed his finger over his lips, a grin hovering. "Well, not exactly making this one bigger, but having two clinics. This one and one in Hillsboro."

Trina shook her head. "That would be a lot to keep track of."

"Yes." Again a chuckle rumbled. "And even someone as tall as Marc can't be in two places at once. Actually, his ideas aren't bad. I think you'll find them interesting."

Trina offered a slight shrug. "I'll wait, then, for him to talk to me."

"Probably after the holidays," Dr. Groening said with a nod. He lifted his gaze toward the window when the sound of a truck's engine intruded. "There's your ride. Have a good Thanksgiving, Trina."

The holiday wouldn't feel right without Graham. Last year right before Thanksgiving, he'd made known his intentions to court her. Now they were miles apart. She swallowed. "I'll do my best, Dr. Groening. You have a good weekend, too."

She slipped her arms into her sweater and headed outside. Tony waited with the engine running. Climbing into the warm cab felt good after her brief time in the nippy November breeze. She sat quietly as Tony turned the pickup toward Sommerfeld, her heart pounding as they approached the spot where the man's pickup had crossed the line and hit Graham's car.

Each time she drove past the accident site, she looked around carefully. Over the past month, the place where the ground had been scuffed by the rolling car had smoothed out. Except for a few bare patches of missing grass and the occasional wink of broken glass, you could hardly tell something monumental had occurred there. But Trina still knew. She lived with the consequences.

She sighed, sending up another silent prayer for Graham's recovery. Although she wrote to him every day and called every Saturday, it wasn't the same as having him close enough to talk to or to touch. The telephone conversations were far from satisfying. She sensed Graham's impatience to be done, yet they wouldn't release him until he could pull himself into a standing position. *Hurry, Lord, and bring healing,* Trina's heart begged. She needed Graham home so things could return to normal.

Suddenly, from behind the steering wheel, Tony erupted in a hysterical giggle, which he quickly squelched.

Trina sent him a puzzled look. "What was that all about?"

He pinched his lips together and didn't answer.

Trina stared at him for a few minutes, but when he kept his eyes on the road, humming to himself, she turned her gaze forward. Silence reigned until they reached the Sommerfeld turnoff. Then, as Tony made the curve, another snort of laughter burst out.

Trina bopped him on the arm. "Stop that!"

"Stop what?" He giggled nearly uncontrollably.

"What's so funny?"

"Nothing." Yet the giggles continued in spurts until he pulled up in front of their house. Then he cleared his throat several times, pasted on a serious face, and said, "Well, let's go in."

Awareness prickled down Trina's spine. "Tony?"

But he just hopped out and jogged up the sidewalk as if he hadn't heard her. She followed more slowly, holding her sweater closed against the bite of the wind. When she reached the front door, Tony was waiting, a goofy grin on his face. He swung the door open for her, and she cast a sidelong glance at him as she stepped over the threshold.

The moment she entered the room, an exultant shout rose: "Surprise!"

Trina staggered backward, connecting with the doorjamb, as dozens of people—family and friends—popped from various locations. She pressed her hands to her chest and stammered stupidly, "W-what?" And then a movement toward the back of the group captured her attention. The bright flash of light on steel forced her to blink, and when she opened her eyes again, her heart fired into her throat.

"Graham!" She raced across the short expanse of carpet and grabbed his hands, which were curled over the padded bar of a silver walker. "You're home!" Oh, how she longed to catapult into his arms, to press her lips to his, to feel his arms wrap around her and hold her close forever. But the frame of the walker created a barrier, so she had to be content to lean as close as possible and beam into his face. "Oh, it's so good to see you! When did you get back?"

"Late last night." He looked older, thinner, haggard. But his dear blue eyes were as warm as ever as he tipped his face toward hers and placed a kiss on her forehead. "Did we surprise you?"

"Yes!" She sent an accusatory look in Tony's direction. "Although Tony tried to give it away by giggling."

Tony assumed an innocent expression, and Andrew gave him a teasing smack on the back of his head. Everyone laughed. Mama stepped forward and put her arm around Trina.

"It was Graham's idea not to tell you he was coming home so you could be surprised." Mama's smile bounced back and forth between Trina and Graham.

Mrs. Ortmann stepped beside Mama, her round face glowing. "And not to be outdone, *we* have surprises for both of you. Sit down."

Trina walked beside Graham as he made his painstaking way to the sofa. His steps were slow, measured, his feet scuffing against the floor. But Trina's heart pounded in happiness at the sight of her Graham on his feet, in her house back in Sommerfeld again. She held her breath as he maneuvered the walker in a small circle before lowering himself to the sofa. Once on the cushion, he released a huge breath, and Trina allowed her air to whoosh out, too. Then, with a smile, she snuggled as close to him as she could get without climbing into his lap.

The others gathered near, surrounding the sofa. Beth and Sean stepped forward, and Sean held out a black leather case. "Trina," Beth said, "now that Graham is home, we know you won't want to spend your evenings at our place on the computer, so. . ."

Sean placed the case on the sofa cushion next to Trina and unzipped it, folding back the cover to reveal a slim, black laptop computer. Trina gasped.

"You can take this wherever Graham is and do your assignments. You'll need to establish Internet connection, but then you can send your assignments from home—wherever that may be." Beth's eyes twinkled. "We're so proud of your accomplishments, Trina, and we wish you much success as you finish your education."

Applause broke out from the group, and several people gave Sean pats on the shoulder as he stepped back. Beth leaned down to give first Trina then Graham a hug, and Trina was too stunned to even protest the extravagant gift.

Deacon Reiss pushed to the front. Mama, Dad, and Graham's parents flanked him, as if forming a wall of support. An air of expectancy filled the room, and Trina took Graham's hand, pressing it tightly between hers.

Deacon Reiss spoke. "Graham and Trina, over the past months, we've seen you exhibit great dedication: dedication to following God's will in your lives and dedication to one another. You have been an inspiration to all of us in facing difficulties with faith and fortitude." He linked his fingers together and pressed them to his middle, a prayerful stance. "We know this accident has created a hardship for you to see your plans through."

Graham flicked a glance at Trina, his brow furrowed. Trina looked back, as puzzled as he.

"There aren't any guarantees when Graham will be able to return to full-time work, yet Trina's college classes will go on. There will be costs involved to pay for school, maintain a home, and meet your daily needs. So. . ." The man drew in a great breath, sending his gaze around the circle of faces before looking at Graham and Trina again. "The deacons and minister met last Sunday afternoon; then they paid visits to every family in the fellowship, and we have gained commitments to contribute a small love token each month for your use. When these tokens are combined, it totals an amount that should meet your monthly needs until Graham is able to work full-time again."

"But we couldn't–," Graham started.

"Oh, but–," Trina started at the same time.

Deacon Reiss raised his hand. "No arguments. We're your family, we love you, and we want to help. Besides–" His lips curved into a smile. "When Trina comes back as a veterinarian, she'll be meeting our needs. You'll have the chance to repay us then."

Tears burned behind Trina's nose. She looked at Graham, and he blinked repeatedly, moisture glimmering in his eyes. She waited for him to decide whether or not to receive this gift. Finally, he swallowed, cleared his throat, and lifted his face to the waiting audience.

"Trina and I appreciate your love and support. Thank you."

Another cheer rose from the group; then everyone crowded close, offering hugs and words of encouragement. Slowly they drifted out the door, leaving Trina, Graham, and their parents. Mama crooked her finger, and the four adults moved to the back half of the house, leaving Trina and Graham alone.

The moment the room was vacated, Trina raised her arms to throw them around Graham's neck. She remembered in time the need to be gentle and cupped his cheeks instead. "I've missed you so much!"

"Me, too," Graham said, turning his face to kiss her palm. "I never want to leave you again. It felt like forever."

Trina pulled back, feigning shock. "You mean it *wasn't* forever?"

Graham laughed and shifted against the couch cushion. He sighed. "Oh, Trina, it's so good to be home."

Very slowly, Trina leaned sideways until her head rested lightly on his shoulder. He tipped his head, pressing his cheek to her cap. They sat for several long minutes, simply enjoying each other's nearness. But then Graham lifted his head and gave a gentle nudge with his shoulder, dislodging her. She sat up and faced him.

"There's much we need to talk about," he said, his expression serious. He took hold of her hands.

Trina nodded. "I've been so worried about finances—how we'd make it." A lump filled her throat. "But we'll be all right."

He sighed. "The financial support is a blessing. That's for sure." His thumbs traced lazy circles on the backs of her hands. "But I'm still not sure where we'll live. I—I can't climb stairs, so the upstairs rooms at Mom and Dad's won't work. On the way home, Mom suggested we take the back downstairs bedroom at their house, and we could, but it won't give us much privacy. It's right off the kitchen."

"It won't be for long, you know. And being right off the kitchen means it'll be easier for us to get midnight snacks."

Graham smirked. "Midnight snacks?"

"Studying makes me hungry," Trina said, grinning. "And besides, I need to fatten you up." She shook her head in mock dismay. "Didn't they feed you at all while you were gone? You're as skinny as a scarecrow."

Graham made a face. "Food never tastes good when you're far from home. Now that I'm here, I'll put the weight back on."

"I'll see to it." There was much Trina would see to—his therapy, his meals, his emotional needs. She squeezed his hand, sending a silent message.

"And I'll help you with your studies," he said. His fingers convulsed. "About our wedding. . ."

Trina sat bolt upright. "We aren't postponing it." Heat flooded her cheeks at her own audacity. Had she just told her future husband what to do?

Graham gave her hands a tug. "I'm not asking you to. Between the hospital and rehabilitation center, I've spent six weeks away from you. I'm as eager as ever to make you my wife." He lifted her hands to his lips and kissed her knuckles.

Trina nearly sagged with relief. "Then what?"

He patted the walker, which waited beside his legs. "I want to stand in front of the guests without leaning on this thing. It will take a lot of work to strengthen the muscles in my back and legs enough to make that possible, and we don't have many weeks to spare." He licked his lips, his fervent gaze pinned to hers. "Will you help me?"

"Of course I will! Whatever you need, I'll do it."

"But it takes time, Trina, and you spend your days at the clinic and your evenings studying. I don't want your other responsibilities to suffer."

Trina leaned forward and planted a quick kiss on his lips. Cupping his cheeks with her hands, she whispered, "Graham, there is nothing more important to me than you. You put aside your own wants and needs to help me achieve my goal. Well, I can set aside some of my activities to help you achieve yours."

Graham closed his eyes a moment. When he opened them, tears glittered in their deep blue depths. "Together, Trina, I think we can accomplish it."

"Together, with God's help," Trina agreed, "we can change the world." She smiled, her lips trembling, as a burst of laughter came from the kitchen. "He's already made big changes in our small corner of it."

Twenty-nine

Graham eased back on the pile of pillows propped against the headboard of his bed and released a sigh. The sliding glass door across from the bed allowed in a healthy dose of early afternoon sunshine, but he could see gray clouds building in the east. Would they have snow for Christmas? He hoped so.

The month between Thanksgiving and Christmas had disappeared in a rush of activity that often left Graham's head spinning. Thanks to the unusually mild winter weather, the men in town had been able to build an addition to the back of Graham's parents' house, doubling the size of the bedroom he and Trina would share after their marriage. The addition included the sliding glass door and a small deck with a ramp, making it easy for Graham to roll his wheelchair in and out of the house rather than struggling up the front porch stairs with his walker.

A week after coming home, he had returned to the lumberyard half days. He worked on the floor, serving customers, rather than out in the warehouse, but at least he felt as though he was earning his keep. He used his wheelchair part of the time and the walker part of the time, making himself walk until tiredness forced him back to the chair. But his walker time was gradually increasing, giving him hope that eventually he would be able to set aside the wheelchair for good.

He spent a couple of hours napping in the afternoon, something he despised, yet his body demanded the time of rest. Before falling asleep, he read passages from the Bible and prayed. He fingered the edges of the Bible, still open to Jeremiah 29, where only a few minutes earlier he had underlined the words, "For I know the thoughts that I think toward you, saith the LORD, thoughts of peace, and not of evil, to give you an expected end."

A smile found its way to his face as he reflected on that promise. The Bible-reading routine helped remove the impatience and frustration that often twisted through his belly. He missed the days of being whole and healthy, yet he'd never had such a large block of time to commit to Bible study and prayer. He discovered a true blessing in being able to rest in God's Word on a daily basis.

Each evening after supper, Trina came over and kept him company while he did his muscle-strengthening exercises. She brought her laptop, and it always made him smile to see her in her Mennonite cap, dress, and tennis shoes, carrying the leather briefcase—such an unusual picture, yet somehow fitting. He'd come to expect the unexpected when it applied to Trina, and he wouldn't have her any other way.

He looked ahead to this evening's visit. Andrew had driven her into El Dorado to take the first of her semester exams. When she returned, depending on how things went, she would be either in a celebratory mood or in need of comfort. Whatever she needed—whether cheering on or cheering up—he would provide it. Graham clamped his jaw, regret striking. How he'd wanted to take her, to offer encouragement and a kiss before sending her through the door to the classroom. But he wasn't allowed to drive yet. The money from insurance waited in an account at the bank for the day when he could drive again. Hopefully before their wedding, since Trina hadn't yet learned.

He emitted a soft chuckle, remembering the day he'd tried to teach Trina to drive. They'd try it again—probably in the spring—and this time he'd stick with it until she mastered it. She could master it, he had no doubt—his Trina could do anything she set her mind to.

A yawn stretched his face, and he settled a little lower on the bed. His back ached, but he'd grown accustomed to that and could block it out most of the time. Closing his eyes, he muttered, "Strengthening rest, Father. Give me strengthening rest."

"So how do you think you did?"

Trina smiled at Andrew's question. It was similar to the one Graham had asked after the midterm exams. She replied, "As well as I could."

Andrew nodded. "That's all anyone can do."

Trina leaned her head against the seat's headrest and sighed. "I'm glad the tests are over, though, and I'll enjoy these next weeks of no studying."

Andrew shot her a puzzled look. "No studying for weeks?"

"During January, they take special classes on the campus, but none are offered online. I wouldn't have signed up for one anyway. My wedding is coming"—a jolt of eager anticipation doubled her pulse—"and I want to be able to focus on it."

"I understand." Andrew shifted his hands on the steering wheel, his lower lip poked out in thought. "How long before you'll need to start taking classes on campus rather than online?"

"At least two years, maybe three, depending on the course work," Trina said. "With veterinary science, there are a number of classes requiring laboratory assignments." She grinned. "I can't do those over the Internet."

"I imagine not."

"But for as long as I can, I'll do online classes and keep working at Dr. Groening's—oops! Dr. Royer's." She grimaced. "I'm not sure I'll ever get used to that change. It's been Dr. Groening's Clinic my whole life."

Andrew sent her a short, speculative look. "Are you getting along okay with the new vet? I've heard he's knowledgeable but not quite as personable as Dr. Groening."

Andrew had heard correctly as far as Trina was concerned. She toyed with the ribbons of her cap while she answered. "I admit it has been hard for me to warm up to him. He has a way of looking down his nose at me that sets my nerves on edge. But he knows what he's doing. I wish he were more like gentle Dr. Groening in the way he relates to me, but he is good with the animals. That's what matters most." She sighed, admitting, "And even though I still wish I could have taken over the clinic, this has worked out best for Dr. Groening. I'll just have to trust that God has something else planned for me."

Andrew nodded. "His plans are always best, even when we people try to mess them up." He offered a sheepish look. "I'm sorry I tried to mess yours up, Trina."

Trina gave his shoulder a brief squeeze. "It's okay. You had a heartache, and it colored your judgment." She paused then braved a question. "How is Livvy doing? She doesn't say much."

Andrew shrugged. "There isn't much to say. Wishing things were different won't change them. She can't have children, and that's all there is to it. But I haven't given up hope. We've looked into adoption, but it's pretty expensive, so I'm setting money aside each month. When the time is right, if we're meant to be parents, God will open the door."

Trina sat quietly, thinking about Andrew's statement about timing and God's doors. She'd seen such evidence of God's hand at work in hers and Graham's lives over the past several months. Andrew's words had proven true for her; surely they would also prove true for him.

"I'll pray to that end, too," she said. "You and Livvy would make wonderful parents."

He smiled, giving her hand a pat. "Thanks, Trina. Just pray for God's will."

"I will." She yawned then giggled. "All that studying has worn me out."

"Well, close your eyes and take a little nap. Before you know it, we'll be home, and you can go over and tell Graham all about your examinations."

Trina settled more comfortably into the corner. "Sounds good." The hum of the tires on asphalt provided a lullaby, and sleep claimed her. In no time, someone shook her arm, bringing her to wakefulness. She sat up and peeked out the window, sighing in satisfaction when she realized they were home. Then she noticed a vehicle parked in front of her house, and her feeling of well-being fled.

Andrew pointed. "What's he doing here?"

Trina's mouth went dry. She licked her lips. "I'm not sure, but I hope I haven't done something wrong. . .again."

"Do you want me to stay?" Andrew's concerned tone offered encouragement.

Trina, knowing neither of her parents was home, nodded. It wouldn't do for her to be alone in the house with Dr. Royer. "Please."

They opened their car doors in unison, and at the same time, Marc Royer swung his door open. He glanced at his wristwatch, a silent reprimand, then met Trina on the sidewalk.

"I've been waiting for you. Can we talk?"

"Of course. Come on in out of the cold." She scurried up the sidewalk, Andrew and Dr. Royer on her heels. Once inside, she gestured to the sofa. "Make yourself comfortable." She sat in Mama's overstuffed chair in the corner, and Andrew moved to Dad's chair.

Dr. Royer perched on the edge of the cushion, with his elbows on his knees, and fixed Trina with a serious look. "I need to visit with you about my plans for the clinic."

Suddenly Trina feared her job was in jeopardy, and she involuntarily sucked in a fortifying breath.

"I believe, to better serve the area communities, I need to expand to two locations—keeping the Lehigh clinic and opening a second one closer to Hillsboro." Dr. Royer plunged on, seemingly unaware of Trina's concerns. "Obviously, this involves quite a financial undertaking, and it isn't something that will occur overnight, so to speak, but it is my long-term goal. I have put together a strategy, based on Dr. Groening's past several years' records and a demography of the area, and I believe within the next five years, I will have the funds to establish the second clinic."

Trina blinked rapidly, absorbing the man's words. If he was preparing to fire her, he had chosen an odd way to do it.

He sat upright. "Of course, with two locations, hiring a second veterinarian becomes necessary. That's where you come in."

Pressing her hand to her throat, Trina gasped, "M–me?"

"If you're interested."

"If?" Trina curled her hands around the chair's armrest to keep from leaping out of her seat and hugging Marc Royer. His timing couldn't have been better if she had planned it! Five years down the line, she'd have her veterinary license in hand, and working at the clinic would let her stay right here in Sommerfeld, just as she and Graham wanted. Swallowing, she forced a calm tone. "Oh yes. I'm interested."

"Good. Then I will refrain from seeking prospects elsewhere. There will be other details to discuss, naturally, but we can cover those at another time." Dr. Royer slapped his knees and rose.

Trina bounced up. "Thank you, Dr. Royer, for giving me this opportunity. I appreciate your confidence in me."

He lifted his chin, peering down his nose in his normal manner, yet somehow it didn't seem condescending this time. "I know I can count on you, and the people of the community already have a relationship with you. So hiring you is in my best interest." He held out his hand, and Trina shook it. "After the first of the year, Groening Clinic will change to the Royer Clinic for the Treatment of Livestock and Domesticated Animals. When you have your degree in hand and our partnership is official, we'll add your name behind mine. Royer and Muller."

"Royer and Ortmann," Andrew corrected. Dr. Royer sent him a puzzled look. Andrew added, "She's getting married in February."

"Ah. Yes. Royer and Ortmann, then. Well." He crossed to the door then paused, his hand on the doorknob. "Keep up your studies, Trina. You'll make a fine veterinarian." He headed out the door.

Trina stared at Andrew in amazement.

"The Royer and Ortmann Clinic for the Treatment of Livestock and Domesticated Animals." Andrew carefully enunciated each word of the clinic's future name and then whistled through his teeth. "Whew, that's a mouthful. I feel sorry for anyone who has to write all of that on a check."

Trina laughed. "I know. But Dr. Royer is a man of length. . .in all ways!" She spun a happy circle, her clasped hands beneath her chin. "Oh! I can't wait to tell Graham!"

Christmas morning, Trina awakened before the sun's rays slipped over the horizon. Her first thought was *"Happy birthday, Jesus,"* followed by,

"*Merry Christmas, Graham.*" She would miss him today after seeing him nearly every day since his return from Nebraska, but they had agreed they should spend this day with family. Their time for Christmases together was near—they could wait.

She slipped a robe over her nightgown and crept to the kitchen on tiptoe, intending to start breakfast. But the lights were already on, and a wonderful aroma greeted her. Mama straightened from checking something in the oven.

"What are you doing up?" they both asked at the same time.

Trina, laughing, gave her mother a hug. "Merry Christmas. I was going to fix breakfast."

"Too late." Mama grinned. "I've got an egg casserole in the oven." Trina sniffed appreciatively, breathing in the scent of eggs, ham, peppers, and onions. Mama put her hands on her hips. "I whipped it up last night after you'd gone to bed so I could surprise everyone."

Trina selected a mug from the cupboard and poured a cup of coffee. "There have been a lot of surprises in Sommerfeld lately."

"Good ones and bad ones," Mama said on a sigh. She stirred cream into a cup of coffee then faced Trina. "But mostly good, I guess. It has been quite a year, hasn't it?"

"A year of change, that's for sure." Trina held the thick mug between both palms. Steam swirled beneath her nose, enticing her to take a sip.

"And more changes coming." Sorrow tinged Mama's voice.

Trina took another sip of the hot coffee and used a teasing tone. "Yes, just think—no more Trina underfoot in another few weeks."

"Well, now," Mama blustered, putting down her cup and swiping her apron across the clean countertop, "I don't think anyone's ever complained about having you underfoot."

Trina's heart turned over, recognizing her mother's penchant for covering deep feelings with brusqueness. "I'll miss you, too, Mama."

For a moment, her mother paused, peering across the kitchen at Trina with her chin quivering. Then she gave a nod and swished her hands together. "Yes, but it's the way of the seasons. Children grow up and move on. It wouldn't be natural any other way."

"I'll make some toast," Trina offered and, at her mother's nod of approval, set to work.

In time, the good smells drew Dad and Tony from their beds, and the family enjoyed a pleasant breakfast. When dishes had been washed, they carried coffee mugs to the front room, where, as had been the tradition for as long as Trina could remember, Dad read the Christmas story from the Bible. Then they prayed together and opened their gifts.

Always practical, Mama and Dad had purchased Trina a set of good cooking pans, and Mama had sewn a half dozen new aprons. Trina gasped when she opened her gift from Tony—a book on the anatomy of cats. He had ordered it online with help from Beth, and he blushed crimson when Trina assured him it would be very helpful.

Afterward in her bedroom to change for the big family get-together at Grandpa Braun's farm, Trina reflected on the fact that this would be her very last Christmas living under Mama and Dad's roof. Sadness brought a quick sting of tears, but anticipation washed them away. She had a grand future awaiting—a future that included being Graham's wife and following her heart's call. A future designed by God's perfect hand.

Someone tapped on her door. "Trina?" Tony's voice. "Dad's got the car warmed up. Are you ready to go?"

Trina smiled. Oh yes. She was ready to go. With a song in her heart, she called, "I'm coming!"

THIRTY

The Friday evening before her wedding, Trina turned over the little sign on the café door to show CLOSED. She turned and sent her mother a huge smile. "Now the fun begins."

Mama laughed. She slung her arm around Trina's shoulders and led her to the storage room, where a box waited. "Let's get busy."

They spent an hour rearranging the tables to clear a wide aisle and leave a space at the far end of the dining room that would accommodate the minister and the wedding party. Trina scrubbed the tables and booths clean, and Mama draped every table with a white linen cloth. The café took on a festive air when Trina placed a glass bowl filled with colorful mints in the center of each table.

When the dining room was finished, they lined up Crock-Pots along the worktable in readiness for tomorrow's dinner. Although many Mennonite families chose to forgo the wedding dinner, Mama insisted that for her only daughter's wedding they would celebrate with fellowship *and* food. Trina didn't mind.

"I'm sorry you'll only have the weekend before you have to go back to your routine," Mama said as she and Trina walked home. "It would be nice if you and Graham could at least get away for a day or two."

Trina shrugged. She and Graham had discussed the situation, and neither resented returning to their routine, as Mama had put it. They felt fortunate that they were able to follow a normal routine considering how different things could be had the accident been more serious. "Graham and I will have our time away from everyone when we go to a campus. In the meantime, we enjoy being here with our families."

Mama released a sigh that hung heavy on the frosty evening air. "Ah, Trina, it will be strange not having you at home. But I couldn't be happier for you. Graham is a good man, and I believe God will bless your union."

Trina curled her arm around Mama's waist, and Mama pressed her cheek briefly to Trina's temple. Then, in typical Mama style, she tugged loose and scolded, "It's cold. Let's hurry."

Saturday dawned bright and cold. No clouds cluttered the crystal sky, and even the wind stayed calm, providing a wonderful day for Trina's wedding. She slipped the light blue dress over her head, smoothing the skirt over her hips. When she'd modeled the dress for Beth, her friend had snapped a photograph.

"Capturing a moment in time," Beth had said.

Remembering the comment, Trina wished she had a photograph of her with Graham—her in her wedding dress, he in his suit—just to know what they looked like side by side in their finest clothes. Then she closed her eyes and created her own image in her mind. She smiled. Perfect.

"Trina?" Dad stood outside the door. "If you want a ride, you'll need to hurry. Your mother is eager to get to the café and put the food in the Crock-Pots so everything will be hot by dinnertime."

Trina called, "Just let me get my shoes on!" Instead of her typical anklet socks and tennis shoes, today Trina wore flesh-toned tights and black satin slippers. Dad had insisted she remove the little ribbon bows that had decorated the shoes, saying they were too ostentatious for a good Mennonite girl, but even without the bows, Trina thought the slippers made her feet appear delicate and feminine.

"Trina!"

"I'm coming!" She snatched up her coat and dashed out the door.

When they reached the café, several cars and two buggies already waited on the street, and the people followed Trina's family inside.

"Just find a seat," Mama instructed, hurrying Trina into the kitchen away from the others. She whispered in Trina's ear, "Stay in here out of sight. I'll let you know when Graham arrives."

Trina perched on a stool in the corner and listened as more people filled the dining room, their voices cheerful and loud and full of celebration. She smiled to herself. Only a few months ago, she had felt as though the community would never accept her choice to break tradition and go to college. Now here they were, turning out by the dozens to wish her well not only on her wedding day but on her future.

"Thank You, Lord," she whispered with heartfelt gratitude.

A hush fell in the dining room, followed by a wave of excited babble, and instantly Trina knew Graham had arrived. She jumped from the stool, her heart pounding, gaze glued to the doorway, awaiting his appearance.

Mama rushed over. "It isn't quite time, Trina. Another ten minutes. Sit back down."

Her limbs trembling, Trina climbed back onto the stool and twirled the ribbons on her cap around her finger repeatedly. It occurred to her that after today, she would snip away the white ribbons and replace them with black, a symbol of her new status of wife. *Wife.* A shiver shook her frame, but she knew the cause was excitement. Only a few more minutes, and she would be Graham's *wife*!

The last minutes passed so slowly Trina wondered if the clock had stopped ticking, but finally the voices from the dining room ceased. Mama stepped into the kitchen, her eyes sparkling with unshed tears, and crooked her finger at Trina. Trina skipped across the floor on black satin slippers and delivered a kiss to Mama's cheek.

Mama whispered, "Be happy, my daughter."

"Always," Trina whispered past the lump that suddenly filled her throat.

Mama placed a white Bible trailing with pink and blue ribbon into Trina's waiting hands. Then she took hold of Trina's shoulders and turned her toward the dining room.

Through the open doorway, Trina glimpsed Graham. Her groom. Seated in his wheelchair, attired in a black suit and white shirt, his hair neatly combed and face shining. His eyes met hers, and his lips tipped into a sweet smile of anticipation. She stared, mesmerized, almost neglecting to breathe, as he leaned forward and swiveled the footrests of his wheelchair out of the way.

The soles of his black lace-up shoes met the tiled floor, and he braced his hands on the armrests of the chair. Then his shoulder muscles bunched beneath the black wool fabric as he pushed, and Trina's breath released in a rush when he stood in front of the chair. His dad stepped into Trina's line of vision and offered Graham his walking aid—a cane carved from a length of sycamore, handcrafted by an Amish artisan to resemble a post wound with ivy.

One hand firmly grasping the cane, he held the other out to her, his smile triumphant. With a little cry of joy, she raced to his side. Tears distorted her vision as she slipped her hand through the bend of his elbow, but she blinked the moisture away, determined to memorize every sight and sound from this special day.

Graham pressed his elbow against his rib cage, giving her fingers a squeeze, and then—on two sturdy feet, with the assistance of the beautifully crafted walking stick—he escorted her slowly through the center of the café to the waiting minister. Trina felt the gazes of their gathered guests, but her eyes remained riveted on Graham's strong, proud profile until they reached the end of the aisle.

The minister cleared his throat, and Trina turned her gaze forward. She listened attentively, aware of Graham's pulse pounding through the sleeve of his jacket, surely matching the eager beat of her own. The familiar Bible passages from Ephesians and 1 Corinthians took on a greater meaning when read during her wedding ceremony and applied to her God-given duties as Graham's mate.

She prayed silently, *Let me honor You, Lord, by being obedient to my call as wife and, if You see fit, mother.* At one point, Graham's eyes slipped closed, and Trina sensed he, too, offered a silent prayer. Her heart seemed to double in size, unable to contain all of the joy and gratitude and anticipation of the moment.

At last, the minister asked them in solemn tones to repeat the selected vows. So many had already been put to the test—for richer, for poorer; in sickness and in health—and they had emerged triumphant. Trina's voice trembled with fervor as she vowed to love, honor, and obey Graham from this day until the day she died or Jesus returned. Listening to Graham's deep, tear-choked voice as he promised to love, honor, and cherish her filled her with such a tumble of joyous emotion that she could no longer control her tears. They spilled down her cheeks in warm rivulets.

But she smiled through the tears, laughing out loud when the minister announced to the waiting guests, "I present to you Mr. and

Mrs. Graham Ortmann. What God hath brought together, let no man put asunder."

Trina tipped her face up to Graham and begged, "Kiss me, please."

And he did. Willingly.

Hours later, Graham's parents dropped him and Trina off at the house. His mother hugged Trina, kissed her cheek, then said, "Welcome home, my dear."

Tears appeared in Trina's dark eyes, but a smile lit her face. "Thank you. I'm so happy to be part of your family!"

Dad helped Graham into his wheelchair and started to wheel him to the house, but Trina rushed forward.

"No, no!" She laughingly pushed in front of Dad, taking control of the handles. "He's my husband—I'll do the honors."

Mom and Dad climbed back into the car with Chuck, and they pulled away with waves and smiles. When they'd first mentioned spending the night at Graham's grandparents to give him and Trina complete privacy their first night as husband and wife, Graham had protested. They shouldn't have to leave their own home. But when he'd mentioned it to Trina, she'd exclaimed, "Oh, that would be wonderful!" So he'd told his folks to go ahead and make the arrangements.

Now, as she pushed him around the back of the house and up the ramp to their own little deck, he was glad he'd told his family to go. Being alone with Trina—his wife—was a blessing beyond compare. They reached the glass doors, and Trina scampered around the wheelchair to slide the door open.

A pang of regret struck, and he sighed.

Trina paused, looking over her shoulder. "What is it?"

He pinched his lips into a brief scowl. "I wish I could carry you over the threshold."

Trina stared at him for a moment, her eyes wide. Then she hunched her shoulders and giggled. "Okay." With a graceful swirl, she seated herself in his lap and wrapped her arms around his neck. "Carry me in!"

Graham hooted with laugher. He grunted with the effort of pushing both of them over the slightly raised threshold, but he made it, and they celebrated his success with a kiss that lasted longer than Graham knew two people could kiss without losing consciousness.

Finally, the cool breeze through the open sliding door forced Trina off his lap. Once she'd closed it, however, she came right back and made herself at home again.

Graham curled his arms around her waist, relishing the feel of her cheek against his shoulder. They sat for long moments, their hearts beating in synchronization with each other, even their breathing finding a matching pattern that made Graham feel as though they truly had become one, just as the minister proclaimed them to be.

He whispered, his lips brushing the organdy cap of their faith, "I love you, Trina."

She released a breathy sigh, her lips curving upward in a sweet smile of contentment. "Oh, I love you, too."

Then slowly, he lifted his hands and removed the pins that held her cap in place. Trina sat up, staring at him with her eyes wide and lips slightly parted, as he slipped the cap free and laid it on the end of the bed. Reverently, he smoothed the ribbons into a line over the edge of the coverlet. Raising his hands to her head, he went on a second pin hunt, popping them loose one by one until her hair fell in tumbling, walnut-colored waves across her shoulders.

He smiled, his heart catching at the sight of Trina with her hair down. "As beautiful as I always imagined it." To his ears, his voice sounded husky.

"Oh, Graham. . ." Trina leaned forward, meeting his lips with hers.

He crushed her close, breathing in her scent, twining his fingers through her silky hair. She shifted in his lap, and a shaft of pain shot through his lower back. Involuntarily he grimaced.

She pulled back in alarm. "What's wrong?"

"A pinch in my back, that's all."

She hopped off at once, slipping to her knees beside the chair. "I hurt you?"

The concern in her eyes brought tears to his. She was so sweet. He cupped her cheeks. "Not you. Never you. It comes and goes. But I don't want you to worry about it."

She remained beside the chair, clinging to his hands and peering up at him with love-filled eyes. "Of course I worry about it. I'm your wife. That's what wives do—worry about their husbands."

He grinned. "Is that right?"

She nodded, her hair bouncing. Her long lashes swept up and down in a beguiling blink. "Wives are very busy people. In addition to worrying, they also cook for their husbands, and clean, and mend socks, and do laundry, and—"

"That all sounds very monotonous," Graham said, pretending to yawn.

"Oh, not at all," Trina protested with an innocent expression. "It's pure joy when you love the person very, very much."

"The way you love me?"

"Of course."

Graham chuckled. "So what else do wives do?"

Slowly, Trina shook her head, her eyes twinkling with mischief. "Oh no. Now it's time for you to tell me what husbands do."

"Ah." He nodded, narrowing his eyes and trying to appear wise. "The husband's duties. . ." He stroked the length of her hair, catching a silken strand and twisting it loosely around one finger as he recited, "Husbands provide for their wives and protect their wives and listen to their wives and—" He gently tugged Trina close and whispered a husbandly privilege in her ear.

She jerked back, her eyes wide, and gasped, "Graham!" But then she erupted into giggles.

His laughter rang, too, and when it died out, she rose and held out her hands.

"You said husbands listen to their wives, so. . .come out of that chair, Mr. Ortmann." The love light in her eyes sent a shaft of warmth through Graham's chest. He pushed himself free of the chair, and she tucked herself beneath his arm and walked him to the bed.

He sat on the edge of the mattress, and she curled next to him, nuzzling her face into his neck. All teasing left her voice as she murmured, "Of all the blessings of the past year, Graham, you are the one I treasure most."

Graham wrapped his arms around his wife—his greatest blessing. He searched for words to convey everything his heart felt, but in the end, the only thing that found its way from his lips was the simple statement, "How I love you, Trina."

And her smile told him those words were enough.

Discussion Questions

1. At the beginning of the story, Trina is acting in obedience to her parents and is engaged in a meaningful occupation, yet she has an underlying feeling of discontent. What was the basis of her discontent? Did she handle the churning emotions appropriately? Why or why not?

2. Graham professes to love Trina, yet he fails to support her desire to be something more than wife and mother. Why did he have such strong feelings concerning her desire to be a veterinarian?

3. Trina sought a support system. Who offered the greatest support? Why did this person react differently than others in the community?

4. Trina expected support from her cousin Andrew. Why did Andrew fail to offer it? Were his actions understandable given the circumstances?

5. In her quest to fulfill her heart's desire, Trina's actions became devious. Should we ever do wrong in order to do right? Why or why not?

6. Although initially obstructive, Graham eventually changed his mind concerning Trina's desires. What brought about his change in attitude? Have you ever experienced a similar heart-change due to reading God's Word?

7. Trina faced many stumbling blocks in seeing her dream become reality. Which was the most difficult to overcome? Why do you feel that way?

8. Each main character in *Blessings* was forced to do some growing and stretching. Discuss the changes seen in Deborah Muller, Troy Muller, Trina Muller, Andrew Braun, Graham Ortmann, Beth Quinn McCauley. Which character changed the most? The least? What do you believe was the motivation for change? What, if anything, prevented characters from changing?

9. Following Graham's accident, Trina briefly relinquished working toward her goal even though she believed it was God's will for her to be a veterinarian. Have you ever strayed from God's pathway? What brought you back on course?

10. Many characters sacrificed their own desires to allow someone they loved to grow. In your opinion, which character made the greatest sacrifice and why?

11. Trina's father was concerned that allowing Trina to step outside of the sect's rules would negatively impact the community as a whole. Were his fears grounded? Change generally brings both positive and negative consequences. Which do you believe will be more prevalent in Sommerfeld—negative consequences or positive consequences? Why?

12. Following God's will is always the best course but isn't always the easiest course. Trina made a few mistakes in her quest to follow God's will. What could she have done differently? What did she do right? How can you apply Trina's lessons to your own life?

ABOUT THE AUTHOR

Kim Vogel Sawyer, a Kansas resident, is a wife, mother, grandmother, teacher, writer, speaker, and lover of cats and chocolate. From the time she was a very little girl, she knew she wanted to be a writer, and seeing her words in print is the culmination of a life-long dream. Kim relishes her time with family and friends, and stays active in her church by teaching adult Sunday School, singing in the choir, and being a "ding-a-ling" (playing in the bell choir). In her spare time, she enjoys drama, quilting, and calligraphy.